G000075296

2023

WORLD WAR III

CARL BERRYMAN

Author ReputationPress®
Creativity & Branding

Copyright © 2021 by Carl Berryman.

All rights reserved. No part of this publication may be reproduced, distributed, or transmitted in any form or by any means, including photocopying, recording, or other electronic or mechanical methods, without the prior written permission of the copyright owner and the publisher, except in the case of brief quotations embodied in critical reviews and certain other noncommercial uses permitted by copyright law. For permission requests, write to the publisher, addressed "Attention: Permissions Coordinator," at the address below.

Author Reputation Press LLC
45 Dan Road Suite 5
Canton MA 02021
www.authorreputationpress.com
Hotline: 1(800) 220-7660
Fax: 1(855) 752-6001

Ordering Information:
Quantity sales. Special discounts are available on quantity purchases by corporations, associations, and others. For details, contact the publisher at the address above.

Printed in the United States of America.

ISBN-13:	Softcover	978-1-64961-162-8
	Hardback	978-1-64961-164-2
	eBook	978-1-64961-163-5

Library of Congress Control Number: 2020921286

CHARACTERS

Allison, David, Secretary, Department of Health and Human Services

Atkinson, George, Vice President to Jason Thornton

Anderson, Robert, General, U.S. Army

Berry, Nathan, Colonel, USMC, Shuttle flight Commander

Bradley, Robert, DVM, MPH, ACVPM, AFIP pathology preceptor, Member of the investigating team in Korea.

Brown, Thomas E. U.S. Ambassador to Pakistan, Chapter

Burgess, Frank, MC, 0-6, USA, Cdr. Medical Intelligence, Unit, Ft. Detrick Preventive Medicine Officer.

Bustamante, Enrico, President of Mexico

Carlson, Cpl. Texas Dept of Public Safety, Brewster County, TX

Carter, James, FBI special agent guarding Diane Foster

Chang, Mao Lin: Chinese Chief of Staff, People's Liberation Army Navy (PLAN).

Chavez, Romero, SSG, on CPT Sabata's team

Chen, Hsein, Wo: Commissar, Chinese Security Council Member, National People's Congress

Chan (Ito) Chinese agent under cover as COSCO shipping clerk.

Chernikov, Vassily, President of Russia.

Choi, We Hin, mathematician and computer scientist, DARPA

Collier, Hugh, US Attorney General under President Thornton.

Consaida, Caesar, SSG, on CPT Sabata's team

Corning, Larry. Software design engineer, Ph.D. for NASA.

Cowart, Republican, Senate Minority Leader, under Pres. Thornton

Craig, Ronald, General, U.S. Army, Chairman, Joint Chiefs of Staff

Cunningham, Jim, Director of Central Intelligence under Pres. Dorn

Dickenson, Sam, Lt, U.S. Border Patrol, HQ in Marfa, Station Chief.

Dorn, Henry, U.S. Democratic President 2004-2012

Estevez, Manuel, SFC on CPT Sabata's team

Fairchild, James, FBI Director under Pres. Dorn

Farrel, Christopher Republican Speaker of the House under President Thornton

Fletcher, Gregory, Commander, USN, engineer, astronaut 2nd in command, shuttle

Fong, Cu-chen. Commander, Army Front IV, Africa.

Foster, Diane. Computer engineer, Ph.D. Lawrence Livermore Labs.

Gardner, Ralph, National Security Advisor to Pres. Thornton

Gateway, Fred, Director of FBI under President Thornton,

Gomez, Mexican spy for Miguel Monzani

Gutierrez, Roger, naturalized Mexican American, Secretary Homeland Security Agency.

Hatcher, Robert. Propulsion physicist, Ph.D. MIT.

Hernando, farm manager of Jesus Gonzalez

Jacobi, Frank, Captain, East Los Angeles Police Department

Johnston, Mel, USN, Rear Admiral, CBG USS Ronald Reagan

Jahrling, Robert, Agent, U.S. Border Patrol, Dickenson's partner.

Kennely, Alfred, Senate Majority, Leader, and US Senate Armed Services Committee

Klein, Frank, House Minority Whip, Democrat, under President Thornton

Koon, Chan He, Captain, ROK infantry. Bradley's escort.

Lee, Robert Wha: Secret Service Agent, Chinese –American, bodyguard to the President Aka Robert Zin Wang

Leng, Sha We: Commissar, National Security Council, National People's Congress

Leonard, Mark, General, USMC Commandant

Ling, Ch'ing Chan's man in Jesus Gonzalez's camp

Lui, Lien-chang, Chinese Army Commander, *Army Front I.*

Matthews, Curtis COL, US Army, BA, DVM, MD, pathologist from AFIP

McCall, Roger, White House Press Secretary for Pres. Thornton

McCluskey, Ed, Director, DCI under Pres. Thornton

Monzani, Miguel, waiter in Mexican restaurant, Long Beach, CA gang leader,

Nash, Bart, Secret Service, US Treasury Department,

Neville, James, SECDEF under Jason Thornton

Pak, Whin-yu, North Korean diplomat in USA

Park, Nan Hin, SFC, Republic of Korea Infantryman

Parsons, Peggy, Secretary to the President Thornton

Paterson, John Colonel, US Army, Brigade Commander, 82nd Airborne Division

Perchay, Pakistani ambassador to US

Perez, Miguel, SFC, on CPT Sabata's team

Peterson, John, COL, 2nd BDE Cdr, 82nd Airborne

Po, Ling Tai, Member, Chinese Security Council, National People's Congress

Sabata, Rodrigo, CPT, US Army Ranger, team to investigate Gonzalez

Satcher, Adam, U.S. Border Patrol, Ruidoso, TX.

Shelton, George, General, Chief of Staff, USAF

Shen, De-ming, Commander, Chinese *Army Front III*

Sheng, Kuan, Chinese Ambassador to USA

Sivaji, Indian Minister of Defense

Slayton, Cathy, LTC, USAF, astronaut, shuttle boom operator

Stark, Frank Robert, Admiral, Chief of Naval Operations, USN

Stearns, Roberta, Deputy Undersecretary of State for Far Eastern Affairs,

Su, Teh-shen. Admiral, PLAN, *Army Front IV*

Sung, Chiang, Prime Minister, People's Republic of China

Talbott, Margaret (Marge), Secretary of State under Pres. Thornton

Thornton, Jason, President of USA, elected in 2012

Timmons, Rodney, MD, epidemiologist with CDC

Tsai, Teng-wen, Chinese General, *Army Commander Front II.*

Tolsten, Zachary, Secret Service Agent

Turner, Susan, US Representative to UN

Wang, Robert Zin, hidden identity of Robert Wha Lee

Weber, Carolyn R. USPHS Surgeon General

Whitefield, General, USAF, Commander, Space Command.

Withers, John, Aide to President Thornton

Wrangell, Ed, Supervisory Special Agent, FBI Task Force in Los Angeles

JESUS GONZALEZ'S TEAM LEADERS

> Fiero
> Felipe
> Gordo
> Ramon
> Francisco
> Luis-secretary, aide-de-camp to Gonzalez

CHAPTER 1

"WALLED TOWNS, STORED ARSENALS AND ARMORIES, GOODLY RACES OF HORSE, CHARIOTS OF WAR, ELEPHANTS, ORDNANCE, ARTILLERY, AND THE LIKE; ALL THIS IS BUT A SHEEP IN A LION'S SKIN, EXCEPT THE BREED AND DISPOSITION OF THE PEOPLE BE STOUT AND WARLIKE. NAY, NUMBER ITSELF IN ARMIES IMPORTETH NOT MUCH, WHERE THE PEOPLE IS OF WEAK COURAGE; FOR AS VIRGIL SAITH:

'IT NEVER TROUBLES A WOLF HOW
MANY THE SHEEP BE.'"

SIR FRANCIS BACON

"AN ELITE WITH LITTLE LOYALTY TO THE STATE AND A MASS SOCIETY FOND OF GLADIATOR ENTERTAINMENTS FORM A SOCIETY IN WHICH CORPORATE LEVIATHANS RULE AND DEMOCRACY IS HOLLOW."

Robert D. Kaplan
The Coming Anarchy

"**S**ince you were retired for disagreeing with the President over the Panama Canal situation, General, perhaps you can speak freely here. Enlighten us with your opinion as to what has happened, beginning with some background material and observations."

"Certainly, Senator. First, I wish to thank you and your committee for inviting me here. I will be glad to express my opinion, which caused my relief in the first place." The General thought wryly to himself, *You old bastard, you just want to make political hay at the expense of your political opponent when you run for President.*

In his early fifties, looking young for his age and bluntly outspoken, Ronald Craig, the retired Chairman of the Joint Chiefs of Staff sat ramrod straight before the Senate Armed Services Committee. A former field artillery officer, he served in the First Gulf War as a battery commander, a battalion commander in the post Second Gulf War with Iraq, liaison officer to the Indian Field Artillery School, Field Artillery Regimental Commander and Assistant Division Commander for Maneuver as a Brigadier and the Commander with the 101st Division, he was much more of a field soldier than a politician. The third and fourth stars had come quickly. They came, however, partly as a result of lack of capable competition. The army had grown small, very small. He was the Chief of Staff, Army for only a year when he was selected to be Chairman of the Joint Chiefs. He had worn the fourth star a little less than two years. He was wearing a civilian suit, white shirt and tie rather than his uniform.

The General cleared his throat and began, "After the end of the Cold War, the United States committed its usual strategic error. Politicians decided how much the government wanted to invest in defense and planned from there. The United States had done this after every conflict since the Civil War. We allow our defenses to erode, ignore our position in the world, engage in self-denial and self-delusion, for which we pay a terrible price in the form of the next war. The United States has never practiced the much saner strategy of defining our strategic interests, then defining what is necessary to protect them, investing adequately and simultaneously in research and development of future weapons systems, procurement of those systems, training and manning the force. The price of this failure is always paid in the next war. As the Commanding General of British

Army Forces in World War II said, 'Preparation for the preservation of our freedom must come in peacetime, and we must pay for it in money and inconvenience. The alternative is blood and extinction.'

"The first Gulf War seemed to confirm the usual approach, as it has been practiced by every administration and congress since. With the initial phenomenal success of the so-called Second Gulf War with Iraq in 2003, the concept of the classical principles of war, indicated by the acronym MOSS COMES, standing for Mass, Objective, Surprise, Security, Command, Offense, Maneuver, Economy of Force, and Simplicity, were no longer considered valid. They were considered as holdovers from Napoleonic wars, and their demise seemed entirely vindicated. The concept of war, the information war, the digital war, was validated by all the current military theorists. Very small forces, precision strikes with precision weapons within minutes of target acquisition from a variety of platforms worked wonders on a second-rate military power that utterly lacked similar information capabilities. No politician saw any massed challenge on the horizon. What little discussion of a massed threat existed only at levels lower than battalion leadership which was ignored by senior officers and squashed by politicians that did not want to offend the People's Republic of China. Leaders of the New China lobby in the 1980s and 1990s, led by a former Secretary of State, did their work well."

Obviously irritated, the senator snapped upright and leaned into the microphone. "Would you care to explain that comment about the New China Lobby, General?"

"Certainly, Senator. After the Cold War, American business regarded China as the ultimate market. To satisfy the employment needs of their tremendous population, China adopted the policy that if you wish to sell it here, you must manufacture it here. Consequently, American manufacturers took their expertise, techniques in manufacturing and management to China. China learned quickly, adapting new methods, technology, and efficiencies. They were less concerned about the environment, labor unions and labor organization and other aspects than they were about forging ahead into the 21st century as at least the leader in Asia, if not the world. The New China Lobby helped them in their initial endeavors by acting as an intermediary. They quickly and efficiently acquired the manufacturing and management capabilities, so they grew exponentially. Once they started, there was no reasonable way of stopping them. They were willing to pay whatever price was required to establish dominance in Asia and over the entire Pacific littoral. They surpassed both the US and Western Europe in total number of vehicles owned and operated in this decade; small, but efficient and of modern design. Their trade with us established such an overwhelming deficit with the United States that we could not possibly even hope to dig our way out. Their profits went into their military machine, unrecognized by the west."

"General, you are a recognized authority in military matters. That is why you are here. You are not recognized as an expert in politics or business. Please confine your remarks to the military situation."

Smiling at so easily invoking the ire of the Chairman, the General responded with a wry smile, "Politics and military affairs are inseparable, Mr. Chairman. Political, economic and military capital, or power, cannot be strategically separated. The immortal Clauswitz addressed that with his classic remark that 'war is politics by other means.' Soldiers don't make policy, we don't declare war, we go where we are told and do what is expected of us to the best of our ability with tools that you have provided us. Our resources, our weapons systems, our personnel, our training, our state of readiness, our morale, and our overall wellbeing are all controlled by you politicians. Our job is to provide the muscle for the decisions you politicians make governing our relationships with the rest of the world."

Two years earlier, a similar confrontation had occurred between a Chinese Colonel General, the equivalent of the Chairman, Joint Chiefs of Staff, the People's Liberation Army Navy, or PLAN, and the Security Council of the National People's Congress.

Chang, Mao Lin was Chief of Staff, People's Liberation Army Navy. He attended a military academy during his teen years, sort of a combined high school and junior college together. He demonstrated a propensity for foreign languages and mastered English, French and Spanish with ease. Upon graduation, he served briefly as a junior officer in the People's

Army. His talent was recognized, and he was offered the chance to study abroad. He jumped at the chance. He was accepted at Oxford University where he earned his Bachelor of Arts degree reading western history. An exceptionally brilliant man, he was allowed to continue pursuit of higher education in the west. He received a Master of Arts from Harvard University in western civilization. His doctorate came from the University of California at Berkeley, in political science.

While at Berkeley, he came to consider pacifist California with its economic woes as typical of most of the entire United States. Since he was immersed in both of them, he recognized the significant differences between the east coast philosophy and the west coast philosophy and regarded those differences as both amusing and quite disruptive. Of the two, he believed the country would not be able to philosophically re-unite, possibly even splitting apart. He looked at the United States and wondered about its Balkanization. He believed that, ultimately, the California influence would win out, if they ever did reach a confluence. "After all, California has been the cutting edge of American culture for decades," he used to say with a smile.

While in America, he acquired a taste for many things American. He especially enjoyed dating Chinese American women, most of whom found him exceptionally charming as well as brilliant and rather good looking. He also liked American fast foods and had to watch his diet in order not to gain too much weight. He continued practicing Shaolin Do karate several nights a week just to maintain his skills and keep his weight down. At five feet ten inches tall, he was slightly taller than the average man from North China. He acquired a taste for scotch whiskey. He was always very careful not to become intoxicated except when he was alone in his apartment. He never consumed alcohol in the company of others. He made many American friends, both male and female. Many of his fellow students were slightly envious of his brilliance and impeccable charm. Inwardly, he held what he called both the California and the New York subcultures in contempt. He wondered if there was anything other than money that kept America united.

"Comrade General Chang, why do you think this enormous endeavor could possibly be successful? It is overwhelming in scale, it is tremendously complicated, it risks destroying the very ultimate things that we seek, which are markets for our goods, food for our people, health and prosperity. How will America respond to this? What guarantees do you offer of success? What will be the end point of such a tremendous undertaking? Aren't we destroying or risking the destruction of the very things we covet? Anything of this magnitude is doomed to failure. This is an insane plan."

"Comrade Commissar, I would point out to you that seventy-five years ago, a small island nation of less than one hundred million accomplished this much in less than fifteen years. They only failed because they overextended themselves in attacking the Americans. They failed to stop and consolidate what they had gained. They went as far west as the Indian State of Assam, and as far south as New Guinea, taking the entire Malayan peninsula. They seized what was then called Manchuria in 1931. They slaughtered our people by the millions. Had they not awakened the sleeping giant that was America, they would be our masters now. Mongols on horseback in the twelfth and thirteenth centuries invaded and conquered China in 1220, then went as far west as Baghdad, where they slaughtered millions of Iraqis. They went through Russia and placed the so-called Mongol yoke upon them. Recall that Timur the Lame stood children against a wagon wheel. If their heads were higher than the axle, they were decapitated. He built caravansaries of their skulls that still stand today in the Central Asian Republics."

"What, General, makes you think that this won't awaken that sleeping giant once again to unleash its wrath on us? Bear in mind that they still have a considerable nuclear force and rocketry to deliver it? This is insanity."

"The America of today is not the America of seventy-five years ago. The American man on the street does not comprehend realpolitik. The American government has historically been dishonest with its people. Administration after administration has adequately failed to explain the fundamentals of their foreign policy. Their foreign policy changes with every change in the administration. Indeed, they deliberately shield the facts from the people for political gain. While the politicians profess democracy and freedom, particularly in the Middle East, they have supported repressive regimes. Their hypocrisy is overwhelming and is not lost on the rest of the world, but not appreciated by the American public. They hope to control events without explaining the forces that create such events. Academics, journalists and comedians across America are left to espouse their views on foreign policy to fill that void. Fortunately, much of academia is very anti-war, social welfare and liberally oriented. They, academia, in conjunction and supported by socialistic elitists and especially by the media moguls and Hollywood, are a reflection of the perspective of the British politicians between 1918 and 1935. In that period, they disarmed, refused to establish their leadership role in the world, engaged in self-delusion and dreams of economic prosperity. America has done much the same since the end of what they call the 'Cold War.'"

"Please elaborate, Comrade General."

"Basically, the American man on the street, particularly the well-to-do, the middle of the middle class and the upper middle classes, see their primary issues as domestic ones, of economic and social improvements in their society. With occasional blips, American politicians in both major parties have been moving towards a socialist society. Government provided services have dramatically increased since the 1960s. In that time frame, increased social welfare was a means of buying off the support of the American people for an unpopular war in Vietnam. It did not work, but the American lower class certainly liked the carrot of welfare. Their politicians found they could buy votes by promising to feed the masses at the public trough. Now, they even provide school clothes for the lower classes, along with free medical care, housing, food in the form of redeemable coupons called food stamps, and unlimited health care for the elderly. Many of these things our government provides, but the Americans do it while accumulating individual wealth. Consequently, they have difficulty in paying for all of these programs. What they do is simply print more paper money, backed by nothing more than the world's faith in it. Their economic system of a floating currency with constant inflation at varying rates will be their downfall. They are a tremendous debtor nation. The day is not far off when they will not be able to pay their debts, their bonds and loans. All they can do is print more paper money.

"Another factor in our favor is that America's population is skewed towards middle age and the elderly. They cannot maintain adequate military forces through volunteers and refuse to reinstate conscription. Indeed, of the Anglo-Americans, they are seriously obese and not physically very strenuous or athletically inclined anyway. The Europeans call America 'the land of the pigs' behind their backs because so many of their young and middle-aged middle class are so fat. Conscription would be political suicide for any of their politicians. They would never be re-elected. This is why so many of their soldiers are foreign born. Their politicians do not explain any of this to the American people. Rather, they continue to increase their national debt. Now, that has come to haunt them, really overwhelm them. Their politicians reduce defense expenditures to buy votes by providing more and more welfare services. The very rich get richer, the middle class is terribly squeezed economically, and the lower class grows by leaps and bounds.

"What they call the baby boomers are now retired and expecting many social services. This places a tremendous drain on their economy. Out of a nation of three hundred million people, an estimated forty million are aged sixty-five are older. That is closing on fifteen percent of their population. They expect full health care at government expense through their MEDICARE and MEDICAID programs. This is not only for the treatment of acute diseases, but chronic diseases and long term institutionalized geriatric care, what they call 'assisted living.' Their families warehouse them at government expense. This number will double by the year 2042, if not sooner. We, on the other hand, have made the difficult choice to limit medical care provided to the elderly and those in the advanced stages of AIDS. We simply cannot afford to squander medical resources on those who no longer contribute to our society.

"These elitists and academics believe all that is necessary for defense is information technology and management, allowing them to control weapons from afar, especially via satellites. This is an outgrowth of what their political scientists and some military chiefs call their Revolution in Military Affairs. They see little need for large land forces and only marginal requirements for naval forces. Incredibly, they somehow believe that you should be able to wage war without bloodshed. Of course, this is nonsense, but you will recognize the fact that they have forced the Department of Defense to squander precious resources on the research and development of non-lethal weapons. Unbelievably, they have appointed their most efficient and aggressive organization, the United States Marine Corps, as the lead agency in research and development of non-lethal weapons. The elitists think war is a game. The Marine Corps does more than twenty-five percent of their defense mission, such as it is, on ten percent of their Department of Defense budget. Not only are they unwilling to accept their own casualties, but they believe you should not harm any of the enemy either.

"Many of these elitists are not nationalists but consider themselves as internationalists. They do not profess any significant loyalty to the United States. They claim, rather, that the entire world should be considered as one nation. The environmentalists are also very supportive of this point of view, and the two groups, the environmentalists and the advocates of a New World Order, are very overlapping, with most of each group belonging to the other. Hollywood is a tremendous psychological factor in this respect. Most of the prominent American movie stars belong to this movement and have provided us with a tremendous psychological edge over their fans, especially people between the ages of ten and forty. They have been taught by Hollywood that they, the elitists, are too good to serve in their armed forces. Their attitude is the same as expressed in the days of their Vietnam conflict. Let some other mothers' sons serve. Not my son! They have no patriotism. Very few members of the American Congress have ever served in their armed forces. They have no personal experience to draw upon. Only for their Air Force do they see significant requirements. At one time, politicians wearing the US Air Force blue uniform had so brainwashed some of their congressmen, that those congressmen actually thought the US did not need a navy or land force. They thought only air power was necessary and could accomplish all missions. Again, this is what the British thought in 1918. The military revolution at that time consisted of the tank, the airplane, and field radio. Britain thought they could control ground forces from the air. Americans should have learned otherwise from Vietnam. They did not. They repeated this again in the Balkans. Of course, after the Balkans affair of the 1990s, that view was somewhat modified. Even now, they define air power essentially as the Space Command with the United States Air Force.

"We owe a great deal to the United States Air Force. For the last decade, they have convinced their American Congress of the superiority of their needs and assets over the other branches of the armed forces. With the budget constraints imposed upon them, the micromanagement by Congress, the attitude of the politicians to 'protect the defense jobs in my district,' whether or not they are necessary for defense, is practiced by virtually all members of the American Congress. The Air Force, and to a lesser extent the Navy, have the high value technological weapons systems that result in high paying jobs in their design and building. Deploying them is something else. The Americans, however, have reduced their military manpower as one means of funding these expensive weapons. Technology is worthless without people who have the knowledge and skills to use it. They do not retain their skilled people in the military due to micromanagement by careerist superiors, overburdening workloads, that is, do more with fewer resources, extended overseas assignments and lower compensation than the civilian markets.

"The less technical forces, the Army, the US Marine Corps, and the U.S. Coast Guard, are woefully unprepared to interfere with our plans. By purchasing very expensive highly technical weapons, especially planes and satellites, they can buy fewer of them. When these high value weapons systems are attrited, they have nothing left. The Americans today believe that mass is no longer a principle of war. Ironically, some Congressmen might look at our endeavors with a concealed glee."

"Why, Comrade General, would they consider such plans as you have proposed with glee?"

"They would rejoice because of the destruction, or at least the interruption of, competition in heavy manufacturing. The American steel and metals industries have suffered for decades from cheap, competitive imports. Americans do not even manufacture their own clothes or footwear. We manufacture most of these items for them. Most of their consumer electronics goods are made overseas or are assembled overseas from parts manufactured in a variety of countries. By the mid 1980s, over 40% of the electronic components of American weapons systems were manufactured overseas. Today, that is much closer to 80%. We manufacture a great deal of them ourselves, as subcontractors for the major American defense companies. In point of fact, we manufacture the great majority of the computers in use in the United States, at all levels, from home use through the highest Department of Defense supercomputers. These people would see the possibility of a return of heavy manufacturing to the United States, especially steel, automobiles, appliances, and others. This translates into jobs in their sagging economy. In the 1980s, American economic theorists surmised that their economy would shift from a manufacturing economy to a service economy. They were right in that regard, but they were wrong in the outcome. They predicted the service economy would be more than capable of providing adequate employment for all. Indeed, they even predicted that more jobs would be created than there are workers to accept them. We all know that this turned out not to be the case. In the 1990s, service jobs began to migrate in large numbers from America to overseas locations as well. Financial services, communications, and processed foods were especially affected. Many of them went to our province of Taiwan, our Southeast Asian neighbors, Central and South America and their offshore islands. Labor is cheaper there, even for service employment.

"There is one other interesting psycho-social factor that is now being expressed by a few minor sociologists and psychologists in the United States. They have begun to ask: for what will America fight? Americans are no longer tied to the land, with the great majority of Americans now in urban and suburban environments. They have no allegiance to anything higher than their own materialism and economic well-being. Some of the more adventurous political scientists in the United States are even predicting a breakup of their country along regional-economic and racial lines in less than fifty years, perhaps much sooner than that. Already, strains of regional conflict are evident and growing if one cares to carefully look for them."

"Comrade General, you do not see this as potentially devastating the American market for our goods? You know they are by far our biggest market. We must not do anything at all which will disrupt our trade with the Americans."

"Comrade, where will they go? They have few other places to trade for even their basic needs other than food. Europe? Europe is hardly in a position to complain or to take our place. They are almost as reliant upon us Asians as the Americans are. South America? Half of South America is in the hands of drug lords who employ private armies to grow, refine and transport drugs for the American and European markets. With South America's growing population, they are more concerned with growing food than manufacturing. Many of the South American countries are suffering borderline instability. Several of their national governments are expected to collapse within the next few years. None have significant military resources. No, it will take years for America to restore their manufacturing capacity. In the interim, they have no choice but to continue to trade with us. By the time they even make the decision as to how to respond, our endeavors will be over. No doubt that a great public debate will occur as to how to best approach the situation. It would not be unreasonable to expect demonstrations, even riots in the streets of America. America is no longer a unified country. They have many cultural centers, many beliefs, and now many histories and languages. There are no longer any unifying factors in the United States. The current political leadership is far less decisive than in the recent past.

"Even if the Americans choose to militarily respond, they have few forces capable of doing so, at least as regards to our main objectives. After the Americans left Iraq in 2005, so many of their military personnel, especially in their Reserve and National Guard units, left their armed forces that they have not been able to reconstitute their reserves. The majority of personnel that remained in the armed forces are, for the most part, considered to be of mediocre quality, and they are stretched very thin in their current commitments. That is not to mean that they don't have some quite brilliant people; they do, but the mass of enlisted personnel is not of the same quality. Their only significant option is nuclear, and they will not let that genie out of the bottle. No, Comrade, the Americans will realize they have no choice and acquiesce to our strategic plans. After all, this momentous effort will guarantee us the resources we so very much require in order to continue trade with both America and Europe. If America goes to war outside its own borders again, it is as likely to go to the aid of Israel as anywhere. I shouldn't even mention the threat that an unstable Mexico poses. The Americans made a secret treaty with the Israelis to come to their aid if the Egyptians and other Arab countries attacked them when they reduced their foreign aid program to both nations.

"What, Comrade Commissar, will be the decisive factors in America not resisting us are, first and most importantly, the lack of a national will and secondly, the inability to adapt to our countermeasures to their supposed technological superiority. In fact, we are very close to them in the technological aspects of their concept of the Revolution in Military Affairs. We can already easily counter their technological weapons, neutralize them, so to speak, today.

"Another subtle but very significant factor occurring in American society is what they call the cultural war. Indeed, that is what it is, with political overtones. The American middle class is the primary tax paying class and has some religious beliefs and values. The elitists, of whom I just spoke, do not necessarily share that middle class value system. This class war is sometimes expressed as political correctness. The elitists have been, for years, attempting to remold American society through legislation and the courts as they think it should be. In so doing, they are attacking the religious, cultural and economic bases of the middle class. As one banker put it in economic terms, 'The rich and the poor gang up on the middle class to pay the taxes. The rich aren't going to pay them, and the poor cannot.' It is most evident when their movie stars make forty million dollars a motion picture, while an average family struggles trying to pay all the bills on thirty thousand dollars a year and cannot afford health insurance. The parallels between the United States today and Rome in its last few decades are amazing."

"Comrade General, will this plan not unite Islam against us?"

"No, Comrade Commissar Chen, I do not believe it will. In fact, I anticipate that it will initially unite the Muslim world behind us. Islam is not a cohesive force. There are many sects, and the major divisions of Sunni and Shiite revile each other. Only three things tend to unite Islam. The first is the perceived threat that western cultural values have upon Islam. The second is a united hatred of Israel. Third is their hatred of Russia. To a lesser extent, is the belief held by many older Muslims, especially in Europe and America, that although they are not ready to take up the sword, so to speak, that no religion other than Islam should exist on the planet. I would point out that the Madrassas, funded throughout the world by the Saudis, have taught that there are three demons, Jews, America, and Russia. The nations of Southwest Asia have no economies other than the export of petroleum. They are being overwhelmed by their own population growth. Saudi Arabia's population growth exceeds 3.5% a year. Over 50% of the population of the Muslim Middle East is less than twenty years of age. They have little education outside of the Madrassas and no jobs. Our surreptitious funding of militant Islamic groups through various front organizations has bought us temporary friends. They have used these resources to wage guerilla warfare against Russia, against the Hindus of India and Kashmir. The resources that we have provided have been much too modest to be any significant factor in resisting us."

"As you pointed out, General, the Mongol invaders of the twelfth and thirteenth centuries slaughtered Muslims by the millions. Will they not regard this invasion in the same light?"

"That is possible, Comrade Commissar Chen, but I do not think so. The Central Asian Republics are composed of diverse peoples, Mongols, Turkic peoples and others. They are fractious among themselves. Our goal here is not to conquer peoples as a resource, but rather to eliminate them as obstacles. They are too weak as individual nations to offer us much resistance, and they have never been able to unite to form a strong coalition for opposition.

"All of the populations of the Central Asian Republics exceed ninety percent Muslims. Our own Uighers have looked to them for guidance. Elimination of these irritating populations at the same time would be favorably considered in some western circles. The terrorist war Muslims have carried out against the western powers, particularly the United States, Great Britain and France, has generated a considerable anti-Muslim backlash in these countries. Indeed, Muslim American organizations have even sued the U.S. Attorney General and the American Government for perceived bias. Unlike Germany, which expelled its Turkish immigrant workers, the elitists in control of the legal system in America demanded, and the U.S. continued, to accept Muslims immigrants from countries essentially inimical to U.S. interests. Why they have done so escapes me and any logic. Nevertheless, they have in their midst a classic fifth column.

Most of them are in supportive roles, supplying money, intelligence, hiding places and weapons to the active terrorists. Many Europeans will cheer, along with Americans, at what they perceive as a reduction in the power and the threat from Islam.

"Egypt, largest of the Islamic nations, is in turmoil, disintegrating with ethnic strife. Radical Islamism rules, with food and water shortages, massive over population, a very youthful population of young men in their teens and twenties who are unemployed and unemployable, suppressed women, and a government that is barely functional. In an attempt to appear even-handed, the United States reduced its commitments to both Egypt and Israel under the previous administration. The Egyptians were receiving conquerable amounts or were close to Israel in the amount of foreign aid they received. This reduction in aid has resulted in a tremendous outburst of anti-U.S. sentiment. Israel has had to fortify Gaza as a result, to deal with constant infiltration attempts. With no settlement on the West Bank or Gaza, Egypt is boiling over against the United States and Israel.

"The only potential difficulty I see is interference by Iran. Our nonaggression pact with them has lowered their guard. It has allowed us to put thousands of our people within their territory for development of their resources and aid in their manufacturing. These are a truculent people who have been warlike throughout history, before the days of Xerxes. They continuously interfere, intervene, and disrupt the internal affairs of their neighbors. They have sufficient unrest within their own population, in spite of their attempts at crushing their internal dissenters over the last few years. Most importantly, our presence there has supported internal turmoil and civil strife by funding various factions within their society. Indeed, we have funded and supplied small arms to both the hard line mullahs and those who wish a more open society. As you are aware, they have begun to kill each other in the back alleys. The mullahs remain in control and still believe in establishing a puritanical Islamic state throughout the world. Our agents in Africa report that the Iranians even have active agents in several countries. It is possible, even likely, that they will declare a Jihad against us at some point in time. If they do come against us, it will be our pleasure to send them to meet Allah. They will find that they do not have the resources to guard the Persian Gulf, threaten their neighbors, and resist us all at the same time. They have a limited number of nuclear weapons, of small yield size, some of their own that they have built, and some they have acquired on the black market from somewhere in the former Soviet Union. If they attempt to use biological weapons, we will respond in kind or with tactical nuclear strikes ourselves. They do have rockets capable of delivering such weapons to a range of one thousand kilometers. That is not sufficient to reach major targets in our country. Our resources are scattered to some extent. While much of our manufacturing is located close to our shoreline, much has also been dispersed throughout the country in the last fifteen years.

"What they have is sufficient to threaten all of their neighbors and the U.S. forces positioned offshore. Indeed, they are potentially a greater threat to us than the United States, as they are not afraid of their own deaths or certainly not of killing infidels. Iranian Islam is something of an unknown in terms of our proposed endeavors. The Iranian mullahs are unstable, and therefore unpredictable. Should they choose to interfere prior to our reaching their borders, I do not think anyone will come to their aid. They are the true pariah of the western world. There will be no nation from the east capable of helping them by that time.

"The Muslim world has no idea of our designs. Once the Arab part of the Muslim world realizes that all of the U.S. forces are tied down in response to our initial actions, or more appropriately, those of our allies, it is conceivable that they will briefly unite to launch an attack on Israel; if they do, so much the better for us. The United States cannot fight a two-front war, one in the western Pacific Littoral, and one in the Middle East, if they choose to fight at all. I am confident that they will not. In that regard, Islam is more likely to, at least initially, consider us an ally."

"Do you consider it likely, Comrade General, that the Arabs will attack Israel at this point in time?"

"No, Comrade Commissar, I think it is most unlikely but not out of the realm of possibility. If it occurs, it will be fueled primarily by Iran and Syria but conducted by Egypt."

"Will you inform the Arabs of this plan, Comrade General?"

"Most certainly not, Comrade Commissar Chen. The Arabs are utterly untrustworthy. They have historically been known to change sides in the middle of a battle, according to who pays the highest bribe. They have no honor. They have no central organization. Rather, they are organized into movements based on their religious sect and/or cause. These organizations are often at odds with, and fight, each other. If the Arabs know of our plans, the western governments will soon know of them as well. No, we will not rely on any support activity by them, but if it occurs, we will regard it as most favorable to us."

"Comrade General, why do you believe that the Muslims will not wage guerilla war on our rear areas as they did to the Americans in Iraq? How will you stabilize your lines of communication?"

"Comrade Commissar, there will be no guerilla operations on our lines of communications simply because there will be no one to conduct such operations. One of our primary objectives is the annihilation of potential adversaries. There will be no civilian population to support any such activities. We will leave no enemies behind. We will consume everything in our path. There will be no food, fuel, haven, or civilian population to support them. They cannot hide without starving or freezing, there will be no bases for them from which to operate. Quite simply and bluntly, this is a true scorched earth campaign that will leave no conquered people. They will simply cease to exist as they did under Timur the Lame."

"And what of other Asian nations, Comrade General?"

"Your policy that began in the closing decade of the twentieth century that continues to this day has served us very well, indeed, Comrade Commissar. Our political leaders over the last twenty years have successfully wooed on an individual basis all the nations of Southeast Asia. By pointing out American perfidy, the lack of will and resourcefulness, that America has only been here on a transitory basis, when it serves their economic interest and advantage, you have undermined any further strategic alliances that the United States might have forged and eroded previous ones. The 'China is here forever' strategy has been enormously successful. We have won many friends in Southeast Asia by declaring war on the rampant piracy on the South China Sea, the Philippine Sea, in the straits of Malacca and the Yellow Sea. Our naval forces that patrol these waters and attack these pirates have made shipping so much safer and cheaper that many are indebted to us and look upon us as a big brother.

"America's Asian allies fail to agree in theory or practice for concerted defense. The Philippine Republic has been fighting a two decades old guerilla war with Muslim insurgents with little success. They are initiating negotiations with the Muslims. The United States has abandoned the Philippines in disgust to prevent another version of Vietnam for them. Singapore has no army, Myanmar, or Burma if you prefer, is a basket case. Vietnam is modestly militarily strong but economically and politically very weak. Due to AIDs, drugs have replaced sex as the primary economic commodity in Thailand. They expelled the Americans because they interfered too much with the drug trade. Who will survive against us?"

"Comrade General, this Committee demands that you keep us informed of your plans as they progress. Is there any difficulty you see in complying with that demand?"

"Of course not, Comrade Commissar. The People's Liberation Army Navy is absolutely forthright with the Security Council of National People's Congress. We will keep you informed as plans unfold." *Like hell we will,* silently thought General Chang, Mao Lin.

CHAPTER 2

"Holy Mother of God, Jesus, where do you find such toys?"

Jesus Gonzalez just grinned. Jesus Gonzalez wasn't his real name, of course. He really wanted to be called El Diablo, but he hadn't achieved anywhere near the necessary recognition for that. No, early in his criminal career, he had been a petty thief, graduating to a drug runner, then a coyote smuggling aliens from Mexico, Central America, and the Far East across the American border. The last endeavor was far more difficult than the others. It had become dangerous since American citizens living along the border had begun to shoot wetbacks on sight, no questions asked. Local law enforcement generally looked the other way, now that the shootings had become so widespread. The federal agency boys still frowned upon it, but after some embarrassing moments in which they were brought to task by local vigilante groups, and two of them were shotgunned, they generally turned a blind eye to the shootings. The governments of the border states were not very supportive of those elitist Yankees sending their storm troopers, that is, the FBI, down and interfering with the security of their citizens under the excuse of protecting the civil rights of illegal aliens.

Jesus made good money smuggling illegal immigrants. He knew the desert pathways and the way of the desert. He occasionally lost a few along the way, those who strayed, those who complained and suffered a bullet in the head for their complaints, but overall, he was one of the better coyotes along the border. His organization had grown from fifteen disgruntled Mexicans to more than fifty. Now, he intended to expand his operations. His new friends had provided him with many toys. These included not only firearms, but devices such as night vision goggles, bionic sound detectors, infrared binoculars and radar detectors of various radio frequencies.

The vehicles, the vans, pickups and sport utility vehicles were nondescript on the outside but were carefully overhauled to make them extremely rugged and dependable in the desert environment. Each had oversized tires, four-wheel drive, limited slip transmissions, heavy duty suspension systems, extra gas tanks, and gun racks. Inside, each vehicle carried four five-gallon jerry cans of water and a case of Meals, Ready to Eat, colloquially called MREs in the American Army. These can be purchased commercially in the United States, which is exactly what he did. Several members of his band had jobs just across the border. Their job was essentially intelligence gathering. Some were women. Each day, they trudged back and forth, from Mexico into several small towns, such as Nogales, Arizona, where they had day jobs. At night, they returned to Mexico, usually carrying food, whisky or other supplies. They came to know the border patrolmen manning the gates, who allowed them to pass without question. Most carried their lunches with them. Occasionally, there was a small packet of heroin hidden in a sandwich, or bottom of a thermos, or in the hollow heel of a shoe. While small, it provided ready cash to purchase those items not readily available except on the black market.

"Each man will be provided with a new AK-47, Luis. We have plenty of ammunition. I expect them to learn their new toys in a week. We will have a class on the basics of the rifle, on rifle shooting and on safety in the morning, and practice in the afternoon, just before the sun goes down. The day after, we will have another class on field stripping and cleaning and care. I want no failures because someone did not know their weapon. Of the rocket propelled grenades, we will have a class on them, too, as well as the machine guns and the hand grenades. I do not want to lose any men to accidents or stupidity. For now, issue each man one rifle, one magazine, but no ammunition. They are not to load the rifles. They are, however, to carry them at all times, and even sleep with them."

"What, Jesus, do you plan to do with all these weapons?"

Jesus grinned. "My friend, when the time comes, you will be among the first to know. For now, pass out the guns. No one is to leave this camp until I say so. Our brothers who are in other locations are not to be informed of our new toys or our plans."

Now, thanks to his new friends who had given him new ideas, as well as new toys, Jesus Gonzalez was about to launch his new career as El Diablo. As the evening faded into darkness one week later, he called his band together in the open packing shed of his Mexican farm that served as their headquarters in Chihuahua. On a tripod he had a map of Ruidoso, Texas, which is a very small town on state highway 2810. His advisor had strongly suggested he start out small, and as his success grew, so would his fame and fortune. Such a small village seemed an ideal starting place.

"We will enter the town from the north, east, and south. Luis, you are responsible for Highway 2810 as it enters the town. No one is to enter or to leave. If anyone causes you any difficulty, they are not to be given a second chance. You can rob any vehicle attempting to enter the town. If you like the vehicle, you can confiscate it as a war prize. The occupants are not to be of any concern to you. You can indulge yourself with them as you choose. Hermosa, your orders are the same as Luis's. You will block Highway 170 as it enters the town from the south. Miguel, you are to do the same from the north. It is not likely anyone will come from Candelera, but it is best to be safe. Each of you will be a team commander. There will be two vehicles under your command for each team. The van will have a machine gun mounted in the rear, such that when the doors are open, you have a free field of fire. The second vehicle will be a pickup truck or a sport utility vehicle. Keep all of your weapons out of sight as any vehicle approaches. Let them think that you are a group of braceros looking for work that has broken down on the road. Park such that you are blocking the road. When they stop, have several of your men who have been hiding along the edge of the road approach their vehicle from the rear. Make the occupants get out of the vehicle and sit in the desert so that they cannot escape and give any alarm. Search them for any cell phones and weapons as your first measure. You can release them after we have finished our business in Ruidoso, that is, if you want to release them. Consider that they will have a good look at several of you. Bring none of them with you when you depart, which will be on my signal on the citizens band radio in each vehicle. Also, you are to cut all telephone lines leading into the town. Communications in and out of the town must be kept to a minimum."

No one said a word. Jesus continued, "We have several targets in Ruidoso. There are several rich Americans whose homes we will visit. There is a sporting goods store which will have firearms and ammunition. There is a food store that also has liquor. Francisco, you will be a team leader. Pick three men not already chosen. Your objective is the sporting goods store. Take the guns and ammunition, GPS units, binoculars, radios, knives, camp stoves, fuel and lanterns. Fiero, you are also a team leader. Your job is to fill your pickup with food. Get a mix of canned foods, fruit, both fresh and canned meats, and several cases of liquor. We must have a party upon our triumphant return. I will lead three men to visit our rich American neighbors after we have disposed of the county sheriff and the border patrolman who live there. They are my first targets. Do not hesitate to defend yourselves, or to shoot anyone who even appears to attempt to resist our efforts. I want all aspects of the operation completed before noon. Questions?"

"What of the women, Jefe? It is very lonely out here in the desert."

"Hernando, you and women! There will not be time to pick and choose. There will probably not be any time at all to enjoy such delights. The best opportunity to enjoy a woman is if one is stopped on the road. The greatest possibility of that will be on the highway to the east, coming from Marfa. Therefore, you are to be on Luis's team. Any other questions? Then see that the vehicles are filled with gas, that there is plenty of water in the jerry cans, and the radiators are full. There is to be no drinking of alcohol or smoking anything other than ordinary tobacco from now until the raid is over and we have returned to camp. Everyone must have a clear, cool head. We will have a light breakfast and leave before dawn. We have a long day, starting with a three-hour drive ahead of us."

The wounded were the first to arrive at the Presidio County Hospital in Marfa around four o'clock in the afternoon. They came in ones and twos, driven in sport utility vehicles and vans by family and friends. They came to the Emergency Department entrance, with horns blowing. Several women jumped out of the passenger seat simultaneously, bolting for the door.

Juanita Garza dashed through the door and to the desk, followed by Deborah Wagner close on her heels. Jan Johnston stood up with a look of alarm from her place behind the admittance counter.

My husband has been shot, so have many others! John is in the back of my truck, and he is bad!"

"What happened?" asked Jan, her countenance changing.

"You ask what happened when I tell you my husband is bleeding to death in a car outside? Idiot! Call the doctors! There are others, I don't know how many, but I know of at least eight that have been shot. Call the doctors." Juanita turned, and spying a clean gurney pushed against the wall, grabbed it and started pushing it out the door as fast as she could to bring her husband inside.

Jan, in exasperation, punched the hospital paging button. "All physicians report immediately to the Emergency Department. We have a mass shooting! All nurses who can be spared immediately report to the Emergency Department. Bring gurneys."

Juanita was desperately trying to get her husband, John, who could not stand, on the gurney. A passerby ran over and, putting his arm under John's shoulders, lifted him onto the gurney while Juanita struggled with his legs. The woman companion of the man gave Juanita a hand. The emergency room began to fill with nurses and the two physicians present. The hospital administrator came out and instructed Jan to call the third physician of the town and to bring their nurses.

Jan nodded yes and picked up the phone. As soon as the administrator turned away, however, rushing to push a gurney and help load a patient, she dialed a friend at the local television station. "Jimmy! Get your mobile broadcasting station over here to the hospital quick. There has been a mass shooting somewhere, and the wounded are pouring in. At least eight wounded according to one observer."

Incredulous, Jimmy responded, "Yeah, right! What do you think this is, April Fool's Day?"

Jan, now quite excited and exasperated, shouted, "You asshole, this is no joke! I'll call CNN," and slammed down the phone.

Five minutes later, a van with a satellite dish on the roof pulled up outside the Emergency Department door. At that moment, a fourth vehicle with a wounded woman pulled in. The TV station van was blocking the drive. The driver of the Ford Explorer laid on the horn. Jimmy looked behind him and casually climbed back in his van and moved it over to the edge of the drive. At that moment, he saw John, soaked in blood, being wheeled inside. "Holy shit! She wasn't kidding," he thought, and opened up the back of the van. Manuel jumped out of the passenger seat and began setting up to broadcast. He contacted their major network so it would be a live broadcast. Jimmy grabbed a microphone, hooked the receiver on his belt, plugged in his earphone, and ran inside. In two minutes, he heard Miguel say, "You're live" in his earphone.

"This is Jim Rodriguez broadcasting live from the Presidio County Hospital in Marfa, Texas. There are now four vehicles unloading wounded people as I speak. Here comes another victim now." Manuel panned the portable camera as a gurney went by with a woman moaning softly, her abdomen drenched in blood. Approaching Jan, he asked, "Can you tell us what happened here?"

"All I know is all of a sudden this woman dashes in and says there has been a shooting. She knows of at least eight wounded. We have called in all medical personnel in town, all the doctors and Emergency Medical Technicians and nurses, all twenty of them. I don't know anything else."

Miguel pointed the camera into the Emergency Department clinic area, where John was being jabbed with intravenous set needles in both arms. The lady who had just passed them on a gurney had a sheet pulled over her face, and she was rolled off to the side. Another man came in, with an obvious leg wound. He was supported by two others. A nurse sat him in a chair in the hall and tied a tight bandage around it to stop the seepage of blood. Then she went back to the clinic area. Several of the others were dead on arrival. One rather attractive young woman was being helped, half carried, by two others. She obviously had suffered a severe beating.

"What happened here?" James Rodriguez asked of one of the men who helped settle the beaten woman in a chair.

"Apparently, a bunch of Mexican bandits raided Ruidoso, about 60 miles from here. They sealed off all roads in and out of town, shot the deputy sheriff and border patrolman, raided several stores and homes, shot anybody who resisted, and raped a couple of women. We found her," he said, nodding to the lady, "alongside the road on the way here. I guess it was her husband she was clinging to. He was shot in the head and dead. I guess they were tourists. I don't recognize them. They were just lying there on the shoulder of the road, no car in sight."

"Can you describe the perpetrators?"

"No, I was just coming into town from the ranch when I saw the lady and the dead man. Then these other people came whizzing by. One stopped, the man with the leg wound driven by his son, and said a lot of people were shot by Mexicans. You'll have to get details from somebody else."

Their network made a scoop. It was immediately broadcast across the nation, as the network cut into live programming. The Associated Press wire service picked up the story for the newspapers. Rodriguez made hourly reports which were often broadcast live. The headlines across the country went "Mexican Bandits Conduct Raid in South Texas! Many wounded and killed." Jim Rodriguez's latest broadcast was played again on late night network news across the country. By morning, the Border Patrol, two Texas Rangers, Department of Public Safety Officers, the county sheriff and three deputies, the county attorney, along with people from the state crime laboratory were in Ruidoso to investigate. Initially, there was some heated discussion as to who would take the lead in conducting the investigation. The Border Patrol, the Texas Rangers, and the state police went at it. The Governor, sensing a debacle and having the nose of a politician, ordered the Rangers and state police to support the Border Patrol, who would be the lead agency. A federal agency in the lead would bring in more resources. Also, if another raid occurred, the heat would more likely be directed at the feds for not preventing it.

Thirty miles north of Presidio, Jesus Gonzalez led his column off Highway 170, crossing the Rio Grande at a very shallow place. Actually, it was something of an underwater bridge he had made his men build last year for this very sort of enterprise.

Jesus Gonzalez was celebrating. He had made his mark. A new career was launched. He had conducted the first significant raid as the leader of Mexican bandits since Poncho Villa raided in 1915. He never heard of Black Jack Pershing. After forty-eight hours, the body count was nine dead, thirteen wounded, two women and one twelve-year-old girl raped.

Gonzalez made everyone stay in their temporary camp. They used it occasionally and hid it well. Vehicles were driven inside three-sided buildings. Fresh water came from a very small spring higher up the mountain. That night, they built a fire and roasted the fresh meat they raided from the grocery store. Liquor flowed freely. Tales of prowess, of the struggles of the women who resisted, of the skills of marksmanship, and their fearless courage, regaled into the night.

"My friends, my companions, today was just the beginning. We will now return to our homes for a few weeks. I will send word to you when to come together next time. Next time, we will do even better. Next time, there will be mucho more money as well as food, liquor, women, and fine guns. In the meantime, be very careful, at the risk of your life; tell no one, not your mother, not your girlfriend or your wife, or your children, and especially not your priest what we did today!" That brought a round of laughter. "Now, I have a little money for each of you. If you can line up, Fiero will give each of you one hundred American dollars that we collected."

At that, a spontaneous cheer arose, and they half staggered, half fell, to the table where Fiero handed each of them one hundred American dollars after they signed their name to the ledger. When one tried to collect twice, Fiero looked at Jesus and nodded. Jesus promptly stepped up and butt stroked the man in the side of the head with a rifle. No one tried to collect the reward a second time.

———— •••••• ————

Sam Dickenson, Lieutenant of the U.S. Border Patrol, studied the site along the highway where the young tourist couple was molested. The blood from the gunshot to her husband's head formed a dark stain partly on the pavement and partly on the sandy shoulder. He noted a shred of cloth hanging from a greasewood brush ten yards off the highway that was blowing in a faint breeze. The tracks on the sand covering the hardpan were not difficult to follow and showed the woman resisted as she was dragged into the brush. Faint heel prints in the desert indicated that several men wearing boots participated. The Lieutenant put the shred of cloth in a plastic bag as evidence, although he knew it would hardly be worthwhile. They had enough semen collected by vaginal flushing during the rape examination that indicated she had been penetrated by four different men.

He knelt down, studied the tracks, stood, and pointed down at the tracks for the laboratory folks. The crime lab boys took photographs of the prints and then plaster casts of the boot prints. Samples of the blood-stained sand were scooped into a plastic bag. They also took castings of the tire tracks in the sand where the Mexicans had turned the car around and driven off.

Dickenson was an old hand, approaching nearly thirty years with the border patrol. The last twenty of it he spent along the Rio Grande. Out of the office in Marfa, he was the first on the scene, he and his junior partner, Rod Jahrling. As soon as they had interviewed a few people at the hospital, they returned to the office. He put in a call to the next higher headquarters, drew an M1A Springfield, four magazines, a hundred rounds of .308 Winchester cartridges, a hundred rounds for his issue sidearm, a Beretta Model 96 .40 Smith and Wesson semi-automatic, and a Deer Hunter version of the twelve gauge Remington 870 pump shotgun., along with a box of 00 buck for the latter.

Jahrling drew a box of 50 rounds for his Beretta 96, but drew his Remington 700 varmint synthetic stocked rifle in .308 Winchester cartridges in its aluminum case from the trunk of his privately owned vehicle. He took fifty rounds of match ammunition from the ammunition locker. On top of the rifle sat a Burris Black Diamond T-plate variable power telescopic sight. With its twenty-six-inch barrel, he could keep five slowly fired rounds in a six-inch circle at five hundred yards. It was a sniper rifle in the guise of a varmint rifle. He had purchased it two years earlier out of his own pocket. In fact, he had made it to the national finals in the long-range rifle match in the Border Patrol shoot off the previous year.

It was dark by the time they reached Ruidoso, but they began a systematic interview of everyone who had been involved or was a witness. After 22:00 hours, they checked into the single motel at the edge of town, one of the enterprises that had been robbed by Jesus. No one was hurt at the motel where they only took money from the cash register. By morning, others from various law enforcement agencies had begun to arrive. First were two Texas Rangers, followed by two Department of Public Safety highway patrolmen. The laboratory boys had flown in and landed their light plane in Marfa late that night, rented a car, and drove down the next morning.

The first stop was the home of the Border Patrolman, Adam Satcher. According to his wife, he had just stepped out on the porch to go to the local coffee shop where he usually ate breakfast. She heard a rifle shot while in the bedroom. She ran to the living room only to find him sprawled on the front porch in a pool of blood on the other side of the screen door. He had been shot in the middle of the chest. He was instantly killed. This was to be his last year. He planned to retire on 31 December. He had ridden the river for many years, and this was considered a relatively non-hazardous assignment, patrolling up and down the deserted highways. Only occasionally would he find illegal aliens. Sometimes, he would scare them back into the brush by firing a few shots, occasionally, he would take one or two into custody, or if he was in a good mood, ignore them. He felt that he had done his duty for many years but was never supported by national policy. Always so much duty, so much time, so little resources; most of his career he was going in harm's way without a partner. Therefore, he didn't feel much of an obligation to his duty anymore. When he had made his intentions known, he was moved from the Marfa office to Ruidoso for his last year. Dickenson, the number two man in Marfa, took the job as section chief. Dickenson thought it was time the old man retired. He didn't seem to want to leave the office anymore, only shuffle papers and be a petty bureaucrat. It was decided that Satcher would maintain the rank of Lieutenant. They justified moving him to Ruidoso to regional headquarters by claiming it was a hotbed of smuggling activity and a dangerous section that required an experienced man. The regional office was well aware of the circumstances and winked at the move. There was insufficient manpower, and really no reason, to allow him to maintain a partner in Ruidoso.

Dickenson was beginning to have brief periods of the same attitude, and they were coming more and more often. He tried not to let Jahrling see it so he would not influence the young officer. Dickenson searched the area and found a rifle cartridge across the street from the Satcher's home. According to a neighbor and confirmed by Mrs. Satcher, a white van was seen driving away from the scene. The neighbor and his wife loaded Satcher's body in the bed of their pickup and put Mrs. Satcher between them in the cab. They drove off for Marfa. They saw the roadblock on the highway and turned around. Afraid to go back into town, they drove into the desert and hid behind a low hill for several hours until the roadblock left. By then, most of the other wounded had also been loaded into various vehicles and the convoy formed for Marfa. It was obvious they knew Lieutenant Satcher's habits and were waiting for him. Dickenson bagged the rifle cartridge and called the lab boys on his cell phone, as if they couldn't find the house on their own in such a small town.

Their next stop was at the home of the local deputy sheriff to pay their respects to his wife. He had been ambushed in his office. Apparently, two Mexicans walked into his office, and as he looked up from his desk, drew hidden pistols and opened fire. A Winchester .30-30 rifle case was found outside as well.

Two people were shot at the food store. Two employees and a customer were murdered in the hardware store. The home of the owner of the food store had been burglarized. The owner's wife, a lady of sixty years of age, had been beaten into unconsciousness but recovered consciousness in a few hours. The house had been ransacked from top to bottom. They even removed a small color television. She managed to drive herself to the doctor's office in town. His office had also been burglarized, as had been the drug store next door. They took most everything on the shelves. The pharmacist had been pistol whipped, suffered severe contusions and a mild concussion, but was otherwise unhurt.

The physician, a middle-aged family practitioner in his fifties, had made his millions in the city of Bayonne, New Jersey. He moved to Ruidoso to escape the big city life and very quietly practice where his skills were truly needed. He was beaten into unconsciousness for objecting when his nurse turned office girl Friday was held across her desk and gang raped. He offered no violence, only verbally objected to her being raped. His nurse, shaking all the way, drove him to Marfa in her pickup. Radiographs revealed his jaw broken at the symphysis, in two places of the left mandible, and a fracture of the right maxilla where he had been pistol whipped. He was treated with morphine and hospitalized. One of the physicians called a friend at El Paso General and scheduled him for facial reconstructive surgery in two days. His nurse was treated for rape, put on antibiotics for possible venereal infection, blood drawn as a baseline, and hospitalized for the night. She would receive counseling the next day for psychiatric trauma and the possibility of HIV infection. If she would go to El Paso General with her boss, she could receive an experimental vaccine against human papilloma virus, as could the other rape victims.

CHAPTER 3

esus had filled the gas tanks of three vehicles he was immediately commanding, then robbed the only gas station in town. He shot the owner when the man demanded payment for the gasoline. A witness said that Jesus smiled and said, "Die, you Gringo son of a bitch!" in clear English. Jesus then shot the witness, but it was a shoulder wound from which he was expected to recover.

One of the deceased was found dead on the corner of a side street. He was known as something of an old desert rat. He lived alone a few miles out of town in an old shack. He did odd jobs when he could and helped out on the ranches in the county when they needed an extra hand. Apparently, he pulled an old lever action .30-30 rifle out of his gun rack and fired at the raiders from across the hood of his pickup truck. The response was that he was raked with automatic weapons fire. They counted forty holes in his pickup truck, and four in his chest. Nobody knew that he inflicted a lethal wound on one of the raiders. After they pulled off state route 70, Jesus ordered the body of his dead man stripped of all belongings and clothes, taken two hundred yards off the track and placed in a coulee. There, the coyotes and buzzards would make quick work of it. The clothes and belongings were burned back at camp.

The twelve-year-old girl was physically more mature than most girls her age. She just happened to be in the hardware store at the wrong time. She was there when they walked in and was immediately observed. Two dragged her down the aisle and into a corner where she was attacked. Stricken with fear, she offered little resistance at first. Then, she began to fight back. They beat her, raped her, and because she appeared to be Mexican, they let her live.

One rancher had the unlucky fortune to be driving his new pickup into town for a load of barbed wire and fencing staples. Unaware of the robbery occurring, he walked into the store only to be faced with a shotgun. One raider asked if that was a brand new truck, and when informed it was less than a month old, the raider demanded the keys. Reluctantly, the owner surrendered them. "Gracias, Señor," was the response, along with a twelve-gauge shotgun blast to the chest.

Interviews with forensic artists over the next few days resulted in composite drawings of a number of the raiders. These were computerized and broadcast across the southwest and to all FBI and Border Patrol offices nationwide.

No convoy of the assorted vehicles was noted passing through any of the adjacent towns. Dickenson then concluded that the raiders had turned into the desert somewhere. He sent Jahrling back to Marfa to hitch one of the station's two horse trailers to their Dodge and load their two saddle horses, two pack horses, saddle bags, and bedrolls. Dickenson continued questioning witnesses, everyone he could find until virtually all of the citizens of Ruidoso had been interviewed.

Jahrling arrived the next morning with the horses and trailer. They put the horses in a local corral and bought dried foods at the local store, enough for three days. Then they drove out of town looking for any indication of where the raiders had left the highway. When they found multiple tracks turning south off Highway 70, they pulled the trailer off the road two hundred meters and unloaded the horses. They unhitched the horse trailer, filled their canteens, packed two panniers on one pack horse and four five-gallon cans of water on the other. Dickenson checked his cell phone, put fresh batteries in his saddle bags, put their rifles in the scabbards and began tracking across the desert. It wasn't hard to follow so many automobile tracks, even across the hard pan. It wasn't long before they noticed the buzzards circling. They found a body, already partially devoured by coyotes, foxes and vultures.

Periodically, Dickenson would scan the landscape with binoculars, looking for any indication of an ambush. The second day out, they stopped at the Rio Grande. They were at the river's edge before they knew it. Dickenson immediately turned them around and backed off four hundred meters. "Unpack the pack horses, keep your rifle within arm's reach at all times. Keep our saddle horses ready in case we have to high tail it out of here. I'm going to the river for a closer look." When he came to within one hundred meters of the river's edge, he sat behind a mesquite tree and carefully surveyed the far side of the river. He thought he could discern where the vehicles had left on the far side. He was particularly interested in places within four hundred meters where a rifleman could hide to ambush anyone who dared cross the river. He crept slowly back to the camp.

"We'll move back behind that small rise and make camp for the night. Keep your rifle handy. I'll cook, and you picket, feed and water all of the horses." Dickenson began to gather dried mesquite wood by digging roots out of the ground. When he had enough, he built a small fire and set a pot of coffee on a camp grill along with a pot of water to boil rice and beans, to which he added a can of tuna fish. After supper, as the sun went down, they took their rifles and binoculars, and Dickenson led Jahrling down to the river. Dickenson took a GPS reading of the crossing site after glassing the area again. He telephoned the location in to his office and informed them they were camping for the night. The information was passed up the chain of command. Thirty minutes later, Dickenson's cell phone rang. He was given explicit orders not to cross the border but to maintain vigilance there for as long as they had sufficient food and water. Their job was to monitor any activity. An aircraft would be dispatched in the morning for photographic purposes.

When the information continued on up the line, the State Department informed the Mexican ambassador of what had occurred and that the raiders had been tracked into Mexico. Would the Mexican National Police please pick up the trail and continue the search? The Mexican ambassador was only too glad to agree to such accommodation. The National Headquarters of the Border Patrol requested aerial surveillance of the area from the U.S. Air Force. The President ordered a long dwelling drone equipped with high resolution and infra red cameras to be flown just inside the U.S. border but to take photographs for one hundred miles inside Mexico for any sign of the raiding force. Unfortunately, by this time, all the vehicles were parked inside Gonzalez's packing sheds. Aerial reconnaissance revealed nothing unusual.

———————•—•◦•—•◦•———————

Henry Dorn, second term Democratic President of the United States, called to Roberta, his secretary, to get the Mexican President on the phone.

"Good Morning, President Bustamante."

"And a good morning to you, President Dorn." Bustamante knew why Dorn was calling him but waited for him to breach the subject.

"I trust you heard of the cross-border raid on Ruidoso, Texas yesterday. We have circumstantial evidence that the raiders originated in Mexico. What do you make of it?"

"Most unfortunate, Mr. President. We are deeply troubled here in Mexico that such violence occurred. Our sympathies go out to all of the families whose loved ones were lost and wounded or otherwise injured. But tell me, what evidence is there that the raiders were from Mexico or that the raid was launched from Mexico?"

"For one, Mr. President, the vehicles were tracked from where they left the highway to where they crossed the Rio Grande. Our officers did not cross into Mexico to continue pursuit. Indeed, they chose to respect the sovereignty of Mexico."

"Please pass to those officers my respect for their professionalism. If they can identify the location, perhaps our officers can, as you Americans say in your western movies, 'pick up the trail.'"

Dorn gave Bustamante the coordinates reported by patrolmen Dickenson and Jahrling.

"I will have my officers on it immediately, both on the ground and in the air. We shall do our utmost to bring these murderers to justice. One problem I see, however, is a Mexican law that we cannot extradite criminals to a country where the possibility of capitol punishment exists. The state of Texas executes more felons than any of your other states. When we capture these vicious killers, some other arrangement will have to be made."

34

Dorn winced at the thought of the political fallout of such an arrangement. The demand for execution by the public would be intense, particularly in Texas. That might cost the Democratic Party Texas in the upcoming presidential election. Labor unions and nationalists were already making noises about tightening inspections on goods originating in Mexico. Some were beginning to float the idea of revoking the North American Free Trade Agreement. With the unemployment rate steady at 9%, it was gaining credence. Dorn certainly did not wish to return to trade wars and tariffs. That would make the international economic playing field lopsided once again, a theory near and dear to liberal hearts.

"Mr. President, I am certain that appropriate arrangements can and will be made. When you catch them, and the sooner the better, we will request extradition. I'll have our Attorney General look into it and get in touch with your people through your embassy here."

"President Dorn, I assure that Mexico will do all that is necessary to bring these rabid dogs to justice. Again, the most sincere condolences from the people of Mexico to the grieving families."

"Thank you, President Bustamante. I will immediately call again if there are any further developments on this end."

"Victory is the main object in war. If this is long delayed, weapons are blunted and morale depressed. When troops attack cities, their strength will be exhausted.

The worst policy is to attack cities; attack cities only when there is no alternative.

There has never been a protracted war from which a country has benefited.

They carry equipment from the homeland; they rely for provisions on the enemy. Thus, the army is plentifully provided with food.

Hence the wise general sees to it that his troops feed on the enemy, for one bushel of the enemy's provisions is equivalent to twenty of his; one hundredweight of enemy fodder to twenty hundred weight of his.

Generally in war, the best policy is to take a state intact; to ruin it is inferior to this.

When you plunder the countryside, divide your forces. When you conquer territory, divide the profits.

Set the troops to their tasks without imparting your designs; use them to gain advantage without revealing the dangers involved. Throw them into a perilous situation and they survive; put them in death ground and they will live. For when the army is placed in such a situation, it can snatch victory from defeat.

It is the business of a general to be serene and inscrutable, impartial and self controlled.

He should be capable of keeping his officers and men in ignorance of his plans."

> Sun Tzu
> The Art of War
> 500 B.C.

Chief of Staff of the People's Liberation Army Navy, Chang, Mao-lin strolled across the stage, arms at his side. Everyone in the room came to attention. "Generals and Admirals, be seated," he announced. "You have been called here to inform you of the first great military operation of the twenty-first century. As professional military officers, every commander among you is hereby relieved of your commands. Each commander is promoted. Each of you is about to receive a new command. Many of you that are chiefs of staff will also receive a command; most of you will replace your commanders in the regular army that I just relieved. Your packet contains your orders and the promotion order of your new rank. Commanders, your new commands are exclusively of the militias of the various provinces which are now assigned to you. You are called together for this briefing to provide you with the overall scope and intent of our plan. Much of what I say to one of you as an individual applies to all of you. Each of you will have considerable freedom of action in this undertaking. It must be that what is discussed here is not to be discussed with anyone except your respective staffs no lower than corps level on pain of death.

No one outside this room is to grasp the significance or enormity of this operation. You are to squelch any and all rumors regarding the nature of this war by any means necessary until all of our forces are in motion. The People's Liberation Army Navy is leaving many of the details to you on how you conduct the war in your particular area.

"As you know, as a nation, we are under tremendous pressure of population, insecurity of food supplies, questionable sources of raw materials for our industries and energy requirements to continue at our current levels of production and population. Above all, there is tremendous restlessness in our rural areas. Therefore, the People's Liberation Army Navy has devised a plan to expand our geographical base to include sources for all of our required raw materials, petroleum, and foodstuffs for the foreseeable future.

"Generals and Admirals, another major goal of this operation is to acquire land for our Han Chinese people. In this regard, your primary mission will be the elimination of the current occupants of your area of operation. Your primary troops will be the militias which you have so aggressively trained. Your reports all indicate that your militia units are fully trained, manned, equipped, and psychologically prepared to carry out their assignments. We shall soon see.

"Your Army fronts will vary somewhat in size, according to the difficulty of your mission. Terrain, your opponents, the significance of the front, transportation, logistics, seasons and weather and so on have all been taken into consideration. Some of you will have more significant resistance than others. Those areas of operation will receive priority for logistical support. All forces of the People's Liberation Army Navy will be fully involved, although many units will be held as a strategic reserve. Your forces will, in effect, be expected to live off the land which you are responsible to seize. As you are all aware, our food reserves and transportation capabilities are our most potential liabilities.

"Without discussing lesser details, the major thrusts will occur after our allies initiate their actions to tie down potential western adversaries. This will preclude the Americans from bringing their weight against us. We have a firm belief that they, the Americans, will not risk nuclear war under the circumstances. We do believe that they might commit limited resources to their previous treaty obligations, but will not extend any efforts to our major thrusts. All of our intelligence and indicators strongly support this belief that the Americans will not interfere with our major operations. In fact, they lack the capability to do so, and no one knows this better than they do. We do not anticipate any other body, such as the United Nations, to contribute anything more strongly than words against our actions.

"We are making major thrusts to essentially conquer much of Asia and half of Africa. One front will be responsible for the Malayan peninsula. Another front will engage the Indian subcontinent. A third front will engage the Central Asian Republics.

This will be the most difficult and largest front of all and will, consequently, receive the greatest logistical support. Fifty million militia personnel will be assigned to this front, and more will be available as required. This front has tentatively, as its final western geographical objective, the Caspian Sea. The Caspian Sea, that is, unless the Iranians decide to engage us. We do not anticipate any difficulties with the Russians. We will make clear to the Americans, Japanese and the Europeans that Iraq and Saudi Arabia and their oil belong to them. This we will guarantee. This should reduce the potential for their involvement.

"The last front will be Africa. Actually, we believe that this will be the least difficult front of all. Africa is devastated by famine, wars, anarchy and AIDs. The People's Liberation Army Navy will begin landing forces on the east African coast and continue to do so according to our limited seaborne transportation assets. We have converted a fleet of merchant ships into troop carriers. We will land a battalion a day as a minimum at each beachhead. There are a number of beachheads all along the coast, according to intermediate objectives. These troop ships will make round trips until the entire front is delivered. The initial battalions are expected to seize and protect their assigned harbors. Thereafter, each battalion is expected to immediately move inland to make way for the next day's arrivals. Our Chief of Naval Operations has accordingly worked out the naval strategy and will discuss it with the individual African Front Commander.

"The Southeast Asian Front, the Malayan area, also has naval assets assigned for its protection. This Front Commander will work in consort with the Chief of the Peoples Navy.

"Perhaps some of you have guessed over the last few years that this concept was being planned as a result of the establishment of the depot system in the various districts in the west and south.

"While all of the strategy and some of the operational details have been worked out, each of you will be called to the People's Liberation Army Navy Headquarters to discuss your individual assignments over the next few months. For the most part, the tactical and some of operational aspects will be left to you. This is what will be discussed with you at these meetings. Your individual fronts are assigned code names that are known only to yourselves as the Commanders, and to the PLAN. Chemical weapons are authorized down to the divisional level. Our air armies are modest in size and capability. Many are aware we have concentrated on building and acquiring ground attack aircraft. Land forces will be supported to a limited degree by our air forces; each front commander will have an assigned numbered air force. The land force commander will have overall command and responsibility for the air force supporting him.

"The Central Committee and the Joints Chiefs of the PLAN recognize that this is a tremendous undertaking, a historical but not quite unprecedented event, not even in scale. Warriors a thousand years ago, and more than once, did what we are about to do, and did it very well. We can, and will, do no less. I will take a few questions from the assigned commanding general of each Army Front at the end of the general guidance.

"Lights out, first presentation, please."

The PowerPoint projection on the screen showed a map of Asia. On it were drawn three large red, curving arrows, flowing out of China to the west and south. "I will call upon each of you new commanders in turn, so that you might know who is on your flanks, what your boundaries are, and what the strategic objectives for each are. We, the Chinese people, are about to ensure the future of our nation and our people as the greatest power on earth in this twenty-first century. This is a massive undertaking, one that will be on par with the Great Revolution and what the west calls

World War II. This entire operation is to be completed within an absolute maximum of eighteen months. Twelve months is desirable, but in some cases, that might be somewhat unrealistic.

"General Liu, Lien-chang, you are hereby promoted to Army Front I Commander. Your region of responsibility will more or less be the Malayan peninsula. You will recall we signed a treaty with the Republic of the Philippines, Vietnam, Malaysia, and Brunei in 2001 called the Treaty of Conduct of Parties to settle all claims of territory in the South China Sea. We are now abrogating that Treaty Conduct of Parties in the South China Sea, without telling the other signatories, of course. Our economic and military assistance programs over the last ten years in Burma, Laos and Cambodia have provided us with excellent intelligence. Their armies are modest but reasonably equipped, mostly as light infantry, as you know. One of the major goals of our agents has been the infiltration of the Islamic militant groups throughout the region. I am happy to report that this effort has been most successful. These people are to be eliminated above all others. The necessary information on these groups, the Guragon Mujahideen, Wau Kah Rah, the Kampualan Mujahideen, and so on, will be in your office in twenty-four hours.

"We acceded to the Association of South Eastern Asian Nations, ASEAN, by signing the Treaty of Amity and Cooperation, in which we pledged to resolve all disputes by peaceful means in 2003. We are about to absolve that treaty as well. Your westward boundary, General Liu, will be the Irawaddy River. You are to include the cities of Rangoon and Singapore in your endeavors unless other arrangements are made at the last minute. They are the prizes at the end of your long march. Do not invade the Philippines or Sumatra at this point. Rather, consolidate your gains; eliminate the great majority of the population, as many as you can. Eliminate all of the ethnic Vietnamese. Spare no one. There are two million Chinese and people of Chinese descent in Vietnam. These are to be spared if at all possible. Their loyalty has always remained with our mother country, and they will be an asset. Indeed, they have supplied us with much intelligence. Malaysia has six million Chinese, and Singapore holds two million Chinese. Those of Singapore might be more difficult to sort out. Many Vietnamese will retreat to the western highlands with the intent of conducting guerilla warfare as they have so successfully done in the past. That is not to be allowed. This is why the Irawaddy River was chosen as your western boundary. You have both flanks of the highlands. International borders are meaningless. You are to kill them by whatever means, making special effort to do so before they can retreat to the interior highlands. You will not have any heavy weapons to speak of at your disposal. Limited mortar and light rocketry will be your artillery. Your air forces will be quite limited. Therefore, you must rely almost wholly on your light infantry; indeed, that is essentially your total force. Your men must, to a considerable degree, live off the land. Your area of responsibility is a major rice producing region of the world. Take advantage of it. Your lines of communication will be long. Commandeer whatever civilian transport is available that you choose. Dependable resupply for your area could be questionable as a result of the lack of transportation assets, particularly if you do not swiftly complete your mission.

"We have, more or less, one year's supply of food for your armies. We have modest medical supplies in storage as well. Stockpiling of anti-malarials, antibiotics and surgical consumables has been a modest priority. Your medical battalions are reasonably well staffed. A number of your units, however, are composed of HIV infected personnel. You must consider the results of expending food and medicines on your wounded and ill soldiers who suffer from an incurable illness against completion of your mission. What guidance you give to your medical personnel in this regard is up to you. Abandoning such will not be frowned upon. Whatever your decision is in this respect, make absolutely sure that your policy is rigorously enforced. Do not hesitate to use the complete and absolute authority we are giving you to conduct this mission.

"You must complete your mission prior to the consumption of that reserve of food and medicines. There must be no support base for the conduct of guerilla warfare. Hence, you must show no mercy in destroying the elements which would support any guerilla warfare. Each village is to be raided, all of its food seized, and its inhabitants killed. Your armies will be composed of the armies of the following provinces that are listed in your orders, chief among them are Yunnan, Kwangsi, and Kwangtung. We estimate that totals about fifteen million men. Since we have never had

41

organizations higher than regiments in our militia units, they are arbitrarily being assigned into divisions, corps and armies. Officers will be promoted to the appropriate ranks for these higher levels of organization. Your staff and your corps and division commanders have been arbitrarily and initially selected for you, many of them you know. Your staff is composed of regular People's Liberation Army Navy generals. They are among the best we have for their particular specialties. Many of your higher militia commanders will be initially insecure, indecisive and hesitant. They will probably lean very heavily upon you and your staff and upon their staffs. It is up to you to work with them and bring them to the appropriate level of their commands as quickly as possible. Do not take a great length of time, however, to do this. If any of them are slow to respond or less than capable, it is your responsibility to immediately replace them with someone who is. Ruthlessness is to be a primary consideration in their selection. A bad decision is considered better than no decision.

"If you need to make a very modest amphibious assault along the coast, coordinate with Headquarters of the People's Liberation Army Navy. We can, at best, mount a two-division sized force for an amphibious flanking movement. We would prefer not to have to do that, but we recognize the possibility that it might be necessary, especially around the larger port cities such as Haiphong.

"Do you have any questions at this time, General?"

"Yes, Comrade General Chang. If our new commands are to be exclusively of these militia units, what role will the regular People's Liberation Army Navy play in this war?"

"An excellent question, Comrade General. The regular army will be held as a trained reserve. There are elements to this plan that are not to be revealed today. We anticipate that they will not be utilized, at least, that is our hope. Nevertheless, we have a trained, standing army ready, if necessary, to meet any contingency. Any further questions?"

"No, Comrade General. Thank you."

CHAPTER 4

"General Tsai, Ting-wen. You are hereby promoted to Commander, Army Front II. You have a very large territory to conquer and possibly an extremely tough opposition to overcome. We have faith that you will accomplish your mission with speed and skill. Your objectives include the Indian peninsula and the destruction of the remains of the Indian and Pakistani armies. You will attack after those antagonists have exhausted themselves. Your eastern boundary is the Irawaddy River. You will invade through Assam and sweep west and south. Your westward boundary is just east of the Iranian border. Pakistan and Afghanistan are yours, but you are to approach no closer than 150 kilometers to the Iranian border. We do not wish to excite the Americans too much. Your northern boundary is the Himalayas, the northern borders of Nepal and Bhutan. These small states are of little consequence, although you might have some minor irritation from the many retired Ghurkas still living there. Much of the guidance which I just gave to General Liu also applies to you. Elimination of the population is the primary objective. Under certain circumstances, specific individuals in India are to be spared, if they can be identified before their demise. Those to be spared when possible are scientists and engineers, faculties of technical institutions and universities and the like. This does not apply to any Muslims anywhere. We will not allow any jihads to be waged behind our backs.

"Your job might become extremely complicated. At the appropriate time, Pakistan will attack India in Kashmir. It is quite possible, indeed likely, that a nuclear exchange will occur. We anticipate that India and Pakistan will attrit each other, either by nuclear fires or conventional warfare. We anticipate that India will be the winner. With luck, their air forces will destroy much of the other's forces, both ground and air. The ground forces of both are heavily armed with man portable surface to air missiles, thankfully supplied by the United States. Such an exchange is expected to last but a few weeks. Only upon the order from the People's Liberation Army Navy are you to give the mobilization order to your forces. I repeat, you do not issue the mobilization order until you are ordered to do so by this Headquarters. That is imperative. Your job is to pick up the pieces, such as they will be, and ensure that neither will constitute a threat, nor be able to conduct any form of guerilla warfare. We believe that Pakistan has about twenty-five nuclear warheads that range from five to twenty-five kilotons in yield, and perhaps twenty-five more that are up to one hundred kilotons in yield. It is possible, even likely, that a number of Indian cities will disappear under mushroom clouds. Most likely, so will Karachi, Rawalpindi and Islamabad, Lahore, and perhaps Peshawar in retaliation. If the latter disappears, your job will be much easier. The Khyber Pass will be open to you, provided, of course, it has not been closed by landslides. How you deal with radioactive areas and contaminated resources is up to you. You are to conquer Afghanistan. Their practice of revenge must be greatly respected. It is important, therefore, that no Afghan lives. What and how your troops treat or do to these people is of no consequence as long as you kill them.

"You will have approximately twenty-five million people to accomplish your mission. They are the militias of the provinces of Hopeh, Anwhei, Hupeh, Kweichow, Hunan, and Szechuan.

"Any Questions, Comrade General?"

Tsai stood, came to attention, and responded, "Comrade General, how will this Indo-Pakistani war be initiated? The timing here can be very crucial."

"You are absolutely correct, Comrade General. Certain events will be initiated to ensure that this conflict is started at the appropriate time.

Pakistan will enter into the war full of confidence due to a secret treaty we have with them. We have what they call the Sino-Pakistan Mutual Assistance Treaty, which guarantees we will come to each other's aid in the event of war with India. We have supplied Pakistan with small amounts of plutonium and technology so that they have manufactured a modest number of artillery and aerial deliverable tactical nuclear warheads, as well as intermediate range rockets, as part of this treaty. By doing so, the International Atomic Energy Association and inspectors have no knowledge of the size and capabilities of their nuclear arsenal. This has bolstered their confidence in our participation in such a conflict.

"Any further questions, Comrade General Tsai?"

"None, Comrade General Chang."

"General Shen, De-ming, you are hereby the Commander of Army Front III. Your mission is perhaps the most difficult of all. At least, you have the greatest distance to travel." This brought a chuckle from the group of generals.

"We have chosen you because you are the most able of the commanders that we have. We are assigning you the majority of our resources, men and material. You have one of our greatest objectives to achieve." General Shen bowed his head to General Chang for the compliment. Chang continued, "Your objective, General Shen, is the Caspian Sea basin. You are to capture the oil fields intact. We want the oil, not a fire fighting mission as occurred in Kuwait in the first Gulf War. Your axis of approach is that of the old Silk Road. Anxi will, of course, be your initial line of departure for your main axes of approach. General Wun, Chief of Ground Forces, has determined that your forces will move along the roads both north and south of the Takla Makan desert. The provincial commander there will fall under your command once you cross into his province, the Xinjiang Uygur Zizhiqu. His forces are modest and composed of local Han Chinese. No Uigher Muslims are included. They are well trained for the environment from which they came. I am sure you will use them accordingly. Commands from some of the eastern provinces will also come under your command to ensure that you have sufficient manpower to accomplish your task.

"You will skirt both north and south of the Takla Makan basin in your southern axis. You will drive north of the Tien Shan Mountains as a separate axis. Put your most able commander in command of this axis of approach. Depots have been built and stocked along your routes of march for your constant supply. We have made the greatest logistical planning and effort on behalf of this mission.

"Perhaps this is the most important objective of all. It includes the states of Kazakhstan, Uzbekistan, Kyrgyzstan, Turkmenistan, and Tajikistan. We must seize the Caspian Sea oil reserves. Your southern boundary is that of 150 kilometers from the border with Iran. If Iranian forces attack you, by all means, respond in kind, or better still, kill them ten times over. Iran is far more heavily armed in terms of heavy forces, missiles, and aircraft than your forces will be. Consequently, you will receive a significant upgrade in handheld surface to air missiles, anti-tank missiles, heavy machine guns, self propelled anti-aircraft units, trucks and heavy mortars. If they attack, it will be along your lines of communication. If they deploy nuclear weapons, we will annihilate all of their cities with nuclear fires launched from here in China. Therefore, you must destroy their local population, pursuing them and living off the land as necessary. The Iranians have not realized that heavy forces can be a liability of sorts. Your northern boundary is more or less Russia. Russia does not have the capability to offer you any significant resistance, and we believe that they will be intelligent enough not to do so. Indeed, we will propose to them that this is an opportunity to subdue, once and forever, their breakaway province of Chechnya. After all, they owe much harm to Chechnya for all of the terrorist activities against Russia.

"The former Soviet Union's Confederation of Independent States is so loosely bound that its members cannot organize a united front against you. Their military establishments are very weak and extremely poorly trained. Graft and corruption reign in all of them. They should not present you with any serious obstacles. Indeed, they might provide you with an additional source of weapons.

"There are a number of larger cities in your area of responsibility, along your axis of attack. You are to isolate these cities by destruction of their transportation nets but not by siege; cities such as Alma Alta, Pishkek, Dushanbe, Tashkent, and so on. Starve them out. Whenever possible, isolate them, reduce their populations when it is convenient. Starve them, dehydrate them so that they die of thirst, or whatever, but do not become bogged down by laying siege to them. Cut their lines of supply. If you let them escape out of the cities, it is easier to kill them in the countryside than in the cities. The arid environment there is not conducive to the survival of large numbers of people. Completely cut off all food, water, relief, and whatever. Practice a scorched earth policy. Indeed, there will be no other choice in order to feed your troops. We do not have sufficient food reserves for more than twelve months of campaigning. Turn your back on rapes, but do not allow pillage and plundering for anything but food, water and weapons. Leave nothing to sustain the enemy. We canot tolerate guerilla warfare being waged against our logistical lines of communication.

"I suspect the Iranians will give you the greatest difficulty if they enter the conflict. We think, but do not know for certain, that Iran has built a substantial supply of chemical weapons. It is therefore imperative that at first indication of their use, you annihilate any units, depots, manufacturing facilities, and so on that contribute to their use. Tehran and Tabriz will probably be your most difficult cities with their large populations. Make use of captured enemy weapons wherever possible. You will have little heavy artillery support. That is another reason to bypass the cities. We do not expect any of them to be able to withstand not being supplied for a year. No doubt they will turn to cannibalism in some instances. That would be the moment to reduce the population. Environmental war will play a significant part of your successful campaign. Your troops will be vaccinated against cholera, typhoid, our engineered strains of tularemia, and paratyphoid. These biological weapons will be made available to you in the form of liquids for contamination of water supplies, wells, reservoirs, what have you, should you decide to deploy them. In any case, your troops should disinfect and boil all water from questionable sources before consuming it to ensure that we do not infect ourselves as the Japanese did in World War II. Tularemia will be provided as aerosolized sprays from aircraft to aid in reduction of urban areas. If necessary, aerosolized bubonic plague, engineered to produce the pneumonic form, will also be made available. All of our troops will be vaccinated against our own agents. It is transmissible between people, so we expect it to spread through their urban populations. We anticipate these will be your major weapons

47

systems against the cities. Chemical agents, nerve agents, both persistent and non-persistent, will also be available for unusual tactical situations. Guard these supplies carefully. Your weakest area will be the very modest air support available to you. You must use it wisely and sparingly.

"The Caspian Sea is, itself, a significant problem. Be very careful on this. Skirting it on the north means going close to the Russian frontier. At this time, we do not wish to engage the Russians. Therefore, we will halt at the eastern side of the Caspian Sea. If things go extremely well, then we will consider flanking the Caspian and entering the Caucasus region. No doubt the Russians would dearly like to see us destroy all of the people of the Caucasus, especially those in Chechnya, but they might fear us even more. We have already initiated subtle talks with the Russians. We have not indicated our plans at all, but rather are attempting to divine their perceptions and possible reactions. Recall that the Russians have been fighting the peoples of the Caucasus off and on for almost two hundred years. The initial war of Russian conquest of Chechnya lasted nearly half a century. The Caucasus peoples are fanatical Muslims. The oil fields on the western shore, however, are a prize worth considering. Your militias will come primarily from Honan, Shansi, Shantung, Shensi, and Kansu. Do you have any questions, General Shen?"

"What of the satellite imagery and communications of the Americans, Russians, Japanese and French that will track us? Is this a concern?"

"At the appropriate time, their satellites will be blinded. Their communications will be severely crippled. They will essentially be ignorant of your progress."

"Not shown on this map is another front; we will take southern Africa. Some of your other Army Front Commanders might be involved in this particular operation as well. It is possible, General Liu, and General Tsai, that when you have demonstrated your considerable skills by completing your peninsular conquests ahead of time and with relatively modest losses, your armies will be transported by the PLAN to the eastern shore of Africa. The mineral wealth of southern Africa is tremendous. It is sufficient to guarantee many of our mineral requirements for the remainder of this century. Contingency plans have been made.

"Admiral Su, Teh-shen is in command of the naval task force for the invasion of Africa. Troops will embark from our southern ports and disembark at Dar Es Salaam, Mombasa, and Tanga. With foresight, Singapore, Haiphong and other peninsular ports will be available. This will be a continuous amphibious operation, with transports traveling in circles, constantly feeding in fresh battalions. These naval forces will be under constant guard by our submarine forces, destroyers and cruisers. Admiral Su will be in complete command of this naval operation while at sea.

"Generals Liu and Tsai, in this operation your troops will remain under your command, but you will be subordinate commanders to the Army Front IV Commander.

That is you, General Fong, Fu-chen. All that I have said regarding the other front commanders applies to you as well. You are to drive across Africa until you reach the Atlantic Ocean in Angola. Once you have divided Africa, you are to turn your troops south until you reach the Cape of Good Hope. You will find very little military resistance. Anarchy reigns over most of Africa; famine, AIDS, brigandage, and revolts rage across the continent. Africa is so riddled with HIV infection that your troops should be strictly disciplined regarding sexual experiences with the Africans; not that most of your troops aren't already AIDS infected. This constant feeding of battalions to your front should allow you to have an army stretching across Africa. When you reach Angola, they can do a left face and march south. If it becomes necessary to forage earlier, then they can turn south at your discretion. The timing of this operation is such that the grain harvests should just be in or about to be harvested in most of your theaters of operation. A major concern is that those we are about to conquer do not destroy those foodstuffs in a scorched earth policy. We do not want a repeat of either Napoleon's or of the Germans' retreat in World War II from western Russia. Hopscotch your battalions for rest if necessary, but continue the attack as relentlessly as possible to preclude destruction of these food stocks.

"We have armed and are feeding small paramilitary units in various African countries. Most are company sized, a few are of battalion size. These units do our bidding and have prepared much of the way for you in some areas without realizing what they have done. At the appropriate time, you are to eliminate these units by any means you find necessary. We will stop our food shipments to them several weeks prior to the debarkation for Africa. Most of them will be half-starved by then. They will have relieved the populations in their areas of all foods to feed themselves. Most will greet you as allies and liberators. That is a convenient time for their elimination. Disarm them, and then kill them.

"Questions, General Fong?"

"None, Comrade General."

"Good. Each of you Front Commanders will be supplied with limited amounts of several different nerve agents for use as area weapons. You will have limited aircraft for their application after you have seized local airfields. Use them wisely, not as routine weapons, but only on special occasions. Perhaps persistent nerve agent would be indicated for several of the urban environments that cause you difficulty. We will go to great lengths to avoid the use of nuclear fires. We do not wish to destroy that which we intend to occupy. We have identified nuclear storage areas as priority targets in the event that our enemies have any left after attacking one another.

"For those units which will experience cold weather, appropriate cold weather clothing will be supplied to your units after they are assembled. They are to be instructed in cold weather injury prevention at the time of issuance. We will not repeat the mistakes of the Germans at Stalingrad in Operation Barbarossa. Further details will be discussed with you individually.

"Generals, I wish you all the success in your missions. Dismissed."

CHAPTER 5

"**Y**ou are pleased with the results of, shall I say, your expedition to Ruidoso?"

"Oh, most certainly, Señor! A very good time was had by all," laughed Jesus Gonzalez.

"Well, when do you think you will be ready for another adventure?"

"Soon, Señor Ito. But let me ask, why is it that you are interested in minor annoyances along the American border? What is the reason for all of this to you?"

"I have my reasons, but they are of no concern to you. What is important to you is that you make money and gain prestige. What now is the size of your army?"

"I can call fifty men in twenty-four hours. There are many more who would join us. I hear of many inquiries, but I have not been interested in accepting people of whom I know little. It is dangerous. One never knows who is a Federale or an American of Mexican descent that has turned his back on his mother country."

"Do you think you could put together an army of one hundred and fifty, or perhaps even two hundred men?"

"This I can do, if I have support. Support costs money. This many men must be fed and trained and equipped. This is no small matter. Then there is the cost of transportation. These hills and deserts are large. Places to go are far between. To move men in such numbers requires many vehicles. I do not wish to use large trucks that are easier to identify. Rather, I wish to use pickups and vans that can blend into the community. If I put no more than four men in a van and three in a pickup, that is many pickups and vans. Where will I get such a number? We must also expand our base here. We will need several more buildings, maybe even another well. This many vehicles must be hidden from the air. That means packing sheds to double as garages. I will need mechanics to care for them. Fuel will be required for them. How can I control that many men unless I can keep them in camp when we are not out on our business? It is too easy for men who are new at this to talk too much. All of this means a bigger base. It can be here on this farm, but it must be enlarged. Then there is the question of weapons and ammunition. I do not have nearly enough for so many men."

"All this I understand, El Jefe. I have brought money for these very things. You are to have an underground fuel storage tank installed. More packing sheds are to be built. You are to recruit your men. More vehicles will be purchased and driven to you. Several mechanics are to be hired by you to maintain the vehicles. A new dining hall is to be built. It will be well equipped. You are to hire cooks of your choice. A word of caution. Have your lieutenants check out each of these people who will join you. In three months, you are to have all this completed. In this suitcase is the money to have your new packing sheds, fuel storage tank and mess hall built. Get started immediately. Weapons you will receive. You will receive five new tractors, farm implements and spare parts. With them will be more automatic rifles, a large quantity of ammunition, half a dozen machine guns, rocket propelled grenades, and hand grenades.

"There is also much money here for the police. Pay them what is necessary to ignore your activities. In fact, if at all possible, purchase information from them on your new recruits. Do not be penurious. Pay them well. It is better to have them on your side, whatever it costs.

"Another thing, I noticed marijuana growing adjacent to some of the tomato plants close to the road. Get rid of it. There is to be no marijuana or drugs grown on this operation. We do not want the American Drug Enforcement Agency or their lackeys in the Federales out looking for marijuana, which they can detect from airplanes. We are not here to compete with those who make their money in this way. Rather, our business is relieving the Americans of their money in other ways. Your new men are not to bring their wives, children, or girlfriends. If necessary, hire a dozen girls to service your men and keep them here on the base. This is very important if you wish to rise to be a leader in the image of Poncho Villa."

Jesus Gonzalez chuckled to himself. *Who is this arrogant Japanese asshole who thinks I can rise to be the equal of Poncho Villa who commanded an army of fifty thousand and captured Mexico City?* Still, the thought fascinated Gonzalez.

"If you can furnish me with the money to do all of these things, they will be done. First, we must have the buildings. We will identify our recruits. When the building is all done, we will call in the new men and begin training. Is there any particular place in Yankee Land you wish me to visit? It takes time to plan and determine what is there that is worth taking and how best to take it."

"Your next objective will be Alpine, Texas."

"Ah, this is a worthy, as you say, objective. It will take at least two hundred men, perhaps more. We can cause much confusion and terror. Still, if I have more than two hundred men, how much more could I do."

"Recruit who and what you need. Here is two hundred and fifty thousand U.S. dollars to initiate your program. A week from now, vehicles will be arriving at this place. At first, there will be just a few. As the packing sheds are finished, more will arrive at a much faster rate."

"How Señor Ito, can I contact you?"

"You cannot. My people will keep me informed as they deliver the pickups and vans. This they will do one or a few at a time. If you have a message for me, give it to one of them. Make it in a sealed envelope so that they will not read it. One other thing, on your next raid, no one is to be left behind. Certainly, no one is to be left behind alive. Do you understand my meaning, El Jefe?"

"Si, Señor. The dead cannot talk."

"Precisely. Adios, Jefe Gonzalez." With that, Ito and his two bodyguards climbed into their air-conditioned van and drove off.

"Hernando," Jesus called to his farm manager. "Pull out all of the marijuana plants. Leave not one. Do it today, before the sun sets."

53

"All of them, El Jefe? We made some nice money with the last crop, selling it to the dealers in the next state, Sonora."

"Yes, Hernando, all of them. We will not do any drugs of any kind anymore. Our other operations are expanding, and we do not want any trouble from anyone over what, in comparison, will be modest income for us. Take what men you need to do this and chop it up and mix it in with the cattle feed. Let the cows get high, if they can. Do not burn it. We do not want to send any smoke signals to anyone. Things will be a bit different around here from now on. We are expanding all of our other operations. We will have new buildings, a new dining hall, a new garage, new men, and new tractors coming. These are not things to be advertised. Go now and take care of the marijuana."

Jesus Gonzalez drove into Ojinaga and then into Texas to discuss and order the construction company to dig for an underground five-thousand-gallon fuel tank. He spent the next three days discussing what he wanted with a contractor. He explained that he was acquiring the adjacent farms and wished to consolidate all these previously separate operations in one location. The existing sheds on these other farms were too dilapidated to bother moving. None had a dining facility of note. He stopped at a fuel distributor and discussed with him that he wanted to order a new fuel tank, to have it installed and filled as soon as possible. He was enlarging his farm and he wanted to ensure that he always had fuel on hand. No, he was ordering a new fleet of gasoline driven tractors, and many of his other farm implements used gasoline. The irrigation pumps consumed a considerable quantity of gasoline each month. He raised tomatoes, cucumbers, melons, broccoli, and alfalfa on irrigated land, and had a small feedlot operation. Therefore, he wanted gasoline, not diesel fuel.

He gave the name of the construction company to the fuel distributor so that they could coordinate their work. The contractor said he could have the hole for the fuel tank prepared in two weeks, the packing sheds in four weeks, the mechanic's garage in ten weeks and the dining facility in eight to ten weeks, depending upon delivery of the refrigeration units. The fuel distributor would have the plumbers install two fueling islands with two pumps each. The fuel dealer thought it very strange that anyone would want to purchase gasoline driven tractors instead of diesel engine tractors, strange indeed. Why would a farm require four pumps for gasoline, even such a large one? A five-thousand-gallon fuel tank would require about a month for construction and delivery from Los Angeles if he phoned in an order that day. Since they all agreed that all work would be paid in cash in American dollars with a sizeable down payment in cash and paid in full upon completion, and much of the money would not be entered into the books, both the construction contractor and the fuel distributor decided not to pursue this question with Mr. Gonzalez any further.

———————————•◦•◉•◦•———————————

Ito returned to Long Beach, California. His real name was Chan, Daling, and he was a minor shipping clerk in the COSCO shipping company. He composed a hand written message in Mandarin requiring the shipment of five tractors, three plows, three cultivators, two discs, three hundred AK-47s in semi-automatic mode only, two hundred and fifty thousand rounds of ammunition, twenty rocket propelled grenade launchers, one hundred rocket grenades, and two hundred hand grenades. The weapons were to be packed with the tractors and implements and labeled as spare parts. The tractors and implements were to be of Japanese manufacture, shipped to China and repackaged with appropriate re-stenciling. The bill was to specify delivery to COSCO at their Long Beach terminal warehouse but from Yokahama as the port of origin. From there, they would be trucked to a non-existent dealer in Tijuana, Mexico. Since the ultimate destination was Mexico, it would pass directly through the American inspection system without being opened or inspected in any way. Half of the records for such inspections were still generated on paper, and only half on computers. The inspectors simply had too much to inspect all those which had a destination in California for farm implements destined for Mexico and so would wave them on through without a second thought. He delivered the message in a sealed envelope to his COSCO boss who was attending a party that night where he would pass it to a Chinese intelligence officer from their embassy who was in the guise of a chauffer.

Then Ito and his bodyguards went to lunch at their favorite little Mexican restaurant. Ito told Miguel, who routinely waited on them, that after they were served in a small back room, they should have a little chat. Miguel smiled, knowing that this meant a little more business for the organization of which he was a member. After they finished their meal, Miguel joined them.

"Miguel, I trust there are people in your organization who know much about automobiles?"

"Indeed, we have a number of men who specialize in automobiles." Miguel smiled to himself. A number of men in his organization had been or were still active as professional car thieves. They would steal cars throughout the American west and Midwest and drive them into Mexico. When necessary, chop shops would alter vehicle identification numbers and repaint them. Forged titles were a routine part of the business.

"I want your people, four of them who are very knowledgeable of automobiles, to purchase, not steal, a number of used automobiles for my company. We are only interested in used vans, sport utility vehicles and pickups that are in good condition. We are especially interested in four-wheel drive vehicles. We wish to build a fleet of these. Are you interested?"

"Of course, Mr. Ito, we are interested." Miguel saw an opportunity here. They could steal a number of them, forge the Vehicle Identification Numbers and titles and sell them to Mr. Ito's company at a substantial profit. A mix of legally purchased vehicles and stolen ones would be good cover. They could claim that they had no knowledge that some of them were stolen.

"How, Mr. Ito, do you wish to accomplish this?"

"I will provide you with cash. I expect a very strict accounting. Do not attempt to steal from my company. We will pay you very well for your services, and that should be enough compensation."

Miguel saw a veiled threat here, and he looked at the two bodyguards who always accompanied Mr. Ito. He knew they were very good at their profession. Their knuckles were capped with connective tissue, and the outside edges of their hands were hard as horn. In the times they had come in short sleeved shirts, he observed that they were very muscular, very lithe, and their eyes constantly darted around them. Nothing missed their gaze. When they came in sport coats, he occasionally observed a handgun imprinted under the jackets. He had no doubt they were very well trained in the martial arts. Since Mr. Ito never identified exactly who he was or what company he represented, he had initially assumed that Mr. Ito must be a very big man in a very big company to have such guardians accompany him everywhere.

"When do you wish this to begin, Mr. Ito?"

"In two days, we will come again and bring money. Again, all purchases are to be legal. Not one of your people is to buy more than one vehicle at the same place. Ideally, you will buy them from individuals who advertise them in the newspapers and neighborhood flyers. It is permissible to occasionally buy one from a dealer, but that is not to occur very often. These vehicles are to be delivered to a parking lot of which I will inform you when I bring the money. The lot will be locked. I will give you four keys to the padlock, one for each of your men. The vehicles are to be immediately parked and left in the lot. They are not to be used for any purpose by your people whatsoever. A duplicate ignition key and door key, if required, will be made and placed in the glove compartment of each vehicle. Each vehicle is to have a spare tire in excellent shape. If a spare tire is missing, or is not in good condition, then have it replaced. Each gas tank is to be filled. Your people are to do all of this before parking the vehicle in the lot. They are to keep receipts for everything. Our bookkeepers must insist on total accountability. Again, you will be more than amply rewarded for your efforts. Is there anything you do not understand?"

"How many do you wish to purchase, Mr. Ito?"

"Ultimately, we wish to have a fleet of twenty four-wheel drive pickups, and forty vans or sport utility vehicles, also all four-wheel drive. This is to be accomplished over the next eight weeks. When this is done, I will have more work for your organization."

"We will be glad to assist you in establishing your fleet of vehicles, Mr. Ito."

"Good, then we will be back in two days. Please tell the chef to put more chiles in my tacos next time. I like spicy foods." Mr. Wan smiled and left thirty dollars on the table for lunch. One bodyguard preceded Mr. Wan out, the other followed him.

—•◦•◦•—

Jesus Gonzalez returned to his farm, slept with his mistress, and presented her with a bottle of perfume and a new dress that he purchased in Texas. Then he packed a suitcase, took twenty thousand dollars in cash from his safe, and left for Alpine, Texas.

In thirty days, Jesus Gonzales had a fleet of forty vans and twenty pickups. Mr. Ito's people began delivery before the packing sheds/garages were completed. Within a day or two of their delivery to the parking lot, they disappeared. Mr. Ito did not want Miguel's people to learn their destination.

On various previous occasions, Miguel had different gang members follow Mr. Ito until they learned the location of his office at the China Ocean Shipping Company, or commonly called COSCO. Subtle inquiries of Mexican American workers at COSCO revealed to Miguel that Mr. Ito was a senior clerk in the shipping section. Nobody really knew exactly what aspect or cargo that he managed, only that they were considered high value items. Electronic goods, stereos, televisions, optics were not included in the categories of shipments he managed. When this was reported to Miguel, his suspicions were further aroused. Shipping clerks did not usually have bodyguards for routine dining. Miguel had the vehicles followed to the Mexican border. Using cell phones and different vehicles, switching them off, Miguel's people ultimately determined their destination as Jesus Gonzalez's farm. To be certain, Miguel had a transmitter placed in a Dodge Ram pickup.

When delivery of more than thirty vehicles had occurred, Miguel selected a particularly bright and ruthless but promising gang member for a particular job. Gomez was an illegal alien who had illegally entered the U.S. five years earlier. His command of English was as good as that of a second generation Mexican American. As a teenager, he worked as a field hand growing and picking tomatoes, cucumbers, peppers and melons.

Now twenty-six, he was skilled with a knife and his bare hands with four murders to his credit.

"I want you to return to Sonora for a few weeks, but not your old haunts. Here is ten thousand dollars. Buy a car in Nogales - legally. Then find a small town to hang around in for a week or two. After you have acquired the local flavor, drive to Ojinaga in Chihuahua. Spend a few days there. Your cover is that you used to be a bracero who tried running a bar and grill in Juarez but failed. Now you are looking for work of any kind. Ultimately, I want you to get a job on the farm of one Jesus Gonzalez. You are to find out what is going on there. Your communication will be only with me. I realize I might not hear from you for a couple of months. Memorize my cell phone number or hide it among some other numbers or something. I want to know what is going on at that farm besides farming. Be careful."

"You are pleased, Señor Ito, with your vehicles? All of them are in excellent condition, as you requested, with good spare tires and full gas tanks."

"Yes, thank you, Miguel, you have done well. The receipts have balanced, and so here is payment for you and your people. Lunch was good today, as usual." One of the bodyguards handed Miguel a small overnight bag filled with twenty-dollar bills. Miguel had not heard from Gomez since he left a month ago, but he was not worried.

The following day, Chan and his bodyguards drove from Long Beach to Tucson, AZ. The following day, they drove through El Paso to Fabens, TX. They arrived at Jesus Gonzalez's farm on the afternoon of the third day. "Perhaps we could consider flying next time to El Paso and renting a car, rather than a six-day round trip drive, Mr. Chan," asked one of his bodyguards as they pulled onto Jesus Gonzalez's road.

"That would require scrutiny at the airports, records of flights and car rentals, and provide an easily discerned pattern and trail. No, we will drive when a visit is necessary and pay cash for all the amenities and necessities along the way."

"Forgive me, Honorable one, I was not thinking." They left the car and walked to the office where Jesus Gonzalez was going over the tomato production figures. He looked up.

"Well, Mr. Gonzalez, are you satisfied with the way things are progressing? I see new packing sheds, your fleet of vehicles, the garage and dining hall almost finished, but how are you doing with recruitment?"

"Ah, Señor Ito. I hope you had a pleasant trip. It is a pleasant surprise to see you. I have made many contacts, or perhaps it would be better to say that many have contacted me. We have many men, now over two hundred and fifty, who are awaiting my call. As soon as the facilities are completed, we will bring them together. We have concentrated on recruiting young single men. There are many, and rumors of many more, who wish to join us. A few are true revolutionaries who think we are fighting Mexican corruption and American imperialism. Many are hungry and desperate. Others seek thrills and adventure. A few are truly criminal. We have collected names and phone numbers and addresses, such as they are. My secretary, Luis, has devised the mechanisms to notify them when we are ready. They will be presented with an application for employment during notification and provided a time and place to report where we will pick them up. Word of mouth about us has spread widely after Ruidoso. A few have managed to locate us on their own. These we have put to work as field hands while we scrutinize them and check their backgrounds. If they are genuine, then they are probably smart enough to be of real use to us. Only those who have been with me for a time, however, and who have my trust will be my lieutenants. Only these will know more than the most minimal of details.

"The tractors and guns have arrived. We have stored them separately from the explosives and ammunition. Bunk beds and mattresses are to arrive in a few days. By next week, we should be assembling our men. I have visited Alpine, Texas several times now. The students at Sul Ross State University will start returning in mid-August. We will conduct our business the first week of August to avoid any complications with students."

"Very good, Señor Gonzalez. Do you require any assistance with the weapons and explosives?"

"No Señor Ito, the manuals are very explicit. My compadres and I are ready to start training our men as soon as they arrive. We have built a rifle range and two classrooms. We will practice with the rifles and master them, but I am reluctant to train with explosives, as that could attract attention that we do not want. We have already worked out training schedules and training teams. These teams will be maintained in the field, a basic premise of leadership, Mr. Ito."

"Is there anything else you require, Señor Gonzalez, in order to complete this operation?"

"More ammunition and magazines for the rifles would be desirable, Mr. Ito. With two hundred and fifty men and two hundred and fifty thousand rounds of ammunition, that is one thousand rounds per man. Half, perhaps much more than half, will be consumed in training. I wish every man to be proficient and have his own dedicated rifle. We will probably have enough for Alpine, but a reserve would be desirable. Also cleaning supplies for the rifles and one hundred handguns, revolvers, preferably, and pump action shotguns. It would be easier for the men to learn revolvers than semi-automatics. Also, some Stinger type missiles for the highway patrol helicopters and Border Patrol aircraft, should they decide to interfere."

"Very well. That seems reasonable. You will receive the extra rifle magazines, the ammunition; Soviet made shoulder fired anti-aircraft missiles and shotguns in a month or so. The handguns will take a little longer. Perhaps not in time for Alpine but for future use.

"You are prepared to carry sufficient gasoline, food and water and supplies for a round trip?"

"Indeed, Señor Ito, including feeding the men on the return trip so there will be no stopping. I have one other concern, though, Señor Ito."

"What is that, Señor Gonzalez?"

"There are many who know of this place. Some of the American suppliers might be suspicious even though they have been well paid. We used middle men for all of our American purchases, except for the underground storage tank and pumps. Their workmen installed the tanks and pumps."

"Is that unusual for a fuel tank to be installed for a farm of this size?"

"No Señor Ito, many farms have such tanks, although this is probably the largest. What is unusual is that this is for gasoline rather than diesel fuel. No one uses gasoline tractors anymore. I have explained it is for irrigation pumps, trucks to haul produce, and other equipment. Still, it is a minor concern."

"I would not be too concerned, Señor Gonzalez. If any Mexican officials become too investigative, bribe them. If such becomes necessary, inform me of them with their names, positions, addresses, and amounts involved. Do not be at all concerned about the Americans. Is there anything else of concern?"

"No, Señor. It is now the first week of June. We will be ready and strike the first week of August. It will be the biggest raid on American territory since Poncho Villa raided Columbus, New Mexico."

"Excellent. I will leave one man with you to observe how things are going. You can reach me only through him. He will be something of a shadow to you. Learn to ignore him. Instruct your men to do likewise. He is not to be interfered with in any way. Do not try to hide anything from him. I will not visit you again until after Alpine."

On the return drive to Long Beach, Chan decided the best way to provide revolvers was to have the Chinese embassy in Brazil purchase two hundred medium frame .357 magnum revolvers for testing purposes. These would be without serial numbers or markings of any kind so as not to influence the military ordnance officers conducting the testing. They were to be delivered to the embassy in Brasilia. From there they would be delivered by diplomatic pouch to the Chinese embassy in Mexico City. A truck would deliver them to Jesus Gonzalez.

CHAPTER 6

Jesus Gonzalez carefully studied the map of Alpine, Texas. He marked the targets, routes of escape and approach for each team: the police station, the county sheriff's office, the West Texas National Bank, the Fort Davis National Bank, the Texas National Bank and the two sporting good stores.

He called his lieutenants together. Each was assigned a specific objective. He gave each five hundred American dollars and told them to visit Alpine independently of one another. Under no circumstances were they to acknowledge each other. For those whose objective was a bank, they were to take particular note of the vault, whether or not shaped charges were indicated, and their security arrangements. He expected to bring home over a million dollars between the three banks. Different escape routes were to be utilized by each team. Some would escape via Highway 90 through Marfa, twenty-six miles away, then south along Highway 67 into Mexico. Another team would head east the twenty-two miles into Marathon before turning south on Highway 385. They would cross into Mexico at Castalon. Still others would flee westward to Van Horn, Texas, and continue on to cross in Esperanzo. Others would travel Highway 28 out of Marfa and return via the underwater bridge.

Each team leader was assigned to either the sheriff's office in the courthouse, the police station, one of the three banks, or one of the sporting goods stores. Based upon their personal surveillance of the town and the assignment of their target, they were to devise the assault plan for their target. They were to refer to their assignment simply as "their target." Gonzalez would not establish roadblocks around Alpine. Rather, they would establish ambush sites on each road leading into the town to prevent the intrusion of any law enforcement officers from surrounding communities. To these teams he would issue Rocket Propelled Grenades as well as AK-47 rifles.

Jesus Gonzalez stood before his handpicked lieutenants, his team leaders. He had a large map of Alpine, Texas hung on the wall behind him. Guards kept all others away.

"Vehicles will travel at intervals of no less than five minutes, no greater than ten minutes apart. We will cross into the U.S. using our underwater bridge and travel south on Highway 170 to Presidio, then north on Highway 67 to Marfa, then east on U.S. 90. Again, do not bunch up. We do not want to present the image of a convoy. If you stop anywhere for whatever reason, it will provide the gringos with the opportunity to recognize and remember you. Each vehicle has its own gas and water cans and a cooler full of sandwiches and food.

"The county sheriff's office, police station and the Border Patrol office will all be attacked at 14:00 hours. Team leaders, co-ordinate your attacks with your shortwave radios. Do not use cell phones. At 14:05 all the banks will be simultaneously robbed. The sporting good stores are not so critical. They are to be robbed between 14:05 and 14:15. Keep radio use to a minimum. Your men are not to know the town or their target. Only that it is a building which might have armed men who will resist inside. Each of you will have a team for which you are responsible for training. Luis will assign you classroom time and range time. Your men are to become proficient with the use of their weapons. You have six seeks to prepare them. They are not to know when we will go until the morning of our departure. Designate two or three of the men on your team as demolitions experts. They have the least amount of time to develop this additional skill. You study the manuals as well. Know what they know and more. The police are to be killed without hesitation. Killing others is to be limited to those who resist in any way. We do not have time to pleasure the gringo women in this adventure. We must wait for other opportunities to indulge them. There is to be no alcohol or drugs consumed for twenty-four hours before this raid. We cannot depend or trust those who are addicted to drugs. These people are to be turned over to Hernando as grave diggers - their own graves. You have complete freedom to summarily execute any member of your team who jeopardizes your mission by balking, attempting to argue with you, or anyone you believe is an informant. It is not unexpected to have one or several informants among us. They make good fertilizer for Hernando.

"Our primary objective here is to collect all the money in the banks. If any vehicle breaks down, take the Vehicle Identification Number off it and set fire to it. Take another from the Gringos. You, my lieutenants, will wear camouflage face masks. If your men wish to be masked, let them wear bandanas.

"Each of you memorize your plan. No one except you is to have a cell phone. Luis has initiated the notification system. If all goes well, we will have at least one hundred and fifty new men in addition to the fifty we already have. Trust none of them.

Luis, start making phone calls."

Luis dispatched two dozen large vans to a dozen different small towns within one hundred miles of the border the next morning.

The bartender told Gomez about a large farm hiring many new workers. "There is more to it than that," he said to Gomez, "but I don't know what." He heard a rumor that men with a tendency toward violence were preferred. He shrugged, "I know nothing else," he said.

There were eight men waiting in the cantina, all casually eyeing Gomez. When Luis's driver came in, the bartender nodded at him and said, "There is the man you should see." The driver informed Gomez that yes, they were hiring young men in good condition as field hands, nothing more. Yes, the van was there to provide them transportation to the farm.

"I have my own car, so I will follow you," said Gomez. The driver shook his head no. "No, Señor, you will ride with me in the van or you do not come. I cannot tell you why that is so, only that El Jefe wishes it."

"What do you expect me to do with my car? I need this job. I cannot leave it here; it will be stolen."

"I do not care what you do with your car. If you can afford a car, you do not need this job."

Gomez put his arm around the shoulders of the man and led him toward the bar out of hearing range of the others. "I stole it from the Gringos," he whispered in the driver's ear.

"In that case, I suggest you sell it. I will leave in thirty minutes, with or without you." The driver sat down at the bar and ordered a Corona. Gomez walked to the other end of the bar and motioned to the bartender. "Can we talk in the back for a minute?"

The bartender looked around, and seeing only the driver at the bar, who was appeased for the moment, motioned for Gomez to follow him out the back door.

"I have this very good automobile which is not stolen. I purchased it legitimately. I will make you a good offer for it.

"I paid four thousand Gringo dollars for it a month ago," stated Gomez matter-of-factly. "I will sell it to you for twenty-five hundred dollars. The legal title I have, and I will sign it over to you."

"Why are you willing to sell it so cheaply then, to lose so much money?" asked the bartender.

"I am wanted by the Rurales. It would be good for me to disappear for a while. This job you talk about will provide a refuge for me."

"Where is the car? I will drive it before I consider it."

"It is on the street, in the front. It is the blue Ford. Let us go drive it." He handed the bartender the keys and walked back through the bar and out the front door. The bartender climbed behind the wheel, Gomez in the passenger side. When they were a mile out of town, the bartender mashed on the accelerator, and the Ford leaped forward. He mashed on the brakes; the Ford skidded to a stop in a straight line. He accelerated gently, moving the wheel from side to side to test the steering. They returned to the cantina.

"Show me the title?" he asked of Gomez, who promptly pulled it out of the glove compartment. "I will buy your car for twenty-five hundred dollars cash."

"Agreed. Please pop open the trunk." Gomez got out and removed a small duffel bag from the trunk. The bartender led Gomez back to the backroom of the bar.

"Fill out the title while I tend to the customers and get the money." Gomez sat down at the desk to complete the title. As the bartender gave another Corona to the driver, he whispered to him what transpired as a warning of caution for Jesus Gonzalez about Gomez. He returned to the back room and opened a small safe. He withdrew a cash box and counted out the agreed sum. He locked the safe, handed the money to Gomez, and they returned to the bar together.

"I sold my car," he said to the driver. The driver eyed Gomez warily, looked at the men standing around, then back at Gomez. He simply said, "Get in," and walked to the men's toilet. As the men climbed into the van, Gomez noted that all of the windows save for the windshield were tinted sufficiently heavily that it was hard to see out, let alone in. The driver started off and turned on the air conditioner. "We have a long drive, sleep if you can, we will eat when we arrive late tonight." With that, he sped out of the town. The pickup hour was deliberately late so that most would sleep and not take notice of the route. All of them slept.

None of the new men had ever handled an AK-47. Very few had ever handled any sort of firearm. Fiero gave all of them a demonstration of the capabilities of the rifle. The Chinese had supplied the semi-automatic version only for the troops. The lieutenants had those with the selective fire switch for full automatic fire capability. Fiero had been practicing, and his demonstration was impressive. He selected one hundred meters as the maximum range at which they would fire. He made it very clear that if anyone accidentally shot anyone else, they themselves would be shot or hanged, at the pleasure of El Jefe, Jesus Gonzalez.

They were divided into teams that rotated morning and afternoons, classroom, rifle range, and physical conditioning. Volunteers for handling explosives were called for. Of the one hundred and forty-odd new men, only eight volunteered. It was enough. Experienced drivers were identified and assigned a vehicle to practice driving around the farm. None were to violate its perimeter.

In the classroom, they learned to field strip and clean their AK-47s. Then they learned about aiming and firing their rifles. Each soldier was assigned a number which he painted on the stock of his rifle so each would have an assigned rifle. The teams blocking the roads practiced with the dummy Rocket Propelled Grenades. They stored them overnight in a makeshift arms room under lock and key at night.

Many asked why, what this was all about. They were told that they were now part of a private army. Henceforth, they would be expected to carry out whatever orders were issued to them without question. They would be paid for their services in cash in due time. If they did not agree, now was the time to speak out. Most presumed they would be guarding marijuana fields or engaged in drug smuggling or smuggling aliens into the U.S. Most of them didn't care, but a dozen asked to be released. Jesus Gonzalez concurred, and in the morning, they would be driven back to their pickup points. Two vans transported the twelve five miles over the highway, then they turned off into the desert. Anxiety arose when they left the highway, and they asked why. The driver told them they were picking up others from a different site. A mile off the road, the two vans stopped, and the drivers got out. They opened the doors and said, "Everybody out." As the vans emptied, the two drivers climbed in and drove off. Felipe and Gordo and Ramon emerged from the brush. Without speaking, they opened fire with AK-47s in full automatic mode. A few started to run, but Fiero was hiding in the arroyo and killed them with a shotgun as they ran past him. The four then pulled the bodies into the arroyo as vulture and coyote feed.

The return of the vans without their passengers was observed, and the word that there was no out quickly spread among the new men. Some resolved to escape at the first opportunity, but only a handful. Some laughed at the irony of their situation, but most simply decided to go along.

The first week of July, Jesus Gonzalez ordered the mechanics to check each of the vehicles. Brakes, tires, steering, anti-freeze/coolant, air conditioners, four-wheel drive transmission, and overall condition were assessed and brought to good order.

The last week of July, he ordered the tanks filled with gas. Four five-gallon jerry cans filled with gas and ten gallons of water in coolers was placed in each vehicle. He directed the cooks to make six sandwiches per man and hold them in refrigeration. Breakfast was at 06:00. At 07:00, each man drew his rifle, one grenade, and four thirty round magazines filled with 7.62x39 millimeter ammunition. At 08:00, the teams were assigned to vehicles, and they were on the road, headed across the desert for their underwater bridge. There, they spaced themselves five to ten minutes apart. They passed through Marfa at 13:00; they were in Alpine by 13:45. The roadblocks, road guards really, were set up with two vehicles on each side of the road on every road leading out of town. There were three men per vehicle. Weapons were kept out of sight. Each roadblock had at least one pickup truck, in the bed of which were two armed rocket propelled grenades.

At 13:55, each entrance to the courthouse and the police station had a vehicle parked to cover the door. Team leaders walked into each establishment, pulled a grenade from out of his shirt, let the spoon fly, holding the grenade so that it was out of sight, and tossed it into the office. They turned and ran. As soon as the grenades exploded, four men ran in and began shooting everyone in the office. A few took the time to remove the Sam Browne belts with their equipment from the dead officers. After firing ceased, the Team Leaders went back in to survey the destruction and search for weapons. They seized several Kevlar vests, broke into weapons lockers, and removed tear gas grenades, gas masks, AR-15 rifles, and .308 Winchester rifles with large telescopic sights. The surprise had been complete. The two Team Leaders radioed Jesus Gonzalez "mission completed."

The explosions of the grenades alerted the town. People came outside of their shops and homes to see what happened. At 14:05, the Team Leaders led their teams into the banks. Alarms were immediately set off, to no avail. No one was left to answer them. Several citizens attempted to call the sheriff's office and the police, but their calls would not go through. Team members assigned to clean out cashiers' drawers did so at the counters and drive-up windows. One bank manager attempted to swing the vault door closed but was immediately shot down. The second bank had the door closed but not locked. A quick-thinking lady cashier spun the handle, locking it when she saw armed men piling out of a van. The third bank was inadvertently prepared with its vault closed and locked, simply because the manager was late in returning from lunch. Gordo demanded the middle-aged vice president open the vault. He refused, begging that he did not have the key and combination. The Team Leader hit him across the mouth with his pistol. It broke off his four incisors and fractured the mandibular symphysis. Gordo put his pistol into the man's bloody face and demanded he open it. He tried to explain that he could not, that he lacked both key and combination as best he could, half dazed and through bloody lips and gums. Gordo put his revolver to the man's forehead and pressed the trigger. The Vice President's blood, brains and bone fragments splattered over his desk. Gordo motioned to his explosive expert to blow open the vault. He ordered those with bags of money from the cashiers' drawers outside to cover any approaching police officers or obviously armed citizens.

Quickly calculating that the walls of the vault were a foot thick, the explosives expert packed half a pound of C4 around the combination dial. Then he put another pound on the vault wall just around the corner closest to the hinges of the vault door. He inserted a blasting cap in the larger block and connected the two with Primacord. He unreeled the electrical wire back to the main entrance of the bank, connected the wires to a hand generator and crouched behind a desk. He yelled, "Fire in the Hole!" just as he had read was the proper procedure in the manuals. Everyone dropped to the floor. Mister Explosives twisted the handle of the generator which sent an electrical charge into the blasting cap. The back half of the side of the building which faced the charge collapsed in a cloud of dust. The force of the blast blew Gordo through the main entrance door. Mr. Explosives lost his head. He was peeking around the corner of the desk looking at the vault when he detonated the C4, and it decapitated him with a chunk of concrete. Everyone present was killed with the blast overpressure that ruptured lungs. Their van was rolled over in the street. The two who scraped clean the cashiers' drawers were standing in front of the double glass doors and were cut to ribbons by flying shards of glass and concrete from the front door and vault. One body slammed into a vehicle and the other skidded down the street. The bank across the street had its windows blown out, as did other nearby buildings. Several other gang members outside were blown several meters through the air and rendered unconscious. Ramon, in the nearby bank, stepped outside and observed the consequences of the explosion. He deemed that the cash from the cashiers' drawers was sufficient. He would not try to blast open the vault. Ramon ordered his team out of the bank, to pick up the unconscious team members, and load them into the van. He radioed Jesus Gonzalez, who was waiting on the edge of town, that Gordo had blown himself, his team, and the bank apart. No, Gordo did not penetrate the vault; he could see the vault still standing, intact, in the center of what was the bank. No, he didn't believe that there were any survivors. The vault in their bank was locked, and he wasn't going to repeat Gordo's experience. He was pulling his team out now.

The sporting goods stores provided better success. No one was killed this time, and no women were molested. One astute citizen called the Presidio County Sheriff's Office in Marfa to report multiple explosions and automatic gunfire. The Presidio County Sheriff tried to call the Brewster County Sheriff and then the Alpine Police Department without success. He then called the Texas Department of Public Safety in Marfa. They raised the State Patrol Officer assigned to Alpine on the radio.

DPS Officer Corporal Carlson was in his cruiser on Highway 118 forty miles north of Alpine when he took the call. Three miles outside of Alpine, he noticed a pickup truck and a van on each side of the road, all four vehicles facing forward and spaced fifty meters apart. Several men seemed to be standing around each one. He slowed down to thirty miles per hour to ascertain if they were armed. He didn't see any weapons. When he was between the spaced cars and ten meters past the first pair, two men, one on each side of the road, suddenly appeared. One of them was pulling on a rope stretched across the highway. It was a string of pyramidal tire slashers that ripped into his tires and flattened all four of them as he drove across the chain. He was boxed in. Immediately recognizing it as an ambush, he floored the accelerator. With flat tires, he couldn't go very fast. He saw the men ahead reach into the back of a pickup bed and come up with AK-47s.

OK, you SOBs, he thought as they raised their weapons to fire. He suddenly swerved onto the right shoulder of the road to see the look of surprise and fear on the face of one Mexican as he hit him, smashing him against the rear of the pickup truck. The other was bowled over like a billiard ball by the side of the pickup truck as a result of the collision of the two vehicles. The two men on the other side of the road, taken by surprise at the collision maneuver, regained themselves and began to spray the police cruiser with fire from their Ak-47s. The officer had, however, already thrown himself down on the passenger seat, opened the door and was sliding to the ground. He saw the dazed Mexican who was bowled over sit up on the shoulder of the road. The officer drew his Beretta .40 Smith and Wesson and shot him twice in the chest. He crawled to the front of his cruiser as the two Mexicans across the road ceased firing. Seeing their legs beneath his cruiser, he maneuvered around the front bumper and opened fire. He shot each of them in one leg. When they fell to the ground, he shot them in the chest. Caught again by surprise, they were unable to return fire before he killed them both.

Crawling over to the dead man that he shot on the shoulder of the road, he came under fire from the van on the right shoulder of the road, fifty meters behind him. He grabbed the AK-47, dropped behind the dead man for cover, and being an ex-marine, returned their fire, accurately and with lethal results. Taking two magazines off the body, he then crept around the front of the pickup truck and engaged the van on the opposite side of the road. His first three rounds shattered the van's passenger window and windshield. Its occupants began to pile out of the door on the passenger side. He shot them dead as they emerged. He expended twenty of the thirty rounds in his rifle magazine when their return fire ceased and he had no visible targets.

Creeping back to the starboard side of the pickup, he didn't observe any motion until movement several hundred meters out in the desert caught his eye. He observed three men running as fast as they could almost in a straight line away from him. He slowly rose to a crouch and approached the passenger side of his cruiser. Observing no motion, he opened the trunk of the cruiser, opened a rifle case therein and removed a Remington Model 700 varmint rifle in .308 Winchester. Sitting down and leaning against the bumper, he racked the bolt to chamber a round from the magazine. Wondering how much to lead them, he held just over the top of the heads of the running men and two feet in front of them. He fired. *Shit, I missed*, he thought, as the man in the center suddenly went down. The other two looked at each other, dove to the ground and started crawling. *Stand up, you sons of bitches*, he thought again. After two minutes, one of them did. He started to run, but the bullet knocked him flat before the sharp crack of the rifle reached him. The third man just continued to crawl. After another three minutes, the officer gave up and radioed Marfa, relating what transpired.

Fearing the worst, Marfa called Headquarters, Department of Public Safety, in Austin. Austin called the El Paso DPS office for an aircraft over flight from that office. Officer Carlson was drinking from a canteen out of his open trunk when he saw a line of cars approaching from the north at high speed. He grabbed his rifle and support bag with binoculars, camera and ammunition and ran into the desert. He was better than one hundred and fifty meters out when the cars stopped to see what happened. Ramon flagged the other vehicles to go on while he investigated. He had observed the officer running into the desert, but figured he was too far out for them to engage one another. Carlson watched Ramon through his binoculars as Ramon checked on the would-be ambushers. When he came to the man Carlson crushed between his cruiser and the pickup, he pulled a pistol and shot the man in the head. *What the hell is he doing?* thought Carlson. Then it dawned on him. The dead don't talk, and it confirmed that those speeding vehicles were part of the Alpine raiders. Carlson put down his binoculars and picked up his rifle. Ramon shot two more of the downed men in the head to make sure they were dead and walked towards his pickup. Almost as an afterthought, he turned towards Carlson and gave him the finger. It was all the time Carlson needed. The 168-grain bullet caught Ramon right in the middle of the chest, rupturing the thoracic aorta and shattering his spine. The driver of Ramon's pickup spun out as fast as he could, leaving Ramon a heap on the road.

By the time the state police Cessna flew over Alpine, the remainder of the raiders had fled. The Alpine airport tower radioed the Cessna that the carnage was over, and it was safe to land. At that moment, Corporal Carlson was entering Alpine at five miles per hour on four flat tires.

CHAPTER 7

Between the three banks, Jesus Gonzalez netted a little over $200,000. While disappointed that it was not in the millions he envisioned, it certainly was nothing to sneeze at. "We must learn more about explosives and bank vaults," sighed Jesus. Also, his men had gained some practical experience. They tasted the thrill of combat, an addictive, adrenaline high. Out of the 130 men who participated in the raid, twenty were killed, most in the bank explosion. The survivors would be more thorough and more careful. Ramon and Gordo would have to be replaced. He would have to observe who demonstrated leadership qualities among the new men. Gomez, who was carefully being watched, demonstrated a natural leadership. He had been on the highway 118 North blocking team, where there was no incident. Jesus Gonzalez was quite suspicious of him, but he had earned only praise during the six weeks of training. The barkeep received a one-hundred-dollar tip for referring Gomez.

Television crews from the major networks scrambled to be the first to broadcast from Alpine. A small network affiliated station from Odessa was the first to arrive with a van to begin broadcasting. An NBC affiliate out of El Paso rented an airplane, loaded it with gear and flew to Alpine with two camera crews. They began broadcasting several hours later. Since bank robbery is a federal crime, the FBI flew in a full compliment of agents and forensic experts. In less than twenty-four hours, a thorough investigation was under way. A Tactical Operations Center, or TOC, was established with the FBI as lead agency.

With the news broadcast over network television on the morning shows, anxiety all along the Mexican border reached new heights. People who did not own guns missed work and waited for sporting good stores to open to purchase them. The phone lines were jammed to the FBI Center in Clarksburg, WV, for purchase approval. Many bought their limit of two guns per month. Some men purchased two and then went home and got their wives so that they could buy two more. Pistols, rifles, and shotguns all sold like fire extinguishers in a fire. Handguns of all types sold out first, followed by semi-automatic rifles and shotguns. Texans became armed as they had not been since the days of cross border raiding of Poncho Villa and the Carrancistas.

The 2020 Presidential campaign had been in full swing for six months. When the Director of Homeland Security was finally notified of the Alpine raid, the Director of the FBI was standing before the President, briefing him in the Oval Office. Infuriated, the Homeland Security Chief called the Director of the Border Patrol to ask why the FBI was giving the President a briefing alone. Why was he not informed in the same time frame as the FBI?

The two-term President called for a meeting at 11:00 hours with the FBI, the DCI, and the Homeland Security Chief, who was to bring the Director of the Border Patrol. Since this was the second raid in six months across the Texas border, the media was already speculating on what it portended. Journalists were interviewing virtually every citizen of Alpine who would talk to them on camera. Many citizens were now openly wearing side arms.

Sul Ross State University, a small state university in Alpine with emphasis on range sciences, animal husbandry and agriculture, began receiving calls from anxious parents canceling their children's registration and demanding a return of fees. Others inquired of what security arrangements were contemplated to ensure student safety. In all, forty-two

Texas citizens and twenty raiders died in the attack. The element of surprise was the main factor in the murder of the law officers.

The Director of the Border Patrol bluntly stated his case. "Mr. President, we have 1800 miles of the Mexican border to patrol. We cannot cover every mile of it twenty-four hours a day, seven days a week. They can easily infiltrate across it both at border crossings legally and across the river and deserts clandestinely singly and in small groups. We don't have enough officers, sensors and money to do that. The haven that Canada is for terrorist cells has put an additional burden on our agency for resources. It is as easy to smuggle people, drugs, weapons or whatever, in from Canada as it is from Mexico. Our inspectors can't even inspect two percent of cargo shipments coming from either Canada or Mexico. Doubling the size of the Immigration and Naturalization Service and the Border Patrol might not even be sufficient resources. Our greatest deficiency, however, is human intelligence. We simply don't know who is plotting what south of the border.

"Part of this problem is the restive Mexican-American population of southern California and the border area, all the way to Brownsville. The agitation of the La Reconquesta movement throughout the Southwest has fomented dozens of cells about agitating for greater political alignment with Mexico. Eight of these organization's cells advocate violence and are of significant size. We don't know if they are perpetrators of either raid. These cells have a surprisingly thorough intelligence gathering capability of their own that covers both sides of the border. Our attempts coordinated with and through the FBI to infiltrate them with our agents have largely been failures. The gangs of the East Los Angeles barrios are major players in this movement and provide a lot of muscle and violence. They are linked to the Mexican drug rings trafficking in a variety of illegal drugs as a means of financing the movement. Mexico is even becoming a major producer of opium poppies. We can't do any more than what we are doing without an increase in resources, Mr. President.

"The alignment of certain politicians with these gang lords is a harbinger of worse things to come, Mr. President. The only way you're going to seal the Mexican border is to have the U.S. Army cover every inch of it. That should turn the heat up on the already boiling pot that is Mexico. Political fallout would be severe, and I can't begin to predict the outcome."

President Dorn looked at the FBI Director and asked, "What's your reading on this? How much of what was just said do you agree with?"

"Director Fairchild was pretty straightforward, Mr. President. We have been watching the situation in East L.A. for some years. It is a growing movement, and it is funded by drug money and possibly other sources."

"What other sources?"

"We have intercepted an occasional small shipment of arms destined for these gangs which originated in Asia. We haven't been able to prove beyond any doubt their origin, but circumstantial evidence points to China. Mostly they have come through the port of Long Beach. We don't know if they are being purchased with drug money, being provided gratis, or some other means of funding. We do know that competition between these gangs has been reduced over the last several years. There is more of an air of cooperation between them, but we don't know if it is a simple division of turf or something more significant, Mr. President."

"You implied that these gangs are engaged in political activities; can you elaborate on that, Mr. Director?"

"Certainly, Mr. President. Certain politicians and community leaders of Hispanic and African heritage are forming alliances with these gangs. Actually, they are morphing into quasi-political organizations at the grass roots level. They provide the muscle to get out the vote, for their candidate of course, and thus influence elections. They intimidate the opposition through threats of violence and occasional acts of brutality. The fact that they are receiving even small shipments of military type armaments is disturbing. These gangs have the potential to become private armies. Several of these gangs number their members in the thousands. They control whole districts, let alone neighborhoods. This is the source of their grassroots intelligence."

"These politicians that you allege are aligning themselves with these gangs, who are they? What offices do they hold?"

The Directors of the FBI and Homeland Security looked at each other. "They are mostly members of your own party, Mr. President. They include local and state officials, as well as several Hispanic-American and black members of the U.S. House of Representatives from California and the southwestern states," volunteered the FBI Director.

"What I am hearing is that in order to stop these raids, the U.S. Army will be required, and that there is the possibility that they are linked with political turmoil along the border, centered in southern California. Their foreign ties seem to be with China or Asia, rather than the Middle East."

Jim Cunningham responded, "That's about it, Mr. President," while the others simply nodded in agreement.

"How many men did you lose?"

"I lost twenty men, Señor Ito." Jesus Gonzalez did not find that particularly disturbing. It was only the loss of Gordo and Ramon that bothered him. The fact that a sharp shooting Texas Highway Patrolman killed Ramon was what irritated him. If he could find a way to exact revenge on the Texas Department of Safety in his next raid, he would do so.

"And did you make much money, Señor Gonzalez?"

"Alas, what the news people say and what we recovered are vastly different. I suppose the bankers skimmed off a great deal. We only relieved the Americans of one hundred thousand dollars between all three banks, not the five hundred thousand they allege. They are lying and pocketing large sums. These Yankee bankers are stealing and blaming us." Jesus Gonzalez had carefully concealed the actual amount of cash from Chan's agent.

"The vaults of two of the banks were locked. Our tragedy happened in trying to dynamite one open. That is why we only took one hundred thousand dollars instead of millions. It was the vault of the smallest bank that was open. We know better next time."

"And you left no wounded behind?"

"In this, the reporters are accurate. We left only the dead."

"And there are no attempts to locate or follow you?"

"To locate us, yes, to follow us, no."

"Our friends at the border crossings are well paid. They see nothing and tell us what they see and hear. And their American compatriots tell them much. We left by a variety of routes. This the Americans have not figured out. Some think we are based in Texas. Others think in Mexico, but they do not know how we come and go."

"You are satisfied with the performance of your men?"

"Si, almost all did well. Only three ran, and the Yankee policeman shot them in the desert." Jesus Gonzalez read of the finding of two bodies in the desert, shot by Corporal Carlson. He didn't know if the third was also killed and being denied by the Americans to arouse concern, or if he escaped to die in the desert, or lived to return home. He would have to send someone to visit the man's home to find out. Jesus Gonzalez was not about to admit to Chan that one man was unaccounted for.

"How soon will your army be ready to raid again, Señor?"

"In a few weeks, perhaps. A little more training is needed. Why, is there any rush? The Americans will be looking for us. Is it not better to wait for a while? Texans are very upset with us. I now am more concerned about Texans in general than their mostly incompetent police."

"You have several capable, trusted lieutenants, I presume, Señor Gonzalez?"

"Unfortunately, I lost two of my best. They will be hard to replace, but I will make sure of the new ones. You must have something in mind, Señor Ito."

"Yes, I do. First, I want your best lieutenant to form a small raiding band. His mission is to conduct small raids in Texas. He is to have a free hand in killing, raping and robbing. How he does it is between the two of you. Isolated ranches, truck highjacking, causing train wrecks so that they can be looted of their goods, ambushing policemen on the highways, carjacking and robbing at gas stations, convenience stores, and whatever. While he is doing his business in Texas, you and the bulk of your army will be busy elsewhere. Do you think you could conduct a raid fifty-five miles north of the Arizona border? It would require much careful planning."

"Yes Señor, I think we could do that, if there are not a lot of police units involved. Our one brief battle did not create battle hardened troops."

"Good. The next raid will be more of a logistical problem than the previous one. It will also require closer coordination between your teams. Your next target is Benson, Arizona. To ensure your safe return to Mexico, you will have teams take out the border crossing guards at two locations.

You are to capture, not kill, your own Mexican guards, but you are to kill the American Border Patrolmen at Douglas, and Naco, Arizona.

"I suggest you dynamite Interstate Highway 10 west of Benson to block traffic on that highway and cut off any reinforcements the police might send from Tucson. If you destroy the Number 302 intersection of I-10 and Highway 90, you also prevent assistance arriving from Sierra Vista. Be prepared and conduct this raid in one month. Here is money to bribe the Mexican officials into cooperating at each border crossing. Of course, you must handcuff them to provide them with an adequate excuse. Pay them well. Here is five thousand dollars for each of them to ensure their cooperation. This suitcase also contains a bonus of one hundred thousand dollars for you and your men. Two larger trucks will be provided to you by the usual method to ensure that you carry enough food, water, gasoline and ammunition to accomplish your task. Your men are to be given free reign in looting, killing and raping for the excellent job they did at Alpine. Now, if there are no more questions, I would like a private word with my man."

Jesus Gonzalez took the suitcase with the one hundred and fifty thousand dollars and thanked Señor Ito. Chan motioned to Ling, Chi'ing to follow him outside.

"Did you accompany our friends on the raid, Ling?"

"No, Honorable Chan. I did not think it wise. If I were killed or captured, the presence of an ethnic Chinese would raise questions."

"Good thinking. What of the amount of money they stole from the banks?"

"I do not believe him. I think it was much more. I think he hid some of it on the way back, both from his men and my lowly self. I do not trust him."

"It is well that you do not. You know how to contact me if necessary. I do not need to remind you to be cautious."

Ten days later, two trucks were delivered. One was a five-ton cargo truck that carried Meals, Ready to Eat, an operating table, medical supplies and bottled water. The second was a 5000-gallon tanker truck of gasoline. An envelope contained instructions to establish a bivouac site on the Mexican Highway 2 between Aqua Prista and the Naco road junction.

The raid was to be conducted the following day. No wounded were to be left behind. In a separate car, a surgeon and a surgical nurse arrived with the trucks. The surgeon was under indictment in Mexico City for revolutionary activities. It was easy enough to convince him that his skills were needed, and a place of refuge, along with a generous amount of money, awaited him for serving in a revolutionary army.

Jesus Gonzalez sent Felipe and a team of five men to discuss the border crossings at Naco, coming and going at the appropriate time. After a week of identifying all of the assigned guards and their residences and families, they were approached, and discussions were opened. No threats were made if the guards declined their generous offer. They were not told what would happen to their American counterparts, only that everything had been previously arranged with them. Since they were offered five thousand dollars as well, it was not to be discussed with the Americans; otherwise they would demand two times that of their Mexican counterparts. None of them declined the five thousand dollars, which constituted a year's salary for them.

Francisco and his team did the same at Aqua Prieta with similar results.

A month later, as planned, they bivouacked overnight, and then crossed into Arizona by driving into the desert between Naco and Douglas without headlights along a route surveyed by Felipe and his team and marked by metal fence posts with flags tied to them. By 10:00, a company of one hundred and fifty men descended upon the Arizona town of Benson, population 5300.

Most of the citizens who were killed were those who attempted to protect their wives and daughters from gang rape. Several women tellers from the bank were dragged at gunpoint into the vans where they were repeatedly molested. The same happened to attractive women caught on the street or in the stores. When the raiders departed, they simply threw the women naked into the street.

Virtually every business in town was robbed. Law officers were shot on sight. Most were caught in their offices as had occurred in Alpine.

A number of the wounded citizens died because the medical assets of the town were overwhelmed. Sporadic gunfights between individual citizens and the raiders accounted for the deaths of twenty-seven raiders and over two dozen wounded. After the initial exchange of gunfire, some of the armed citizens survived by fleeing rather than continuing the fight. Two citizens died fighting when they ran out of ammunition. Others began sniping at the raiders with high powered rifles from the edge of town. Several merchants climbed to the roofs of their building to snipe at the raiders. Two were killed, one wounded, and two were unscathed. These five men accounted for over a dozen of the dead and wounded raiders.

Each team leader was responsible to account for each of his men. If they were critically wounded, a chest or head wound, they received a bullet in the brain. If an abdominal or limb wound, they were loaded into vans or pickups with a topper. The county high school was not disturbed.

As they retreated towards Naco and Douglas, Jesus Gonzalez, leading the column, radioed Francisco at Aqua Prieta to initiate action. They handcuffed the Mexican guards after having them disrobe. Donning their uniforms, Francisco calmly led his team to the American guard booths where they opened fire upon them. One American Border Patrol officer who was inspecting a car managed to shoot two of them with his Beretta 96 before going down. Another Border Patrolman shot down two more with a shotgun when he saw them draw their sidearms en masse. Francisco went from Border Patrolman to Border Patrolman, calmly shooting each in the head as he had been instructed. He examined his own four wounded and dispatched them likewise. People on both sides of the border fled their cars as the shooting began. Francisco and his men waved Jesus Gonzales and Miguel's team through the checkpoint and into Mexico.

Felipe had somewhat better luck. He only lost two men. Of course, the traffic at Naco wasn't nearly as heavy as that at Douglas.

<hr />

When word of the Benson raid reached the national news media, the feeding frenzy was orgasmic. Television journalists were commenting that federal action must occur. These raids were intolerable. The Army must be brought in. Reporters from Tucson were on the scene in a matter of a few hours. They had live broadcasts of dead and bleeding wounded citizens lying in the streets. They had the unmitigated bad taste to show live some of the battered and raped and nearly unconscious nude women.

The next morning, the Governor of Arizona announced he was activating the National Guard military police and infantry units, both mechanized and light. Their mission: patrol the border and reinforce checkpoints. Infantry Fighting Vehicles would be stationed at all border checkpoints. Illegal aliens attempting to cross into Arizona would be fired upon without warning. Arizona civilians had his authority to shoot illegal aliens attempting to cross the border, irrespective of their civil rights and the legality of it, and the ACLU could go to hell if they didn't like it. Civil Air Patrols would monitor the border from the air. The American Civil Liberties Union immediately protested and filed a lawsuit against the Governor's order to shoot illegal aliens attempting to sneak across the border.

Phone calls, faxes, e-mail messages, and telegrams flooded the White House and office of every U.S. Senator and congressman whose districts stretched from California to Brownsville, Texas.

That night, President Dorn called a meeting for 08:00 the next day with the Director of Central Intelligence, Director Gateway of the FBI, the Secretary of State, the Secretary for Homeland Security, the Attorney General, the Joint Chiefs, and the senior senators from the Border States as to how to best respond to the cross border raids. The governors of the Border States were invited, and all made overnight flights into Washington to attend. Since the integrity of the U.S. had been breached, the Attorney General expressed the opinion that the Posse Commitatus Act would not apply. If it went to the courts, the Department of Justice would fight it through the Supreme Court. If the court overturned it, the President could declare Martial Law, which would allow deployment of federal troops.

The Joint Chiefs accepted the recommendation of the Chief of Staff, Army, that the 101st Airborne Division be deployed because of their organic helicopter fleet. It would be much easier to resupply outposts and patrols, coordinate air and ground patrols, and establish outlying bases with a force already task organized.

The Governor also requested federalization of the National Guard units, which would augment the brigades of the 101st. Airborne Division.

The Adjutant Generals of California, Arizona, Texas and New Mexico would coordinate with the Commanding General of the 101st. In this way, there would be more than one soldier per mile of the border; 1800 miles long, and the federal government would shoulder the financial burden.

The general consensus held that these cross border raids, drawing upon the historic raids of Pancho Villa and bandits in the early part of the twentieth century, were the result of a nascent Revolutionary Army seeking funds to expand its activities in Mexico.

President Dorn had his secretary, Roberta, place a call to Mexico's President, Enrico Bustamante. "Mr. President, I am sure you have heard of the raid two days ago on Benson, Arizona. The American public is howling for protection and revenge. Do you have any idea as to the objective of these raids, who is conducting them, and where they are hiding?"

Bustamante hesitated and then responded. "No, Mr. President, I do not. My federal officers were all captured with none killed, as you know. Interrogation of them has revealed that they are totally ignorant of what happened. Are you certain these raiders are Mexican nationals and not Americans of Mexican descent pretending to be Mexicans?"

He's a little upbeat, thought Dorn. "Quite a number of our citizens in this region are, as you say, of Mexican descent, Mr. President. Consequently, most of them are bilingual, fluent in both English and Spanish as spoken in Mexico. Quite a number of our surviving Mexican American citizens have remarked that most of the raiders spoke with an accent native to Chihuahua. Are there any rebel armies or bands of brigands currently operating in Chihuahua?"

It was a bluff, but Bustamante didn't know it. "No, Mr. President, there are not. Of course, one could have formed in these last two months that we have no knowledge of at this point in time."

Like hell you don't, thought Dorn. "There has been a band of revolutionaries who turned to banditry to support themselves running loose in Chihuahua for at least ten years. They hire out to drug lords as a private army on occasion, when the drug lords wage turf wars on one another. Even our agents know that much.

"President Bustamante, I have the unfortunate duty to inform you that I am now ordering the U.S. Army to initiate patrolling of the border, and a greatly increased crackdown on the flow of illegal immigrants into the U.S. across our mutual border. It is with considerable reluctance that I do this. It is better for our federal government to do it, however, rather than state militias. As you have probably heard, yesterday, the Governor of Arizona ordered the Arizona National Guard to active duty to patrol the border. He personally and expressly gave the order to shoot on sight anyone attempting to illegally cross the border into Arizona."

Bustamante cringed. The use of federal troops to tighten the border would increase the hazards to, and reduce the flow of, drugs and people into the U.S. Mexico's economy would be severely hampered if federal forces were effective for very long. His political party would lose millions of dollars in a very short time.

"President Dorn, I will pursue this very vigorously. We cannot allow bandits to harm our long standing and mutually beneficial relationship."

"Thank you, Mr. President. I am sure your efforts will be thorough and effective. Give my regards to Mrs. Bustamante."

"And ours, from myself and Mrs. Bustamante, and Mexico, to your lovely wife."

Now, why would all of the Mexican officers be unharmed while all the American Border Patrol agents were killed, mused Henry Dorn. *Don't tell me it wasn't a setup!*

CHAPTER 8

The meter reader for the power company thought it odd that so many vehicles were parked at the Taylor Ranch in Brewster County, Texas. *Must be a family reunion,* he thought, *all of the license plates are from California.* As he was reading the meter, Felipe saw him out the window. Simultaneously, the meter reader saw him. Felipe smiled. He turned to two of his men eating at the table. "Go quickly now, kill the meter man before he escapes."

They picked up their AK 47s from the table and ran out the door. They opened fire as they rounded the corner of the house and saw the meter man open his truck door and start to climb in. Half a dozen bullets in his back slammed him against his truck. He fell dead with a bullet through his heart.

———— •◦●◦●◦• ————

Robert Taylor was lying dead in the living room. Two braceros, ranch hands, living in the house trailer were also murdered. Felipe sent four men against the trailer while he and six others assaulted the house. It was 07:00, and all at the Taylor ranch were eating their breakfast. The braceros had little wealth. They found a Timex watch on one, and they had twenty dollars between them. New blue jeans and work shoes and a chore coat were divided among the raiders.

"What shall we do with the woman, Felipe?" Jose had asked. Jose, barely 20, decided he would have her. He had been a virgin until he sampled the prostitutes maintained at the base. Now, being curious how the older woman would look and feel, decided he would have her. He did. Jose disinterestedly heard her begging as Jose ripped off her clothes and tied her to the bed. When he finished, he asked, "Does anyone else want the woman? The two who murdered the braceros did.

Felipe shrugged. "What would you do? How good a look did she get of your face?" When they were finished with her, Jose shot her in the head.

Felipe and his raiders made themselves more breakfast and had a hearty meal. They were just finishing when the meter man appeared.

"Jose, fill all the vehicles with gas from the farm gas tank. Miguel, refill the water cans, Manuel, gather food and restock the trucks."

The meter reader wasn't missed until after 18:00. He didn't answer his radio or cell phone. The power company supervisor began calling those on his route plan for the day. Several had seen him. His fourth stop was the Taylor ranch, where no one answered the phone.

Felipe and his team moved north and east into Terrell County, Texas. They cut the fence on a lonely stretch of highway and drove their two vans and pickups with toppers into the desert out of sight to camp for the night. The next day, they drove back roads, seeking isolated homes and ranches. They found easy victims every other day. They would fill their gasoline and water cans at the ranches or in small towns where they would buy food as needed, always pretending to be migrant workers looking for work.

At 20:00, the supervisor called the sheriff's department to report that Herman was four hours overdue. The sheriff's department notified the Department of Public Safety officer for the county. At 21:00, Herman's wife called, demanding to know why her husband was so late returning home. The supervisor postulated that he was broken down in some back road in an arroyo where he couldn't be reached by radio or phone. She didn't buy that. She thought his boss was covering for him while he was out drinking or visiting some woman with loose morals.

When shift change occurred, the night shift supervisor informed the dayshift supervisor coming on duty. He didn't like it at all. He called the Texas Department of Public Safety and asked if there was aerial surveillance in the area. All aircraft were flying further south along the border was the answer. The day time supervisor checked out the newest truck, filled it with gas, took a five-gallon can of gas, a thermos of coffee, and purchased a six-pack of bottled water, a dozen donuts and four sandwiches at the convenience store. He started driving Herman's route beginning at his last known location. At 14:00, he reached the Taylor ranch. One hundred meters from the house, he recognized Herman's truck and saw his body next to it. He stopped, quickly glanced around, and called the sheriff's office on his cell phone. At 16:00, the sheriff, three heavily armed deputies and the county coroner arrived. The supervisor had not moved from where he had stopped. Upon entering the house and trailer, the sheriff notified the Department of Public Safety, who passed it on to Austin, who notified the Border Patrol and the FBI. By 22:00, a full-blown investigation was underway. The sheriff decided to make a news release that a ranch family had been murdered without identifying them. That would have to wait until next of kin were notified. It was repeated on area radio and television all the next morning. South Texas had been put on alert.

Friends began to call friends. By the fourth day, three other ranch raids were found. Texas Rangers plotted them on a map and determined the route Felipe followed. State patrolmen and Texas Rangers began interviewing gas stations and convenience stores, motels and other likely stops along the route. A number remembered a caravan of two vans and two pickups with about a dozen men. A huge circuit up to Odessa was identified. Law enforcement agencies throughout Texas were very closely following events. It was postulated that the suspects would turn west through Loving, Reeves, and Culberson counties, or northeast towards San Angelo.

Since their pattern was to strike isolated ranches, two likely routes emerged. An All Points Bulletin was issued. Twenty-four hours later, a DPS trooper observed them at a roadside picnic area just outside Sterling city. The officer drove past them as he radioed their location and turned off the road where he could observe them. DPS troopers and county sheriffs' departments moved quickly to block each of the six highways leading in and out of Sterling City. The city of San Angelo contributed a five-man SWAT team and twenty officers. When Felipe's team moved south on Highway 163, the Iron County Sheriff's Department set up a roadblock north of the junction of 163 and 2469, and waited. It didn't take long.

When Felipe saw the roadblock ahead, he pulled on the shoulder. The others followed. That's when he noticed the train of police cars behind them without lights or sirens. He immediately drove off the road and plowed through a four-stand barbed wire fence. It slowed him down some, as posts and wires finally snapped, but didn't stop him. Now, all units began a chase across a recently combined sorghum field. A DPS helicopter arrived, and the officer in the passenger's seat opened fire with a Barrett semi-automatic fifty caliber rifle. The engine in Felipe's truck exploded on the impact of the 750-grain full metal jacket boat tailed bullet. His truck quickly plowed to a stop. He jumped out, as did the other raiders. Reaching behind their seats, they pulled out their AK-47s. The other raider vehicles drove past them, with the police 50 meters behind them in close pursuit. The doors of the last van flew open, and two gunmen opened fire with their AK-47s. Their bullets struck the windshield and radiator of the leading police cruiser. It veered off to the side. The police officer riding shotgun in the second cruised was leaning out the window with a fighting shotgun. As soon as the first vehicle cleared the field of fire, he opened fire. His first two rounds were with BBs, the third with #1 buckshot, the fourth, fifth, and sixth rounds with 00 buck, the seventh and eighth with one-ounce slugs. He didn't miss with any of them. The two gunmen fell out of the truck with numerous pellet wounds. The 00 buck and slugs ripped through the seat and into the other occupants. The trooper was reloading when the van came to the very small irrigation ditch. It didn't quite fly across it, but the driver and front seat passenger flew into the windshield as the front end of the van dropped and crashed into the far bank.

Felipe and his driver, firing at the helicopter, ignored the dozen police cars until it was too late. Both fell dead to officers emulating Roy with the shotgun. Somewhat spread out, the next three police cruisers had driving officers firing hand guns out their windows while the officers in the passenger seats were firing with a Mini-14, a lever action Marlin .30-30 and a shotgun. Some of the rifle bullets penetrated the gasoline cans in the next van. A moron raider pulled the hand grenade pin and released the spoon just when #4 shotgun pellets hit him in the hands, face and chest. He dropped the grenade and fell back on the second seat. The grenade rolled forward and detonated under the driver's seat. Two milliseconds later, the ignited gasoline exploded as a ball of flame. The windshield saved the officers in the cruiser immediately behind them from flash burns. The last pickup slowed to a stop under the intense fire from the helicopter re-engaging it with rifle fire. The police caravan came to a halt, with the lead police vehicle passing the last raider vehicle before stopping. The windshield was shot out, the cab was filled with bullet holes, and so were the occupants. Of the twelve raiders, none were alive. The two who impacted on the windshield died of subdural hemorrhage and broken necks before medical assistance arrived. A search of the unburned vehicles revealed much of the loot taken from their victims. Their raid had lasted a little over three weeks.

Jesus Gonzalez heard the news of the deaths of Felipe's team on the local nightly news broadcast out of El Paso. Several of the older members, those who had been with Jesus Gonzalez for more than a year, aspired to leadership, so Jesus selected them as new lieutenants. Jesus Gonzalez's prowess as a bandit leader and revolutionary spread by word of mouth. Many more were looking to join his little army, more than he could accommodate.

With the deployment of the 101 Air Assault Division, Jesus Gonzalez didn't know what to do with his army. He knew that he was a toad of a Mr. Chan, a Chinaman pretending to be a Japanese Mr. Ito, but to what purpose all of this was, he could not comprehend. He certainly wasn't going to fight the U.S. Army on American soil.

Now, helicopters equipped with machine guns, radar, night vision devices and sometimes rockets patrolled the skies day and night. Ten-man patrols tramped up and down the border. The illicit flow of drugs, people, stolen cars and stolen everything else slowed to a trickle. The addicts and drug lords were screaming. The street cost of drugs doubled, tripled, and then quadrupled. Drug suppliers began scrambling for new sources of drugs. Many heroin addicts attempted cold turkey withdrawal. Some made it, most did not. Armed robbery, burglary, and drug related crimes soared throughout the United States commensurate with prices. Drug lords experimented with new methods of smuggling and explored new routes with new partners. Canada and Florida took on a renewed meaning for the Cuban axis.

———————— •◦•◆•◦• ————————

A shipping crate arrived, but Jesus Gonzalez had not ordered anything. He had it moved into a packing shed. Two days later, Mr. Ito arrived.

"Have you received anything lately, Señor Gonzalez?"

"Yes Señor Ito, a large crate arrived two days ago. I had it moved into a packing shed but have not opened it since I did not order anything. I suspected it came from you but thought I would wait until you confirmed or denied it."

"Well, let's go and open it."

"Luis, get several men and open the present from Mr. Ito."

They walked to the shed with small talk. Inside the crate were thirty brand new Russian made, synthetic stocked, bolt action sniper rifles. Each had a huge scope mounted on it that featured a range finding reticle and target turret adjustment knobs for windage and elevation. Smaller crates of ammunition and cleaning supplies in plastic kits accompanied the rifles. Mr. Ito handed Jesus Gonzalez a rifle and picked another out of the rack in an opened crate.

"These are among the most accurate in the world. Look through the scope."

Jesus Gonzalez did so and saw it was filled with circles and lines that grew smaller as one went down toward the bottom of the reticle.

"Instruction manuals accompany each rifle. You are to select your best marksmen and train them in the use of these rifles," Mr. Ito told Jesus Gonzalez as they walked out of earshot.

"Señor Ito, forgive me, you have paid me much money to do things I wanted to do, had a good time in doing, and would do again, but doing battle with the American Army is not one of them. Even I am not that stupid."

Ito smiled. "First, you can kill a man over half a mile away with one shot from any one of these rifles. They are that accurate. Second, you can do it from your side of the border, because the Americans will not violate the border to pursue you. Third, you do not have to do it yourself. Give a one-hundred-dollar reward to the shooter every time he hits an American. It does not matter if he wounds or kills the American, so long as the bullet strikes him. I will also give you one hundred dollars each time an American soldier is wounded or killed by one of your men. It will cost you nothing, you have nothing to lose, and you stand to gain a good deal of money. It all depends upon how well you train your men."

Jesus thought about it for a moment, then asked, "How do you know the Americans won't cross the border to come after us, or shoot us with their tanks or rockets?"

"First, relations between Mexico and the Americans are already strained, so much more since you initiated your cross-border activities. President Dorn will do nothing more than irritate President Bustamante. That would be very bad for business. Second, the law forbids it, and the Americans are very conscious of the law and generally abide by it. Third, it would create a serious public relations challenge for them if it became known they were breaking the law to shoot up another country. Fourth, if they cross the river to come after you, you can shoot them with AK-47s, with rocket propelled grenades, and throw hand grenades. Fifth, their rifles, M-16s, are essentially varmint rifles. They do not have the range or accuracy these rifles do. Sixth, your men can be scattered over several hundred miles of the border. The Americans won't know where to concentrate their forces."

"Why not just kill them with rocket propelled grenades and be done with it?"

"Because RPGs leave a very visible trail of smoke that reveals your position. This way, they do not know where the men are who are shooting at them."

Jesus Gonzalez thought about it for another minute, then decided to himself, *I can give the men fifty dollars and keep one hundred and fifty dollars for myself. One dead American a day at that rate is pretty good business. If the men are pursued, we can surprise them with the RPGs.*

Jesus Gonzalez smiled. "Señor Ito, we will do it." As always, I am grateful for your generosity."

"If the soldiers go away, you will, of course, begin your excursions across the border, will you not?"

"Oh, most certainly. In spite of our losses, the men find it both intoxicating and profitable."

Ito smiled. "You have done well. Another ten thousand dollars in my car is for you." What he thought was nothing to harass the Americans and keep them occupied.

Roberta's voice came over the telephone. "Mr. President, President Vassily Chernikof is on line one."

"Thank you, Roberta." Hello, Vassily. How are you this day?

"Well, Henry, all things considered, not too bad. All family is in good health, and I am sure that you have heard that as of yesterday we have successfully concluded the prosecution of one industrial ring of organized crime that was exploiting the mineral wealth of our country."

"Yes, Vassily, I heard. Congratulations! Your prosecutors and police investigators are to be commended. Let us hope they continue their good works."

"We have heard of the raids you are experiencing, and I am calling to offer my condolences to the grieving families of those killed by these bandits. We, too, as you know, have been experiencing similar episodes for some time, especially from Chechnya."

"Thank you, Vassily. I will have our public relations guru issue a press release that you and the people of Russia have called with their condolences. I am sure it will be appreciated by all."

"We are still very much in America's debt, Henry. Your former President Bush was very helpful in expanding our trade with you as much as possible some years ago. Purchasing our products has done as much as anything in assisting us in fighting the organized criminal elements here. He understood what we were faced with in Chechnya much better than the so-called human rights activists of your country.

"Unfortunately, as you know, we have experienced considerable difficulties with the Islamic states on our southern border which used to be part of our old empire conducting similar raids. Chechnya, in particular, still part of Russia, has been a most thorny problem. Still, the other Islamic states send armed bands into our country, waging what amounts to low-grade banditry, brigandage, or terrorism, depending upon your point of view. Now, with the problems you have with raiders from Mexico, I believe many more Americans understand what we have experienced over the decades in Chechnya and more recently from these independent Islamic states."

"I'll be sure that Mike includes a paragraph or so to call attention to your years of experiencing a similar situation. Perhaps it will help that segment of our society who feels that this is just the work of poor starving Mexicans striking out in desperation."

"Thank you, Henry. Again, our condolences from Russia; we also hope that you bring these bandits to swift justice. My regards to Mrs Dorn."

"Thanks again, Vassily. Our warmest regards to Alexandra and the kids."

CHAPTER 9

The summer of 2019 was one of intense campaigning for the Democratic Party. Half a dozen candidates were serious contenders for the Democratic nomination. In the end, it was Senator Henry Kenneley who won the Democratic Party's nomination at the Chicago convention in July. He campaigned during both the primary and general election on the standard social welfare police state rhetoric of the Democratic Party. Jobs, greater standardization and federal control of education, protection of the environment, socialized medical care for everyone, regardless of health insurance or lack thereof, public housing, expansion of the food stamp program, and clothes for school children, and the promise that greater police protection would denigrate the need for personal ownership of firearms. All would be provided to immigrants and their families as they "took jobs Americans shun."

Jason Thornton was something of a dark horse. He was a Jeffersonian Democrat in disguise of a Republican. Thomas Jefferson believed in the independent farmer, merchant, tradesman, and craftsman who had an inherent distrust of government. Independent minded citizens who would accept responsibility for their own welfare and held an inherent distrust of government were the fundamental beliefs of what is now termed Jeffersonian Democracy.

Jason Thornton harbored a terrible vision that some day the United States would no longer be a Republic. Like Rome from the First Century

A.D. onward, he reasoned, it depended too much on imports, on "slave, read foreign" labor, on having to rely upon foreign mercenaries to man their armies, foreign sources of food, that a tremendous gulf separated the poor and the remainder of society. The only major difference was that the timeline was being tremendously compressed. The middle class would be economically squeezed, with the great majority being forced into the ranks of the poor. The cream of the middle class would rise to the upper class rich, while the remainder of the middle class would be terribly diminished. As one economic advisor told him, "The rich and the poor always gang up on the middle class. The poor can't afford to pay the taxes for all these social welfare programs, and the rich have the power to see that they themselves don't pay for them."

On a budget provided primarily by the center of the middle class and the upper middle class, he borrowed a few issues of the Democratic Party. He stressed that he would create a greater stewardship of the environment, far better than previous Republican administrations. Being something of a hunter, he saw the need for hunting as a means to control selected wildlife populations, such as white-tailed deer that had overgrown their ecological niche in many eastern states. He also campaigned for private ownership of firearms in the west, where the significance of such was brought home as a result of the Mexican raids.

He promised greater border security, tightening of immigration restrictions, limited tariffs and other forms of protection for American manufacturing to counter foreign imports and protection of American jobs. By 2003, 96% of all of the clothes worn by Americans were manufactured overseas. He stressed a return of the clothing and shoe industry to the U.S., especially in the south where cotton was grown and textiles were manufactured, and in the northeast where the garment industry used to exist. He promised greater support to agriculture, since America's greatest exports were grain and beef. Much of America's fruit and vegetables were now imported from Central and South America. Much of the processed foods industry had moved south over the last ten years because the labor was so much cheaper. Manufacturers could make and ship processed foods frozen cheaper from Brazil, Argentina, and Mexico than they could be processed in the United States. Factory workers in China were making seventy-five cents per hour, while American manufacturing workers were being paid an average of twenty-one dollars per hour. U.S. made goods could not be found on the shelves of almost any store.

In the rust belt, he promised tariffs against imported iron and steel until those industries could make another "adjustment" as they had in the opening years of the twenty-first century.

In foreign policy, he railed against the historical Bretton-Woods agreement, in which the underlying policy concept was founded that economics was the cause of world wars. He preached how this concept of leveling the economic playing field worldwide led to the decline and economic prosperity of the United States. The U.S. trade deficit was approaching 10 trillion dollars, up from 3.5 trillion in 2003. While the United States declined in economic power and other countries increased in wealth, there had been no effect whatsoever in reducing wars and international tensions. Africa smoldered, flared and burned in numerous civil wars based on tribal, religious and ethnic grounds, as well as between countries over boundaries, oil, gold and diamonds. The Central Asian Republics became even more dictatorial through ethnic strife, tribalism and Islamic fanaticism; one tyrannical government replaced another. The Middle East was on the brink of deploying weapons of mass destruction, as democracy was being rolled back on many fronts.

With demographic predictions indicating that in thirty years or less, over one half of the U.S. population would be foreign born, mostly Hispanic, his threat of immigration limitations sparked civil strife in many cities. Barrios in Los Angeles, San Antonio, Houston, Phoenix, Tucson, El Paso, Dallas-Fort Worth, Omaha, Chicago, and New York demonstrated against his so-called "racism." The La Reconquesta movement of Mexican Americans came out in the open as an organized political force supporting Senator Kenneley.

Mexico began to experience small riots and an increase in lawlessness. Small bands of revolutionaries, which the government labeled as "bandits with lawyers" emerged among the native American populations in the states of Yucatan, Jalisco, and Durango. The movement in the state of Durango had an urban element to it as well as a rural one, centered in the city of

Durango. The common theme was against corruption in government and a more equitable distribution of resources, particularly land.

Selecting Los Angeles as a site for the Democratic convention backfired on the Democratic Party. Selected to show Democratic support for Mexican Americans, many of the city's Latino citizens responded with riots and violence against the Democrat's National Convention. La Reconquesta bussed in Mexicans from nearby border towns to swell their numbers. They provided them with free meals, cigarettes, and massive campgrounds around the city in support of their demonstrations. In the end, the riots of East Los Angeles, the numerous deaths, the destruction of more than a dozen square blocks of the barrio by fire resulted in a backlash originating in the middle class. When it was over, every middle-class person who had a job or even hoped for one voted Republican. The working population of both white and black Americans felt tremendously threatened by the influx of more immigrants, of losing their jobs, of further exportation of service industries, and the very few remaining manufacturing jobs. In a unique movement, middle class Black America voted Republican. Iowa, Minnesota, Washington, and Maine went Republican in the Electoral College. It was enough to swing the election to Jason Thornton.

Jason Thornton's immediate problems were the relationship with Mexico and the selection of his cabinet. As of the swearing in ceremony, he was still debating on several cabinet positions. Continued long range sniping at soldiers from the Mexican side of the border resulted in pulling American forces a kilometer back inside the U.S. In spite of this, sniping continued. Mexican snipers then began to stalk the American soldiers on American soil. Thornton's response was immediate. The day after he took the oath of office, he ordered Army sniper teams to retaliate. Counter sniping became the order of the day. Army two-man sniper teams began to cross the Rio Grande at various points and hunt down and kill any armed Mexican civilian they saw. After seven Mexican snipers were eliminated and their rifles collected, the Mexicans stayed on their side of the Rio Grande.

When Mexico's President Bustamante discovered American soldiers were violating Mexican territory, he angrily denounced in public American intrusion of Mexico's Sovereignty. Mexico's ambassador filed a formal protest and called upon President Thornton. Jason Thornton calmly replied to the Mexican ambassador that if Mexico didn't like it, all they had to do was stop the cross-border raids and sniping. Until then, the United States would take whatever action it deemed necessary to protect its sovereignty and its citizens. President Thornton's last words to the Mexican ambassador were, "If those responsible for cross border raids were not brought to justice in the near future, it is conceivable that the United States will take appropriate action to see that the responsible individuals are brought to the United States for trial or killed, even if it is on Mexican soil. That is my position, Mr. Ambassador. Please give my kind regards to President Bustamante."

Somehow, Jason Thornton's words were leaked to the press without his knowledge or consent. They made a splash in Mexican newspapers that aroused a wave of Mexican nationalism. In the United States, they aroused a wave of support for Jason Thornton.

——————————•••••——————————

The October day was cool, the nighttime temperature dropped into the upper thirties, Fahrenheit degrees. The day had been overcast, but no rain. The coming day promised to be similar, only cooler. The humidity hung around 50%. It was 02:00 local time. A ten mile an hour wind was steadily blowing from the north. Gusts of 15 miles an hour occurred frequently. The 100-odd four-man teams emerged from various tunnels and cautiously edged towards a fifty mile long stretch of the fence of the demilitarized zone. All four members of each team carried what appeared to be self-contained breathing apparatus on their backs. The steel tanks were painted dark grey, and the faces and hands of all of the men were painted with earth tone camouflage paints. Foliage was secured in helmet nets. Four hundred meters short of the fence, the four men of each team spread apart, one man every one hundred meters. When they reached the fence, each man extended a collapsible wand ten feet into the air and opened the valve on his tank. Each tank made a low hissing sound as it emptied its contents. It took fifteen minutes to empty a tank. The men turned and slowly crawled back to the tunnels from which they had emerged two hours earlier.

The first cases were reported three days later. At first, the soldiers reported to their battalion aid stations. They were running a high fever, experiencing tightness in the chest, and some reported difficulty in breathing. In the next twenty-four hours, the ranks of the ill swelled. By the fifth day, as much as fifty percent of some units were in sick bay. On day five post release, some began to die. Many were shipped the thirty-odd miles from Camp Casey to Seoul. The abandoned American bases simply could not handle the enormous number of ill South Korean soldiers. Initially, the South Korean government attempted to keep the epidemic quiet. The outbreak was noted in Seoul a week later and reported on international television. CNN spread the word of another attack of the Asian influenza. The World Health Organization committed teams of virologists, bacteriologists, and epidemiologists. The Centers for Disease Control and Prevention in Atlanta, Georgia, was invited to send its teams to Seoul.

The quick and dirty preliminary epidemiological investigation supported the contention that sixty to seventy percent of the South Korean troops on the DMZ were experiencing the disease. The case fatality ratio, that is, the number dead among those ill seemed to be about twenty-five percent.

Curtis Matthews, MD, forensic pathologist, removed his gloves, placed them in the biohazard materials bag, followed by his mask and gown. He peeled the tape off his pant legs which were stuffed into his disposable booties and deposited them as well. Now naked, he opened the airlock and stepped into the shower. The warm water flushed over him as he scrubbed himself from head to toe. He turned off the shower and turned on the disinfectant spray, allowing it to play over him. The next shower was with clean water to remove any disinfectant. Dripping wet, he moved to the next small area where he toweled dry. Then he moved into the locker room and donned his class B uniform. The eagles of his shoulder boards indicated he was a Colonel in the American Army, a representative of the Armed Forces Institute of Pathology on the Walter Reed campus in Washington, DC.

Christ, he thought to himself, *if I were back in veterinary practice, I would say this was one hell of a case of Pasteurella pneumonia,* the cause of shipping fever in a calf. Dr. Matthews had been a veterinarian before he became a physician. After several years of a mixed veterinary practice in Nebraska, with several cattle and hog feedlots in his practice, Matthews decided there had to be an easier way of making a living than delivering calves in March blizzards at minus twenty degrees Fahrenheit. Going back to Medical School at his alma mater, the University of Missouri, Columbia, was tough. It cost him a great deal emotionally and physically. It cost him his marriage. His wife, an attorney, would not stand for losing her husband to studying. His second year of medical school, she took their son and left for Denver. That year, he signed on for an Army program that commissioned him as a second lieutenant in the US Army. It paid for the next three years of medical school.

He discovered his niche in pathology his sophomore year. His clinical skills were good but not outstanding his last two years. He was promoted to captain upon graduation, as were the other members of the military program. He did an internship at Walter Reed Army Medical Center, then was accepted as a pathology resident there. After three years of residency training in pathology, he was promoted to major. He passed his pathology boards examination the next year and was promoted to lieutenant colonel. He was assigned to Irwin Army Hospital at Fort Sill, OK. After two years at Fort Sill, he returned to the Walter Reed campus as a staff pathologist at the Armed Forces Institute of Pathology. He was assigned to the respiratory diseases branch of pathology where he specialized in diseases of the lung. After two years, he became branch chief. Now at 42 years of age, he had no social life. He occasionally wrote his son and visited him once during the Christmas holidays his first year of residency. He did not know his son, who now considered himself to be the son of his stepfather.

"What do you think, Curt?"

"It's hot, whatever the agent is. I took plenty of tissue samples out of that Korean kid. Bacteriology should have some answers in three or four days. I don't know why the Koreans haven't at least figured it out down to the genus level. The hematoxylin and eosin slides I looked at earlier this morning from other cases are suggestive of a red hot bacterial pneumonia rather than a virus. The Koreans are sophisticated enough to figure that out."

"Any bets as to genus?" Dr. Timmons, an epidemiologist from the Centers of Disease Control and Prevention asked as they strolled out the hospital.

Matthews thought for a moment and looked Timmons in the eye. "Look, are you thinking it is a released agent, a biological attack or something?"

Timmons shrugged, "I doubt it, but then, you never know. North Korea's leaders are a crazy bunch. They are capable of anything. They have bluffed before and backed down at the last minute. They have pursued nukes and bioweapons in spite of everything we have done to prevent it."

As an epidemiologist, Timmons asked questions others were slow to consider. "Why only here? Why not in China, Indonesia, the Philippines, Japan or some other crowded place as well? Maybe it came out of China, and they are sitting on it, although that is extremely difficult if not impossible in today's world of information. China today is a far more open society. After the SARS episode, the Severe Acute Respiratory Syndrome with coronavirus in 2003 and 20024 plus Covid-19 in 2020 they learned their lesson about sitting on epidemics and trying to hide them. No, it does seem very suspicious. Hell, we can't even determine if it is transmissible. It's odd, but there don't seem to be any secondary cases associated with caregivers or others. It seems to be extremely infectious but nontransmissible. The fact that the majority of cases initially occurred in line units along the DMZ is very, very suspicious.

"Cases now showing up down here in Seoul indicate that it is a very hardy agent, highly resistant to the environment if it is nontransmissible. It would have to be windborne, lasting for days, not affected by humidity and sunlight. Cases here in Seoul seem to appear in pockets. I have asked meteorologists to look at wind patterns blowing out of the north. It does seem to have a much-generalized center; it is that part of the city that receives the breezes coming out of the Imjin Valley. Far fewer cases appear on the surrounding mountainsides. While we are still doing a lot of case finding, our early distribution maps and epidemiologic curve indicate that it suddenly appeared along a hundred- and fifty-mile front all along the

DMZ. Extremely abrupt in its appearance, in a linear distribution, it is very suggestive. It is also very disturbing."

"Well, if it is the opening shot, we'll know soon enough. The tanks will roll, and we will be in the proverbial polluted pond. In the meantime, let's get some lunch over at the officer's mess. I'm hungry."

"How can you eat after doing a postmortem on a kid like that? Ugh!"

———————•●◆●•———————

The city of Seoul was extremely quiet. Very few people were on the streets. All public meetings were cancelled; businesses were, for the most part, closed. Only the food stores and street vendors selling vegetables were open and out. The officer's mess was understaffed, and it took thirty minutes for them to get a sandwich. A few other officers were scattered about; almost all were Koreans. There were two other Americans in uniform. Their insignias indicated they were colonels of infantry and artillery. Nods were exchanged, but the physicians remained to themselves.

"Are there any other epidemiological indicators which you can share with me as to the nature of this beast, Dr. Timmons?" Matthews asked.

"Well, the veterinarians recently forced us to accept a veterinary epidemiologist on our team. Now, I am glad we have him. He went looking for cases in livestock, found a bunch in goats and sheep, and a few cows. Widespread too, up along the DMZ. Seems like the Koreans decided to establish a small ruminant industry a few years ago. They began to import dairy goats to establish a possible market for goat cheese, and sheep for wool and meat. He did some necropsies and brought back samples, fresh tissues for microbiological and virological culture and isolation, as well as some formalin fixed. His pathology reports indicate a red-hot pneumonia very similar to the descriptions you doctors of the dead are detailing. He says he has seen something like it before in the veterinary files at AFIP when he was a pathology preceptor there. He says it most closely resembles a red-hot strain of tularemia, one from what he called the paleoarctic branch of Francisella, or something like that."

"You say this vet is a pathologist as well? If so, I would like to meet him."

"Yeah, he was a veterinary pathologist preceptor at AFIP but isn't boarded. He has specialty boards in veterinary public health, specializing in epidemiology. He has kind of a funny personality though, almost paranoid around the rest of the team. He doesn't seem to have much of a sense of humor concerning us physicians. He's cynical, almost antagonistic towards us MDs. He seems to think veterinarians are our equals. He has a real attitude problem."

"Hmm. I guess you didn't know I was a veterinarian before I was a physician. Veterinary school was harder than medical school. Veterinarians have a saying that physicians are just veterinarians who specialize in one species. I remember a gross anatomy test that was two questions long and took two hours. 'Trace a drop of blood from the third phalange of the fifth digit of the dog through the entire circulatory system, naming all possible routes and variations.' The second question was 'compare that in the horse, pig, and cow and name all possible variations.' Veterinary medicine today has almost as many subspecialties of human medicine. Small animal medicine today is only a few years behind human medicine in specialization and competence, Doctor."

"I'll have to take your word on that, although that does tend to deflate the ego somewhat. As to Veterinarian Major Bradley, I don't know where he is right now. Probably off again, running around the countryside. One thing about him, though, he raised hell about wanting to carry a weapon. Seems he wanted a firearm of some kind, for his own protection, he claims. Says there are still bandits running around the countryside in South Korea, and he feels that it is likely that the North will come down screaming and running. He wanted both a rifle and a pistol, but the team leader nixed that. Instead, the Koreans gave him two armed guards, both of whom speak English very well, and an old Chevy Blazer to run around in. He seemed quite pleased about that. He says these Korean Rangers are the toughest in the world, and never, ever, get in a fight with them. Seems he did a tour here when he first came on active duty. Knows something about the people and the country. He said he wouldn't at all be surprised if we are at war within a week. Of course, most the team thought he was full of crap. Now, I am not so sure of anything."

"Where did he take his samples, do you know?"

Timmons shrugged. "I don't know for sure. I believe I heard him remark that he split his samples, half to go back to AFIP and half to the Korean Veterinary Institute. He didn't want much to do with the World Health Organization folks who are around here. I think they have a pathologist here, too, but I am not sure. I think they are over in Pusan. You might run over to the Korean Veterinary School here in Seoul and see what they say. We should be able to get you a driver and interpreter to get you there. As an American officer, they tell me you never, ever want to drive in this country. No doubt they speak English in that veterinary institution."

The Korean colonel in charge of liaison with the American team looked at the eagles on Matthews's shoulder boards and the gold caduceus on his blouse and nodded his head in a slight bow. In perfect English, he asked, "What can I do for you, Colonel?"

"I understand our veterinary officer has discovered similar cases in animals and taken samples to your veterinary institute. Is it possible to have a car and driver take me to your Institute of Veterinary Medicine, so that I might confer with them on what they have found?"

"It is most reasonable Colonel, and a car and driver you shall have." The colonel motioned to a soldier standing by, uttered something in Korean, and then turned to Matthews. "If you will accompany this soldier, he will see that you are immediately assigned a car and driver."

Matthews saluted, "I thank you, Colonel. I hope it will be of benefit."

Matthews studied the hematoxylin stained tissues Major Bradley, U.S. Army Veterinary Corps, had submitted to the Koreans as well as those the Korean Department of Agriculture collected. The tissues revealed identical pathology in all cases. He observed the species related differences between human, porcine, bovine, and caprine tissues. It dawned upon him that veterinary medicine just might surpass human medicine in its breadth and depth of knowledge. In spite of the tissue differences, however, the reactions to the infection were essentially the same. After two hours of reviewing the tissues, he decided that the agent was a zoonoses, a disease agent common to both animals and man. He thanked his Korean hosts, bowed at the waist, and left. En route to the former American compound at Yong San Dong, Yong San Ku, Seoul, Matthews decided to discuss his observations with Timmons over supper.

CHAPTER 10

At 03:30 the next day, from bases all along southern North Korea, six squadrons of North Korean Mig 29s, a Soviet made first line aircraft very similar to the American F-16 Fighting Falcon, and equipped with look-down shoot-down radar and missile systems, rolled out of revetments along highways that doubled as runways and took off. They rendezvoused with six squadrons of Sukhoi Su-27s, the Soviet equivalent of the USAF F15 air superiority fighter, and three squadrons of Mig -31s. Their mission was to provide air cover for the squadrons of ground attack aircraft, the Mig -27 Flogger Ds, the FC-1Dragons and Sukhoi-24D Fencers, whose mission it was to destroy the South Korean Air Force on the ground. They flew at treetop level across the DMZ. Osan Air Base and Seoul International Airport were among the first targets destroyed. It was seven air seconds from North Korea to Seoul.

Some of the South Korean F-16s from the more northern bases made it into the air and made a worthy showing for themselves. In the end, however, they were overwhelmed by sheer numbers. They did buy time for their colleagues from more southern bases to get into the fight, though. The South Korean aviators accounted themselves well. They were better trained and far exceeded their northern brethren in aerial combat. The cost, however, was tremendous, as North Korea had amassed a larger air force than anyone realized. The look-down shoot-down radar systems and the newer Mig 31s were responsible for most of the South Korean losses.

The Mig 31s were purchased from Russia in spite of denials by the Russians that they were selling modern weapons to countries such as North Korea. The North Koreans controlled their aircraft from the ground, vectoring them into the foray in the classic Soviet style. The South Koreans flew in sections of two aircraft, often attacking as many as six of their opponents at once.

At 03:35, a distant rumbling, like thunder, suddenly reverberated over the horizon. The ground along the DMZ seemed to be vibrating. Seismic sensors went off all along the DMZ. At 03:45, battalion after battalion of T-64, T-72 and T-80 Soviet model tanks poured out of the tunnels starting on the northern side of the DMZ. The T80s had British style Chobham armor which made them resistant to direct hits from most anti-tank weapons. A rolling artillery barrage from Soviet made 122 mm howitzers pounded the terrain 500 meters ahead of the tanks. Soviet style armored personnel carriers, BTRs and BTMs, were mixed among the tanks.

Satellite infra-red imagery at 05:00 showed a massive assault launched down the Imjin River valley. Smaller thrusts occurred farther to the east, all along the Korean peninsula. Light infantry in trucks moved south along the Pukhan River, and the road from Panmunjom was bumper to bumper with tanks, armored personnel carriers and supply trains. A major thrust from Kosong moved along the eastern coastline. The objective of this thrust was to occupy the road that led to Pusan and ultimately capture that port city. The South Koreans moved quickly. The roadblocks, consisting of massive stone carvings piled lengthwise along the shoulders of the highways in the northern part of the country, were dynamited, allowing the huge carved octagonal and squared cylinders four feet in diameter to roll onto the highways, blocking them for the onslaught of armored vehicles. All of the highways of Jinsang Ri, especially Route 324 paralleling the Imjin River, were bumper to bumper with North Korean combat vehicles. Hastily constructed bridges were thrown across the Imjin River near Yachon to tie into the South Korean road net at a loop of the river. Another Bailey type bridge was hastily constructed at Baembal Ri, and a third at the old Ferry site at Jingpa Ri. Armored vehicles spread out on both sides of the Imjin.

Route 3 is the major north-south hard surface highway, connecting Seoul with the DMZ. Highway 3 is west of Highway 325, running through Tongduchon. Highways 349 and 368 are parallel hard surfaced highways west of Highway 3. Farther east, Highway 43 divides at Unch-on, where a spur turns west to link with Highway 325. Highway 43 continues south where it intersects Highways 327 and 322. The North Korean 2nd Armored Division poured south out of Idong Myon. The Taebak Mountains caused the North Koreans to split their forces into two massive movements, similar to that of General McArthur in the summer of 1950 after the successful landing at Inchon.

The South Koreans blew the bridges on Highway 322 across the Imjin River just north of Mapo-ri and between Jensang-Ri on the east and Mudeung Ri on the west. Slightly to the east, an armored brigade poured down Highway 3 from Sinmang Ri. The city of Jeon-gog was overrun by the second hour, and the city of Tongduchon came under immediate attack while follow-on forces bypassed it en route to Seoul.

The telephone lines were overwhelmed as the call went out for all South Korean men and women in the reserves to report to their martialling areas. All South Korean women and girls were trained in first aid and nursing through high school to at least the level of the American licensed practical nurse. All able-bodied South Korean males studied Tae Kwon Do and military tactics while within the educational system. Any Korean male who could not achieve at least the brown belt level was considered a disgrace. All received basic training in infantry tactics and weapons as part of their normal high school curriculum. The biggest difference between the South Korean soldier and the North Korean soldier was one of hate. The North Korean was raised on a diet of hatred for Americans and for their South Korean brothers. "South Koreans are the running dogs of the Americans" was the slogan they had known from cradle to grave. Their cruelty and disregard for human life was unmatched since the Japanese cruelty of World War II. Much of that Japanese cruelty was inflicted upon Koreans. It was kept alive by tales from the grandparents of what they had suffered and observed as children. They had not forgotten.

Many of the civilians not involved in the defense immediately took to the roads, evacuating the northern cities and towns. Within hours, the highways out of Seoul became utterly clogged with civilian traffic. Those who did not have vehicles moved on foot, carrying what luggage they could. Tremendous traffic jams occurred, hampering South Korean units attempting to move north along the same highways. Traffic slowed to a snail's pace, even those in vehicles couldn't move faster because of the pedestrians. In frustration, one South Korean tank company commander even ordered his tanks forward to plow through the civilians blocking the road. Another company commander of mechanized infantry ordered his lead M-113 armored personnel carrier to clear the road by machine gun fire into the civilians. Under such circumstances, people fled to the surrounding fields or to the shoulder of the road as quickly as they realized they were being fired upon.

South Korean artillery from the former American bases such as Camp Casey and Red Cloud opened up with pre-registered fires. Air-fuel bomblets from tube artillery rained on the North Korean armored columns. Within minutes, the lead elements of the North Korean columns were in flames. Highly flammable fuels from the bomblets were immediately vaporized and then ignited. The result was a flashing explosion and searing heat, reaching 5000 degrees Fahrenheit. The ammunition and fuel within vehicles were immediately ignited and the crews incinerated. They never felt a thing. North Koreans responded with counter battery fire, and Soviet made Sukhoi-25 ground attack aircraft, NATO code named Frogfoot, zeroed in to destroy the firing batteries. South Korean soldiers with Stinger missiles guarded the artillery batteries and took their toll of the Sukhoi 25s. Many of the Sukhoi 25s took a missile hit in one of their external engines and went limping back to North Korea in flames. Others went down in flames.

Mobile surface to air missiles hidden in camouflaged revetments targeted the Migs as they flew across the DMZ, and everywhere there were no friendly aircraft in the skies north of Seoul.

North Korean armored columns poured down Highway 3 and into Tonguchon along the Imjin Gong (river), the classic invasion route to Seoul. Other columns poured down parallel Highways 325 out of Chorwon, down Highway 43 out of Kalmal, down Highways 374 and 368, and down through Idong Myon. Bridges were hastily thrown over the Injin

Gong near Yach On to tie into South Korea's road net at a loop in the Imjin north of Tongduchong. Follow-on forces poured across the bridges thrown across at Baembal Ri, and at the ferry at Jingpa Ri. Columns moved south on both sides of the Imjin. On each serviceable road, North Korean tanks, armored personnel carriers and self-propelled artillery moved, stopping only when under intense fire. Sights fell off of some of the North Korean artillery pieces when they fired. Others failed to register accurate fires. Still others simply broke down. These were pushed off the road and abandoned.

North Korean battalions linked up across east to west Highways 322, 349 and 37. Thus, they isolated whole sections of northern South Korea. In these sections, small South Korean units, platoons and companies, and even as individual soldiers, fought and fought well. Many died, but they bled the enemy with small arms and man portable weapons. They put mortar fire and Light Anti-tank Weapons (LAW) against the infantry fighting vehicles, and rifle fire with their excellent Dae Woo rifles against individual enemy soldiers. They knew history well. In the Korean War of the 1950s, North Koreans slaughtered entire villages of men, women and children, whom they suspected of being sympathetic with South Korean government. Many died of excruciating torture. The South Koreans knew it would be the same this time. Only this time, they were better prepared. They were armed, trained, and ready, knowing that it would be weeks, if ever, before American or United Nations' help could arrive. They knew they had to hold, as there was no other option. To other South Koreans, the attack was a horrifying shock. Many felt that there was no necessity for a treaty with the United States to return in case of an attack. In disbelief, they cringed with the realization that their northern relatives were attacking and would destroy much of their country in an effort to unite the peninsula under a totalitarian government.

For the last several years, Kim, Jong-un now in his 50's, had played a dangerous game of political advance and retreat, each time seemingly becoming a little less belligerent and a little more reasonable. At each conference, with each proclamation, Kim, Jong-un seemed to offer opening the door of North Korea a millimeter wider to the outside world. Yet real improvements in transparency and relationships never materialized. Weapons systems such as aircraft, tanks, armored personnel carriers, and artillery, and Russian 122 mm howitzers were purchased from Russian enterprises, owned by organized crime, and shipped disassembled as machinery parts for assembly in underground factories inside North Korea. It was a tremendous source of exports for Russia.

Physicians Matthews and Timmons heard distant explosions but didn't realize their nature. When a two-hundred-kilogram bomb landed on the building that housed the former United Nations command on the Yongsang Dong compound, they were shaken out of their beds. They dressed as hurriedly as they could. Matthews, being short sighted, had brought only Class A and Class B uniforms, which were the formal and daily office dress uniforms. He packed no battle dress uniforms. Timmons was exclusively a civilian. A product of suburban Maryland, Timmons was a member of the liberal wing of the Democratic Party. The thought of developing any type of outdoor survival skills was anathema to him. He particularly loathed firearms and the right for civilians to own them.

"It seems your veterinarian was right, Mark," remarked Matthews as he pulled on his pants. "I hope to hell he isn't up there on the DMZ."

"Well, if he is, he is probably toast by now, literally," responded Timmons. Neither said anything more as they moved out the door. At that moment, cannon fire from a Frogfoot raked their building.

At the same moment, Major Robert Bradley was in a Korean inn in the town of Hwach'on, on the road north of Ch'unch'on. He and his Korean guards were pulling on their camouflage Battle Dress Uniforms, known colloquially as BDUs, as fast as they could. "We have to get the hell out of here," yelled Bradley, over the noise of the North Korean aircraft. "I think we should head south toward Ch'unch'on. What do you gentlemen think?"

The Korean captain shouted, "I think you are right on both counts, Major. We need to get the hell out of here, and we need to head south. This road was extended into North Korea in the 1990s under the sunshine program. North Korean armor is probably already moving south on it. We couldn't be more than a few kilometers ahead of it." The Korean sergeant vigorously shook his head yes. With that, they all dashed out to their camouflaged painted Chevy Blazer. The sergeant drove, the Captain rode shotgun, and Bradley sat in the back seat. He reached behind him and pulled three MREs from the open case. One was beef ravioli, one was chicken tetrazzini and the third vegetarian bean and burrito. He kept the beef ravioli and handed the other two to the captain. The captain looked at the labels and put the vegetarian bean and burrito between the sergeant's legs as he drove. The sergeant glanced down just long enough to read the label. "Thank you, Sir," was the sergeant's response. Civilian traffic was already moving south along the road.

At 04:00, a phone call went to the White House. "Mr. President, Mr. President!" The aide's hand shook the President from a fitful slumber. He opened his eyes to the dim light, looking into the face of his aide. "Mr. President, North Korea has attacked South Korea. They are attacking in force at several points across the DMZ."

"Oh God!" was the only comment heard from the First Lady at the President's side.

"Put all American forces on full alert. Alert all reserve and guard units as well as active forces. I want breakfast in twenty minutes, a meeting with the National Command Authority in one hour, and the Joint Chiefs of Staff to join us in two hours." The President liked breakfast. He felt that he could function better on a full stomach and a clear mind. He showered quickly, dressed in slacks and dress shirt, put on a necktie, and sat down in his private quarters to a breakfast of bacon and eggs, toast, jam, orange juice, milk and coffee.

At 60, Jason Thornton was still slim and trim. He worked out in the White House gym and swimming pool on a daily basis, even taking Tong Soo Do lessons twice a week, sometimes more. He was the first Republican president after eight years of Democratic Party administration, during which the Democrats controlled both the houses of Congress. One of the planks in his platforms was to restore some military capability. While never having served in the armed forces, not even in the reserves, he read history as a hobby. One of three children, he had an older brother and a younger sister. He was raised in the Presbyterian Church and on the two hundred acre family farm where they grew corn, sorghum, alfalfa for hay, raised hogs and fed out about thirty head of steers each year. His older brother was the real farmer in the family. His parents wanted him to be a veterinarian, but his sister turned out to pursue that profession. In fact, after graduating with her Doctor of Veterinary Medicine from Iowa State University, she did an internship followed by a residency in equine medicine. She made quite a name for herself as an equine practitioner.

Jason had earned a Bachelor of Arts in political science at Iowa University and an L.L.B. at the same institution. After graduation, he served as a junior partner in a law firm in Davenport, Iowa for four years. After not being offered a full partnership, he moved to a small town in Iowa and started his own general practice. After two years, he was elected county attorney. After four years of county attorney, he was elected circuit court judge. Following this, he was appointed as a federal district judge. Being dismayed with the irresponsible legislation which he was bound to follow, he decided to do something to change it. Then he was elected to the House of Representatives. After four terms, he ran for the U.S. Senate. He was elected for two terms, which was his springboard for the presidency.

Now, in his first six months of office, his worst fear had come true. He was being put to the most severe test of all - whether or not to commit U.S. forces to battle on the Asian mainland and lead the country into war. From reading history, he saw parallels between the United States and the Roman Empire in the first century, in Great Britain after World War I, and the failure of the United States to prepare for world leadership after World War II. He recognized the consequences of these failures of World War II by the British failure to assume leadership, the United States failing between World War II and the Korean War, and the failure to maintain that leadership after the demise of the Soviet Union and the end of the Cold War.

The South Korean reserve battalions were tertiary targets for the Sukhoi 25s. Their higher priorities went to air bases, anti-aircraft and artillery assets, radar sites, communications nodes, and the headquarters units of active forces of regiments and divisions. Those reserve units which had so far escaped targeting were essentially formed by 08:00 and had drawn their weapons. By this time, the second wave of North Korean aircraft were making themselves felt. They attacked the South Korean convoys headed north as targets of opportunity.

Inchon was taken within the first 96 hours after heavy house to house fighting. North Korea mounted a division-sized amphibious operation, landing north of Inchon and cutting off that approach to the city. On the second day, a second division was landed as reinforcements, and on the fifth day, a third division to begin encirclement of the city. North Korea was not about to let a repeat of McArthur's famous landing in 1950, notwithstanding that the United States had neither the forces nor the will to do so. Rocket propelled grenades, RPGs, of the North Koreans, and Light Anti-Tank, or LAW, handheld missiles of the South Koreans took a terrible toll on their respective enemies. The South Koreans used their LAWs on the North Korean vehicles, especially the armored personnel carriers, like snipers. They fired from buildings, from behind bushes and trees and walls, any place there was cover. When the North Korean infantry dismounted from their vehicles, they were met with a fusillade of semi-automatic rifle fire from the South Koreans Dae-Woo rifles and grenade launchers. Neither side held their fire when civilians were caught in the crossfires.

The roads leading from Uijongbu and Kaesong into Seoul became so clogged with burning North Korean vehicles that they became a formidable roadblock themselves. Pushing them off the road slowed the North Korean advance. North Korean commanders from the company level up, frustrated by the fierceness of the resistance and the resultant slow progress towards Seoul, berated their troops to move even faster. The North Korean soldiers who reached the edge of Seoul after forty-eight hours of heavy fighting, were awed by how modern the city was, by the shops, the material goods, and the apparent health and wealth of the civilian population. While as soldiers, they were well-fed, they knew full well that their own civilian population was again on the brink of mass starvation. The more intelligent and educated among them were troubled by their observations. This was particularly true of the company grade officers. They said nothing, however, of their observations to their enlisted personnel. Some of the enlisted men began to loot. The more fanatical of their officers shot those they caught looting. Other officers beat, slapped, whipped and kicked their troops back into the battle.

CHAPTER 11

The Secretaries of State, Defense (SECDEF), and Homeland Security, the Director of Central Intelligence (DCI), the Director of the FBI, the Chairman of the Joint Chiefs of Staff, the National Security Advisor, the President and the Vice President compose the National Command Authority. Except for the Secretary of Defense, who was fishing in Wyoming and the Secretary for Homeland Security, they were all waiting as the President walked in. The Assistant Secretary of Defense represented him.

"Ladies and gentlemen, who has not had breakfast?" Somewhat surprised by what they viewed as slightly irreverent by the President at the moment, they all raised their hands. The President turned to his aide, "Johnny, call the kitchen, have them send up some bacon and eggs and ham, pancakes, toast, juice, coffee and milk and all the fixings for our guests, ASAP." John Withers nodded and walked to a phone in the next room to place the order.

"Folks, if you are not aware of it, North Korea attacked South Korea at 03:30 this morning. I've ordered a helicopter to pick up the SECDEF in Wyoming. He'll fly by jet out of Casper. He should be here by this afternoon. In the meantime, we will proceed without him. Ed, can you give us a brief update of what happened and current status?"

Ed McCluskey, the Director of Central Intelligence, said, "We have limited information at this point. We know that the North led the attack with several massive waves of aircraft, while armored units attacked along several axes. Intermediate objectives have been identified as Inchon, Seoul, and Pusan as a final one. Our satellites picked up these waves as they took off and headed south. Intense fighting is going on all along the peninsula. The South Koreans have initially given a good account of themselves. The question remains: is this an all-out push or an attack of limited objectives? None of our intelligence indicates that this is anything but an all-out attack to unite the peninsula under domination by the north.

"We have two aircraft carrier battle groups presently in the Pacific. One is in the South China Sea, and the other is south of the Indonesian Archipelago. A third is present in the Indian Ocean, standing south, off the Straits of Hormuz. Our liaison office is in Yongsan Dong, Yongsan Ku, at our old Eighth U.S. Army Headquarters. We have lost contact with them. We expect that that base has been heavily attacked. We do have other people over there in other offices, and we have contacted them by cell phone, via satellite relay. Our satellite imagery reveals that the North Koreans are at least three echelons deep above Corps level. I put in a call to the Director, National Reconnaissance Office for a measure of North Korean traffic headed south, on all radio traffic at the division level and higher, and anything else they have on the situation. I am waiting for a return call on that on my secure phone. In the eastern part of the peninsula, where it is more mountainous, they will have to move slower. They can't utilize their massive armor brigades as efficiently. It is more of a light infantry conflict. That will be tough.

"We don't know how much support the North Koreans will receive from the Chinese or Russians. It is far more likely that that China will support them. Russia should have no stake in it. We do have confirmed reports that the Russians have been selling them armor and first-line aircraft at varying rates and models for the last two decades. This seems to be a matter of the Russian mafia that runs the manufacturing plants rather than official Russian government policy. I'll send classified memos to everyone present as the situation develops and more information is available."

"Marge, what have you heard from your State Department folks over there? Any word at all?" Marge Talbot, Secretary of State, frowned. "We had an initial communication that came in at 03:45. It said that a wave of North Korean aircraft had attacked Seoul. We presume other points, targets north of Seoul, have come under intense fire as well. Our message was sent in the clear. Apparently, they saw no justification to encrypt it. I don't see any reason either. Our response was a request for more information, but we haven't been able to raise them. It is not unreasonable to assume our embassy was a North Korean target; no doubt a stray bomb, quite by accident, destroyed it, of course! I anticipate we will receive an apology when things quiet down a bit. Things have been pretty quiet over there for the last six months, so we didn't know if the North had calmed down or what. Apparently, they were trying to play it cool while they finalized their plans and amassed their forces. That's all I have at this time, Mr. President."

"General, what do your folks have to say?"

Ronald Craig, Chairman, Joint Chiefs of Staff responded. "I put in a call to the Chief of Naval Operations as soon as my aide awakened me. He told me that he would immediately order the carrier battle groups in the region to steam towards the Korean peninsula. He seemed to think it would be a good idea to put one group on each side of the peninsula, the Sea of Japan and the South China Sea. I concurred. One should be on station in twenty-four hours, and the other could take as long as two days. All naval forces worldwide should now be on alert through the office of the CNO, per your order earlier this morning.

"The South Koreans are tough and determined. I do not know, however, what the outcome will be. As Ed said, it will probably hinge on how much support they get from China, and whether or not they will use tactical nuclear weapons. If they do go to nukes, all bets are off. We left enough tactical nukes there when we pulled out for the South Koreans to eliminate the north. On the other hand, nobody wants to make a glass-lined, radioactive parking lot out of land they covet. Still, the North Korean leadership is crazy enough to do anything. If it goes badly for them long enough, it would not surprise me to see North Korea let the nuclear genie out of the bottle.

"This pretty well confirms, at least to me, that the massive illness experienced by the South Korean troops up on the DMZ is the result of a biological attack. The last word I had from our medical boys at Fort Detrick was that the organism appeared to be a genetically altered strain of tularemia. Extremely infectious, but not contagious. Apparently, this organism is very easily genetically manipulated and can be tailored for a particular situation. They have been doing DNA analysis comparing it to all known related organisms. It seems the North Koreans engineered resistance to all commonly used antibiotics into it. While it is certainly lethal enough, killing about fifty or more percent of the victims, it does not seem to be transmissible person to person. Rather, it results in a significant illness that takes a long time for recuperation. That tells us that they want to reduce the potential for infection in the civilian population, especially in Seoul. I would suggest that they want to preserve the brain talent in that city. That's where most of their national expertise lives. That biological attack, in itself, might constitute a declaration of use of weapons of mass destruction. The South Korean strategy is to attrit the attacking force initially, bring it to a standstill along a line roughly halfway down South Korea, then launch a counterattack that will take them all the way to the Yalu. That is another story. Nobody knows what will happen when, or if, the South Koreans get that far. Nobody knows if the Chinese will get into it the way they did in the fall of 1950 when they attacked NATO forces south across the Yalu."

"Ladies and gentlemen, you are all aware we are under treaty to come to the aid of South Korea. General, what land forces are immediately deployable and how soon can we get them there?"

"Mr. President, we have our two premier divisions, the 82nd Airborne, and the 101st Air Assault. It will take about 24 hours to get task organized, draw sufficient ammunition from the stores, and get them to the ships. We might be able to airlift a few battalions in, but that is about it. Our air fleet is incapable of moving any significant heavy forces. It will only be light forces that we can immediately deploy. It will take two weeks for us to get heavy forces to the coasts and on ships and started. A major logistical problem exists in that we don't have enough organic sealift. We will have to contract with many foreign vessels in order to provide any sustainable logistical support, the way we did in the first Gulf War. Our seven fast roll-on roll-off ships won't get an intact heavy division to the battle in time.

We only have two of the new San Antonio class LHD assault ships in the water. I can have the 18th Airborne Corps out of Fort Hood, TX ready to roll in twenty-four hours, ready to board the ships in Galveston, but unfortunately, we won't have any ships for them to board. In all, it will be about a month before we have heavy forces on the peninsula. The Marines have an expeditionary brigade afloat in the Indian Ocean. It would take about five days to get them into the battle. Thirty-five hundred Marines and a dozen aging Harrier aircraft aboard half a dozen ships screened by one submarine aren't going to make much difference. They would more or less be a sacrificial lamb. Nevertheless, they are steaming in that direction. The war could well be over – or go nuclear - by the time our heavy forces arrive. We have to decide then whether or not, if that nuclear genie escapes from the bottle, we want to commit to a nuclear battlefield. Almost certainly, our leading elements as well as our logistical support will receive nuclear fires under such circumstances. The CNO tells me that if it goes nuclear, our ships will probably be hit while they are several hundred miles out to sea to preclude any rescue or support of any kind."

"Marge, are there any indications at all, even the most trivial hint, of how the Chinese will act in all of this?"

"No, Mr. President, there isn't the slightest hint. The Chinese toned down the rhetoric just before the last national elections and haven't turned it up again. They have been most polite, even almost accommodating. I find that a bit disconcerting, given their rhetoric and minor irritating actions over the last few years. I don't have a good feeling about them."

"Marge, do we have anything at all from our so-called friends and allies?"

"The British called to let us know that they are standing by their red phones if and when you decide to call, Mr. President. Germany simply sent us a secure fax stating that they are aware of the North Korean invasion. Nothing more, nothing less. No one else has responded in any way."

"If any of you have any subordinates with expertise that might be of value that you want to bring into the discussion, call them now. Ed, call the Recon Office and find out what they have at the moment."

"Yes, sir." Ed McCluskey and Margaret Talbott scooted their chairs back and reached for their cell phones as they moved to the foyer. Talbott called her office, while McCluskey called the National Reconnaissance Office for an update. Talbott told them to get Roberta Sterns to the White House ASAP. "Send a car for her, with an armed guard, and be quick about it."

Breakfast for the meeting was wheeled in on several carts as the two returned from the foyer. The President said, "Let's eat, folks. We can think and talk while we chow down." The President had once deeply regretted to himself that he had never served in the military service of his country. Now, he saw the value of it and vowed that if he could, he would change the constitution to require that the President of the United States serve at least two years of active military duty. The cabinet members quickly filled their plates and returned to the table. Stewards served hot coffee and tea as they ate. The President and Marge Talbott preferred tea to coffee, so there was always hot tea available.

Johnny Withers walked to the President's chair and whispered in his ear. "Bring him in, Johnny."

"Yes, sir" said Johnny Withers as he briskly walked out of the room. In a moment, he returned with an oriental visitor.

"Ladies and gentlemen, I'm sure you know Mr. Pak, Whin-yu, the North Korean delegate from their Consulate here in Washington."

Mr. Pak, Whin-yu, bowed graciously from the waist to the President, and glanced at the table. "I am so sorry to interrupt your breakfast, I did not know you were eating, or I would have waited outside."

"Nonsense, Mr. Pak, we are glad you are here. We are most certainly interested in everything you have to say."

"Thank you, Mr. President. I have been instructed to hand you a letter from our Kim, Jong-un, regarding the current circumstances in our homeland." Pak, Whin-yu removed a file folder from his case and handed it to Johnny Withers who handed it to the President. He carried the document in a simple polyvinyl case. He did not like being searched by the Secret Service Agents who would not allow him to carry anything in without intense scrutiny, including radiographing it.

"I will wait outside, Mr. President, while you and your Cabinet discuss it, in case you so desire to reply. Thank you for seeing me." Pak, Whin-yu bowed again, took two steps backward, turned and walked away. Johnny

Withers escorted him to an outside waiting room, offered him some coffee or tea and breakfast Danish rolls and returned to the Conference Room.

The President read the letter out loud as the Cabinet continued to eat.

> "Dear Mr. President: Our wonderful country of Korea is about to be re-united under one government. We are one people, not two, and shall go forward from this day as one. It is in the best interest of all concerned if this is accomplished without outside interference. It is a problem exclusively of the Korean people and will be exclusively resolved by the Korean people.
>
> Any outside interference will not be tolerated and will be considered an act of war. We, the People's Republic of Korea, are fully prepared to utilize any and all means at our disposal, including weapons of mass destruction, against any nation or nations that attempts to interfere in our internal affairs. The consequences of such interference are so severe that that interference should not even be a consideration. We will utilize all means at our disposal to attack both the military forces and the homeland of the nation that sends them.
>
> We feel confident that the United States will act in its own best interest in this matter. We look forward to having a warm and working relationship with the United States in the future."
>
> Kim, Jong-un
> President, People's Republic of Korea

The President glanced around the room, then turned to Johnny Withers. "Tell Mr. Pak Whin-yu that we have no reply for his government at this time. We will send for him as soon as we have formulated a response."

"Yes, Mr. President." Johnny Withers walked away. The President glanced at the faces in the room. He noticed his personal bodyguard, Win, James Ho Lee (alias Robert Lee) a second generation Chinese American, stood with arms across his chest, looking out into the foyer where Withers disappeared.

"Comments, people," said the President. No one spoke. "Myron, as Assistant SECDEF, get your top dog military medical intelligence guy up here, right now. I want everyone to know the latest about biological weapons of mass destruction."

"Yes, Mr. President, it will be a couple of hours. We will fly him in from Fort Detrick, at the Medical Intelligence unit where he is commander. I'll send a helicopter after him." Ed McCluskey left the table once again, this time to call Andrews Air Force Base to dispatch a UH-60 Blackhawk helicopter, with gunship escorts. Then he called the Medical Intelligence Unit Commander at Fort Detrick on a hot line. "Colonel, I'm sending a helicopter after you. It should be there in an hour. Pack a suitcase. You're wanted at the White House, and you might be here for several days to weeks. That is all." After he heard a "Yes, sir" for response, McCluskey hung up without waiting for further conversation and returned to the conference room.

Frank Burgess, Colonel, Medical Corps, U.S. Army, Defense Medical Intelligence Unit, Commanding, hung up his red phone. He picked up his routine phone and called his wife. "Honey, I have to go to Washington. Turn on the news. North Korea just attacked across the DMZ. I'm sure that is what this about. Pack me a couple of bags, with two Class A uniforms, three or four uniform shirts, underwear, ditty bag, raincoat, and a couple of civilian outfits, you know the drill. I have to go to D.C. and might be gone for a week or so. I'll send a car over to pick them up. Put my Beretta 96 in as well, along with my Kydex holster and my shoulder holster and magazine pouch with an extra magazine. I'm sure I won't need it, but you know the Washington, D.C. area." The Colonel had applied for and received a federal pistol permit from the FBI based upon his position in the Army. He really didn't like going armed in the nation's capitol, but it was better to be safe than sorry.

Johnny Withers strode over to Marge Talbott and whispered in her ear. Marge spoke, "Mr. President, Roberta Stearns, my Deputy Undersecretary for Far Eastern Affairs, is in the foyer. She has been preaching something like this for the last couple of years.

The President nodded to Withers, "Bring her in, Johnny."

Roberta Stearns, at thirty-five, was a rather attractive woman. Slim, auburn hair brushed back, tall, even lithesome, with blue-grey eyes, she moved very well. She was rather plainly dressed in squashed heels and hose, a loose skirt and a half-sleeved blouse. June in Washington, D.C. can be quite warm. Being from a somewhat modest family, she joined the Army out of high school for three years as a way of paying for college. It helped. She served as a clerk in the logistics shop, traffic management office, for XVIIIth Airborne Corps at Fort Hood, TX. She was an E-4 at the end of her three-year tour. She acquired a bachelor's degree in business administration from a central Midwestern university, but found it somewhat inane. She enrolled in a dual master's program for history and political science in a major north central university in a large metropolitan area. She found the coursework in particular and the program in general so liberally biased and politically correct, she dropped it after three years. Her disenchantment with the program, combined with a disappointing love affair, caused her to decide to move west for a change of scenery and perhaps philosophy. She applied and was accepted into law school at the University of Wyoming. Completing her Juris Doctorate in only three years, she found that government service offered the most promise of steady employment where her skills could be applied and she would earn an acceptable income. Her parents were ecstatic, as they were both quite proud of their only daughter and almost bankrupt in financing her graduate education. She had also borrowed a great deal of money the last three years so that she could concentrate on her law studies.

———— •◦◆◦• ————

Roberta Stearns followed Withers into the conference room. "Have some coffee or tea, or rolls, or breakfast, anything on the table, whatever you like; don't be bashful, you can eat and talk, we are extremely informal here. We would all like to hear anything you have to say on the current situation."

"Thank you, Mr. President. A cup of tea will be fine." The steward looked at her, they exchanged glances, and she said "Two lumps, no lemon, thanks." The steward smiled and served her hot tea as she took an empty chair at the end of the table.

You are probably aware of the North Korean attack across the South Korean border in a pre-dawn attack this morning. We are awaiting an update of details, but it appears to be a full-blown hell-bent-for-leather attack to re-unite the peninsula. That view was confirmed a little while ago by the North Korean ambassador, Pak, Whin –yu, whom I suspect you have met."

"Yes, Mr. President, I have met Pak, Whin-yu, and I do not trust him or his government. I am not surprised by the attack. I have expected it for some time."

"Can you tell us why you have expected this attack, Ms. Stearns?"

"Yes, Mr. President. I have had a very unpopular theory for several years that China is orchestrating a massive war on several fronts. I see that they must attack in order to avoid a combination of mass starvation, economic stagnation due to a strategic long-term shortage of energy and selected raw materials. Their economic growth has not kept up with their population growth, in spite of long-term attempts at population control. In my opinion, they have kept their true population demographics secret. I believe that this is only the opening move on a chess board. The Korean peninsula is but one maneuver."

"This is going to be interesting. Please go on, Ms. Stearns."

"First, the Chinese have established a tremendous trade deficit with us, one which will be difficult for us to overcome. We have become dependent on so many Chinese goods that it will be quite difficult to find other sources for our goods or to initiate manufacture of them ourselves. We have become so very dependent on China, literally, for much of our manufactured goods in all endeavors. Everything, from electronics to heavy appliances, to the routine, mundane things we use every day. It will take years to build the plants, train the workforce, and re-establish their manufacture in the United States. Europe is not all that far behind us in the same regard. The Chinese are well aware of this. China has become the manufacturing center of the world.

"Second, over the past several years, the Chinese have been more than friendly, even appearing to bend over backwards, so to speak, to present the image of a benevolent behemoth. This is consistent with their psychology of war, as first elucidated by Sun Tzu. 'When you are strong, appear weak, when you are weak, appear strong.' They have deliberately presented a most benign façade. This façade also served the purpose of duping the United States in to reducing its military capability, so that we could not respond to any crisis that they might generate. As certain politicians like to say, 'Where's the threat?'

"Third, the weather gods have been against the Chinese for the last decade. Our estimate of their grain reserves in 2007 was around 350 million metric tons. Due to several years of floods, then five years of severe drought, plus an increasing and youthful population, we believe these reserves are almost exhausted if they are already not depleted. Now, India's population is nearly that of China's. China now has to compete with India for food. India itself is acutely aware that the next green revolution has not materialized as many expected. The results have been quite disappointing on that issue.

"Fourth, intelligence sources indicate that China has been building a tremendous military type truck fleet, with an emphasis on a fleet of medium duty trucks. These are something like our classic military trucks that carry up to two and a half tons; hence its military nickname of 'deuce and a half.' To go along with this, road building programs through western and southern China have taken on an added impetus in the last five years. They have had major construction programs in western and southern China. To go along with the road building, they have been laying railroad tracks big time. What is there in western China that requires four major parallel rail lines? The answer is the oil of the Caspian Sea area.

"Many claim that this is simply an indication of growing internal commerce and transportation. Most of those trucks, however, have been camouflage painted, or painted in dull military colors.

"Fifth, when China put pressure on North Korea to end their nuclear program early in this decade, North Korea complied, somewhat too willingly to my way of thinking. I came to the conclusion that the only way that China could persuade North Korea to end its uranium enrichment, allow inspections of its facilities, and present a go-along face to the west was to promise, or provide them, with fissile materials or perhaps ready made Chinese nukes. We know that they also supplied oil and food to North Korea. This allowed North Korea to have its cake and eat it, too. They could develop nuclear power for domestic consumption and still have nuclear weapons.

"Sixth, North Korea has one of the most sophisticated and advanced biological weapons programs in the world, if not the most advanced. Intelligence reports, while few and far between and somewhat generalized, suggest that they have weaponized a number of pathogens for release on any major opponent.

"Seventh, they, China, have modestly trained and equipped a tremendous military reserve at minimal cost, while keeping their standing army at modest levels in terms of equipment and manpower. This reserve has been concentrated in rural areas, but also some of the population centers along the coast. Estimates of the size of this reserve vary from one hundred million men to two hundred million men. We really don't know how big it is. While Mr. Pak, Whin-yu has told me that this is a method of keeping peace in the rural areas, to prevent roving gangs of marauders seeking food, raping women and the essentials of life, I believe they have a more sinister primary purpose.

"Eighth, they have created several consortiums with Pakistan. One of which has built their new joint venture, multi-role jet aircraft, the FC-1 Dragon. Pakistan has built quite a number of these aircraft in the last few years, as has China. How many, we don't precisely know. As a multi-role aircraft, they appear to be a bit superior to the European Tornado, with an emphasis on ground attack. Additionally, Pakistan has also emphasized building a quite large fleet of medium-sized military trucks. Ammunition plants in both China and Pakistan have been producing substantial amounts of small arms ammunition for about four years. It is stored in various depots in both countries.

"That, Mr. President, in a nutshell, is what I think about this attack."

"If China is behind this, Ms. Stearns, why aren't they pouring across the Yalu to assist the North Koreans?"

"Very simply, Mr. President, I believe the Chinese are going to use North Korea as a surrogate, and possibly others, and utilize their tremendous reserve manpower to attack in other directions."

Margaret Talbott seemed to explode. "Ms. Stearns, this is what I have heard from you before, but you offer no concrete proof of this. How you can draw such conclusions that China will attack its neighbors without more definitive evidence is not the way to conduct the affairs of state! When I sent for you, I did not expect that you would present such a full-blown theory against the Chinese. Rather, that you would limit yourself to known facts."

The President waved a hand to quiet Marge Talbott. "Please go on, Ms. Stearns, I find this quite fascinating. Far-fetched, yes, but not outside the realm of possibility. Anything is possible. Please, go on."

"Well, the road building program to the west and south, the military truck procurement program, their shortage of oil, their massive buildup of reserves and small arms ammunition all suggest to me that they plan to move west and south. Perhaps they will go through the Malayan peninsula, perhaps to eliminate India as competition for food and as a threat, one or both."

"Ed, what do you make of Ms. Stearns theory?"

"Mr. President, it is quite far-fetched and extremely unlikely, yet everything she has said regarding the reasons is factual. However, I don't think it will occur. It is so unlikely that I think we can dismiss it."

"Anything else you would like to say, Ms. Stearns?"

"No, Mr. President, I have said more than enough. Still, I feel obligated to express my theory, however it is regarded. That is what I am paid to do."

The President smiled. "Indeed, it is, Ms. Stearns, and I appreciate it. If you would please stay close. I might wish to confer with you later. Leave your cell phone number and any other numbers where we might reach you with my secretary on your way out. Don't leave town. I appreciate your candor and your prompt response."

"Thank you, Mr. President." Roberta Stearns got up and was escorted out by Johnny Withers. Withers smiled and said to Stearns, "That was a pretty good show you put on in there. Stick by your guns, lady, you have done better than you think."

Roberta smiled and said thanks, and Johnny left her in the presence of the President's secretary.

Johnny Withers walked to the President. "Sir, the Joint Chiefs are assembled in the war room in the basement."

"Let's adjourn down there and join the Chiefs," said the President. "Have the Director of Homeland Security join us in the war room, Johnny, as soon as he arrives." After the President stood, so did all the others, and they trooped downstairs, led by the President and trailed by his personal bodyguard, Robert Lee. Withers directed the Homeland Security Chief, who had just arrived and was in the waiting room, to join them.

CHAPTER 12

Multiple video screens were on the wall, displaying live satellite images of varying points around the world, but mostly on the Korean peninsula and the surrounding waters. Most disturbing were the massive columns of armor, men and trucks moving across the DMZ into South Korea at numerous points. Another screen depicted the air battles going on all over the peninsula. Another portrayed the Sea of Japan, while another, the Yellow Sea.

"Ed, do you have any update from your people in Seoul?"

"No, Mr. President, I do not. Apparently, they are overrun, as our liaison office there has been bombed, all telephone communications are being jammed at the local level through microwave interference there, and the South Koreans are in general too busy to respond. What information we have, Mr. President, is what is presented on the screens right here."

"General Craig, how do you read it?"

"The South Koreans were slow to respond the first four hours. They took a pretty good beating, but they are stiffening now. The reserves were a bit slow in getting mobilized, but they are getting their act together, and the attack has slowed a bit. That is partly due to the roadblocks being dropped in place, several bridges being blown, and the roads having artillery delivered mines scattered on them. Heavy fighting is going on around Seoul. From what we surmise, the South Korean forward artillery did a pretty good job, but they were overrun, or at least silenced, about an hour ago. The South Korean Air Force has suffered significant losses. They were caught on the ground initially, but their pilots are far more skilled than their North Korean counterparts. They have taken out a number of North Korean aircraft. A few North Korean aviators, however, seem exceptionally skilled. They probably were trained out of country. Trouble is, all of the South Korean air bases got hit pretty hard. They took a lot of rocket hits as well as strafing by the North's air force. We tracked their incoming missiles by satellite. I must say, they were surprisingly accurate. We don't know the current condition of the South's air bases. They were hit as far as south as Pusan. We don't know if we can get in or not."

The President handed Withers the North Korean letter, "Generals, we have heard from the North Korean ambassador. Johnny, make copies of this letter for everybody. After you read it, I'll hear your opinions."

After ten minutes, the Joint Chiefs glanced at each other, recognizing the feasibility of the threats stated in the document.

"Roger wasn't able to join us initially upstairs, so this letter is also new to him. Roger, what's your take on the letter from the North Koreans?"

Roger Gutierrez, Secretary for Homeland Security, took off his glasses. "It's a viable threat, Mr. President. God knows it is so easy to smuggle anything into this country at any time, across any of our borders. They could have nuclear weapons here, or worse, biologicals. Either could be tactical or strategic, depending upon the nature of it, where it is deployed, and under what conditions. The real questions are: is it a bluff or is the threat genuine, and will they carry it out? God knows, they are the world's masters at brinkmanship. They should realize, however, that we can, and probably will, blow them off the face of the earth with nuclear retaliation if they should unleash a biological weapon or detonate a nuke here. That is something we must force them to understand, regardless of our course of action."

Roger Gutierrez had come into the United States as a seven-year-old illegal immigrant with his mother, a single parent. Working in the shadows, his mother Elena scrimped and saved at every opportunity. Realizing the necessity for money to send her son to college so that he might succeed, she sometimes did so in an immoral manner. She did not initially speak English but forced her son to do so. He quickly learned

English on the street, joining a gang of street scamps to help him. Elana made him teach her what he learned when they were home together, which was not often. In two years, he had a passing knowledge of the language. At the age of eleven, he enrolled in a public school, presenting a false address, birth certificate, and claiming the legitimate Mexican American neighbors as his parents. Living in the barrio of East Los Angeles, he spent all his free time at the library learning everything he could. He went to a public high school, where he graduated with a perfect 4.0 grade point average. Rather than play sports after school, he worked for a local grocery store to help supplement the family income. He was a good worker, and the store manager who, on rare occasion and unknown to Roger, engaged the services of his mother, gave him a discount on all his food purchases. Roger strongly suspected what his mother did to supplement their income, but he chose to ignore how his mother made the money for his schooling. Instead, he was grateful and loved her for it. It made him study all that much harder.

Roger applied for, and won, a scholarship in mathematics to San Diego State. He graduated cum laude with a Bachelor of Arts, which was well enough to be accepted into a master's degree program in mathematics and computer engineering at the same institution. At this time, he presented himself to the Immigration and Naturalization Service and applied for citizenship. They turned a blind eye to his history and counted the time he entered high school as time towards his naturalization. After acquiring his M.S. degree, he went to work for Boeing aircraft in Wichita, KS. He became a full-fledged United States citizen. While working in classified unmanned aerial vehicles design, he earned a master's degree in administration at Washburn University. There, he was noticed by the Federal Aviation Administration and hired by the FAA to work on control of unmanned passenger aircraft systems. He quickly moved up the bureaucratic ladder. When Jason Thornton was elected President, he needed to balance his Cabinet with a suitable number of minorities in order to achieve the politically correct balance. His choice of Roger Gutierrez was a good one.

"Admiral Stark, where are our forces, and how soon can we get the carriers there to help out?"

"One battle group was west of Diego Garcia in the Indian Ocean, doing picket duty. It's headed towards the Yellow Sea now but won't get there for at least three days. We have another east of Taiwan. That group can be in the Sea of Japan in about twenty-four hours. The Marine Expeditionary Brigade off Diego Garcia isn't large enough to really make any difference. It is only the carrier air wings at this point that can lend any real support to the South Koreans. Both carrier groups have squadrons of F-18E Super Hornets, and the MEB has about six of the new Joint Strike Fighters. Both are capable of ground attack, but that is really the specialty area of the Strike Fighters. We only have three squadrons in the Navy and two of the Marine's version in the Marine Corps right now."

"General Shelton, what can the Air Force do at this time?"

"Mr. President, our AWACS are flying about fifty miles out to sea, covering the entire peninsula from fifty thousand feet. I have given the order for them to retreat at any indication that they will come under attack, as they are unarmed, and we can't get fighter escorts to them in a timely manner. They are monitoring the air traffic over the peninsula. We are not sending any data to the South Koreans from them at this time, which is probably why they haven't been attacked.

"With the retirement of a number of the B-52s three years ago, and the F-111s last year, we have very limited long-range bombing capabilities. There are about thirty B-52s that are combat ready. We do have two squadrons of long range B-1 bombers on the west coast and a couple of squadrons of B-2s that can take off from Whiteman Air Force Base in Missouri, refuel in Hawaii, refuel again by air over Japan if we can get tankers airborne ahead of them out of Hawaii, but it will be tough. Only about 30 of the B-1Bs and sixteen of the B-2s are combat ready. Without any land base anywhere except Guam, we are hurting. I'll bet right now both the Koreans and the Japanese are wishing that they hadn't thrown us out. We sure could use Okinawa. Ditto the Philippines. Without land bases, we might be able to fly no more than a squadron-sized strike every twenty-four hours due to lack of refueling capabilities. Diego Garcia has limited capabilities in this regard. Perhaps as important is the fact that the British own Diego Garcia. With their current anti-American Labor Government, I don't know what to expect. We have to have their permission before we can utilize the base there in time of war, even though we built it. They don't store a heck of a lot of JP-8 fuel for our aircraft, at least not in terms of extended combat operations. Perhaps enough for two weeks of round the clock combat. If we start hauling aircraft fuel to the Navy's carriers, we might be able to conduct a dozen or so strikes before we run the well dry. The last administration regarded our renting modified 767s from Boeing for use as tankers as a sweetheart deal for Boeing. With the cancellation of the contract, we lack any strategic depth in aerial refueling."

"Why are so few of these bombers combat ready, General?"

"Sir, the last administration raided the OPM, the Operational and Maintenance, funds for other purposes so that we don't have enough spare parts for one hundred percent maintenance. We cannibalize the down aircraft as necessary to keep the others in the air."

"Marge, go upstairs and get on the horn with first the Japanese, then the Filipinos. Find out if they will let us reopen our old bases there and use them as refueling and maintenance bases. Then call the Brits and see if they will permit us to use Diego Garcia. How long, Admiral Stark, will it take to get those bases operational, using your Sea Bees?"

"To be honest, Mr. President, I don't know. It will depend upon their condition and how much of a security problem we will have. The Islamic extremists will most certainly regard this as a bonanza of a target in the Philippines. Okinawa, maybe three weeks to a month, depending on how fast we can get the Japanese out of there, our own people in, and get to work. We can use Guam as an intermediate staging area. We can get a couple of tankers started in that direction, but we won't know the status of the pipelines, storage tanks, valves, and so on until we inspect them. Lastly, the Navy is down to three battalions of Sea Bees. We're strapped for manpower."

"What about this Mobile Offshore Base ship or concept that was in the news last year? Where do we stand on it?"

"There is a lot of confusion and public misconception over that, Mr. President. Funds were allotted only for proof of concept. Construction really hasn't begun. It is a hundred-billion-dollar deal, and Congress wanted absolute proof before they voted funds to build a floating island you could land a C-130H on. No support ships, let alone the main landing ship, have been funded nor construction initiated."

"Admiral, order that carrier battle group with the Marine Expeditionary Brigade to stand by off Pusan. If we go in, we must have that port. We will need the Marines there. We will hold Pusan regardless of the cost."

"Mr. President, I should point out that it appears that the North Koreans launched an amphibious assault in the Yellow Sea, and we think their objective is the port of Inchon. It doesn't seem to be a large invasion force at this time, perhaps a division or so in size, but it could cause us trouble. It does present a target for consideration for this carrier battle group. The Marine Expeditionary Brigade can continue on to guard Pusan if you so order."

The President pondered for a moment, then said, "Good suggestion, Admiral, but I deem Pusan more important. I want that carrier air arm and naval gunfire in complete support of the Marines if we go. Pusan is of the most strategic value right now, at least until we get further information about the situation on the ground."

The Admiral picked up the red phone in front of him and gave the order. "Pusan is the objective of the Carrier Battle Group III and the Marine Expeditionary Brigade accompanying it."

The President spoke. "A little while ago, I heard an interesting theory from one of Secretary Talbot's people. She believes the Chinese are orchestrating this and that it is only the opening move of a series of thrusts that will ultimately be made by the Chinese. She thinks China will strike south and west. India would be the logical target of the western thrust, and she didn't express an opinion on the objective of the southern thrust. What do you gentlemen think China's role is in this? General Leonard?"

"Mr. President, my Marines and I think it is entirely plausible. Our folks have never felt comfortable with China since the early 1930s." General Craig and several of the others smiled at Mark Leonard's homily.

"What, General, do your folks think?"

"Well, Mr. President, my intelligence people think that the real objective of China might be Caspian Sea oil. The Korean peninsula, maybe even Taiwan, and less likely India or Vietnam, could be strategic feints. Rather like the Japanese attempt to draw us off to Alaska and then take Midway, only on a far grander scale. Who knows, maybe they want it all. Certainly, they intend to bring Taiwan into the fold, sooner or later, one way or another, peaceably or by force. It could be that the Korean peninsula is a way of tying us down while they make a major move."

"General Anderson, what's your opinion, comments, recommendations?"

"Mr. President, we have, as you know, ten active divisions, and ten now in reserve. Those reserve divisions are not up to snuff. We are prepared to fight a limited war, but nothing like the massive capabilities of the Chinese should they enter the foray. We can have all the information we want, but without the firepower necessary to do them, we can only watch them on satellite computer screens. In order to meet any kind of mass the Chinese are capable of fielding, we would have to go nuclear."

"Well, what about the peninsula?"

"We lack the strategic airlift to get there in any kind of timely fashion, Mr. President. It takes 600 to 750 sorties with C-17s and C-5As to get an entire heavy division into the battle. We will have to move by sealift. That will take several weeks. So, it boils down to how fast South Korea is overrun, whether or not the South can hold out until the cavalry arrives, and if enough of it arrives in time."

"Admiral, what is the threat at sea? I don't believe the North has any kind of a Navy that can threaten our sealift, do they?"

"Our concern in that area, Mr. President, is the submarine threat, and we believe it is substantial. We will be operating close to the mainland, well within range of the latest, state of the art diesel submarine fleet in the world. We know the North Koreans have purchased several Kilo 636s from the Russians. We also believe, but have no firm evidence, that they might have acquired several more from China. We know that the Swedes, Germans, and French have sold them the latest in diesel submarine engines and technology, sonar and detection gear, guidance systems for torpedoes and so on. We now have three Virginia class submarines as our first line submarine fleet. We have twenty-five of the Los Angeles class submarines still in service, and those platforms are all thirty-five years old or older. They are noisier, however, and not as well equipped as we believe the submarines the North Koreans have purchased are."

"You mean to tell me, Admiral, that we are behind some lousy third-rate lunatic dictator in submarine capability?"

"Yes, Mr. President, in the littoral or brown water environment, their submarine capability exceeds ours. I would not be surprised to lose a number of our Los Angeles class nuclear attack submarines to theirs in an undersea battle. Our surface anti-submarine research has lagged for over a decade due to under funding. Our anti-submarine capabilities have atrophied over the last twenty years due to lack of funding. Our antisubmarine warfare assets are in worse shape than our submarine fleet. We might have a difficult time detecting them with air or surface assets. We have been trying to ferret them out in the Yellow Sea to record their individual characteristics, but more often than not, they give us the slip or show up tracking us without our knowledge until they are well within kill parameters. We can't seem to track them very well with the Los Angeles class boats. We found in war gaming in the late 1990s and the early years of this century that the latest diesel-powered boats were more than a match for our Los Angeles class boats, especially in the littoral environment. In point of fact, a Chilean submarine escaped our detection in 1996. A Russian Oscar submarine trailed our USS Coronado without detection for two days in 1997. Australian submarines penetrated our best defense efforts during the war game RIMPAC 2000. Since then, our antisubmarine warfare capability and submarine fleet have deteriorated even more.

"Now, our new Virginia class submarines are a different story. They were designed and built for littoral operations. We can nail enemy submarines with those, but unfortunately, we only have three of them at this time. We were supposed to get one a year, but the previous administration saw no need for them and cancelled the contracts. One of them is in the North Atlantic, the other two in the Arabian Sea. You will recall our Sea Wolf submarine program was cancelled late in the last century. That was a superb, multi-mission, do everything, super stealthy submarine that was deemed too expensive. Now, we could use about 50 of them."

"Well, just how many submarines do you think they have, Admiral?"

"Our estimates vary widely, Mr. President. Our best guess is that they have about thirty in total. There might be more to this story, however, Mr. President."

"You mean more good submarine news, Admiral?"

"Mr. President, a major concern has been the People's Liberation Army Navy, or PLAN, of China. In 2004, they began purchasing a variety of the latest diesel submarine technology from the Germans, French and Swedes and tested them. They contracted in 2007 with the Germans for their technology under license. The Germans sent hundreds of technicians and engineers to China to teach them how to build their latest model. We have unconfirmed reports of a massive submarine construction program ongoing in China. We really don't know for sure, but some intelligence sources indicate they have been building five to ten boats a year for the last several years in different shipyards. These ships have a variety of state-of-the-art weapons systems and stealth technology. They can accurately shoot cruise missiles without having to surface. In fact, they can shoot from significant depths. If China supports North Korea with submarine forces in the Straits of Taiwan or the Yellow Sea or the South China Sea, we could have very grave problems.

"We have been in communication with our Joint Task Force, JTF-519. The Commander of this JTF is also the Pacific Fleet Commander. The Pacific Fleet has five carrier battle groups assigned to it. We retired a sixth two years ago. Two of the five Pacific Fleet's carrier groups are on the west coast for refueling and refitting. Many members of their crews are scattered across on the country, on extended leave. They will be of little immediate assistance. The carriers are undergoing nuclear fuel rod exchange that takes weeks to months. The Commander of the JTF has ordered all ships under his command, that is all the ships in the Pacific Theater, to steam towards Korea.

"The Central Command Naval Commander is holding steady in his positions in the Arabian Sea awaiting orders."

"All right, back to the immediate business of the Korean peninsula. What is our formal game plan, and when was it last updated, General Craig?"

"Our last update was three years ago. The previous administration decided we would not honor our agreement of coming to the aid of South Korea because they threw us out. Without the tripwire force there to create a strong emotional reaction, he felt that there was no way the American people would support another war in Asia. When we left, we left them fifty tactical nuclear warheads, mostly in the one quarter kiloton to ten kiloton range. We believe the South has produced several of their own that are larger than that. Additionally, the South Koreans have purchased intermediate range rockets from the Japanese and built some short-range rockets of their own, all capable of delivery of warheads in this size range. In short, Mr. President, we have left the South Koreans out there by themselves. Of course, they brought it on themselves. Our treaty with them is worthless, and both we and they know it."

"Well, I wonder what the United Nations has to say about this attack. Johnny, call our ambassador in New York City and get some feedback. This has been underway now for some hours, and surely the UN has started their ball rolling. I wonder why Dick Griffith hasn't checked in with us. See what you can find out. I'm going back upstairs. General Craig, give me a routine report every four hours via a messenger on how it is going unless something really significant happens, like mushroom clouds. Secretaries, we will meet again here with the Chiefs at 14:00 hours. Marge, see me in my office for a few minutes. Oh, one more thing, in addition to the Presidential Daily Brief, I want this group to meet every Monday, Wednesday and Friday mornings for breakfast at 07:00 until further notice. The brain power here is far more synergistic than individually. OK, Marge, let's you and I go back upstairs, and everybody else, back to the grind."

Back in the Oval Office, Jason Thornton plopped in his chair and bit his lip. "Marge, I'm a bit troubled about Roberta Stearns's theory. I wonder if the North Koreans would dare do anything without the permission of China. Call the Chinese ambassador, let's keep it low-key today, but try and find out what they think, what they are doing about this. Have a report ready at 14:00 hours for all of us."

"Yes, Mr. President. I'll call their ambassador immediately." With that, she nodded and left the Oval Office.

Jason Thornton picked up the phone and punched the number to the war room. An aide answered. "Let me speak to General Craig, or better still, put me on the speaker," said Thornton. "Gentlemen, I want you to keep an eye on any indicator of mobilization by the Chinese. Anything at all that looks suspicious let me know. Call our folks there and see if there is any indication of any kind of mobilization."

"This is General Craig, Mr. President. We will contact you as soon as there is any indication of anything at all. We have people in several cities, and we will contact them. We will also monitor via satellite."

"Thanks, General. Talk to you later." Jason Thornton hung up his phone, leaned back in his chair and thought of the consequences of Chinese involvement.

———————

Johnny Withers looked into the Oval Office to see his boss lost in space. He knocked on the doorframe to announce his presence. "Mr. President, The Assistant Secretary of Defense is here with a Colonel Burgess from Fort Detrick."

"Bring them in, Johnny."

"Yes sir. Gentlemen, this way if you please." He ushered the two into the oval office.

"Mr. President, this is Colonel Frank Burgess, Medical Corps, and Commander of our DOD Medical Intelligence Unit at Fort Detrick. You asked for him to come a couple of hours ago."

"Yes, please have a seat, gentlemen. I am particularly interested, Colonel, in the possibility of a biological attack on the United States by the People's Republic of Korea. What can you tell me about North Korea's capabilities for such an attack?"

"Frankly, Mr. President, they are extremely good. North Korea has quite an offensive biological weapons program from what we can gather. A defector two years ago made it to South Korea, where we had the opportunity to interview him on a number of occasions. The North Koreans have weaponized a number of biological agents. This guy was really a virologist, working on some novel viruses; actually, he was especially involved with genetically engineering an influenza virus to make it resistant to the two antibiotics amantidine and rimantidine. He said he was quite successful in enhancing both its virulence and pathogenicity. He is aware that they also have genetically engineered a number of other agents, including anthrax and tularemia and a couple of others, but he has no details of them. Each section was very exclusive, and no contact was supposed to occur between working groups working on the different organisms."

"Colonel, you used two terms, virulent and patho- something. What do those mean?"

"Mr. President, virulence refers to the severity of the disease caused by an organism. Pathogenicity refers to its ability to cause disease without reference as to the severity of the disease. Pathogenicity implies, but doesn't specifically state, a high degree of transmissibility."

"In other words, Colonel, he was working to engineer an influenza virus that caused a lot of severe sickness and was highly contagious?"

"Precisely, Mr. President. He indicated that they hadn't field tested it yet, but they did try it on a number of political prisoners. He said the case fatality ratio, that's the number dead over the number ill, was quite high, in the neighborhood of sixty to seventy percent."

"You mean they tested this on people?"

"Mr. President, according to what this defector said, they took about five hundred people and put them in an isolated maximum security prison in a rural area, then sprayed the organism in the ventilation system. Virtually everyone was exposed, even some of the guards, although quite by accident. It survived in the environment longer than they thought it would. They didn't feed these prisoners anything for two days after exposure, thinking the virus would all die. It didn't. When they went in after forty-eight hours, it was still quite viable, and a number of the prison staff also became ill. They had to disinfect the whole facility with formaldehyde. The incubation period was about five days. A week after everyone was ill, they executed all of the survivors and cremated everybody. He didn't know how many were ill from the virus, or how many were ill from the formaldehyde disinfection. They sprayed everything with a solution of it, then aerosolized it and pumped it around as a gas. They even laundered the prisoners' clothes in formaldehyde. That is pretty toxic stuff in itself. They wanted to make sure the virus didn't get loose into the environment."

"So, you think this virus could be here in the U.S.? How would they get it here, how would they maintain it if it is vulnerable to the environment?"

"Mr. President, it is ridiculously easy to smuggle a biological weapon in enormous quantities into this country. We import hundreds of thousand of tons of frozen foods every year. Everything from frozen meat from South America, fresh frozen fruit juices, chilled fruits, and so on are brought in under refrigerated or in the frozen state. The virus is viable for decades if it is kept frozen at very low temperatures. It is far easier to smuggle in biological weapons than it is nuclear weapons."

"How then, would they disseminate the agent?"

"Mr. President, dissemination could occur by a variety of ways. Aerosolization is by far and away the best. It can be put in aerosolized canisters, in large spray tanks, delivered by aircraft such as a crop duster, as insecticide control sprays in city streets, it could be released in ventilation systems of large buildings, in subways, and so on. If the agent is contagious, and you could figure out a way to expose a large number of people on a single exposure, such as at a professional football game in an enclosed stadium, then it could spread like wildfire among the population. It is really limited by the imagination.

"Some ten years ago, a regional epidemiologist from a rural state sent a letter to the White House with a scenario for a smallpox attack that was quite feasible and as scary as they come. It was a plane load of revelers leaving Honolulu after the Christmas and New Year's holidays. An enemy agent put aerosolized smallpox into the aircraft ventilation system. Four hundred plus people were infected. When they landed in Atlanta, they got on two dozen commuter flights and went all over the Midwest and east coast. In two weeks, we had hundreds of outbreaks over half the country as a result of secondary cases in this scenario."

"How then, could they maintain this agent in the frozen state if they brought it in this way?"

"That is relatively easy, Mr. President. It can be maintained in home deep freezers supplemented with dry ice. That will keep it at minus twenty degrees Fahrenheit for years. Just renew the dry ice periodically. They could rent lockers in cold storage areas for modest-sized quantities, or somewhat bizarrely, in bovine semen containers."

"What?"

"Our veterinarian informs us that every rural county in the country has at least one, and likely several bovine inseminators for insemination of both dairy and beef cattle. Each of these commercial inseminators maintains tanks of liquid nitrogen which hold bovine semen at minus seventy degrees Centigrade. They usually have a number of such tanks and can store good-sized quantities of a virus agent in these tanks."

"Jesus Christ!"

"It gets worse, Mr. President. It seems the neighbor of our informant was also a virologist who is working on smallpox. Our informant learned from this neighbor that they have a red-hot strain of smallpox that they acquired from Russian scientists they hired after the breakup of the Former Soviet Union. They hired these Russian virologists for nice salaries and high positions with lots of benefits who have been continuing their work in North Korea for some years. What I said about the influenza virus also applies to smallpox."

"Do you have any other good news, Colonel? What about vaccinating our people against smallpox?"

We don't know if the vaccine we have will be effective against this strain. Mr. X doesn't know much about it. You will remember that in 2002 and 2003 a number of people wanted to initiate a national mass vaccination campaign against smallpox, but the people down at the CDC scared the living crap out of both the medical community and the general public about adverse reactions to the vaccination. They claimed they could vaccinate the county in a few weeks in the face of a release of smallpox. It won't spread so fast they can't control it , so they claimed. So, the entire country is at risk if we are attacked with smallpox. It takes a week or two to build immunity after vaccination. There is some evidence that some degree of immunity is immediately conferred, but it probably isn't sufficient for protection in the face of exposure to a large dose. Smallpox, too, is spread by aerosolization, but you have to be relatively close for person to person spread. That's generally considered to be six or eight feet. Some people cough, and then spread millions of the virus from their throats when they do."

"What else do you want to tell me, Colonel?"

"I don't know what information would be of benefit to you at this time, Mr. President."

"Alright, make sure you leave your phone and fax number outside in case I can't get ahold of you through Secretary Neville. I presume you have a secure phone arrangement at your office?"

"Yes, Mr. President. I have a secure hotline. I can be reached any time, day or night, at my office. I live about twenty minutes from my office and can be there if I get a heads-up call."

"Thank you, Colonel. I appreciate your candor and your immediate response in coming."

"Thank you, Mr. President. I wish I had better news." Johnny Withers escorted them out. The President's personal bodyguard, Robert Lee, standing in the corner, with his arms folded across his chest, watched them through narrow eyes as they left.

CHAPTER 13

J ohnny Withers came in. "Well, Mr. President. The word is out. There is a media feeding frenzy in the press room. They are clamoring for a statement. CNN and all the other channels are broadcasting live from different locations in Korea. It seems that CBS and NBC reporters headed south out of Seoul in a hurry, at the first flight of aircraft. CNN stayed in Seoul and is broadcasting from there. It looks pretty ugly over there."

"Turn on the television, Johnny, CNN, but no volume; I just want to see the pictures, please."

Withers picked up the remote control from the top of the television, turned on the digital TV, laid the remote on the President's desk and walked out to the antechamber.

The intercom rang on the President's desk; he answered it. It was Air Force Chief of Staff George Shelton. "Mr. President, we just received word that all the airports in Pusan are down. Their runways are sufficiently cratered that nothing can get in or out. This cuts the possibility of air delivery of reinforcements into Pusan until those runways are repaired. The air battle is see-sawing back and forth. No clear-cut picture as yet on that, Mr. President."

"What are we talking about, in terms of getting those airfields repaired, General?"

"Well Mr. President, if the South Koreans are up to snuff, about eight hours. The North Koreans copied our catering bomblets munitions. The runways are filled with hundreds of holes that will tear the landing gear off any aircraft, landing or taking off. Unfortunately, with continued wave attacks, it becomes a battle between repair and destruction. I can't predict who will win that one. I have no idea how much repair materials and manpower and equipment the South has dedicated to this function. If the North Korean ground attack aircraft take out the people and equipment, it is probably a done deal."

"Anything else, developments of any kind that I should know about, General Shelton?"

"No, sir, nothing more at this time."

"Thank you, General," and Thornton hung up the phone.

Johnny Withers came in. "Mr. President, Roger has a prepared statement, very brief, acknowledging to the press that South Korea is under attack. Do you want to take a look at it?"

"No, Johnny, I'll trust Roger. I am sure he has not identified what our response will be. Neither should he identify that we haven't formulated one at this time. If he is that stupid, I'll fire him, if I don't wring his neck first. Let him rip."

The President glanced over at the television, where a CNN reporter was standing inside the White House Press Room. Roger McCall, the White House Press Secretary, strode confidently to the podium. The President turned the volume up with his remote.

The phone on the President's desk rang. He turned down the television volume. "Mr. President, Marge Talbott. I was just on the phone with our ambassador in London. Things don't look good. Seems the Brits have been debating their role in this for a couple of hours now. The Labour government is deeply opposed to any kind of British participation at all. Near as our guy can figure out, there are a couple of things that the British find disturbing. They are afraid of terrorist retaliation on the home islands, by whom, I am not sure. Perhaps more importantly, they look at it as perhaps the final solution to the Korean problem. Let the peninsula be reunited under whomever and then deal with whichever government is the winner. They certainly aren't going to commit any of their whopping three divisions to it, and they are even debating whether or not they should allow us to use Diego Garcia. As soon as the dust settles, our man will send us a secure fax."

"Do you think a phone call from me to the Prime Minister would be of any benefit, particularly in regard to Diego Garcia?"

"I asked that question, and our man said right now their P.M. is engaged in a hot and heavy debate; maybe later today, but not now. He never was very friendly to us Americans. He is leaning against us on all fronts at the moment. He wants to see how the political wind is blowing with the natives first, at least that is what our man thinks.

"One more thing, Mr. President. The French Ambassador can hardly retain his glee at our dilemma. It seems the French want to see us get our comeuppance. I don't think we will get any support at all out of the French, formally or informally."

"Thanks, Marge. Keep me informed of anything of use that you hear, as I am sure you will. Oh, give our Russian friends a call at their embassy as a matter of courtesy. Ask them what their position is on the North Korean invasion this morning. Let's see what their take is. Talk to you later."

Jason Thornton turned the volume up on the television, just in time to hear NBC's latest beautiful lady reporter ask Roger, "What will be the United State's response to this invasion?"

Roger just smirked and said, "Do you think it would be wise to tell an extremely lethal and unpredictable enemy how you will react to his aggression? Don't you think he might prepare for any response you would care to identify? Perhaps you would like to be part and parcel of whatever our response is? I am sure that the troops in one of our first response ground units, should we choose to militarily respond, would certainly be happy to have you embedded with them." The double meaning was not lost on the reporter, and her blush was obvious on camera. Jason Thornton laughed to himself, glad he had selected Roger McCall. Neither of them had much use for antagonistic journalists, and Roger, obviously, could be just as sarcastic as the best of them.

By noon, a dozen or so demonstrators had gathered outside the White House. None of them were favorable to involvement. The placards they carried, obviously home made, carried various slogans: NO WAR! U.S. STAY HOME! NOT IN ASIA! KEEP US OUT! and so on. They were

2023: WORLD WAR III

marching, circling peacefully under the watchful eye of a dozen Washington, D.C., and National Park police officers and some men in civilian clothes who had small radio receivers clipped to their ears.

The Vice President called from his office, just to let Thornton know that various Congressional Committees were meeting on Capitol Hill to discuss the invasion.

Margie Talbott called again. "Mr. President, I just spoke with the Japanese ambassador. He has received no guidance from the Japanese government. His personal opinion, however, is that a major re-alignment will result. Japanese forces are on alert, and their militia units have been put on stand-by notice. I'll let you know as soon as he gets back to me with any formal response.

"The Taiwanese delegation was also here and just left. The Taiwanese have gone to full alert. They are concerned that China might use this as a cover for invasion. They are not taking any chances. Their ships of the line are putting out to sea in the Strait now. They have armed their missiles. We think they are going to establish an Aegis destroyer picket line. Our AWACs over the Strait haven't picked up any indicators of unusual ship or military air activities."

"Thanks, Marge. Talk to you later." Thornton hung up the phone. *Frigging great*, Thornton thought to himself. *If the Chinese do go for Taiwan, how in hell are we going to respond to both Korea and Taiwan?*

Thornton dialed the war room. "Anything changing down there? Secretary Talbott just told me that Taiwan is on full alert and moving their ships into the Strait."

"Admiral Stark here, Mr. President. Yes, sir, we are monitoring their movement into the Strait. They are scared. We are listening to their conversations in real time, and they are very unhappy campers."

"Anything on any kind of movement or response from the Chinese?"

"No, Mr. President, nothing in terms of any movement. One of our naval attaches noticed, however, something a little odd. It seems that over the last month, a large number of Chinese freighters have been tied up in Chinese ports, big and little. Probably a hundred or more of these freighters have been pulled off the oceans and seem to be just sitting in ports."

"Odd, what do you make of it?"

"We don't have anything but wild guesses right now, Mr. President. We told one of our people over there to start sniffing around and see what he can find out. The Port Authority Traffic Management Office said, 'We have noticed about a fifteen percent drop in Chinese ships coming into our ports on both coasts over the last five or six weeks.' That would tie in with their ships staying in home ports, but why, they don't know either."

"Thanks, Admiral. For your information, the folks on the Hill are yakking at each other, and the protestors are already marching outside the gates up here. See you after lunch." Jason Thornton hung up the phone.

At 11:30, Marge Talbott called again. "The South Korean ambassador just left my office. He hasn't received any official word from Seoul yet, but on his own he is putting out feelers about possible military support from us. He fully realizes that our departure from South Korea was a mistake. Both the government and the people never dreamed the North would invade again. He has less of a clear picture than we do as to how the invasion is going."

"What did you tell him, Marge?"

"Nothing concrete, that it is being discussed in the White House and Congress. I told him that the only immediate option was that if you used your authority under the War Powers Act there could be any kind of an immediate response. That immediate response wouldn't come for several weeks at the earliest. It might require deliberation by Congress, with a vote to go to war to do it according to our Constitution. I told him I could not say what, when, or how it would go. He left a very disappointed and anxious man."

"Good job, Marge. I don't know myself how all of this will fall out. I am still troubled by Dr. Stearns's concept. I'll see you at our 14:00 hours meeting." Thornton put down the phone and leaned back in his chair. "What in God's name should our response be?"

14:00 Hours, White House War Room

At 13:45, the cars began arriving at the underground entrance to the White House as the Joint Chiefs began arriving from the Pentagon and the Department Secretaries who are members of the National Security

Council from their offices. Everyone was seated by 13:55 when Jason Thornton came in. In previous meetings, the President indicated that no one should stand in these meetings when he entered. Jim Neville, the SECDEF, had arrived, having been briefed en route over a secure net by his staff.

"Ok, folks, let's get started. Jim, what do you have from your end?"

"Well, Mr. President, the North is still moving south, albeit a lot slower. Twenty-two hours post attack, the South has suffered considerable attrition of its air forces. The ground forces are retreating more slowly, making it far more costly to the north. The Pusan area air bases are still down, suffering repeated attacks; their air reserves are doing well, however, with old F-4 Phantoms in the ground attack role. They are hitting the North Korean columns really hard and have launched several strikes north of the Thirty-Eighth parallel into the North with good results. A couple of them even made it up to strike in Pyong Yang. They did pretty good, albeit the strike was small. They hit their Pentagon, so to speak, and Kim, Jong-uns' palace. We don't think they got him, as he went on television and radio an hour after the strike and said he wasn't injured at all and that it was an example of South Korean aggression.

"The Taiwanese have established a picket line of Aegis destroyers in the Formosa Strait. All Taiwanese forces are on full alert. We haven't detected any movement or unusual activity on the part of the Chinese so far.

"Admiral Stark tells me the carrier battle groups are making good time, and one will be standing by in less than twenty-four hours. He has ordered them to take up stations one hundred and fifty miles off the Korean peninsula. We will have one on each side and one on the southern tip in two days. We had a couple of planes destroyed at the Seoul International Airport. Our game plan was to evacuate our embassy people with those. They are now cut off. Secretary Talbott might have more on them."

"Marge?"

"We didn't get our people out, Mr. President. We did hear from them, however, on their satellite phones. They destroyed all of the communications gear and files in our embassy to prevent them from falling into the North's hands. We couldn't let them have such an intelligence windfall. They have joined the throngs flocking south along jammed highways, blending in with the South Korean civilian population."

"Marge, I want those people who stayed behind and destroyed all those records and communications gear decorated. Write them up. If they get out, I want to personally decorate them in the rose garden. Sometimes our statesmen don't get the recognition they deserve. What else do you have?"

"We have heard from the Australians, Mr. President. They say we can use the training areas we utilized in World War II as staging bases if we decide to go in. They will not provide troops, logistical support outside their home country, or military support at this time. They are waiting to see what the other Commonwealth nations do.

"I have also heard from the Japanese. They are still debating what role they should play in all this. They have tremendous investments in South Korea they want to salvage, but they don't want to send any troops according to their unchanged constitution. They are leaning towards the perspective that a united Korea will be easier to deal with in the future. Of course, they are counting on the South winning. I'm not sure they realize that means the South going north clear to the Yalu and cleaning house. They can't seem to make up their minds about our use of our former bases in Okinawa. Worse, they haven't debated what their picture is on the role of China, if any, is in this affair."

"Jim, generals and admirals, put your heads together. How quickly can we move substantial ground forces to Hawaii and Guam as forward staging areas? I mean whole divisions. I want the 82nd and the 101st on Guam as quickly as possible. Air transport them. I realize that the helicopters of the 101st will have to be moved later by ship. Then I want the remainder of the Eighteenth Airborne Corps, the 1st Infantry Division, the 10th Mountain Division, and whatever is left at Fort Hood, TX, moved to Hawaii as quickly as possible. We won't wait for the Japanese or Philippines to make up their minds. It will be more costly to do this. It could also be that we will get some answers while they are en route, and we will then be able move them directly to Okinawa and our old Philippine bases. Get that ball rolling this afternoon. Start moving our air assets in the same direction. Our emphasis will be on tactical air, air superiority and ground attack. Our F-22 Raptors cost us sixty million dollars apiece and our Joint Strike

Fighters forty million. It is time to make them pay for themselves. Whether we go in or not, we will certainly give the North Koreans reason to pause and think. General Shelton, I hate to say this, but do what you have to do to get tanker support for mid-air refueling.

"General Anderson, with the 101st Air Assault scattered along the Mexican border, why not just gather them up and head for Los Angeles or San Diego as ports of debarkation?"

"Can do, Mr. President. What about those Army National Guard units that are supplementing them in border duty?"

"How many are we talking about, how soon can we get them into the system? Do they require anything else in terms of support that the 101st Air Assault has and they don't?"

"We have a reserve division and multiple National Guard battalions, mostly from the southwest, doing that duty. We can't ship them all at once, Mr. President. In fact, it will take a couple of weeks to get task organized, line up the transportation assets, and issue basic supplies. I suggest we give them two weeks leave at home to prepare, and then move them to Los Angeles for overseas movement."

"Make it happen, General."

"Yes, Mr. President."

"General Leonard, I am not going to use your Marines as cannon fodder on a holding mission until the major forces arrive. When, and if, we go in, we will do it en mass, not piecemeal. That much about military strategy I know."

"Roger, Homeland Security. What are we doing here?"

"Well, Mr. President, I have raised the alert level to yellow just for public awareness. I don't really expect any kind of sabotage or anything until, or if, we declare our intent to support South Korea. I don't think they want to do anything that we would consider an act of war first. Besides, they would lose tremendous propaganda value by being the aggressor. They certainly don't want to give us any excuse, like "Remember the Maine!"

"This might sound a little stupid, Roger, but if it hasn't been done, I want you to prioritize possible terrorist targets by category and by location. In other words, what are our most vulnerable and our most valuable assets, and where we stand on protecting them? For example, our power grid, our communications system, our transportation system, especially broken down into subcategories such as rail, air, road net, waterways with our dams and locks, and so on. Outline it, so putting things into subcategories applied to all aspects and categories. Put your staff on it today. I want a thorough study, rather than quick and dirty. I won't put a time limit on it, but I don't want it to drag out, either. If any agency gives you any resistance, tell them to call me. If that doesn't get you positive response and support, you call me, and we'll get it straightened out in a hurry.

"Fred, work with Roger, will you? I wouldn't be surprised if you FBI folks haven't already done this, or at least a lot of it. Don't hold any information back that his staff feels that he needs."

Fred Gateway, the new Director of the FBI, merely nodded his assent.

"It is impossible to keep a news blackout on our mobilization efforts, so we will neither deny nor confirm them. Let the media have their frenzy. Maybe it will just add to North Korea's angst.

"Ed, what does the CIA have? Anything at all on China's reaction to all of this? I have a very bad feeling about this."

"No, Mr. President. None of our folks in China have given us any indication of Chinese mobilization or anything other than detached interest by the Chinese leadership. It might be that China, tired of supporting North Korea, just might let them dig their own grave."

"Marge, through official channels, try and find out what the Chinese reaction to all of this is."

"Already have, Mr. President. I faxed our folks in Peking over a secure line early this morning, after you expressed interested in Ms. Stearns's theory. I don't have any response at this time. I am hoping to hear something by close of business, so to speak, today."

Jason Thornton smiled. He liked people who could think and act ahead. *So,* he thought, *we have an official line and the CIA boys both working to see what China is thinking. Hope to hell it is nothing drastic.*

"Anybody have anything else they want to bring up? Oh, one more thing, Ed, have your CIA boys in China find out why all those commercial freighters or whatever ships are being held in China's ports."

"Yes, Mr. President, I'll get that out via our Peking boys." Ed McCluskey was the Director of Central Intelligence. In that role, he ran the Central Intelligence Agency.

The President rolled the pencil around on the table in front of him. "I find Ms. Stearns's concept very disconcerting. It really bothers me. I can't believe that the North Koreans would not do this without Peking's blessing, or at least acquiescence. It is very disturbing that the Chinese just might be backing this play as a diversion for taking Taiwan or something else."

"One thing, Mr. President. How are we going to pay for this, shall I say, limited mobilization?", asked Marge.

I'll have one of our supporters in each of the House and Senate introduce legislation for limited emergency funding. I don't know, or even how to estimate, how much what we just decided will cost. I'll have the number crunchers from the Office of Management and Budget get with your staffs. Try and have the figures by 12:00 tomorrow. Is that a feasible time limit for something quick and dirty but still be in the ballpark?"

All nodded in the affirmative.

"I'll have our supporters in both Houses of Congress in for coffee and give them the numbers late tomorrow afternoon. Any other related issues that we need to talk about right now?"

"No, Mr. President," was unanimously voiced.

"Then let's go to work. Thanks to all." The President scooted back his chair and left the room. Robert Lee was waiting outside the war room door for his charge.

"Mr. President, the Russian President, Vassily Chernikof, is on the line."

"Thanks, Marge, put him through. Funny he didn't call on the red line. Guess he didn't think it was a hot enough issue." Jason Thornton picked up the phone.

"Good day, Vassily. I appreciate your call, and I will get right to the point. What is Russia's perspective of the difficulties on the Korean peninsula?"

"And a good day to you, Jason, although I know it is a most hectic one. We in Russia are not at all surprised. In fact, we have expected it before this but had nothing but vague signs upon which to base our judgments. It does not portend well for either of our countries. I know you have a treaty with South Korea, but your predecessor made it a known fact that he would not honor it after the South Koreans rather rudely expelled you from their country. Their leadership and their students did not believe the North would ever become sufficiently belligerent to come south, militarily speaking.

"Our main concern about it is whether or not the Chinese will come to their rescue as they did in the Korean War of the 1950s. We don't have a good feel for that. There have long been signs of a slow, long militarization in western China, signs of infrastructure to support an invasion, but we don't think they are aimed at us. Rather, they seem to be aimed more at India. Still, the development of rail lines, depots, and water storage basins in such a dry region do have considerable peaceful applications in development of that region. If China were to become involved, I would have expected expansion and mobilization along their border with North Korea."

"Your points are all very valid, Vassily. I am afraid that, at the moment, I must agree with you. Is it possible that the weapons you have sold to China have been made available to the North Koreans?"

"That is possible, Jason. Those sales have contributed greatly to our stability and economy. As you are well aware, we have a gargantuan wrestling problem with the criminal element here, trying to get them at least under control if not entirely eliminated. We have not been as successful as we hoped in that endeavor. They can sell sophisticated weapons because of their tremendous influence in all areas of our society and economy. I hate to admit it, but they are as strong as the government here. Our intelligence has revealed that one criminal organization sold the blueprints of our latest submarine design to the Chinese. We are pursing that now, but short of assassination of these irresponsible individuals, our judicial system might not be able to bring them to justice. Our judicial system is corrupt, but that is another problem we are trying to deal with. No, I don't think they could have, or would have, passed those on to North Korea. Certainly, North Korea would not have had the time to build, equip, man, and train such a submarine, let alone a fleet of them. In that respect, I do not see the North as a threat to your naval presence in the Yellow or South China Seas."

CHAPTER 14

"**M**r. President, one of the Mexicans trying to escape after the raid in Benson, Arizona that the Texas Highway Patrolman shot a month or two ago has been recovering in El Paso General Hospital. He has decided to talk in exchange for immunity. He thinks we might even let him become a U.S. citizen.

"He has revealed that these raids have been pretty much the work of one gang that approaches a military company in size, organization, financing, and logistics. He's not sure of the precise location of their base. He comes from farther south in Mexico. He thought he was joining a revolutionary band at first. We have it down to a general area inside Mexico, where it is disguised as a fruits and vegetables farm of considerable size. The soldiers work as field hands between raids. He's been with the gang for about a year.

"Some Orientals visited the farm a couple of times in the year he has been there. He thinks they might be supplying the weapons and cash to conduct these raids. At one time, they also grew a lot of marijuana, but right after a visit of these Orientals, they had to pull it all out and grind it up and mix it in cattle feed. Apparently, they have a cattle feeding operation of modest size. He has observed that they go on a raid a month or two after these Orientals come calling. He says they drive a nice, large air-conditioned car. It looks like there is one boss and a couple of bodyguards each time. The car has a California license plate. They were all given their own, brand new, semi-automatic version of an Ak-47 rifle. There are no markings on the rifles that we recovered, but their manufacturing quality suggests that they are newly made and of Chinese origin."

"OK Fred, anything from any of our drones that help pinpoint where this base is?"

"We have some leads that indicate it is about fifty miles inside the Mexican border in a relatively isolated area. The lead suspect farm has its own deep wells for irrigation which makes for a large, intensively cultivated patch of ground in an otherwise relatively isolated and desolate desert."

"Anything else this guy has revealed?"

"Yes, sir. He says some months ago, a whole bunch of SUVs and pickups began arriving one or two at a time over the course of a month or so. They all had California plates. They have a regular garage where the mechanics check them over and equip them with whatever is necessary. Water cans, CB radios, gun racks, seats, and so on, so they can use them in their raids. They, apparently, have large underground fuel storage tanks that were installed by Americans some months ago. I am having our boys check all along the border for the purchase of filling station sized underground tanks. That might give a definite location of this base."

"What, Fred, do you think the Mexican authorities know of this?"

"I think they must know an awful lot, Mr. President. Certainly, the local and probably the state authorities know of an operation of this size. I have no doubt a lot of payoffs occur."

"Johnny, would you excuse us, please? No recorders, notes or anything else. I want a totally private discussion with our FBI Director. Are you uncomfortable with that, Fred?"

Fred Gateway smiled, "Mr. President, I am at your service." Johnny Withers joined Robert Lee outside the Oval Office until summoned.

"Fred, it really bothers me when all the American Border Agents are killed at their posts and all the Mexican officials are merely handcuffed when they crossed back into Mexico. That tells me it was a setup."

"I agree, Mr. President. That has bothered me as well. I have been wondering just how to address that."

"Do you have anything in mind?"

"I have thought of kidnapping a couple of those Mexican agents who were involved. I would like to look at their bank accounts and perhaps engage in some other illegal investigations of them. Of course, that would all be illegal and if discovered would result in another emotional outburst from Mexico about their sovereignty."

"Do you have the people you can trust to pull this off? People who are willing to take the heat and say they acted on their own, perhaps as an act of revenge for the killing of their fellow officers?"

Fred Gateway's smile cracked a couple of centimeters. "Mr. President, the line of volunteers would be a block long."

"Well then, Fred, if there is no other business this morning, why don't you get to it?"

———————————•═◆═•———————————

After thirty minutes of fleeing south towards Chu'nch'on, Major Robert Bradley tapped the Korean Captain on the shoulder. "Let's stop over there and eat these MREs and fill the gas tank from a jerry can." The Captain nodded first to Bradley, then the Korean sergeant driving. The sergeant nosed the Chevy Blazer over on a wide shoulder of the road. Bradley set up three small stoves, took each of their MREs, poured water from the water can into the MRE entree pouches to re-hydrate the meals, ignited the fuel tablets and set the pouches on the stoves. In the meantime, the Captain had taken their only rifle and patrolled down the road, while the Sergeant filled the gas tank with diesel fuel from one of the three jerry cans. After a few minutes, the meals were ready, and Captain Koon reappeared. They ate in silence, each lost in his thoughts. Captain Koon picked up the trash from his MRE, threw it into the back of the Blazer and, turning to Bradley, and said "I think I will walk down the road around the bend. We seem to have outrun the civilians on the road. I didn't get very far ahead, so I'll see what's around the bend while you finish." With that, he picked up the Sergeant's Dae Woo Rifle, put on his field hat and walked off. Three minutes later, rifle fire erupted. That different calibers were being fired was obvious. Bradley and Sergeant Park jumped to their feet and ran to their vehicle. Park started the engine. Captain Koon was running towards them. "North Koreans were mining the road ahead, but I got two of them. A couple of others jumped into the brush about two hundred meters ahead."

"Will they attempt to ambush us?" Bradley asked.

"I don't know, but I don't think we should stay here. Let's move on south." Bradley resumed his backseat position, while Captain Koon leaned out the window with the rifle. "Go fast for about a hundred and fifty meters, and then slow down. Look for fresh diggings in the dirt, where there might be mines." Sergeant Park nodded a yes sir, and did exactly that. At twenty-five meters, the Sergeant saw where they were digging for an anti-tank mine that was still in its wooden box. He skirted the mine at fifteen kilometers an hour, straining to look ahead for others.

"I don't see any bodies. Are you sure you hit two of them, Captain?"

"Yes, Major, I saw them go down. They must have dragged the two casualties into the brush for first aid or to hide them if they are dead."

From one hundred meters up the hill on their left flank, the North Koreans opened with rifle fire. Sergeant Park mashed on the accelerator. Bullets penetrated the rear of the vehicle just behind Bradley. One of them hit two of the diesel fuel jerry cans. Another round hit the case of MREs. Sergeant Park swerved, shifted gears, and the Blazer shot forward, swerving around the curve. From the sound and small volume of fire, Captain Koon judged that it was the two remaining in the road mining detail.

Captain Koon shot a quick glance at Sergeant Park, and seeing he was not hit, swiveled around to see about Bradley. "You hit?" he asked.

"Nope, but it was damned close. I wish I had a rifle and this vehicle had a radio so we could report it."

Captain Park just nodded, then added, we'll stop at the next village or whatever and see if we can telephone it in."

"I don't like all this diesel fuel back here. We better hope those rounds didn't hit the tank as well or we are in for a long walk." Now, several gallons of diesel fuel had leaked forward under their feet. Their boots were soaking it up. The two Koreans looked down at the floor and just looked at each other. If they had to walk out, they would leave a trail of diesel vapor a baby could follow.

They had reached a few miles north of Ch'unch'on, when Captain Koon told the Sergeant to pull over. He leaned over the seat and told Bradley, "The road forks here in Ch'unch'on. One goes southwest to Seoul, the other southeast, but then curves northeast to tie into the coastal road at Sokch'o. The North Koreans are undoubtedly driving hard south along the coastal road, making for Pusan. Undoubtedly, our best bet is to head for Seoul, but it is probably already under heavy attack by air, and armored columns are undoubtedly driving for it. The risk of coming under attack by air is increasing with every mile. Additionally, we are just north of the bridge over the Soyang Chosuji, a reservoir on the Pukhan Gang, a rather large river. We better be very careful from here on. If I were the North, I would have a team out to seize and hold the bridge. I better explore ahead a few hundred yards, and then you, Sergeant, drive forward on my signal. I'll take the rifle with me."

With that, he climbed out of the Blazer. Holding the rifle at port arms, he held close to the shoulder of the road, scanning both sides of the road very carefully as he walked. After three hundred meters, he motioned for the Blazer to come forward and wait where he was standing. As he walked another four hundred meters, the bridge came in sight. He slipped off the roadside and into the brush and went halfway up the hill on the left side. Crouching, he snuck forward until he could scan the panorama before him. Traffic on the bridge was nonexistent. It seemed unusually quiet to him. Without binoculars, he couldn't pick up a lot of detail. Smoke from a dozen fires was rising from the city. A group of three individuals in uniform were standing at the close end of the bridge. They turned and walked to the south end of the bridge. Captain Koon couldn't make out their uniforms, other than that they were in some camouflage pattern. He edged forward, slowly, still in the crouched position, around the hill. Movement in the brush just off the edge of the road below caught his eye. He froze and listened. He observed for a few minutes, saw more movement on the side of the road that he was on. Slowly, he picked out several camouflaged positions stretched over fifty or so meters, each manned by two or three men. He dropped to his abdomen and crawled forward ever so slowly. Voices were directly ahead of him. He peered carefully through the brush. Ten meters ahead were three North Koreans in a fox hole to prevent any flanking move of the roadblock below.

Bradley began to worry. He looked at his watch. "Christ, he's been gone for forty minutes. What's going on?"

Sergeant Park said, "Sir, I suggest we move away from the vehicle. It is a target for aircraft, and if any North Koreans are in the area, they will come to investigate. I suggest we move up the hill a ways, so we can observe the vehicle and be out of sight ourselves."

"Good idea, Sergeant Park. I'll grab a few MREs, and we'll cut a chogi up the hill." Bradley opened the back door and grabbed an unopened case of MREs and said, "Lead the way, Sergeant." After ten minutes of sitting up on the hillside, Captain Koon came dog trotting into view.

"North Koreans hold the bridge. A roadblock is set up as an ambush about five hundred meters ahead. They have flanking positions on the hill. We will have to flank around them and follow the river into Seoul. I wish we had a couple more rifles and ammunition, canteens and your American MREs. We are going to get thirsty before we get back. We have perhaps a hundred-kilometer march ahead of us. If we stay near the river, it will be longer than going overland, but we won't get lost and at least have water, however contaminated or dirty it is. You can bet there is a terrible battle going on for Seoul. We need to reach Seoul before it falls, or we will truly be trapped behind the lines. Time, therefore, is very important. What do you say, Major, are you up for a little stroll?"

With a wry grin, Bradley said, "Captain, you and Sergeant Park are the experts here, not me. Consider me a lowly private." With that, he took out his Gerber folding knife from its sheath on his belt and cut off the sewn on badge of rank, the gold oak leaf on his right collar. "Lead on, gentlemen."

A regiment of North Korean paratroopers had seized the bridge at Ch'unch'on in the predawn darkness. The battle was relatively brief, overwhelming the regimental sized South Korean reserve force that lived in Ch'unch'on. The South Koreans couldn't get organized quickly enough to present an effective defense. As should have been anticipated, the armory was an objective as well as the bridge. Many South Korean reservists were killed as they reported to the armory to draw their weapons. One North Korean battalion seized the bridge, while the remainder of the division swept through the town. Males in the town who appeared to be between fifteen and sixty years of age were shot on sight without question or remorse. The roadblocks, so common along the highway, were not dynamited into place. The fifteen foot long hexagonal columns of carved rock, three feet in diameter, piled three or four deep, were supposed to roll onto the highway, blocking it when their concrete cradles were obliterated by the light charges of explosives placed in them. They still sat in their cradles.

It was obvious to Captain Koon that the North Koreans intended to drive down through Ch'unch'on in a flanking movement on Seoul. He figured the North just shot up the town, took out the reserve unit, and moved on. They might have left a battalion or two in town, but he knew that they were more interested in a blitzkreig operation rather than seizing and holding urban areas. The battalion's job was to make sure the road was open for follow on forces. He didn't tell Bradley that, but he knew that Sergeant Park realized it. Sergeant Park just looked at his captain and said northing. Enlisted men do not question the decisions of their officers in the Army of Republic of Korea; to do so results in a severe beating and loss of a month's pay. Discipline. Sergeant Park also realized they had little choice. The North Korean columns would soon cut them off.

"Sergeant Park, take point. Major Bradley, bring up the rear. We will be about one hundred meters behind you, Sergeant. Major Bradley, follow me by about ten meters. I don't want all of us to go down in an ambush." He gave the rifle to Sergeant Park and nodded. "Henceforth, we will not talk unless absolutely necessary, and only then in whispers. Major, it would be very beneficial if you did not speak at all. Your English would be an immediate giveaway. Sergeant, take off." Major Bradley nodded his assent.

They crept forward up to the bottom of the crest of the hill, then slowly down the other side. The brush was thick, and there were mature pine trees growing on the hillside. The pines had been planted under the arbor program to hold the soil and to establish a source of national timber. When the Japanese occupied Korea, they cut down every tree on the peninsula and exported it to Japan. Curving around the hill, they skirted around the ravine on the far side. After two hours of slow movement, mostly in a crouch, Robert Bradley's legs and back ached. Carrying the case of MREs didn't help. He wished he had spent a lot more time in the gym. Commuting two to three hours each way every day back and forth from Pennsylvania to Washington, D.C. however, left him little time for physical fitness. He could not find a place in the Washington, D.C. metropolitan area that he felt was safe enough for his family, so he commuted from Pennsylvania, as did many others assigned to the D.C. area. After another hour, he absolutely ached, and wondered how Captain Koon and Sergeant Park were able to move so well. On a hillside two hundred meters above the road, Sergeant Park stopped to allow the other two to catch up and take a break. They carefully kneeled in the brush. All were quite thirsty. Captain Koon had indicated they would move downhill to the river for water when they heard the traffic. They kneeled back down. After five minutes, an armored column of North Koreans came into view. Tanks led the way, and then tanks and personnel carriers alternated, with truckloads of infantry apparently mixed in a random manner. It seemed to Bradley that there were a lot more trucks loaded with infantry than there were tanks or armored personnel carriers. It took fifteen minutes for the column to pass. Captain Koon estimated it was a brigade-sized force.

Captain Koon motioned to the other two to quickly follow him, with the rapid up and down movement of the forearms with a closed fist. They quickly crept down the hill and stopped ten meters short of the road. "Sergeant Park, go first, quickly; we will follow in short intervals, with you, Major, next. I will bring up the rear." Park crept to the edge of the road, looked both ways and, in a crouch, ran across. Bradley followed in thirty seconds after a nod from Koon. Once across the road, they slid down the hillside to the river, pausing in the brush along the bank. All surveyed the opposite shore for any sign of activity. Captain Koon motioned to Park to go first and drink. He did so; Bradley followed as soon as Sergeant Park crept back to their position. Captain Koon did likewise as soon as Bradley returned. Then they went halfway up the hill, staying between the river and the road. Major Bradley checked his compass on his watchband. They were steadily traveling in a generally southerly direction. By nightfall, they had covered almost fifteen kilometers of rugged terrain.

Captain Koon led them down to the river's edge and said, "We have done well. We will rest. It is better to travel at night, but one needs moonlight. We will take three-hour watches. The watch will have the rifle. Sergeant Park, you will take the first watch, Major Bradley the second, and I the last. We will move when the moonlight is sufficient or at dawn if it is not." Captain Koon indicated to Bradley to break out the MREs. Major Bradley never realized just how good a hot MRE could taste. After they had eaten, they gathered the paper and plastic waste and scraped a shallow hole with their hands in which to bury it. Bradley and Koon promptly fell asleep. Sergeant Park moved to a tree to lean against with the rifle across his lap, so that he could watch the riverbanks.

At 23:00 hours, as he was about to wake Major Bradley when another convoy of North Koreans moved down the road. Sergeant Park heard it coming and rolled over onto his stomach and covered the road with the rifle. Awakened by the noise, Major Bradley and Captain Koon rolled over on their stomachs. "Keep your face down, Major," Koon whispered to Bradley. It shines very well even in the dark. It will be easy to see, even at fifty meters from the road. Bradley put his face into the dirt. Captain Koon carefully and slowly smeared dirt on his face and continued to watch as the column passed. It was larger than the first. It, too, had tanks, armored personnel carriers, trucks with infantry, and a number of covered trucks. Bradley raised his head so that his eyes were just above his forearm bent in front of him. He figured it must be another regiment or brigade sized unit, only it had more covered trucks; more ammunition, fuel, and food he thought.

Sergeant Park handed the rifle to Major Bradley, who accepted it without question and assumed the position the Sergeant previously occupied. Fifteen minutes later, multiple explosions occurred to the southwest. Two ancient South Korean F-4 Phantoms streaked overhead. The glow in the sky indicated the Phantoms had struck pay dirt in attacking the column. Bradley wanted to jump for joy, but the immediate thought of all those North Korean infantry now on the ground between them and the safety of the south was immensely sobering.

"What do we do now, Captain? Advance? Do you think the enemy will come back this way, or what?"

"No, Major, I do not. I think they will push their wrecked vehicles off the road, put their wounded on the side of the road, and continue to advance. We wait here for an hour, and then we keep heading south. Maybe we can pick up some weapons, canteens and so on from some of the dead. If it doesn't look promising, we'll skirt the attack site. It should be three or four kilometers from here." Bradley looked at the dirt on the captain's face and thought that might be a good idea, add a little camouflage. He did the same around his cheekbones, chin and forehead. Captain Koon just smiled. Bradley and Sergeant Park went to sleep. An hour later, Captain Koon shook them awake and led them out. Major Bradley picked up what was left of the case of MREs and fell in.

Five kilometers and two hours later, they approached the site of the attack. Sergeant Park said nothing, just pointed to himself and then out to the road where wounded and dead were laying. Captain Koon nodded his head yes and pointed to Major Bradley to stay put. Sergeant Park began to crawl forward slowly, up the hill, towards the road. Captain Koon followed his Sergeant by about ten meters to cover him with the Dae Woo. The dead and wounded had been laid out in a neat row all along the shoulder of the road for their medics. The unit had otherwise moved on. The dead and wounded stretched for as far as Park could see in the dark. Sergeant Park calculated that those two F-4 Phantoms must have inflicted several hundred casualties in strafing the trucks of infantry in the narrow defile.

Sergeant Park saw a couple of their medics fifty meters away attending the wounded towards the other end of the road. He crawled up on the shoulder and approached the first body. The man was still breathing but had an abdominal wound and appeared unconscious. Sergeant Park laid the man's rifle aside, pulled his own bayonet from the sheath, put his hand over the man's mouth, and stabbed him in the heart. The body jerked for a couple of seconds, and then lay still. Sergeant Park removed his web gear and picked up the rifle lying adjacent to the body. He crawled over to the next body, perhaps two meters away. This man was dead. As he was removing the web gear, a wounded soldier on the opposite side of the road sat up and yelled. Sergeant Park silenced him with a single shot from the AK-47. The medics looked around, as did many others. Park put his face down and did not move, as he was lying right alongside the dead North Korean. After several minutes, things returned to normal. Apparently, the medics decided that someone was in too much pain and committed suicide. Park finished removing the web gear, with its ammunition pouches filled with magazines for the AK-47, a canteen, and several hand grenades. He slipped over to the next body and picked up a third AK-47 and ammunition belt. He slowly pushed himself backwards down the hill feet first, watching for any sign of alarm, then crawled back with Captain Koon to where Major Bradley was waiting.

Captain Koon put on a set of web gear, slung the Dae Woo on his shoulder and handed one of the AK-47s to Major Bradley along with the other set of web gear. Captain Koon led them back four hundred meters around the last curve, then across the road and halfway up the hill, and then they skirted the kill site. Grey light was just a hint of the coming dawn. Captain Koon wanted to put some distance between the carnage and themselves. In a half crouch, he led them forward at a rather fast pace through the brush. An hour later, the sun was well up on the horizon, but not over the mountain. Koon carefully searched the terrain for a place they could hide for the day. He chose a rocky outcropping, the front of which was covered with brush. The overhang screened them from view above, and the brush from below. Captain Koon figured they had covered about twelve kilometers in all since midnight. At least they had some water in the canteens, and now each was armed. They all heard another convoy coming from the north. They lay in the brush until the convoy past.

Bradley, thinking he was starving, sat up and pulled three MREs from the case he was carrying. He looked at the menus, selected his own, and handed one each to Captain Koon and Sergeant Park. Captain Koon said, "From now on, we eat two meals a day. No noon meal, only breakfast and a late supper after we stop moving." They ate in silence, each facing a different direction, and then gathered their trash to bury it. Koon indicated he would take the first watch, Park the second, and Bradley the last. Koon figured Bradley needed the most sleep right now and would be more refreshed for the last watch before dark. He was right.

At 16:00, Park shook Bradley from a sound sleep. Bradley nodded, sat up, rubbed his eyes, and crept forward a few feet. In effect, he and Park traded places. At 20:00 hours, Captain Koon sat up, rubbed his face, and shook his Sergeant awake. They ate another meal in silence. Captain Koon noted there were only three MRE's left, so he pointed to them and then to each of themselves. Bradley understood and gave the other two a meal. He put the third in his BDU trousers cargo pocket. Captain Koon slowly surveyed the immediate area in all directions, and then led off. Another convoy passed them.

They took a break at midnight. Bradley and Koon promptly fell asleep. After thirty minutes, Sergeant Park shook them both awake. Koon took point again, the others following at ten-meter intervals. Yet another convoy passed them in the dark. At dawn, they were overlooking a village adjacent to the roadside. Civilians were milling about, and smoke curled from a few fires. Several burned buildings were obvious. It was obvious from several bodies lying in the dirt that the North Koreans did not consider South Koreans of this village to be fellow citizens. Apparently, the last convoy that passed them lingered here for a few hours. They watched the village for an hour, and then approached it in bounding overwatch. Captain Koon identified himself as an officer in the South Korean Army, which the villagers immediately recognized by his uniform. The North Koreans had committed numerous rapes in the village during their brief stay. The head man of the village informed them that a tremendous battle was raging for Seoul. Before the North Koreans came, they were watching some of the battle on their television sets. The head man advised them to turn due south and stay in the hills. They filled their canteens at one of the houses. The villagers provided them with two kilograms of rice each and asked them to hurriedly move on. Captain Koon thanked the villagers for their kindness and led off to the south. They had no more reached the brush when another battalion-sized convoy moved down the road. One kilometer and half an hour later, they found a suitable place for a layover. Now in a routine, they ate their last MRE. Captain Koon took the first watch while Bradley and Park slept.

At 18:00, all three were awake. Sergeant Park began to gather brush for a small fire. The two Koreans each poured a cup of water into his canteen cup and put a handful of rice in it. Bradley emulated them. In a few minutes, Sergeant Park had a small fire going which he fed with dead wood so that there was a minimum of smoke. After twenty minutes, they each set their cups of rice on the edge to boil. After eating their supper, they wiped out the canteen cups with leaves and put them back in the canteen covers. Bradley drank about half of the water left in his canteen. Captain Koon slowly led them down the hill towards the river. By now, it was twilight. They filled their canteens and moved back up the hill.

One kilometer later, they spotted a North Korean truck broken down alongside the road. They looked at each other but said nothing. They crept closer. Barely able to see it at one hundred meters, they observed that there was only a driver and an assistant. No other North Koreans appeared in the area. Both were leaning against a front wheel. Captain Koon whispered to Sergeant Park, "I'll shoot the one on the right; you shoot the one on the left as soon as I fire." Two shots rang out, and both North Koreans slumped with bullets in their chest. Sergeant Park moved out in a crawl, then a crouch. He attached the bayonet from the web gear to the AK-47 and dashed across the road. He bayoneted both in the chest. Their rifle fire had caused a flat in the truck. He quickly dragged the two bodies over the hill out of sight.

Bradley and Koon rushed the truck to examine the contents. It contained a mix of food and ammunition. Captain Koon broke open a box of magazines for the AK-47s, handed Major Bradley half a dozen, took as many for himself, and broke open a case of food. He shoved several packages into his shirt, handed Bradley several more, and opened a case of grenades. He hung or stuck one in every possible place about his body. Bradley jumped down, Koon handed him several more grenades, food and magazines for Sergeant Park. They heard an approaching truck as Sergeant Park appeared around the front from disposing of the bodies. All three quickly slid down the hill into the brush.

The truck stopped. The driver called out but received no answer. Park and Koon each slowly pulled out a grenade. The driver got down and with a flashlight, shined it around the truck. He noticed the flat tire and the pool of blood from the two dead Koreans. He yelled. A squad of North Koreans dismounted from the truck. Park and Koon pulled the pins of the grenades, held them for two seconds and threw them. All three ducked. The grenades exploded against the second truck, and Bradley opened fire with his AK-47. All three of them jumped up and fired into the truck and the North Koreans. It lasted perhaps ten seconds. Eight dead North

Korean infantrymen and four drivers accounted for the total. The second truck also contained food and ammunition.

"Quickly," said Koon, "get more grenades and magazines from the first truck and move up the hill." Bradley climbed into the rear of the truck and handed Park a handful of magazines, a case of food, and grabbed several more grenades. Together, they ran up the hill. Captain Koon led them on a brisk walk, upright, just below the ridge of the hill. They didn't stop moving for two hours. Bradley thought to himself, *Christ, I might just have killed a couple of men, if the grenades didn't get them. Several were still on their feet when I opened fire. I don't feel any remorse about it. Why should I? They were the bad guys. Humph. I wonder if they will give me a combat Infantryman's badge for this little stroll.*

Now, in the distance, they could hear what sounded like thunder. It was very faint, but like thunder. All realized it was artillery and bombs from the battle for Seoul. The South Koreans were not going to surrender their capitol and largest city without a tremendous bloodletting.

CHAPTER 15

"**M**r. President, my colleagues and I are deeply disturbed that you are considering going to the aid of what you call the Republic of Korea, or the South Koreans. Certainly, this will require a declaration of war. The invasion of South Korea by the North is not a direct threat to the United States. After all, the South Koreans threw us out after fifty years of safeguarding their freedoms and allowing them to become one of the economic power houses of East Asia. The Koreans danced in the streets with our departure. Remember the Koreans throwing rotten vegetables and eggs on our troops as they marched out? This did not go down well with the American public. For you to attempt to invoke the War Powers Act and order forces into Korea would be in violation of our constitution."

"Tell me, Senator Kennely, will the Senate support a declaration of war to go to the aid of South Korea?"

"Mr. President, the only way the United States will enter that conflict is under the aegis of the United Nations. You know better than I that the chances of that are almost nonexistent. With the tremendous debate on whether or not the United States should even remain in the UN, and your earlier campaign remarks about moving the United Nations out of the United States, it really came down hard on a number of international nerves. The UN will not go to South Korea's aid simply because you wish it to do so. They are not willing to field a nonexistent international force that they cannot afford. More importantly, there is a general fear that China might have something to do with this, and they do not wish to confront Chinese troops as occurred in the first Korean War."

"Senator, will your party support a bill for the Declaration of War to go to the defense of South Korea or not?"

"Mr. President, I fear that not only my party, but a large number of your party, will not support it either. After being bogged down in the Balkans, in Afghanistan, and a tremendously expensive and essentially unsuccessful excursion into Iraq, I don't believe that we can afford it or that the American people will support it. Not only that, but I, personally, and a number of my colleagues agree with me, question whether or not we would be militarily successful against the overwhelming forces that the North is throwing against the South. They are pouring over a million men into the South. We have only eight divisions nearby. What will you do if the Chinese enter into the war as they did before? You better be prepared to answer that question before anyone introduces a bill for a Declaration of War. I think about the best you can hope for is support for getting whatever American citizens are there out of there as quickly as possible."

Turning to the Senate Minority Leader, a leader of his own party, Jason Thornton asked, "What do our party colleagues of the Senate say, Senator Cowart?"

"Mr. President, we are pretty much in agreement with our Democratic colleagues on this one."

"Congressman Farrel, or do you prefer Mr. Speaker, what is your opinion of this, how does the House feel about our assistance to South Korea?"

"I'm afraid, Mr. President, that the House very closely reflects that of the Senate. The Koreans threw us out; now they are paying the price for it. No more American blood should be shed for a land war in Asia. No, Mr. President, I don't believe there is any way that the House of Representatives would even consider passing a Declaration of War. If South Korea needs help, then let the Asian Tigers help. Where is Japan? Where is the Republic of the Philippines, where is Singapore? What are they doing? The hue and cry of the public would be worse than what we experienced in the days of the Vietnam War. There is no public support for another Korean War at all. No, I don't believe this will get anywhere except get all of us thrown out of office. In point of fact, Mr. President, I even heard mention of impeachment if you attempt to put us in there under the War Powers Act. Look out your window, Mr. President. On only the second day of the attack, there are hundreds of demonstrators against our involvement walking the sidewalk out there. Do you see any supporters for our involvement? I don't. Recall that the last President of our party was voted out of office after one term because of anti-terrorist commitments in Iraq, the Philippines, Indonesia, and against the drug lords in South America."

"Congressman Klein, what do your Democratic colleagues in the House of Representatives say?"

"I'm afraid, Mr. President, that the consensus is almost unanimous. This is one we can't win and should walk away from. It isn't worth American blood. If the North wins, as they are likely to do, they will, over the course of the next twenty years or so, just run the entire peninsula into the ground. It will be a first-class basket case, and then, and only then, can change be effected. That change will have to come from inside, most likely in the form of a revolution. The Old Guard can't keep the rest of the world out forever. Sooner or later, the people will learn and rebel. In that interim, they can continue to be a drain on China, who is supporting them with food and oil."

"Well, Gentlemen, I thank you for your candor, and your time. I will seriously consider your advice. In the meantime, I intend to get our Americans out of there as quickly as possible, by any means necessary."

"Mr. President, I don't think you will have any difficulty, politically speaking, with that. I'm sure the public will support your attempts to get our people out of there as quickly as possible. Most certainly the Congress will."

"Thank you, Gentlemen. Give my regards to the Senate and the House. I do respect our Constitution as the highest law of the land."

The Senate Majority Leader, Minority Leader, the Speaker of the House and House Minority Whip rose and shook the President's hand. They nodded tritely and were escorted out by Johnny Withers.

The President picked up the phone and punched the appropriate button for the phone that rings on Secretary Talbott's desk. She answered.

"Marge, where do we stand with our people? What have you heard? Where are they that we can get them out?"

"Mr. President, I have had several reports earlier today. Most are headed for Inchon, Ascom City, to be precise. If we can get some helicopters in there, we should be able to get them out. Most of them won't get there until late tonight or tomorrow, as they are walking out with the flood of refugees from Seoul. The pre-arranged pickup point is one of which they are all aware. They are gathering there and await rescue."

"All right, Marge, tell them that as soon as our Marines are close enough, we'll send in some Sea Stallion helicopters to pull them out. Wish them luck from me." He hung up the phone.

"Peggy, get me Admiral Stark on the phone," the President said into the intercom. Two minutes later, the President's phone rang. "Admiral Stark here, Mr. President."

"Admiral, what is the estimated time of arrival of that Marine Expeditionary Brigade into the Yellow Sea? How soon will they be in helicopter range to evacuate American personnel from Inchon?"

"They should be within round trip flight time and distance in about thirty hours, Mr. President. I strongly recommend, however, we wait until daylight before attempting to affect a rescue. I wouldn't want to send the choppers in at night, having to look for people, especially with a lot of Koreans around who just might want to hitch a ride."

"OK, Admiral, that sounds reasonable to me. I'll leave it in your hands. I believe you have the necessary details?"

"Yes, sir, Mr. President. The helicopter crews are in briefing as we speak. Gives them plenty of time for preparation."

"Thank you, Admiral." Jason Thornton hung up the phone. He turned on the television to Fox News Channel. Live broadcasts of anti-war demonstrations were coming from Los Angeles, San Francisco, Houston, Philadelphia, Chicago, and Detroit. It seemed that everyone everywhere in America was against American involvement. The screen played to live broadcast from Seoul. The reporter appeared to be a few hundred meters behind the fighting. Black smoke was everywhere, and the noise was deafening. The reporter pointed to South Korean jet attack aircraft streaking north to bomb the invaders. Two M-60 tanks rolled behind him, making it impossible to hear what he said. House to house fighting, urban warfare, military operations in urban terrain, by whatever name, was the most costly in men, material, infrastructure, and civilian casualties. Ambulances came crawling past him, and several wounded soldiers were seen staggering towards the rear behind him. An artillery shell exploded against a building fifty meters away. The blast and debris laid the reporter and cameraman on the ground. The camera kept rolling while they regained their stance. The reporter was obviously dazed, wobbling on his feet. The cameraman wasn't much better. Someone, probably the sound man, came forward and helped the reporter limp away under the eye of the camera. It appeared that Nam Sam Mountain overlooking Seoul was falling to the enemy. The cameraman panned to the air battle in the sky. The sound man now was talking; taking the place of the reporter.

"The South Korean Air Force has taken its toll on the North Korean Air Force. There is no question that the South Koreans have superior pilots and fly superior aircraft and have superior training. They have almost swept the skies free, at least here over Seoul today, of North Korean planes. Their nemesis, however, is surface to air missiles. We have seen a number of South Korean fighter planes go down in flames from surface to air missiles. They appear to be shoulder fired surface to air missiles. Any time one of the South Korean ground attack aircraft swoops in to strafe the North Korean forces, a dozen stinger type missiles are fired at it. The North also appears to have mobile anti-aircraft guns in excess. They are like four heavy machine guns mounted on a tank chassis. I'm told they are Soviet built ZSU-24s. We have reports that they are using them to attack fortified South Korean positions as well as using them against aircraft. We're going to have to pull back from here a bit. The North Koreans have broken through the Nam Sam tunnel. Small arms fire is beginning to rake the area. Back to you, Bill."

"Shit," thought the President, half aloud. He looked at his watch. 16:30. they had another update meeting in thirty minutes. He punched in Marge Talbott's number again.

"Marge, get ahold of the North Korean representative. Tell him we plan to evacuate our people by helicopter in thirty-six to forty-eight hours. The evacuation point will be in the Inchon area. We request that no hostile fires be directed against our aircraft. It would not help their cause to shoot at our folks while we are trying to evacuate American civilians. Especially stress that would be a factor in tilting American participation in this war."

"I have already done that, Mr. President. I took that liberty and told him where and how but didn't have a time reference for him. I'll pass that on immediately to him. If there is nothing else, Mr. President, I will see you in thirty minutes."

"I knew there was a reason I picked you for Secretary of State. See you in thirty minutes."

The attendees were in the War Room when Jason Thornton entered.

"Marge, what is the international scene like? Anybody for doing anything other than sitting on their thumbs?"

"Unfortunately, Mr. President, that's about it. There are significant demonstrations in London, Paris, Stockholm, Berlin and a few lesser ones scattered around. It seems nobody wants to go to this war."

"Admiral Stark, where do we stand with getting our carrier groups in range?"

"The Marine Expeditionary Brigade has been making excellent time. As I earlier stated, we can affect a rescue in thirty-six to forty-eight hours. Another twenty-four hours after that and all three carrier battle groups will be within striking range of one hundred and fifty miles or less."

"The unofficial word I have on the hill is that neither house of congress is willing to go along with this one. I am in quite a quandary. General Craig, what is your overall view of this war? If the United States jumps in to help South Korea, do we stand a chance of pushing the North back to the 38th Parallel or back to the Yalu?"

"Forgive me, Mr. President, but what are the chances of the Chinese jumping in?"

"Damn it, General! I wish to God I knew. Marge, can you give us anything on that? Any indication about Chinese intentions?"

"Well, Mr. President, I have a sinking gut feeling that they have known about this for some time. Maybe that's why so many of their merchant ships are tied up in port. They aren't as inscrutable as they like to think they are. Just reading body language of some of their embassy folks my staff and I met with this morning is that they are jumping up and down inside with glee. I don't like it. I have a sinking gut level feeling about this."

"General Craig, how are the South Koreans doing?"

"About as well as can be expected, Mr. President. Ultimately, though, I don't know. The North has so many men under arms, well over a million, that they might overwhelm the South by sheer mass. The South Korean satellites are in orbits of close proximity to ours, and they are seeing the same pictures we are. They don't look good. Forces are still pouring down all of the roads out of the North into the South. The initial onslaught was down the roads by mechanized forces. We are starting to see follow-on infantry forces spreading out through the countryside while mechanized forces continue to pour down the roads. They know that if a battalion or larger force concentrates, they might catch a small tactical nuke. Therefore, no formations larger than a company are moving either on the roads or through in the rural areas. With the exception of Seoul, the North is making better time in the western part of the peninsula, where it is flatter, than they are in the eastern mountains. That is to be expected. The North has made a pretty good dent, although they are slowing down. The South Korean Air Force has taken very serious losses. I don't know how long they can sustain them. If they lose air support, it will become pretty much a ground pounders war. Light infantry will be slugging it out toe to toe. It tends to be that way in the eastern part of the peninsula anyway. Having said that, the North can form a solid line across the peninsula and march south. They have the manpower to do that. What that means is that the South doesn't have the manpower under arms to match them under those conditions. South Korean units will be isolated and destroyed in place. If it comes to that, the South will probably lose. I would like to remind you, Mr. President, that we have only eight active divisions in the area, and most of our reserve and National Guard Divisions are hollow. That especially applies to our Army and Navy reserves. I am not so certain that our concept of Network Centric Warfare will stand us in such good stead under these conditions."

"Johnny, go out in the hall and call the Secretary of the Treasury, Wall Street, or whoever the hell else you can think of, and try and get a handle on the size of the American investment in South Korea. I want to know how many billions of dollars American investors are going to lose if South Korea falls."

"Yes, Mr. President." Johnny Withers moved to the hall where Robert Lee was waiting for his charge. Withers made his calls.

The President studied the video screens depicting the battle from the satellite broadcasts. "Comments, anyone?"

No one spoke.

"At this time, I don't see how we can do anything but sit this out. I don't know what the long-term consequences will be, but I'm damned sure they won't be good. We don't have the support of the international community, support from the American people is in doubt, Congress won't support it, you tell me now that mass has somehow been restored as an important principle or war, and that we lack mass, transportation assets, trained reserves, and I don't know what else. Does anyone see it any differently?"

No one spoke. "All right, we will move our carrier battle groups into position off the peninsula, but we won't get involved. We will rescue our own people and monitor the situation. I hope they don't go nuclear, but if Seoul gets desperate enough, would they take out Pyongyang? Or vice versa? Will the North nuke the South if there is a reversal? General Shelton, you have a comment?"

"Mr. President, I don't see the North using nuclear weapons against the South, at least not unless South Korean forces pass north of the 38th parallel. In that case, I think the North would use them on anything that crosses the line. They want the South, its industrial capacity, its trained work force intact and its food-producing capability. I don't think they will cut off their nose to spite their face on the south side of the line."

"Point well taken, General. All right, if no one has anything else, then we will be bystanders off the coast. All we want are our people. Marge, make sure you transmit this to both the North Koreans and the Chinese. We will not enter into this conflict, at least not as long as we have our people out of there, safe and sound. If any harm comes to the several thousand Americans there, the story might change."

"I will transmit that message in person by calling upon both embassies before I have supper tonight, Mr. President."

"General Craig, have our forces stand down a notch. No use keeping the red flag up if we aren't going to war."

"Yes, sir."

"Anything else anybody wants to add or say? Ed? Roger? Jim? No? Then meeting adjourned." Jason Thornton had a very sinking feeling in the pit of his stomach. He returned to his office upstairs and poured a large rye over ice, to which he added Coca-cola from a small refrigerator in the back of his office.

There is a difference between doing what is right when you can afford to do it and doing nothing when you cannot. I'm not going to throw the lives of American military personnel on a useless, unsupported quest. Good God, my own political party won't even support me. Well, we aren't going to be the world's policeman anymore. It will just have to grow up or die on its own, thought Jason Thornton.

"Peggy, get Roger McCall in here," he more or less yelled to his secretary. Peggy, recognizing the irritation in his voice, didn't hesitate to call Roger. In two minutes, Roger was standing before the President's desk in the Oval Office.

"Roger, at another time, I would offer you one of these," he said holding up his drink, "but you are going before the cameras in an hour or so. This is a press release that the United States will affect a rescue mission of American personnel, military and civilians, from the Republic of Korea within forty-eight hours. At this time, the United States does not intend to enter into the current Korean conflict. Dress it up however you want. You can field any questions that you choose and ignore those that you choose. It is your call. Neither the House nor the Senate will support our entry into the conflict. The Republicans won't support it any more than the Democrats. Anti-American participation seems to be universal. You can call the press conference when you are ready. Give yourself plenty of time. The wolves are always howling around feeding time."

"Yes, Mr. President. Would you like to review it before I go on the air?"

"Hell no, Roger. That's why you got the job. You don't need me to do that. You know how I feel about it, but there is nothing I can do. I am not a dictator of America, let alone the world. That cesspool out there is your ballpark. Get on with it." He waved Roger out with his drink in hand.

"Yes, Mr. President." Roger had already drafted half a dozen versions to cover all contingencies. He walked into the press room and announced that there would be a press release at 20:00 hours regarding the Korean conflict. Turning on his heel, he left as abruptly as he came. He went to his office and pulled the appropriate dialogue. He simply wanted to review what he had already written, shave with an electric razor, and put on a fresh shirt and deodorant.

The Marine Expeditionary Brigade reached station north of the Island of Tokchok in the Yellow Sea. She moved to fifteen kilometers off the coast. Standing five kilometers off their portside were three North Korean destroyers of the Luhu Class, purchased from Red China in a sort of lend-lease program.

The USS Bataan, a Wasp Class Amphibious Assault Ship, detected the submarine laying quietly on the bottom just off her starboard bow, two thousand meters out. The Chinese-built North Korean submarine did not detect the USS Virginia lying three thousand meters off its stern.

At dawn, twelve V-22 Ospreys launched from the decks of the USS Bataan. Almost immediately, two Super Cobra helicopter gunships lifted off to form on the flanks of the Super Stallion formation. Five minutes later, two AV-8B II Harriers took off from her foredeck and streaked towards land. They climbed to fifteen thousand feet and began circling, providing fighter cover for the helicopters below should any North Korean hothead decide the Americans were easy pickings. Two more Harriers launched to provide cover for the amphibious group. Below the flight deck of the Bataan, 1200 Marines stood by in landing craft should it be necessary to fight their way in to rescue the Americans, mostly civilians. The next wave, composed of six Super Stallion helicopters, was lifted by elevators to the flight deck.

The first flight of V-22 Ospreys landed in the American compound and warehouse complex not far from the docks. Several American export companies had rented warehouses and a small office building close to the docks of Inchon. The Americans, mostly in an orderly fashion, put their children on the first flight. All twelve of the Ospreys were filled, carrying almost three hundred children. They lifted off without incident. The flight leader radioed in that all aircraft were filled and outbound. Fifteen minutes later, the second flight landed. Koreans, seeing the helicopters evacuating the Americans, began to climb the fencing and push against the compound gates.

The next two flights evacuated the women, of which there were about two hundred. On the third flight, many Koreans were inside the compound, pushing and shoving aside the American men. Those who spoke English demanded evacuation. Those who did not pointed at the helicopters and began shouting in Korean. The crowd was becoming more and more menacing. The American civilian men formed an impromptu cordon around the landing field. Several Koreans reached the helicopters and tried to climb aboard. Many of the American men were forced into fist fights with the Koreans in their attempts to restrain them. Since Korean males are required to study Tae Kwan Do through high school, very few of the Americans were a match in hand to hand combat, and quite a few were knocked flat or cold. There were about four hundred American men still to be evacuated. The air crews managed to kick a few off, but there were too many. The mob gained on the first two air crews; the Koreans fought back to remain on board. The Marine aviator flight leader in the first helicopter ordered weapons drawn. One Korean lunged for the crewman, who promptly shot him. Two more lunged at the crew member, but they were shot by the other crewman. General panic broke out. The aviator called to the gunships for assistance. The first Marine Cobra buzzed the now collapsed gate, but it did little except to cause the mob to duck for a few seconds. The second ship radioed the Bataan for instructions. The order came back from the Air Squadron Commander, "Do what you have to do to get the Americans out. If that includes the use of deadly force, so be it."

Other air crews began to resort to their pistols for self-defense. The OV-22 flight leader radioed to the Super Cobras, "You have to get the mob pressure off of us. They are pulling Americans off our craft."

The gunship section leader responded, "Roger, Evacuation Leader. Chicken Hawk II, take position on my port side. Fire upon my command."

The Super Cobras in tandem flew in low and hovered inside the gate. "Upon my command, spray a five second burst of .30 caliber." Each sprayed a five second burst of 7.62x51 mm. machine gun fires into the mob as it poured through the gate. It was the evacuation of Saigon all over again in miniature. Screams and curses arose from the Koreans; some shook their fists at the Americans. The gunships rose up and began to circle again. The mob was delayed only momentarily. Another surge brought more Koreans into the fray.

The helicopter flight leader radioed to the Bataan. The Super Cobras landed again in front of the gate and, this time, held the position. The next flight of six helicopters carried two platoons of an armed Marine infantry company to restore order and ensure the evacuation. As they landed, the Marines deployed around the landing zone and set up a fire line. The mob was coming in from other gates and over the compound walls. When they saw the Marines, they only hesitated momentarily. The Captain in charge of the Marine landing party gave the order through a bull horn, "Pick your targets, fire at will." Marines commenced sporadic rifle fire upon threatening Koreans, and those who were engaged in struggles with the Americans. After fifty or so rounds were fired into the crowd, a semblance of order was restored.

The Marine Captain ordered the platoon leader in the center of the line to have three squads get the American men loaded in the nearest aircraft and get them airborne. Quite a number of dead and wounded Koreans, men and women, lie on the ground. The Marines held their position, most in prone, in a circle around the landing zone. The civilians helped their comrades who were injured in fights with the Koreans. Several of them were dead. The Harriers remained aloft, just off the coastline, not wanting to provoke some hot-headed North Korean into a dogfight. The Harrier is designed primarily as a ground attack aircraft and has aerial combat as its secondary role. Still, with two sidewinder missiles, it is a worthy opponent for most aviators of other countries. As Chuck Yeager said, "It is the aviator, not the machine that wins the dogfight." The Company Commander ordered the bodies of the deceased Americans loaded on the last flight out.

After four hours elapsed, all identified Americans in the compound were airborne. The Marines mounted their flight and looked down upon those they killed as they lifted off.

CHAPTER 16

After the first week of intense fighting, the North had captured about one fourth of the city of Inchon even though it was surrounded by the end of the week. Their mass of North Korean personnel was too large, although they suffered tremendous casualties. The North was advancing faster in other areas of the south. The North was moving mobile forces along the roads, bypassing intermediate towns and cities, aiming to control critical road and transportation junctions. Behind these mobile forces came a horde of infantry, moving much slower, but coming as a solid wave, combing the countryside and seizing control of the local population.

Rumors of North Korean amphibious assault at Inchon on the second day began to surge through the South Korean forces. Some units in Seoul panicked, fearing being cut off and trapped between enemy lines. Some turned and ran, first as individuals, then squads, then platoons. Officers at the company level attempted to restore order and discipline, in many cases, by on the spot executions. For the most part, they were successful, and the battle for Seoul continued, growing ever more costly.

The temperature was in the low nineties, and the humidity was approaching 85%. It was hot and sticky, even for the first week of June in the Seoul area. *I've never been thirstier in my life*, Timmons thought. Timmons and Matthews were drenched in sweat as they walked south out of Seoul towards the road to Inchon, joined by tens of thousands pouring onto the road. Ten miles later and still in the metropolitan area, thirst began to be a major factor for everybody. Stores and shops were inundated with thirsty people. Where no shop keeper was in attendance, the crowd helped itself to whatever was on the shelves and then some. Timmons ached all over. Carrying a suitcase in each hand, his shoulders felt like his arms were pulling them out of the sockets. At five feet ten inches tall and two hundred pounds, Timmons wished he was in better physical condition. Matthews appeared to be in somewhat better shape. *Maybe that's because he's Army, and they have to do all that physical training stuff,* thought Timmons.

"Wait a minute, Curt," said Timmons. They moved to the side of the road where Timmons opened both his suitcases and started going through them, trying to decide what he could discard. Finally, he settled on two spare shirts, two pairs of pants, a windbreaker and all his socks. He put them in the larger suitcase and abandoned everything else. Matthews was wearing what amounted to a Class B uniform, with his tunic in his suitcase and a spare pair of lace-up shoes that the Army calls low quarters. Two miles later, Timmons was limping. They moved to the side of the road and stopped, where Timmons took off his loafers and socks to examine his feet. There were blisters on his heels, the balls of his feet and his little toes were swollen.

Others were taking breaks all along the road. As aircraft zoomed overhead, everyone looked up to see whose they were. Matthews was wishing he was in better physical condition and that he had his Battle Dress Uniform and combat boots rather than Class A and B uniforms. He would give his eye teeth for his pistol belt with a canteen on it. He would feel even better if he had a pistol to put on it. His service cap offered no protection or shade for his eyes. He wondered if he wouldn't have been better off wearing a change of civilian clothes. Still, he figured if he was in uniform, and the United States did declare war, he would be treated as a Prisoner of War if captured, whereas in civilian clothes, the North Koreans could declare him a spy for execution.

Both men were hungry, in fact, ravenously hungry. Neither Matthews nor Timmons had ever gone twenty-four hours without eating in their lives. Now, they had a sampling of what much of the world suffers. By nightfall, they had covered a little less than twenty miles of the route to

Inchon. The shoulders of the highway were crowded as darkness fell. A few fires were lit, but fuel was scarce. Some families had a cooking pot over their fire. They remembered stories from their grandparents of the 1950-1953 Korean War and had thoughtfully brought food with them. Food was in very short supply then for many of the civilians. A number of unattached young men had formed into loose bands, and they were looking for easy prey in terms of procuring food from some of those who had it. Timmons and Matthews witnessed one such loosely organized gang attempt to assault a family in the midst of the stopped refugees in the adjacent field, but a number of other Korean males joined in the defense of the family. The result was five severely roughed up young men. Two were beaten into unconsciousness, and three staggered off to lick their wounds; one had an obviously broken arm, another had blood running down his face from a club applied to his head. Timmons's mouth was so dry he couldn't swallow. It took several hours for him to fall asleep because of the aches and pains and thirst. Aircraft continued to fly over them, with an occasional air battle occurring, which woke many. Several planes went down in flames, but in the darkness, it was not obvious who the victors were. A few more hardy souls continued to march down the road in the darkness.

With dawn, the mass of people began to stir. With the sun halfway up on the horizon, many had resumed the march to the south. Matthews sat up, looked around, scratched his head and face, and noted the smell of urine and feces. He shook Timmons awake. Timmons groaned and rolled over. Matthews shook him harder this time. He sat up, looked around, and saw the mass of humanity moving, something akin to an ocean wave breaking on the beach. *Oh God*, he thought and then asked, "How close are we to Inchon?"

"Near as I can tell, about ten or twelve miles from the city. I don't know where in the city the depot is located, however, and how far it is from the edge of the city. I only know that it is close to the port, so we need to find that out as we get closer into Inchon. I think it is really at some place called Ascom City, which is a part of Inchon. We don't need to walk any extra miles because we don't know where to go." Timmons was so stiff he could hardly move. He looked around for his suitcase. Sometime in the night, someone had stolen it. Matthews still had his because he'd used it for a pillow. *It's just as well,* thought Timmons, *Because I couldn't carry it today anyway.* "OK, let's go," he said to Matthews. Matthews noted the loss of Timmons's suitcase, but said nothing. He picked up his own and the walked back onto the road.

By ten o'clock, both men knew Timmons was in trouble. By noon, he was struggling from severe dehydration. Matthews half-carried him into the shade of some roadside buildings. He eased Timmons down against an outside wall and entered the building. It was deserted and had pretty much been ransacked of whatever was of value that could be carried. He found an empty plastic jug with a lid on it. He sniffed it, and near as he could tell, it once had bleach in it. He noted a small stream, more of a ditch with running water, out the open back door, took the bottle, and went down and filled it with water that did not appear too clean. *OK,* he thought, *so there is probably hepatitis, typhoid fever, classical Salmonella, amebic dysentery, Shigellosis, toxigenic Escherichia coli, and God knows what else in this water, but we need water or we die anyway.* He took it around to Timmons and made him sip it slowly. Timmons never knew plain water could taste so good. Over the next thirty minutes, Matthews and Timmons had consumed all four liters that the jug held. Matthews went back to the stream and filled the jug again. He noticed others drinking from the stream. Matthews pulled Timmons to his feet, and they rejoined the marching throng. Not having eaten for almost two days, the stomachs of both men were undergoing painful contractions. Matthews moved to the shoulder of the road, pulling Timmons with him. He opened his suitcase and took out his tunic. He stuffed his spare socks in the pockets, changed shirts, and walked back on the highway, abandoning the suitcase. The closer to Inchon they came, the more the sounds of battle grew in intensity. By nightfall, they were on the edge of Inchon, and it was painfully obvious that Inchon was also under attack.

With no major roads running south out of Inchon, some of its citizenry was pouring across the countryside in a southeasterly direction, towards Anyang and Suwon. They had not encountered any other Americans, or Europeans for that matter, since leaving Seoul. Matthews began questioning Koreans where the depot was located. All he got was shrugging shoulders and heads shaking no. They stopped at what passed for a gas station. Timmons slid down the outside wall for a rest. Matthews entered and, looking around, found what he presumed was a map of Inchon on the wall. He could recognize the harbor area, but the depot was not labeled. He took a stool and tried to smash the frame off the wall with no success. He found a tire iron and used it to pry the frame off. He folded the map and put it in his hip pocket, cursing because he did not have a compass. He knew from the rising sun which way was west to the harbor, but that's all he knew. *Hell,* he thought, *what good would a compass do me anyway? I haven't read a map or used a compass since the Medical Department Basic Course with a one-hour lecture on it and a one-night practical exercise in the field at Camp Bullis. If I make it out of this alive, I am going to make damned sure my grandkids are in the Boy Scouts and learn this stuff! That is, if I ever have any or live to see them.*

With Timmons in tow, he headed west down what he presumed was a main thoroughfare, since it was four lanes wide. No vehicles were in sight, and the masses of people from Seoul, now realizing Inchon was under attack, had begun to drift to the southeast across the countryside. There were still many individuals, and people in groups of two or three, on the streets. It appeared to Matthews that many of them were looters, or those who had opted to stay in their homes rather than flee the city. It was obvious to both of them that Timmons was near the end of his endurance. He needed rest, food, and above all, good water. Matthews stuck his head in the door of what appeared to be an apartment building. He knocked on the first door on the first floor, and when no one came, he went upstairs to the second floor. At the first door, he knocked and called again. No answer. He tried the knob. It was locked. He kicked it hard, and it broke open. He called a loud "hello." Again, no answer. He entered and quickly sought the kitchen.

In the refrigerator, which was still running, he found several dishes, some rice, some summer kimchi, sauces and some kind of meat in a stew. He tried the water tap at the faucet. It worked. He filled the kettle on the stove and soon had boiling water into which he put a tablespoon of tea. He went downstairs and half-carried Timmons up. He sat Timmons at the table and gave him some of the cold rice and stew to eat with a spoon he found in a drawer. He poured them both a cup of hot tea. After they ate, Matthews rummaged through more kitchen drawers where he found several rather dull knives. He stuck one in his belt on his left side, and gave one to Timmons, who said nothing, but stuck it in his belt like Matthews did anyway. Since it was late afternoon, Matthews said, "Perhaps we ought to sleep here tonight and get a good night's rest, then search for the depot tomorrow. We don't know what the situation is here, and I'm not sure it is a good idea to be floating around here after dark."

"Sounds good to me; we both know I am exhausted. It would do us both good."

Matthews put a pan of water on the stove to boil and dropped in all the eggs he found in the refrigerator. He was thinking they would keep better this way, and they could carry them in their pockets if they had to. He didn't want to take a chance on losing water or electricity or the bottled natural gas on the stove. They drank the rest of the tea, and Matthews made more. Then they both crashed on mats on the floor of the bedroom.

At dawn, both men awoke with the sun in their eyes. As they were drinking tea and eating the remainder of everything in the refrigerator, Timmons suddenly groaned and bent double. He pushed away from the kitchen table and bent over, made for the bathroom. He had got his pants down and squatted over the floor level toilet when he lost control. Fluid feces squirted from him and splashed his pants and the floor. The Asians don't use a sit-down toilet as is universal in the west. Their classical toilet is an oblong depression in the bathroom floor, phonetically called a "banjo" in Korean. They believe sitting on a common toilet seat leads to the spread of enteric diseases. Timmons passed about a liter of fluid before he was finished. He wiped himself with toilet paper and weakly stood up. He rinsed his hands as there was no soap obviously available and dried them on a towel. He was still cramping. Matthews remained at the table, wondering when it would hit him.

A rumbling noise grew louder, proclaiming the presence of a heavy vehicle. Matthews looked out the window to see a North Korean T-72 tank rolling down the street, with infantry along each side of the street. No one else was present. North Korean soldiers were checking buildings as they progressed. Matthews went to the bathroom and said, "We have company. North Koreans are moving down the street with armor and infantry. They seem to be checking buildings as they come. They will be here in about five minutes. How are you feeling?"

"Shitty, thank you, doctor. What the hell are we supposed to do?"

"I don't know. I don't know if we should try and run, which with your condition would be rather futile, or just surrender ourselves and hope that they treat prisoners better than they did in the last war. I really don't think we have much of a chance with your condition."

"Do what you think will give us the best possible odds for survival, Curt. I'll go along with whatever you decide."

"OK, I think I will go talk to the North Koreans and see what they say."

Matthews went downstairs and stepped into the street with his hands raised. Several North Koreans ran up to him. One of them butt stroked him in the abdomen with a rifle, which buckled him to his knees. He was about to deliver a butt stroke to the back of Matthews's head when a shout from a Korean lieutenant stopped him.

Matthews looked up and asked, "Do you speak English?"

The officer nodded, and said, "An American?"

"Yes, I am a physician who was sent here to study an epidemic that broke out two weeks ago. I was in Seoul when you attacked. We walked here from Seoul in the hope of being evacuated from Inchon. We didn't know you attacked here as well."

"Americans are very smart this time. Much smarter than before. America has not entered this war. Americans are gathering at the depot. We have been ordered to direct westerners to the depot whenever we encounter them. Several hundred have probably already gathered there. You should go there immediately."

"Can you tell us where it is?"

"You said us, and we. Are there more than you?"

"Yes, I have a friend who is sick upstairs."

"You and your friend should go quickly. Evacuation is scheduled for today or tomorrow. If you do not make it, you will be left here. I can offer you no transportation. You will have to walk about fifteen kilometers west of here, and you will find the depot. Take your friend and go now."

"Thank you. We will do so. You are?"

"I am First Lieutenant Soo, Choi He, and do not thank me. If I had the choice, I would kill you here and now. If you encounter more victorious North Korean soldiers, ask for an officer and tell them you are Americans looking for the depot for evacuation. They have orders to give you directions. Go now."

Matthews nodded and rose to his feet. Holding his abdomen, he went back into the building to get Timmons. Timmons was squatting over the banjo again.

"Come on, Americans are being evacuated at the depot about twelve miles from here. We have to make it today, or we don't get out. We have to walk it, diarrhea or not. We need to go now."

"OK." Timmons wiped himself again and pulled up his pants. He was sweating, Matthews noted. Timmons took the roll of toilet paper off the holder. Matthews went into the kitchen and picked up the hard-boiled eggs and a salt shaker. Timmons, especially, would need salt and other electrolytes. Together, they stumbled down the stairs and into the street. Matthews headed them west, in the direction Lieutenant Soo had indicated.

By noon, Timmons was running a high fever. Not quite delirious, he was in obvious distress. They had stopped four times for his cramps, but he could pass nothing but mucous tinged with blood. His gastrointestinal system was empty. Still, he kept walking, if somewhat unsteadily. Due to the short incubation period, judging from when they drank water from the ditch, Matthews made a tentative diagnosis of shigellosis, commonly called bacillary dysentery. He wondered when he would break with it. Maybe he had not already because he was in better physical condition than Timmons, that he wasn't overweight, that his immune system was better, or maybe he just didn't get as large an infective dose. Whatever the reason, Matthews prayed that he would not be affected, at least, not until they got out of Korea and he could have proper medical attention. Half-carrying Timmons, they stumbled on for two more hours when Timmons finally collapsed. Matthews carefully eased him down against a building wall. He knew they were close to the depot because he suddenly became aware of the sound of helicopters. "Come on, Rod, we've come this far, we have to make it. It couldn't be that far." Timmons was closer to unconsciousness than consciousness. Matthews tried to pick him up but couldn't. Timmons's legs were like rubber; they couldn't support his body.

Matthews thought, *Damn, what the hell do I do now? If I leave him, he'll never make it. If I don't go now, I won't get out of here, and neither will he. Do I go for help? Where? Where exactly is the depot? Who will help? Certainly not the South Koreans watching us; sure as hell not the North Koreans who would just as soon shoot us.* Matthews struggled with Timmons, finally getting him to his feet by bracing him against the wall. He took Timmons arm over his shoulder and held his arm while he grasped him around his waist, holding onto his belt. He made it a few more blocks. He could see a crowd gathered, at what appeared to be a high wall. Some people were attempting to climb the wall, others were pushing and shoving trying to get through what Matthews surmised was some sort of gate. Then he heard the machine gun fire. The crowd broke for a few moments as Matthews watched, then it surged forward towards and through the gate again. Two large helicopters lifted off, and Matthews sensed an immediate change in the mood of the mob. The pushing and shoving stopped; the din immediately died down, and Matthews struggled on, half carrying, half dragging Timmons. When they reached the rear edge of the crowd, many of the Koreans smirked at them, a few spit on them, others just stood aside. Many Koreans had now entered the compound, where many bodies lay. People were bent over their loved ones, crying and wailing. Others were running into the warehouses to see what they could find. Matthews estimated that there must be fifty people down, some dead, some wounded. One South Korean man, seeing the two Americans, leaped up behind Matthews as he passed and karate punched him in the kidney. Matthews groaned and went down to his knees, letting Timmons slide to the ground. The Korean walked around to face Matthews, and then kicked him in the solar plexus, then under the chin. At the third kick, a roundhouse kick to the temple, Matthews blacked out.

When he regained consciousness, it was night. Matthews's head felt like it was going to explode. He sat up and almost vomited. *Slight concussion*, he thought. Propping himself up on his hands, he looked over at Timmons. He could see in the moonlight that his face was a bloody mess. Apparently, the angry Korean man had stomped on his face. Matthews felt his pulse.

He didn't have one. He was dead. Matthews looked at his watch. It was gone. He felt for his wallet. It too, was gone. They had been robbed while they were unconscious. Matthews sank back down and laid his head on Timmons's body. *Sorry, Rod, that I couldn't do better,* he thought as he slipped into unconsciousness again.

* * *

"Ed, we have had a complete failure of intelligence on this whole fiasco. The international order is in serious danger, and we haven't learned crap about it. I know you are new in your job as DCI, so I don't hold you personally responsible. Get your best people together and determine why we have had such a catastrophic failure. Why didn't we recognize the biological attack by North Korea for what it was? Why didn't we recognize North Korean mobilization? How did they hide it so well? How will the Japanese react to this? What is China's role in all of this? What the hell is our intelligence community doing?"

"I can tell you some of the answers right now, Mr. President. I'll have to talk with my folks to ascertain the others. As a generalization, the C4I concept, the high-tech boys have dominated the scene since September 11, 2001. That stands for communications, command, control, computers and information. We have collected so damned much information so fast, we can't begin to analyze what we collect. We don't have enough linguists; we don't have enough people who can think independently. Perhaps more importantly, we don't have people who think in both realms, that is technologically and the political-human experience realm."

"What do you mean political-human experience realm?"

"I use that to describe people who are technically competent and can correctly interpret what information they have garnered when they receive it. The two fields have not meshed together. A computer scientist, Electronics Warfare Officer in the Pacific can gather the information, but it has to go to some analyst back here in Washington, where it often sits for months before its meaning, or possible meanings, are deciphered. It becomes tactically and operationally useless because it can't be applied to the situation in a timely manner. For the last ten years, the technology folks have come to the fore in the military. They tend to think we can do everything with information, à la network centric warfare. They have left out many, if not most, of Clauswitz's classic principles of war. We're at the beginning of a learning curve, learning the hard way that they are still valid."

"Be more specific, Ed, what are we talking about?"

"If you remember the old acronym, MOSS COMES, Mr. President, you will have them. M stands for mass, be it people, fires, weapons systems, or whatever. O stands for objective. What is your objective? S stands for surprise. You can overcome tremendous odds if you can strike with complete surprise. The second S stands for security. You must not allow your enemy to understand your intentions. You have to keep him guessing, keep him off balance. C stands for command. That is one of our major areas of failure. The second O is for offensive. You don't win battles or wars by being primarily defensive. The second M is for maneuver. Anytime you become fixed in your position you are inviting destruction. You must be able to move. E stands for economy of force. You have to win the battle decisively while preserving your own force to fight another day. What good is it to win the battle if your own forces are destroyed doing it? The last S stands for simplicity. If your plans are too complicated, there is too much room for misunderstanding. Too many things go wrong.

"These technically oriented people never appreciated the value of human intelligence. You have to be able to interpret the information you receive in the way your opponent thinks. We look at it from one perspective, while it usually means something quite different to them. To paraphrase Liddell Hart, the former military historian for the Encyclopedia Britannica, you have to crawl into the mind of the enemy commander. You have to know what he thinks, why he thinks it, and how he will act. You have to know what is important to him, what his value system is. That is how you determine what is called his concept of operation. What are his objectives? This was a major reason we failed in Vietnam and failed to detect this attack in Korea. We couldn't grasp their concepts of war. We tried to fight as if we were on the plains of Europe, not the jungles of Southeast Asia. We didn't want to fight by their rules, but by our own, which were invalid against their doctrine.

"Back to the C4I bit, Mr. President. This dominating military thought didn't pay enough attention to the other factors. They failed to address the moral issue, for one. As Napoleon Bonaparte once said, 'The moral is to the physical as three to one.' Leadership is another major factor. The admirals and generals paid leadership lip service while they continued to micromanage all their subordinates instead of giving them learning room, letting them make mistakes and grow and develop leadership skills. Many, if not most, of our senior officers are micromanagers. You could put them in business suits, and you couldn't tell them from corporate executives. They are careerists, afraid they will suffer for minor mistakes made by their subordinates. All the information in the world is useless on the battlefield if it is misinterpreted, if doctrine is unsound or inflexible.

"Entering into this is the belief that war no longer has to be bloody. We have wasted good money on nonlethal weapons research. Sun Tzu said 3500 years ago the art of war is making the other guy surrender without a fight if possible. If that's not possible, then Georgie Patton's principle applies. That principle is to apply maximum lethality with whatever weapons you have at hand as quickly as possible to the enemy. Our strategic think tankers have gone soft, Mr. President. They don't really want to kill the bad guys anymore.

"The high techie concept of a battlefield is nonlinear. In spite of what they say, it is centralized thousands of miles away as an amorphous field, without lines, where long-range weapons will dominate. The battle will be fought on video screens by generals who control computer linked weapons and people. Our soldiers only need to be a few and far between, according to them. The job of the battlefield warrior will primarily be as information gatherers on the battlefield, feeding it back to some armchair general who will launch weapons systems while he is sipping coffee. They haven't truly experienced information overload. Information will be bombarding our analysts and armchair generals faster than they can process it. They won't separate the wheat from the chaff in a timely manner. This is going to cause our more timid leaders to hesitate until they have a complete or bigger picture of the battlefield before they act. That is likely to have disastrous consequences. Then, our armchair generals are going to try to act upon it themselves instead of passing it down the chain of command to the operational and tactical levels where lower echelon commanders should be making those decisions on the battlefield. The fog of war will never go away.

"Training is another failure, Mr. President, although this falls more into Jim Neville's territory. We have too much damned training on simulators and not enough field training. After we were kicked out of Korea, we reduced our training exercises because they were too expensive. We spent a lot of time and effort training people in using the network centric high-tech toys, so we have soldiers that can't build a campfire or skin a rabbit or kill a chicken in the field.

"As for North Korea's deployment of tularemia as a genetically engineered biological weapon, we totally missed the boat. We were grossly misled by the Centers of Disease Control and Prevention who thought this was a new, novel, emerging disease coming out of Asia, like the old SARS episodes in 2003 and 2004. They thought it might be another scrambled version of influenza, with the virus mixing its genes from bird, pig and human strains into something new. That's why we sent a number of our scientists to study it when we received the initial reports. Nobody wanted to address the possibility of a biological attack. It is just too horrendous to think about. They wanted absolute, scientific proof via identification of the organism. We learned the hard way. We didn't crawl into the mind of the North Koreans and see they don't care about human life.

"As for China's role, well, we are still working on that one. Our embassy people there are going night and day trying to decipher China's role in all of this. That's about what I have right now, Mr. President. I'll dribble information in to you as soon as we come up with loss or assorted facts of significance."

"Thanks, Ed. It is the China thing that bothers me the most."

"What scares me the most, Mr. President is just how reliant we are on the concept of Network Centric Warfare. We have put our eggs all in one strategic and doctrinal concept. Hackers from all over the world go at us thousands of times a day. If they should find a portal we missed, they could bring the whole system down like a house of cards. Digital networks just might not be as secure as we think they are. We are supposed to disrupt the enemy by electronically attacking his computer and communications networks. What makes us think ours are invulnerable? Our national security depends on computer digital networks right now. That just isn't limited to our Defense Department either, Mr. President. Everybody knows it also controls our communications networks, transportation nets, financial institutions, power grids, water supplies, and just about everything else. If had my way, I would have special teams of highly trained people who would hunt down the more sophisticated of these hackers, worldwide, the ones most likely to break into our systems, and put an end to their hacking. Of course, that would be illegal and violate their rights to life and liberty. The ACLU would have a field day with that one."

God help us, thought Thornton. "OK, Ed, I'll wait with bated breath for anything you come up with. Have a good one."

"Thanks, Mr. President. I will try."

CHAPTER 17

"**W**e do have some good news, Mr. President. We got a lot of our people out of Ascom City, there, just outside of Seoul. The Navy and Marines did a pretty good job of helicopter evacuation. We believe there are some souls still stranded there, but we don't have a handle yet on how many and whom."

"Thanks, Jim. We could use some good news. Keep me posted on the recovery of any stragglers, will you?"

"Roger, Mr. President. I just hope that if they are in the hands of the North Koreans, they will be treated a lot more kindly than were our POWs in the Korean War. I'll call as soon as we hear anything."

The Secretary of Defense was an outdoorsman at heart. He almost secretly wished that he was Secretary of the Department of the Interior rather than Defense. He loved to hunt and fish, but he had a deep love for nature and things outdoors. The last Republican administration had initiated the rape of the environment in the name of being independent of foreign sources of energy. As a result, everyone who ever spent any time out of doors voted against his re-election. Even the Green Party of Europe united with the Sierra Club and every other major environmentally oriented organization, which together, made a concerted effort to publicize his active and proposed violations of environmental regulations. It was a major plank in the Democratic Party's platform. The threats to the National Parks that the President had parceled out in the form of permits for the mining and timber industries were particularly odious. That cost him an election.

Secretary of Defense James Neville was the last of President Thornton's cabinet to be appointed to his office, taking office only in the last week of May. After a vigorous debate, it was his scientific and military background that made the difference. Growing up in small town West Virginia, he had the love of outdoors and hunting and fishing innate to that state. He graduated from West Virginia University with a bachelor's degree in electronic engineering and computer sciences. After a four-year stint in the Navy, mostly on submarines as an Electronic Warfare Officer, he returned to college for two years for a Master's in electrical engineering at Stanford, courtesy of the Navy. After another five years of active duty to repay the Navy for the higher education, he faced a difficult dilemma. The first two of those years were aboard the USS Ronald Reagan, the last of the Nimitz class carriers. The Naval War College resident course followed. The last two were in the Office of Naval Research, where he was Assistant Director for Antisubmarine Warfare Weapons research. While Neville loved the research and the management of the programs, he hated the politics of the job. He spent almost as much time in the Pentagon and before Congressional Committees as he did studying and determining which research efforts had the greatest potential payoff for the money. Now, at the rank of Lieutenant Commander, Grade 0-4, with eleven years of service, he couldn't decide whether to remain on active duty or "go commercial" and become a beltway bandit. The six-figure income offers from several defense contractors seemed very lucrative. In the end, he struck a deal with the Navy. He would attend Georgetown University part time to work on a Ph.D. in physics and computer engineering while working in the Office of Naval Research.

His interest was the conversion of signals from the marine biosphere into a variety of detectable signals and the integration of those signals into weapons systems by computers. What can marine life tell us about submarines and mines in their environment? How can that be translated into detectable signals and interpreted by computers? Consequently, he found himself immersed in biology courses as well. He discovered the old adage that physics is applied mathematics, chemistry is applied physics, and biology is applied chemistry, to be quite accurate. Five years later, with a new Ph.D., he found himself in the Fleet Anti-Submarine Warfare Command, as Director, Division of Submarine Detection Systems. His thesis was widely read with great interest around the world in marine research laboratories, but hardly funded by the United States Navy as a result of congressional budget decisions. For the next four years, he argued for funds to field submarine detection systems. The submarine community itself tended to disregard his research and theories as too radical. Many senior submariners were convinced they could counter any current diesel submarine threat in the littoral environment by more traditional means since they had practiced against the USS Trout and the USS Dolphin. These two diesel submarines were among the last diesel electric submarines the U.S. Navy built. Technologically speaking, they were 1950s vintage technology and were a very far cry from the much advanced non-nuclear air independent propulsion submarines built by a variety of nations in the closing days of the twentieth century and the first decade of the twenty-first century. Practicing against the ancient vessels only created a false impression of proficiency.

At twenty years of service and the rank of Captain, Grade 0-6, and convinced he would never make flag rank, he had had enough. He resigned his commission and took a research and teaching position at Massachusetts Institute of Technology. Constantly chided for his perceived militaristic stance, he took a dare from some of the more liberal members of the physics department at MIT and filed to run on the Republican ticket for the U.S. House of Representatives. His platform was increased defense to be paid for by reductions in the federal government's welfare programs, increased environmental protection, particularly the marine environment, and fiscal responsibility. The federal government should balance its books, primarily at the expense of the welfare state. To the surprise of everyone, especially James Neville, a very close race ensued. Congressman Neville won the office with a two percent majority of the vote. It was the threatened middle class that supported him with money and votes.

As a freshman in Congress, he was appointed to several of the more scientific committees. He was elected to a second term in 2020. Thornton had noticed Neville at once, and his stand on the issues. Numerous

Republican Party elites wanted the office, but Thornton offered the job to Neville. A great deal of heartburn was generated when the offer was made and even more when Neville accepted. He was considered too much of a scientist and not enough of a politician for most of his party colleagues. Now, after just having won his second election, resigning from his congressional seat after only a few months, being sworn in as the Secretary of Defense, and re-aligning his own staff, James Neville decided that he and Mrs. Neville needed a relaxing vacation fishing in Jackson Hole, Wyoming. Mrs. Neville was also an outdoor enthusiast and an ardent fly fisherwoman in her own right. Together, they had decided that they would retire to the Rocky Mountain west when he finished public service.

Bradley, Captain Koon, Sergeant Park and five South Korean reservists spent a cool late July night under the rocky ledge in the Taebok Mountains. Running and hiding since mid-June had taken its toll on all of them. Bradley had lost twenty-five pounds, Koon and Park, perhaps ten each. All eight were now lean, tired, dirty, unshaven, and determined to kill as many North Koreans as possible before they, too, died.

Captain Koon was a native of Seoul, while Sergeant Park came from a small town in central South Korea. As children, both heard stories of the atrocities of their northern brethren in the last Korean War from their great grandparents and great uncles and aunts. Now, they had witnessed what they had been told. Bradley soon adopted the skills of ambush, camouflage, night attack and use of the knife from Koon and Park who were truly professional soldiers. They tutored him well in the subtleties of killing. In turn, they admired his shooting skills with a rifle. With one of the more accurate Dae Woo rifles, Bradley consistently demonstrated he could score a casualty at four hundred meters. Captain Koon was the natural leader of the group. Bradley was quickly picking up the Korean language, as Koon and Park repeated everything in English and Korean. Several of the reservists had modest English skills.

During the second week of the war, several stray South Korean militiamen who were wandering around in the mountains after destruction of their units joined them. The skills of the militia were not up to those of Koon and Park, but they were eager learners. As guerillas, they depended a great deal on the surviving local population to feed them and provide intelligence. Now eight men strong, they were quickly developing sufficient skills and strengths to ambush small North Korean patrols. This, in turn, provided more weapons, ammunition and food. They operated out of an isolated mountain valley that had been mostly bypassed by the major thrusts. Captain Koon made it a matter of policy never to attack the North Koreans in their valley, as it would invite reprisals on the several villages in the valley upon which they were so dependent.

The following late July night, they found a T-80 tank and two trucks parked on the shoulder of a gravel road not too far from a small village in the next valley to the west. Captain Koon quickly and quietly laid out the plan of attack. The militiamen were to cover the sleeping personnel while Park and Bradley eliminated the sentries. Sergeant Park knifed the sentry at one end of the sleeping camp, while Bradley took out the sentry at the other. Three North Koreans were sleeping next to the tank. Sergeant Park put his hand on the first sleeping North Korean's mouth, his knee in his stomach, and plunged his bayonet directly into the man's heart. He died with little more than a few kicks. Sergeant Park went to the next and the next. Bradley killed another in a similar manner before Captain Koon quietly slipped on top of the tank and dropped a hand grenade through the hatch. When it exploded inside killing the sleeping crew, Sergeant Park, the five militia men and Bradley sprayed the remaining North Koreans with automatic rifle fire as they rose from their makeshift beds. Twelve North Korean infantry and three tank crew members died. Captain Koon's command suffered no casualties.

The truck was a support vehicle for the tank, loaded with fuel, food, and North Korean ammunition. They surmised the North Korean unit had the mission of questioning the villagers and perhaps destroying the village during a dawn attack. Several shoulder-fired surface to air Stinger type missiles were in the truck. These were given to the militia men. Each man took fifteen kilos of food and fifteen kilos of ammunition.

With the additional sixty-six pounds to their loads, they moved slower, so they decided to return to their valley hideout to cache their new food and ammunition. The food consisted mostly of rice, dried peppers, dried fish, dried seaweed, and a few sacks of fresh vegetables they apparently confiscated from another village, as they still had dirt on them. Captain Koon rigged the tank's ammunition as a booby trap. Whoever next opened the hatch would pull the pin from a grenade set under several high explosive tank rounds.

Each time they returned to their base, they approached from a different direction. Two always circled it completely, meeting on the far side, then passing each other in a wider circle to ensure that no ambush was waiting for them. Then, one soldier would approach their shack and examine the door and interior for booby traps. Once it was determined to be clear, he would signal the others to come. Captain Koon made them establish small caches of spare rifles and ammunition in several locations, a few hundred meters from their shack. These were hidden under rocks or placed in shallow pits and covered with whatever materials were convenient, and a few centimeters of dirt.

Their greatest need was for communications equipment. They had a very modest supply of medical supplies taken from North Koreans. Several short-range radios, "walkie-talkies," were what they desired. A lookout posted part way up the mountain had a clear view of both ends of the valleys. With powerful binoculars, a sentry would observe any enemy approaching from either direction. A small radio would provide communications between the sentry and the shack.

Bradley estimated that their ambushes, since the militiamen joined them, in one form or another, had resulted in killing over two hundred North Koreans. Why, Bradley wondered, had the Army never trained to conduct guerilla war? What better way to develop the doctrine necessary to counter it? They laid mines in roads, set up roadblock ambushes, used L shaped ambushes for small patrols along mountain paths, and once, even started an avalanche on a squad of North Koreans.

By mid-August, North Koreans began to appreciate the effectiveness of Captain Koon's little group operating against their lines of communication. Captain Koon began to expand their area of operations, conducting ambushes farther and farther away from their base. A North Korean helicopter surprised them as they were about to ambush a convoy of trucks. One of the militia men shot it down with his surface to air missile. As infantry began to dismount from the trucks, another militia man fired his missile into the lead truck which instantly exploded. Other militia men put rocket propelled grenades against the remaining trucks. A few infantry and the drivers scrambled away to survive the ambush. As they fled up the hill, one of the North Koreans sprayed automatic rifle fire. Bradley returned the fire, killing the North Korean. One of the militia was badly wounded by the North Korean's fire. His companions dragged him under concealment behind a clump of bushes. Young trees were growing on the hillside as a result of the tree planting programs of the nineteen seventies added to shielding them from aerial observation. The wounded militia man took a bullet through his right kidney, which exited through his liver. He was severely bleeding. Bradley quickly examined him, shook his head, and whispered to Koon, he might live fifteen minutes, at most, depending upon how much damage to the kidney and liver. Koon nodded, and simply said, "We can't take any chances. We can't carry him out of here." Bradley knew what he meant, so he just nodded in agreement and walked away. Koon knelt next to the man and whispered a few things to him. The militia man tried to smile through his grimace and nodded that he understood. The militia man closed his eyes while Captain Koon put his pistol an inch from the man's temple and euthanized him. Koon reholstered his pistol. Sergeant Pak passed out the dead man's weapon, ammunition and pack to the others. He put the dead man's personal effects in his own pocket. They all shouldered their loads and crept up the hill with no talking.

———•◦◆◦•———

"Everybody get some breakfast and let's get started. Marge, you lead off. Tell me about the latest Mexican complaint."

"It seems, Mr. President, some of our soldiers not only returned the sniper fire across the Mexican border, but they crossed the border in pursuit. Killed two Mexicans and captured one. The protest the Mexican ambassador lodged was against our crossing the border. The prisoner talked his guts out. Now, Jim might be able to tell you how they got this Mexican sniper to talk, all I hear in that regard is rumors," she said with a broad grin and resumed eating her bagel with cream cheese and strawberry jam.

"OK, Jim, what do you have."

"Marge is right on the details that I have, Mr. President. The soldiers involved in the incident were on the Texas side when they came under some pretty accurate sniper fire. One soldier was wounded in the leg. A sniper team observed the bad guys' location and returned the fire. They took out the shooter and killed another dumb enough to rise up and look to see who was shooting back. A couple of soldiers flanked them and caught two of them. One put up a fight that lasted about two seconds. The second was taken uninjured. Now, nobody will testify, but I think this live one almost drowned in the river, apparently on the trip back when he didn't talk. It appears they 'rescued' him from drowning when he tried to cross back into Mexico.

"We now have a precise location of the camp, Mr. President, and a good idea of the size of their operations. It is really a reinforced guerilla company. They have between 250 and 300 men. They even have ladies of the evening for entertainment on a permanent basis in a separate building. The detainee volunteered that they are armed with Stinger missiles, machine guns, AK-47s of new manufacture, and explosives. They have a regular training camp and regimen. They have a fleet of pickups and SUVs they use for their raids. They even have a huge garage to service the vehicles. They have security cameras around the fences and monitoring the roads. They are taught weapons and tactics in classrooms, even have firing ranges. It is obviously financed by big money, but we don't know whom. The whole place is disguised as, and actually is, a working vegetable farm, with irrigation and everything. Between raids, they grow vegetables for the American table. Now, the question is what we do about it."

"I'll tell you right now what we are going to do about it. Jim, you put some Army Rangers down there. A whole company of them, or a battalion if you think that many are needed. Let's get some Mexican American ranger volunteers to scout this outfit, people who speak the lingo and are tough as nails and not afraid to kill any of their ancestral kin. How deep into Mexico are they?"

"About fifty miles, across mostly desert in the Mexican state of Chihuahua, Mr. President. It is pretty isolated country down there. I had our drones photograph the place from high altitude. It is pretty innocuous looking from air until you recognize the rifle range."

"When your Rangers are satisfied that they have everything they need, turn them loose."

"Mr. President, do you mean you are going to authorize a military raid into Mexico?"

"You bet your bippy, Marge. We aren't going to take the chance of them conducting any more raids."

"But, Mr. President, such a raid is a significant violation of international conduct. Why don't we let the Mexican authorities handle it?"

"Marge, you know as well as I do that within a couple of hours of our informing the Mexican authorities about it, that camp will be vacated like jack rabbits being chased by coyotes. They aren't going to get away with it. What are the Mexicans going to do about us raiding it anyway? Authorize or conduct more raids across our border? I don't think so. It should be an object lesson they won't forget. Mexico is a huge trading partner, and if they give us any crap, I'll slap enhanced inspections on them for everything crossing the border. I'll tighten down their truck emissions, inspections of their fresh fruits and vegetables, and order that all illegal aliens crossing the border will be regarded as foreign agents liable to be shot on sight. We aren't going to have any more of these raids into our territory. End of discussion."

"All right, what else do we have?"

Vice President George Atkinson motioned with his hand, which the President acknowledged with a nod.

George Atkinson was unquestionably the most taciturn of the administration's bureaucracy. He very rarely spoke unless spoken to. Born in the mountainous western part of Virginia into a poor family that the locals referred to as poor white trash, he established a reputation as a quiet boy as a result of ridicule, but one when pushed too far, would become a fierce fighter. Bullies on the grade school playground soon learned that he was more trouble than they could handle. In high school, he was quite shy, afraid of the girls, but more determined than ever that some day they would wish they had paid attention to him. A moderate athletic, he earned two high school letters in track and was awarded one as a guard on the basketball team his senior year, more for his aggressive spirit than for his skills. He graduated as one of several with a perfect grade point in his high school class. It was enough to earn several modest scholarships at the University of Virginia. He worked part time at various jobs and carried between twelve and sixteen units a semester, taking five years to earn a Bachelor of Arts with dual major in history and economics from the College of Arts and Sciences.

The University of Kansas at Lawrence offered him a position as a laboratory instructor while doing graduate studies, again with the dual major of economics and history. To Roger Atkinson, economics and history were inseparable. To him, all wars, famines, earthquakes, fires and floods were the result of politicians attempting to control the economies of their home nations and influence the economies of others to their own benefit. The American Civil War fascinated him. At the University of Kansas, he avidly read all the library held on the Civil War guerilla raids and border warfare between the states of Kansas and Missouri. His Master's thesis explored the relationship of the economies of the two states and how it influenced their outlook as secessionist and abolitionist states. As a sudden impulse at the beginning of his fourth year in graduate school as a new Ph.D. candidate, almost as a lark, he applied to several law schools. Surprised by his acceptance at the University of Missouri at Columbia, he found himself enrolled as a freshman the following fall. Three years later, he left Columbia with an LLB.

He went to work for a small law firm, a partnership of two lawyers in Jackson County, Missouri. They assigned him the more mundane cases at first, the bankruptcies, the divorces, and the occasional small litigation case. It wasn't long before he began to enjoy the trial lawyer's role. After three years, he developed oratorical skills that surprised and surpassed the two senior partners. When he approached them about a partnership, the two owning attorneys decided that they were not ready for a junior partner. In actuality, they were making considerably more money than his salary off his skills in the courtroom. Partly out of spite, and partly out of frustration, he accepted a job as deputy county attorney for Jackson County, a county of 675,000 citizens. He handled most of the criminal prosecution cases assigned to him with aplomb. His forensics skills were quickly realized. After four years, he couldn't decide whether to run for the county attorney's job or remain as an assistant county prosecutor and run for state senator as well. He chose to remain an assistant county attorney and run for the state senate. He won.

On the floor of the state senate, he realized his true calling. At age thirty-four, he was beginning to overcome his inhibitions regarding the fairer sex. He began to seriously date. Modestly handsome, he suddenly discovered he was much in demand. After flirting around for two years, he finally married a thirty-year-old accountant. After four years of the Missouri Senate, he ran for the U.S. Congress. He won. Arguing for his assignment to the House Ways and Means Committee at his own request, making cogent arguments because of his educational background, he was awarded the coveted seat over more senior party members. It was most unusual for a freshman of the Congress to land such a plum. Elected to four terms in the House of Representatives, he was a powerful force to be reckoned with regarding economics. He was a fervent crusader for a balanced budget, fiscal responsibility, and reduction of government entitlements. That brought him to the attention of Jason Thornton. When offered the position of Vice President on the ticket, he wasn't sure if he should take the chance. Jason Thornton persuaded him that he was needed to appeal to the fiscally conservative voters, that he could still work behind the scenes with members of both the house and Senate toward fiscal responsibility. The party needed him. He could bring in both the southern and Midwestern votes. There would likely be many tied votes in the Senate on spending bills that he could make or break. Reluctantly, he accepted Jason Thornton's offer.

"The figures on unemployment for the last quarter will be released after the stock exchange closes on Friday. They aren't good. Employment dipped a little again over the last quarter. We're pushing eight and half percent unemployment. Frankly, I think it is higher than that. The Social Security account doesn't look any better, thanks to all the baby boomers who retired over the last five years, and our trade deficit with the rest of the world jumped another half a percentage point in just the last month. We have been trying to control the economy for years by raising or lowering the interest rates, but that just seems to add to inflation in the long run. I don't know what we can do to create more jobs in this country. The wages are so depressed now from foreign competition and so many aliens coming in that our welfare system will probably collapse if we don't turn it around. We are discovering that many of those retired baby boomers are beginning to take low paying machts nichts jobs because they can't make it on their retirement plans. That just puts an even greater squeeze on the youngsters just entering the job market."

"George, you and your economic news are always so cheerful. What do you think we should do? Repeal the North American Free Trade Agreement? Pull out of the World Trade Agreement? What?"

"Mr. President, perhaps we should consider doing those very things you just mentioned. It just might be in our interest to enter bilateral trade agreements in the future instead of broad all-encompassing ones. We just can't compete with the cheap overseas labor. We don't have any manufacturing left in this country except very high-tech stuff, and we are in intense competition with that. Airplanes and agriculture are our best exports, and the world market is about saturated with airplanes. Well over half of our farm workers are now aliens, really closer to two thirds. The American family farm is just about a thing of the past.

"Interim measures might include reducing or withdrawing from the World Bank. That has been a black hole for money from the git go. Most of it has wound up in the foreign bank accounts of petty tyrants and bureaucrats of the countries we have tried to help. In the end, though, the bottom line is jobs and we just don't have enough of them and can't create enough new ones in the foreseeable future. The day is coming in not too many years when we won't be able to pay off our U.S. Treasury bonds. When that happens, the world economy will collapse."

"What do you suggest we do about this?"

"Sooner or later, we are going to have to devalue the dollar. Sooner or later, the world will select another currency as primacy. It wouldn't be a bad idea to go back to a commodity standard, like the gold standard. It doesn't have to be gold, although that is an excellent one. This concept of one currency being valued against another with their floating up and down that we have been working off of for fifty years just isn't working over the long term. It is just leading us deeper and deeper in to the print more money, borrow more money, creeping inflation cycle that sooner or later will break our piggy bank. Sooner or later, the inflation bubble has to burst. Remember what happened to the Weimar Republic of Germany after World War I and what it led to. We don't want that to happen."

"All right with the good news and theories. Anybody have anything else?"

CHAPTER 18

"**I** need about five minutes, Mr. President, to discuss a minor issue."

"Ok, Fred, hang around. I'd like to hear what the FBI has to say."

After everyone left, Fred Gateway poured himself a cup of coffee, and said, "You remember your authorization of us, shall I say, talking, with a couple of the Mexican border agents that were bound and gagged but unharmed when all of ours were shot in the head?"

"Go on."

"We had a little talk with two of them. We examined their bank accounts and found that they were suddenly several thousand dollars richer a week or so before that raid where our agents were killed. The raiders bought their escape through the border crossing station at Naco, just southwest of Bisbee, Arizona. They were given the option of cooperating and being paid to cooperate, or their families would be killed. They each received a whole year's salary as that bribe. They claimed they didn't know the American agents would be killed. They thought our Border Patrol agents had also been bribed to let those raiders cross without difficulty. Whoever is behind this is well financed. They bribed half a dozen Mexican agents and made it stick. Two who didn't buy into it were found murdered along with their families. There is some powerful force behind this. A lot of money has been passed around, even for Mexico. They claim they didn't know who was behind it all. We showed them some photographs, but they didn't recognize anybody, or claimed they didn't.

"With what we got out of that raider that Corporal Carlson shot but didn't die, the one that spent so much time in an El Paso Hospital that we kept under wraps as a crime victim, we pretty much got down that an Asian is supplying them with money, and probably everything else. The one says it is a Japanese man who goes by the name of Ito; says he overhead their leader whose name is Gonzalez call him that. The Japanese referred back to him as 'Señor Gonzalez.' That's probably an alias, but no way to know at this time.

"Any chance some of my boys can play in this raid?"

"Nope, Fred, I'm going to keep it an all military operation. Too many cooks spoil the stew, so to speak. I'll let the chain of command handle it. We sent the Marines into Vera Cruz and Blackjack Pershing out of Texas down there in 1915, it'll be interesting to see who gets to play the current version. You know, I read a book about that expedition a few years ago. We went after Poncho Villa for raiding into the United States; never did catch him, but we sure as hell shot up a lot of Villistas, his supporters. I think they learned then, and they are going to relearn that lesson, real hard. What have you done with the wounded Mexican from the El Paso General?"

"Oh, we're holding him under wraps, keeping him away from lawyers, telling him he is in protective custody. He told us that their policy was to leave no one alive, so he appreciates the three square meals a day and his very comfortable cell with its television in an isolation cell block in a secure federal prison. The ACLU would accuse us of violating his rights, sure as hell, but we are keeping him alive and talking under the circumstance."

"Captain Sabata, how would you like to volunteer for a mission that has a rather surreptitious nature?"

"I am your man, Colonel." Captain Sabata graduated from West Point, class of 2006. A second generation Mexican American, he was an all-star football player in high school in Las Vegas, Nevada. He played linebacker at the Academy and was noted for his hard tackling. He thought about professional football off and on, but decided the Army held more and greater challenges, like Ranger School. He thought about Special Forces, but decided not to go that route, as the specialization in one culture and language would curtail a broader range of activities in the Rangers. At twenty-seven years of age, he was bench pressing two hundred pounds in sets of ten repetitions. At six foot one inches tall and 200 pounds, he was all muscle and sinew that was hard to hide. His body fat content hovered around five percent. Unmarried, he didn't have much time for anything but the Army. His second tour of duty was in Korea, just before U.S. Forces were withdrawn from the peninsula in 2008. "Screw the duties" became his motto while in Korea. He spent four hours a day in the gym taking Kuk Ki Do lessons. When he left Korea twelve months later, he was a first Dan, a true black belt. Kuk Ki Do is the form of karate that is mandatory for all of the guards of the Blue House, South Korea's version of the White House. All of the elite guards must be Kuk Ki Do black belts. Kuk Ki Do is not a sport, but a deadly art. It has only one philosophy, to kill, maim or completely incapacitate your opponent as quickly and quietly as possible.

"Do you have a couple of Mexican Americans in your battalion you would like to join you? We're thinking about a four- or five-man team. Final number is up to you."

"Yes, sir, I can pick four easily. I have a couple in my own company, as a matter of fact, that will do nicely for whatever needs to be done."

"Good. They must be fluent in Tex-Mex, have completely Mexican names, willing to go undercover unarmed and in civilian dress. Have them in my office at fifteen hundred hours."

Three hours later, Captain Rodrigo Sabata, Sergeants First Class Manuel Estevez, Miguel Perez, along with Staff Sergeants Caesar Consaida and Romero Chavez stood before the Ranger battalion commander.

"This gentleman will brief you now and alone," stated the Lieutenant Colonel, indicating the man dressed in casual clothing and sitting in a chair against the wall. The Lieutenant Colonel left the room.

"The five of you must commit now, without hearing any details at all of what you are tasked to do, or you are dismissed as of this moment."

No one said anything, but all except Captain Sabata had a slight smile on his face.

"Very well. You five are going undercover into Mexico to investigate, and possibly join, the organization or organizations that have been raiding across the border in Texas and Arizona the last year or two. You will leave Fort Benning tonight. We will fly you to El Paso, where you will buy a car and proceed into Mexico as braceros looking for work. You are to travel separately, unrecognizing each other until you join up at the Motel 8 on Interstate 10 outside El Paso. Reservations will be made for each of you under your own names. Each of you will be given $3000 cash at the end of this briefing. Captain Sabata, you will have an additional $10,000 out of which you are to purchase a dependable used car for travel into Mexico. I have reviewed your field 201 Personnel Files. You have somewhat diverse geographic backgrounds, coming from different areas of the southwest. That is fine. Your cover will be that you met and formed friendships while working the sugar beet fields in central Wyoming. That's far enough from the border that no one there will hopefully have any details of that area. Each of your packets has information on the Big Horn Basin. After you memorize it, burn it, and I mean burn it before you leave here tonight. You are traveling unarmed, at least until you get to El Paso. No firearms there, but I don't object if you get a good fighting folder out of your pocket money. You each worked and saved for a year in the sugar beet fields to accumulate your pocket money. You decided you didn't like the cold Wyoming winters and wanted to return to the southwest. Together, you traveled south but your car, a tan, 2002 Chevy Impala with a small engine and an automatic transmission, caught fire and burned along the highway just north of El Paso, so you abandoned it and bought another in El Paso. You heard a rumor in a bar in El Paso that the farm in question was hiring, so you thought you would check it out. So, go to a bar together in Ciudad Juarez and establish your presence with the bartender. It doesn't seem to matter which bar.

"Basically, the farm in question is believed to be the base for these raids. What scanty information we have is that some Asians are backing these raids with money and guns. The Mexican government just calls them bandits. Maybe, but we don't think so. We want to know whom and

211

why. Try and get hired. If not, just hang around the area and see what you can pick up. If you don't get hired, you have a month to gather collateral information. Travel around the area if you think it is indicated. When the month is up, report to Fort Bliss, Adjutant of the Commanding General. We will have further instructions for you then. Your information packet has a collect call phone number that is manned 24/7. Aerial photos and descriptions of the place are in your packets. These people are absolutely ruthless killers. If you think they are on to you, bug out. Pack light. You have four hours to prepare. Questions? None, then here are your packets and money. You depart here at 19:00 hours. A bus will pick you up at this office. Good luck."

Captain Sabata and his four companions drove slowly past the fenced area. Sergeant First Class Perez was driving, while the other four scrutinized the road. At first, they paid no attention to the small boxes attached to the fence posts about every quarter mile, until Staff Sergeant Chavez noticed that sunlight was reflecting off what appeared to be a camera lens. Then they noted the little boxes every four hundred meters.

"This must be the place, with security like that," said Captain Sabata. At that moment, a tractor drove past them from the opposite direction. After driving a few more miles, they turned around and drove back to a wide gate that was electronically controlled. They pulled up to the gate, and Sergeant Perez looked into the security camera.

A voice from a speaker asked, "Who are you?"

"Just a couple of amigos looking for work. We heard that there was a farm somewhere around here, hiring. We are looking for that place."

"Someone will be with you in a couple of minutes. Be patient." The speaker fell silent.

"Gomez, you and Hernando go look them over. Chat with them for a while. See what you can find out. We could use some good men, but don't take any chances."

Gomez picked up his AK-47 and a .357, Hernando took a .357 magnum revolver from his top right-hand desk drawer, got up from his desk and together they climbed in to a Ford pickup truck outside the office. Sabata and his team waited for five minutes until Gomez and Hernando in their pickup truck came to the gate, opened it, and got out of their truck and walked over to the soldiers. Both Hernando and Gomez had their handguns in their waistbands hidden under untucked shirt tails. Gomez walked to the driver's side and looked in. Hernando stood relatively close to his pickup, with the AK-47 in the front seat.

"So, Amigos, you are looking for work? What kind of work do you do?"

Sabata spoke for them. "We have been working sugar beet fields up north but didn't care for the cold. We thought we would come to where it is warm again. It is good to be in a place like this."

"You are field hands, then. Can you all drive trucks of different kinds, tractors, operate combines and other machinery?"

"We can do many things, all of those which you mention. We can do many other things as well."

"What other things can you do, Amigo? Many skills are appreciated here. Can you weld? Are you a mechanic who can fix automobiles and farm machinery?"

"Caesar is a fair mechanic, Romero did a little welding, not all that good perhaps, but he knows to heat the metal before you push the welding rod. We had heard you were looking for other skills as well."

Gomez's sense of danger came alive. "What skills do you speak of? We have no special requirements on this farm. We do have feedlot cattle. Perhaps you do veterinary work?"

"Manuel knows a little of medicine. He might be of use to you. He has pulled a few calves, done a little surgery, he knows to wash his hands. We have heard talk that you have need of other skills as well."

"Amigo, I do not know of what you speak. Where have you heard this talk? What is this talk? I do not understand you."

"We were in a bar in Juarez two nights ago. We heard men talking that you were looking for adventurous men, men who were willing to do a little extra in order to earn a little extra money. We are very much interested in a little extra money. There are five of us, and none of us have families, but we would all like to be able to afford one some day."

"Let me look at you. Step out of the car, let's see if you are big and strong men, or are small and weak."

The five dismounted from the car, as Hernando and Gomez carefully sized them up. "I am foremen for one of the crews, the one that works the feedlot. We have cattle to brand, castrate, vaccinate and dehorn in a couple of days. I will talk to the general foreman and see what he says. Come back tomorrow at the same time. I will tell you then what he says."

Sabata and all of his men noted that Hernando stayed close to the pickup and kept his arms crossed across his chest. This tended to pull in his shirt a little, which allowed his revolver he had stuck in the front of his pants to be imprinted by his shirt, his right hand near the butt.

"We will return tomorrow at this time. We hope you have work for us. We are good workers," stated Consaida as they climbed back into their car. They drove carefully away, so as not to raise a lot of dust.

"What did they look like to you two?" asked Jesus Gonzalez.

"I don't like them," said Gomez.

"I liked them," said Hernando.

"Interesting," said Gonzalez. "Why didn't you like them, Gomez?"

"Because every one of them had very short hair, every one of them was very well built, very muscular. They have not suffered lack of eating, but they are not at all fat. They have the physique of people who lift weights and work out regularly. They look like soldiers. Only the leader spoke until the very end. That smacks of military discipline. Each of them inspected us as we inspected them. They are very observant, these men. They did not smell bad enough. They have all bathed and shaved recently. None of them even had a mustache. The piercing eyes of the leader bother me. He was looking right through me. I have seen that look before."

"All that Gomez says is true. Perhaps that is why I liked them. Our reputation has spread very far. Perhaps they are police or soldiers as Gomez suggests. This I do not know. Certainly, they are not from around here. Their Spanish is different. That might mean that they are from a different region or that they are Federales or perhaps Americans, if Americans would dare to do such a thing. We know the American drug agents do these things, but soldiers? Perhaps they are what they say they are. Who knows?

Jesus Gonzalez thought about it for a minute, and then said, "Do not hire them. We are not planning any big raids for the time being. Our snipers are busy, but we have lost several of them. We could not find the bodies of two, so maybe the Americans have them. The timing is not good. Tell them to leave their names and check back in a couple of months. We might be hiring then."

"I will tell them when they return tomorrow. I told them come back tomorrow so we could think about it; maybe have someone watch them for a while if they stay around in town."

"That is a good idea, Gomez. Take one or two of your better street fighters. Go into town tonight. Find out where they are staying. Have your man start a fight with one who is not the leader. See how well they handle themselves, if they come to the aid of their man if he needs it. Do not use any weapons, but bare hands. We don't want any unnecessary trouble. If you find their car in a place where you can search it without difficulty, do so. Perhaps there will be some clues as to how they act. They will probably eat at a cantina, and so be easy to find since there are only two in town."

Captain Sabata and his four men strolled into the cantina and selected an empty table adjacent to the far wall. From their table, they could watch the front door, the bar, and the back door that opened at the end of the hall along the bar. They had strolled around the back of the cantina before they entered it in order to orient themselves and identify possible escape routes. They ordered a meal of tamales, chicken quesadas, frijoles, tortillas, and a pitcher of Corona beer. The beer didn't last long. Captain Sabata drew an American five-dollar bill from his wallet and threw it on the table. Staff Sergeant Consaida picked it up and walked to the bar with the empty pitcher. He handed both to the bartender without saying a word. He placed both hands on the bar top while the bartender refilled the pitcher and gave him a dollar's change in pesos. As he picked up the pitcher, his arm was rudely shoved from behind. Consaida looked at the man who shoved him in the mirror, then turned to face him, as he sat the pitcher on the bar. Consaida shook the beer off his hand, looked at the bartender and then asked for a bar towel. The bartender, recognizing the offending man, gave Consaida the towel without saying anything, then began to wipe up the spilled beer with another.

"Why don't you be more careful, Amigo?" said the individual, who slightly weaved as he stood. Consaida looked into his eyes and saw that they were clear. The man was not drunk as he pretended. He also read a degree of malevolence. The Sergeant immediately recognized the challenge.

"Si, I'll do that," Consaida said as he turned to the bartender and said, "Please fill it again, Amigo, throwing down the peso he had just picked up as change. When he started to pick up the pitcher, the man hit his arm again. All the time, the four other Rangers were watching. They had observed who sat with whom, who was paying attention to the altercation at the bar, and who was not. So far, no one else had moved in the direction of Consaida and the offender. They continued eating while observing carefully the surroundings.

"Don't do that, Amigo, it is not good to waste good beer."

"Then, you can lick it off the bar, can't you?"

"Amigo, I do not want trouble. Do not carry this any farther. Let me go in peace."

"You will lick the bar, or I will put your head in, on, or through it, Señor."

"That is what you will have to do."

The man made a grab for Consaida's neck with his left hand, but found his left arm pushed up by Consaida's right hand as Consaida ducked under it. A fierce left jab to the man's left bottom rib, followed by a powerful right jab to the man's left kidney left him sinking to his knees as he uttered an agonizing "ugh" from his cracked rib and terrible kidney pain. The man held onto the bar with both hands as he slid downwards. Consaida grabbed a hand full of the man's hair and whispered in his ear as he sank to the floor.

"I do not think it is healthy in here, for you, Amigo. I suggest you leave now before bad things happen to you. Do not make me hurt you again. I can, and will, do terrible things to you, so why don't you just leave. Do you understand me?"

The man nodded yes, as he winced in pain.

Consaida turned loose of his hair, picked up the pitcher of beer and walked casually back to the table as the man pulled himself up to the bar and staggered out the door.

"I think we have just been tested; one of the two men whom we met at the gate is sitting in the far corner, taking this all in," said Captain Sabata with a smile. "Either we have been made or we just passed the test. Do not think any more about it. We shall see tomorrow."

Gomez dialed the cell phone number of Miguel. "I think bad things are going to happen down here in the not-too-distant future. I think we are under close surveillance by our friends from the north. There are five men looking for work who are not workers, but well-trained people from across the river. I think it is close to time to come home."

"I will leave it to your judgment not to stay too long but remain there as long as it is not too threatening. I need to know what is developing. It has taken the gringos long enough to figure things out. There might be a way for us to make some good money over this. If I need to contact you, I will leave word in a sealed envelope at the desk at the hotel there in town." Gomez heard the click as Miguel switched off the phone. He went back into the bar to further observe those whom he perceived to be American agents of some nature. After they retired to their hotel rooms, he broke into their car and thoroughly searched it. He found nothing unusual or incriminating. He collected the man who picked a fight with Sergeant Consaida and drove back to the farm that night. The man moaned frequently but softly the entire trip. He took the man to the infirmary and left him there. Since it was so late, he reported to Jesus Gonzalez in the morning his observations, more convinced than ever that they were American agents. The nurse reported to Gonzalez that the man had two broken ribs and a bruised kidney. His urine would be tinged with hemoglobin over the next several days. He had to remain at bed rest until his urine cleared and his rib fractures stabilized.

Gonzalez pondered his courses of action. He could hire them and then kill them before they could report anything. He could hire them and keep them under observation to confirm that they were American agents and then act, or he could refuse to hire them. He decided the first course of action might bring even more agents and closer scrutiny, the second might allow them to see too much, and so decided on the third course. "Refuse them employment. Tell them we do not need any more help at this time, but to come back in three months if they are not well situated elsewhere and we will see then."

Not willing to accept returning to Fort Bliss without information, Captain Sabata and his team drove back across the border and called his commander with a request. He wanted computers, binoculars, small arms, video equipment and more money. His request was denied, and he was ordered to return to Fort Benning via Fort Bliss. He dutifully drove back to El Paso and sold the car to the dealer from whom he purchased it at a $400 loss. They went to the USO, where they all took the shuttle bus back to Ft. Bliss. From Fort Bliss, they flew to Fort Benning in a C-130H just in time to make a practice jump.

CHAPTER 19

The South Koreans were fighting desperately, but slowly being pushed backwards by the sheer mass of manpower. After two weeks, Seoul was outflanked on the east and south, essentially surrounded. The main roads were more or less controlled by North Koreans, although isolated pockets of South Korean infantry continued to cut the roads and ambush convoys in a very irregular fashion. Moving more slowly, the North Korean infantry was overwhelming the countryside in the eastern portion of the peninsula. In places where the civilian refugees blocked the road by sheer mass, the North Koreans opened fire on them with automatic weapons, or in a few cases, simply drove T-64 and T-72 tanks over them to open the roads. Peasants were always easier to replace and in steady supply than skilled industrial workers of the cities.

At the beginning of the third week, North Korean destroyers began shelling Kunsan. North Korean armored forces were just outside of Taejon. The North had formed a line more or less through Ch'ungch'ong Namdo, running to the northeast towards Samchok. North Korean armor halted along the Choch'won –Ch'ongju road for rest and reupply, while the infantry to the east moved ten to twelve kilometers a day. Infantry units hopscotched around each other as they cleared the countryside of all resistance. Any village which offered resistance was destroyed by killing the inhabitants and burning the village. None were spared, not even children. Ch'ongju fell before the week was out. Many in the western part of the country fled into the low mountains to the east, where they would ultimately come into contact with the advancing infantry.

By the middle of the fourth week, South Korea was squeezed into a line roughly running from Kunsan through Chonju to Taegu to Pohang. Three fourths of South Korea was now held by North Korean forces.

From an island south of Mokp'o, an intermediate range missile with a Global Positioning System Guidance system streaked to P'yongyang. It carried a twenty-kiloton warhead. When it detonated, it was one thousand feet over the political center of the city.

The tremendous machstem, the backpressure composed of eighteen hundred mile an hour winds of the explosion, wreaked havoc and destruction for four thousand meters in every direction. The heat ignited fires such that the entire circumference of the blast was revealed by satellites to be a huge blackened spot upon the earth. The blast was slightly larger than those dropped on Hiroshima and Nagasaki.

Jason Thornton's phone rang. It was General Craig. "I just informed the SECDEF. He asked me to give you a direct call. Sir, the South Koreans launched a nuclear strike on Pyongyang. Our satellites just picked it up. The nuclear genie is out of the bottle. We think it was around a twenty-kiloton weapon detonated as an aerial burst. The electromagnetic pulse was pretty significant, but it seemed to be tailored more towards the heat and blast aspects of the spectrum. Thank God, we didn't have an AWACs in there. The South Koreans did, but it seems to still be flying and reporting. We can't say at this stage where the fallout will go for certain, but the winds are generally from the south and the west this time of year. China should get some of it, if not the majority of the fallout. We also picked up some ominous transmissions from the South Korean leadership to an elite artillery unit. We think they might be going tactical nuclear as well."

"Is there any response from North Korea or China?"

"No, sir, we haven't intercepted any at the moment, but things can change at any second."

"Very well. Keep me informed of anything and everything of significance."

"Yes, Mr. President. I or one of the staff will call you in seconds of anything occurring."

In the ten-minute interval of flight time to cover the three hundred miles, a phone call went from Peking to an underground bunker complex two hundred feet below a granite mountain. The call was taken as the warhead exploded. In the phone call, the launch site was identified, it's plotted trajectory, and the size of the warhead the missile carried.

At the same time, just north of Taegu, three maneuver battalions of the People's 24th Infantry Regiment were converging for an assault on the critical road junctions of the Taegu and Hayang road. The South Korean self propelled 155mm. howitzer battalion received the fire order. The battalion commander checked the classified message against his code, had the special munition loaded into his Jeep and drove to Alpha battery, his "Go-To" battery, and informed the battery commander to load and fire it. "Captain, you are to personally check the firing data and lay of the firing gun yourself. You know what the warhead is."

Very grimly, the Korean artillery captain nodded, "Yes, sir, I do. I just hate to use it over our own soil."

"I know, Captain, we all do. There is little else we can do. The North is at the final line of resistance. We will retreat no more. Without United Nations or at least American support, we will cease to exist in a week if we do not use all of our assets. Fire the damned thing." The Captain did as he was ordered. The special warhead was loaded into the 155 mm. howitzer, and fifteen seconds and twelve miles away, a one-half-kiloton nuclear weapon detonated over the North Korean Peoples 24th Infantry regiment at an altitude of five hundred feet. A very small mushroom cloud arose in a matter of seconds. Fires began to rage on the north side of Taegu. The southerly breezes began to gently move the cloud of alpha particles northward. The 24th Infantry Regiment of the Peoples' Army no longer existed. Those in the supply trains who survived the initial blast and heat would die in forty-eight hours of gamma radiation poisoning, in seventy-two hours to ninety-six hours of bacterial infection of their massive third degree burns, all in spite of the anti-radiation pills issued to them by their government.

Ten minutes after the phone call from Peking was received, the North Korean leadership gave the launch order. The first missile struck the South

Korean missile launch site. The island and the city of Makp'o disappeared under a ten-kiloton blast.

Jason Thornton's phone rang again. Thornton dreaded picking it up. He knew what it meant and was overwhelmed with apprehension.

"What do you have, General?" not knowing for certain with whom he spoke.

"Mr. President, the North has retaliated with a nuclear strike on the South Korean launch site. We have no idea how many exchanges will occur before it ends. This one was a rather small blast, smaller than the one the South hit Pyongyang with. We figure in the ten- to twelve-kiloton range. The launch site was a small island off the southwest tip of South Korea. The provincial capital of Makp'o will get a good dose of the fallout, and sure felt the heat and blast. Damage assessment with greater detail will take a couple of hours pending analysis of satellite photos after the smoke clears. The fires will obscure the pictures to some degree. We believe the North Korean leadership was not in Pyongyang, but rather are orchestrating the war from an underground bunker deep within a mountain. There are several such possible sites, and we don't know for sure which one they are at. It might be that different divisions of the leadership are in different ones; the military in one, Kim, jong un in another, other aspects of government in others."

"I will have the Press Secretary call you for whatever details you think are appropriate for a press release. I would like to get that out in thirty minutes, before the news networks scoop us again. Have a list ready, and Roger McCall will call you in about fifteen minutes. I'll leave it to your discretion as to what constitutes pertinent details."

"Yes, Mr. President, I'll have something together in the next few minutes. Thank you, Mr. President." Jason Thornton hung up the phone. He punched his intercom button for his secretary, Peggy Parsons. "Peggy, get Roger McCall on the phone. Have him call General Craig at the Pentagon bunker right now. I mean, right now!"

Thirty minutes later, a second missile launched by North Korea streaked one hundred and twenty miles into space where over half a dozen satellites were orbiting overhead.

The small nuclear blast of three kilotons was designed to maximize the electromagnetic pulse of the nuclear explosion. All the satellites within three thousand miles went blank. Their cameras were burned, their communications circuits fried by the electromagnet energy from the pulse of the blast.

———————•◦•◆•◦•———————

Roger McCall was giving his press briefing on the first exchange when President Thornton's red phone rang again.

"General Craig here, sir. It has escalated. The South took out a North Korean regimental sized unit with a battlefield sized nuke, Mr. President." There was a pause, some yelling was heard in the background, and then a hush, followed by a loud "Oh, shit!" from General Craig came over Thornton's phone.

"Sir, the North just launched a missile into space. It took out our satellites over that region as well as the South's. We're pretty blind as of right now, sir! It took out some of our Global Positioning Satellites as well as some of our observation and communications satellites. I'll order an AWACs into the area ASAP, Mr. President, but it might be several hours before we can get something there. Right now, we're blind."

"How much will this hurt South Korea, General? I suspect it is a devastating blow."

"It is, sir. It should have affected the South Korean AWACs as well. We presume it is still in flight, circling around fifty thousand feet, but we can't detect that. This loss of satellites also crippled our carrier battle groups standing in international waters. We're waiting on reports from those carrier battle groups on damage assessment from the electromagnetic pulse right now. Reports would routinely come over the Integrated Link 16 Network where we would all receive the same information simultaneously. Now, without those satellites, it might have to be transmitted the old way, and up through the chain of command. If our Link 16 is down, we're back to Cold War level war fighting, Mr. President, at least for that area of the world."

As General Craig was speaking, a flight of three Mig 31s was climbing to fifty thousand feet altitude and engaging the South Korean AWACs with air to air missiles. The AWACs went down in flames after the missile hit the fuselage just behind the port wing. The entire plane was engulfed in flames and disintegrated. No parachutes opened.

"I'll call Ed McCluskey and see what he can get out of the National Reconnaisance Office for replacements or repositioning some of our other satellites. I'll get back to you, General."

At that moment, Peggy Parsons walked into the Oval Office. "Mr. President, the DCI is on the line for you."

"Thank you, Peggy." Thornton punched another button on the phone. "I guess you just got the word, Ed. What's your assessment, or is it too early? You couldn't have had more than five minutes."

"Less than that, Mr. President. The Director of the National Reconnaisance Office just called me. We're pretty blind at the moment. He and his staff are working on an assessment and how we can best get back online, so to speak."

"Ed, do we have to have a meeting here, or would the time be better spent working on solutions with the various staffs? Your people at CIA and the National Recon Office boys, doing your thing, I hope together. You know I would rather have people working on the problem than sitting in a meeting jawing about potential solutions."

"I appreciate that, Mr. President. For right now, I think it is better if we have time to get our potential responses and alternatives together. We need a little time down here, but if you feel the need, we can fly up there from here in Langley."

"No, Ed, stay down there and let me know when you feel a meeting is appropriate. I am sure you will liaison as required with the Joint Chiefs. They are mad as hell, I'm sure. I don't like our carrier battle groups sitting out there blind. While there is no threat to them that I am aware of, I don't like them compromised in any way."

"Roger that, Mr. President. I'll get back to you with something ASAP. I'll get on the horn with the Joint Chiefs for their input."

"Thank you, Ed." Jason Thornton hung up the phone. "Peggy, get Roger McCall in here, ASAP," Thornton spoke into his intercom. Three minutes later, McCall was standing before the President.

"Roger, the North Koreans just took out a bunch of our satellites, along with South Korea's, with a nuclear blast in space."

McCall whistled. "That's why all the cell phones on those reporters in the press room starting going off as I was leaving. They want to know why their communications are down. What are we going to do, Mr. President?"

"Well, for starters, we are going to tell those news vultures out there that a North Korean missile aimed at South Korea's communications satellites also took out ours. At the moment, we are compromised on communications with that area of the world. We are working to restore those communications by alternative means as soon as possible. Military requirements will, of course, have precedence. Civilian communications satellites will have to be addressed later. You are authorized to release that to the public. You will be bombarded by questions of how severely we are hurt, how long to get communications back up, both military and civilian, yak yak yak. Tell them there will be more details released as solutions are implemented. Don't really let them know how bad we are hurt. Go to it, Roger."

"Yes, Mr. President." Roger McCall went back to the press room. Johnny Withers poured the President a cup of tea and set it on his desk in front of him and just stood there. Jason Thornton looked back, and then nodded. Withers took the hint and returned to the antechamber.

The President's phone rang. Again. This time it was Marge Talbott.

"Mr. President, the Chinese Ambassador just arrived at my office. He would like to meet with you and me immediately at your office, if that is possible."

"By all means, Marge, get your butts over here." That was the first time the Secretary of State heard the President speak in street language.

Thirty minutes later, the Secretary of State and the Chinese Ambassador were escorted in by Johnny Withers.

"Mr. President, it is my pleasure to see you again, even though it is under these unfortunate circumstances," said Kuan, Sheng, the Chinese Ambassador, bowing at the waist.

Johnny Withers set two chairs in front of the President's desk.

"I am very glad to see you, Mr. Ambassador. Your presence is most reassuring in these troubled times. Please continue, Mr. Ambassador."

"My government has been asked by the People's Republic of North Korea to extend to you their most sincere apology for the damage inflicted upon your satellite system in their area of the world. It was not deliberate, but the target, as I am sure you are aware, was the satellite system of South Korea. Your satellites were, shall I say, unfortunate victims of the fortunes of war."

"Those unfortunate victims of the fortunes of war were very, very expensive, Mr. Ambassador. If the People's Republic of Korea survives this conflict, I can assure you, they will get the bill, and we will demand replacement cost, to include launching costs, for them."

"Rest assured, Mr. President. The People's Republic of Korea has requested my government to inform you that they will compensate you at full replacement costs once the current unfortunate conflict is resolved."

"Please pass on to the People's Republic of Korea my thanks for their offer, and we look forward to full reimbursement as soon as possible. I would like to add to that, once again, the thanks of our government to the People's Republic for not interfering with the evacuation of American civilians from the Republic of Korea.

"What is the feeling of the People's Republic of China towards all this unpleasantness in your area of the world? The United States and the rest of the western nations are very concerned about this and how it will affect many things, including security arrangements, future trade, the flow of goods and oil and capitol and people."

"Mr. President, the People's Republic of China is greatly disturbed over this nastiness. We had no knowledge of Kim, Jong-un's intent. We are working diligently to persuade the People's Republic of Korea to end hostilities immediately if not sooner. Unfortunately, Dear Leader is bent on reuniting the peninsula under himself. We wring our hands in frustration as well as you. This is most unfortunate for my government as it is for yours."

"Express my thanks and appreciation to your government for their efforts to end the conflict as quickly as possible and for being as kind as to act as a benevolent intermediary."

"It will be my pleasure to express your wishes to both my government and to pass them on to the People's Republic of Korea, Mr. President." The Chinese ambassador arose, along with Marge Talbott, and bowed at the waist to the President.

"Johnny, have my chauffer take the kind ambassador to wherever he wishes. Marge, remain for a while. I would like to discuss a few matters with you."

"Thank you, Mr. President, but we arrived in our separate automobiles. It will not be necessary," said the Chinese ambassador.

"Of course, Mr. Ambassador, how thoughtless of me." What Jason Thornton was really thinking was that *Of course, you did. You didn't want any recordings of any conversation you had with Marge Talbott en route, did you.*

"What do you think, Marge? What's your reading of the Chinese ambassador on this?"

"Mr. President, I have a gut level feeling he knew it was going to happen all along."

Twelve thousand miles away, another series of important messages was being relayed. These went from Chang, Mao Lin, Chinese Chief of Staff, Peoples Army Navy, to the Army Front Commanders.

———————•◦●◦•———————

"What is the word from the National Reconnaissance Office Ed? How soon are we going to get our satellites going?"

"Something seems wrong, Mr. President. We have a number of sleeper satellites and dual-purpose satellites which have remained quiet just for this contingency. These are in addition to the several we repositioned. The NRO tells me they are all malfunctioning."

"What the hell do you mean, malfunctioning? Be specific, Ed."

"They aren't responding to the signals, Mr. President. We don't know why."

"Any idea as to when we will have it figured out, Ed? Damn it, we need those satellites now. AWACS are good, but not nearly as capable as those satellites. As soon as you have some idea of the problem, call a meeting for here with the NRO, the National Security Council, and the Joint Chiefs. Ride the asses of those people over in the NRO until then. Find out about using commercial satellites as surrogates if any are ready for launch until we are up and running. Get back to me on that ASAP."

"Yes, Mr. President. The people at Livermore are working on both aspects as we speak. I'll call you as soon as I hear anything. Ron Weber is over at NRO now trying to kick butt!"

"The commercials will probably want a pretty penny for their efforts, maybe even a guarantee on a contract. It wasn't just our military satellites, but some of the commercials that were on the Pacific Rim went down, too. They will have to reposition some of them, maybe even change orbits. That means they will have to cut short services for some other customers already contracted for."

"Damn it, Ed, that's it. Get your people over here at 08:00 tomorrow. Bring as many answers and people and theories as you can or think necessary."

"Aye aye, Mr. President. We'll be there." Both men hung up, and McCluskey started calling the NRO, Livermore Lab boys and a few others.

"Peggy!"

"Yes, Mr. President?"

"I want an NSA meeting with the Joint Chiefs tomorrow at 08:00. Ed is bringing some extra people. We'll meet in the war room. Set it up, breakfast for anybody who wants it, tea, coffee, donuts, and the usual fat pills. Let them know we will host breakfast as usual."

———————————— •—•—• ————————————

Jason Thornton was utterly convinced that everyone worked better on a good breakfast. Some simple carbohydrates to provide blood glucose for brain food are always in order.

Most people were eating when Jason Thornton walked into the meeting. All began to stand. Thornton waved them down. "Sit and eat, people. I know some of you commuted over an hour to get here, and others had a late-night flight. What I know about our satellite capabilities over East Asia is that we don't have any. Now, I would like to hear what you know and what our options are. The DCI brought some of his experts with him, so Ed, I'll hand it off to you and yours to get us started. Ed."

"Thank you, Mr. President. Our guests are Doctors Diane Foster, computer engineering, Lawrence Livermore Laboratories; Robert Hatcher, propulsion systems, Massachusetts Institute of Technology; and Larry Corning, Software design and engineering, NASA. Dr. Corning, can you give us some ideas or possibilities of what happened to our backup satellites?"

"Mr. President, people. There are several plausible explanations of what happened. Solutions, of course, depend upon which explanation actually occurred. First is that our satellites were attacked. Take that as fact. Mechanisms of attack include a massive burst of electromagnetic pulse that fried all the microcircuits. This could occur by delivery of a very small but tailored nuclear blast in the immediate vicinity of our satellites. It is noteworthy that other satellites positioned over the same region suffered the same fate. The burst could be so powerful and so short that it would occur in microseconds and wouldn't be registered by other instruments here in the States. This is the most plausible explanation, but also unlikely. We easily observed the first attack with EMP, I doubt that they could do so again to the degree that it wouldn't be registered by the observable flash from the burst, even in daylight or picked up peripherally by our ships at sea or other nations.

"Less likely but equally effective is that they were attacked by a laser beam of the appropriate wavelength and energy level. Properly regulated, it would have the same effect but not necessarily explode them. Third is that the codes were changed, scrambled, if you like. This wouldn't damage the satellites but render them useless. They would be transmitting nonsense. This seems to be the case. This outcome requires that whoever changed the codes had to have the original ones in order to introduce changes. We are attempting to recover radio signals the 24 hours before the satellites went down to see if any have received a similar code. We don't have ground-based listening stations in the right places on land anymore to detect such signals, so this is a long shot."

"Dr. Corning, forgive my ignorance, but you are saying that someone could have changed our codes by radio signal to our satellites? Secondly, is there any reason for the twenty-four-hour criterion?"

"Actually, in the first case, yes, Mr. President. In response to the second question, if someone had the original codes, they could have sent the signal, that is, planted it by a worm, to change or scramble the codes at any time or to initiate other changes at any other time."

"It sounds, Dr., like searching for the proverbial needle in the haystack of space."

"That is exactly right, Mr. President. That's what it amounts to."

"How many people would have access to these codes?"

"It is usually about two dozen people per satellite, with a core of five or six for most satellites. The others vary with the sponsoring agency and the mission of the satellite."

"These five or six core people, would they have access to all of those codes of the individual satellites?"

"Yes, sir. These involve the programmers themselves, the software designers and engineers who write the programs and build the appropriate interfacing hardware and controlling devices. I don't think, Mr. President, that any of these people would in any way have anything to do with malfunction."

"Ed, I want you and Fred to work very closely on this one. As soon as we are finished, I want an extremely thorough but behind the scenes investigation of those core people. No exceptions. If you don't turn up anything, expand your investigation to the others. Don't sacrifice thoroughness and accuracy for speed. For our good doctors here today, you must understand that your vows of secrecy extend to everything you see and do here. When you walk out that door, this meeting never happened. I want to make that very clear to you. I don't care if anyone or all of the others is your mother, brother, wife, sister or lover. The consequences of a single slip could be personally and nationally very catastrophic."

No one said a word. Never before had Jason Thornton unleashed such a naked threat. "Please continue, Dr. Corning."

Stammering, "Well, Mr. President, those are the three most likely explanations of what occurred. We can't be sure which of the three, or if something we haven't considered, has occurred, without physically examining the satellites to see what physical damage they experienced."

"Ed, can we recover one or several of these repositioned satellites for examination? Can we get them down with a shuttle flight, or maybe even examine and repair them in orbit?"

"I'll pass that one off to Dr. Hatcher, Mr. President. He has current knowledge of our launch schedule and capabilities. Dr. Hatcher."

"If we push it, carefully, we can have a shuttle launch with a recovery mission in about a couple of weeks, Mr. President."

"Do we bring them down or examine them up there?"

"If we have capable members on board the shuttle, I am not aware of why initial examination couldn't occur while in orbit. If it is fried, we can always bring it down. If it is a scrambled code, it would require reprogramming. That, in turn, requires a super huge computer that really won't make it on the flight."

"Dr. Corning, can the completely new software be built or programmed down here, and simply switched out with the old code up there?"

"There is no reason why that wouldn't work, Mr. President." Corning thought to himself, *The President is sharper than I ever thought.*

"How many people would have to know about the new codes to have it done in ten days? I presume that Dr. Foster would be one of them?"

"She is absolutely critical to it, Mr. President. It would require those core six and perhaps one or two of the second tier programmers. The problem would come in testing it. That would take as long as or longer than building it."

"Joint Chiefs, for war fighting, which satellites are the most critical?"

"Mr. President, that is best answered by the Commander, Space Command, one of General Shelton's major subordinate commanders, General Whitfield. He isn't here right now," said General Craig.

"General Shelton, get on your secure phone right now and put that to your subordinate commander. I want an answer in fifteen minutes. When you reach him, put him on the speaker phone here."

General Shelton picked up his red phone and started punching buttons.

"Doctors, I have bad news for you. The three of you are working for Ed McCluskey, as of this minute. You are going to run this mission and you three alone. You will write, create the program, new software, and build new hardware, whatever it takes. You will do it, I am sure. Ed, coordinate with General Shelton and his people. No one outside this room is to know who these three are and what they are up to. They have maximum use of any and all resources they need, across all agency lines."

General Shelton came back into the conversation. "I have General Whitfield, Commander, Space Command, on the speaker, Mr. President. Go ahead, General Whitfield."

"We have identified two critical satellites, Mr. President. One will intercept electronic emissions in a wide spectrum. The second will be live television, infra-red and several other areas of the electromagnetic spectrum. We call them Big Eye and Little Ear."

"Thank you, General Whitfield. General Shelton will fill you in with details before the day is out. Chiefs, Secretaries, Directors, anybody have anything to say?"

The answer, "No, Mr. President" was virtually in unison.

"Well, then, let's get to it. I hope you all enjoyed breakfast."

CHAPTER 20

The missile launch was not detected by any of the now scrambled satellites over the South China Sea. It was initially recognized in the Tactical Operations Center aboard the USS Ronald Reagan when it reached twenty-five miles into the atmosphere. The twenty-year-old sailor on her first cruise screamed "missile incoming" in panic the second it appeared on her radar screen. The Lieutenant Commander on the watch dashed to her workstation. The computer, calculating the launch site by tracing the trajectory, determined it to be launched from the Yellow Sea. The trajectory took it directly over the carrier battle group, fifty miles into the atmosphere. There, the nuclear warhead, tailored to maximize the electromagnetic pulse, exploded.

Electronic and communications gear throughout the carrier battle group popped, fizzled, and went blank. Ship to ship communications died. Every computer operating in the carrier battle group was fried. The lieutenant commander picked up the intercom phone to the bridge. "Admiral, every piece of electronic communications gear, radar, sonar, are all down. Everything that was operating went blank at once. The entire Navy Marine Corps Intranet is down over the Yellow Sea, the South China Sea and extending into the Arabian Sea. That blast was tailored to provide the maximum electromagnetic pulse."

The blast and heat were felt by those on deck as a flash of sudden bright light and a blast of strong wind a minute later. All those on deck looked around to determine what it was and its source. Those operating tractors for towing aircraft and munitions suddenly found their engines would not start. Others, observing nothing unusual, returned to their tasks at hand with considerable apprehension. A few guessed it was a far off atomic blast.

Aircrews of aircraft providing air cover for the carrier battle group suddenly found they could not communicate with their carrier or each other, or anybody else. The section leader mentioned to his wingman by hand signal to return to the carrier. The two F-18 Super Hornets did a fly-by and waggled their wings as a signal for the intent to land. The Captain ordered the ship turned into the wind in order to affect their recovery. The Carrier battle group commander, Rear Admiral Mel Johnston, ordered the Carrier Air Group Commander, the ship's Captain and the Executive Officer to meet in the TOC.

"What the hell happened, Commander?" asked the Admiral.

"We picked up a missile launch from the Yellow Sea. It had a heading directly for us only fifty miles high. It fried all of our electronics. Every computer on this ship that wasn't heavily shielded is probably fried. It was the equivalent of sending one hundred thousand volts through the computer chips. Their circuits are melted together. We can't communicate outside this ship by electronic means. I have asked all sections to report weapons status. What I am getting is that all of our radar-controlled weapons systems are down, as is our sonar."

"What of the computers that were not turned on? Are they fried as well?" asked the Admiral. "What is our level of redundancy?" A sudden ominous thought struck him. He turned to the Captain, "Double the watch, sound general quarters. This might be the opening move of an attack. It appears that this is a deliberate electronic attack on this battle group."

The Captain asked, "I presume this also applies to the other ships in this command. Is there any way we can communicate with them?"

"Not electronically, Admiral. It is back to Morse Code by lights and signal flags."

At that moment, the intercom interrupted the Admiral. Bridge to Tactical Operations Center. "We are receiving in Morse Code messages from other ships that they are experiencing massive electronic failures. They are asking are we under attack?"

The Admiral looked at the sailor and said, "Send this signal. Prepare as if we are."

Turning back to his staff, the Admiral asked the Electronic Warfare Officer, (EWO), "How soon can we get some kind of notification to Pacific Command in Hawaii?"

"We'll test some of the spare computers and signal equipment. If they are not damaged, we will be back in business to some degree, in a matter of hours. I can't guarantee how many hours or what degree of business, but we should be able to restore some of our capabilities. Hopefully, shielding protected about 50% of our capabilities that weren't in operation. I don't know what magnetizing effect this has had on some of our motors. I have sent runners throughout the ship to determine that. My people are already testing the backup computers."

"What of passive detection measures?"

"Admiral, we can, by anomalous means, detect any torpedo launch. By sound wave magnetics, we can pick up any incoming aircraft or missile that is subsonic. If they are supersonic or hypersonic, we can't detect them in time."

"Very well, Commander. Let's get to it. Keep me informed of every development."

"Aye aye, Admiral."

To the Commander of the Air Wing, the Admiral said, "On second thought, double your air patrols using drones rather than piloted aircraft if their motors are not frozen as soon as you can control them, but keep our emissions to them at an absolute minimum. What assets are in the air now?"

"We have two F18E Super Hornets airborne, Admiral."

"Get them down by signal light or other visual signals. Let's be prepared to counter any attack from submarines or air attack from land-based aircraft. I am going to take a considerable risk, gentlemen. Signal all ships that they are to use visual signals and passive detection means only, even after restoration of all electronic systems. Electronic emissions are to be kept to an absolute minimum, as in none at all other than our drones.

I want the enemy to believe we are entirely crippled. Let's draw out the culprit, be it North Korean or Chinese, and kill him. Only after incoming will we light up the skies with emissions. Be prepared for a maximum launch of strike aircraft on a second's notice of any attack from any quarter.

"Captain Johnston, as our Medical Officer, prepare a handout sheet on possible signs and symptoms of radiation exposure. Measure the ship for any alpha particles. Get readings from our instruments on beta and gamma radiation so you will know what level of exposure has actually occurred and write your handout accordingly. Post it on all bulletin boards. A personal copy is to go to every sailor who was on deck at the time of the blast. Publish and distribute it in four hours. I don't want any sailor to think he or she is going to be sterile or impotent as a result of this exposure. Get on it. I don't want any anxiety attacks that can be avoided.

"All officers not standing watch are to report to their ready rooms for briefing in forty-five minutes. XO, prepare that briefing in thirty minutes. Be accurate, objective, and have a prediction as to how soon we will be fully operational again. Get with the EWO for his approval on accuracy.

"Air Wing Commander, to maintain the façade, launch a Greyhound to the nearest land base, the Republic of the Philippines, where we have an embassy, to inform CINPAC (Commander-in-Chief-Pacific). Request the intelligence officer send it via code of an electronic attack and to warn other carrier battle groups and go up the chain of command.

"I will address the ship over the intercom. Thankfully, someone had the good sense to hardwire this ship and shield many of its electronic suites from non-ionizing radiation. That's all for now. Let's get busy, people."

The yeoman blew his whistle into the intercom. "Now hear this, now hear this. The Admiral will address the ship."

The Admiral stepped up to the microphone. "Sailors, marines and airmen of the U.S.S. Ronald Reagan, this is the Admiral. The flash of light and sudden gust of strong wind that those of you above deck felt was the result of an electronic attack on this carrier battle group. A nuclear device, tailored for a bust of electromagnetic pulse was detonated directly over us at an altitude of approximately fifty miles. For those of you who were on deck, the Medical Officer will issue information and instructions in a matter of hours. It is extremely unlikely that anyone will suffer any harm whatsoever from radiation. Do not report to sick bay unless you have actual physical symptoms. All of you have received basic training in nuclear, biological and chemical warfare. This attack should come as no surprise.

"The result is that much of our electronic equipment and weapons systems have been seriously, but only temporarily, degraded. I have ordered immediate repairs and a complete blackout of electronic emissions of every kind. When communications are restored, no one is to send any signal, e-mail, or phone call, even from personal cell phones, from this carrier battle group. Our intent is to let the enemy believe that he has completely crippled all of our communications and weapons systems in the hope that he will expose his intentions and himself. When he does, we will engage him and kill him. Until otherwise indicated, consider us at war from this moment on. Be prepared to man your battle stations at a moment's notice. That is all."

The Electronic Warfare Officer approached the Admiral in the wardroom, with a grin and salute. "Admiral, our electronic capabilities were fully restored in sixty-three minutes. No overt attack has been detected. We are still standing down on emissions. Is there any change in the orders of emissions blackout?"

"No change in orders, Commander. Well done."

The hastily called press conference was broadcast on all networks, interrupting all programming. Roger McCall was standing grim-faced before the cameras when he announced that nuclear war had broken out on the Korean Peninsula.

"The only knowledge we have at this time is that there has been a nuclear exchange of atomic weapons. So far, indications are that they are all smaller than those used against Japan in August of 1945. Unfortunately, these nuclear blasts have also crippled our communications satellites, so that there is a dearth of information forthcoming. We have no further details at this time. I cannot take any questions as we have no other information. Thank you."

McCall pivoted on his heel and abruptly left the room with reporters shouting questions after him. The broadcast was played and replayed every fifteen minutes over all the networks. America wondered what would be the nation's reaction.

Marge Talbott sent a secure telex to the American ambassador in Japan for information on the Japanese reaction. Later that evening, television reports came in of demonstrations and rallies that approached riots in numerous Japanese cities. The ambassador's response came in at 23:00 that night. "Japan is transfixed. It doesn't know what to do. It now realizes that its lack of militarization might, probably will, result in Chinese dominance over Japan. Korea is most likely ruined as any kind of entity, politically, militarily or economically. Japanese observation aircraft flying at high altitudes off the Korean peninsula have recorded numerous small tactical weapons being deployed. Japan is now concerned about their own physical and economic survival. The Chinese ambassador to Japan has said nothing. The only good note is that the Prime Minister has suddenly offered to share its latest anti-submarine technology with us. Apparently, they are much farther ahead than we realized. I have been told that they know where we are, and that they are at least five years ahead of us in research but have not fielded any weapons, only tested them on various platforms. The Diet wouldn't support their deployment.

"There is a bonus here, Mr. President. The Japanese Prime Minister informed me today that they want to purchase a dozen DDX destroyers and want to build two dozen more in Japan under license. He assures me that there will be no difficulty with the Diet funding the purchase and their building their own under license. Not only that, but he strongly suspects that they will also fund purchase of several dozen new Joint Strike Fighters. He hasn't discussed that aspect yet with the appropriate leaders in the Diet and his own cabinet, but he personally is all for it."

Jason Thornton's smile just increased about one meter: American jobs and rejuvenation of the American shipbuilding industry, American aircraft ruling the skies, and above all, American jobs. Just what the economy needs. For decades, the American shipbuilding industry languished, with most American ships purchased from shipyards overseas. South Korea,

Japan, Singapore, Norway, Denmark, and even Poland built ships for the U.S. merchant lines.

"You tell the Prime Minister we will sell him all we can. We will build them as fast as we can. We will pull out all the stops and put workers going on them around the clock. We will work with them on the latest technological information for anti-submarine warfare, anti-mine warfare, undersea unmanned vehicles, and any other damned thing he wants. They smell war coming, and so do I. Have him contact the appropriate companies and write the contracts; tonight, if he wants. Pass this on to Jim Neville. Have him get right on it with his Japanese counterparts. Let's rebuild our Navy and our anti-submarine capability."

———————— •◦•◦•◦ ————————

Curtis Matthews had never been so tired in his life. He thought he would never quit walking. He had seen the mushroom clouds, small ones, on several occasions. He felt the strong machstem winds that they generated. He was hungry. He could not remember when he had last eaten. The nights were getting cooler, but the days were still warm and muggy. He had trudged southwards with the mass of refugees. No one would share food with him. He was drinking water whenever he could find any that looked halfway potable. He was thirsty enough that even ditch water looked good. He knew it was full of urine and feces, and it was all he could do to restrain himself from drinking it as he witnessed hundreds of others drinking it.

Corpses lay all along the route of their march. The young and the old, as in most cases of such severe societal disruption, were the first to collapse. Hunger, dehydration, and now radiation poisoning was adding to their distress. He observed many corpses with no obvious physical wounds. Many others had radiation burns and flash burns from tactical nuclear weapons. Others, he attributed to infections, particularly bacterial meningitis by Neisseria meningitidis. He scratched his head only to notice that a number of scalp hairs came away with his fingertips. He recognized it as a sign of radiation poisoning. The sound of battle was never far away and often continuous for hours, first in one direction, and then another.

He surmised that it was mostly small units, patrols, squads, platoons and companies that were skirmishing, but at other times, it was apparent that at least battalion-sized operations were under way. He left the roads and headed south across the countryside, guided only by the sun and stars. Each night, he would find the North Star as he was taught in the Medical Department Basic Course and orient himself due south. It was about all he remembered of the extremely meager field craft they were taught at Camp Bullis. Sometimes, he would just lie down wherever he was and sleep. In some fields, there were still a few vegetables that he would dig out with his hands, wipe the dirt off them and eat them raw on the spot. He had no means to make a fire, no pot to boil anything, no means of washing his food, so he ate it raw.

Sometimes when he found more than one Chinese cabbage, he would put a few in his shirt, at least what was left of his shirt. Chinese cabbage is one of the mainstays of kimchi, the horrendously hotly seasoned national dish of Korea. He had tried fresh summer kimchi, which is the mildest variety, in a Korean restaurant just before the war started, and couldn't get the fire out of his mouth. The Koreans learned to hide their food from the Japanese by burying it in large earthen crocks. To keep it from spoiling, they would add large quantities of hot peppers and vinegar-like solutions. In time, it became the national dish and referred to as winter kimchi. In summertime, it was made fresh daily. Winter kimchi, however, was fermented with terribly hot peppers. Koreans who ate it reeked of it for days. When the Japanese occupied Korea after the Russo-Japanese War of 1905, they raped the entire peninsula in every respect to the maximum extent they could. Hardly a tree was left standing. School girls of all ages were raped coming and going to school. That gave rise to the national dress for women. They all dressed as if they were in the last trimester of pregnancy to avoid being gang raped.

Curtis Matthews, MD, recognized that he was suffering to some degree of radiation poisoning. He just didn't know to what extent. Masses of people were now moving in all directions, attempting to get away from areas impacted by nuclear fires. North Koreans had observed him on several occasions, since he was taller and a different shade of skin and an obvious Occidental. More than one threatened to shoot him, and then laughed as he ducked and ran. One did fire several shots at him but missed and hit civilians that were around him. He witnessed human predator-prey reactions around the periphery of the masses, as several gangs of young South Koreans robbed others for whatever food or valuables they could find. On one occasion, the mob reacted to the beating of an elderly Korean. They caught one perpetrator and chased the remaining would-be bandits away, throwing whatever they could find at them. The mob beat, stomped, and kicked the bandit, breaking bones and causing internal injuries until he was unconscious and left him for dead, which he nearly was. The perpetrator did not live through the night.

"Mr. President, we have formulated a plan of operation to take out the Mexican raiders' base of operations in Chihuahua. The SECDEF told me to give you a call whenever we're ready. We are ready to present your briefing any time you like. The Service Chiefs suggest we get this operation underway immediately, given the international situation. We don't want anything to interfere, one with the other."

"I agree, General Craig. Have Peggy schedule it in as soon as possible. I'll send your call back into her."

A few minutes later, Peggy Parsons walked into the Oval Office. "We can have that briefing tomorrow morning, Mr. President, as part of the usual tri-weekly meeting. There should be enough time. General Craig tells me it will take about thirty minutes."

"Schedule it in, Peggy. I am anxious to get it on the road."

The next morning at 08:00, General Robert Anderson, Chief of Staff, Army, initiated briefing the President and his Secretaries. "Mr. President, Secretaries, this is the operational plan to launch a surprise raid into Chihuahua, Mexico to capture or kill the Mexicans who have been raiding into our southwestern states. It will utilize two maneuver battalions, one of the 82nd Airborne, one Ranger battalion, and one transportation battalion. There are many political considerations that we have not addressed, but which I will mention as we progress through the briefing for your consideration and decision.

"Both maneuver battalions will be delivered by Hercules C-130Hs out of Fort Bliss, TX. Our cover is that it will be a routine desert training exercise. The officers and noncommissioned officers only will be briefed on the operation twenty-four hours before deployment. They will have a low-level static line jump that is from 500 and 700 feet, in order to achieve complete surprise. The flight plan calls for the aircraft to drop below radar level before crossing the Mexican border. The 2nd battalion, 82nd Airborne, will cover the northern half of the drop, with the 1st Ranger Battalion covering the southern half. They will drop 500 meters into a complete perimeter around the camp. Apache gunships will provide covering fire if it is necessary. Our information is that they have the older variety of Stinger missiles. We don't want any of our aircraft shot down, so they will have a free fire zone at any possible target that might deploy a shoulder fired anti-aircraft missile.

"The transportation battalion will be accompanied by four Bradley infantry fighting vehicles to provide fire support and security screening. The transportation battalion will also have a company of Military Police attached to arrest those captured and transport them in two- and one-half ton trucks back to the United States. This brings the first political question to mind. Mexico will be howling mad that we raided into their country and, I am sure they will call it "kidnapping" of their citizens. The second political question here is putting them on trial. In what state or federal court will they be tried? The third question is, will the death sentence be invoked? Those are questions we cannot answer, Mr. President.

"We anticipate minimal to moderate resistance, with the possibility of two hundred prisoners. We have initiated building a compound to hold them at Fort Bliss for trial or whatever dispensation.

"The transportation battalion will also collect and transport back to the U.S. all weapons, explosives, personal goods of their American victims, and any information that is found. The transportation battalion will travel as a convoy out into the desert, using the same underwater bridge the raiders use in a remote location to cross the Rio Grande River. They will depart several hours earlier, such that they arrive on site fifteen minutes after the parachute drop. Estimated time from the parachute drop to vacating the site is four hours, with a maximum of six hours, Mr. President. Unless you object, we will destroy the premises."

"General, as I understand it, this is also truly a working farm that produces a considerable quantity of vegetables and has a feedlot. Are you sure you have the right place?"

"Yes, Mr. President. This is a working farm that produces a considerable quantity of tomatoes, cucumbers, lettuce, broccoli, peppers, and other vegetables. They have a small feedlot that variably contains 200 to 500 head of cattle. We have had this place under surveillance for several months now. We have aerial photographs from unmanned aerial vehicles of them training in small arms, explosives, and company sized tactics. There is no doubt that this is a terrorist camp of some sort. The working farm presentation is perfect cover."

"Then let's not destroy anything that can produce food. If you find something that has strictly military application, then by all means, blow it away. Perhaps we can make a gift of it to the Mexican government as a work camp or something, to assuage their ruffled feathers. I hope you can find a lot of intelligence information on this operation as a result of this raid. Why are they doing this? Is it strictly for money, glory, to finance a revolution, or something else driving this train? Is there an Islamic connection? I trust you have selected a commander for this operation. Who is he?"

"It is the Commander of the 2nd Brigade of the 82nd, Mr. President, Colonel John Paterson. He is a tough old bird at forty-three years of age, Mr. President. He has well over one hundred jumps and a third Dan black belt in Ai Ki Do. He can show the kids a thing or two as well as keep up with them. He leads from the front. The 2nd Battalion of the 82nd is part of his routine outfit. The transportation battalion is also part of the 82nd and has worked with the 2nd Brigade in the past. The Rangers had a little heartburn working for the 82nd, but they decided they could do that when the choice was not to participate, with the 1st Battalion of the 82nd going instead of them. Colonel Paterson wasn't too happy about taking the Rangers, preferring to have two of his regular battalions, but he appreciates the Rangers' skills and desire to participate. The Ranger battalion has an integral sniper platoon which was an excellent selling point. They will set up around the perimeter. Those soldiers can take out an enemy on the run at 800 meters as a matter of routine. Their mission is to prevent escapees making it into the hills."

"What about innocent farm workers on this place? They are going to scatter like quail."

"Mr. President, we can assume that everybody there will claim to be an innocent farm worker without any knowledge of any raids ever occurring. We have to assume, therefore, that they are knowledgeable and all raiders. We sent a team down there to snoop around as braceros, but they wouldn't hire them for whatever reason."

"How soon can you go after I give the word?"

"Mr. President, we can launch this operation within twenty-four hours of your OK."

"Alright. Mr. Attorney General Hugh Collier, what do you say, other than it is as illegal as hell?"

"That says it all, Mr. President. I also say that we have a more fundamental obligation to protect our citizens by any means necessary, including invading another, even friendly, country, to remove a threat to life, liberty, and limb, not to mention economic destruction that these raids have cost. The Governors of the southwestern states are still hopping mad. Some of our Mexican American citizens have been shot down without cause, and shootings of the illegal aliens crossing the border have been increased twenty times over since the first raid. Sales of firearms in the Border States have increased a thousand percent in the last year, and the Hispanics of those states are up in arms. The La Reconquesta movement is making all kinds of noise about the shootings, especially through their representatives, most of whom are members of the opposite political party."

"Can we take the political heat on this with our Mexican friends, Marge?"

"I have seen the light; we don't have any Mexican friends, Mr. President. We have only acquaintances. The façade is paper thin. We all realize that secrecy is paramount here. That place used to be a major producer of marijuana and could easily be so again. If we let the Mexican government in on this, that operation down there will be closed down in hours and all evidence removed. Mexico is so close to being a narco-government that it is difficult to draw the line anymore. Other Central and South American governments will, of course, side with Mexico. There's no love lost there, either. Their big fear is the precedent this sets; that they might be next. As for the United Nations, I wouldn't be surprised if Mexico filed an official protest with them. I think we can defend our actions on the floor of the UN. If we can't, and are sanctioned, what is that worth?"

"Jim, what do you think of the operation?"

"Mr. President, as Secretary of Defense, I think it is a go. It is time to remind certain elements around the world that we still have some fangs, and maybe a little venom."

"Let me put it this way. Is there anyone here who objects to this military operation, or thinks it is a bad idea? If so, speak up now."

Nobody said a word.

"General Anderson, the word is go, and I will leave it to you as to when you go."

The phone on Jason Thornton's desk rang. "Good news, Mr. President. The South Korean Navy is doing pretty well against the North Koreans. We just found out that they have sunk a half dozen of their submarines off both coasts and taken a pretty good toll of some of their surface craft."

"That is good news, Jim. How come they are doing a better job than I have been led to believe than we can do?"

"Well, sir, the Japanese spent a lot of money on their surveillance towed array sonar, called ULTASS. The Japanese sold it to the South Koreans who integrated it into a couple of their subs and their several Aegis destroyers and smaller patrol ships. They fed the data into their torpedoes and antiship missiles automatically so that they were fire-and-forget within seconds of detecting the enemy subs. We didn't hear about any of this until today as a result of our communications losses. It seems the South Korean torpedoes were very deadly against those quiet diesel submarines. Some of them had apparently been lying submerged off the South Korean coastlines for a week or more. The South Korean studies and mapping of the ocean floor off their coastline apparently had identified every rock more than three meters in diameter. When the South Korean subs painted the ocean floor with sonar, they knew exactly what was already there in the way of rock formations and so on, and what were quietly laying submarines. They blasted the hell out of them. We should survey our coastline like that!

"It seems they sunk a number of surface craft during the North's amphibious assault on Inchon as well. The North didn't pull it off near as well as McArthur in 1950. They didn't get it right before those twenty-foot tides changed, with the consequence that a lot of their landing craft got stuck and became sitting ducks. The South Korean destroyer escorts and patrol boats slaughtered them with long range naval fires as they stuck in the mud. The rapid fire automatic 155 mm AGS guns with high velocity guided munitions that they put on their patrol boats did it. I'm glad to say that we sold them those guns. The North lost a lot more men and equipment than they ever imagined. We didn't know the South Korean Navy was that sophisticated. Their destroyers and destroyer escorts sailed out of the area for a day or two playing chicken, to return in time to wallop the North Korean Navy when things were most pressing."

"What's the latest word on how the ground forces are doing?"

"Things are turning around, Mr. President. Since the nuclear exchange, the South Koreans have given the North a lot stiffer resistance than any one expected. They have launched a guerilla type effort that is showing signs of increasing organization. This is especially true in the eastern part of the peninsula, in the Taebok Mountains. Company- and battalion-sized South Korean units, acting independently, have begun to attack and defeat regimental sized North Korean units. South Korean civilians are beginning to take part in the fighting. The civilians are giving the South Korean Army their food and anything they think can help. It seems the North Korean logistical train has broken down, with their forces running out of food, fuel, and ammunition. There are indications that some North Korean units are beginning to retreat. We don't know if they are doing this under orders or on their own as a result of pressure from the ROKs. Some of them are retreating through hot areas where tactical nukes were used, apparently unaware of the danger. A lot of them are going to unwittingly commit suicide in doing so. From what we can gather, the ROKs are pursuing them up to those hot areas and then stopping. Consequently, the North Koreans are spending more time in them, to rest and regroup, considering it a respite from the pressure of the ROKs. The ROKs are obviously quite content to let them maximize their own dose of radiation poisoning. It strongly suggests that the North didn't train its troops very well in NBC, that is, Nuclear, Biological or Chemical warfare." (NBC, or sometimes referred to as CBR, for chemical, biological and radiological warfare).

CHAPTER 21

When the SpaceX Dragon rocket with the new shuttle clamped to it began to roll out of its hangar at the Florida launch site, some observers began to call the base. Word was passed to a local newspaper that a shuttle flight might be in progress. A call to NASA by the local paper informed the inquisitive reporter that they were merely rolling it out to do some open-air testing. Being somewhat suspicious, the newspaper put a van with a cameraman and reporter on the perimeter to monitor what was happening. When six astronauts were observed through the powerful lens of the telescope, the cameras began to whirl. A second call went to NASA headquarters in Houston, but again, the response was the same. The crew was going aboard to test several systems rather than in the simulators. New space suits needed to be tested on board to ensure their integration into the shuttle's onboard systems. NASA told the inquisitive reporters that each suit was tailored to the individual astronaut and their position on the shuttle, so they had to do that under outdoor simulations.

Larry Corning, Diane Foster and Robert Hatcher were all excited and scared out of their wits. Marine Colonel Nathan Berry, Mission Commander, laughed to himself but just grinned at his charges. "Relax folks, this is the most enjoyable ride you will ever have in your lives. Greg and I will give you the view of a lifetime." Commander Gregory Fletcher, US Navy, second-in-command, computer engineer and navigator, just looked at the passengers and grimaced to himself. He didn't want them to observe his concern for their preparation with only a two-week crash course on being astronauts. The third member of the crew, Cathy Slayton, Lieutenant Colonel, USAF, aerospace engineer, with several shuttle flights to her credit, had already proven herself a capable astronaut and boom handler extraordinaire. The two gals had immediately bonded.

One hour later, the shuttle lifted off. In thirty minutes, it was orbiting in the same orbit as their first satellite objective. Colonel Berry fired the maneuvering rockets that slowed the shuttle, then gently brought it within meters of the satellite. LTC Slayton opened the shuttle bay and maneuvered the arm to very gently rotate the satellite to bring its "handles" to the appropriate position so that it could be securely grasped. Commander Fletcher donned his space suit for a brief space walk. He went through the airlock while LTC Slayton was securing the satellite. He fired his backpack rockets, which gently propelled him to the satellite. There, he quite carefully folded the solar panels into place. He checked the boom hands to ensure the satellite was properly locked in place. He turned towards the shuttle and gave LTC Slayton a salute. Slayton heard him say, "OK, take it away!"

Now securely locked in position by the boom, she gingerly brought it into the cargo bay of the shuttle. She closed the shuttle bay doors. Commander Fletcher entered the bay with the shuttle, more or less riding on the boom. Slayton then pressurized the bay so that the three passengers could examine the satellite in the bay without having to make a space walk. Fletcher went back through the airlock to climb out of his space suit to give the three scientists room to do their job.

"Ok, people, let's go take a look at your satellite and see what you can do to fix it," said Colonel Berry, as he un-strapped himself from his seat. "I'll stay in the command cockpit while you folks do your thing."

Drs. Hatcher, Foster and Corning slowly guided themselves over to the hatch leading to the shuttle bay. Once in the shuttle bay, they slowly examined the external surfaces for damage. Seeing none, Dr. Corning began to unscrew the cover plates which covered the computers. He placed the screws in a magnetized dish which he placed on the boom arm. Removing the two computers, he unplugged their hard drives and handed them to Diane Foster. He then began to examine the solar panels by unfolding them and examining them one at a time. Visual inspection suggested the wafers were burned out. He would have to test them for confirmation. They would require replacing if seriously damaged.

Dr. Foster moved back into the shuttle where the necessary instrumentation for testing was located. Twenty minutes later, Corning followed her in with one section of a solar panel. He removed the wafers and connected them to a micro voltmeter. Nothing. They were dead, fried, burned out. He moved back into the shuttle bay and, snapping himself in place by his belt lines, began to remove all four of the burned-out solar panels. He secured them to the bay wall with bungee cords equipped with T hooks that mated in small slots in the structural ribs of the bay. He then opened a long but very shallow locker along the bay wall. He removed the new solar panels one at a time and very carefully folded them, then screwed them in place on the satellite. They were far too big to remain unfolded in the shuttle bay. The panel locker would protrude too far into the shuttle bay if they were stored folded. After replacing all four panels, he floated back to the hatch by giving himself a gentle shove off the boom.

Hatcher came into the shuttle bay to examine the positioning rockets and their controls of the satellite. These were what moved the satellite from orbit to orbit or rotated it to achieve the proper viewing angle. He found no problems with any of them after one hour of examination. He replaced small bottles of liquid fuel for each of the rockets, then moved back into the command area of the shuttle.

Dr. Foster was engrossed in examining the lines of codes. The readings she got indicated that they had been scrambled. All circuits were working normally, they were just sending nonsense signals that could neither be received nor read.

"This is deliberate. This is sabotage of the highest order. I don't know who had access to these command modes, but they have been deliberately scrambled. Somebody built a worm into this that made it an unintelligible mess upon receipt of a signal. They all have to be replaced. It will take hours on a mega computer, bigger than anything we have on board, hours, and maybe days, to unscramble it and identify the worm. We need to put the new codes in and get that satellite back in working order. We'll take these boards with us and see what they reveal back on Terra Firma." She wrote "scrambled" on the hard drives and packed them in a small lock box. Then she removed two new hard drives and handed them to Corning. He looked at her with a fixed stare. Then she realized why.

"Don't worry, I programmed this myself. I am the only one who knows the codes in these, and I have secured the only copies of them where no one else in the world knows."

"OK Di, I believe you. I'll go stick them in the satellite right now so we can get out of here. This weightlessness bugs me." He grinned and pushed himself away from her computer screen towards the hatch. He carefully replaced the computer hard drives in the satellite and returned to the command area. "How soon can we get out of here?" he asked.

COL Berry just grinned, and said, "We are coming up on an orbital path in about an hour and thirty minutes. We'll touch down in Houston in no time."

Berry turned to Slayton and said, "Let's get that satellite back in orbit, Colonel. I think the man here must have a hot date tonight." Cathy Slayton grinned, knowing that it was really Berry who had the hot date.

"Aye aye, Colonel," she replied with a grin and wink. She checked the airlock and hatch doors, then strapped herself into her seat and began to open the shuttle bay doors. Once fully opened, she carefully raised the boom arm to its maximum height, then opened the claws of the boom to release the satellite. When the claws opened, they gave the satellite a very gentle shove, which sent it a few meters away from the ship and the boom arm. Carefully, she lowered the boom back into the shuttle bay, then closed the bay doors. "Satellite free, boom secure, bay doors closed and locked. Do you want to test it while we are here, Dr. Foster?"

"Absolutely," she cried. She spun her chair around and sent a simple maneuver signal to the satellite, which caused the rockets to ignite and send the satellite a mile higher. Then she positioned the satellite to focus on earth and initiated its television camera. The image she received on her computer screen was bright and clear. Next, she signaled the infra-red camera to initiate photography. The image was clean and crisp.

"Big Eye is back in business!" she exclaimed, then realized what she had said. No one however, seemed to pay any attention at all.

"How do we know, Di, that it won't be disrupted again?"

"It will take another nuclear blast with a large EMP pulse to do it. I redid the codes differently than before. It won't respond to any signal but mine. It disregards all others. That way, nobody can interfere. Regarding another EMP event, it will have to be up here in space, pretty close to the satellite. I lined these circuit boards with a gold over layer to ensure that far off pulses won't screw it up. Anything below 50,000 feet shouldn't interfere with it at all."

"Smart girl," Berry said. He had been admiring her figure from afar for the last two weeks. She smiled in return.

"Alright, back to business. Coming up on the orbital re-entry point. Everybody in your seats. Get buckled and double check." He spun around, buckled himself in, tugged on them, and then began throwing switches as Greg went down the checklist. Cathy Slayton began to double check their entry data.

"Re-entry point in ten minutes," stated the LTC navigator and boom girl Friday. Greg kept going down the checklist, while Slayton checked in with NASA in Houston. They confirmed her readings and gave them a go. At the countdown, Berry ignited the shuttle rocket and positioned the shuttle for a glide path to Houston. Forty-five minutes later they touched down at NASA.

After coming to a stop, Dr. Foster put the damaged hard drives in her carry-on bag. They deplaned, so to speak, to a waiting vehicle who took them immediately to NASA. The first thing Diane Foster did was to hand the hard drives over to the Flight Director. "I need maximum computer power. I don't know what you have here, but I will need about one million gigabytes computing power to do this in hours. Otherwise, it will take days."

"And you shall have it. When do you want it? I suggest you shower and eat, and maybe even sleep for a while, before tackling this."

"No, I'm too excited to sleep. I'll eat and shower, but then I'll start on this."

Once out of their space suits, they all showered and moved to the chow hall. It was evident they already considered themselves a team, the three scientists and the shuttle crew.

At the console, Diane Foster plugged in the hard drive and began to decipher the codes. Three hours later, she fell asleep. Three hours after that an alarm went off which awakened her. The computer identified a worm that was programmed in when the program was written. She copies that information on a thumb drive and then continued. She found a second worm embedded in the program as a back up, in case the first worm failed. She put that on a separate thumb drive. Another hour went by, and the nanoboard had been completely scanned. She plugged in the second hard drive and had her answer six hours later. It was clean. She called the Flight Director. "I need a secure phone, now."

"I have one on my desk you can use. You can punch in a direct dial to the President, to Fred Gateway or to Ed McCluskey if you like."

She nodded in agreement, and said, "Let's go to your office." Once there, she said, "Excuse me, but I must make this call to Ed McCluskey in absolute privacy." He picked up the phone, punched some buttons and handed it to her. When she heard the voice on the other end, she said "Siphonoptera" as a code word only the two of them knew. He replied with "Quintus Atillius," a response that only he knew. They each knew they had the right party.

"What do you have, Doctor?"

She sighed, "I hate to say this, but we have a mole in the organization. Only one hard drive had been reprogrammed, and it was done on the ground floor. Someone in our organization who has the highest of clearance did this. Only a handful of such people had access. I can't identify who for sure, but I have some ideas."

"NASA has a Lear jet there. Put Mike back on, and I'll have the three of you here in a couple of hours."

She put down the phone and walked over to the door. Flight Director Mike Shannon was leaning against the opposite wall of the corridor. "Ed wants to speak to you."

He walked in and picked up the phone. "This is Mike."

"Mike, get those people on your Lear, and get them here as quickly as is safely possible."

"I think I can get them airborne in about forty-five minutes. About three hours' flight time, I'll have them there in time for supper. Anything else?"

"That's it. Thanks, Mike."

Mike punched a number into his phone. "Get the Lear ready and warmed up as quickly as possible. Flight plan is for Andrews Air Force Base. Let me know ten minutes before you are ready. Call me on my cell," and he hung up. "Let's round up the rest of the crew." Four hours later, the Lear landed at Andrews, where a three-car escort was waiting for them. All three cars had deeply tinted windows and looked alike. The cars played shuffleboard across the tarmac as a somewhat feeble effort at the old game of pea under the shell.

Fred Gateway, Jim Neville and Ed McCluskey were waiting for them at Langley, CIA headquarters. Drs. Hatcher and Corning were warmly greeted by the three and congratulated, but then escorted elsewhere for debriefing. Dr. Foster accompanied the three to a separate room where two other men whom she did not know were waiting. They were not introduced, so she did not ask.

Ed McCluskey opened with, "What did you find, Doctor?"

"The big news is a worm. The solar panels were also fried by an EMP but easily replaced." She produced the hard drives and stated, "This drive was programmed with two worms. This second drive is clean. With the exception of me, the same people did not work on both drives. That narrows our field down to about four people, those who worked only on this drive. Whoever did this had to know the type, configuration of both the hardware and software, and access to these drives of the onboard computers. I am sure you will put those people under intense scrutiny."

"Is there anyone in particular you suspect, Dr.?" asked Fred Gateway. She lowered her head as she thought. She had suspicions but was reluctant to express them as she had no proof, only a gut level feeling. Out of concern of leveling possibly false charges which might do irreparable harm to one's career and possibly their life, she finally said, "No, there is no one I particularly suspect."

"Can you tell us why these worms were not picked up before the satellite was sent into orbit, Doctor?"

"There are over 2.5 million lines of code on each of these hard drives. To do so would require a computer review of enormous magnitude. Very few computers in the world have enough power to do that. Even so, it took six hours for NASA's largest to find these two worms. It is virtually impossible to detect them. The initial worm was actually broken into several parts so that it would appear as an error that the code writer failed to erase or correct. The result was that the individual pieces would cascade together as they received their signals. The individual pieces would appear as nonsense and not be worth the effort to dig out these pieces, possibly damaging other codes. You would most likely do more damage than good. You could almost liken it to a piece of DNA in a gene whose function was not recognized nor appreciated. Maybe a better illustration would be a piece of shrapnel in a critical anatomical location in a wounded soldier that would result in greater damage removing it than if you left it in place."

The three looked at each other. Then the Secretary of Defense asked, "Is there anything else you can tell us, or would like to say, Dr. Foster?"

"I don't know what else I can say."

"Doctor, your efforts have been Herculean. We appreciate that. You have done your country more than Yeoman service. I can assure you that your efforts will be recognized and rewarded. I will have a jet fly you to Lawrence Livermore and a car to take you home. Director Gateway will assign a team of agents as your bodyguard until this is over. You will be under our wing until the mole is caught."

"Thank you, Mr. Secretary, but I don't want any bodyguards."

"Nevertheless, you are going to have them. You are too valuable a resource. We cannot risk anything happening to you. You can take a vacation within the United States if you like or return to work. You will hardly be aware of your escorts. They are very well trained. Whatever you do, you will be in our care. That is final, ma'am."

Diane Foster smiled weakly, knowing she had no choice. "Well then, it's home for me and a day of rest perhaps, then back to work. On the other hand, I am not sure I want to go back and look at my colleagues' faces, knowing that one of them is a traitor."

"An agent now outside the door will be with until you return home. There, a team of FBI agents, very special ones I would say, will be waiting for you. They will be your guardian angels. Again, we can't thank you enough." Diane Foster nodded, as Ed McCluskey stood and escorted her to the door, where the waiting agent nodded and smiled to Dr. Foster. McCluskey closed the door and returned to the desk where he turned to face the two unidentified men in the room. "Well, Doctors, what do you think?"

Dr. Stangness nodded to his colleague as a signal that he should offer his opinion first. "She has suspicions of the traitor but is afraid to voice them for lack of evidence, for fear of harming an innocent if she is wrong. What do you think, Doctor Realms?"

"I agree with you completely, Doctor. Her body language suggested some degree of guilt in not coming forth. I am of the opinion that her gut level instincts will turn out to be correct. They usually are. We need her opinion. Perhaps one of her bodyguards can get close enough to her for her to share her opinions."

Fred Gateway shook his head affirmatively. "One of them is a handsome, intelligent and single agent in his thirties. The rest are all married men. I'll order him to very gently court her and see what information he can develop. I thank you two distinguished psychiatrists for your assistance. You know the usual rules apply."

<hr />

"Mr. President, I have some more good news."

"What is that, Marge?"

"The Japanese ambassador just informed me that they have launched a new communications satellite over the area. Apparently, they were getting ready to replace one of their older satellites and were close to a launch anyway. They are getting excellent resolution from the television cameras, in the one-meter range from 125 miles up. They are offering to relay their broadcasts to our major networks if we approve of it. We can't keep the situation quiet forever. I told them absolutely, but I would check with you and get back to them in case you had any objections. Our major network people in their Tokyo offices found out about the offer and aren't sitting on their hands. They will likely go ahead with or without our governmental approval. I didn't ask, but I bet the Japanese offered to share with the Europeans as well. They are scared, Mr. President. The ramifications are coming home to them. They can start sharing broadcasts in minutes."

"Good, Marge. I have no objections. Let's let the American people see what it is like to be in a war zone again, not just some police action governed by surgical strikes. I think I'll call Ed McCluskey and see where we are with another of our satellites."

That night, pictures of nuclear devastation on the Korean peninsula penetrated every American home on the evening news. Retired military personnel appeared on every network as experts in nuclear war. Maps projecting fallout patterns were displayed along with rates of fallout, estimated times of fallout in zones. Maps showing the centers of detonations with Zones I, II, and III depicted. Meteorological data was brought into the equation to describe how current and near-term wind patterns would disperse it. Most of the blasts occurred in South Korea. Much of the fallout would settle in North Korea. Predictions showed that China would receive only modest amounts of fallout, as the blasts were small, almost all less than three kilotons. Only Pyongyang received a sizeable bomb in the north. Chinese armed forces actively engaged and repelled all North Koreans who attempted to cross into China. The border was sealed. The Japanese satellite revealed the armed conflict. The American public became very subdued.

"Everybody saw the results of the nuclear exchange in Korea on TV last night. You all know those signals were relayed from a Japanese satellite. I don't like being upstaged by the Japanese, but Marge informs us that the Japanese had one almost ready for launch as a replacement. Where do we stand, getting more satellites up, either as commercial or military?"

"I talked with representatives of several of the commercial satellite companies about that two days ago, Mr. President. I meant to bring it up yesterday but got bogged down and failed to mention it. COMSAT says they have put one together from strictly off-the-shelf parts that will do the job. Perhaps it is not quite as good as a specifically tailored one, but one good enough. They say they will have it ready in about a week. They will initiate testing it tomorrow. They were going to have the Chinese or Japanese launch it, but I nixed that. I checked with NASA; they can put it up using the SpaceX Dragon rocket. They are working on the rockets and will have them ready by the end of this week. The Navy recovered the various stages of our previous launch, and NASA is overhauling them for future launches as well. As usual, however, NASA said they are working over budget and need more funds. They want to get back to the space station. If they can get it up to snuff and put a crew in there, they can handle our low orbit stuff a lot easier and cheaper. An attack on it would be a declaration of war with the U.S., and everybody knows it. So, they feel comfortable in trying to sell this approach. NASA says they have some volunteer astronauts willing to man it."

"Thanks, Ed. God Bless American heroes! We'll go with the cost be damned. Ed, get it rolling. General Craig, you and Ed work well together; the two of you work it out between your organizations ASAP. I don't like depending on foreign broadcasts that can be used as filters for information being fed to the American public, let alone the egg on our face of having to depend on foreign resources. Let's try and get the American military and the civilian community to work together once again for the common good."

"Mr. President, are you talking about the satellite launch or the space station or both?"

"Both, of course. Let it be known that we will obliterate any nation on earth that attacks the space station. From now on, it is not an International Space Station, it is exclusively an American Space Station. Make sure that the Chinese understand that. They are about the only ones that can challenge it, but don't specifically mention them by name. We don't want any miscommunications on this issue at all. Any rockets come anywhere close to it, any nuclear blasts in its vicinity, accidental or otherwise, will result in enough American nuclear firepower being launched to destroy a continent. You can quote me on that to the journalists."

Robert Lee's pulse raced at those words. He needed a vacation. Perhaps a week off to fish in Labrador would do it.

"Secretary of Defense Neville, you're a physicist, what do you and your science boys say about fallout from the Korean nuclear exchange?"

"Mr. President, Korea doesn't experience the monsoon winds that Southeast Asia does. Nevertheless, the prevailing winds will carry a lot of fallout over the Pacific. Japan, in particular, will receive a lot of it. Summer rains will bring down a lot of the particulate matter, to which alpha particles are attached. Alpha particles are really doubly charged helium atoms. This is a helium atom with both of its electrons removed. They tend to stick to dust particles; hence they are truly the fallout particles; when the dust settles, these charged particles come to earth's surface. That's the real threat at this time. The beta and gamma radiation are a done deed. They are much more powerful and are instantaneous at the time of the burst. Beta rays are simply electrons. For the gamma radiation, we're essentially talking X-rays, Mr. President. Gamma rays are an electromagnetic wave that is the same to a little higher frequency than X-rays.

"All three are ionizing agents, but they differ in their ionizing ability. They ionize other atoms when they collide with them, by knocking their electrons out of place, that is, their orbits. All other factors being equal, they vary considerably in their ionizing power. It is all relative. The gamma ray will ionize one atom to a beta particle's one hundred atoms to an alpha particle's ten thousand atoms. That alpha particle gains and loses electrons at a tremendous rate as it passes through material. Ultimately, it will gain and retain two electrons and become a normal helium atom again. The threat it poses is then over.

"Hopefully, a lot of the alpha radiation will come down over the Pacific during rainstorms before it reaches the United States. Still, some of it is bound to reach North America. We just can't predict how much at this point in time. In order to get a better handle on it, we need the Navy to monitor what's going on out in the Pacific. We can send some ships out of Pearl Harbor with the specific mission of doing just that. We can also put some aircraft flying around to monitor various levels of the atmosphere and stratosphere to determine the height and concentration of radiation in time and place. That will give us good prediction data. We do have some data from our tests in the South Pacific, but it is very limited. We didn't have the sophistication at the time of those tests to monitor it the way we do now. The Navy has been drilling for NBC warfare for thirty years, so I don't see why they can't do this.

"The Japanese are paying very close attention to this. They have issued public advisories to stay indoors as much as possible. It is particularly important to stay out of the rain. The rain will wash those contaminated dust particles out of the air. Ultimately, those will wash into the seas around Japan. That might be a long-term problem for Japan in terms of radioactive sea foods. The southern Japanese islands will suffer more than the more northerly ones. They can expect to see a rise in cancers over the next few years. I doubt though it will be nearly as bad as what they experienced after World War II. If you study the data, the rates did significantly increase after Hiroshima and Nagasaki, but the total number of cases weren't near as bad as anticipated, even thirty years later."

"General Craig, get with Admiral Stark and make that happen. I want very close monitoring of fallout. California is going gaga as we speak. Some of those folks are partying like they won't live tomorrow, others are fleeing the west coast, some are headed for the hills to try and ride it out. We need good information to predict just what and where and how much.

"Secretary of Health and Human Services Allison, have Surgeon General Carolyn Weber prepare whatever public information you deem necessary to inform the public of the risks, what they can do to prevent undue exposure, personal protection, and so on. I don't want any panics like Three Mile Island back in the 1970s. The public didn't comprehend a dang thing then. Let's hope we can do a better job of informing them than we did then. Utilize every available media. Help the press get it right for a change."

CHAPTER 22

T he trucks pulled out of Fort Bliss at 08:00. They were well equipped with spare food, water, ammunition, explosives, fuel, medical supplies, the Military Police Company and military journalists armed with camcorders. At the last minute, Colonel Paterson added an engineering company with two bulldozers and a road grader to the column, just in case. The engineering platoon would handle any demolitions, the Emergency Ordnance Disposal any booby traps, assist in collection of weapons, and provide a mass grave for the Mexicans who died in combat. They camped that night out in the desert off of state highway 2810 after a two-hundred-and-fifty-mile drive. That night, the convoy personnel who were not previously briefed were informed that this was not just a routine training exercise, but that they were in support of a "hot" military mission. The battalion commander established at the camp what was, in effect, a FARP, a Forward Arming and Refueling Point. It would serve to provide fuel for the helicopter medical evacuation company to evacuate any wounded soldiers by air to any one of several civilian hospitals or the medical center at Fort Bliss. The helicopters would arrive at 06:00 for refueling. The civilian hospitals would not be informed of any anticipated wounded until the time the parachute drop began. The Division Surgeon of the 82nd had conducted a surreptitious evaluation of the surgical capabilities of the regional hospitals which might be able to offer critical surgery, rather than evacuating wounded all the way back to Fort Bliss, outside of El Paso. The battalion surgeons would triage the wounded.

Boots and saddles sounded at 04:00. Camp was broken by 05:30, and the convoy began to slowly move across the desert. At 06:30, the flight of C-130H Hercules appeared over the horizon from the farm of Jesus Gonzalez. At 06:35, paratroopers from both battalions hit the silk in a perfect circle surrounding the farm. The drop was timed for when it was presumed that the great majority of the workers would be in the mess hall. They were. Many rushed to the door to see why aircraft were flying so low. At that same moment, paratroopers came tumbling out of the aircraft. They were on the ground in seconds. They rolled their chutes, pulled their rifles out of their cases, formed into their platoons and began advancing in an ever-tightening circle. Captain Sabata's Ranger Company was on the southern end of the camp.

The sniper platoon set up operations as fifteen two-man teams on small rises where they had relatively good views of the operation. They had free fire orders. Anybody who got through the cordon of paratroopers was fair game.

Most of the Mexicans decided either to attempt to escape or to surrender, but a few decided to fight. They dashed to the arms room to grab their rifles, but the double padlocked door delayed them for several minutes while someone went to Jesus Gonzalez's office to get the keys. The locks and hasps were reinforced to prevent their being pried off. By the time they acquired their rifles and bandoleer of ammunition, the Americans were within two hundred meters and closing fast at a dog trot. So far, not a single shot had been fired. Those Mexicans who decided to fight found the closest cover and opened fire. A dozen paratroopers were immediately hit. The remainder dove to the ground and returned fire. Under orders to fire individual rounds in the semi-automatic mode from their M-4 carbines and M-16A3 rifles rather than full automatic fire, the paratroopers delivered a more accurate, aimed fire. With advanced combat optical sights on their M-16s and M-4s, the Americans quickly inflicted severe casualties on the fighting Mexicans. Most of the Mexicans who were shooting were spraying rounds in the general direction of the soldiers, rather than aimed fire. Most of them were killed or wounded before they recognized the accuracy of fire from the Americans. A few Mexicans threw hand grenades at the soldiers that inflicted several deaths and serious casualties among the soldiers. By coincidence, none of those who threw grenades survived the ensuing return rifle fire.

Using fire and maneuver, each company commander closed the circle towards the central part of the compound. Moving from building to building and securing each in turn, as practiced at Fort Bragg, they quickly secured the compound. Most of the Mexicans had fled the mess hall but quickly ran into the wall of Americans. Most surrendered on the spot, those who were armed dropping their rifles and raising their hands. Others attempted to run through the American lines. Those who did were shot as soon as they passed through the lines to the point where friendly fire would not inflict any casualties. Those few who did manage to pass through the American line and evade rifle fire from the paratroopers were shot by the sniper teams. A few Mexicans armed with sniper rifles engaged the Americans from various positions. They proved to be the most difficult to overcome. They inflicted a dozen casualties before they were eliminated. One Ranger sniper observed his Mexican counterpart firing from an obstructed position and shot him in the head from one thousand meters out with his Remington .308 Winchester sniper rifle.

"Well, there's a runner, Sarge. Kinda scruffy looking at that. He's about 700 meters out. He's running maybe twenty-five or fifty meters, and then falling down playing dead until he thinks the coast is clear. He's at our 2:00 o'clock. Think you can take him?"

"Specialist Stone, if I couldn't take him, I wouldn't be here. I don't pick him up with the naked eye or in the rifle scope, so he must be down right now."

"Right you are, Sarge, he's just behind a little ground swell there. If you let him get to the irrigation ditch, he might just get away. Oops, his head just came up. See him?"

"I got him, Corporal; I figure you're right at about 700 meters. I'll get him as he gets to his feet."

"If you miss, it's my turn. I want to see if I can pick him off on the run."

"Keep your cool, Corporal. I still have ten minutes left on the gun before I take over on the spotting scope. Anyhow, I won't miss. Another second, there he goes."

As the Mexican rose to a crouch and looked around in preparation to run, the 173-grain bullet launched at 2550 feet per second smashed into the center of his chest. He crumpled to the ground.

"You got him, Sarge! Switch with me now, so maybe I can have a shot!"

Sergeant E-5 Thomas Worth looked at his junior partner with a wide grin. "Sure, why not." He crawled behind Corporal Stone, who merely rolled over to assume the prone position behind the Harris bipod rested rifle while Sergeant Worth took up surveying through the spotting scope.

"Corporal, there's some guy prone behind some boxes next to the warehouse. He's using a scoped rifle and seems to know what he is doing. He is firing slowly and methodically, picking his targets. I don't like that. Can you pick him up in the scope? He's on his elbows with a rifle with a bipod. He's only partially exposed."

"Yea, Sarge, I saw him raise up and fire and then duck. All I got now are his legs."

"Well, I'll see what I can do to shake him loose with my M-14. If we can get him to move, you might get a clear shot when he stands. Be ready."

"Sarge, I'm ready. Go ahead and do him. Let's see if you can get a hit at this range with that scoped M-14."

Sergeant Worth took careful aim and squeezed a round. It hit the box behind which the sniper was hiding. It had no effect. Worth squeezed off a second round. It hit the building behind him and just over his head. On the third shot, Worth scored a hit, just grazing a gluteal muscle on one side that was slightly higher than the other. The target raised his head, took a quick look around at the direction of the fire, and raised to the knee on his wounded leg and planted his other foot in preparation to run. As he stood to run, the Corporal's bullet caught him square in the chest, just an inch away from the heart. He fell backwards and lay still.

Due to their engine noises, the approaching American convoy didn't hear the firing until they were less than a kilometer away. They reached the locked gate a few minutes later. The engineering platoon leader quickly ordered the bulldozer unloaded and the gate bulldozed open and out of the way.

Some of the Mexicans had run out of the mess hall with their hands raised. Others remained in the mess hall lying on the floor. When Captain Sabata and company advanced, those who exited the mess hall were motioned to lie on the ground spread eagle. Captain Sabata's Rangers trained their rifles on those just outside the mess hall as other Rangers went through the mess hall doors to cover those inside as well. Captain Sabata shouted and was repeated in turn by his Spanish speaking Rangers, "Any movement will result in your being shot."

The convoy drove to the center of the compound. Mexicans who attempted to run but were turned back at gunpoint as prisoners were herded to the area around the mess hall. The Military Police Company quickly moved in, ordering each prisoner to stand in turn to be searched and then secured with plastic hand ties. Then they were taken to the trucks and loaded in for transport across the border. As a truck became full, it departed. The trucks filled rather quickly, so that a truck departed every few minutes. A military police specialist rode shotgun in the cab in each truck, and two MPs armed with shotguns rode in the back. Talking was not permitted. The MPs told them in Spanish not to speak. When one Mexican in the first truck decided to disobey by making a smart remark, the MP rose from his seat adjacent to the tailgate and butt stroked him across the face. The man's head arched backwards and slammed into the canvas of the truck. With bloodied lips and several broken teeth on the left side of his mouth, he sagged forward but did not quite pass out. The prisoners looked at one another but said nothing. There would be no reports of brutality by the MP Specialist, and no recrimination.

Meanwhile, the MP Company Commander and Colonel Paterson were briefly going through Jesus Gonzalez's office in a quick review. All papers, file cabinets, ledgers, and even the safe were packed and loaded into a truck. They found a forklift to handle the safe and file cabinets. The forklift was too small to go through the office door, so the engineers simply chain sawed the door large enough for it to fit into the room. Captain Sabata was ordered to report to Colonel Paterson.

"Captain, have your men quickly question who is El Jefe here. We want to be sure to capture him. Carry on."

Captain Sabata told his Rangers to ask each prisoner in turn as they were stood by the MPs to be searched, who was the El Jefe and other leaders. Word was quickly passed to the Hispanic members of the 82nd to question all about El Jefe. Many mentioned the name of Jesus Gonzalez, but as they turned to look for him, none of them could identify him. Half a dozen, however, identified Luis as Gonzalez's secretary and bookkeeper. Three others identified Fiero as one of the team leaders. An MP was assigned to individually guard each of them.

Alpha Company, 82nd Airborne loaded all weapons from the arms room into trucks. Other Alpha company members were collecting AK-47s from the dead and wounded. Three paratroopers were assigned to guard each truckload of weapons as it was filled and drove away, headed for Fort Bliss.

The battalion surgeon reported to Colonel Paterson there were eleven American dead, twenty-six wounded, nine of them seriously. He had called in the air ambulances that would be arriving any minute to evacuate the nine. The body count for Mexican dead and wounded was still ongoing. He had forty-seven wounded Mexicans to date, eighteen seriously.

"Doctor, the critically wounded American soldiers will go out of here first on the air ambulances. I don't want to hear one word of humanitarian bullshit about some Mexican being more severely wounded and having a higher priority than any American soldier. If I do, I will personally kick your ass so hard that you will never walk again. My soldiers have the highest priority, understood?"

"Sir, I must protest. I have to triage all the wounded without regard to which side they are on."

"Doctor, you are relieved of your command. Get your Number Two in here."

"You're not my commander, Colonel. I'm only attached for this operation. I'm in Health Services Command. Only doctors can command doctors."

"When we get back to Bragg, you can file all the official protests you want. I think you will find there is no room for you in the 82nd Airborne and probably not in the United States Army. I will spread the word that you value the lives of Mexican raiders more than you do the United States soldiers in every newspaper in America, now get out of my sight!"

The Major, Medical Corps, swallowed hard, turned on his heel, and walked out. The Colonel didn't hesitate for even one second to give him the chance to reverse his course. He knew that his military career was over. Having served as a General Medical Officer for five years, he had just been selected for a residence in surgery at Walter Reed Army Medical Center. He also knew Colonel Paterson could pull enough strings that his residency selection would be withdrawn. He heard rumors that several very good friends of the Colonel's were highly placed in the Army Medical Department. It had something to do with the invasion of Iraq in 2003.

The UH-60 air ambulances came in and set down fifty meters apart behind the mess hall. They were quickly loaded with the critically wounded. A Captain, Medical Corps, reported to Colonel Paterson.

"Captain, I want you to re-evaluate Major Johnson's triage. I'll tell you the same thing I told him. American soldiers have first priority on those air ambulances. I don't give a damn how badly wounded some Mexican is. After the seriously wounded Americans are air evaced, you can take out the seriously wounded Mexicans if there is still room on the air ambulances, but not before. Let them ride in ground ambulances. Do you have any trouble with that?"

"No, sir, I don't."

"Fine, I have relieved Major Johnson. You are in command, and your word is law. Anybody wants to argue, I'll send a couple of MPs they can argue with. Go to it, Doctor."

The MP Company commander reported in. "Sir, I have 176 prisoners. We have thirty-eight dead Mexicans. I don't know how many wounded. I have ordered the bodies brought to a ditch the engineers are digging for a mass burial should you give the order to do so. Otherwise, we can stack them in the packing sheds. They will get awfully ripe in this heat very quickly in the packing sheds, so I don't know which is better. In 24 hours, they will be grotesquely swollen, maybe to the point of exploding."

"To hell with the ditch; no mass burial. Put them in the packing sheds and let them stink. That way the Mexican government can't accuse us of covering anything up, literally or figuratively. Their loved ones can identify and claim them, provided anybody loved them in the first place and they haven't rotted beyond recognition by the time any relatives or friends can get here."

"Colonel, we have also collected 332 AK-47 rifles, two dozen sniper rifles with fine telescopic sights, several unopened crates of grenades, thousands of rounds of small arms ammunition, several unopened crates of handguns without markings, RPGs, cases of dynamite and Simtex, and four Stinger missiles. We are making an accurate inventory of everything."

"Excellent, Captain, if there is nothing else, carry on."

The ground ambulances pulled out with four wounded and a medic in each one as they were loaded.

The sniper teams reported in. They had accounted for sixteen dead Mexicans. No wounded Mexicans were included in their report. They brought in weapons from several of the dead Mexicans who had broken through the cordon in various locations. Two HUMVEEs were sent to collect the dead Mexicans and deposit them in the packing sheds where the bodies were being laid out in a row, heads towards the aisle to make identification easier. When they were finished, the drivers hosed the blood and debris out of their HUMVEEs. One MP who could speak and read Spanish was going through each row, searching the bodies for any papers or identifications. Personal items were left on the bodies after they were noted along with any identification papers. A video camcorder recorded each deceased as any identifying papers were read aloud or personal identifiers described. Only any information of military value was removed.

Colonel Paterson, accompanied by the two battalion commanders and the MP company commander, toured the farm. They found nothing that was of particular military value except the firing ranges. Colonel Paterson decided they weren't worth destroying. Perhaps the Mexican police or army could use this place as a future training ground, he decided.

"It gripes my ass that we don't have the leader of the operation."

"It might be that he wasn't in town, so to speak, Colonel," opined the MP Captain.

"Possibly, Captain, but I still don't like it. Run some of the prisoners who haven't left yet through the dead in the packing sheds. See if they can identify him among the dead. Get to it, Captain."

The Colonel and his party returned to Gonzalez's office. The Ranger Lieutenant Colonel commanding the Ranger Battalion decided to use the bathroom in the building to pee. In so doing, he noticed that the rug on the floor adjacent to the shower didn't scuff when he caught it with the toe of his boot. He gave it a kick. It didn't move. "Must be glued down," he thought. He looked at it again, curiously. He reached down to grab it but when he pulled on it, it was surprisingly heavy. He immediately unholstered his personal handgun in Kimber Classic .45 ACP, opened the bathroom window and called, "Soldier, in here on the double" to the nearest trooper. A PFC reported into him, saluting Colonel Paterson as he walked past.

"Trooper, I want you to take hold of that rug and pull it up when I give you the nod. Stand in the shower while you are doing it and pull it towards you." He took a Mini-Mag penlight out of his blouse pocket turned it on, pointed his .45 and the beam of light at the rug and nodded at the soldier. A trap door came up with the rug, revealing a tunnel.

"Colonel Paterson, I believe we have something of interest in here. Would you care to come and look?" he shouted over his shoulder, not taking his eyes off the tunnel entrance.

Colonel Paterson stepped around LTC Sharp and looked into the tunnel illuminated by the flashlight. "Well, I'll be damned, an escape hatch. Let's get somebody down there and see what we find. Where's that MP Captain? Let's see if he has any CS2 or flash-bang grenades. Soldier, find the MP company commander, tell him what we found, and what I want. Go to it."

Five minutes later, Captain Williamson appeared with three specialists, two gas masks, two CS2 grenades and two flash-bang grenades. He called down in Spanish for anyone there to surrender before they threw in the grenades. No answer. He nodded, and the MP Specialist tossed in a CS2 grenade and slammed shut the trap door. No sounds were forthcoming. The Specialist donned a gas mask, as did the second Specialist, who opened the door and threw down a flash-bang grenade and quickly closed the trap door. After it went off, both Specialists quickly entered the hole, armed with 9-millimeter Berettas and flashlights. After ten meters of tunnels, they came to a closed door. They banged on it with their handguns and called out in Spanish, "Come out, or we will dynamite the door." The door slowly opened and out came Jesus Gonzalez, hands on his head. One Specialist put a gun to his head, the other into his back, as they squeezed him past them in the narrow tunnel and pushed him towards the trap door. Jesus Gonzalez looked up into the smiling faces of Colonel Paterson, LTC Sharp and Captain Williamson.

CHAPTER 23

"When you're lying wounded on the Afghan plains,
And the women come out to cut up your remains,
Just roll to your rifle and blow out your brains
And go to your God like a soldier."

Rudyard Kipling

On a very early spring night in 2021, the specially trained Chinese mountain soldiers, wearing the traditional dress of a not too distant Pakistani Pushtun tribe of the Northwestern Frontier Province, spread out and moved quietly on the outskirts of a small Hindu village at the foot of the Panjal Range. Wherever they found peach, plum or apricot trees, they girdled it with saws so that it would die. While one squad, armed with submachine guns and grenades, formed a perimeter around one side of the village to cover their retreat, another stealthily moved into the village. Underneath their waistcoats, they carried Beretta semi-automatic nine-millimeter handguns with suppressors screwed on to the end of the extended barrels. It was 02:00 local time, and no villagers were awake. A few dogs barked but were quickly silenced by bullets in their heads from suppressor equipped pistols. As they came upon the cattle scattered throughout the village, they shot them in the head as well. One bullet was sufficient. They had practiced shooting cattle at the abattoir and had become thoroughly familiar with the anatomy of the bovine head. There, the heads were sectioned on a band saw after each cow was killed so that they would know the path of the bullet they fired, and how effective was their bullet placement.

Previous visits to this village by Chinese agents identified the most attractive young woman residing there. After they completed their mission of slaughtering cattle, they entered her house. The woman was held down with her mouth taped shut with duct tape and made to watch as her husband was beaten. Keeping their faces covered so that their race could not be determined, and speaking only Pashto, they beat her husband into semi-consciousness. Then his hands were tied behind his back and his feet at the ankles. His wife was then tied spread eagle to the bed. Over the next hour, the dozen men gang raped her and then beat her and left her tied and gagged so that she could not immediately raise an alarm. At dawn, the village discovered over fifty cattle slaughtered and left to rot in their yards, pens and streets. Several hours later, her husband managed to free himself and crawl through the door to seek medical help for his wife and himself. He could only describe the attackers by their waistcoats, turbans and language. Some authorities prefer the spelling and pronunciation of Pakhtun and Pakhtunwali to that of Pushtan or Pushtun.

Three weeks later, an old, heavily laden donkey was led alongside a mosque in Jabori. The mullah was calling to the faithful for evening prayers. The man tending the donkey poured a little grain on the ground along with a few pieces of vegetables, hobbled the donkey, and went around to the front of the mosque to join the others in prayer. Only, he didn't enter the mosque, but instead blended to the far side of the entering throng, then turned abruptly and walked away. One alley away, a man on horseback with a British Enfield .303 rifle slung over his shoulder held the reins of a second horse. The donkey man mounted it, and together they slowly rode for another three blocks. Reaching down into a saddle bag, the horseman removed a remote-controlled radio device. He flipped a switch, pointed the antenna at the mosque, and pushed a button. Seventy-five pounds of Simtex loaded on the donkey exploded. The wall of the mosque collapsed.

The rider replaced the radio back in the saddle bag, and the two riders casually trotted their horses away.

Over forty Muslims were killed in the blast; another hundred were injured to various degrees. Among the dead was the elder, the khan, of the Shinwari clan. The Pushtuns are a very proud people with a rich cultural heritage. Part of that cultural heritage is Pakhtunwali, or Way of the Pakhtuns. It is a code of the most demanding honor, of culture, of their society, of life, that is governed by three primary obligations. The most important of these obligations is revenge, known as badal. The others are melmastia and nanawati. Nanawati requires the Pakhtun to offer shelter and to protect, even at the cost of his own life, anyone in distress, even an enemy, who demands it. Melmastia requires the Pakhtun to feed and shelter anyone who comes to his home. Compared to that of revenge, the other two of hospitality and asylum pale to insignificance. Badal requires revenge for the slightest of insults or even a perceived insult, even if it requires a hundred years. Badal is usually extracted in blood and murder.

The district commissioner initiated an investigation. The provincial governor telephoned Islamabad, requesting more Pakistani soldiers to expand patrolling in the district. Fearing an escalation and more bloodshed, Islamabad promised an investigation team as well as more soldiers. Since there is a modest arms and accessories industry in the district, every civilian man is armed with at least a rifle and a blade of some nature. Provoking the Shinwari clan, a fierce and close-knit clan, vowing badal, guaranteed further violence. The only question for the Shinwalis was in which direction to unleash it.

Witnesses not attending the mosque described the two horsemen riding away. They were overheard conversing in Hindi. The horse holder looked and dressed like a Hindu. Neither man was recognized as being a local citizen. At the last sighting, they were observed approaching the line of control that separates India from Pakistan in the Kashmir.

Within the week, the track immediately in front of a trainload of Hindu pilgrims who were making their way up the mountain to a shrine was dynamited as the train rounded a curve at forty-five kilometers per hour. The momentum of the train carried each car along. The entire train plunged down the mountainside. Hundreds were killed, with hundreds more injured. Investigation led to the discovery of several pamphlets in Pashto at the site.

An Indian patrol was wiped out by mortar fire coming from the north. An Indian Chetak SA 319B helicopter, bringing supplies to an isolated mountain post on the Pakistani border, was shot down by a shoulder fired surface to air missile.

A mosque in the Northwest Frontier Province of Pakistan was obliterated by fire from a heavy mortar barrage as prayers were attended. Investigation revealed the firing site, along with scraps of pork sandwiches. Identification markings and language painted on the cases which contained the mortar rounds were found to be in Hindi and English.

When a Muslim woman is raped, she is considered defiled. Her life is ruined. No Muslim man will have her for a wife. She is condemned to a life of shame. One of the greatest insults is to impregnate a Muslim woman and force her to carry the baby of the infidel. So shamed, some Muslim women commit suicide. The Indian police and paramilitary police, mostly Hindi, inflicted extremes of rape and torture on Muslim separatists and Sikhs of all ages to repress the Sikh rebellion and to cower Muslim Kashmiri separatists. The Pushtuns and the Sikhs are among the most fierce, aggressive, and violent people in the world. They will remember an insult or a perceived wrong for one hundred years in order to honor badal.

The company-sized group of infiltrators was composed of irregulars but led by a Captain of the Indian Army who had intimate knowledge of the area. Most were members of the Border Security Force, a poorly disciplined but well equipped police force renowned for their barbarous behavior against Muslims. The captain was a devout Hindu, who believed the only answer to peace and Indian possession of Kashmir was total annihilation of the Muslim population. A few kilometers from the outpost where the Captain was assigned, they slipped across the Line of Control. Their objective was a small Muslim village along the Kishaganga River just west of Anzbari Mountain. They crossed at night, using donkeys to carry supplies, in itself quite a dangerous undertaking. Their intent was to kill the males of the village and rape all the females.

They invaded the village shortly after midnight. Initially, the homes were invaded one at a time. Knives were used to silence the men and children of both sexes as they slept. The women were bound and gagged to be left until the small village had been completely captured. Three fourths of the way through the village, a woman screamed which alerted the remainder of the village. Thereafter, automatic weapons came into play. The response of the raiders was immediate. All who stepped outside their homes were shot on sight. Grenades were tossed through doors and windows of the homes not yet violated. All means of electronic communication in the village were actively sought out and destroyed. With no telephones and radios, the village was completely isolated. Only the women survived. Girls as young as twelve were repeatedly raped. An hour before dawn, the raiders retreated along a different route, leaving over sixty dead villagers and a number of impregnated girls and women.

The Indian town of Tangmarg lies almost due west of Srinagar, India. Srinagar has a population of 500,000, almost exclusively Hindus. It is on the banks of a feeder stream to the Jhelum River in the Vale of Kashmir. It is perhaps forty kilometers, or twenty five miles, inside Indian territory from a modest salient in the Line of Control. The battalion of Pakistani Pushtuns took two days, traveling only at night and sleeping under camouflage covers during the day to reach the town. Each man carried nearly seventy pounds of ordnance and food. Each man carried either belts of machine gun ammunition, road mines, fifteen pounds of plastic explosive or two mortar rounds in addition to his basic load of hand grenades, ammunition, personal weapon, rain gear, sleeping bag, cooking gear or camouflage pup tent, and four days supply of food.

Three miles from the town, they bivouacked on the third day. A shepherd and his family were killed to ensure all would remain quiet. The battalion commander set his headquarters in the modest stone, mud and stick house of the shepherd family. At 22:00 on the third night, they infiltrated the town in the guise of civilians. Previous intelligence had identified the police stations, the mayor's home, the Indian army barracks, the telephone exchange and the power station. Posing as Hindu pilgrims, a number of individual Pakistani agents had made a thorough reconnaissance of the town. A platoon was assigned to annihilate each of the police stations, two companies to the army barracks, a squad to the mayor, one to the telephone exchange, and a squad to each Hindu priest and his family. At 01:00, all commenced in a coordinated attack. Civilians were killed on sight, indiscriminately. The signal section of the Indian Army detachment stationed there radioed part of a message that they were under attack before the hand grenades ripped him and the radio apart. By 04:00, several hundred people lay dead and wounded. The mayor, the priests and their families all murdered. The barracks, telephone exchange and power substation were blown to pieces. The battalion commander ordered a withdrawal.

Alerted by the partial message, a relieving battalion-sized force of the Indian Army was immediately ordered into trucks. Helicopter forces were informed at 04:30 of the attack and ordered to stand ready for an attack as soon as light permitted at 07:00. Traveling the road in the dark resulted in the convoy experiencing several accidents along the road. As they approached the town from the east, the second truck in the convoy exploded over a road mine. Fifty meters further, a second truck exploded. As the convoy entered the city and soldiers dismounted, they ran into tripwires connected to explosives. Pushing on through the town in pursuit as dawn emerged, the Indian commander noticed fresh diggings in the road. Ordering a halt in the column, he had mine detectors brought forward. After the first five holes were found to be empty, he started the convoy again. When a truck hit the tenth hole, it exploded in a ball of flame, killing all eighteen men on board. Seething in frustration, the Indian lieutenant colonel ordered each digging to be checked for a mine. As the lead truck rounded a curve on a hillside where the road showed no signs of being disturbed, the front bumper of the truck caught a monofilament tripwire. Five pounds of plastic explosive ignited, blowing the truck and its contents off the road and down into the stream.

At 08:00, the retreating Pushtun column was observed by the scout helicopter of the Indian helicopter force. The retreating Pushtuns were at the base of Mount Abharwat, 4143 meters above sea level. The scout helicopter circled above and a kilometer behind them while excitedly radioing their position. The Pushtuns were waiting for the attacking helicopters. As the attack helicopters swept low, Pushtun soldiers with portable surface to air shoulder fired missiles emerged from previously dug spider holes and from behind rock barricades. They launched a barrage that virtually swept the skies free of Indian attack aircraft. The troop-carrying helicopters of the aviation detachment swept in to rake the positions of the Pushtun archers with their door machine guns. More stinger missile men emerged from other hidden positions to engage the troop-carrying helicopters. At only three hundred feet off the ground, the helicopters could not avoid the missiles. Four more were shot down. The remaining helicopters retreated to a kilometer away to discharge their squads who advanced on foot.

Having expended most of their ordnance, the Pushtuns, now with much less burden, made better time, although fatigue was beginning to set in.

Upon receiving word of the loss of most of his aircraft, the Indian Major General commanding the division at Srinagar notified the Chaklala airbase and requested an aerial strike upon the retreating Pushtuns. Calling the Indian High Command, authorization was granted in fifteen minutes. A flight of four Jaguars, configured for ground attack, took off. Pakistani radar quickly picked up the four aircraft as they rose above two thousand feet. Informed by radio of incoming jet aircraft, the Pakistani lieutenant colonel ordered immediate dispersal of his command, with the remaining shoulder fired missiles to be ready to respond within minutes. In ten minutes, they were over the target. As the lead aircraft passed, a heat seeking shoulder fired missile streaked from the ground and went directly into its engine. The aircraft exploded immediately, sending flying parts over several hundred square meters. The following second and third aircraft delivered Geneva Convention-outlawed 200-kilogram napalm bombs that seared the broad defile. Many of the Pushtuns died a horrific death. Those who made it up more than five hundred meters above the valley floor of the defile survived.

Suddenly, breaking over the mountain ridge, a flight of four F-16A3 Fighting Falcons of the Pakistani Air Force appeared. In a no-contest aerial battle, the remaining three Jaguars went down in flames in seconds. Waving their wings to the few survivors below, the Falcons streaked back to their air base. Artillery fires from just inside the Line of Control covered the remainder of the retreat of the Pushtun battalion. When the Pushtuns crested the mountain ridge, the Indian soldiers broke off the pursuit.

Word of the raid, its aftermath and the loss of so many aircraft infuriated the Indian Prime Minister and his cabinet. Previous battles in the last several decades had occasionally escalated to division-sized engagements, but now India was much stronger in all respects than Pakistan. The Indian Ministry of Defense wanted to immediately retaliate. The Prime Minister refused, with the concept he would take the problem, once again, to the United Nations. Details were sent to the Indian delegation to the UN. Two days later, India called for condemnation of Pakistan for the repeated raids, and especially the fiasco of Tangmarg. As usual, the United Nations General Assembly listened politely to both sides and did nothing.

The Indian Ministry of Defense, seething at this last military insult, quietly discussed a general onslaught of Muslims in Kashmir. The concept of pushing several hundred thousand Muslims out of Kashmir and into Pakistan had considerable merit. The refugees would create a calamity for Pakistan. The sixteen-hundred-kilometer border between the two countries, running from Kashmir to the Arabian Sea, cannot be defended by Pakistan.

The Indian Prime Minister, bitterly disappointed in the United Nation's lack of response, called a meeting of the Union Executive, which consists of the President, the Vice President, and the Council of Ministers, which is chaired by the Prime Minister. The Council of Ministers is composed of the Prime Minister, Cabinet Ministers, the Ministers of the various states and deputy ministers. On this particular occasion, the Service Chiefs of Staff and the political affairs committee of the cabinet attended.

"In view of the debacle we have recently suffered regarding Tanmarg, and the failure of the United Nations to take no action whatsoever, I wish to discuss our options to see that such a raid does not occur again. With the audacity to attack a town so close to one of Kashmir's major cities, having over 500,000 population, Brahma only knows what the Pakistanis will next attempt. So, gentlemen, let me hear your opinions, starting with you, Minister of Defense Sivaji."

"We have a number of options, Prime Minister. For one, we can exchange them tit for tat in conventional raids. I cannot predict where such an exchange of blows will end. Second, we can declare all-out conventional war. Pakistan's response will quite likely be a nuclear attack on our forces, government, and cities. Third, we can initiate nuclear war by striking first with small nuclear bombs that will take out their nuclear capabilities with a reasonable chance of success. Fourth, we can initiate a major attack limited to Kashmir with the objective of terrorizing the Muslims and forcing them out. In past episodes, Pakistan activated their nuclear forces under such circumstances, but of course, things were always calmed down by outside pressures before any nuclear exchange occurred. Naturally, we would have to have a full alert all along our mutual border. Pakistan is so weak in all areas relative to us that they have little option to being defeated under conventional means. That means they will have to go nuclear to have a creditable response to any significant attack we mount. Fifth, we can go to general quarters all round, that is, full alert and deployment along our border to see what their response is; a bluff, as they would say in American western movies. Pakistan would probably view this as the intent to launch an all-out attack on them. This would give them the excuse for a pre-emptive attack on us. Sixth, we can do nothing. Pakistan is very, very shaky indeed."

"What other options are available? Does anyone else have any other thoughts they would care to express? Certainly, everything should be considered and nothing dismissed outright."

No one said a word. The enmity between Pakistan and India, Muslim and Hindu, Sikh and Pushtun, had grown too strong.

"Very well, then. Of the options Defense Minister Sivaji outlined, the last is too bitter to contemplate. This was a raid of sufficient magnitude that it cannot be ignored. The public is clamoring for retaliation as I have never heard before. The Bharatiya Janata Party is demanding the resignation of myself and this Cabinet. The people seem to be in favor of it if we do not respond. Of the other options, I question how much outside help can Pakistan receive, and from whom. Will other Muslim nations come to their aid? Will the United States assist them in any way? The United States has armed them to a considerable degree in the past. After supporting Pakistan for several years, only to find that Osama bin Laden and the Taliban core cadre were being protected in a mountain redoubt, the United States most likely feels duped and humiliated. Certainly, Russia will not provide aid to Pakistan. Given the difficulties they have had over Chechnya, and the cross-border raids from the Islamic Central Asian states, I am confident they would like to see Islam crushed. That only leaves China, in my opinion, which might provide some assistance to Pakistan. If so, how much and in what form will China provide aid? How concerned is China right now with the situation in Korea? The North Koreans have been severely bloodied and are retreating. Pyongyang is now in the hands of the South, and it appears that in spite of the nuclear exchanges, a united Korea ruled from Seoul seems to be the ultimate outcome.

"What are your opinions, gentlemen? Minister of State, what say you?"

"Mr. Prime Minister, Pakistan is acting in a most arrogant way. Is it a bluff, an attempt to provoke us into war? Are they acting according to Sun Tzu, 'When you are weak, appear strong'? I do not know for certain. They can be attempting to hide insecurity, but I doubt it. As serious as this raid was, I don't believe they would undertake anything that would lead to war unless they were assured of considerable outside support. As you suggest, I see that only China could or would provide such support, but I very seriously doubt that the Chinese are that stupid. The Chinese, I am sure, understand just how fragile and weak Pakistan is. Our agents continue to report on the large number of Chinese businessmen and advisors there. They should know Pakistan. I don't think they would want to back a loser. Why should they pour resources down a black hole? How will they provide massive support? Whose territory would they cross? Tajikistan? I don't think so. No, I think Pakistan will have to go it alone if war breaks out. My conclusion, therefore, is that this was a massive raid to tweak our nose, demonstrate their capabilities, and show the world that they are something of a regional power. Perceptions are sometimes more important than reality. In the final analysis, however, I believe they will back down rather than commit to a war they cannot win."

"Minister of Justice, what are legalities here?"

"Constitutionally, we should have a Declaration of War from both Houses of Parliament, of the House of the People and the Council of States. Certainly, even calling a closed meeting of Parliament under the circumstance would destroy any chance of surprise."

"Chiefs of Staff, what do you feel is militarily possible? Let me establish a parameter. We will not be the instigators of nuclear war. While we might suffer the first atomic blast in anger since World War II, we will not initiate it. If Pakistan unleashes a nuclear device, we will launch a complete and catastrophic attack upon Pakistan, with both conventional and nuclear forces. In that circumstance, our objectives are to first destroy all their nuclear capabilities, followed by destruction of all their armed forces, and third, annihilation of their political leadership."

The Service Chiefs looked at each other and nodded, already having reached mutual agreement. The Chairman spoke. "Mr. Prime Minister, we can, and will, do whatever you and the Executive Union decide. We can militarily defeat anything the Pakistanis can mount. It is only the political fallout that is a concern, and that is something with which you must deal."

"Given the optimism of our military establishment then, our option will be the conventional invasion of Kashmir. We will drive the Muslims out and seize control of the headwaters of the major river systems originating there. Jammu and Kashmir belong to India. We will settle this question once and for all. Minister Sivaji, put all our defense forces on maximum alert, but did not move them to the border below Kashmir. We will not give them the impression that an all-out invasion is under way. If you wish to move them to martialling areas from which you can launch an all-out attack according to previous planning, all well and good, but hold them in those areas. Pakistan will be hard pressed to defend a 1600-kilometer border with us. Have our nuclear forces prepared, however, to launch immediate retaliatory strikes at the first indication of a nuclear assault upon any of our forces or territory. Your targets, of course, are their major force deployments, their command and control nodes, their governmental leadership, their weapons depots and their industrial centers. While we will not be concerned with Islamic civilian casualties, all of our weapons will be of small yield for the sake of precision. Who knows, if nuclear war develops, perhaps what is left of Pakistan will once again be united with India."

CHAPTER 24

"Vassily, it's Jason Thornton here. I trust you are aware of the Indian mobilization in the Kashmir region."

"Yes, Jason, we are closely monitoring the situation. It is of grave concern to us. If it goes nuclear, we are very much concerned about where the fallout will settle and about the refugee problem it will create. It is quite possible that it will create a domino effect. Kashmiris will flee to Pakistan; Pakistanis will flee to Tajikistan and Afghanistan. Those countries cannot support them and will quite possibly pass them on to other Central Asian states. While still a long way away from our southern border, they have the potential for tremendous turmoil and possibly violence. Who will feed them?"

"Yes, Vassily, I must agree with that. The world's food supply, or at the moment, its distribution, is sufficiently in jeopardy as it is. With displaced peoples, the pressure on that supply only increases. That is not the most hospitable region of the world, either. Winters, I understand, can be very harsh, and potable water will be a major problem."

"This time of year, the winds blow from the south, off the Arabian Sea. The Indian monsoons will continue into September. If there is much fallout, millions of square miles can be contaminated, depending upon the yield of the weapons used, the height of the burst, how the nuclear devices are tailored for effect, and the nature of the terrain in which they are detonated. Now, that will change in several weeks, but who knows if they will restrain the nuclear genie for that long?"

"Are you taking any precautions at this time, Vassily? Are you ordering an alert of your military or something, or giving out iodine tablets or anything at all?"

"No, Jason, at the moment we are very uneasy, but doing nothing more than monitoring the situation. Have you made any decisions? Will you commit to any peace process, arm twisting, as you call it? You still have some influence with Pakistan, I take it?"

"No, Vassily, we have not initiated any action at this time. As you, we are closely monitoring the situation. We find it most disturbing, but it does not directly impact upon us, at least not at this time. Your point about the winds carrying fallout, though, is appropriate. We recall the Chernobyl accident you experienced some years ago, and how the winds carried some of it across the Pacific. All of our satellites are not back in order, but we do have aircraft offshore observing and listening. But no, we have not committed to anything. I will certainly inform you of any proposed action before we initiate it. After all, that is your back yard."

"Russia will do the same. We will inform you of any steps which we might take. It has been pleasant speaking with you, Mr. President. Russia sends her best. Thank you."

President Thornton punched his intercom button, "Peggy, get me Secretary Talbott on the phone, please. Thanks."

A few minutes later, Marge Talbott was on the line. "Marge, I want you to have a runner send over the files on our ambassador to Pakistan, and on the Pakistani ambassador to us. Pick someone who knows both men to come over tomorrow. Peggy will set up the appointment. I want to get a feel for them. Then I want to meet the Pakistani ambassador in a day or two. Please keep me up to date on anything you hear on what's going on with Pakistan and India."

"Yes, Mr. President. I'll have the files there within the hour. I'll have to feel around to see who knows both men. That might take me a while, but I'll get right on it. I'll call Peggy when I have something set up."

"Thanks, Marge. Talk to you later."

Punching his intercom button, "Peggy, have Johnny get me a map showing India, Pakistan and that region of the world. I want to look at the geography." Johnny Withers, sitting in Peggy's office, heard the word, waved to Peggy, and went to the White House library. He was back with the maps in ten minutes. Jason Thornton studied the map with a magnifying glass, concentrating on Kashmir. The requested files arrived within the hour. After he read them, Jason Thornton set them aside, and his concern increased.

At 16:00 that day, a middle-aged bureaucrat who had served as an assistant to the Ambassador to Pakistan six years ago stood before President Thornton.

"Yes, Mr. President, I know both our current ambassador to Pakistan and the Pakistani ambassador. Both are quite knowledgeable and suave individuals. What can I tell you about them?"

"Thank you for coming, Mr. Tremble. How is it that you know both men?"

"I was the Science and Business Attaché to Pakistan from 2004 to 2008. As such, I dealt a lot with the business and scientific communities of Pakistan. I had frequent contact with Mr. Perchay, Pakistan's current ambassador to us. I met him frequently both informally and formally. He was educated at Princeton where he earned a master's degree in physics. After that, he went to Wharton School of Economics to study management. He was always trying to entice American business to invest in Pakistan. He is a very intelligent and shrewd individual, Mr. President. He bears watching.

"I know our current ambassador to Pakistan less well than I do Ambassador Perchay. After our invasion of Afghanistan, he studied Pashto at the Department of Defense Language School at Monterey, California. He already spoke fluent Farsi, which impressed me. He came to Pakistan in 2007, so we had a year overlap. When I left in 2008, he went to Pakistan as the Deputy Ambassador because of his linguistic abilities. After our ambassador there retired in 2010, he was promoted into the position. He, too, is extremely ambitious. He is also very smart."

"I want to get a feel for the potential for Pakistan to go to war over Kashmir. As you know, there is an exchange of gunfire going on as we speak. I am concerned that Pakistan might go nuclear because of the overwhelming superiority of India. How can our ambassador to Pakistan best convey our concerns? I want absolutely no miscommunications here. Secondly, I am going to invite the Pakistani Ambassador to meet with me in the next day or so. Since you know him, I would like to have you present. Are you good at reading body language? Can you interpret between the lines of what he says for me? That is what I am asking."

"Yes, Mr. President. I would be delighted to be present. I will do my best to 'read' what Ambassador Perchay is saying, or perhaps not saying. We had numerous meetings, both formally and socially, so I know him rather well. While I have never considered myself an expert at reading body language, I will do my best. As regards to our own Ambassador Brown, he will have no difficulty in conveying your precise meaning to the Pakistani government, Mr. President. I have long felt that Pakistan and India would ultimately come to nuclear blows over Kashmir."

"Why, Mr. Tremble, do you think it will be nuclear war over Kashmir?"

"Mr. President, Jammu and Kashmir has been the fire hot emotional push-button issue between India and Pakistan since they separated in 1948 to become the Muslim state of Pakistan and the Hindu state of India. The west simply cannot appreciate the intensity of the emotional attachment of both sides over who controls Jammu and Kashmir. The emotional aspect is every bit as important as the population, perhaps the paramount issue. Jammu and Kashmir controls, or perhaps I should say, contains, much of the sources of water for South Asia. Who controls the area literally has control over south central Asia. They are willing to deploy nuclear fires on each other over who owns the Siachen Glacier. It is not inaccurate to say the area is intensely thirsty. The religious intolerance between the Hindus of India and the Muslims of Pakistan is equally contentious."

"Mr. Tremble, if it goes nuclear, who, in your opinion, will launch the first bomb?"

"I am confident that the answer to that, Mr. President, is Pakistan. That is because they will feel severely threatened and have no option but to launch a first strike. Their first targets, naturally, will be the Indian nuclear-capable units and sites, followed by their conventional military forces."

"Anything else you would like to add, Mr. Tremble?"

"No, Mr. President, unless there is something specific you would like to ask?"

"Thank you very much for coming. Please leave all of your phone numbers with my secretary, Peggy, so she can get ahold of you to set up the meeting with Ambassador Perchay, Secretary Talbott, and myself."

At 14:00 the following day, President Thornton welcomed Ambassador Perchay, Secretary Talbott and Mr. Tremble into his office.

"Mr. Ambassador, can I offer you a cup of tea, or perhaps something else?"

With a very gracious smile, "Yes, thank you, Mr. President. That would be lovely. It is nice to meet with Mr. Tremble again. I am sure he has told you that we had many pleasant and interesting meetings when he was in Pakistan. It is also nice to meet you again, Mr. President. I certainly enjoyed myself at your ambassadorial ball."

Tremble was right, thought Thornton. *He is a smooth son-of-a-bitch!*

Johnny Withers and a waiter brought in a tea service and served everyone while Mssrs. Tremble and Perchay conducted small talk, asking and informing each other of what had transpired with them since their last meeting. After Withers and the waiter left the room, President Thornton spoke. "I'm sure you know why I invited you here, Mr. Ambassador. We are greatly concerned over the hostilities between Pakistan and India in Kashmir. We certainly hope it will not expand and most definitely would like to see such hostilities cease. Can you tell us how this will play out?"

"Mr. President, Pakistan absolutely has no wish to go to war with India or anyone else. We certainly cannot match India in any strategic category. For us to go to war would be the utmost folly. No, we will do almost anything to avoid such a conflict."

"How then, Mr. Ambassador, will this current hostility end?"

"Mr. President, I cannot predict it, but if we, Pakistan, can, we will end it today. All we ask is that we be left in peace. These raids by Hindus into our territory and their persecution of Muslims in Jammu and Kashmir must cease. We will do nothing more than is needed to protect our people and our territory."

"Will your nation and India ever peacefully settle the question of boundaries in the region?"

"Frankly, Mr. President, that is too much to ask for. No, I see us being at odds over this issue until some great power which can exert absolute control over both of us forces the settlement. I see no great power in our region which can do that. Perhaps in the next century, if a one-world government comes into being, with sufficient military power to enforce its will, a settlement might be imposed. We are as bad as the Jews of Israel and the Palestinians in this."

"Will Pakistan use nuclear weapons if a full-scale war erupts, Mr. Ambassador?"

"Heavens no, Mr. President! Pakistan will never be the first to, as you Americans say, 'let the nuclear genie out of the bottle' in our region. We completely agree with America on that issue. With the nuclear devices detonated on the Korean peninsula and the destruction they have wrought, what we see in Korea is certainly a lesson for all of us. Unfortunately, their use could potentially become widespread, especially since technology has allowed the development of much smaller, tactical nuclear weapons as we have seen deployed."

"And does Pakistan have such small, tactical nuclear weapons, Mr. Ambassador?"

"Our weapons are few in number and crude, Mr. President. For us to use nuclear weapons against such a powerful foe as India would surely result in our total destruction. No, the best we can hope for, should war come, is a stalemate in conventional warfare. Barring that, we hope the conquerors will be generous in their victory and our defeat. We do not wish to cease to exist as a nation."

What the ambassador was thinking was, *You have no idea with what and how our friends, the Chinese, have supplied us. They will come to our aid as they promised to eliminate the common enemy. India will be beaten back into the age of the Mughals.* Ambassador Perchay did not know just how very well China had supplied them. Only General Chang and his staff knew.

Ambassador Perchay smiled and set down his teacup. He thought to himself, *Straight from the hip, up front and direct. No political nuances here. This old boy must be a Texas cowboy at heart.* Instead, he said, "Mr.

President, I am sure your CIA operatives have informed you of every move Pakistan makes in the nuclear weapons field. You know the size and location of every nuclear device in our arsenal, its status, its design and how it will be deployed, if it ever is. I must add that they will be deployed only in defense of our territory. Only to save ourselves from being overrun will such weapons come into use. We know full well that India would respond in kind, and that they have many more, and theirs are better developed than ours."

Thornton smiled. "Mr. Ambassador, I only wish our CIA was as effective as you credit it to be. Let us hope that Pakistan and its neighbor quickly and quietly settle the current unpleasantness before it gets out of hand. If the United States can be of any service, as a negotiator, arbiter, or go-between, we will most certainly and gladly do so."

"Mr. President, I thank you for your kind offer on behalf of my country. I will immediately convey your concerns and offer to Islamabad. If there is any opportunity to settle the current distress amicably, Pakistan will assuredly do so."

"Thank you for coming, Mr. Ambassador."

"The pleasure is all mine, Mr. President. I have enjoyed the opportunity to see my old friend, Mr. Tremble. Good day to you all." With that, Ambassador Perchay was escorted out of the room by Johnny Withers.

"Well, Mr. Tremble, what do you read of your 'old friend?'"

"He either has the best façade I have ever seen, or he is overconfident, Mr. President. Either he is holding an ace or two he thinks we don't know about or he is confident that the matter will soon be over."

"What kind of aces do you think Pakistan might be holding, Mr. Tremble?"

"If the Pakistanis are as farsighted as I consider them, their intelligence service might have already planted nuclear devices in a number of strategic locations within India. Of course, the same holds true for India planting them in Pakistan. Or, they might have other weapons of mass destruction, such as biologicals, about which I have no information; or peace talks might already be under way; or Pakistan might have something up its sleeve that we have no knowledge or even guessed about. Don't ask me what."

"Marge, what is your reading on all this?"

"Mr. President, I haven't any. I don't know what to make of Mr. Perchay other than he is extremely charming. I don't have information from my folks on their weaponry. I sent a secret telex two hours ago to Ambassador Brown for an update but haven't received a response."

"Mr. Tremble, you are the voice of experience here, what is your gut feeling?"

"I don't like it, Mr. President. I don't like it at all. It scares me."

Thornton scratched his bald spot, sighed, and said, "Thanks to both of you for coming."

———————•◦◆◦•———————

Indian forces began to martial from twenty to fifty miles behind the Pakistani border. Armored and mounted infantry regiments martialled twenty-five kilometers inside the Great Indian Desert. Should general war be declared, four heavy divisions had as their axis of advance a drive through Moro and Dadu to cross the Indus River and on to Sonmiana Bay with the objective of cutting off the rectangular area that contains Karachi.

Indian brigades of mountain infantry loaded in trucks began to advance out of Srinagar. Trained for infantry operations at high altitude and in intense cold, they moved towards the Line of Control. Mountain infantry, some with pack animals, crossed the Line of Control in Kashmir and initiated combat with Pakistani outposts. The little village of Chakoti, on the apex of a salient, was the first to feel the weight of the Indian attack.

Pakistan responded with an intense artillery barrage against invading Indian units. Man-portable trajectory plotting radars identified the location of the Pakistani batteries, revealing some in new positions. Within minutes, Indian Mig-24Ds, purchased from Russia in the opening years of the new century, placed improved conventional munitions on the firing batteries, followed by Geneva Convention-outlawed two-hundred-kilogram napalm bombs to ensure their complete destruction. Twenty minutes after the Mig-24Ds departed, Pakistani FC-1 Dragons attacked the Indian infantry with napalm. The losses on both sides were substantial. Several companies of Indian infantry and two batteries of Pakistani artillery were lost. Most died of burns.

Twenty-four hours later, car bombs loaded with explosives went off outside government buildings in a dozen Indian cities. Each car was packed with a thousand pounds of dynamite and did considerable damage. They were detonated by remote control in periods of rush hour traffic to maximize casualties. News of the bombings dominated television networks throughout the world, but especially in India.

Forty-eight hours later, similar car bombs were detonated in Karachi, Multan, Bahawalpur, Sukkur, and Shikarpur, Pakistan. Civilian casualties were again very heavy.

Pakistan, already on yellow alert, ordered general mobilization. Four hours later, a Chinese agent received a seemingly innocuous signal in the guise of a radio commercial played for the first time on a particular station. Located near the center of the city, the timer was set for a four-hour delay to give the agent sufficient time to escape. When he threw the switch to turn the timer on, the explosion was instantaneous. A five-kiloton weapon detonated, destroying most of Sargodha, Pakistan. A second blast of similar size destroyed Mardan, Pakistan a few minutes later.

The explosions were reported to the Indian Prime Minister in New Dehli within minutes. He immediately called the Minister of Defense Sivaji, who denied all knowledge of the origins of the explosions. Sivaji denied having given any such order, nor to his knowledge, had any of the Indian military commanders. Nuclear weapons had not been released from their arsenals.

"Call together the Cabinet, immediately," he ordered his secretary. "We must avert nuclear war. We will meet in the shielded bunker." His next call was to Islamabad, to the leader of the junta.

"General, I understand that two nuclear detonations occurred just minutes ago in your country. Did you have nuclear accidents? I want to assure you that India had nothing to do with such disasters!"

"Prime Minister, we have had no nuclear accidents. We did not have any nuclear devices of any nature anywhere near either Sargodha or Mardan. Surely you do not think we are naive enough to believe this is not the handiwork of India? Since no aircraft or missiles were observed entering our country, you must have had agents in our midst who planted the bombs."

"General, most assuredly, India had nothing to do with these explosions. I have no explanation for them. Our objective was to push Muslims out of Kashmir with conventional forces. We have no wish to engage in nuclear war. The world has already seen far too many nuclear bombs. Both of our countries are already in jeopardy from such explosions. We cannot afford any more catastrophes. In such a circumstance, there are no winners, only losers."

"In that, I agree with you, Mr. Prime Minister. If Pakistan will cease to exist, so will India as you know it." With that, the line went dead.

Before the Cabinet members arrived, Pakistan launched six intermediate range ballistic missiles and a dozen short range ballistic missiles. Their flight times to their targets varied from five to fifteen minutes. Indian AWACS and other monitoring systems observed their launch. The warning simultaneously went out to New Dehli and various military installations. Among them were all the bases which housed nuclear weapons. Judging from the early stages of their trajectories, the AWACS crew predicted the targets were Bangalore, Nagpur, Ahmadabad, Madras, Kanpur, and Kota. The smallest weapon detonated was twenty kilotons, the largest, fifty kilotons. None were particularly clean weapons, and most were detonated three hundred meters above the surface of their respective targets to maximize the effects of heat, blast and radiation. Little attention was given to the effects of their electromagnetic pulse, or EMP, which magnetizes motors, overloads some electrical equipment and computer circuits and thus destroys virtually all communications equipment which was in operation.

One minute after the multiple Pakistani launch, Indian electronic warfare officers whose equipment still functioned picked up a communication sent in the clear to all Pakistani units that nuclear war had been initiated. The message read, "Nuclear war has been initiated. All forces, conventional and special units alike, are to fight independently for as long as possible. Your objective is the destruction of any and all things Indian."

When the message was read by the Indian Prime Minister, he sat down at his desk and put his hands on his head. He knew the outcome. He picked up the phone and called Minister of Defense Sivaji. When Sivaji answered, he simply said, "Do what you must to save India," and hung up.

By previous secret mutual aid treaty, China agreed to come to the aid of Pakistan if war with India should break out. China willingly filled the void left by the retreating Americans. The previous administration of the United States called it disengagement due to corruption, military dominance over the entire society and culture, concern over human rights, and continued surreptitious support for Islamic extremists in both Pakistan and Afghanistan. In terms of the treaty, China agreed to respond with tactical nuclear weapons aimed at agreed upon designated targets in India if India initially deployed nuclear weapons against Pakistan, thus opening a two-front war for India. The devastation of the new nuclear war was expected to be horrific. It exceeded all expectations.

Ten minutes after the Pakistani message declaring all-out war was broadcast, a one megaton hydrogen bomb was detonated in Islamabad. For all practical purposes, this blast destroyed the government of Pakistan. There was no escape for most of the citizens of Islamabad. The blast affected both Pakistani and Indian troops and civilians alike in Jammu and Kashmir. The searing heat melted parts of many of the glaciers in the region. Troops of both countries saw the tremendous mushroom cloud, felt the heat and the tremendous machstem winds, exceeding two thousand miles per hour. All knowledgeable people knew what it meant, most of all, the Prime Minister of India. Now, there was no one left with whom to negotiate a truce. Pakistani missiles from various sites, including some mobile launchers, launched as soon as they were ready. All had pre-determined targets. Most had independent inertial guidance systems. They carried intermediate sized warheads, mostly in the ten to-fifteen kiloton range. Most were aimed at Indian cities. New Dehli, Bombay, Kakinda, Mysore, Haora, Calcutta and a score of others were all attacked. Over the next two hours, over thirty nuclear tipped missiles were exchanged. A few weapons of similar size were delivered by aircraft. Pakistan had far more nuclear weapons than anyone had surmised. Much of the Indian communications network was destroyed within the first four hours. Consequently, nuclear equipped forces on both sides continued to fire at pre-designated targets until they had no nuclear fires left to deliver.

By nightfall, it was as if Pakistan had been plunged back into the twelfth century. India suffered tremendous destruction in many of its major cities and ports. The mountainous areas were spared from the immediate effects of blast and heat more than the plains. The skies were darkened for the next six days as millions of tons of earth were sucked upwards and slowly returned to earth as radioactive dust particles. Alpha radiation was overwhelming, as none of the weapons were particularly "clean." Dose-dependent deaths from radiation poisoning began in twenty-four hours and continued into the ensuing months. Floods washed away many small villages along riverbanks throughout the area as a result of the melting of glacial ice feeding some of the largest rivers in the world. The Monsoon winds and rains carried lesser amounts of fallout into Afghanistan, Turkmenistan, Uzbekistan and Kazakhstan. Surface waters, livestock and crops were contaminated by the falling radioactive dust particles. Livestock and people suffered subsequent radiation poisoning from handling and consuming contaminated crops and forage. With depressed immune systems damaged by radiation, many began to weaken and die from infections which otherwise would have been inconsequential. Bacterial meningitis alone killed tens of thousands. Skin infections became life threatening and resulted in septicemia, or blood poisoning. Common colds resulted in fatal pneumonias. Bodies generally lay where they fell. Those still alive were too sick to gather and bury the dead.

Two weeks later, elements of the Chinese Second Army Front moved across the fifty-mile border with Jammu and Kashmir. The Chinese built north-south road across Aksai Chin proved its strategic value. Farther south, Chinese HIV battalions moved all along the border.

———————————•◦•●•◦•———————————

The Mexican prisoners were herded into a tent city surrounded by a twelve-foot cyclone fence topped with razor wire. A ten-meter fire zone of bare, plowed ground separated the cyclone fence and coils of intertwined razor and barbed wire. Sensors were at each corner that detected motion and sound. Laser beams oscillated between various heights every few seconds that would ensure no one could cross them without breaking the light beam. Low guard towers with a spotlight on a swivel were manned by two soldiers, each armed with a machine gun and a rifle.

Many of the prisoners' hands were blue from lack of circulation. Their restraints had been removed once, when they were allowed one stop to relieve themselves, drink water, and then were re-cuffed with plastic ties and placed back on the trucks for an otherwise nonstop drive to their new home in a desert corner of Fort Bliss, far away from prying eyes.

President Thornton didn't get the phone call from President of Mexico Enrico Bustamante until almost twenty-four hours after the raid.

"Good morning, Enrico. I know you are upset with me, but go ahead anyway," Jason Thornton could hardly keep from laughing out loud.

"Mr. President, how dare you invade my country! What have you done? You have killed many poor people, merely farm hands trying to make a living growing vegetables and beef to sell to your country. How could you do this? Don't you realize the implications of this outrageous behavior? The United Nations will hear of this on the floor of the General Assembly tomorrow."

"Of course they will, Enrico. We expect no less. On the other hand, we have collected quite an assemblage of weapons, of explosives, of personal effects of American victims of their raids, more than a million dollars in cash, and some very interesting documents. We are quite prepared to explain our side of the equation on the floor of the General Assembly. I regret that we couldn't involve your government, but we gave security our highest priority. For that, you have my most sincere apology."

"You have kidnapped over a hundred Mexican citizens. What have you done with them? Where are they being held? I demand that you return them immediately!"

"Nonsense, Enrico. They will stand trial for murder, rape, and robbery under the charge of brigandage. I understand that some of them are already talking. It is really amazing the things they are saying. They will have a speedy trial here. We are going to put them on trial, and we will hang them if they are found guilty. I assure you that they will have the legal guarantees that apply to them. I think it will be the same ones that apply to piracy on the high seas. I really don't give a damn what the international lawyers say about the legality of this raid. After all, Poncho Villa set the stage, followed by our Blackjack Pershing. We will not return them to Mexico where they will serve only a few years of incarceration, if any at all, only to be turned loose to extract vengeance on anyone. As we speak, they are being photographed, fingerprinted, and blood samples drawn. We will do DNA matching on the rape cases and circulate their photographs to all of the citizens of the towns that were raided for individual identification. Should any of them not be convicted, they will be returned to Mexico. You had the opportunity to put an end to this, and you did not. You had months to do it. We gave you specific information, and you refused to act. You have no one to blame but yourself and your government, Enrico. You forced us to conduct this raid. We will make public the dates, locations, testimonials, recordings of phone calls and so on for the benefit of the circus that is the United Nations. You can rest assured, you will have egg on your face on the international scene if you go public, Enrico."

"No country in the world is safe from United States imperialism! What gives the United States the right to play judge and jury and to invade other nations? Who do you think you are?"

"The right to defend our citizens against Mexicans raiding on American soil gives us that right. Tell you what, Enrico. Why don't you ask the Chinese ambassador to Mexico those very same questions? Ask them why they are invading India as we speak. Why are they pouring down the Malayan peninsula? Please inform me as to what his response is? I don't hear you, Enrico? Are you there?" The line went dead.

Jesus Gonzalez was taken to a hidden remote location that was kept secret. His operations files and paperwork were thoroughly scrutinized. Spanish speaking attorneys were recruited and sworn to secrecy until relief would be granted by the U.S. Attorney General, the Honorable Hugh Collier.

True to his word, two days later, the Mexican ambassador to the United Nations delivered a scathing attack on the United States for raiding into the sovereign state of Mexico. It lasted for over an hour. The United States representative blithely listened to the Mexican representative while he called for censure of the United States.

When called upon the U.S. Representative, Ms. Susan Turner admitted without hesitation that the United States did, indeed, conduct a raid three days previously into Mexico to end a threat of future raids and to bring to justice those guilty of previous raids. She produced pictures of the arms and explosives, the rocket propelled grenades, the rifle range and training grounds, personal valuables taken from American citizens during previous raids, facsimiles of telexes with the President of Mexico, copies of phone calls between the Presidents of the respective countries discussing it, vehicles involved in the raids, and lastly, some early testimonials in the form of affidavits of the participants. Her closing words were "The United States makes no apology for conducting this raid into Mexico in order to prevent future raids and bring these criminals to justice."

The General Assembly voted overwhelmingly to condemn the United States.

Susan Turner rose and said, "Mr. Speakers, delegates, I ask you why you censor the United States for conducting what is merely a tactical raid into the soil of a neighboring country, while China invades numerous neighboring countries at the cost of millions of lives, and nuclear detonations have occurred over the Asian subcontinent. This body is the greatest collection of hypocrites in the history of civilization." With that, she turned and walked out of the United Nations.

The next morning, Jason Thornton called the General Secretary of the United Nations. "Mr. Secretary, we are withdrawing from the United Nations, based upon the General Assembly's actions yesterday. As a result, the United Nations as an organization is no longer welcome in the United States. Since we have historically paid a minimum of twenty-five percent of the UN budget, provided you with office space on premium real estate, you will very shortly be handed a formal letter telling you that you and your organization are no longer welcome on United States soil. Thirty days hence, we will close the United Nations building. We built it, we maintain it, it is on our soil, and we own it. You have until then to find somewhere else to conduct your meetings. Perhaps your home state of Libya will provide your organization with appropriate support."

"I must protest, Mr. President. There is no way we can move such an organization in so short a time. Literally tens of thousands of personnel are involved, records, computer networks, communications equipment, furniture, everything will have to be moved. It will take years to move."

"Mr. Secretary, in thirty days we will revoke the privileges and status of every member of the United Nations. Their passports and exemption from our laws will be revoked. It will be our choice as to who goes and who stays and when. Frankly, I don't care where your organization goes as long as it is not on United States soil. I have already ordered, as of 09:00 this morning, to freeze all payments to all branches and sub-organizations of the United Nations. So far as the United States is concerned, the United Nations is no longer a legal entity in this country. Unless some of your delegates want to spend a little time being interrogated by the FBI about their activities, they will leave very quickly."

"Mr. President, I must protest, this is impossible."

"You can protest all you wish, but it is to no avail. There is no further need of discussion. Get up and get out. Take your organization and all of its people with you. Good day, Mr. Secretary General."

———————— ·•◆•·· ————————

FBI Special Agent James Carter introduced himself and the three other members of the first team, Richard Walker, Martin Rand, and Mel Givens. "We will establish a perimeter around your place. Ma'am, we will be in an adjacent apartment all of the time. I am sorry that it is necessary to invade your privacy to some degree, but your safety is our charge and paramount to national interests. I truly hope you will bear with us and work with us. We will try to be as unobtrusive as possible. One of us will keep you in sight at all times. I strongly suggest that you go about your daily routine as best you can and totally ignore us. I can appreciate how difficult this might be. We will try to be as innocuous as possible. In the meantime, it would be most helpful to us if you make us a list of your acquaintances, along with their telephone numbers and addresses. If you have any recently-made friends, male or female, please highlight those for us. It could save us a lot of time."

"Agent Carter, do you truly think I am in any danger?"

"Ma'am, I cannot say one way or the other. Most certainly we will do everything possible to ensure your safety under all circumstances. I hope you haven't planned any vacations lately; that would certainly complicate things for all concerned."

"No, Agent Carter, I am not planning on doing anything except sleeping, resting, reading, and getting some exercise. Then I am going back to work."

"In that case, we will get out of your way for the moment." Agent Carter nodded his head and walked to the apartment next door. He didn't tell her that they also occupied the apartment directly above hers as well as the adjacent one. A microscopic fiberoptic camera had been inserted into a wall or ceiling of each room so that they could be simultaneously monitored. Only the bathroom was spared.

Not a bad-looking woman, Carter thought as he entered the FBI's apartment. *Brains and beauty in one woman; not bad if she has her mind right and not out on some loony fringe of religion or philosophy. This might turn out to be the most pleasant assignment I have had to date.* When she undressed in the bedroom and headed for the shower, Agent Carter was impressed. Three days later, Agent Carter invited her to supper at his favorite Italian restaurant. She accepted.

CHAPTER 25

General Chang briefly pondered with some inward trepidation what he had just launched. His coded message to each of the Army Front Commanders would put Asia in a war that at least equaled, if not exceeded, World War II. His concern was not for China. China is forever as Han Chinese. No, he knew he was doing the right thing. *Han Chinese must be allowed to expand*, he thought. *Allowed by whom?* he asked himself. *Han Chinese have the oldest history, culture and civilization in the world. For four hundred years, we have been on the bottom of the world's hierarchy. Now, particularly through my efforts, that hierarchy is about to be reversed. China will again become the Middle Kingdom. China will rule from the Pacific to Eastern Europe and the southern half of Africa. Who could oppose us? Not Europe, not the United States, most certainly not South America. Without our ruling hand, Africa would flare and burn for a hundred years.*

Most interesting that the American President was smarter than we thought. We had hoped the American President would commit U.S. forces to save the Republic of Korea. Perhaps it was their Congress that was the smart one and wouldn't support him in committing to their defense. Still, while a setback, it is only a minor one. We put the Americans in a difficult position with two choices, each to our advantage no matter which position they took. If they went to help South Korea, it would have been with their best troops, and they would have been bloodied. If they remained outside, they destroyed their own future along the Pacific Rim. Now, the world knows the Americans will not stand by their treaties if it is against their best interest to do so. The United States can do nothing to stop us. They are not willing to employ nuclear weapons and risk total devastation. Our ambassador will make certain the American President understands the options. A nuclear winter and a destroyed United States will serve no one. No, even a united world would have difficulty in controlling our China. It is too vast. With close to two billion people, almost one-third of the world's population, we have overtaken Western Europe in production, we rival the United States and India in research, turn out more scientists, mathematicians, engineers, chemists and physicists than any other nation in the world. No, the Twenty-First Century is the century of China. This is our century.

The only weak spot in this operation is that we are committing our militias piecemeal, at least to some degree, due to a lack of transportation. Our rail lines will run in circles in our drive to the west, also to the south. Our ships will sail in a huge circle to transport our troops to Africa. At least we are committing division-sized forces at each time. Once we cross the border, they will disburse anyway. No doubt about our younger brothers, the Vietnamese. They will be our toughest opponent man per man in Army Front I. Still, we will overwhelm them with mass. Our HIV battalions will lead the assault. The Vietnamese will be flattened by our steam roller. They have no idea what is in store for them. The loss of our HIV battalions will be no great thing; it will actually be a plus, a purge of our society of the carriers of a fatal, noncurable disease. We are spared the tremendous expense of anti-retroviral drugs for them. It will be rare, indeed, for any commander below the regimental level to visit or become acquainted with all of his troops. It will be the company and battalion commanders who carry the real burden of command. The duty of our higher echelons is to support those to the best of their ability with the distribution of resources. Ultimately, that rests with the Front Commanders and the Chiefs of Staff. That means me.

The Army Front Commanders began broadcast faxing down to the battalion level in their commands. All personnel were to report to their units seventy-two hours from receipt of this order at battalion headquarters. All personnel were to wear one uniform, bring their spare, and draw weapons and ammunition upon reporting. The trucks would move in a continuous circle, carrying troops to their line of departure on all fronts.

Part of the mobilization order read, "There are no organizational changes at the battalion level and below. Organizational structure above the battalion level will be regimental, divisional, corps, army, army groups and army front. Commanding officers and staffs have been appointed to fill these positions above the battalion level. In contrast to the Regular People's Army, the number of battalions in the regiments of the People's Militia Army is hereby tripled that of the regular People's Army. The number of regiments per division is hereby tripled. The number of divisions per corps is hereby tripled. The number of corps per army is hereby tripled. Armies are formed into army groups. Army groups are formed into army fronts. Army front commanders are assigned a various number of army groups, depending upon their mission. The next senior officer in your chain of command will visit you in the next seventy-two hours to issue you your orders verbally. All battalion commanders are to brief their subordinates on the ultimate objectives and concept of operation. General orders shall include the following:

1. No unit in the field is to move in any formation or order larger than a company. To do so will invite massed fires.
2. Companies can bypass each other in the field upon coordination with the battalion commander.
3. Companies and battalions are to be disbursed over large areas, governed by terrain, weather, opposition, and the judgment of the company commander."

Enclosed is a message from the Chief of Staff, People's Liberation Army Navy.

"Militia of the People's Liberation Army, hear me! For five hundred years, foreigners have invaded our soil, dominated our government, used our labor for their own profit, infected us with their poison of opium and other drugs in order to gain control of our minds and our economy, dictated to us, told us what we cannot do to protect ourselves, claimed parts of our country as their own, despoiled our women, and forced us into economic and moral slavery. They have surrounded us with their so-called policy of containment. Now, since our Great Revolution, we have grown in strength, gained the will, earned our self respect, and surpassed our enemies in moral cause. Our enemies and their running dogs that are our neighbors have, for too long, denied us our rights as one of the great nations of the world and our place in current history. No more. Now, the People's Republic of China is claiming its place in the world. That place is that of the greatest nation in the history of the world. It is your duty to see that our leadership of the world can no longer be denied. This is your legacy.

You have been well trained and equipped for your mission. You are motivated soldiers, the great backbone of your country. Each of you has a mission as a soldier of your country. Your leaders are well trained and dedicated and know each of you. You are formed into units that ultimately form great armies. Your battalions are formed into regiments. Your regiments are formed into divisions. Your divisions are formed into corps. Your corps are formed into armies. Each Peoples Army is part of an Army Group. Army Groups constitute an Army Front. Each Army Front has been assigned a specific mission. Your mission, as individual soldiers of your nation and of your Army Front, is to defend your country! In the course of events, our great nation has forged alliances with our friends. Our friends are now defending themselves against military attack on all fronts. India is attacking Pakistan. South Korea is attacking North Korea. Vietnam is raiding across our border. The United States and its allies are supporting India and South Korea in their attempts to conquer our allies. The Americans, Germans, Japanese and the British are attempting once again to establish colonialism in Africa in the name of free trade. They are committing the same atrocities against the African Peoples that they committed against us for over two hundred years. Our African friends have nowhere to turn! They cannot defend themselves from the slavery being forced upon them. They are crying out in terror for our help. We will not permit these western nations to inflict their harm and greed on other peoples of the world as they have done to us in the past. The Americans are attempting to keep us in our place by choking off our supplies of petroleum and other forms of energy from the Middle East. They are demanding that we trade them our finished products for raw materials at prices that are so excessive that we will be forced into economic subservience once more.

They demand that we pay ever increasing prices for raw materials until they cost more than our finished products.

It is your duty to prevent our friends from being conquered. It is your duty to defend our borders. It is your duty to see that we do not become economic slaves again. It is your duty to obey your officers and your commanders. You have been trained only in the offense, because there is no option in defense. It is your duty to perpetually attack. You are to attack without ceasing. You are part of the greatest force in the history of the world. You are invincible! Now is the time to see that our enemies never rise again to threaten us. It is your duty to eliminate the aggressors – all of them. This is not the time to feel pity for the enemy. You are to attack without mercy. This is the time to wipe the enemies of China from the face of the earth. You will not stop in your march until you have accomplished your mission. Take what you need from the enemy. Whatever the enemy possesses that will assist your victory is now yours. Take his grain, take his livestock, take his food, take his vehicles, take all that he has that will help you accomplish your mission, and most of all, take his life. Spare no one. Let none of them have heads to again raise against China for eternity.

Chang, Mao Lin
Chief of Staff, People's Liberation Army Navy

———————— •••••• ————————

Settling into his chair, he pondered on his meeting with the Supreme Council that morning where his concept was finally presented in totality. General Chang poured himself two fingers of scotch. *Too bad we can't go to Scotland as well*, he thought.

"Comrade General, five years ago, you organized rural militias at considerable expense against the better judgment of this council. You explained at that time that the purpose of these militias was to provide manpower in the event of invasion by India, either separately or in consonance with the United States. It appears now, that your purpose of such organization was to provide an invasion force rather than a defensive force. Is that not correct?"

"You will forgive me, Comrade Commissar, if I admit such culpability. I and the remainder of the leadership of both the People's Liberation Army Navy felt very strongly on this issue. It was felt necessary to deceive this council in order to maintain the utmost secrecy of long-range planning. Any hint of their true purpose would have given our enemies an indication of our intentions. This way, they are much less prepared.

"As you are well aware, Comrades, between seventy and eighty percent of our population is still rural. Historically, a peasant could grow enough food for his family on two to three acres in a good year. In bad years, they starved. Our floating population is mostly rural and is approaching two hundred million out of a total population of approximately two billion, essentially ten percent of our total population. Most of these people are less than thirty years of age. Now, as a result of decades of female infanticide, our population is skewed heavily towards young men who flock to the cities, looking for work, wives and wine. The institution of certain modern medical practices into the rural areas, such as amniocentesis and ultrasound, allowed the sexing of fetuses in utero. Couples had the female fetuses aborted so that they might have sons. Couples also bribed many local officials into falsifying death reports of infant sons so that they could have more than two children, all males. Lacking the essential population of young women to become wives for this population skewed towards young men, prostitution flourished. Along with it, a massive HIV epidemic with its tremendous economic burden has also flourished, as we are all aware.

"Many of these young people still in rural areas are out of work, roaming the countryside. Banditry, assaults and rapes have tremendously increased in the countryside. Rather than imprison or kill these people, the People's Liberation Army decided to put them to good use. We have channeled their excessive energies into a useful purpose. By paying them a very lowly monthly sum, providing them with food, clothing, both civilian and uniforms, and teaching them military skills, we helped reduce the population pressure on our cities, especially along the coastline. This effort more or less tied them to their home villages.

"In a way, this has allowed our efforts at establishing collective farms to increase, a notable effort of this council. This mechanization and economy of scale has been a two-edged sword. Intensive manpower is no longer needed for agricultural production. With increases in education and awareness of the world and its material goods, the lure of a lifestyle above subsistence cannot be denied by many of these young men who are an excess population in our countryside.

"Not only are the rural militias well equipped, they are superbly trained and exhibit considerable unit cohesiveness. Everyone knows everyone else in these units, their strengths and their weaknesses. They have learned to adjust, to compensate, and have welded themselves into hardened, integral, cohesive units. We initiated a psychological campaign along with their initial organization that grew in complexity, intensiveness, and purpose. These units are now very aggressive, believe we are under imminent attack, and are fully prepared to do their duty. Such units allowed us to maintain very modestly-sized 'regular units' while building up a two hundred-million-person reserve. Our purpose here was to hide our capabilities from our enemies more than from this council."

"How well, Comrade General, have you succeeded in disguising your efforts from the west, as well as our neighbors?"

"Comrade Commissar, we organized these units on a district basis. They are almost exclusively light infantry. We determined that any program to build armor, tube artillery, any heavy forces at all would send a strong signal to our opponents. Instead, the People's Liberation Army put all of our efforts into logistical support for these units. We have amassed a tremendous truck fleet of the latest, most rugged design; we have developed underground storage depots along the axes of attack, calling them catchment basins for water, which is, of course, a function they also fulfill. Dehydrated foods, small arms munitions, limited medical supplies, spare parts, maintenance shops and so on, have been established right up to our borders. In some cases, we have extended a small number of these depots across our borders by bribing local officials, employing some of their people as guards, and providing them with small arms."

"Comrade General, if the People's Liberation Army has not invested in heavy forces, tanks, armored personnel carriers, artillery, how will you provide fire support for them?"

"Easily enough, Comrade Commissar Po. Each of these battalions will have several truck-mounted light rocket launchers. We found that mortars and small rockets could effectively and cheaply replace heavy and expensive tube artillery. The launchers are easily reloaded in a few minutes and can be reloaded while moving, albeit at reduced speeds. This helps avoid counter battery fire. We took a lesson from the Americans in that these launchers are computer-controlled ground radar effective and can initiate counter battery fire with accuracy of plus or minus five meters at a range of twenty miles. They are far less expensive than tanks or tube artillery and are mass produced as a single rocket. One does not have to worry about the proper powder charge, or so on. They have various warheads, from anti-armor, high explosive, smoke, and anti-personnel. They have greater range than the American 105- or 155-millimeter tube artillery, which has been purchased or supplied to most of America's so-called allies. Incidentally, the American artillery has the shortest range of any Army in the world. It was their doctrine, tactics and training that made them so effective in the two Gulf Wars. Now, they have suffered inadequate training for years. They study tactics on computers but have no money to practice them in the field. Due to budgetary constraints, the Americans do not often drill in units larger than a battalion. When they do, it is merely as a brigade. The American Army of today is one more of theory, not of practice. They think they can do everything through their concept of what they call C4I; that is communications, command, computers, control, and information. They use simulators rather than field exercises because it is so much cheaper. They have not recognized the difference between video war games and real war.

"As regards to the People's Liberation Army Navy, the decision was made to expand the state-of-the-art diesel submarine force in the last decade of the last century. Our latest models are the quietest in the world, virtually undetectable from the air, by surface forces, or other submarines, unless you are within one kilometer of them. We now have a fleet of over one hundred such late-model submarines, due to our underground and undersea submarine pens at Qinhuangdo and Yingkou. Being in close proximity to the steel works and coal mines of Shenyang made this possible. Our enemies believed all of the required metals went into railroad stocks for the further development of the Northwest Provinces, what the west calls Manchuria. The electrical, computer and ceramic industries of

Shenyang were also valuable resources. We sold a few submarines of our latest model without the more sophisticated systems to our North Korean allies, to assist them in their endeavors. Those submarines we sold were built at our very modest facilities of Dandong. Not even the North Koreans are aware of the enormous size of our submarine fleet."

"And Comrade General, do you expect this enormous submarine force to offset the Americans strength in aircraft carrier battle groups? Do you expect these submarines to engage these groups and destroy them?"

"Yes, Comrade Commissar Ling, with tremendous assistance from our North Korean allies, and others, we do. Actually, we anticipated the Americans would support South Korea under their treaty obligations. Their order of battle calls for two carrier battle groups in the Sea of Japan and two in the Yellow Sea. When or if we make our threatening gesture towards our province of Taiwan, the Americans will have to commit two more of their battle groups to the Straits of Taiwan. The Americans cannot sail more than six battle groups at any one time. In fact, they will find it extremely difficult to have five battle groups at sea all at one time. Too many of their ships are being retrofitted, crews are stretched to their limits, and due to extended time at sea, the American Navy suffers a tremendous shortage of qualified sailors. The American Navy is now one-fourth of the size it was in the 1980s. Their navy now totals less than three hundred ships, many of which are obsolete, are logistically oriented, and by that, I mean antiquated freighters, and smaller craft rather than capitol ships of the line. They have not kept pace with building warships to replace those which become obsolete or too expensive to retrofit. Since the end of what they call the Cold War, they have reduced the number of their carriers from thirteen to eight. They lack sufficient numbers of destroyers, cruisers and frigates. The design of their first line Los Angeles class nuclear attack submarines is now more than forty years old. When we begin our attack, should any of the American Navy choose to engage us, those American ships still remaining afloat will be attacked by our submarine and surface ships and air forces. We have the advantage of land-based aircraft, as opposed to the carrier-based capabilities of the Americans. It was our hope that, with any skill at all, the North Koreans would have very seriously degraded the American air fleet at sea. Still, even though the Americans did not come to the aid of South Korea, they are stretched logistically to the breaking point. They fear our invasion of Taiwan, and so guard it zealously.

"This submarine force is aimed not only at the Americans, however. It is also aimed at the growing Indian Navy in particular. They patrol the Indian Ocean as partners with the American Navy. The Australians might choose to support the American efforts but are of little consequence. They have few submarines, some older cruisers and destroyers, and a few frigates. They have little of the Aegis capability of the Americans and not very much of the network centric computerization. They will be sunk by our submarines waiting for them if they sail out of their harbors to engage us. Our ally Pakistan has little naval capability to counter the Indian Navy. We will fulfill that role for them while Pakistan neutralizes the Indian Army. Kashmir will again become part of Pakistan. Or so they think.

"The Japanese failed to take Australia, stopped by General McArthur in New Guinea in World War II. The Japanese learned the value of submarine warfare the hard way. Now, they are more advanced than the Americans in the anti-submarine warfare aspects that are detection and discrimination. Fortunately, they have never put any such technology or forces into capitol ships. We can continue to trade with Australia for the time being, rather than attempt to conquer it now, as it has such relatively small defenses, but that is a decision for a later time."

"Comrade General, will you please elaborate on these rural militia forces? I am very much interested in them, particularly the role of the women in them."

"Certainly, Comrade Commissar Po. These forces are organized as five-man teams, three teams to a squad, and three maneuver squads to a platoon. Each platoon also has a machine gun section, a mortar section, a medic, a communications-computer-radio technician, and a noncommissioned officer chiefly as an administrator. It is led by a platoon commander. There are three such maneuver platoons to a company. Each company also has a motor pool section with its organic trucks, a mess section, a communications section, two additional aid personnel, and so on. There are three such maneuver companies to a battalion. The battalion controls the rocket artillery. It also has its own headquarters company for administrative purposes, mess facilities, and so on. It provides logistical support for the companies. It is responsible for moving ammunition from the regiments to the maneuver companies. The regiments are composed of three companies and a regimental headquarters. The regiments are the highest of units in the militia. There is at least one regiment per district. These regiments contain approximately 3000 personnel. The depots are under a different organization and command. They will support the regiments as required. Any regiment can draw upon any depot.

"Women are an integral part of each unit, beginning with the platoon level. Most of the truck drivers, mess personnel, medical personnel, clerks, and so on are women. Some platoons, however, have incorporated women into their infantry squads. All reports indicate that the women do almost as well as the men in infantry functions and often exceed the men in the support and ancillary functions. Many of our snipers are women. They have finely-honed motor skills, are extremely patient, dedicated, and well trained in the arts of field craft and camouflage.

"We do not care if couples form within these units. Pregnancy, however, is not permitted. Abortions are free but frowned upon, as it takes the female soldier out of duty for a time. Rather, birth control methods are freely distributed by medical personnel without question. Given the lack of a number of suitable young women for wives in our society, many of these young female soldiers enjoy the affections of many of their male comrades. While this has caused some problems with unintentional bonding, it has not led to many serious difficulties. Discipline is swift and harsh whenever it is required, which is very infrequently, as everyone understands their position. Some of the platoon leaders and even a few of the company commanders are women. All are quite capable.

"For those personnel who are infected with the HIV virus, we have pooled them in each district into special battalions. These battalions are composed exclusively of HIV infected people. Each of these battalions has a full complement of people. In some cases, they are over staffed. This has occurred in the districts with high rates of HIV infection. Some prostitutes are in these units. This is of no concern to us, as all concerned are already infected with HIV. We do require that they limit the practice of their trade within their own company. We do immediately treat any cases of usual venereal diseases simply because it reduces the effectiveness of the soldier. We do not provide any medications at all for their HIV infection. When their infection becomes too severe for their duties, we try to find a less difficult position. For example, an infantryman might become a truck driver, or a truck driver a weapons maintenance specialist, something less physically demanding. When they can no longer perform any useful function, they are given the option of being released from service or voluntary euthanasia by chemical means; simply an overdose of sleep-inducing drugs."

"Comrade General, will you please elaborate what your specific goals are with this overwhelmingly ambitious war that you feel we should engage in? Why are you suggesting that we engage multiple countries simultaneously in a terrible ground war? How can we possibly accomplish so much simultaneously?"

"We have, Comrade Commissar, only a little better than ten percent of our population in the militia. They total approximately two hundred million soldiers. We have the population to spare. We can double this militia force over the course of two years, or even less if required. Our regular forces can be held to be utilized if, and when and where, they are needed. These militia forces will, to a great extent, live off the land as they march. While not exactly a scorched earth policy, they are to destroy the target populations in order to have what the Germans of World War II called 'lebensraum.' This is room for our Han Chinese people.

"Comrade Ling, we have a number of objectives which we feel we will accomplish all at once with this plan. I have just explained a most significant one, that of what Hitler called 'lebensraum', or room to live. Also chief among them are seizure of the oil and gas fields in the Central Asian Republics. This is necessary to ensure that our economy will have sufficient petroleum and energy supplies to continue to grow.

"While the iron ore from T'ung-hua and the coal from Fu-shen have created the largest iron and steel industry of Asia, they are becoming depleted. The coal mines of Fu Shen will not last forever, and the oil contained in the oil shale there is particularly difficult and expensive to extract. New sources of coal and iron from overseas will allow inexpensive delivery via ocean vessels to our Darien-Port Arthur industrial complex.

These seaports and the raw materials that this operation will provide, inexpensively shipped via ocean going ore carriers, will result in an expanded industrial complex that will become the heavy manufacturing center of the world.

"Not only do we need the oil for the present and future, but burning oil as opposed to coal will lessen the severe impact coal burning technology has on the quality of our air. As everyone is well aware, the atmospheres of our cities are so polluted with smog from burning coal to generate electricity and vehicle exhaust as to constitute a serious health hazard for all. Therefore, our second goal is new sources of energy.

"Our third goal is to gain arable land for further food production. The total population of the planet is approaching eight billion people according to the United Nations. It is expected to reach nine billion by the year 2050. India's population is now the same as ours, or very close to it. According to the United Nations, India will surpass us in population in ten years. That means half of all of the world's population will be in China and India. If you add the other populations of east and central Asia, then two-thirds of the world's population will live on this continent. The Islamic world is also rapidly expanding. Muslims average five and a half children per family, worldwide. The competition for food will be enormous in the coming decades. Our own population exceeds 1.8 billion and growing, albeit slower than in the last three decades. Nevertheless, it is more than we will be able to feed in the coming years. We cannot afford mass starvation or a repeat of the turmoil and dangers of the Cultural Revolution, especially as that occurred in the summer of 1966.

"The second green revolution has not occurred as many have hoped. In the 1960s, population explosion was predicted, and it would outstrip food production. Then, the first green revolution occurred. Plant genetics provided the tremendous increase in production to keep pace with the growing world population. Our agronomists tell us there will be no second such great leap forward, particularly in grain production. We have reached the point of diminishing returns. Indeed, soils are wearing out around the world. This is working to our advantage in this plan. The demand for meat protein is dramatically increasing in our own population. We must have grain to feed to meat-producing livestock. Africa, in particular, is suffering tremendous famine, disease, social unrest in the form of revolutions, and brigandage. There is little or no organized resistance to stop our African acquisition.

"Of course, we do not intend to conquer all of Africa. That is unnecessary. We will concentrate on Africa south of the Sahara. Over thirty of these countries south of the Sahara have HIV prevalence rates above thirty percent. Some are approaching prevalence rates of fifty percent. The prevalence rate is the percentage of the population that is infected at any given time. The infection rate is increasing exponentially in some of these countries. A number of these nations have incidence rates approaching fifty percent, that is, the number of new infections in a year's time, of those for each year of birth below the age of twenty-five. They really are no longer nations, not even city-states, but have deteriorated to the point of no governmental control, only local autonomy and perhaps not even that. Banditry, famine, and anarchy reign in many places. Many of those infected are in full-blown disease development, fully incapacitated with AIDS. Our agents tell us that in many locales they are so devastated by AIDS, they cannot even bury their dead. The populations of these countries are dominated by orphans. Most of these orphans are also AIDS infected as a result of transmission at birth or in early infancy. They have little to live for except the smallest of pleasures of their day to day existence. They have little chance of resisting us. In fact, in some states, we have organized them into bands ourselves. They will be useful to us for a limited time. We have determined major methods to eliminate these bands and what other little resistance we encounter at the appropriate time. In the meantime, we provide them with small arms and food, and they do our bidding. We have had thousands of agents in Africa for years. We fully comprehend that situation; what we can and will do is to eliminate any opposition. We expect that the African question will be settled in less than a year, most probably within six months after our invasion begins. What depopulation AIDS has not already accomplished, we will. At the appropriate time, we will deny them any more weapons, ammunition and food. This will guarantee the concept of Hitler's lebensraum for future generations of Han Chinese in the finest lands of Africa.

"The weather gods have not been kind to us these last few years. With alternating drought and floods in our northern plain, the tremendous erosion and dust and sandstorms, we have reached the point where food production has been a major concern. Our industrialization program of building a factory in a rural area, then a town around it, has consumed considerable quantities of our more productive farmland. Nowhere is this more pronounced than in the lower Yangtze River Valley, our most agriculturally productive land. This has happened in Japan, South Korea, Taiwan, and other developing countries. We should more carefully consider consolidation, rather than dispersal, of our industries. At any rate, in one to two years, especially if drought continues, we will not be able to feed the population we have today. Again, this is a fact of which we are all acutely aware. This plan will give us the tremendous rice growing areas of Southeast Asia, particularly the Delta of Vietnam and other great rivers. I do not have to remind you of the long-standing difficulties we have suffered with this southern neighbor that was once a province of China for a thousand years. With this plan, such difficulties will cease to exist, as the Vietnamese as a people will cease to exist. This area will also provide us with rubber, tin, some iron and coal, and a secondary source of petroleum. Of course, the Spratley and Paracel Islands are included in our plan.

"The North Indian plain will become part of China. We need this tremendous grain producing area. The demand for grain for human food will be approximately 47% greater in the year 2025 than it was in 2010. The demand for grain for livestock will increase by more than ten percent. Poultry and pork are the most efficient converters of grain energy to animal protein. This opens the way for large, commercial animal protein endeavors. The Hindus of India worship cows and will not eat them. We will eat their cows.

"Our fourth goal is the tremendous wealth south of the African equator. One fourth of the world's necessary minerals for continued growth are in this region of Africa. There are deposits of chromium, manganese, molybdenum, uranium, gold, diamonds and oil, especially Angola is rich in oil and diamonds that are of much value. We will control the major sources of these minerals between what we acquire and what we already possess. We will be the manufacturing center of the world. We will control much of the heavy manufacturing for durable goods for the world. Our automotive industry is but one such indicator and successful undertaking. We will be able to produce household goods for our own people to enjoy the way America has enjoyed them in the past. This will be the century of China when we can do this.

"A fifth goal that will never be admitted anywhere but this innermost circle of the National People's Congress and our highest command is to reduce our population pressure. It is disturbingly skewed towards young men, angry, unemployed, hungry young men. To reiterate, much of this is a result of female infanticide over the last three decades. In a way, this has helped reduce our population, as fewer women are available to give birth. This will help in bring our population back into a reasonable balance. It will also reduce our AIDS burden, as we will utilize many HIV infected young people for our conquests as possible. We will direct these battalions primarily to the south.

"A sixth goal, relative to the others but not as an important goal, is to control waters. We have proposed a dam on the upper Brahmaputra River. This will be a tremendous undertaking. It will allow us to regulate water flow into what is now Bangladesh. We will increase the rice production of the delta. It will allow settlement of Han Chinese in this area. Of course, once we clear the area of its current occupants. The Muslim population of Bangladesh will not be a formidable obstruction in any event. This dam will be below the Namchbawasham Mountain and will provide considerable water for several irrigation systems."

"Comrade General, what reaction do you anticipate from the Russians?"

"Comrade Commissar Leng, your question is most excellent. Today, Russia is a government that essentially exists in name only. Ninety percent of all Russian businesses pay extortion money to organized crime. Organized crime controls over fifty percent of the Russian economy. Even their armaments industry is heavily influenced by the cabals of organized crime. The Russian government sells most of its latest weapons production to us. A few other countries also buy some of their weapons, notably our ally, North Korea. Russians lack the logistics, transportation and most importantly, a consensus, a national will, to come to the aid of their former socialist republics today called the Central Asian Republics, a former part of their vast empire. Indeed, many, if not most Russian citizens would believe that these Central Asian Republics are getting what they deserve for fragmenting away from the Former Soviet Union. As long as we do not attack Mother Russia itself, there will be no rallying cry, no emotional reason for the Russians to interfere. We will make it extremely clear to the Russians that we will very strictly honor their territory. I am sure we will remain, as our generals are ordered, at least one hundred kilometers away from Russia's borders. If any refugees flee into Russia, then it is up to Russia to seal their border. This will leave any refugees in a sort of no-man's-land."

"Still, Comrade General, this does not address our basic relationship with Russia in the aftermath of our seizure of the Central Asian Republics. What does the People's Liberation Army Navy see of our relationship after this endeavor?"

"Comrade Po, our subtle inquiries, nothing explicit, with the various cabals, suggests they and the Russian government have little to say about it. They realize they cannot prevent it. They are realpolitik. They understand they must have the oil and minerals themselves and will have to purchase them from whoever possesses them. It is most notable that the great majority of the wealth from mineral extraction in Russia has wound up in foreign bank accounts of members of the cabals rather than being reinvested in Russian infrastructure. The country is essentially bankrupt. All that is left of moral equivalents is nihilism. The cabals that do not flee still have Siberia to exploit. Tremendous oil and gas reserves there have only been recently discovered, of which the world is unaware. Announcement of these reserves will not be forthcoming until the appropriate powers, the criminal cabals, have secured them, both legally and literally. The cabals indeed do employ modest private armies, mostly of battalion size, but a few of regimental size. They are equivocal to paramilitary light infantry forces, lacking heavy weapons. They are of no consequence.

"The cabals would actually welcome political stability on Russia's southern borders. They have great fears of Islamic militarism, as displayed by the Chechnyans. They do not care who provides it since they cannot. Our controlling presence will eliminate the possibility of revolution or civil unrest of any sort to their south.

"No, Comrade Commissar, the only potentially significant threat I see after destruction of the regular armed forces of the Central Asian Republics is limited guerilla warfare, aimed at production facilities, pipelines, and our personnel associated with petroleum production, transportation, and general occupation forces. I say limited, because it will not long survive."

"How will you address this guerilla threat, Comrade General?"

"Comrade Commissar, we will not control it. When I said limited guerilla warfare, I was referring to limitations in time. The People's Liberation Army Navy will eliminate it. Historically, it is a proven fact that guerilla warfare cannot succeed without the support of the local population. A truism recognized by our own great Mao Ze Dong. By the total elimination of the civilian population no guerilla effort can be sustained. Those few communities which survive our initial onslaught will be intensively scrutinized. At the first indication of resistance, they will be eliminated. Additionally, the harsh environment of the Central Asian Republics, essentially desert with intensely cold winters and intensely hot summers, will not support independent guerilla operations of any worth. They will be too busy merely trying to survive.

"As an added factor, our organized communes are trained to their particular assigned areas of endeavor. You might regard them as colonists trained to inhabit and practice agriculture in their assigned environment or district. In about a year, they should be self-sufficient in food production. In three years, manufacturing initiatives for light industries will be introduced according to locally available resources."

"When, Comrade General, will these forces be ready for deployment?"

"Comrade Commissar Po, they are ready at this moment."

Slightly irritated, Po rose from his chair and walked to the General's table.

"Comrade General, can you tell us when they will be deployed?"

"Yes, Comrade Po. They are being deployed now. We initiated mobilization early this morning.

"Regarding possible Russian involvement, the General Staff of the People's Liberation Army Navy has drafted a communiqué for you to deliver to our ambassador in Russia within the next few hours. It should be delivered to the Russian President by 08:00 tomorrow morning. We cross the frontiers at that time. A copy of the message is now being handed to you by an adjutant. It reads:

1. The People's Republic of China will respect Russian territory and remain a minimum of one hundred kilometers from the Russian frontier.
2. The Central Asian Republics are our areas of interest. If Russia should choose to enter the conflict on behalf of former Soviet Republics under the Mutual Aggression Treaty, Chinese forces will defend themselves with maximum effort. Such an endeavor will place the entire Russian nation at risk.
3. The People's Republic of China wants nothing more than amicable relations with its huge and significant neighbor of the north and west. We look forward to a long and prosperous and a peaceful relationship with the people of Russia and her government.

"We have prepared a similar message for delivery to our ambassador in Tokyo. It informs the Japanese that the People's Republic of China is reclaiming the Loochoo Islands which they took from us by force in 1878. Japanese renaming them the Ryukyu Islands and Okinawa in no way changes the fact that they were Chinese until they were seized. In the name of avoiding bloodshed, we advise the government of Japan to evacuate all Japanese citizens prior to our imminent arrival."

CHAPTER 26

A knock on the door broke into General Chang's thoughts.

"Enter."

General Shen, De-ming, Commander of Army Front III, stepped up to Chang's desk and delivered a smart salute. Chang returned the salute and motioned Shen into a chair with a flourish of his hand.

"I'm afraid you will have your hands full with your mission, De-ming. It is the most difficult of all, which is why I gave it to you. I know you and your staff have been planning for months. I am glad you took my advice to ignore the northern half of Kazakhstan in your planning. Our interest lies in driving across the southern half which is abysmally lacking in roads. We appreciate that re-supply of your forces will be most difficult. Your logistical tail will be extremely long and difficult. With Uzbekistan and Turkmenistan being essentially desert, water for your troops might well be your greatest problem. With their small populations, there should otherwise be little resistance from them. The Kazakh city of Atyrau on the northern coast of the Caspian will be your ultimate objective, and letting the Russians know it should assuage some of their fears. We will make it perfectly clear to the Russians that they are of no interest to us. In fact, we are taking the approach that we are doing them a favor, eliminating the Islamic terrorist threat that has long plagued their southern border.

"I have forgotten my manners. Can I pour you a scotch?"

General Shen, De-ming nodded, smiled, and picked up a glass from a tray on the table adjacent to the desk. He held out his glass while Chang, Mao Lin poured two fingers of scotch into his glass.

"As long as you seize the road net around Almaty, you can bypass the city and let the Muslims starve or die of thirst. Tajikistan will be a modest prize, with its hydroelectric output of energy, much of which we have been purchasing. It is imperative that you leave absolutely nothing for any of these people to eat. Those who do not starve to death will die in the remaining summer heat or the coming winter cold.

"Kyrgyzstan might well be your toughest nut. Being the heart of the Tien Shan mountain network, having extremely few roads, severe winters, being tremendously enthusiastic hunters and rugged mountaineers, they might be your worst guerilla warfare nightmare. Thank God, there are only about five million of them. When you seize all of their livestock and agricultural harvest, you will put them in a tremendously bad way. They will have to rely on seizing your logistical support in order to survive. You know what that means. Every mountain pass is an ambush, an avalanche, or a roadblock. They might be as bad as the Pushtuns guarding the Khyber Pass that extracted tolls from the British troops in the nineteenth century! Perhaps persistent nerve agents will cure that problem. I understand your staff is recommending passing through once in a scorched earth policy, then abandoning the area. The terrain simply favors the defense too much. An excellent strategy, I think. Destroying the road and rail links around old city of Frunze, which they renamed Pishkek, is an excellent idea. Isolating that city will put them in a world of hurt. The old Russian military academy that used to be there would be of interest to our historians, I am sure.

"I understand they raise excellent horses around Lake Issyk-Kul. Would it surprise you to see horse mounted cavalry? Guerilla irregulars on horseback possibly? Perhaps you might find a good mount for yourself, a good way to keep the boots clean, eh, De-ming? I know you enjoyed equestrian activities at the academy. Your staff will find you a good mount, I am sure."

De-ming merely grinned and shook his head at the thought of riding up and down his troop columns on horseback. What an imagination his superior must have. It is also obvious that someone on his central staff besides himself was keeping him well informed of the planning.

"Tajikistan, what can I say? A smaller version of Kyrgyzstan? Over half the country is above 3,000 meters high, with peaks over 7,000 meters. The agriculture production of their fertile valleys is the key. Seize it all, take it with you, and starve them out. All of them Muslims, with allegiance to Allah!

"Ah, General Shen, if Iran were only in our grasp. With the world's third largest known reserves of petroleum, of massive, perhaps the world's second greatest reserves of natural gas, over 65 trillion cubic feet, we would be energy sufficient for a hundred years."

"Perhaps General Chang, the Iranians will accommodate us by attacking our forces."

"I almost wish they would, De-ming. I am afraid with a population of 65 million, and as truculent as the Persians are, and with the terrain, it would be most difficult. It is certainly not as severe or rugged terrain as in Kyrgyzstan or Tajikistan, but rugged enough. I anticipate that our HIV battalions will be exhausted by the time we reach the Caspian, and our regular forces will have to then be engaged. Then there are the Americans and the Europeans. These Europeans can agree on nothing as they fight for the leadership of Europe. They have nothing but token forces. They couldn't even handle the Balkans without the Americans. It is possible, however, that seizing Iran would be considered such a threat by them that they would unite with America to form a tremendous coalition against us. Remember that America still has several thousand nuclear weapons. We cannot hope to stop them all. They might even attack our homeland as well as our forces in the field. It is too great a risk. Europe and the Americans will understand that we are leaving them Saudi Arabia, Iraq, Iran and the Trucial States as sources for their oil."

"All the more pity, the irony, that is. A coalition of Europe and the United States would come to the aid of Iran, a nation which has preached the overthrow of the United States as the Great Satan for decades."

"One thing about Iran does vex me though, De-ming. In the early 1990s, we began selling them technology, especially missile technology. This was done to cause consternation and anxiety to the Americans. It did have the desired effect of diluting their military and economic strengths by forcing them to deploy more forces to the Persian Gulf region. This put a tremendous strain on them. After the second Iraqi war, the loss of personnel in the All Volunteer Forces, as they call their armed forces, was profound. Still, using the missiles and technology we supplied, the Iranians advanced their own designs and models which might be turned against us. That is why you will reserve the lion's share of anti-missile defense warfare systems for your final area objective. Our factories for these weapons have been ordered into round-the-clock production. We hope to keep you well supplied with our trucking assets, but I cannot promise anything. We have our own version of the American General Patton's Red Ball Express in World War II.

"Ignore the fallout from the Indian-Pakistani nuclear exchanges which are occurring. Don't even inform your troops of the threat. Your HIV battalions will die anyway but take all precautions for yourself and your staff. The fallout might well expunge Afghanistan. Who knows, with no one to grow opium poppies there, China might also assume the role of the world's greatest supplier of refined heroin to Europe and America. Of course, we don't want our markets destroyed, just controlled. We have made tremendous profits from the heroin market in the United States and Europe. We have cycled those funds through the banks of the Cayman Islands, billions of dollars each year. Those funds have bankrolled the inroads we have made in Africa, by supplying guns and food to the various tribal and ethnic groups there, and the same to the Middle East. Our support of Iran, in that respect, has supported much of the dissension between Shiite and Sunni, and a dozen offshoots of both major branches of Islam."

"Do you anticipate fallout to be much of a problem, General Chang?"

"We know the Americans left a sizeable number of tactical nuclear weapons on Korea, some deliverable by artillery fires, others by aircraft. We know the South Koreans have launched their own nuclear weapons research and manufacturing program as well as a nascent biological one. We knew the South Korean line of final retreat at which point they used them. We did not share that information with North Korea. North Korea had sufficient conventional forces to push them to that line. Their opening biological attack was a masterpiece. We have supplied North Korea with a small number of similar nuclear weapons just to keep things even. We assured the North Koreans that we would come to their assistance if the South crosses the 38th parallel, just as we did 63 years ago, but of course, we didn't this time. We lost a million men supporting them in the last Korean War. The destruction they are wreaking on their own country will eliminate them as an economic competitor for another 30 years. Seoul is virtually being destroyed. By then, well, we shall be well established as the hegemon of the Pacific Rim west of Hawaii. Japan and Australia will have little choice but to accept their respective positions. The rice bowl of Malaya shall feed us, as well as the Indian plains and the Valleys of the Indus and Ganges. Russia, in due time, will fall in line. They have no choice.

"Besides, De-ming, we will still take Africa. It will be the easiest plum of all, provided we have the forces left to take it. There will be no local opposition worthy of the name. With southern Africa's oil, gold, diamonds, uranium, tungsten, cobalt, chrome, and vanadium, we will have quite a corner on the market, so to speak."

"Well then, here's to Africa," said Shen, hoisting his glass to his superior. Chang acknowledged the toast by nodding back and sipping his scotch. "And what of the Americans? Why will they allow this?"

"All in good time, De-ming. We have planned accordingly. You know, it is truly pathetic how little understanding of us the Americans really have. They still think their concepts apply to us. We have gained a significant advantage over our enemies. We know how they think. The American elitists suffer a tremendous failure. They lack any idea of their own historical perspective, their history and imagination. They have forgotten how they once acted and thought. They have never grasped the application of our concepts of stealth, deceit and surprise as part of grand strategy. We tie down one of their most effective divisions along the Mexican border. Their active army, as you know, has less than eight total divisions anyway. Even though they did not go to the aid of South Korea, they are still disbursed along an eighteen-hundred-mile border. We manipulate them without their knowledge. India and Pakistan annihilate each other so that they do not compete against us for energy and food.

Korea as an economic power no longer exists. We have the added bonus of occupying their depopulated lands. Our nephews the Vietnamese will no longer exist to resist our suzerainty. They will in fact, no longer exist! It is now early August. The Second Army Front has begun its mobilization. You will begin yours in ten days. You have a great distance to travel and little time before General Winter becomes a foe, or an ally.

"I must admit, though, De-ming, we are finally employing one of our greatest assets, the concept of mass to the battlefield. American military thinkers of the last twenty years thought this concept invalid. Unless they deploy nuclear weapons against our troops while we are on foreign soil, we will prove its validity. This, too, will serve our purpose by cleansing our nation of HIV infected people to a level where we can control, or perhaps even eliminate, the disease.

"Rest assured, the Americans will not respond against us. We have equaled and even surpassed the United States in many, although not all, areas of military technology. Our cruise missiles, for instance, are equal those of the Americans. Our artillery deliverable nuclear weapons are superior to theirs, and our biological weapons far exceed their defensive measures. They do not even have any defensive measures against biological agents that have been genetically engineered.

"While the health departments in their major cities have made modest preparations, many medium and smaller municipalities have not. They have paid it lip service only. They are skeptical. They regard themselves as unimportant enough to make serious preparations. They think the federal government will ride to their rescue like the cavalry in American western cinemas. They believe that if they are attacked, they will be the only ones so affected. Indeed, many rural states have not made adequate preparations or even plans. Those that have planned have not assigned any resources against those plans. They think only in terms of bombs, chemical attacks, and then mostly of attacks on infrastructure rather than the population itself. It is one of these smaller municipalities that has some strategic significance but is inadequately prepared that will be our initial target. We have identified several such cities, each of which has some unique characteristic of significance. One of these will serve, should it become necessary, as a signal of our resolve and of our capabilities."

"What weapons are you referring to, Comrade?"

"Our biological weapons scientists tell me that we have a genetically engineered strain of an adenovirus virus as our first warning. It is extremely infectious, survives well in the environment, is highly transmissible, with very high morbidity, but low mortality. Should this fail, we can utilize a strain of engineered influenza A virus with a much higher case fatality ratio. It is resistant to the antibiotics routinely used to treat other strains of influenza A viruses, amantidine and rimantidine: It, too, could quickly spread across the entire country in a few weeks."

"Has this virus been tested somehow, somewhere, Comrade General?"

"Yes, Comrade, it was tested on an isolated Uigher village fifteen months ago. It was very effective and will serve our purposes well."

"And what of the Uigher village?"

"Alas, Comrade we could not allow the escape of the virus from the village. Our personnel, all vaccinated against the disease, completely isolated the village to ensure no one left or entered. They were a small nomadic group of herders, moving goats and yaks from winter to summer pasture. The survivors are all buried in the Takla Makan. Their physical possessions were buried with them, and their flocks allowed to return to the wild. Of course, this weapon system will only be employed as an indicator, a harbinger of even worse things to come if we are to suffer too much American interference."

"What, Comrade, if the Americans do not accept this attack as a warning? They could take it as an overt act of war, or perhaps claim it is a natural epidemic not released by our agents?"

"De-ming, we have other agents far more severe. Agents which will disrupt their entire society. In such an instance, their entire military capability will come to a halt as well as their civilian sectors. As you know, sixty percent of their military capability is in the reserves. Their all-volunteer force became very hollow after their debacle in Iraq. Many left both the active forces and the reserves, deserted more or less, as soon as they could legally do so. They will be unable to mobilize. Their active forces are stretched very thin as it is. I worry more about their navy than their land forces. With the reserves, any significant military action, certainly one sustainable for more than a few days, without those reserves, is unfathomable. That is all I can say for now, except, more scotch?"

———————•••◆•••———————

Jim Neville accompanied National Security Advisor Ralph Gardner into the Oval Office for the Daily Presidential Brief as the first activity of the morning. Gardner's presentation lasted less than fifteen minutes, as it usually did, just to inform the President of what occurred that might be of national significance overnight. He included comments from the National Reconnaisance Office regarding Chinese movements. Neville listened without comment until Gardner finished.

"Jim, does Ralph need to hear what you have to say this morning?"

"It certainly wouldn't hurt, Mr. President."

"All right, then let's have it."

"The Japanese Ambassador and his naval attaché' walked into my office late yesterday afternoon. They had a most interesting proposal that I said I would bring to you the first thing this morning. They want a mutual agreement pact regarding naval forces. They are offering to share with us their very latest developments in anti-submarine warfare in return for building DDX destroyers and frigates under license in Japan. Their research hasn't exactly overlapped ours but is a bit complementary. We can merge the technologies and put them on the latest of our small ship designs, those of destroyers and frigates. These are the smallest ships I would suggest as transoceanic anti-submarine capable capitol ships. I still think we should go with the small littoral fighting ship but primarily to protect our own coasts. These smaller vessels just don't have the staying power we need to send them across oceans.

"To go along with this, the marine engineers in the Office of Naval Research have developed a higher level of modularity in the design for these two classes of ships, that is, the destroyers and frigates. They think we can contract out these much smaller modules for these ships for manufacture in any of our metal fabricating facilities anywhere in the USA with final assembly in the shipyards of the primary contractors. These modules are small enough to be shipped by rail car. That was part of their basic objective. We can build them a lot faster that way, instead of the two to three years it now takes us to put a quality DDX destroyer together. The most time-consuming aspect of this will be getting the specifications out and letting the contracts. We could have a hundred different plants building different parts and then weld them all together in about a month's time at the yards. It was something along the lines of what we did in World War II in order to get a large enough fleet to meet the demands for capitol ships in both oceans. The electronics and weapons modules are already at the point where they can be built anywhere and incorporated during construction. The concept is that of the old adage, plug and play utilizing commercial off-the-shelf components. It is just a matter of building the components here as opposed to overseas. Too much of our electronics are manufactured offshore."

"Have you talked with Admiral Stark about this? I find it humorous that you are now the boss of your old boss, the Chief of Naval Operations."

Jim Neville grinned. "Well, I retired a Captain, and he was wearing two stars as a Rear Admiral at that time. He holds no rancor and thinks it is kind of humorous, too. I suspect, though, now he wishes he had paid greater attention to what I tried to tell him those many years ago. But to answer your question, no, I haven't discussed it with him. However, I am all for the technology bit. I'll leave the design aspects of their proposal up to the maritime engineers. If you give your permission, I'll take it up with Admiral Stark today."

"Jim, by all means, let's go for it. I wish to God we had two hundred of those DDX destroyers and frigates and littoral fighting ships, right now. If we build them, can we man them? Can we recruit and train the crews as fast as we can build the ships? Let me know what the CNO and his engineers think of it after thorough discussions."

Jim Neville rose to his feet. "Yes, sir, Mr. President. I'm on my way back to the Pentagon. I'll let you know as soon as it is hashed out."

CHAPTER 27

With the recognition of Chinese forces massing on their side of the border, Vietnam ordered a massive mobilization. Vietnamese political leaders recognized the tremendous hordes of personnel lined against them and realized that this was to be a major confrontation over disputed boundary areas. Over a thousand years ago, Vietnam was considered part of China, at least by the Chinese. China controlled Vietnam as a province from 111 B.C. until 939 A.D. The Chinese expanded their influence by bringing education, administration, building roads and harbors, improved agriculture with the introduction of the metal plow, pottery, draft animals, and better methods of irrigation, especially in the Red River Valley of the north. The Vietnamese resisted all efforts of Sinicization in spite of frequent intermarriage. Marked by occasional rebellions throughout the period, followed by almost uninterrupted guerilla warfare against the Chinese in the ninth and tenth centuries, the Vietnamese finally broke free of Chinese domination. The fall of the Chinese T'ang dynasty permitted the final rebellion, marked by the overwhelming Vietnamese defeat of a Chinese army. Throughout the last two thousand years, Vietnam has resisted dominance by China and other, outside influences. Honed in their history, the Vietnamese became the masters of guerilla warfare. Fighting their own kind of war against the Japanese, the French and then the Americans, they demonstrated an almost pathological desire to maintain their independence at any cost.

China held its forces on its side of the Yalu River, the border between China and North Korea, until after the nuclear exchange. Compared to what Pakistan and India did to each other with nuclear weapons, the Korean peninsula fared relatively well. Now, with South Korean forces surging northward, quickly regaining ground over retreating North Korean forces, the Chinese withdrew from their border area with North Korea. They informed the retreating North Korean Leadership they would no longer honor their mutual aggression pact, with the excuse that they did not wish to expose their troops to the nuclear fallout. Those forces moved southwest by rail to reinforce those already along the Vietnamese border.

To the surprise of the Vietnamese, the Chinese forces paused at the border. Instead, massed Chinese poured into Laos. Initially, the Vietnamese did not realize the magnitude of the invasion of Laos and its significance. The rainy season is nearing its end in September. While October is still part of the rainy season in Southeast Asia, the highlands of Laos are not as severely affected by monsoons as are the lowlands of Vietnam. Only after the first two weeks of standing ready did the Vietnamese realize the depth and size of the invasion of Laos.

General Lui, Lien-chang, Commander of Army Front I, did his homework well. With no mutual assistance agreement, each country was determined to defend its own borders and would not come to the aid of its neighbors. In any event, the forces of Cambodia and Laos against such odds were negligible. Each hoped to escape the onslaught. The consequences of such policies were that they were more or less defeated piecemeal. Three thousand inflatable rafts of the Zodiac type that held eight men and their gear were unloaded at the headwaters of the Ou River near the Chinese border. The Ou River is a northern tributary of the Mekong River that empties into it above the major city of Louangphrabang, Laos. Thus, a whole division and one brigade initially moved with surprising swiftness down the Mekong River Valley through Laos and into Cambodia. High waters pouring from the highlands as a result of the monsoons allowed swift movement of the Zodiacs boats down the river. Every motorboat that would hold four or more men and their gear along the river that could be captured was sent upstream to pick up more Chinese soldiers. Platoons and company-sized units, even squads, became independent follow-on riverine forces moving downriver. Whenever fuel or food or rest was needed, the next village or town was attacked.

Thai armed forces did not dare fire on the Chinese flotillas in those areas where the Mekong River formed the international boundary for fear of invoking Chinese invasion of their own country. The Chinese flotillas bypassed cities that held several thousand or more people, leaving them for the light infantry units moving on foot, but smaller villages and towns were not spared. As many inhabitants that could be easily caught were slaughtered in each village. Young women and girls were usually gang raped before being killed.

Ultimately, the Chinese bypassed Phnom Penh, the capitol of Cambodia. It suddenly dawned upon the Vietnamese that part of the Chinese strategy was to cut off any escape route to the west. The Mekong varies in width from half a mile to almost a mile and is filled with numerous islands and rapids that were considered essentially impassable. The numerous islands of the lower Mekong provided rather secure rest stops for the Chinese. The rapids were either bypassed by carrying the Zodiacs around them or paddled through by the more adventurous among the Chinese militia. Thousands of Chinese militia were then ordered off the river to form a phalanx all along Vietnams' western border from the lower reaches of the Mekong River across the border of the Mekong River which is a border into Vietnam below Ho Chi Minh City, formerly known as Saigon. Thus, the northern three fourths of Vietnam were caught in a gigantic vise with the majority of their forces deployed along the northern border. The southern Chinese pincer was reinforced daily with the arrival of more Chinese by boats. Then, as initially anticipated, the Chinese poured across the border into the upper part of the Red River Valley in October, the first month of the relatively dry season.

In the United Nations, Vietnam appealed for help and condemnation of China. China's response was that repeated border raids by Vietnamese prompted the invasion of Vietnam. The question of the boundary between their two nations would also be settled by force of arms at this time.

Appeals by Cambodia and Laos regarding the Chinese invasion of their territory were virtually ignored as the Vietnamese representative raved on. The United Nations finally condemned the invasion after five days of debate over the accuracy of the information. The Chinese delegation shrugged and walked out.

On the day the Chinese riverine forces crossed the border into Vietnam, a dozen of the new Chinese Ma-anshan class of frigates, displacing over 4,000 tons, arrived on station and patrolled the coastline of Vietnam. Equipped with anti-ship missiles, torpedoes, anti-aircraft missiles, radar controlled guns and firing systems, including the Chinese takeoff of the French Crotale point defense missile system, and 100mm guns fore and aft, very few ships of the line of southeast Asian nations could challenge them, let alone unarmed merchant vessels. A number of incoming ships were turned away, but many attempted to run the blockade. Those ships that attempted to continue into Da Nang, Haiphong or Hue harbors were boarded by Chinese marines. They were forced to sail to Chinese shipyards where the crews were held in Chinese jails and their cargoes confiscated as "war prizes." Their cargoes were immediately off loaded, and the shipyards worked twenty-fours a day converting the ships into troop carrying ships. Most were completed within seven days by crews working around the clock utilizing function specific compartmentalized sections that could be lowered into the cargo holds of the ships and rolled into place. There were galley sections, weapons and vehicle storage compartments, troop bunk areas, and fuel bunkers. The officers shared the same accommodations as their men. Those which could not accept the compartments without major alterations were utilized as transports for carrying vehicular mounted weapons systems, such as the Chinese version of the ZSU-24, and trucks. Not appreciated at the time was an outer picket line of Chinese diesel submarines lurking below the surface in case there was a challenge mounted by the U.S. Navy. These capitol ships would soon form the defense perimeter and escort vessels for the troop carriers mounting the invasion of the African continent.

Smaller Vietnamese vessels loaded with passengers attempting to escape via sea, mostly to Australia, Malaysia, or the Philippines, provided target practice for the 100-millimeter guns on the Chinese frigates. Thousands of Vietnamese drowned.

The Chinese HIV battalions poured into the northern end of the Red River Valley of northern Vietnam. Rice planting had started several weeks earlier. In many fields, planting was already completed. The Red River Valley and the Mekong Delta of Vietnam are two of the great rice growing areas of the world. Rice requires long periods of sunshine and yields from 600 to 3,500 pounds of grain per acre. Under traditional, ancient methods, rice can require as much as 400 hours of labor per acre per year.

Chinese battalions poured down the valleys of the Lo and Gam rivers as well. Chinese troops in the mountainous areas and highlands in between were making much slower time. This created a checkerboard pattern of Chinese troop disposition. Many Vietnamese were able to flee the valleys into the hills, only to be massacred by the slower moving Chinese units passing through. With Cambodia and Laos secured by the Chinese and Vietnam about to fall, Thailand initiated pleas for help from the United Nations and the United States. The United States, with six active divisions in the Army and two in the United States Marine Corps, and no bases in the region, could offer no assistance except by nuclear fires. Thailand refused. By December, the Chinese were knocking on the door of Singapore.

Fred Gateway sat quietly in the front corner of the room while the regional FBI Bureau Chief for espionage in southern California, Ed Wrangell, conducted the briefing of a room full of fifty FBI agents that formed Task Force 2.

"We finally made identification on that Chinese guy who was killed in the raid on the Mexican bandit camp. He was illegally in the country. We picked him out of the files of about 5,000 photographs we have been taking of people coming and going in the COSCO shipping company complex down in Long Beach, among others. His hands were calloused on the knuckles and edges. Obviously, he was a well-trained martial artist. The pathologist who did the autopsy said the guy was an absolutely superb physical specimen. Large for a Chinese, he was nearly six feet tall. A body scan showed he ran less than ten percent body fat although he weighed two hundred pounds. We figure he originally came from northern or central China. They tended to be taller than those from the south.

"His immunological profiles indicated he had been vaccinated against, or at some time or another, infected with, a variety of diseases. We figure he was most likely vaccinated. Interestingly, the doc tells me that one of them was an unusual strain of smallpox, at least his serum cross reacted very strongly with the smallpox virus, which is Variola, and Vaccinia, used to vaccinate against smallpox. It wasn't one of the usual strains of Vaccinia virus used to immunize against the smallpox Variola virus but something different. They are trying to work backwards from the construct of the antibodies to get a better handle on the strain of virus used. The consulting immunologist from the Army's lab at Fort Detrick thinks it might reveal immunization against a weaponized strain of smallpox. The Russians are assisting by providing, they claim, a sample of every smallpox strain in their library to the Centers for Disease Prevention and Control. The CDC will coordinate with the military at Fort Detrick. They want to know as much as we do what this guy was vaccinated for and against. Their concern is the same as ours. The Chinese might have weaponized a nasty strain of smallpox. No telling how long that will take.

"There is little doubt that this guy was a bodyguard. Most of the time, he was seen in the company of one man who is supposed to be a mid level shipping clerk. One of the snipers remembers taking him out. He was running with an AK-47 when the sniper dropped him with a hit in the chest. He didn't live long enough to talk. His fingerprints had been removed but were in the process of growing back. Medical forensics tells me that their removal occurred about a year ago.

"Nobody at the COSCO office claimed to recognize him from his photograph. Ten days later, we went into COSCO's personnel shop under the cover of searching for illegal Mexicans and came up with the name of Ling Ch'ing for him. Undoubtedly, that is not his real name. He was carried on their books as a warehouse man. The Chinese legation in L.A. claimed they didn't know him when we offered them the body as an unknown John Doe. They accepted the body, though, they claimed, simply because he appeared to be an ethnic Chinese. Our best guess is that he was a watchdog for COSCO or something like that, in Jesus Gonzalez's camp. We're not sure at this time just who he reported to. His photograph was identified by a number of the Mexican prisoners in the camp. According to those prisoners, he visited the camp in the company of several other men, usually two others, on a number of occasions before he became a permanent fixture there. A couple of the Mexicans timed his arrival with the arrival of those Russian sniper rifles. They thought he was the bodyguard of some Japanese big businessman.

"We put a bug in the outer wall of the coffin that looked like the head of a screw. We got some interesting conversation before they swept the coffin and found it. That was pretty sharp of them to check it out so thoroughly. We figured they would check the body and then cremate it, but they shipped it back to China after they swept it for transmitters.

"We believe the AK-47s originated in China as copies of the classic Russian design. They were all of new manufacture and typical of Chinese handiwork. Ditto for the ammunition. The ammo was as good as any commercial grade, of better quality than the rifles.

"Our tasks now are to identify Ling's contacts, his boss, methods of shipment, and confirmation of how this was all put together. Our theory is that Gonzalez and his crew was motivated primarily by money, both supplied by the Chinese and by what they gained from raiding into the United States. We don't have any proof of that, and that is what we are after. Gonzalez had received a large shipment of farm implements and tractors. We got their serial numbers and paperwork from them. They are of Japanese manufacture, and the Japanese indicated they were shipped to China first, then the Chinese shipped them to Mexico through Long Beach by COSCO. The records we seized from COSCO on the tractors indicate they went to dealers in Mexico from whom Gonzalez purchased them with funds drawn on a Mexican bank. There were very large sums in the account. Gonzalez also had a personal account that we accessed through bribing a bank clerk. The tractors were paid for by another Chinese front company, according to the Japanese. Very convenient. We think the arms were hidden in this shipment, and possibly others.

"Composite sketches of the two men that Ling usually accompanied were made with the assistance of several Mexican prisoners. One of our agents noticed the likeness in COSCO's files of one of them. Surveillance of these two resulted in their photographs. These are the photographs being passed out now of the two men Ling was generally seen in the company of. One, the larger of the two, is also listed as a warehouse man. It is likely that he is a second bodyguard to Chan. The smaller is carried as a shipping clerk named Chan. I want twenty-four-hour surveillance on each of these two men.

"We have traced a number of the vehicles we brought back from the terrorists' camp. They were all legally purchased in southern California over a short and abrupt period of time by a variety of individuals all of whom had Hispanic names. That suggests some kind of a network, possibly a gang connection. Put a team on checking out those who purchased the vehicles. See what you can shake out of the bushes. If they all go to the same source, then we just might be on to something. The fact that all of them were purchased in a relatively narrow timeframe strongly supports the network idea and that they were deliberately purchased for Gonzalez to use in the conduct of his raids. We want to know about that network.

"You are being divided into teams. Those of you with Hispanic roots will be undercover. We are going to send you on the streets to see what you can sniff out. Be careful! Go armed all of the time, but without your box tops. That's my law. I don't want any of you identified by the opposition. Carry whatever you are most comfortable with, but not less than a 9-millimeter or .38 Special. If you get in trouble with the local boys in blue, go along. Don't explain anything to them. We will get you out when you make your phone call. We don't know how deep or where this investigation will lead. Those of you in suits will continue to carry your issue weapon or your standard sidearm, as approved by your supervisors. Your teams are posted on the bulletin board. Supervisory Special Agents are listed as team leaders. This is the first time some of you have worked together. I realize that might cause some of you to hesitate. It shouldn't; you are all here by special selection. I expect you to all be team players and cohesive teams from this moment on. Any questions? No? Then let's hit the streets."

In mid summer of 2021, the Chinese ambassador to Japan called upon the Prime Minister of Japan to hand him a formal note. Foregoing the usual amenities of courtesy, the Chinese ambassador simply handed the note to him. It read:

Dear Prime Minister:

It is our desire to settle certain territorial claims with your government. It is our express desire that this be amicably and most peacefully accomplished. The territories in dispute to which the People's Republic of China are referring are the Senkaku Islands and the Loochoo Islands, which you call the Ryukyu Islands and seized from China in 1878.

Let me assure you that our intentions are entirely peaceful in reclaiming these territories the People's Republic of China lost to you by conquest in the nineteenth century. It would be in the best interest of Japanese citizens to evacuate these islands as quickly as possible. We will assume control of all of the former U.S. military bases there in thirty days' time. Thereafter, we will occupy all the major centers of transportation, utilities, communications and government offices on these islands.

It is our intense desire to offer Japan our protection from further domination by western military and economic interests. Japan has already made tremendous investments in China which are of the greatest importance to both our nations and for which we are profoundly grateful. By uniting our two countries in economic integration, we can form a union that will be the world's largest market, manufacturing axis, and technological center. Together, we will dominate the world economy. There is no need for you to expend your economic power in further development of military capabilities. Our nuclear umbrella and the People's Liberation Army Navy will provide Japan with complete military superiority and protection. With time, other Asian nations might wish to join our consortium to form an even greater economic sphere of cooperation.

Sung, Chiang, Prime Minister
The Supreme Council of the People's Republic of China

Inwardly, the Japanese Prime Minister was seething. In spite of the fact that Japanese high schools do not teach an accurate history of World War II, or only just mention that they were defeated by the Allies, the Prime Minister recognized that it was a replay of Japan's old game plan of Economic Co-Prosperity Sphere in reverse whereby Japan occupied or controlled much of Asia. It led directly to World War II. Indeed, the atrocities the Japanese inflicted upon tens of millions of Chinese in their invasions of Manchuria and China in the 1930s flashed through the Prime Minister's mind. The fear that those atrocities that Japanese soldiers inflicted upon civilians of other nations just might come home to roost, to be repeated on his people, caused him to shudder. He thought of Unit 731, their biological weapons unit that experimented on Allied prisoners and Chinese citizens and in some cases, entire towns and regions. A moment of despair passed over him as he remembered the accounts of Japanese physicians conducting live vivisection on patients without the benefit of anesthesia to follow the course of the diseases they induced in allied prisoners and peoples of various countries to determine if there were any racial differences.

"Mr. Ambassador, surely you cannot believe that we will surrender Japanese territory without a war. We will fight for every square meter of Japanese soil. Neither will we accept Chinese suzerainty. This demand is so preposterous that I must consider it a very morbid and sick joke. Surely Sung Chiang is more responsible than to write this. Surely China would not risk war with Japan, particularly while you are invading the Asian mainland."

"I assure you, Mr. Prime Minister, it is no joke. The People's Republic of China will reclaim those islands. They are Chinese territory and will once again be part of China. I suggest you present this letter to your Diet to see what their response is, Mr. Prime Minister."

"Rest assured, I will call an emergency session for tomorrow morning and do just that. Recidivism has no place in the modern world. China will find that the world will unite against its aggression. Good day, Mr. Ambassador."

The Prime Minister reflected for a moment over expelling the U.S. Marines out of Okinawa, of the Philippines throwing the Americans out after Mount Pinatubo erupted, of Australia's not allowing any American nuclear powered warships into its harbors, of Thailand's expulsion of the Americans from their airbases and wondered if they should have done things differently.

CHAPTER 28

Rest areas were actually depots fully supplied with containerized supplies, configured to specific requirements. Most of these containers were three meters wide by four meters long by three meters high. Those for the light infantry units had small arms ammunition, food, modest amounts of diesel fuel for trucks and water. Those for mechanized infantry contained much more diesel fuel, ammunition for their weapons systems, food and water; those for anti-aircraft platoons had missiles, food and water. The containers are easily set on the back of a flatbed truck where they are quickly secured by numerous nylon straps. Rest stops where both drivers and passengers could rest were located every one hundred kilometers. Large roadside kitchens where the truck mounted troops could dismount and be fed a quick meal were integral to the rest stops. Fuel trucks to supply diesel fuel acted as mobile fuel stations all along the route. Each was a veritable oasis.

Shen, De-ming, Army Front III Commander, gave the order to his HIV battalions to mobilize, along with General Chang's general order. In each village and town in his assigned provinces, the platoons and companies assembled. The assigned transportation assets, troop carrying trucks, gathered the companies to transport them to the battalion assembly points. Traveling mostly at night to reduce observation from satellites, large convoys wound their way westward into Sinkiang. Supplies would be continually ferried forward in convoys that never stopped making a great circle, expanding ever westward. Shen De-ming had studied the Red Ball Express of the Americans in support of Patton's Third Army in Europe during World War II. It has long been remarked in the strategy of attrition warfare in military circles that amateurs think of tactics while professionals think of logistics.

Shen, De-ming was not about to repeat the critically disastrous mistakes committed by the Germans in Operation Barbarossa in World War II. Years of cumulative study of the regions and their peoples, of their resources, transportation nets, beliefs, strengths and weaknesses went into the planning by his staff. The depots were stocked with cold weather clothing, special fuel additives and lubricants for sub zero temperatures, snow goggles, small portable stoves that burned diesel fuel for instillation in fire resistant polyester lined tents, and everything he could think that might be useful in a winter campaign. He had no illusions that it would be a tremendous undertaking, one of the greatest in military history. Starting out as a late summer campaign that would quickly become a winter campaign, crossing over some of the highest and most rugged mountain ranges in the world, to descend into high desert plateaus where strong winds never ceased, winds that sometimes reached hurricane speeds, conditions that would test and destroy all but the most prepared of armies. Myriads of rivers fed by glaciers occurred in steep mountain valleys, rivers would present considerable difficulties in crossing. Lakes were present in some valleys, fed by these rivers on one end, and draining them at the other. These rivers would become raging torrents from melting snows and glaciers in the coming spring. His troops would see temperatures higher than 120 degrees Fahrenheit in the summer months. In winter, the same location could have temperatures as cold as thirty degrees below zero Fahrenheit. Rains could turn the plains into seas of mud. In the central part of Kazakhstan, pastoral peoples mostly lived in small settlements that were widely disbursed. Shen's troops would seize the fall's harvest of fruits and vegetables, of grain and livestock in the mountain valleys. Even mobile slaughter plants on tractor trailers were part of the plan to take advantage of local livestock resources. Meat was becoming increasingly important to the Chinese diet. It was irrelevant if the meat was from cattle, sheep, goats, yaks, camels, or horses. Heavily spiced, no one could tell the difference.

General Shen, De-ming gave the order. The first three vehicles were infantry fighting vehicles, behind which came two Chinese built Russian style T-80 tanks and three trucks filled with light infantry. These were acting as the point vehicles, traveling a kilometer ahead of the main column. Behind them stretched a hundred trucks carrying infantry, tents, extra clothing, food and ammunition. Truck mounted anti-aircraft missile batteries, free rocket over ground launchers on flatbed trucks, quad mounts of heavy 12.7 mm machine guns on light trucks, radar trucks searched the skies as they moved, communications trucks monitored radio traffic, and self-contained galley trucks already began preparing the next meal in cooking containers clamped shut. Already cool winds were blowing, and a light snow fell two days earlier. They drove out of Huocheng, in Sinkiang, headed west. Tanker trucks were interspersed in the column, carrying either diesel fuel or water. When freezing weather set in, pumps and heaters would circulate the water in the tankers to prevent freezing. The vehicles maintained strict discipline, one hundred meters between each vehicle. Engineering battalions with road graders, bulldozers, and recovery vehicles were in each column to clear avalanches, landslides, and roadblocks. Bridging equipment would enable crossing raging mountain rivers where bridges were destroyed.

In the past five years, the market for goose down from China had become more and more expensive, as the military preparations absorbed greater and greater amounts to manufacture down clothing. State of the art synthetics produced in massive quantities also went into the manufacture of tremendous numbers of winter garments, sleeping bags, gloves, hats, and tent liners.

A similar column departed Kashi, approximately four hundred miles to the south. One hour later, an identical column departed behind each of those two columns. Behind that column came another, and another and another. Each column was task organized for its specific mission. The lead columns out of Huocheng had as the first objective the road net around Almaty, the capitol of Kazakhstan. The Kashi columns followed the Wulu-Kyzylsu River road west. Their first major objective was to cut the road net around Dushanbe, the capitol in the center of Tajikistan. All of the villages in the valley were destroyed as the Chinese columns passed.

Homes and barns were searched for food stuffs and then burned. Livestock was shot and eviscerated on the spot by the mobile abattoirs, then hung in refrigerated trucks if not immediately prepared for consumption in the galleys. When one segment of the column stopped to conduct search and destroy or foraging activities, the remainder of the column simply left them the assigned light infantry company for security and moved ahead.

<hr />

"The launch went well, Mr. President. We have three satellites now orbiting over the region, and everybody in the world knows what is going on over there."

Evening television broadcasts on the daily news now came from the several satellites of different nations. The French and Germans had rushed commercial satellites into orbit as well as the United States. Commercial companies always seemed one step ahead of governments in employing the latest technology. Broad band digital satellites launched by private companies in Japan were in place two weeks after the nuclear blinding. Apparently, some of the international satellite companies kept spare satellites on hand, or were ready to launch new models by an act of accidental timing. International satellite companies offered varying commentaries with their television broadcasts. All of them showed the tremendous devastation now, not only of Korea, but of India and Pakistan, from the nuclear exchanges. The effects of fallout were not visible to the television camera of Big Eye, but experts made their comments anyway. A couple of the networks dug out archival films from the Hiroshima and Nagasaki bombings that ended World War II. They showed the tremendous number of humans burned and with radiation sickness. They pointed to increases in cancer deaths, and medical experts were rolled out by the dozen to explain how radiation sickness reduced the body's ability to fight normal infections and how the more rapidly dividing cells were damaged. The damage to the intestinal tract, the respiratory tract, the germinal layer of the skin, the thyroid glands, and lymphatic tissue were all demonstrated time and again. The medical community seemed determined to scare the hell out of the rest of the world.

A few brave, or perhaps ignorant, or too ambitious for their own good, or perhaps uncaring for their own health, reporters from half a dozen countries were now on the ground in southern Korea. They reported with glaring detail the burned landscape, the masses of the dead, the destroyed cities and towns. They broadcast Geiger-Mueller counter readings on a daily basis as they advanced northward with the South Korean Army. They also reported that the surviving South Korean forces were now advancing steadily and making good progress. Inchon was retaken. Seoul was being retaken. Neither side had elected to strike Seoul with nuclear weapons. It was simply too rich a prize with its manufacturing capabilities and being the intellectual center of South Korea. South Korean battalions on their own initiative were bypassing Seoul, moving towards Uijongbu to cut off the retreating North Koreans. South Korean units in the Taebok Mountains were playing havoc with the retreating North Koreans. They did not repeat McArthur's mistake in late 1950 of leaving units and stragglers, often up to battalion size, in their rear to harass their lines of communication. North Koreans were systematically hunted down and killed. Each valley was cleared of North Koreans before moving to the next. Several journalists suggested in every daily report that massive aid, food, shelter, construction supplies, fuel, medicines, and construction machinery, would be necessary if the survivors of the war were to survive the coming winter. As in all wars, it is the civilians that suffer the most.

Street combat in Seoul resulted in thousands of North Korean prisoners. Many small groups of captives were herded into deserted sections of the city and executed without remorse. Everyone was hungry, and South Korean soldiers who had lost families, friends and comrades-in-arms saw no reason to feed those who had done everything possible to destroy their homes and their peninsula. Officers, in particular, often suffered cruel deaths, as they were tortured for information before dying. A few conscripts were fortunate enough to fall into the hands of sympathetic ROK soldiers who treated them as Prisoners of War and placed them in temporary POW compounds. Most South Koreans felt nothing but a deep, unabiding hatred for their northern brothers as a result of the treachery inflicted upon their people.

Captain Koon's little band had grown into a full-sized company as more and more sections, squads, and even civilian volunteers joined him. In the short period of three months, his reputation had grown, and he expanded his operations over the entire district. He promoted Sergeant Park to Lieutenant Park and made him a platoon leader of fifty men and women. Now, he moved northward, harassing the retreating North Koreans. Major Bradley gave Captain Koon his major's insignia and told him he deserved a promotion. The two men had formed the bond of combat. Bradley became more or less his adjutant, an executive officer, and second in command. Now reasonably conversant in Korean through what amounted to deep immersion, Bradley sometimes led platoon-sized raids as diversions while Captain Koon conducted larger hit and run operations.

Tremendous road traffic at night was picked up by Big Eye in Sinkiang. Ed McCluskey informed everyone at their tri-weekly briefing the following Monday morning.

"It appears to us that the Chinese are massing troops all along their western borders. This would tie in with the road and rail construction they have been building for many years. Those water catchment areas, the underground reservoirs they claimed were for agricultural development, the large hangar type buildings they constructed all along the road net, these huge nightly convoys, the massive truck fleet they built over the years, all support invasion."

"Marge, a couple of months ago, last spring, one of your analysts predicted this. What was her name, Starns, no Stearns, wasn't it? On Wednesday's meeting, bring her in. She deserves to be in on this. She called it right, she should get the credit. She probably has better ideas than any of us regarding their objectives and what our responses should be."

Feeling somewhat humiliated, Marge Talbott glumly mumbled, "I'll have her here, Mr. President. I'll give her a call and get her here right now. She is only a few blocks away."

Ed McCluskey gave what he called a rough estimate of the forces being moved westward. He reported on the southward movement of Chinese forces through Southeast Asia. Smoke from hundreds, if not thousands, of fires of varying size obscured detail from the television cameras of the satellites. It appeared the Chinese were advancing through Vietnam at the rate of three to five kilometers a day. Slower advances seemed the norm in the more mountainous westward areas of Laos and Cambodia. There, two to three kilometers a day were the average. In areas behind the Chinese lines, where smoke did not obscure the view, the landscape was devastated. The earth appeared blackened, with nothing left of small towns and villages. Roads clogged with Vietnamese moving south to escape the Chinese were broadcast worldwide. It was reminiscent of the Koreans fleeing south from the onslaught of the north in 1950 and the opening days of the Korean War of 2021.

"Mr. President, President Vassily Chernikov is on the secure phone for you."

"Thank you, Peggy." Jason Thornton picked up the phone. "Good morning, Vassily, or should I say good afternoon, Moscow time."

"And a good day to you, Jason. I am sure you know why I am calling. Your satellites have no doubt observed the massive Chinese movements."

"Yes, Vassily, we have. I find it most disturbing. First, they mass along the Indian border, and then they mass in western Sinkiang. I am told that convoy after convoy is on the move. I don't have any firm figures on how many, but it must be several million if those trucks are full of troops, according to our analysts."

"I'm afraid your analysts are right, Jason. That's what ours say as well. I am relatively confident that they are headed into Kazakhstan, possibly Tajikistan and Kyrgyzstan as well, although I don't know why anyone in their right mind would attack through those mountains this time of year. The logic there escapes me. We have received a memorandum from China through their ambassador here. I had it sent to you via secure fax a few moments ago. Your office should have it by now. It sounds very ominous to me. Our news broadcasts last night picked up on the Chinese movements, and our people are very nervous today. What actions are you going to take, if any?"

"A good question, Vassily. I will discuss it with my cabinet at our meeting right now. It might just be that one analyst was right. They might be after Caspian Sea Basin oil. Do you suppose they intend to pick up the pieces of India and Pakistan along the way?"

"I would not at all be surprised, given the world food situation. There is nothing to stop them from doing so short of all-out nuclear war. If they go through Pakistan, they could sweep northward through Afghanistan and have two massive pincer movements on the east bank of the Caspian. They will have the rice bowl of Southeast Asia and those of Bangladesh and India, now depopulated. Further, the fallout from the Indian-Pakistan exchange seems to be of no concern to them. I don't know what they are telling their armies. It certainly has us concerned."

"Do you think they really have the manpower, or rather, can field that much manpower to accomplish that?"

"Jason, I think they do. What if they decide to go into Iran, and Iraq? From there the Persian Gulf and Saudi Arabia are next door. They could control the world's oil supply if they do."

"If they do cross the line, Vassily, and go into the Confederation of Independent States, what will Russia do?"

"That, Jason, is the major debate going on here. Frankly, our military is very limited unless we go nuclear. That would add even more to the threat of radiation from fallout. With current wind directions, we would contaminate much of ourselves. We could take out much of them, but do we strike only when they are in CIS, especially if they disburse as they most likely will? What would be the result if we hit them in their homeland where they are massed? I am afraid it would be a nuclear holocaust of World War III, Jason. A true nuclear winter might ensue."

"Vassily, you have given me much food for thought. Give my regards to your lovely wife, and we will certainly hash this out from our perspective."

"One other thing, we have decided to supply small arms to our old friends and enemies alike. We are going to provide weapons to the members of the Confederation of Independent States, Afghanistan, and perhaps Pakistan. Thank you, Jason, for the regards to my wife, and the same to you."

Roberta Stearns entered the room, and Margaret Talbott moved her chair a little to make room at the table for the chair that Johnny Withers was attempting to fit in.

"Well Ms. Stearns, welcome to our staff meeting this fine Wednesday morning."

"Thank you, Mr. President; it is a privilege to be here."

"I've invited you because of your excellent assessment of Chinese intentions which you shared with us a few months ago. Now, the Chinese are halfway down the Malayan Peninsula and appear to be massing in the west. Do you have any idea as to what they are up to?"

"Mr. President, I still contend that their major objective is Caspian Sea Basin oil. The thrust through Southeast Asia is, in my opinion, to gain the rice growing areas of that region for themselves. I anticipate they will colonize the entire peninsula. Whether or not they will strike east or west from there remains to be seen. I would not be surprised for them to do so. From the information Secretary McCluskey has provided me, I would suspect they will. It appears they are massing along the Sino-Indian border to move southward into India. After the devastation India and Pakistan inflicted upon one another, both would be easy pickings. That would provide China with the massive river valleys such as the Indus and Ganges and the Indo-Gangian Plain with their rice and other grain producing areas. Also, the northern Indian plain with its wheat crops would make a lot of sense to me. They could practice genocide and be complete masters of those states, expanding them as Chinese territory. In any case, India, Pakistan, and really, Bangladesh, are eliminated as competition for food. With the seizure of the eastern aspects of the Central Asian Republics, they have, or will gain control of tremendous water sources for hydroelectric power. While not as rich in oil or natural gas, there are some modestly valuable mineral deposits in each of them. One thing I have not been provided are estimates of the size of the troops massing in the west, so I can't project for certain just how far they intend to go."

"Ms. Stearns, I'm moving you over to the CIA as an analyst. From now on, you're working for Ed McCluskey. What grade are you?"

"I'm a GS-11, Mr. President."

"Now you are a GS-13, and Ed will find a place for you on his immediate staff. I want you to concentrate on this Chinese puzzle. That might rankle some feathers, but I don't care about that. I want talent in positions where it can be the most effective. Come to these briefings every

Monday, Wednesday and Friday for discussions of the Chinese situation. Congratulations, Ms. Stearns."

"Thank you, Mr. President. I'm very flattered and grateful. One other point I would like to make, Mr. President."

"Proceed, Ms. Stearns," said Thornton with a smile.

"It is just possible, very unlikely from the way things are shaping up right now, but we should not overlook the possibility of an invasion of Taiwan at the same time."

"Jim, from a military perspective, what do the Joint Chiefs say? Do they have any idea as to the ultimate objective of the Chinese?"

"The Chiefs are pretty much unanimous, Mr. President. They all think the Chinese are going for the Persian Gulf as a minimum. If they go into Pakistan and Afghanistan, and there is every indication they will, they will have Iran right next door, be on the Arabian Sea, and could choke off the Gulf."

"Ed, what do your folks think?"

"They are all in pretty much in agreement, and in agreement with Jim's people. They all think the target is the Gulf."

"Well then, the big question comes, what is our response? Opinions?"

Everyone glanced around the room at all the other cabinet ministers and attendees. It was what everyone thought but no one wanted to suggest.

In the next briefing, Roger McCall announced they were preparing for the worst and let the press speculate about that. Intentions soon became apparent. Jason Thornton made no secret that he ordered all remaining intercontinental ballistic missiles restored. In a carefully leaked and planned scenario, missile silos were filmed being inspected and tested. Warheads were removed from storage and replaced on aged Minuteman III missiles being re-installed in the silos. A flurry of such activity occurred in missile silos all over Montana, North and South Dakota, and Nebraska. It was déjà vu, a return to the Cold War days with the strategy of MAD, Mutually Assured Destruction. A public announcement to the world declared that our satellites were off limits. Any further attacks on them would be considered an act of war and result in ICBM launches with nuclear warheads. It would not be a limited attack but all-out destruction of the attacking country. The only question was at whom they would be aimed. That remained unstated, but most presumed it was China. Television journalists repeatedly stood outside the fenced silos before the television cameras and asked, "At whom are these aimed, and who has aimed theirs at the United States?"

China filed a protest through their ambassador, with the concern that China was their target. The Chinese ambassador was most sincere. He had not been informed by his own government, as the Japanese envoys to the United States were not informed of the impending attack on Pearl Harbor in December 1941, of the true situation. He knew from the daily news coverage, however, what his government was doing. The American response was anticipated, and the appropriate counter response was already in place. President Thornton repeatedly asked the ambassador why China was attacking its neighbors. The response was always the same.

"China is settling its territorial disputes once and for all. We have no desire to intimidate anyone, merely to claim for China that which is China's." When asked about the massive troop movements into western China, why, and where they were going, the ambassador denied all knowledge of any such troop movements. He did not have the knowledge, but he had an intuitive, gut wrenching feeling the reports were true, and his country just might provoke a war with the United States. He felt Jason Thornton was being pushed more than he would admit.

Anti-war protestors marched in the streets in many of America's larger cities. The television broadcasts depicted riots reminiscent of the 1960's over American involvement in Vietnam. The American public was almost hysterical that war was coming to the United States, or that the United States would take war to Asia. Senator Kennely was particularly vitriolic against the administration. All over Europe, similar demonstrations formed, declaring that the American President was a trigger-happy idiot. The citizens of France were particularly concerned that Jason Thornton would launch a nuclear holocaust.

Experts from various institutions, academics, retired military personnel, physician radiologists, climatologists, physicists, and so on, were all recruited by the media networks for their testimony. They claimed that the millions of tons of ash would circle the globe, reducing the amount of sunlight filtering to the earth. This would change crop and agricultural patterns, the glaciers would expand, warm areas would cool as the temperature dropped an average of perhaps as much as five degrees Celsius or more. Ports and harbors would be affected as the shorelines receded due to massive increases in the amount of sea ice and polar ice caps. They predicted whole regions of Asia would be uninhabitable for centuries. They expressed the opinion that the ozone layer was dramatically damaged. It would take decades, if not centuries, for the ozone layer to be restored. This would be an additional, possibly synergistic, effect, resulting in higher rates of cancers, particularly of the skin. Children would be most vulnerable to radiation sickness, as multiplying cells are most seriously affected. Some so-called authorities recommended that people should consider taking Vitamin D supplements, get more artificial sunlight, and guard their thyroid glands; milk supplies should be closely monitored for Iodine[131] and Strontium [90.] The former concentrates in the thyroid gland and the latter replaces calcium in bone deposition. People should spend as little time outdoors as possible until assured that the majority of fallout had occurred and be washed from the surface of the earth by rains. One obstetrician on CNN recommended that couples delay starting or increasing their families, as they predicted a higher rate of spontaneous abortions, fetal anomalies, fetal deaths, premature births and deformed children.

Monitoring stations were established at various institutions around the country to measure fallout. There was a mad rush on by the American public to purchase Geiger-Mueller counters to measure radiation around their homes and yards. The American public verged on hysteria. In Japan, hysteria became the norm.

———————— •◦●◦• ————————

"What do you have so far on the Chinese bodyguard, Ed?"

"Mr. Director, we moved half a dozen of the more talkative prisoners from the Army's Mexican raid here to L.A. for questioning. We're holding them in our own facility rather than the local one for convenience and to keep them out of the reach of possible harm or identification by unknown others. These Mexican prisoners from our raid into Mexico identified Mr. Chan as the Japanese businessman who occasionally visited Gonzalez's camp in Mexico. Only they said they heard him addressed as Señor Ito. They thought he was Japanese. Our Chan, their Mr. Ito, visited the same Mexican restaurant this week as he did last week. He was accompanied by his usual one bodyguard, of course. He was also identified by the Mexicans as the other bodyguard for Chan. Why does a clerk have a constant bodyguard? One of our undercover folks followed him in, but Chan and company went to a private room in the back. They were waited on by the guy that runs the place both this week and last week. He's known to the local police. He has been identified as an associate, shall I say, of a very large Mexican gang. We don't know his exact role yet, but it might be wise to put a couple of agents on him, just in case. At any rate, as soon as Chan and his bodyguard left, our man slipped in there and pinched their water glasses. He didn't know which was whose, so he took them both. We lifted fingerprints off of them.

"Chan seems to live by modest means; nothing fancy, just nice and comfortable. He lives alone and doesn't seem to go out much during the evenings. His bodyguard drops him off at home each evening and picks him up each morning. He doesn't seem to own a car or drive, as near as we can tell. We don't have enough at this point to ask for a wiretap, but that's something to think about. I doubt that he would conduct any serious business from his office in COSCO. That would seem to be too risky. I suspect he does it at home or elsewhere. We will continue with full surveillance until something breaks."

"OK, Ed. Keep me informed of any further developments." Fred Gateway hung up the phone. *Well,* he mused, *it seems that the Chinese have a hand in these raids. What would be their reason? We deployed the 101st Airborne Division there, didn't we? They created all this mess as a diversion to tie down one of our divisions along the border to delay any possible entry into Korea. Interesting theory. Is this the reason we didn't go into Korea, or a contributing factor? If so, it worked. The President should hear this idea tomorrow morning at the usual staff breakfast.*

CHAPTER 29

"THAT STATE WHICH SEPARATES ITS SCHOLARS FROM ITS WARRIORS WILL HAVE ITS THINKING DONE BY COWARDS AND ITS FIGHTING DONE BY FOOLS."

Thucydides, during the Peloponnesian War.

"Well, people, it is almost Halloween. I don't like nasty surprises. Do any of you see any coming? Ed?"

"Mr. President, the Chinese battalions are now in Mandalay and Myitkyina. They are pouring both north and south along the Irawaddy River. Burma is slower going due to the mountainous terrain. They, the Chinese, crossed into Thailand from Cambodia, Laos, and Vietnam. They will own the entire Malayan peninsula in a matter of a week or two, if not days. In both Thailand and Burma, the native peoples are rioting in the streets, attacking ethnic Chinese wherever they can find them. They are being beaten and often killed. Their businesses and homes are being looted. For that matter, stores are being looted as people gather food for hoarding in the cities. Country people are flooding onto the roads headed south to escape the Chinese onslaught. The Chinese convoys just machine gun them or run over them with their trucks as they overtake them on the roads.

"Vietnam is fighting a delaying action, and they are fighting well; but they are feeling the weight of the Chinese mass. Ethnic Chinese civilians are being hunted down and killed all over Vietnam, even third and fourth generation Sino-Vietnamese citizens.

They are being killed by the thousands everywhere.

"The Vietnamese Army appears to be trying to save that part of the rice crop that has already been harvested. We have pictures of trucks loading grain in front of the Chinese, trying to move it south. I presume they are trying to deny it to the Chinese to keep them from consuming it as they march south. What good that will do in the long term, I don't know. If the Chinese go all the way down the peninsula, they will have to burn what they save to keep it out of Vietnamese hands. Perhaps they think they can reach an agreement with the Chinese at the last minute and feed whatever is left of their population. It would seem, though, that the rice growing delta is the real breadbasket and possible objective of the Chinese from a food perspective.

"The Chinese are now entering Assam and going down the Brahmaputra River roads. No doubt they will own all of Bangladesh in a matter of days. For that matter, they are utilizing every available road. It seems they built a road through every mountain pass in the Himalayas that might be negotiable and along north-south rivers. They are sweeping along the southern face of the Himalayas westward from the northern routes. Those forces that turned south have now flanked east from the southern axes of advance into the mountain valleys all along the border, slaughtering as they go. Slaughtering, that is, what's left of the Indian civilians that they can find. It seems there are plenty left at that. The Indian army has no major units left, nothing seems to be any larger than a battalion, but independent battalions and company-sized units are putting up resistance. They are just being overwhelmed by sheer mass. There isn't much left of the Indian Air Force. The Chinese are amply supplied with surface to air missiles. I anticipate that in a couple of weeks all of northern India will be in Chinese hands, and then those armies will also turn south to conquer the entire Indian peninsula. I don't know when, or if, these two massive

Army Fronts, one on the north side of the Himalayas and one on the south, will ever link up. If they do, it is quite likely to be after one takes Afghanistan and Pakistan. That will be a job in itself. Afghanistan won't be able to offer much resistance without outside support. No one is going to come to their aid. They might be able to conduct guerilla operations for a while, but when they run out of food and ammunition, they will have a hard time surviving in the mountains. With winter coming on, and the Chinese taking every living thing, the only fuel they will have will be animal dung, and there isn't much of that.

"So far, they have fastidiously adhered to their pledge to remain away from the Russian border as they march across Kazakhstan. They have progressed both north and south of Lake Balqash but stayed on or below the road net out of the city of Astana, the Capitol. They have just about taken all of Tajikistan and Kyrgyzstan. It appears they concentrated on getting through the mountains of those two countries first, before winter sets in. Kazakhstan is more open high desert and much easier to cross. They have occupied our old base at Manas International Airport, which is just 19 miles from the capitol of Bishkek, Kyrgyzstan. They have cut off the city, surrounded it, but apparently are not laying siege to it. Convoys detour around it. It remains to be seen which major thrust will take Pakistan; probably the southern one, coming across from India. It will be easier than the northern approach through Afghanistan. Iranians must be trembling in their boots.

"So far, they haven't invaded Uzbekistan, but I have no doubt they will do so as soon as they can re-supply and push forward again. The convoys are continuously rolling. They don't really pause, just slow down for a while as fresh troops and supplies become available. Uzbekistan has the best military of the Central Asian States, but it won't last long against the Chinese onslaught. All of these states are dictatorial, tyrannical. None of these countries have allowed the civilians to keep and bear arms. Their armed forces can't depend upon the civilian population for any paramilitary support, that is, guerilla warfare."

Jason Thornton gazed at the map projected on the wall. *God,* he thought, *don't let us have to offer help to Iran. I'd almost as soon see those*

SOBs overrun by a Chinese horde. Out loud, he looked at Marge Talbott and nodded, "Marge."

"Thailand asked for help last night, Mr. President. I don't know what they expected. They threw us out several years ago, didn't want anything to do with us, became ever more repressive and tyrannical, now they want us to save their butts, and there is no way I can see to do that."

"Mr. President, we have picked up some unusual naval activity. It seems that China has suddenly developed a fleet of large catamarans that are modular in design. They were sighted by Admiral Johnston's carrier battle group about a week ago. At first, it was one or two, now they are seeing more than a dozen. They seem pretty impressive. We had one of our satellites focus on their shipyards. Seems they have suddenly started pulling modules out of warehouses and putting them together. They are about two hundred feet long, of shallow draft, appear seaworthy, and capable of hauling about a thousand tons of cargo at speeds up to thirty knots. They can put together several a week. The question is what will they do with them? The possibility of an amphibious assault in the Persian Gulf to tie in with their overland forces can't be discounted. In fact, that looks very probable."

"When are the Chinese going to run out of manpower? Where did they get all these troops?" asked Secretary Talbott.

The Secretary of Health and Human Services, David Allison, M.D., put in his two cents. "I think I can answer that one, Marge, Mr. President. I had our demographers doing a little calculating. We believe the Chinese were lying about their population demographics over the last twenty-five or so years. Or perhaps the national leaders were being lied to or misled by local and regional party members. As rural health programs succeeded, they reduced the severe intestinal parasitisms: roundworms, hookworms, and schistosomiasis in particular and malaria in the southern provinces. They increased their general nutritional level as a result of better education, which created a greater demand for protein, particularly in their developing middle class. Vaccination programs greatly reduced childhood diseases, such as diphtheria, tetanus, and rubella. Rural potable water and sanitary sewage programs reduced diarrheal diseases such as typhoid, salmonellosis, and shigellosis, or bacillary dysentery if you prefer that term, and rotavirus infections. Consequently, more people lived, and they are living a lot longer. This increased longevity and reduced infant mortality partially offset their birth control programs.

"When the Chinese instituted the one child per family policy, it was widely disobeyed. As amniocentesis and ultrasound became common in the rural areas and allowed for the sexing of fetuses, couples often elected to abort female fetuses in order to have male children later on. Not only did they not adhere to one male child, but they often bribed the physicians and local officials into reporting that the first male child died and then had numbers two and even three. Consequently, their population is heavily skewed towards young men. This created the problem of insufficient young women for wives. This gave rise to rampant prostitution, big time, and severely enhanced the spread of AIDS. We now figure China has a population of at least two billion people. If their AIDS overall prevalence rate is 25%, they have 500 million AIDS cases. Of a population of two billion, 30% are less than thirty years old. That amounts to about 600 million people. If 65% of these are males, they have 390 million young men ready to bear arms. Worse, AIDS prevalence of this population is believed to also be about 25%, or about 98 million men. If they include young women in their forces, this number becomes even larger. If the AIDS cases are in the early stages of HIV infection and not Stages III or IV of AIDS, they can function on the battlefield. They have everything to gain and nothing to lose. Radiation will aid to their demise, depending upon their exposure rates. It will make them much more vulnerable to opportunistic infections. China gets rid of millions of AIDS infected young men, reduces their burden on the health care system, gains territory and food growing capability, brings their population back into balance and secures tremendous natural resources, all at the same time. An absolutely brilliant strategy, if I may say so."

"Mr. President, the truck convoys just keep coming. Every convoy delivers several hundred more troops to each thrust. They run several convoys to each front every day. There are literally millions of Chinese, both men and women. No inequality there!"

That last remark earned Ed McCluskey burning glances from both Marge Talbott and Roberta Stearns. McCluskey had difficulty in repressing a smile at pulling Marge Talbott's chain, although he thought Ms. Stearns especially attractive today.

"Where are we going to draw the line, Mr. President? Are we going to let them go into the Gulf? Into Iran? How far is far enough?"

"Ed, you don't know how much I have been wrestling with that question. It is imperative that they be stopped, one way or another, short of the Gulf. Marge, feel out what is left of NATO, what do our European allies, God, how I hate to call them that, feel about this? What are they willing to contribute? Where do they think the line should be drawn? What are they willing to do beside talk? We have ignored them all too long. Chinese nuclear submarines with nuclear tipped missiles off our coasts scare me. Korea is lost, but we haven't heard much from the Japanese since their offer of anti-submarine warfare technology and proposal for the DDX ships, which we are both now building. Let's get with them as well. Their economy will absolutely crash worse than ours or Europe's if China shuts off the oil. From now on, until this is all over, all the Service Chiefs attend every meeting. Jim, Marge, share whatever the Europeans and the Nipponese say with everyone. Let's continue with 100 percent interdepartmental and hopefully international team effort.

"In the meantime, everyone start formulating your opinion of where we will draw the line. Think of it in terms of where one, we go it alone, two, if we form a coalition with the Europeans, three, if we form a coalition with Russia, and four, a coalition with Europe and Russia and Japan. Each scenario might have a different prospective. What will we threaten and what will we carry through against the Chinese? It will be a primary discussion Wednesday."

"Marge, get with the Russian ambassador in the next day or two. Feel them out about how they would like a coalition with us. Be frank, find out where they are willing to take on the Chinese if we go together, or as a triumvate with Europe or quadripartite with Japan."

"Mr. President, I would like to remind you that China has about 225 cities that have a population of over a million people, while 75% of their population is still rural. Their industries, major brain centers, economic centers, transportation, and so on, are concentrated within fifty miles of the coast. Sort of like our Boston to Charleston, SC corridor, and San Francisco to San Diego corridor. That is where we can hurt them."

"Good thinking, Marge. Any of that kind of information State should share with Defense for targeting purposes. I know the rules of engagement require State to approve any targets that Defense wants to hit. In these targeting scenarios, think long term, not just short term."

"Jim, get us an updated report on Chinese submarine capabilities. Let's have the whole picture, type, class characteristics, numbers, training, capabilities, everything. Can your Navy boys put that together for Wednesday's meeting?"

"Yes, sir, you can have it this afternoon, if you like."

"No, let's have it Wednesday morning and have everybody here. I know all the Service Chiefs are well aware of China's capabilities, but I would like to hear their comments too, after the brief. Henceforth, I want them to speak freely at any time they choose. We are getting too close to a military confrontation. We will not let the Chinese have the Persian Gulf or Iran. As a matter of fact, Jim, let's expand that into a discussion of how to defeat the Chinese submarine fleet in particular and the Chinese Navy in general. Let's go to work, people."

"Peggy, get Congressman Chris Farrel on the line for me, please."

After a few moments, Peggy walked into the Oval Office. "Congressman Farrel is in a House Ways and Means Committee meeting right now, Mr. President. He will interrupt the meeting, if you wish him to speak with you."

"No, but have him drop by sometime before 17:00 hours today. Thanks, Peggy."

At 16:00, Republican Speaker of the House Christopher Farrel was waiting in the ante chamber of the Oval Office. Johnny Withers brought him in as soon as the President was off the phone.

"Thanks for stopping by, Chris. It is good to see you again. How did things go in the House Ways and Means Committee today?"

"Not well, Mr. President. The unemployment figures are too high, closing in on nine percent. Income from taxes is down, and the Health and Human Services budget is way out of control. Social security will not be able to meet its obligations in two years, maybe less. We are going to have to reduce these so-called entitlements, or we will have an economic meltdown. We are so far in debt as a debtor nation that in two or three years we will not be able to pay the interest, let alone the principle on our T-bills, U.S. Savings bonds, and other financial instruments. We're in trillions of dollars of debt as a nation. Remember the Weimar Republic after World War I, Mr. President? Well, that's the financial crisis we are approaching in the next decade. They must have devalued the Deutsch Mark something like a million to one. That financial crisis and massive starvation in the population are major events that gave raise to the Nationalist Socialist Party, and Adolph Shicklegruber, aka Adolph Hitler. So, what can I do for you this fine day, Mr. President?"

"God, Chris. Do you always have to start by painting me such a rosy picture? When are we going to turn it around? You and the Vice President! You must have gone to the same school. Anyway, I asked you to drop by because I want you to write a bill repealing the Goldwater-Nichols Reform Act. It muzzles the Service Chiefs too much. It had some good qualities, but what I see is that only one point of view is summarily presented. I don't like that. I want to hear and learn all sides, from each service arm, and then what the SECDEF finally decides and why. Get with whomever you like to help you rewrite it. Get with Vern Cowart and see what his opinion is on getting it through the Senate. He might want to sponsor the Senate version or have someone else do it. Let's get it written within the next month or two and see how it flies. I know your staff is stretched pretty thin, but I feel we are really going to need reform and soon. Think you can do that?"

"Mr. President, it will be my pleasure. Any other bills you would like to introduce?"

"Someday, I would like an amendment to the Constitution. After what I am experiencing, I believe that we should change the requirements for the Presidency. From now on, every Presidential candidate should have to serve two years, minimum, active duty in the armed forces. No exceptions. The Public Health Service, the Coast Guard, the Reserves, the America Corps and all that crap doesn't cut it. It has to be a military uniformed service, combat arms branch preferred. I doubt that will ever fly, given the current crop of cowardly politicians, but it should be so."

"We'll have to control the House, the Senate, and the Oval Office for that one, Mr. President. Then we will have to persuade enough of our

Democratic colleagues to have the necessary votes. Still, maybe it is an idea whose time has come. It might take a decade after the idea is introduced, but that's all the more reason to get started.

"Our elitist liberal comrades of the Democratic Party still hold the assumption that state power in the proper hands can lead its citizens to a better, even great, society. That concept is alive and well in them. These elitists suffer from the concept of just give me a little more power and I can do so much more good for so many more people. They believe that they are social engineers. Accordingly, many of them also believe they are above the law. Unfortunately, there is no drawn line on the limits of power they crave. The end result is an oligarchy, autocracy, or a dictatorship. In any event, or form, it is still tyranny and the end of the Republic. The thought of a military dictatorship, one they can't control, as opposed to a civilian one, scares the hell out of them. We're becoming more and more like Rome every day."

"Thanks, Chris. I appreciate your take and support on the concept. How great it is to see a lawyer who is both a Constitutionalist and a Congressman. Take care, and I'll talk with you later." Johnny Withers escorted the Congressman out as Peggy walked in.

"Mr. President, Robert Lee wants to take a little leave. He has put his request in through his channels, but the Treasury guys want to know if it is OK with you. They can assign somebody else as your personal bodyguard without difficulty, or two or three if you like. It seems that Robert wants to go fishing in Canada again. He says he has a good deal on a guided trip up in Ontario for pike and muskies the next week. He's anxiously awaiting your decision to make the phone call for reservations."

Jason Thornton smiled. "Of course, Peggy, Robert can go fishing. I wish I could go myself. This job is very tiring. I could use a little vacation, and I haven't had one since I took office almost two years ago. Right now, though, I'm just afraid to do so. Sure, let the poor boy go."

Born to parents shortly after their emigration from Hong Kong in the 1980s, Robert-wha Lee was a second generation Chinese American and a current bodyguard to the President of the United States for the third year. He took several fishing trips a year, usually to Minnesota, Manitoba or Ontario. Sometimes, he employed a guide service, but often he went alone. His parents raised him under the strict hierarchy of the Chinese family. They inculcated a love of China in him from the day he was born. He excelled as a scholar-athlete. He won a scholarship to Princeton on being an outstanding high school football wide receiver with a 4.0 average. At Princeton, he played wide receiver on the gridiron for three years and majored in pre-law with an emphasis on criminal justice. After three years of undergraduate work, he was accepted to and attended Princeton's law school. Upon graduation, he applied to the FBI Academy and was accepted. Upon graduation, he was a field officer for two years and then joined the hostage-rescue team for two more. His athletic prowess and karate skills as a member of the elite FBI HRT unit made him a prime candidate for bodyguard assignments for Very Important Persons. Upon request of the Treasury Department, he was laterally transferred and assigned as a bodyguard to the Vice President for one year, then to the President. He served President Dorn admirably and then became Jason Thornton's personal bodyguard. He also served China very well.

Wednesday, 30 October 2022

"Service Chiefs, welcome once more to our tri-weekly meetings. From now on, you are all invited to attend. I very much appreciate your presence and encourage you to speak freely. At this table, everyone's ideas and comments are important.

I have asked our SECDEF to have the Navy put together a briefing for the cabinet this morning, and I want this information to be understood by all members of the cabinet. It affects everybody, including Health and Human Services, Interior, Treasury, and so on, because it will impact on everybody's budget at the very least. So, we'll lead off with the briefing by Chief of Naval Operations Admiral Stark. Admiral, the floor is yours."

"Thank you, Mr. President. The objective of this briefing is to inform you specifically of the Chinese submarine threat and, more generally, of the Chinese Navy. Referred to as the PLAN, or Chinese Liberation Army Navy, they have more or less a unified command structure. Over the last ten years, the Chinese have pretty much emulated the United States in many aspects. This translates to their forming their version of the

Reserve Officers Training Corps at their universities and colleges. From all appearances, this is turning out quality junior officers, especially for the Navy. Many of these young people are joining the submarine service because it is the bedrock of the Chinese Navy. These people are receiving first rate training, equal in all respects to that which we give our naval officers. Their people are well screened, which provides them with the officers who are aggressive, can think for themselves, show initiative, and can stand confinement in submarines for weeks at a time.

"The Chinese strategy is simply that they believe the best answer to our carrier battle groups is the submarine. They can't compete on the surface, so they feel that stealth is their answer to asymmetric warfare. They have all classes of submarines, nuclear attack, ballistic missile nuclear boats, and diesel attack submarines. It is the last category, the diesel attack submarine that offers the greatest threat to our blue water Navy. The diesel attack submarine is the ideal weapons system for the littoral environment. It can do double duty as a blue-water system as well, provided it can be replenished at sea, or can return to its base every four to twelve weeks, depending upon a variety of factors.

"These submarines and surface ships of the line have been practicing as combined arms teams for the last five or so years. The Chinese have also taken a lesson from the Germans in World War II. These submarines are practicing in hunter-killer groups, the so-called Wolf Packs of the Germans in the North Atlantic. Some of their documents even indicate they are willing to sacrifice their older submarines as bait to lure our Los Angeles Class submarines into attacking them, thus revealing their position to the more deadly Song II submarines lurking undetected in the area.

"Starting in the closing years of the last decade, the Chinese began buying state of the art Russian submarines. In the opening few years of this century, they purchased Project 636 Kilo class submarines, Russia's best. These are air-independent propulsion diesel engine submarines. They can remain submerged for perhaps as many as four or more weeks without having to surface or snorkel. They can cruise quietly at three to five knots at depths up to five hundred meters for weeks at a time. If this isn't enough, the Chinese have developed their own models, what they call the Song II class of submarines. They have been buying diesel engine systems, the best that the world has to offer, from the Germans. Their primary propulsion plant is a 1040-kilowatt diesel engine for recharging their eight membrane cells and surface movement. They have forty-kilowatt Siemens polymer electrolytic membrane fuel cells for underwater power. These are what allow them to remain submerged and quiet for so long. These are among the world's best, if not the best, diesel submarines. They are far quieter than our Los Angeles class nuclear attack submarines. They have applied stealth technology to them, which is particularly hard for our submarines to detect. In fact, we believe that three-fourths of the time, we don't detect them at all. When we do, it has been a matter of luck more than anything. These submarines have a skewed seven-blade propeller, can launch both anti-ship cruise missiles and land attack cruise missiles while submerged, and carry the best Russian torpedoes. Recall the Kursk, the Russian submarine that sank in 2001 with all hands aboard. They wouldn't let us help rescue their sailors because they didn't want to reveal their super cavitational torpedo which was in the research stage. The Chinese have adopted this torpedo. It blows a tremendous air bubble in front of itself, so that it is actually traveling in air rather than water. It has been clocked at 200 nautical miles per hour under water. This is no joke or exaggeration. No ship within ten miles can maneuver fast enough to escape it. Not only have they deployed this torpedo, but they also are equipped with second generation 53-65KE wake homing torpedoes, 73ME wire-guided torpedoes and independent sonar guided torpedoes.

"To go along with the diesel submarine threat, the Chinese have had a marked program of underwater exploration all along their southern coast extending into Southeast Asia. I am referring to underwater topographic map making. This will allow them to identify any submarine lying quietly on the bottom any time they want to scan the ocean floor. This technology is also valuable for mine-counter-mine warfare. There are reports, as yet unconfirmed, that they have also conducted some underwater mapping and exploration off the Indian subcontinent. That information came from the Indian Navy, which no longer exists. The Indian Navy experienced significant losses, many of which are believed to have been to submarines. Unfortunately, there is no way to confirm whose submarines, Pakistan's or China's. Since China and Pakistan had a mutual assistance treaty, it is not unreasonable to regard many of these sinkings as due to the Chinese Navy. They might have conducted these operations for practice against the United States Navy.

"We believe that many of these state-of-the-art diesel submarines are now deployed all around Taiwan, literally in a circle. While they have more or less completed the conquest of Southeast Asia, their navy and army and air forces have significant forces standing by on their coastline, apparently poised for an invasion of Taiwan. If they do launch an invasion, and we go to the aid of Taiwan, these submarines will constitute a major threat to our carrier battle groups.

"In this regard, we are somewhat skeptical that they will launch an attack against Taiwan at this time, but one can never be certain of that. The Chinese have surprised us many times before. Our reasoning for skepticism at this point is that they appear to lack sufficient landing craft and carrier vessels, such as our LHA and LHD classes of ships, like the USS Iwo Jima and the USS Bataan, to launch an invasion. Then, too, their invasion of Southeast Asia and now the Indian peninsula would argue that they are concentrating their land forces elsewhere.

"As if the diesel Song II subs aren't enough of a threat, the Chinese now have blue water *nuclear* attack submarines they call the Type 93. They are similarly equipped with the same torpedoes as the Song II submarine fleet. Their mission is to engage our carrier battle groups in the blue water, before they reach the littorals, where the engagement will continue with the Song IIs. These Type 93 boats are at least equal to our Los Angeles attack submarines and probably approach the capabilities of our Virginia Class of nuclear attack submarines. Our Los Angeles class nuclear attack submarines are all platforms that are between thirty and forty years old. We have twenty-five left in the fleet, spread around the world. They can't be upgraded to include more modern technology. We only have three of the newer Virginia class attack submarines. Congress eliminated the program in the 1990s as a cost saving measure. We believe the Chinese have at least twenty Type 93 attack boats.

"Regarding ballistic missile submarines, the Chinese have what they call the Type 94. It carries sixteen intermediate range, that is, 8,000-kilometer range, and ballistic land attack missiles. These are very quiet boats, evolutionarily derived from the Russian Typhoon missile submarines that used to prowl our coasts in the days of the Cold War. These missiles can be launched while submerged, the same as ours. We are not sure how many they have of these submarines; estimates vary from between two and ten. These missiles carry up to six MIRV, or multiple independent re-entry vehicles, warheads. The warheads can be nuclear or biological in nature. The nuclear warheads are believed to be about twenty-five kiloton yield. We lost this technology, essentially gave it to the Chinese through espionage, through the downloading of critical data from Los Alamos Laboratories onto personal computers about fourteen years ago. That cost us billions and gave the Chinese a twenty year leap of technological research.

"The Russians also sold them a couple of Oscar II Class SSGN, that's ship, submersible, guided missile, nuclear, a couple of years back. The Kursk, that was the sub that sank when they were testing their cavitational torpedo, was one of the first. These are cruise missile carrying nuclear submarines. These are 154 meters along the beam, depth tested to 600 meters, carry 24 'Granite' supersonic cruise missiles with a 550-kilometer range. They carry eighteen missiles or torpedoes in reserve. They have torpedo tubes for both the 650 mm torpedoes and 533 mm bow torpedo tubes. In short, they can fire all classes of torpedoes. They have 100,000 horsepower drive trains and can do thirty-three knots submerged.

"In monitoring sales of technology, we believe all of these submarines have utilized state of the art off-the-shelf technology for digital sonar systems and signal processing.

"In terms of the surface fleet, we have very recently seen large ocean going catamarans which we believe can carry a thousand tons or more of cargo. They appear to be about 350 feet long, double hulled, and probably made of aluminum. We're not sure just how seaworthy these craft are, but they appear to be quite fast, thirty-five knots an hour, modular, and cheaply constructed. We think they might be a supply fleet for a land invasion, but that is speculation on our part. If they remain in the littoral waters, seaworthiness might not be as significant as blue water capability. We don't know how many of these ships are in the inventory, or how many they plan to build.

"In terms of ships of the line, they have been building a fleet of guided missile patrol boats. These are a derivative of our concept of the littoral combat ship. They are fast, up to forty knots, carry automatic multi-purpose 57 mm Bofors guns, two torpedo tubes which we suspect house anti-submarine torpedoes, and four pods of four anti-aircraft missiles each, and two modular anti-ship units with four ship to ship cruise missiles for a total of eight. They have towed array sonar and medium range radar. They have a crew of about 50 men and officers. They pack an awfully lot of firepower in a small package. They have what appears to us to have a very small boom on the back and a rail. These are believed to be for launching and recovering small unmanned aerial vehicles. If so, these give them even greater versatility with over-the-horizon vision.

"In 2002, the Chinese launched the first of several guided missile destroyers, which they call Project 52B. These are 6,000-ton ships that carry up to 48 surface to air missiles, surface anti-ship missiles, what appear to be anti-submarine torpedoes, twin 100-mm guns, and a helicopter. Pictures yield what are believed to be phased array radar. They also have considerable sonar capability. They have been building about eight of these boats every year since then. It would appear that they will be the backbone of the surface fleet. Relatively small for what they carry, they employ considerable stealth technology. With fleets of these destroyers and patrol boats, they pose a considerable threat to invasion through littoral waters. That concludes the briefing. Are there any questions, Mr. President? Anyone?"

"Thank you, Admiral. With that background, it seems logical to assume their primary objective is the Persian Gulf. They have to go through or north of Iran to get the Caspian Basin. Why should they go for the lesser resources of the Caspian Basin when they might be able to take Iran and the Gulf? It seems obvious to me that they are going to control the Arabian Sea. Let me hear arguments to the contrary? Ms. Stearns, you earlier suggested the Caspian Basin over the Gulf. What's your thinking on that?"

"Mr. President, I think that if they go for Iran and the Gulf, they are smart enough to realize they will provoke the United States, Japan, and Europe against them. Russia and the United States have enough nuclear power to annihilate the Chinese homeland, and they know it. The Caspian Sea Basin resources will satisfy their energy requirements for the next twenty-five to thirty years. By that time, they will be able to take the Persian Gulf without a fight, as they will dominate all of Asia and be so overpowering that no one or coalition will dare to oppose them. Another factor is Iran itself. They are extending themselves over thousands of miles on three fronts. How far can they go? Then there are the Iranian people. Iran is one of the most truculent nations or peoples in history. The Chinese have yet to encounter anyone so well armed and dedicated as the Iranians. The Iranians would fight them every step of the way, at a tremendous cost to both sides. I don't think they want to tangle with Iran. Iranians would blow their own wells, I am sure; the devastation and pollution would be worse than the Iraqi retreat from Kuwait in 1991. I think they are smarter than that."

"How do you explain this extraordinary buildup of naval power? How does that fit in with the Caspian Sea Basin as their objective?"

"It is possible that they intend to control the Arabian Sea but not move into the Gulf itself. If they control the shipping out of the Gulf, they don't need to take the Persian Gulf itself. They can establish their bases of interdiction along the southern coast of Pakistan and western coast of India. They will also control the Straits of Malacca which will allow them to choke down Japan any time they choose. Korea is already written off as any kind of power at all. Korea will be a very modest source of food stuffs, provided they can get anybody to go in there and farm rice and raise livestock, given all the tactical nukes that went off on the peninsula."

"Jim, where do we stand in our cooperation with the Japanese on state-of-the-art anti-submarine warfare? How soon are we going to be able to take on these quiet diesel subs and win 90% of the time?"

"We have shared technology, utilizing the latest off-the-shelf hardware and have made good progress in these last several months, Mr. President. Both we and the Japanese have jumped ahead, far better than each going it alone. Overall, I would have to say, though, that we got the better end of the deal. They were farther ahead than any of us thought. Another couple of years, and it will be a done deed."

"Jim, I don't think we have a couple of years. If we have a couple of months more, we will be lucky. I mean, how soon can these new anti-submarine suites be installed on all of our subs, Japanese and American, and crews trained, and be ready to kick ass?"

"That, Mr. President, I am not prepared to answer at this time. I can only hazard a guess of a year for our current Los Angeles class subs, probably a little less if we push full steam ahead. We might do just as well with the new DDX ships."

"Admiral Stark, I want state-of-the-art installed on one submarine of each of our classes today and training of the crews initiated. Call it field testing if you like. If you think it indicated, get Japanese experts onboard with our crews to help. We will do the same for them. Jim, you and the Admiral call on the Japanese ambassador today with that proposal. We can't start soon enough. I think they will be only too eager to share.

"Admiral Stark, what, in your opinion, would be the result of testing our subs against the Chinese mainland's anti-submarine defenses? Would it alert them? Would it help them develop countermeasures? Would we be giving away methods and information we shouldn't?"

"Mr. President, we have been testing our subs against their ring of subs around Taiwan. It has been a mixed bag. We are working and learning, but so are they. I wouldn't care to predict an outcome. We are finding their diesel subs are awfully quiet. We usually don't find them before they find us. They let us know they have us in their sights when they hit us with a ping. I don't like it at all. We just quietly slip away then with our tail between our legs."

"At one time during the Cold War, we had sonar buoys anchored to the ocean floor. They were given away by the Walker family of spies in the employ of the Russians in the 1980s. Can we do something like that again to monitor the most likely submarine approaches to our coast? I realize that we have an enormous coastline, but we should concentrate on the Pacific side. Where will they put their missile carrying submarines? Off our west coast cities, right? Can we, do we have enough of these buoys to employ them off our cities? How far out do we have to put them? I don't know the technical aspects but check into that and see if we can put passive buoys out there. Let me know what you can do. Is a week enough time for you to get some answers on that, Admiral Stark? If it is possible, go ahead and get started, don't wait for my OK. Get it done."

"I'll get some answers to you sooner than that, Mr. President. We will do what we can with what we have while we work on improving and expanding whatever resources we have ready to field."

"What about passive mines? Can we mine our own coast? Do we have mines that can release homing torpedoes against a sub? Can we integrate those with our buoys? Can we program them to not detonate against our own ships or neutral shipping, but against enemy submarines? Can we code them to tell the difference, or will they have to be controlled from shore? I am open to any and all possibilities to protect us against the threat of cruise missiles and ballistic missiles. God, why didn't we fund the necessary research for all this way back in the 1990s?"

Johnny Withers walked into the room and handed President Thornton a piece of paper. The room fell quiet as Thornton read it. He took off his glasses, sighed and looked at his cabinet and officers. "Singapore has just announced that it has reached conciliation with the People's Republic of China. Singapore will become a Chinese city. The Chinese will not occupy Singapore en masse but will 'manage' the city and its economy. It will become another Hong Kong. The Chinese Army will stop its main line of march twenty-five kilometers north of the city. Strict orders have been issued to the Chinese soldiers that Singaporeans are not to be molested in any way. Food, water and raw materials will continue to flow into the city as usual. It is to be considered an open city managed by Chinese officials. Singapore, however, will not accept any refugees."

Thornton looked up. "Well, hell, if the Chinese are stopping twenty-five kilometers out and have been consuming everything in their line of march, where are the citizens of Singapore going to get their food and water anyway? That's a city of several million people. How are they going to keep the refugees out? Turn guns on their neighbors fleeing south? I guess the Chinese will have to feed and water them if they want the city to remain solvent and a center of technological excellence, manufacturing and trade. Singapore has a great harbor as well; it's one of the world's super ports, automated as it can be. I wonder if that has anything to do with this conciliation. Ed, let's keep a close watch on what happens around

Singapore. I can see why they want the city-state and its population intact. It is extremely wealthy, with a highly educated and technologically superior population."

Withers then handed the President a second piece of paper. It was from the British government. He read it out loud. "Given the agreement between the governments of Singapore and the People's Republic of China, Chinese troops will form a protective cordon around Singapore to stop the influx of refugees. Refugees will be fired upon if they attempt to breach the cordon, according to Chinese officials with whom British Embassy personnel had spoken earlier today. The BBC will carry a live broadcast from Singapore on their 22:00 hours news program. The Chinese representatives also stated that civil disobedience in Singapore will not be tolerated." That meant it would make the 18:00 hours, or six o'clock evening news, on the east coast of the United States.

CHAPTER 30

"I guess that means Chinese troops will drive down the highways and establish a line of troops that completely severs the peninsula just above Singapore. The refugees will be caught between the hammer and the anvil, and very few will survive. It also means that the large segment of the population of Singapore that is ethnic Chinese will be protected. That will give the Chinese an excuse to enter the city and break the agreement. If there are no riots, the Chinese will probably create one."

"Are there any indications that the Chinese are entering Korea, Ed?"

"No, Mr. President, at this time there are no indications that they intend to invade Korea. Everything seems oriented towards the west right now. I hope that makes Japan feel safer. The Chinese probably think they won't have any trouble taking Korea any time they wish now, and they are right. Korea, now one country, more or less, is theirs for the taking. It is essentially set back forty years and no threat whatsoever. At the worst scenario, it will be the classic springboard for an invasion of Japan, as described by the Prussian advisor to Japan in the 1890s that led to the Russo-Japanese war, as a 'dagger pointed at the heart of Japan.' That is what the Japanese are so worried about."

"What do any of you think of getting some food shipments to Korea?"

"No way, Mr. President. Their transportation network is destroyed. There is no way to distribute it, no indigenous capability to do so, no warehouses, vehicles or people. Any foreigner who would go into a land that suffered so many tactical nuclear blasts needs his or her head examined. Anybody who does so is an idiot. Then there are the problems with distribution itself even if someone could. I am referring to rioting, black market activities, outright banditry and assault of those delivering and trying to distribute it. Sorry to be so pessimistic, Mr. President."

"That's all right, General Anderson. You have been there as the former UN Commander and know the situation better than anybody. I'm glad you spoke with such finality that you quickly ended that idea without further discussion."

"Dr. Allison, anything you want to say about radiation or any other public health threats? Where do we stand on that?"

"The Chinese planned it very well, Mr. President. Pakistan and India essentially neutralized each other. While there are many initial survivors in the cities, they will die, fast or slow, depending upon the dosage of radiation poisoning, opportunistic infections as a result of radiation induced immune-incompetence, malnutrition, and just the bloodthirsty strong preying upon the weak for meager resources such as food and potable water. The radiation fallout is more or less contained on the Asian subcontinent by southeasterly winds that blow it onto the Himalayas during the rainy season. The rains wash it down the slopes and into the great rivers. Punjab, incidentally, means land between the five rivers, and onto the plains of India and Pakistan. There, it kills millions more and is ultimately washed into the Arabian Sea and Indian Ocean. In the fall, the winds are reversed, blowing from the northeast to the southwest, carrying away any residual airborne particles, blowing it back over India and Pakistan. Their troops march in during the fall before winter begins to a mostly cleansed land to pick up the pieces."

"How many dead are you estimating, Doctor?"

"There is no way to even provide a reasonable guess, Mr. President. Pakistan had over a hundred and fifty million people; India was approaching two billion souls. Those in the hills and mountains stand a much better chance of survival, at least initially, than those of the cities. India suffered greater casualty rates because of the terrain, the climate, winds, population concentrations, and so on. At least they didn't target Afghanistan, or if they have, nobody has told me about it. As for the number and range of yield of weapons exchanged, I haven't seen the data. That will have some influence as well. Sunlight will be reduced for a while, particularly in that region. That will make winter that much more difficult. The nuclear winter theory most likely will come into play on a modest scale. That will make survival harder for those who have made it thus far. Food and uncontaminated water will be an immediate problem. The cereal grains that were not harvested, which constitute the majority of the diet of those peoples, will be severely contaminated. Hunger, infections, increased severity of the coming winter, and psychological depression will all come together. Certainly, the dead number in the hundreds of millions, but how many hundreds of millions is anybody's guess.

"As for radiation reaching the United States, I don't think we will have too much to worry about. While we will see an increase, it will be very modest in size, and much of the radiation will be washed out of the skies by rains over the Pacific Ocean. The public needs to be informed of that, and I had the people at the Centers for Disease Prevention and Control work up another public education program. It will be released later this week so as to educate and avoid any noise about a public panic generated by an ignorant media."

"All right, people, what are we talking about time wise? If they go for the Persian Gulf, land and sea forces, how soon will we know and where is our demarcation line to launch World War III? Jim, what is the opinion of your folks?"

"Generals Craig, Anderson, and Leonard have been meeting on that very subject for the last two weeks. I believe I'll pass that off to General Leonard, since the Marines have more experience in the Central Asian Republics than anyone else, Mr. President. General?"

"Thank you, Mr. Secretary. When you get off the plains and start into the hill country, you get into the Pushtuns, or Pakhtuns, whichever pronunciation you prefer. They are an entirely different animal, Mr. President. They are the fiercest, most war-like people on earth. They are extremely proud, ignorant to the point of superstition, and almost ready to enter the nineteenth century. They are clan and tribal oriented, and governed by three overriding philosophies: badal, nanawati, and milmastia. These are referred to as Pakhtunwali, or the way of the Pakhtun. I mention this because the first, badal, is that they will take revenge, in blood, for the smallest, or even slightly perceived insult. They will fight to the death over badal. They have killed each other, even close blood relatives, over the centuries because of badal. I believe that the Pakhtuns are going to be a far harder nut to crack than the Chinese ever thought about. I have no doubt that they will fight until the last five-year-old kid can no longer pull a trigger. The Chinese are going to have to crawl over every rock, every ridge, and into every cave in order to kill them. They will kill Chinese until they are all dead. The Pakhtuns still have millions of small arms all over Pakistan and Afghanistan. Every adult owns at least one rifle, plenty of ammunition, a dagger, and possibly even a sword from the nineteenth century. Afghanistan and Pakistan encompass, and cut through, many tribal areas. The concept of those entities as individual nations is secondary to them thinking of themselves as tribal entities. They consider the border as arbitrary and unnecessary. Like the Arabs, they are known to switch sides in the middle of a battle, according to who pays them the highest bribe. In the case of badal, however, there is no question. It is the overriding concept in all of Pakhtun life. Anyone who does not practice it is scorned and considered less than a man.

"For this reason, above all others, I believe the Chinese march through Pakistan and Afghanistan will take them several months. Pakhtun life is much more primitive than most of the Chinese now have, even those from the rural areas. They can withstand the harsh mountain winter far better than the Chinese from the coasts and more temperate regions. The Chinese better have lots of tough, well trained troops to sacrifice and lots of ammunition to expend, because the Pakhtuns are certainly going to extract as much blood as possible. While we Chiefs of Staff disagree among ourselves, it is only a matter of degree. General Anderson thinks it will be all over by January. I think the Pakhtuns will hold out until spring, when they will come out of their holes with a vengeance and conduct guerilla warfare like the Chinese never imagined. They will ask no quarter, and none will be given.

"Unfortunately, the tyrannical governments of the Central Asian Republics didn't allow Pakhtunwali to continue. They clamped down on anyone who threatened, or whom they perceived threatened, state security.

Their leaders have been more like miniature Stalins in the early days of the Soviet Union. This is one reason they are being overrun far more quickly than we anticipate Pakistan and Afghanistan will be. Therefore, Mr. President, we have decided to recommend the Iranian border as the line of demarcation for our action. If they cross into Iran, or within a hundred miles of the Turkmenistan or Uzbekistan borders with Iran, there is little alternative for the west."

"Thank you, General. That begs the question, then: can we supply small arms to the Pakhtuns, as you call them? How would we get them in and distribute them?"

"There are several possible ways to do that, Mr. President. One is simply to supply them to Iran and let Iran make the distribution. Of course, Iran will keep a goodly supply, if not all, for itself. Otherwise, we go through the Central Asian Republics. We can go through Turkey and southern Russia, cross the Caspian, and supply Kazakhstan, Uzbekistan, and Turkmenistan. No telling how many they would rip off, even though it would be in their own best interest to pass them on and let the Afghans do the initial fighting. Of course, they might not even make it to Afghanistan or Pakistan. Alternatively, we could air drop them onto Pakistani and Afghani villages directly. That's the only sure way to get them to the Pakhtuns and avoid being ripped off, so to speak. Frankly, I don't think we have all that many left in storage and probably won't be able to crank enough out of our manufacturing system to provide more than several hundred thousand all total before Pakistan and Afghanistan are overrun. The Army has, for several decades now, purchased its rifles from Fabrique Nationale of Belgium. We really don't manufacture most of our own small arms anymore."

Jesus Christ, thought Jason Thornton. *We can't even manufacture our own small arms anymore? We have outsourced even our own military's personal weaponry!*

Instead, he said, "Ed, Jim, get your heads together. Take whatever small arms and ammunition we have in storage and air drop them on Pakhtun villages. Nothing sophisticated. Include explosives as well; I presume those people know what dynamite is. Try and do it as surreptitiously as possible; I don't care how you do it, make it happen. Make sure there are no Made in USA paintings on the crates. If the Chinese detect and protest it, so be it, but get it done anyway! We'll tell them it is humanitarian supplies, food and medicines.

"Jim, get contracts with all of our small arms and ammunition manufacturers to start cranking out our own weapons again. I want round the clock shifts going on ammunition and small arms production. If the Chinese even think about carrying out an invasion of the United States, and that includes Hawaii, I want us to be able to arm every able-bodied male. Maybe the founding fathers' definition of militia was right after all.

"Also, see what we can do about bringing home all the outsourced components of more sophisticated weapons that are manufactured overseas. Why should our sophisticated weapons depend upon components manufactured in China, or, for that matter, Southeast Asian countries that are being overrun by the Chinese? Get with the folks in Silicone Valley and bring home everything, every weapons component that we can in as short a time as possible. If you need to promote somebody to whatever level as an HMFIC in order to get it done, do it over my signature. Budget balancing be damned. I will have to meet with our congressional leaders and see about more funding for defense. If they don't cooperate, we will crash the Health and Human Services funding."

Marge Talbott raised her hand, with a terribly worried look on her face. "Mr. President, do you presume to consider that the Chinese might actually launch an invasion of the United States across the Pacific?"

"Marge, I don't know. Ask the Chinese what their ultimate objectives are. Where are they going, and why? What are all these new ocean-going catamarans for? We must be prepared for whatever they do.

"Jim, you and the Admirals put your heads together and see what you can do about protecting the sea lanes and the continental United States with mines, passive and active. All those things we previously mentioned, and how soon they can be deployed, are to be pursued. In the meantime, everybody be thinking about the possibility of re-instituting the selective service. We just might have to start drafting young people for military service. Peggy, make sure that is an agenda item for the next meeting with congressional leaders, reinstituting the draft."

"If you don't mind, Mr. President, I would like to meet with my flag officers for about ten minutes here right after we adjourn."

"Sure, Jim, you people are going to be extremely busy, and there is no use wasting time meeting somewhere else. If there is nothing else anyone wishes to bring up right now, let's go to work."

The room cleared within a few minutes, leaving the SECDEF and the Service Chiefs sitting around the table. Secretary of Defense Jim Neville made it brief. "On this rifle thing, we will bypass the Defense Logistics Agency. Their bureaucracy is too great and cumbersome. I am appointing the Army as lead agency in the procurement of rifles according to the President's wishes. General Anderson, make the Army Acquisition Corps the action people. Our primary concentration will be on semi-automatic rifles and will be of the M-16 type. We will let the first contracts as soon as possible. Now, don't give away the farm, make the contractors come in with reasonable prices. The rifles can be M-16A3s, M16-A4s, or M-4 carbines firing the 5.56x45 mm NATO cartridge. All will be in semi-automatic configuration only. No design that will allow modification for full automatic capability is to be accepted. Our first goal will be the procurement of five million rifles. I will make that an arbitrary figure. Utilize all possible manufacturers within the United States. Include the little guys who have been making them for the civilian market, such as Rock River, Armalite, Panther Arms, and so on. We won't buy any this time from foreign based firms. If they want to build plants here to produce them, I'll allow for that. All manufacturing will be in-house. I know setting up the appropriate tooling might be a time-consuming hindrance, so let's see who can produce that tooling ASAP for other potential manufacturers. This also means having tight ass inspectors in all of the plants to ensure quality. Everything will be to military specifications or higher. Primary manufacturers can outsource or subcontract for components all they wish, as long as those subcontractors are within the continental United States. I'll set the goal to be up and running in major production runs by the primary contractors sixty days from now with no decrease in quality.

"One exception to the M-16 type rifle I will make will be Sturm, Ruger and Company. We will buy their little Ruger Mini-14 as fast as they can produce them. That is a far better little rifle for civilians anyway.

Certainly, producing the magazines and ammunition will go hand in hand. Make it five magazines per rifle, twenty rounds per magazine, for twenty-five million magazines. On the ammunition account, I know we have been buying foreign made ammunition for the last twenty years. Contact our overseas suppliers and see how fast they can provide us with increased production. The same goes for magazines, especially from Italy where we have been buying a lot of them. We will need it sooner than we need the rifles. Look to Israeli Military Industries in particular. They are among the best and least expensive. At one thousand rounds per rifle, that will require five billion rounds of ammunition. Run our own plants 24/7. At the same time, start looking for storage places in every corner, as in National Guard armories and depots all around the country. If we have to let contracts to build small, secure, temperature-controlled arms bunkers on National Guard and Army Reserve properties, do that as well. If we have to arm the civilian population, then we don't want to have a distribution problem at the last minute.

"General Anderson, expand the Army's armorer training program. Run it day and night if necessary. Double or triple the class size and number of classes wherever your school is. Call for volunteers. If that isn't sufficient, then reassign people in uniform. That goes for the other branches of services as well. Change the Table of Distribution and Allowances for all the maintenance companies in the Guard and Reserves to add the extra armorers for small arms. If we go back to the draft, it will mostly likely be that we will tremendously expand the Reserves and Guard rather than the Active components. This applies in particular to the Army. General Craig for all services and General Anderson, especially for the Army, get with your personnel people and start studying that. Look at the possibilities of adding several million men to the National Guard and Army Reserve. Make plans for rapid expansion in training. No shortcuts are to be taken in their training. The emphasis will be on light infantry. Make the basic training for these folks just the same as the active Army. I don't want to have to go back and retrain multiple divisions as we had to do in the first Gulf War in 1991 when reservists didn't know how to load a rifle or throw a hand grenade. General Leonard, everything I said for the Army applies equally to the Marine Corps.

"I know the recruiting figures are way down. Nobody wants to go fight overseas, especially against the massed Chinese on the Asian continent. Therefore, we should consider planning for a subtle campaign, a propaganda campaign, to introduce the possibility of an invasion threat to the continental United States. I'll check with the President and see if he wants to release the news about the Chinese naval buildup. Then, some unnamed source in the Pentagon can 'leak' the news to a favorite journalist who can imply that the Chinese are massing a potential invasion force, possibly for the U.S. That should get the west coast folks concerned. Of course, the journalist will have to admit to the greater possibilities that the invasion fleet is aimed at the Middle East or elsewhere rather than the continental U.S., but the threat should not be ignored simply on those grounds. 'Uncle Joe' Stalin learned the hard way in World War II that people will fight for the homeland when they won't fight for the government. That is how we will have to play it. Any questions?"

"Mr. Secretary, what of other individual small arms and crew served weapons, such as machine guns, mortars and hand grenades? Certainly, we will need an increase in those weapons for training, if for no other purpose."

"Good thought, General Leonard. We will look at that later. I can see a modest need for an increase in those weapons. Right now, though, we will concentrate on the rifles, as we are about to deplete all our reserve stocks supplying the Afghans and surviving Pakistanis. Any other questions? No, well then, get back to me in a week with progress reports. Thank you, gentlemen."

"Mr. President, the Chinese Ambassador, His Excellency Kuan Sheng, is here for his appointment."

"Thank you, Peggy, have Johnny bring him in, and have tea served for the Ambassador." The President rose from his desk and walked around it to greet Mr. Kuan. "I am glad to see you, Mr. Ambassador. Please have a chair," indicating with a flourish of his hand to a chair at the end of the coffee table while he took another chair adjacent to it.

"Thank you, Mr. President. I am afraid my country is most upset with your letter of concerns about the progress of the Chinese Armies in the field. I have a written answer for you, which we hope assuages your concerns, but also points out certain vulnerabilities of your country. Please view this with an objective concern. China does not at all wish to threaten our greatest trading partner and the first true country of democracy. That would destroy our own economy. Rather, it is to inform you of the price you will be expected to pay if you interfere with China's destiny." The Ambassador handed Jason Thornton a letter. Jason Thornton extended his hand and took it.

Dear President Thornton:

The People's Republic of China is most distressed that you, the President of the greatest nation of the Twentieth Century and our greatest trading partner, would threaten our nation with nuclear holocaust when we pose absolutely no threat to you.

You have expressed concern about the possibility of our invasion of Iran and the threat we pose to the Persian Gulf area, the Middle East in general, and the flow of petroleum to your county, Europe, Japan and the rest of the world. We assure you, Mr. President, and the rest of the world as well, that we do not intend to invade Iran, Iraq, Saudi Arabia or any of the Persian Gulf states. We understand your concern for a continued flow of oil into the world market. We will do nothing to disrupt that flow from these sources. We will do nothing which threatens the United States or Europe unless we are similarly threatened. There have already been too many nuclear explosions over the last six months for eternity. Millions have already died this year over misunderstandings. Let us hope there are no more.

Should, however, the United States declare war, or launch an undeclared war in the form of a surprise attack on the People's Republic of China or her armed forces anywhere in the world, the People's Republic of China will respond with massive retaliation against your nation. You are no doubt aware that we have numerous nuclear missile carrying submarines armed with both biological and nuclear weapons off both coasts of North America. In addition, the garrison in the Republic of Panama is armed with intermediate range missiles that are tipped with multiple re-entry vehicle warheads that have an interesting array of biological weapons as well as nuclear warheads. Each is programmed to strike a different American target should war erupt between our countries. Should armed conflict come between our countries, it is doubtful that the United States will continue to exist in its present state. The leader of so wise and powerful a nation as the United States with three hundred million citizens would surely not put it in the path of destruction when your nation is not threatened.

The People's Republic of China most sincerely hopes you will not regard this as a threat or a challenge, but merely as a matter of informing you of our capabilities. You are the leader of the western world, and it is China's destiny to be the leader of the eastern world. Together, we can ensure that the world will be a peaceful and prosperous world in which to work and play and love.

Most respectfully,
The People's Republic of China

Jason Thornton took off his glasses and rubbed his eyes. He looked at the Chinese Ambassador, who avoided his gaze.

"This memorandum certainly spells it out very clearly, Mr. Ambassador. Your country doesn't want war any more than mine does. Yet you are prepared to go the distance of nuclear war with us if we interfere with your invasion of other countries. To make sure there are no misunderstandings, Mr. Ambassador, I will reiterate. Iran, the Persian Gulf States, Saudi Arabia and Iraq are off limits to China. If one soldier sets foot across any of those borders, make no mistake, we will go to war over it."

"My country fully understands and appreciates your position, Mr. President. We read western military history in China as well as Asian military history. We are acutely aware of the tragedy that happened through miscommunication and misunderstandings of motives that led to the terrible Russo-Finnish War of 1939-1940. The terrible price paid by both sides that could have been avoided through clear communication if each side only understood from where the other was coming and why. I have the highest confidence that our Supreme Council will honor its word and remain a considerable distance from those borders, sufficiently so that you can monitor those said borders from your now many functional satellites. In fact, I have been authorized to invite you to send your observers and representatives to the eastern side of the borders of those named countries. Your people will be treated as our guests with the greatest attention and care to ensure that no harm comes to them whatsoever. They will be provided with vehicles, guides, or whatever they wish to conduct their observations. Or, they can bring their own vehicles and equipment, whatever you and they decide is fine with us. They will not be interfered with in any way. They will have one hundred percent freedom of movement, to come and go, and go anywhere, at any time, as they choose. They can set up satellite communications and convey their findings to you at any time. In fact, we would be delighted to have their company. We find such experts are usually quite intelligent and most amiable. They make very good company. This invitation extends not only to your government representatives, but to members of the western press as well. If I might add, journalists generally do not make quite as good company as your representatives."

"Your offer is most generous, Mr. Ambassador. I will share this communication with the appropriate people in this government. I thank you and the People's Republic for spelling it out so clearly; more so, I must say, than most of your written communications. There is no ambiguity here that we normally find in our written communiqués."

"Thank you, Mr. President. I am also instructed to inform you that similar letters have been sent to the governments of Russia, Japan, and interested European nations. If there are no other subjects of discussion, then I will be on my way to let you continue with your affairs of state. Thank you for the time and the very excellent tea, which, I understand, is a product of my country."

"It is, Mr. Ambassador, and I must admit, the world's finest tea. Give my respects to Mrs. Kuan. Good day, Mr. Ambassador."

Jason Thornton hit a buzzer on his desk, and Johnny Withers came in to escort the ambassador out. "Peggy, come in, please," Thornton called over the intercom. He handed her the letter the ambassador had delivered.

"Peggy, make a copy of this for all of the service chiefs, each member of my cabinet, and the chairs of the House and Senate Committees on Foreign Relations and Defense. See that they all get it before close of business today. I want to discuss it at our tri-weekly breakfast meeting tomorrow. Label it Top Secret, no Critical. Put a memorandum on it from me that they are not to share this with members of their respective committees at this time."

CHAPTER 31

"**E**verybody continue to eat while somebody else is talking. What do you have, Ed?"

"Mr. President, the Chinese Army Front of the Asian Subcontinent has split apart. We have named the Army Group moving south through the Indian Peninsula, Army Group South. The other group going across the to of India, we have named Indian Army Group West. Army Group West is now into eastern Pakistan. It appears to be further subdividing into three armies. It appears that one Army will swing northwest, one group will swing south southwestward in the direction of the Iranian border, and the central army will move due west towards Afghanistan. It appears they plan to link with what we call the Central Asian Army Front. Strictly conjecture on our part, but we think the two Army Fronts will link up somewhere along the Turkmenistan-Uzbekistan border. We have no people on the ground in any of these areas due to the threat of radioactive fallout. All of this information is a result of satellite intelligence and monitoring radio signals between the various units.

"Another interesting fact has come to light, Mr. President. You recall all those merchant ships that were tied up in Chinese harbors? We discovered that they are being converted into troop carriers. That means they are planning an amphibious invasion. Our demographers indicate that they can field several million more people. How well trained they are is anybody's guess. They are using the home guard, so to speak. These home guard units never trained together in units larger than a battalion. Obviously, they have been planning this for years. Each battalion is assigned a line of march and told to live off the land by whatever means. They march until the battalion ceases to exist. Then they throw another one in behind it on the same line of march to continue until they reach the sea or their final objective, wherever that is. Any survivors of the first unit simply join the second unit. The question is: why all those troop ships? Do they plan to bring troops home in them? I don't think so. The fleet of ocean-going catamarans suggests that they intend to have an oceanic sea line of supply and communications. They will have their armies on the borders of Iran on the north and east, so why the seagoing effort? Do they plan to keep them supplied on the coasts by ship? There aren't very many good harbors on the Arabian Sea. Do they intend to take the Japanese Islands? That has the Japanese really concerned, I'll bet. Or, they might take Taiwan and eliminate their population, and then move on to Japan.

"Pakistan? In another month or less, they will be through Pakistan; minimal or no organized resistance there, especially in the central and southern and western parts. There wasn't a city of 100,000 or more that didn't take a nuclear hit of some size. Too many nukes and fallout created real survivor problems. There are small pockets of survivors in the mountain valleys, but who knows how long they will last. The Chinese will find out the hard way about Pakhtunwahli, the way of the Pakhtun, which is the proper term for these people, not Pathan. They will fight for vengeance if it takes one hundred years or until they are all dead. The Chinese will follow the Indus and Sutlej Rivers all the way through Hydrabad and take Karachi en route, provided the fallout has decreased to their definition of tolerable levels. Surviving Pakistani Army units might block some critical passes for a while, but the Chinese will undoubtedly flank south of the Sulaiman Mountain Range and come up on the west side.

"Afghanistan, well, the Afghanis will play hell with their supply lines for a while, they are really Pushtuns, or Pakhtuns if you prefer, as well. The only difference between Afghans and Pakistanis is tribal. They really are the same people. The British in the form of Sir Henry Durand drew the line dividing those countries on a map from mountain top to mountain top in 1893. In so doing, he cut across more than a dozen Pakhtun tribes. If the Chinese go to nerve gas or something like that over wide areas or whole villages, however, they won't last long. Persistent agents, artillery or aircraft delivered, such as VX nerve gas in cooler and cold weather or the use of a mustard formulation in warmer weather that contaminates the land for a week or two will put a major restraint on guerilla warfare. The Chinese might get a couple of hundred million dollars in raw opium out of Afghanistan; otherwise, there isn't much reason for them to pause there."

"Ms. Stearns, do you have any ideas on their ultimate objective?"

"Only conjecture, Mr. President. It would seem the Persian Gulf would be most logical. Still, the Chinese are masters at what appears to be illogical, only to be completely logical in the long term. They think in generations, while we think in months to a few years at most. I don't believe they plan to invade North America, that is so improbable, but you never know." She almost said, *We think only in terms of the next election,* but she bit her lip and thought better of it.

"All right, folks, I have about made up my mind. If they threaten Iran, we have to go. The only way we can go is nuclear. So, where do we hurt them, the Chinese littoral, along the Pacific Rim, as Marge previously suggested, or their armies in the field? General Craig, what are your suggestions?"

"The Romans once faced a somewhat similar situation with an upstart Carthaginian named Hannibal. They couldn't defeat him tactically on the battlefield, so they defeated him strategically. They decided to cut his supply lines and let him wither on the vine, so to speak, that is, in the field. If we take out their major coastal cities and ordnance centers and naval centers, what will the armies in the field do? Soon, they will run out of ammunition. They have practiced a scorched earth policy as they moved, so there is nothing left for them to eat behind themselves, rather like Napoleon's strategic retreat from Moscow in the middle of winter, when most of his army froze and starved to death. If we cut their strategic sources, that is, we take out their production centers, then they, too, will wither on the vine.

"Alternatively, we can try and strategically interdict their supply lines. Remember, though, we couldn't stop the flow of men and materiel down the Ho Chi Minh Trail in the Vietnam war. There is no way we can interdict their overland supply routes. It might apply to the high seas, however. Even if we do interdict them on the high seas, that does not negate their overland supply routes. Oceanic interdiction means we will have to neutralize their fleets of catamarans, troop carrying ships, and their submarine fleet. The order of targeting will have to be, above all, their submarine fleet, followed by their surface fleet of new destroyers and cruisers, then their cargo ships and catamarans. That is not as effective as destroying the manufacturing centers, but then, we have found in World War II, Vietnam, and the Balkans, that strategic bombing doesn't always work either. With the use of nuclear weapons as opposed to conventional bombs, that will in all likelihood change. If we go nuclear after their strategic industrial centers, they won't have time or, hopefully, the means to rebuild in the next five to ten years. We can deliver nuclear warheads via intercontinental missiles and submarine launched missiles, on their centers, but what of our coastal cities within reach of their missile carrying submarines? We don't have a missile defense umbrella over this country. Your predecessor saw to that. Do we give the Chinese another warning that attacking Iran will not be tolerated and surrender the element of surprise, or attack without warning? We have already told them we will not allow the invasion of Iran. What of a declaration of war from Congress before we launch into nuclear war? I see no conventional alternative that would be anywhere effective, and certainly not worth the cost, Mr. President. It will have to be a simultaneous attack on their missile carrying capabilities, their ships and submarines, and nuclear attack on their homeland."

"Admiral Stark, do you agree with General Craig?"

"Yes, Mr. President, I do. His strategic thinking is sound. There is no way to interdict their landlocked supply lines. My greatest concern is that if we go after their sea lines of communication, whether or not we have the Navy to take out the submarine fleet, followed by their surface naval fleet, which is doubtful, we still can't cut their land routes. The Chinese have surprised us with the quality and number of ships and submarines over the last decade, especially the latter, as I indicated in my briefing two weeks ago. We will give it 100%, if that is your decision. We'll make them pay a terrible price. Who knows, maybe after the fallout settles, China will break into seven kingdoms again."

"Marge?"

"Mr. President, if we declare war with an act of Congress, the Chinese will know it within minutes and could launch their missiles at us from their submarines, and who knows, maybe their ICBMs are now fully operational. Still, I would not want to launch my country into a potentially nation-destroying event without the consent of the people through their representatives, the Congress. What happens if we draw the proverbial line in the sand and tell the Chinese where we have drawn it? Doesn't that put the ball in their court?"

The President thought about it for a moment, looked at the faces of his cabinet. He picked these people because they, at least for the most part, had a fundamental belief in the Constitution as it was written. *How does one declare war when such a declaration could result in the annihilation of your country within hours, if not minutes?* he thought. Out loud, he said, "I'll have to ponder that. The rest of you do so as well. I don't know if we will resolve that at this time."

"What are the Chinese doing about the larger cities of the nations they have invaded? Ed?"

"Mr. President, it appears that they are completely isolating and bypassing them, laying siege to them in the barest sense of the word. They are using just enough troops to keep the population bottled up but are not invading the cities. Most of the Chinese armies are marching right past them, while selected units keep the gates shut. It appears their strategy is simply to starve them to death, nothing in, nothing out. Since there is nothing to bring in due to their scorched earth policy, it appears to be a deliberate policy of starvation. Cannibalism will soon take hold, if it hasn't already, in cities like Hanoi. That won't last long in tropical and subtropical heat, even in the winter months. Bodies don't keep in any such environment. Any attempts to escape by sea are sunk by their coastal patrol boats and destroyer escorts."

Robert Wha Lee drove west on Interstate 70 and turned north on U.S. 15 and drove through Harrisburg, PA. Tired, he drove into a Wendy's and ordered their latest sandwich, with large coffee, Coca-cola and French fries. He ate as he pushed northward, turning west on Interstate 90 towards Buffalo, NY. He stopped at a small motel outside Niagara Falls for the night. After supper at Bonanza, he retired to his room for a hot shower. He turned on the television, turned down the lights, and unpacked his suitcase. Carefully removing the suitcase lining that was held in place with Velcro, he removed a civilian passport, driver's license, Elk's Club card, library card, three credit cards from major banks, and a picture of himself with a young lady. He was now Robert Zin Wang, of Washington, DC. He placed his White House and Secret Service credentials very carefully in the sewn in pockets on the backside of the liner and replaced it in the suitcase. He deliberately left his sidearm in his apartment. Canada would not even allow American law officers to enter their country with sidearms. More importantly, it would be difficult to explain if it was discovered in the possession of Robert Zin Wang.

After breakfast, he crossed into Canada at Niagara Falls, drove through Hamilton and Toronto, and turned north on Route 400 towards Sudbury. At the town of Parry Sound, he turned left, toward the Georgian Bay and the Thirty Thousand Islands. He left his car at the resort car park and boarded a boat for the isolated fishing lodge on one of the many islands in the Bay. At the lodge, he was greeted very cordially. He had stayed at the Royal Lodge of the Pines on several previous occasions. He was not a big tipper but left enough for the staff to remember him each time he visited. He arrived in time for a supper of fresh lake trout, white wine, broccoli and mashed potatoes with almond chips. His dessert of ice cream and chocolate syrup was served by a Chinese waiter who greeted him very cordially. Frank Li Yunn was a naturalized Canadian citizen. He arrived nearly twenty years ago from Hong Kong and immediately found employment at the Royal Lodge of the Pines where he had worked ever since. Frank and his wife lived on the island year round. Someone had to care for the resort throughout the winter which could be brutal and damaging to the facilities. It was perfect for the Yunns. They had no children. The island was ten miles out into the Georgian Bay, so it was only natural that the resort had a very substantial short wave radio capability, and Frank was the resident expert with it. He routinely used the radio as a hobby, talking with people around the world several times a week. In his verbal conversations, sent in the clear, he would often mispronounce words, or leave out key words that would make a complete sentence. It comprised a very open, very pragmatic, very innocent, and a very effective code simply to let the powers that be know a message was about to be delivered.

"I hope you are staying all week, Mr. Wang," he said as he served the ice cream dessert.

"I'm not sure how much time I will have, but I hope the fish are biting. It will certainly influence me to stay as long as I can." This message was routine, not only between Robert Wha Lee and Frank, but a number of other occasional ethnic Chinese visitors.

Robert Wha Lee did not ordinarily smoke. He was smoking a cigar that evening as he walked along the beach, staying close to the timber after the sun went down. Frank Lee Yunn stepped out between the trees. "I hope the cigar tastes good, Mr. Lee."

"Yes, it does, but I generally smoke them to keep the mosquitoes and midges away. I don't like smelling like insect repellent. I believe the fish can pick up the molecules of the repellent on the lures after handling them, Mr. Yunn."

The two men stepped back into the trees. It got dark early in the northern latitudes in the late fall of the year. The wind was moderate, but the temperature was hovering just above freezing. Both men wore heavy coats and hats. They spoke in low tones and in Chinese.

"What do you have for me?"

"The American President is becoming very nervous. They have, or more precisely, are attempting to coordinate what will be an appropriate response with allies. That's a loose usage of that word, allies. America doesn't have any. It only has temporary coalition partners. Naturally, Russia is the one nation which has the greatest concern. Anyway, they have decided to drop small arms to the Central Asian Republics and the Pakhtuns in Afghanistan and western Pakistan. It is the hope of the Americans that these forces can wage successful guerilla warfare against us the way they did against the Russians. They could be a thorn in our side, so to speak. Recall that the Russians were defeated after eight years of struggle in Afghanistan. They were supplied by the Americans with weapons and tactics, of course, but still, the Pakhtun concept of badal was impossible for the Russians to defeat. Also, remember it took the Americans several years to root out the majority of the Taliban elements in Afghanistan. Chances are that the Pakhtuns will forget their petty squabbles and work together against us, at least that is what the Americans are hoping.

"They are drawing the weapons from their reserves in stockpile, some from the reserve units and even some active ground forces while letting contracts for new ones. I am speaking primarily of semi-automatic rifles, of the M-16 variety. It is interesting that they should do so. They don't even produce their own rifles for their army. They don't have enough machine guns, grenades, and shoulder fired anti-aircraft missiles as yet to give away. They are essentially disarming themselves for an indefinite period of time, until they can replace them. That might take a year or even several years. On the other hand, they are pushing forward with advanced anti-submarine warfare efforts in co-ordination with the Japanese. That I don't like. They are talking of deploying anchored mines off the west coast to sink our submarines if we go to war. Jason Thornton took the threatening letter from the Council very seriously.

"They will quite likely draw the line at Iran. I can see it in Jason Thornton's mind. If we get too close to the border, they will go to Iran's aid as much as they hate to do so. The generals want to go strategic nuclear against our homeland. The threat to the Gulf oil is too critical not to, in their opinion. Quite possibly, they will employ tactical nuclear weapons against our field forces, although Margaret Talbott suggested they take out our coastal cities as a means of cutting off lines of communication to our field armies. That didn't fly very well, but I think it is in the back of Jason Thornton's mind. No one wants to create a nuclear winter that will threaten the entire world. They will most likely utilize submarine launched ballistic missiles out of the Arabian Sea or Indian Ocean. We should concentrate our submarine fleet there, but of course, that is so obvious that General Chang will immediately do so without my having to mention it. Japan has requested the U.S. to build them as many new DDX destroyers as they can as fast as they can. The United States Navy will, of course, want them all for themselves. The Japanese didn't even ask about the price. They just said build them and we will buy them. The Americans and Japanese will need five years or perhaps more to adequately prepare, even with crash programs. Of course, they don't have that much time. Our offensive should be over by the middle of next summer.

"Marge Talbott has expressed the opinion that the Americans can't go to war without a declaration of war by Congress, according to their Constitution. That should give us both plenty of warning and a good laugh if they are that stupid. The military, obviously, prefers a surprise attack, without warning of any kind. If the U.S. Navy suddenly deploys, then that is the key. The Americans won't commit any land forces to a war halfway around the world. They simply don't have the army for massed confrontation. They can't get the Army there in a timely manner anyway, at least nothing other than one or two light divisions without armor or real artillery to support them. They won't be able to fight our field armies the way they did in the Second Gulf War or Afghanistan. We simply will overwhelm them. In spite of their new doctrine, mass is still a critical element of war.

"It has been an excellent plan to allow the foreign media, especially the Europeans, into the war zone. The nightly news pictures from the various fronts, especially from the nuclear devastated areas, have scared the American public almost out of its mind. At this point, I don't think the American public will support a war at all. As long as they don't feel the American homeland is threatened, they will stay out of our way. Of course, if we get too close to Iran, Thornton will probably launch regardless of the American public's perspective. He might just launch unilaterally, without the support of Europe. McCluskey and Neville would go for that. The European Union and NATO are still essentially paper tigers without any real military force at all. Their economic and military clout was diluted when they expanded to twenty-five nations in 2004. They can't agree on anything that is practical or field worthy. They haven't been able to bring the original EU members up to military snuff, let alone the new members. No, the threat will come from Thornton and his crew, with a little help from Japan. The Hollywood crowd and elitist liberals will howl like beaten dogs."

Unknown to Robert Wha Lee, Frank Li Yunn was wearing a minute recorder just under his coat collar. The microphone was very sensitive, and the recorder put every word Lee said on tape. Early in the morning of the next day, a launch delivering groceries would dock at the lodge. The boatman took a package of mail and other things to the mainland. Among them was a small package that he delivered to a resident of the town. It contained the tape recorded conversation between Yunn and Lee. A small company which manufactured very good but very expensive fishing lures and trout flies would include it in its routine outgoing shipping. Federal Express picked up shipments every afternoon; FEDEX would make sure that it reached an address in Ottawa the following day. Once in Ottawa, it would be immediately delivered to the Chinese embassy by the resident at the address on the package. In the embassy, it would be studied upon arrival, not only for its contents, but interpretation of how Robert Lee said it. The tape and the interpretation would then be placed in the diplomatic pouch and flown to Peking where another independent analysis would be made, and notes compared with the first. Robert Wha Lee's tapes always had first priority for interpretation and discussion. His predictive accuracy was in the 99th percentile range. Six days later, Robert Wha Lee retraced his steps and procedures to cross back into the United States. He brought several photos of himself with fish he caught.

———————— •◦◆◦• ————————

Yang Chi was just a little bit drunk. He hadn't had a woman in a year, and he felt the need for feminine comfort. He was thirty years old and felt that his virility was suffering. His libido had suffered enough. He worked out at a commercial gymnasium five nights a week, and his daily practice in the evenings of martial arts was wearing pretty thin. He didn't work out long at home, only one hour or so most of the evenings. Usually, he just went through the katas to keep in practice. He kept his hands in shape by bare handed punching on the one hundred pound punching bag in the spare bedroom he used as his home gym. He only lifted weights and jogged on the treadmills at the commercial gym. He was under strict orders not to demonstrate his martial arts skills for fear of discovery of his true identity. He was not to attract any undue attention to himself. Leaner than his former partner, Ling Ch'ung, he was still very lithe and muscular.

He had casually observed for some months now the constant stream of men coming and going into the modest neighborhood hotel. He believed there must be a reason, and his assumption was correct. His suspicions aroused, he confirmed his own views after several evenings and weekends of surveillance. Young, quite attractive Caucasian females also came and went. He did not know that they were essentially white slaves provided by the Russia mafia. These were young women who were promised marriage opportunities and jobs in the United States for a price. They were told that ten percent of their earnings and a modest profit of fifteen percent for the company would be collected until the cost of their immigration was recovered. They weren't told they would be forced into prostitution to earn that money under pain of death or torture.

Yang Chi approached the hotel desk and smiled politely at the clerk, a middle aged man of considerable size. He spoke with an accent when Yang Chi inquired about the price of a room for the evening. Yang Chi nodded and placed fifty dollars on the counter. He signed the registry card without saying a word. He rather stupidly put his current address on the card. When the clerk looked at the card to file it, he noticed the local address. Between Yang's accent, appearance as an Asian, and address on the card, lack of luggage, he anticipated Yang wanted more than just a room. He just looked at Yang for a moment, waiting for him to speak. Yang just stood there, slightly glaring back. The clerk could smell the bourbon on Yang's breath. Finally, he asked Yang Chi, "Are there any particular services you had in mind?"

Yang's eyes narrowed, not quite sure how to reply. This was all new to him. "I noticed there are many young women in this hotel. Is there any possibility of meeting one of them?" he asked.

The clerk smiled, "Of course, there is always that opportunity. There are several in the lobby on the left. You should certainly feel free to introduce yourself to any of them that you find attractive. I believe you will find them all attentive to your needs."

Yang Chi proceeded cautiously into the indicated lobby. Before him, sitting around in rather provocative dress, were more than half a dozen young, attractive women. The evening was still young, and business didn't pick up until after 22:00 hours. Blondes predominated, but there were two redheads and two with dark hair. Yang wondered about those with red hair. Were they any different than Chinese girls, he wondered?

He stiffly approached the nearest one and said, "Good evening, my name is Chi, and I am here for a little while on a business trip. Is it possible that we could become acquainted?" The young lady smiled, trying not to giggle, but the other girls all smiled or smirked at the courtesy of his approach. He looked around with a glare at the giggles, which abruptly stopped when they saw the intensity of his gaze.

He turned back to the young lady, who said, "Of course, Chi. My name is Lila. Do you have a room? Would you like a drink?"

"Yes, Lila, on both counts."

"Good, so would I. Would you mind so much as purchasing a bottle for us, along with a six pack of Coca-cola for me? I like to drink my liquor mixed with soda. You can buy a bottle in the bar in the other lobby, across the foyer. I will accompany you." She took him by the arm and led him into the bar. "Jack, will you sell my date a fifth of Jack Daniels, black label, please, and a six pack of cold Coke?", Lila coyly asked of the bartender. Jack smiled and put an unopened fifth on the counter along with a six pack.

"That will be twenty dollars even, Mister." Yang Chi opened his wallet and laid a twenty dollar bill on the counter and picked up the bottle while Lila took the Coke.

"What room are you in?" Lila asked as she led him to the elevator. "You must tell me about yourself. You said you were new in town, what business are you in?" The girls were instructed to glean as much personal information out of their clients as possible. If their client was deemed sufficiently important, it could result in blackmail. Selected rooms were equipped with video cameras that could film at different angles. A control room behind the front desk monitored the rooms from time to time for possible filming.

Inside the room, Lila poured them each a drink while Yang sat on the bed and watched. She handed Yang a bourbon and soda without asking him what he liked. His was mostly alcohol, hers mostly soda. She enticingly fingered the top button of her blouse. "So, tell me, Yang, what do you do? You must be important."

"I am a warehouse man for an international shipping company. I direct people where and how to stack things in warehouses."

"That's interesting. What company do you work for?"

Chang blurted out, "COSCO, a very large international company." He began to gulp his drink.

This one shouldn't last too long, thought Lila as she sipped her own drink. It had just enough whiskey in it to be detected on her breath. "What do you stack in your warehouses?"

"Mostly electronics, computers, televisions, stereo sets, DVDs, those things." Yang was beginning to stutter just a bit. The bouncer monitoring the conversation in the room behind the front desk was becoming interested. This could develop into a source of hijacked electronics. Being Russian, he never cared for the Chinese anyway. He picked up the phone and dialed Yang's room. Lila answered the phone with a hello.

"Get as much information out of him as you can before you seduce him. Let's find out how much he is worth and all about those warehouses," and hung up.

"Who was that?" asked Yang.

"Oh, it was a wrong number," she replied. She poured him another drink. "Your warehouse must be on the docks somewhere, Mr. Yang."

"It is adjacent to the COSCO pier. We have a dozen warehouses there. I just work in one or two."

"You must be a very responsible man to oversee such expensive goods in a large warehouse complex like that. I hope they pay you what you are worth." She sat in a chair adjacent to the bed, letting her mini skirt ride even further up on her thighs, revealing her long, lean legs. She began to fumble with the top button of her blouse.

"They pay me enough." His mouth became dry as she slowly unbuttoned her blouse in front of him. "I am paid well, too, Mr. Yang. I will spend the night with you for three hundred dollars. If you just want an hour of my time, it is only one hundred dollars."

"You are very expensive. Are you worth it?"

She slipped off her mini skirt, then her blouse, revealing a modest bosom in an uplifting bra and all of her long, lean legs beneath slim hips clothed in red panties.

"What do you think?" she asked.

"I think you are worth one hundred dollars. He removed his wallet and laid the money alongside it on the dresser. He then began to undress, but she came over and did it for him. He didn't last five minutes before reaching a climax. Thirty minutes later, he wanted more sex. He wanted something different. This redhead didn't seem all that different from Chinese girls. He rolled her over on her abdomen and attempted to sodomize her. She struggled.

"I don't do that," she cried. The more she struggled, the madder he got. She began to protest in a loud voice. He slapped her on the back of the head with a heavy hand that stunned her. "No, no, I won't do it!"

Yang yanked her up by the hair. He kidney punched her, then rolled her over and slapped her back and forth across the face. The bouncer in the back room jumped up, grabbed the spare room key from the pigeon hole and started up the elevator. When he entered the room, Yang was holding her up in a sitting position, slapping the unconscious girl back and forth across the face. He didn't hear the bouncer enter. George hit Yang with a fist behind the ear. It staggered Yang, who dropped the girl and spun around off the bed. George hit him with a right cross that laid Yang back across the bed. Yang lashed out with a foot that caught George in the groin. George staggered back in agony. Yang came off the bed with a roundhouse kick that caught George on the shoulder and sent him across the room. George got up only to receive a spinning wheel kick in the solar plexus followed by a fist to the chest. George's face went blank. Two more body blows broke ribs and stopped George's heart in diastole. George sank to the floor, dead.

Yang looked around, stunned by what he had done. He quickly dressed, took his wallet and the one hundred dollars he left on the counter and bolted from the room. The desk clerk saw him hurriedly leaving and went to the back room where the monitors had recorded everything. He saw an unconscious Lila and a dead George. He called the police.

Lila and George were taken to the nearest hospital, where Lila was placed in intensive care with a severely damaged kidney and a battered face. Yang's calloused knuckles had cut her face in numerous places as he open-handedly slapped her, but he didn't break any bones. George went to the hospital morgue for post mortem examination.

The police took the videotape and fingerprinted the room after photographing everything. An all-points bulletin went out for Yang. His fingerprints from his whiskey glass were quite clear. They went into the FBI's file twenty-four hours later as a matter of routine for murder cases. Yang's face was sufficiently revealed on the videotape for the police to print a picture from it. His address on the registration card resulted in the police getting a search warrant and surrounding his apartment building four hours later.

The FBI surveillance team observed Yang walking hurriedly and animatedly out of the hotel. As usual, they followed him at a discrete distance. He did not return to his apartment, rather he went straight to the Chinese embassy. The surveillance team called Supervisory Special Agent Ed Wrangell. Then they waited a block from the gate of the Chinese embassy.

Two days later, a computer match reported the fingerprints from the Los Angeles Police Department matched those taken from the water glass of the bodyguard of Chan. The surveillance team, now two different men, reported that they had not observed Chan emerging from the Chinese embassy. Surveillance cameras that recorded every movement of every egress of the embassy did not reveal Yang leaving the embassy. On the third day, a rather large crate was taken from the embassy to the Baltimore-Washington International Airport, where it was placed on a China Airlines Boeing 747D destined for Peking. It was part of the diplomatic pouch. The crate was handled by China Airlines personnel from the moment it reached the China Airlines gate. Members of the FBI Task Force II watched it through the gates as it was loaded on the aircraft.

An inquiry by a "relative" with a heavy accent of the prostitute beaten by Yang gave the police clerk two one hundred dollar bills to answer his questions. "What information do you have on George's killer?"

The answer he received was, "The FBI is on the case. They think he got shipped out of country in a crate labeled diplomatic pouch. They think he's back in China now. He was supposed to work for a shipping company called COSCO. Nobody knows for sure, though."

In China, Yang Chi was sentenced to ten years hard labor, not for killing George or for beating Lila, but for a lack of discipline, for blowing his cover. The Chinese intelligence service immediately dispatched another bodyguard for Chan upon the arrival of Yang Chi. He would enter the United States by a submarine which would deliver him to a Chinese pleasure yacht thirty miles off the California coast.

CHAPTER 32

"**W**e'll start off this morning's breakfast discussion with General Craig, if you don't mind, General. After the Chinese letter about the threat from the Panama Canal towards the USA mainland, we should all know what's down there. I've asked Ralph to bring the Surgeon General along because of the nature of the threat. I think you all know Admiral Weber. What is the military situation in Panama, General Craig?"

"Mr. President, after we turned the Panama Canal over to the Panamanians in the Jimmy Carter administration, the Chinese quickly began to bribe the Panamanian officials for the use of the bases we vacated. The Chinese made millionaires out of a number of high and middle level bureaucrats. They quickly assumed control of the Canal itself through their front organizations, the Hutchinson-Whampoa International Shipping Company, and COSCO, the Chinese Ocean Shipping Company. As such, they assumed control of all the warehouses, locks, dams and everything else. At last count, there were about 20,000 Chinese in the Panama area, mostly in the Canal Zone itself. Many of them are military, but many of them are not. They always provided good service and plenty of warehouse space for anyone and everyone who wanted it. By everyone I mean every international shipper, company or country.

"They even built some new, temperature-controlled warehouses that they maintained for perishable foodstuffs from the Chinese mainland. At least, that is what they claimed they were for. They do cycle many tonnes, that's a thousand metric tons, of food through them, not only foodstuffs from the Orient, but Central and South America as well. We don't believe nearly enough foods go through there to utilize the full capacity of all those warehouses. It is possible they built an over capacity in anticipation of gradually increased business. There are certainly warehouses large enough to house several dozen IRBMs, intermediate range ballistic missiles. Being temperature-controlled would make sense for live biological agents in warheads. They could maintain such agents in the frozen state and load them into warheads in hours, if not minutes. Their IRBMs are sufficiently accurate now to hit any city in North America. They have a Circle of Equal Probability of fifty meters. That is more than sufficient for even conventional warheads. IRBMs are small enough that they can fit into standard sized shipping containers. Even if they weren't, they could be shipped in sections and assembled in the warehouses. If they put them on mobile launchers, they could pull them out of the warehouses with tractors and go over any road in Panama. They easily fit into a grain truck with false sides and roof. That would make them a bit harder to take out as individual rockets before launch. No doubt each missile is individually programmed with a GPS guidance system."

"Ed, what's your analysis and comment on this?"

"Mr. President, General Craig and I concur and have conferred on this on a number of occasions. We estimate that the Chinese could have as many as 50 IRBMs with MIRV warheads in those warehouses. They could probably launch within 15 to thirty minutes of receiving a launch order. Perhaps less if they had a warning order in sufficient time. We have also observed from satellite imagery that the Chinese built several small railroad spurs. They have boxcars sitting on those spurs. These boxcars haven't moved in months, some even in a couple of years. They could house rockets larger than the standard Chinese IRBMs. Our agents have also identified a number of Chinese Army field grade officers in the Canal Zone. They stay pretty close to home, but every once in a while, they will slip out into the night spots where we have spotted them. There are a number of colonels and a few generals wandering about down there. We don't like it. No doubt the Chinese do have IRBMs in place. It is not an idle threat, in my opinion."

"Ralph, what is your input here on the Canal Zone?"

"Well, the input that Fred Gateway, Roger Gutierrez and I have been working on concerns Chinese opium entering the U.S. through the Canal Zone. We have been tracking opium into the Canal Zone aboard Chinese shipping where it is offloaded into specific warehouses. We have many photos of the entire Zone and have identified warehouses which are closely guarded, but little comes and goes. Those we know used for storing opium have a lot more traffic than these I just mentioned. We have been trying to find out what these guarded warehouses contain without success. The Panamanians don't know, claiming they are bonded warehouses managed exclusively by the Chinese. Even the Panamanian stevedores and officials can't get near them. Everything in and around them is done by the Chinese. These are probably the same ones Ed referred to."

"Jim, what do you think of all of this?"

"I don't think we have any feasible alternative, Mr. President. If we don't rise to the occasion, we will be surrendering world hegemony to the Chinese. They will only grow stronger."

"General Craig, do you have any idea how we could neutralize this threat if we have to?"

"Mr. President, we, the armed services, in true joint fashion, have a game plan all worked out. In fact, we have had it on the books for a couple of years, just as a 'what if' situation. It looks like we get to dust it off."

"And of what does this plan consist?"

"It is a surprise attack, Mr. President, which requires full integration of the armed forces in all aspects. It is no small operation. I'll let General Shelton briefly describe the Air Force's role. General Shelton."

"The Air Force will wage electronic warfare to interrupt their signal communications. If any missiles are launched, our fighters along the Mexican border will attempt interception. We will also attempt to scramble the guidance systems of the missiles before they reach our border. We will provide airlift for the 82nd Airborne Division. I'll let Admiral Stark describe the Navy's role. Admiral Stark."

"The Navy will block the Canal at both ends and be in the Canal itself, Mr. President. Navy SEALs will ensure that the locks and dams are free of explosives and munitions that might destroy them. Navy SEALS will be spread too thinly protecting the locks and dams to participate in the on-land raids. Submarines will provide surreptitious entry to the SEALS and some of the Army Ranger teams, if indicated. We will have several ships in the canal full of Rangers and the 101st Airborne Division for invasion at various points along the Canal itself. The Marine Corps will be participating as an Amphibious Assault Group, complete with Joint Strike Fighter support, at each end of the Canal. I'll pass the ball to General Anderson for the Army's role. General."

"Mr. President, the Army will attack with its entire Ranger Regiment leading the way to cut communications centers, take out high priority leadership, headquarters of selected units, secure a couple of airfields, drop in the 82nd Airborne Division by parachute while the 101st Air Assault Division attacks targets along the length of the canal from Navy ships disguised as freighters, for a complete attack and destruction of all Chinese elements."

Oh my God, thought Thornton. *What the hell do we have here, a bunch of cowboys?* Instead, he said, "What are the chances of success; that is defined as taking the Chinese down without any missiles being launched? General Craig?"

"The element of surprise is most critical, Mr. President. With complete surprise, we believe it is much better than fifty-fifty. Without, the issue will be in doubt. No word of this plan can be mentioned outside this room. Otherwise, it will be a slaughter: ours, in this battle and strategically, for our country if they should launch such weapons."

"Marge, your opinion?"

"Mr. President, this game plan is idiocy. We can't risk our entire nation to nuclear and biological war!"

"Surgeon General Carolyn Weber, what's your opinion as if they launch those rockets?"

Carolyn Weber began her career as a Public Health Nurse in Texas. She worked with minorities in the eastern part of the state in a county health department. In frustration with having to deal with physicians who were political appointees as the county health officer, she decided that she would become a physician herself. Her nursing school courses were not sufficient to meet the pre-medical programs of most universities. Consequently, she returned to school to take the necessary courses part time. She supported herself by working as a floor nurse in the University Medical Center. After two years, she applied to the medical school and the college of osteopathic medicine in the northern part of the state, and the Uniformed University of Health Sciences Edward F. Hebert School of Medicine on the Bethesda Naval Medical Center campus. She wasn't accepted at the University Medical Center, which was quite a disappointment, but she was accepted at the federal institution. Four years later, she graduated third from the bottom of her class.

Since the Public Health Service is considered one of the six uniformed services, she elected to join it rather than one of the military services. After an internship at the Public Health Hospital on the Blackfoot Indian Reservation in Browning, Montana, she applied for and was accepted into a residency in community medicine and epidemiology at her alma mater. Biometry was a considerable challenge for her, but she was successful in becoming board certified in epidemiology and industrial medicine. Her work on the Blackfoot Indian Reservation, her experiences with minorities as a public health nurse in Texas, and her residency in community medicine in and around the Washington D.C. area, especially with the homeless, left her with a decided socialistic bent. She believed that medical care should be free to all. Vice President Atkinson and Surgeon General Weber on occasion had some rather heated discussions over how such a program should be funded. Since she never married, the rare remark was heard that her intemperance was due to a lack of male companionship. Jason Thornton often wondered whatever possessed him to offer her the position of Vice Admiral, Surgeon General of the United States. Now that he had her, he felt he was stuck with her.

"Mr. President, I would have to have much more detail in order to give you any kind of rational estimate of casualties if this operation should fail. I don't know the size of these nuclear warheads, to what radiological effects they are tailored, meteorological conditions at the time of detonation, height of burst, and so on. Biological agents are another matter entirely.

They are quite likely a greater threat than nuclear bombs. What biological agents they might contain, and they are probably genetically engineered, transmissible agents against which we have no defense, their persistence in the natural environment, and where they are aimed, are major variables. There are so many variables that it is impossible to give you any kind of a realistic answer. Suffice it to say, in a worst-case scenario, it could be a nation-destroying event."

Thornton reflected on his conversation with Colonel Burgess from the Medical Intelligence Unit at Fort Detrick, Maryland some months earlier. A knot formed in his stomach. He was very aware of the friction between the military medical services and the U.S. Public Health Service. The military medicos considered the Public Health Service and Centers for Disease Control and Prevention people as a bunch of socialist-liberal weenies riding on the back of the military medical community. The military physicians thought they should have representation at this level rather than Doctor Weber, but Thornton wanted a better balance between the military representation provided by the SECDEF and the Joint Chiefs and the more or less civilian medical community. He wasn't sure he achieved it.

"Marge, once again get with the Europeans, the British, Germans, French, Italians, Poles, Swedes, Norwegians, and whoever the hell has a stake in Middle East oil. Feel them out again given the continued Chinese advance. Ask if they are ready to risk war and at what point. What is their threshold threat level? Where will they draw the line? It is your highest priority. Tell them where we stand. We will go to war if they approach Iran, Iraq, the Trucial Gulf States, or any place else on the Persian Gulf. Report to us at Friday's meeting. Make sure they understand that. Will they go to war as coalition allies, or will they expect us to do it all alone? We went down this road before without any results when the Chinese first broke out of their borders. I'll talk to Vassily Chernikov myself.

"Jim, Generals and Admiral, how much lead time do you need for a warning order? I know the more time you have the better, but what is your estimate right now if I give the order to go? How long will it take you to get everything ready to move? What geographical positions can we take without tipping our hand? Get your heads together and let me know ASAP."

"Mr. President, a week would be critically a minimum. The longer lead time, the better job we can do of coordinating, stock piling, mobilizing, and so on. The downside is that the longer we wait, the greater the chance of a leak or somebody figuring out where we are going and when. God knows how good the Chinese intelligence network is. I wouldn't be surprised if they had a bug in this office."

"Could you do it disjointed, a little piece at a time, sneak up on it so to speak, so no one could put it together, General Craig?"

"Possibly, Mr. President, but that entails some risk as well. The major risk is the same, that of loss of surprise. Once committed, we can't back out. We have no missile defense, and if those missiles are launched and get through General Shelton's fighters, God help us all. If the biological agents aren't destroyed in the heat and blast of being shot down, they could easily spread over Central America and Mexico. Transmissible agents dispersed there would be here in one or two weeks under such an occurrence. That would give us a little time to prepare, but not much. Our preparations probably wouldn't be successful anyway without shutting down our entire southern border to include all incoming shipping. It would be almost the same thing."

"Carolyn, what about vaccines for these agents?"

"Mr. President, we have to have the agent first, to study its genetic makeup. We have to know where the parts of the organism are that invoke an immunological response that will be protective. These immunological parts of the molecular surface of the organism are called epitopes, and it requires experimentation to determine which are the appropriate ones. Then there is the problem of manufacturing on a grand scale, enough for everyone in the country. That doesn't include distribution and inoculation of the citizenry. That alone could take weeks. Remember that we have been looking for a vaccine for AIDS for more than thirty years without success. Many of the vaccines we have today aren't all that good either. 70% efficacy is considered a standard. With a highly pathogenic and virulent agent, we would still lose a lot of vaccinated folks with a vaccine that was only 70% efficacious. Therefore, if this operation goes down, we have to be one hundred percent sure those missiles are never launched."

"Jim, is there any way we can be absolutely certain those missiles will never be launched?"

"Yes, sir, Mr. President. We can take them out with small tactical nuclear weapons in a complete surprise attack, launched from multiple sites. That is a 99% plus. Only thing is, the geologists wonder what kind of effect that would have on the geological faults in the area, and if there would be a shift in the tectonic plates as a result of that. That is why we didn't use nukes to build another Panama Canal in another country when we surrendered the Canal to the Panamanians. It is still a valid concern. It could set off a chain of very severe earthquakes. One just might slide California into the Pacific Ocean. Still, if we used small enough nukes, we could probably get away with it, especially if they were tailored for an electromagnetic pulse that would screw up their guidance and control systems."

"We won't respond with nuclear weapons. That's out. So, it becomes more critical as the Chinese armies close in on Iran and the Caspian Sea Basin. Jim, you and your folks review all your plans. Fill in any gaps, revise it, get started doing it, piece meal it; get the units started in training, practice, stockpiling, moving around, as routine training exercises. Nobody is to know the overall plan until the very last minute. We won't wait to see what happens. We will be ready to move if and when the time comes. We'll see how much time those Pakhtuns buy us, how well they practice badal, their code of revenge, on the Chinese.

"Either we go with this operation or surrender our place as the number one power on the world stage and let China dictate its policies to us, even in this hemisphere. We must weigh the risks and decide. If we launch this operation and fail, we could lose tens of millions of American citizens. Alternatively, if we fail to act, or this operation fails, then there will be no one left in the world to stand against them. Europe could never get its act together to do so. There isn't time, even if they could work together for a change. Under those circumstances, the Mongols wouldn't have to stop in the Middle East, Russia, and the Balkans or at the gates of Vienna like the Ottomans. All of the world will be open to them. They won't have to invade in order to control. They could do it through intimidation, coercion, threat of nuclear or biological war, through control of the sea lanes of communication at critical passages such as the Panama Canal, the Suez Canal, the Straits of Malacca, the Straits of Hormuz and world trade. They could dominate the remaining world sources of raw materials. Maybe the biblical description in the Book of Revelation in Chapters Nine and Sixteen might just come to pass, literally, after all. Does anyone see this final scenario any differently?"

Chan visited the Mexican restaurant where Miguel worked. Miguel motioned Chan to the back room with a nod of his head. Chan nodded affirmatively and followed Miguel to the rear room. "Where are your friends today, Señor Ito?" inquired Miguel.

"They are on vacation. I will be dining by myself for a while. I'll have the big burrito today, with a cold beer, and a beef and bean taco as well, thank you, Miguel."

Miguel nodded and departed. In ten minutes, he returned with Chan's order and a frosted bottle of Michelob. After serving Chan, Miguel pulled a chair out and sat down, to the surprise of Chan. "I think we might have a little business to conduct, Señor Ito, if indeed that is your name. I know you are supposed to be a middle level clerk in COSCO, but we both know that is not the truth, don't we, Mr. Ito?"

"What is it you want, Miguel?"

"You were behind, or had some part in those raids across the border that attacked those towns in Texas and Arizona. You had some role in that. Those trucks and vans that we supplied you with were seized in the raid. They are being traced to my people. We don't like that. The FBI has many resources, and many tongues might wag.

It could take much to ensure that no one talks, Mr. Ito. Should I continue to call you that? I know you are not the Japanese citizen that you pretend to be. I know that you are a Chinese citizen, almost certainly a Chinese operative or spy. You must be someone special to be accompanied by two bodyguards most of the time. Something must have happened, or they would be with you now. My friends in the police department have identified one of your guards as an individual wanted for murder. That murder has ignited the enmity of some of the other forces in the area. Surely you do not wish to engage them in any altercations. It seems to me that now you have two forces to contend with: the FBI and the Russians. Which is worse?"

Chan continued eating and took a sip of his beer. "Again, what do you wish of me, Miguel?"

"My people are being questioned by the FBI. I think five hundred American dollars for each of them would ensure their silence. They will each claim that the vehicle was sold, but they did not complete the paperwork, or that they were afraid to go to the police to report it stolen, or that they loaned it to a relative who left the area with it, or some other such thing. There are over thirty people involved, none of which wish to go to jail. Wouldn't you think fifteen thousand dollars is a modest price to purchase their silence?"

"Yes, Miguel, I do. I will speak to my superiors. I must be careful with my contacts. It will take several days to have an answer for you. Do not be impatient. I am sure that some reconciliation can be reached."

Thank you, Señor Ito, I knew you would understand." Miguel dismissed himself with a smile on his face. That night, as he left the restaurant, a 64-grain bullet from a silenced Ruger Mini-14 found its way into Miguel's brain.

CHAPTER 33

"**S**ecretary Talbott is here with a letter from the Chinese ambassador, Mr. President."

"Fine, send her in, Peggy." Marge Talbott came in with a drained look on her face, something between a frown and a scowl.

"Well, what did our yellow brethren bequeath upon us this time, Marge?"

"The Chinese ambassador Kuan Sheng delivered a nice little letter to us earlier this morning, Mr. President. I made several copies for my own office, but I have the original here for your eyes. It isn't very nice." She handed Jason Thornton a single sheet of paper with the Chinese government's letterhead. It was signed by the Prime Minister of China.

Dear President Thornton:

For decades the renegade providence of Taiwan has acted as an independent political entity. This situation can no longer be tolerated. It is time that the Province of Taiwan became incorporated into the nation of the People's Republic of China.

It is in the best interest of all concerned that this integration be accomplished in a peaceful and constructive manner. If it is necessary to bring Taiwan into the People's Republic of China by the use of force, then that is the method that will be used. Let us hope that it is not so. In this regard, interference by outside forces will not be tolerated.

No doubt you would consider it a declaration of war if a foreign power from halfway around the world came to the aid of the state of California if it declared its independence and seceded from the United States. The People's Republic of China regards Taiwan in the same light. We are certain that you and the people of the United States understand and will not interfere. We will defend Taiwan as a part of the People's Republic of China.

As of this morning, we have informed those inhabiting the Island of Formosa that they are, indeed, part of one China and that we will integrate them in all respects into our nation in the immediate future. Letters similar to this one have been sent to the governments of Japan and Russia to inform them of our decision.

Respectfully,

Sung, Chiang
Prime Minister
People's Republic of China

"Swell letter Sung writes," stated Thornton sarcastically. He leaned forward to switch his intercom button. "Peggy, call a meeting of the National Security Council in one hour. Invite everybody. We have some late breaking news here." He leaned back in his chair and looked at Marge Talbott. "What did he say with his body language, Marge? Was he happy, morose or the usual inscrutable Chinaman?"

Marge Talbott grinned at her boss. "He was the usual inscrutable Chinaman, Mr. President. I couldn't tell how he personally felt about it. I suspect, however, he was dancing a jig inside."

When the appropriate departmental secretaries and the members of the Joint Chiefs of Staff arrived, Peggy Parsons passed around copies of the letter from Sung.

After reading it, all of them looked at the President and waited.

"Well, people, is this an objective of theirs, or is it a diversion from another objective? Opinions? Marge, as Secretary of State, you first."

"Mr. President, I do believe it to be a diversion from a real objective of the Caspian Sea basin and perhaps the Middle East. They haven't formed any more armies of which I am aware along their eastern seaboard. Such armies would be absolutely essential unless Taiwan agreed to unconditional surrender. I have had no such reply from the government of Taiwan when I queried them on receipt of this letter. I think Taiwan will fight, and China knows it. The Chinese won't risk war on two fronts, in my opinion. Then, too, they know that Taiwan will hurt them. There could be some truth to the rumors that the Taiwanese have acquired a number of nuclear warheads that formerly belonged to the Soviet Union. At that short range, Taiwan couldn't miss."

"Ed?"

"I concur with Secretary Talbott, Mr. President, for the same reasons, and more. Caspian Sea oil and the Middle East are far more important targets. World energy consumption, demand for energy, is increasing close to 50% between now and the year 2050. No doubt about that. Both India and China were really consuming the energy until the war. The Chinese have to have greater amounts of raw materials, especially oil and natural gas. They are burning tremendous amounts of coal to generate electricity right now. Consequently, many of their eastern cities are so polluted that it is almost dark until mid-morning, or sometimes noon in a few of them. You would think a sandstorm blew in from the desert. It is not healthy to breathe the air in China.

"They can't sustain their current employment without a greater abundance of raw materials, particularly energy, at lower rates than they are now paying. Another point is that all of their coastal cities are easily within the range and accuracy of missiles from Taiwan. We know Taiwan has secretly built intermediate range missiles with nuclear warhead capability. No doubt China knows this as well. I don't know if the Chinese know that the previous administration gave small nuclear warheads to Taiwan or that they acquired some from the former Soviet Union. Although these missiles have never been tested by firing one, there is no reason to believe they won't be highly functional and accurate. Neither have we observed any concentration of Chinese air forces along their coast. That would be essential for an invasion of Taiwan."

Jason Thornton looked at his flag officers, who were all mildly nodding their heads in agreement with their boss. They agreed because they agreed with his assessment, not because he was their boss. His National Security Advisor was also nodding affirmatively.

"Well, it seems to be unanimous. We all agree that, for the moment, this is a political diversion. No doubt that in the future it will be an objective, just as it is spelled out in this letter, but for now, I suspect it is to tie down our naval forces in the Strait of Formosa and Sea of Japan while they invade the Middle East. That is where we will stand. Ed, you and Admiral Stark plan on the naval forces we need to move into the Arabian Sea in the immediate future."

"While we are all here, what has transpired about weapons procurement and shipment? Have you made any progress, General Anderson?"

"Mr. President, we have an open-ended contract with Sturm, Ruger and Co. for all the Mini-14 and Mini-30 model rifles they can build. They have agreed to hire sufficient workforce to produce these rifles around the clock with their current workforce. It will take those about three months to get fully geared up because of machinery requirements to increase production over their current ability. They have to train machinists even with CNC equipment. These two rifles use our standard NATO 5.56 millimeter and the former Soviet 7.62 by 39 millimeter ammunition respectively. This way, we can take advantage of whatever ammunition sources the recipients already have. We have contracted with Colt Firearms, Rock River Firearms, and the Armalite Corporation while Fabrique National of America is negotiating, for all the M-16 type rifles in semi-automatic configuration they can manufacture. Additionally, we have let contracts for ammunition and magazines to fit them. Our contracts have taken these sources quite by surprise. When queried as to who would be the recipients, I instructed our contracting officers to state that we are building a national stockpile. It took a couple of days for the bureaucrats in the Army Acquisition Corps to get their act together to comprehend we wanted these rifles ASAP, as many as we could get. Once they grasped that, they got on the ball. The biggest question remaining regarding procurement is: where will the funding come from?"

"The funding will come out of pots from other departments, not from other DOD pots, I might add. They will be purchased essentially out of the Health and Human Resources budget. We will have to shift some funds somehow, legally or otherwise. I don't want the word out on this just yet. For now, consider they are coming from the public housing funding. Go on."

"We have spoken secretly with the Russian, Polish, and Hungarian military attachés. We are all agreed that arms could and should flow through those states into the Central Asian Republics, Afghanistan, and possibly Pakistan if anyone there is still alive. The Russian attaché has tentatively agreed, pending approval by their government, to allow us the use of air bases close to the CAS borders as bases for C-130s to drop the arms into the CAS and Afghanistan. By flying over the Caspian Sea in international air space, we are keeping international involvements to a minimum. A couple of our people assigned to Afghanistan are doing a little exploring on the Afghan-Pakistan border as we speak, about who is left and where. We have drones over that area, Global Hawks II at 50,000 feet, and over Pakistan watching for movement, especially of regular army, militia or paramilitary organizations. It is ironic we are going to re-arm these clans and tribes who are still in the nineteenth century after we went to so much difficulty to disarm them ten years ago, Mr. President."

Jason Thornton had to smile on that one. "It appears to me that you have accomplished a great deal in one week, General. My compliments.

"Marge, have you heard anything from our so-called Allies in Europe?"

"Yes, Mr. President, and it is a mixed bag. The countries of Eastern Europe are with us, the French are against us, the Germans can't make up their mind, and the British are protesting in the streets, both in front of our embassy and the Chinese embassy. Poland, Hungary, Romania, the Czech Republic, Serbia and even Turkey are with us. They all fear a horde of Chinese overrunning them. Russia is with us one hundred percent. They will go along with anything we want to do. It seems that even the Russian Mafia is taking the threat of invasion very seriously. They are beginning to realize that they could be next. Historically, Russia and China have fought along the Amur River for decades, ever since Russia expanded east in the eighteenth century. Most of those countries I have mentioned are already recruiting and training troops for their defense. Their arms plants are also going twenty-four-seven, Mr. President. I think we can count on them all. I do believe they will no longer accept any foreign yoke of any kind, now that they have tasted freedom."

"Inform them each in turn, Marge, that we are drawing the line. If Chinese forces come within 150 kilometers of the Russian or Iranian borders, we will initiate nuclear strikes against China. It is all we can do. We cannot let them control the Middle Eastern oil fields. There is no recourse. They could plunge us all back into the dark ages by simply shutting off the oil supply. Western Europe and the United States would be resorting to cannibalism before the year is out. I'd rather force them to face a nuclear winter along with us rather than go down alone. Tell them all that and see if they change their minds.

"Now, with the exception of the Joint Chiefs, Marge, Ed, Jim, George and Ralph, I thank you all for coming and hope you have a good afternoon." After the room had cleared except for the named, Thornton asked, "Where do we stand on preparation for taking down the Canal Zone? Jim, let's hear from each of your folks in turn regarding their respective services."

Jim Neville nodded, and said, "Admiral Stark, if you would care to lead off."

The Admiral nodded to his boss and opened the briefing. "We have coordinated with the 101st Airborne, which just arrived at Norfolk for practicing loading and unloading procedures from cargo carrying vessels. We will do that far enough offshore that we are out of observation.

"We borrowed an idea from the Germans in World Wars I and II in that we are converting some of our cargo vessels into what were called Q boats. We can drop open a door in the side of the ship and open fire with five inch naval guns. We are installing them on half a dozen vessels, two guns per side of each ship. They can provide direct fires in support of the 101st ashore.

"I have sent submarines to monitor each end of the Canal, really to search for any submarines that might be there. I have ordered that no action be taken against them at this time, just locate, observe and orient. Navy SEALs are being briefed on the construction of the locks and dams. They are being informed of where and what to look for to prevent their destruction. They will go in just a few hours before dawn and clear any explosive charges. We will have a carrier standing 50 miles offshore in the Atlantic just in case any extra support is needed. That's it for the Navy so far, Mr. President."

"For the Army, I have ordered the Commander of the 101st and his staff to draw up plans for invading the eastern two thirds of the Canal Zone, using the Navy ships as their means of transportation. He will use the entire division of 12,000 personnel less their heavy weapons. They will disembark from the cargo vessels just before first light. He is assigning specific targets and activities to his brigades and battalions. I have left the details up to him. He is very capable, and I have utmost faith in him, Mr. President. I have assigned the western third of the Canal Zone to the Commander of the 82nd Airborne Division. He is to have a brigade of paratroopers dropped into the western one third. He is completing his plan as we speak. These two units will simultaneously attack the majority of the bases. Special Forces and Army Rangers will make surreptitious entry into the Canal Zone on the night before to take down the suspected warehouses, headquarters and communications facilities. Both division commanders have been informed of which of these facilities have been assigned to Special Operations. Spec Ops have increased training by practicing stealth exercises at night, hand to hand combat, weapons firing on the target range, explosives and demolitions, identification and elimination of high priority personnel, and all the other things snake eaters do." He nodded to General Mark Leonard, USMC.

"As far as the Marines go, I have ordered two Marine Expeditionary Units to prepare for both amphibious and vertical envelopment operations. One MEU will be assigned to each end of the Canal. I have ordered the MEUs to add two additional Joint Strike Fighters to each amphibious ship capable of supporting them. The strike fighters will provide close air support on call to the Marines, the 82nd, and the 101st. These two MEUs will undoubtedly command the initial attention of the Chinese. They are, to some degree, a diversionary force. They are also acting as reserves, capable of supporting any of the Army units which run into unexpected difficulties, through vertical envelopment with C-22 Osprey aircraft and direct amphibious assault with amphibious light armored vehicles. No disparagement on the Army, but each unit has 3500 gung-ho Marines who want to get into the action. We will also have a Marine EA-6B Prowler on call on that Navy carrier standing off shore to jam any electronic signal communications if it becomes necessary." He grinned and nodded at General Anderson, who grinned back. General Leonard nodded to General George Shelton, USAF.

"The Air Force has initiated increased training with F-16s as missile interceptors. We are flying three squadrons to bases in south Texas, Arizona and New Mexico. Additional squadrons are being assigned along the Gulf Coast to intercept any missiles fired towards the eastern seaboard. The 82nd will make a low level drop from Hercules C-130 aircraft. We will fly out of Fort Hood, TX, over the ocean at less than five hundred feet to avoid radar detection by any radar units the Chinese might have established. They, a five thousand man brigade, will be dropped precisely at dawn right over their targets. The pilots are practicing now for low-level flights over water at night. Each target is precisely pinpointed for its drop."

Robert Wha Lee enjoyed himself very much. He did like to fish and was good at it. The weather in the Georgian Bay in November can be very treacherous. Consequently, he stayed relatively close to the island. The days were warm, but the nights cold. Sudden winds often whipped the Bay into whitecaps. After catching enough fish for several good meals and sufficient photographs taken by Frank to support his trip, Lee decided he should return to the United States. The night before he decided to leave, the weather took a turn for the worse. It rained heavily for six hours, and then the temperature dropped. The first snow storm of the season blew in during the pre-dawn hours of the morning he checked out of the

Lodge. The launch took him back to the mainland, along with two other fishermen, the last of the season.

He had been driving for about two hours, making relatively good time on the icy road. Large, heavy wet flakes of snow were falling profusely. His windshield wipers set on intermittent were keeping up with the falling snow. Having developed a taste for classical music, he unbuckled his seatbelt to reach into the backseat for his compact disk case. He was thumbing through it to look for Vivaldi's Four Seasons performed by the London Symphony. At that moment, he rounded the curve only to see a moose dash up the embankment and onto the highway from the left shoulder of the road. He swerved to the left to avoid the animal, but the moose slipped and went down on the ice. Its rear legs went under it, but its front legs were straight, so it was in a sitting position. He slammed on the brakes, and the car had just begun to fishtail when he collided with the moose. He was doing forty-five miles an hour when he squarely broadsided the moose just behind its shoulders with the right front fender of his car. The thousand pound moose flew straight ahead and off towards the right shoulder of the road in the middle of the curve while the air bag activated. It momentarily blinded Robert Wha Lee and filled the driver's side of the front seat. The car spun into a one hundred and eighty degree clockwise turn and slid another twenty meters backwards in the left lane, directly into the path of an eighteen wheeled tractor trailer rounding the curve. The driver saw the moose flying off the curve and watched it before he saw Robert Wha Lee's car coming towards him. Immediately before impact by the tractor trailer, the airbag of Lee's car deflated. The tractor trailer was doing fifty miles an hour when it hit the rear of Lee's car. It crushed the trunk and sent the car flying off the road, where it rolled down the embankment of the raised highway and came to rest against a tree. Lee's head snapped back to be stopped by the headrest, but then he was rebounded forward against and over the top of the steering wheel to smash his head into the windshield. The driver of the eighteen wheeler slammed on his brakes and jackknifed the truck, coming to a stop in the center of the road. The tractor was ninety degrees to the trailer, but the entire rig stayed halfway on the highway and halfway on the shoulder of the road. Before leaving the cab, the truck driver put in an emergency call on his citizen's band radio, reporting the accident to the Ontario Provincial Police. Then he left his truck, uncertain whether to see about potential victims in the car or to put out emergency markers. He decided that it would be better from a legal standpoint not to be involved in any more accidents, so he put out the triangular warning signs fifty meters ahead and behind his rig. He felt better about that, as his tractor was blocking much of the right lane, and being on a curve in a snowstorm didn't help.

He ran down the embankment to Lee's car and looked in through the driver's window. He saw an unconscious Robert Wha Lee leaning against the steering wheel with blood on his face. The windshield had a circle of broken glass where he had impacted against it. The truck driver didn't know what to do, but seeing no indications of any fire danger, he looked around, and decided not to attempt to move Robert Wha Lee or provide any kind of first aid for fear of a lawsuit. The trucker ran back to his truck to report that an unconscious and bleeding driver was still trapped in the other vehicle. In thirty minutes, an ambulance and Provincial police cruiser arrived on the scene. The emergency medical technicians worked to extract Robert Lee while the police officer directed the twenty or so vehicles that had accumulated around the accident site so as to have enough room to move the jackknifed truck. Then he guided the tractor trailer driver to straighten out his rig to unblock the road. Traffic resumed flow, albeit it at a much slower pace. He walked over to check on the moose. Seeing it was still alive, but crippled and unable to move its rear quarters, he returned to his cruiser and removed a .30-06. He slowly approached to within ten feet of the bull moose then worked the bolt to chamber a round and sent a 180-grain bullet into the animal's brain, immediately ending its agony. It was something he did not like to do. He had seen too many moose automobile collisions. Returning to the scene, the EMTs now had Robert Wha Lee on a gurney with an intravenous line into his arm, a blood pressure cuff on him, and cardiac telemetry going to the regional hospital.

"How does it look, Fred?" the officer said to the senior EMT, whom he had known for several years.

"Well, he might have a fractured skull, he certainly has a concussion, but he is stable. We'll get out of here in about two minutes. I haven't checked his wallet for any identification, but we can do that when we get him to the hospital."

The officer nodded, and the EMTs loaded Lee into the ambulance, slammed the doors, turned on the lights and sirens while the officer held up traffic to allow the ambulance to pull on the highway. When the ambulance disappeared, he walked over to Lee's car to examine it. The trunk lid was up, and Lee's suitcase was crumpled, with the lid up. His clothes were half out of the suitcase, revealing the false section in the bottom which was bent in half. The documents revealing him as a Secret Service Officer were in view and caught the officer's eye. He searched the rest of the car, then put the suitcase and clothes into the trunk of his cruiser, turned on his lights and pulled onto the highway. At the local police office, the officer removed the suitcase from his cruiser, taking it inside for close examination. When he read the hidden documents, he called his supervisor. His supervisor read the documents, and then called the Superintendent. When the Superintendent reviewed the identity papers, he called Ottawa to report it to his superiors, who in turned called the Royal Canadian Mounted Police and the American Embassy.

The Superintendent then called the hospital to ascertain the condition of Officer Robert Wha Lee. The emergency room nurse stated that no one by that name had arrived. When the investigating officer described him and the accident time and place, the nurse remarked, "Oh, that gentleman has a driver's license and other identity papers under another name. His condition is stable; he has a concussion and is unconscious at the moment. We are radiographing him and running blood tests to determine the extent of other injuries, if any."

Four hours later, a sergeant of the RCMP arrived at the District Office of the Provincial Police to examine the hidden papers. "Fold the suitcase lid down with the false section in place; put the clothes in on top of them, as if these documents were never discovered. Bundle the bag up in double plastic bags." After doing so, he and the investigating officer went to the local hospital where they examined the documents in Robert Wha Lee's wallet. He then instructed the hospital emergency staff to place the bagged suitcase in Robert Wha Lee's room and that it was not to be opened. He called Ottawa to inform them that the victim was traveling under an assumed name with two sets of documents. He took the liberty of suggesting that the American FBI be called. Like bureaucrats everywhere, the RCMP Captain took it as a mild insult that a subordinate would suggest something that he might not otherwise do or be so inept that he would not think of it himself. He did agree that it was appropriate, and so called the American Embassy to report Robert Wha Lee's condition and that he was traveling under a false identity.

The FBI found this somewhat curious and called the Treasury Department. After an hour, the Treasury Department decided to send their own officer to investigate. Close to midnight that same day, Secret Service agent Zachary Tolsten arrived at the District Office of the Provincial Police Headquarters. The investigating officer was called in. Aroused from his sleep, he was not in a particularly good mood but described everything he found and saw. With the investigating RCMP Sergeant, Agent Tolsten requested that they take a field fingerprinting kit to the hospital along with a digital camera. Robert Wha Lee was still unconscious when they arrived. He was fingerprinted and a photo taken. His fingers were scrubbed until all traces of the ink were removed. Although his scalp was shaved and sutured, his features were still clearly defined. The fingerprints and digital picture were transmitted by portable computer to the Treasury Department where confirmation of Lee's identity took less than five minutes. Examining the forgeries, Agent Tolsten also took digital photos of them and all the contents of Lee's wallet and personal belongings. Close examination revealed nothing out of the ordinary. All of the documents looked like those carried by the ordinary American citizen every day. He requested through the RCMP Sergeant that the hospital assign Robert Wha Lee to a private room and that he be recognized as Robert Zin Wang.

The hospital called the telephone number given on the HMO card. The address for the company was listed in Washington, D.C. After a few minutes, the person responding for the HMO said that Robert Zin Wang was fully covered, and that all expenses incurred would be paid by the HMO. No treatment was to be withheld. All invoices were to be sent to the address listed on the card. That certainly satisfied the hospital administrator and the billing department.

At the Treasury Department, it was decided not to reveal Lee's true identity. The emergency room staff nurse with whom the Provincial Police

Superintendent spoke was instructed not to mention any possibility of a second identity to anyone under any circumstance. One of the cards in Lee's wallet was for a health maintenance organization. When the Treasury Department ran a check on it, they found no such HMO actually existed. In an unusual spirit of cooperation in the intelligence community, really to avoid charges of a cover-up within their organization, the FBI was called in to investigate the anomaly of Robert Wha Lee, his HMO, and why he was carrying false identity papers that were not issued by the Treasury Department. As a Special Treasury Agent and bodyguard to two presidents, who had to report all of his travel destinations and difficulties, it was not at all understood why Robert Wha Lee had any need of a false identity. Indeed, he had informed his superiors of his destination of the Lodge of the Pines with its address, phone and fax numbers.

The next morning, a utility van from Robert's Heating and Air Conditioning Company, of Silver Springs, Maryland parked in front of Robert Wha Lee's suburban home. Three men in coveralls emerged and walked to the front door. One inserted a lock pick gun and opened the front door. Another walked around to the side of the house to visually inspect the heat pump. The next door neighbor, something of a busybody, was raking leaves in the back yard. "Who are you people? The owner isn't home there. Maybe I should call the police!"

The man smiled at her, and said, "Not at all, lady. Robert Lee gave us the key to the front door. He asked us to inspect his furnace and heat pump while he is fishing in Canada. He said he doesn't believe it is working right, and he wants to get ready for winter. We are going to clean his furnace, replace all the filters, check it out and make any repairs or adjustments and do the same to his heat pump as well. We're having a special on it this month. Are you interested in having us do the same for you? It is only $99.95 this month only. We do a great job!"

Satisfied that nothing was amiss, the lady shook her head no and returned to raking leaves. The three FBI agents thoroughly searched his house and placed a hidden microphone in each room, sometimes in a ceiling light, sometimes in other locations. His telephone line was tapped outside his house.

When he recovered consciousness, and his mind cleared, Robert Wha Lee panicked. The first thing he asked was, "Where's my suitcase?" The attending nurse informed him that the Provincial Police had it bagged, and it was in the closet. As soon as the nurse left, Robert Wha Lee staggered over to the closet, opened the plastic bags and experienced tremendous relief to see that the secret false bottom was more or less in place and that the documents contained therein were undisturbed. Returning to his bed, he slept for eight hours.

Upon awakening, he was famished. He buzzed for the nurse and requested food. The nurse smiled and said, "Breakfast will be served in less than an hour, can you wait that long, Mr. Zing?" Smiling back, Robert Lee said he could but that he would like to use the telephone. The nurse removed a telephone from the bottom of the bed stand and plugged it into the wall outlet for him. The first call he made was to the Treasury Department to inform them that he had an accident and was hospitalized. He was fine, but would return to Washington in a few days, as soon as he could drive. When they asked where he was, he informed them. He also told them that his private HMO was going to take care of the paperwork and bills. This accident was not incurred in the line of duty, and the government shouldn't have to pay for it. He carried his own supplemental insurance for just such emergencies.

Four days later, Robert Zin Wang was discharged. He caught a bus to Toronto where he purchased a new suitcase and discarded the crushed one. He hid his false identity papers in his wallet under the concept of hiding them in plain sight. Then he caught an airplane to Washington, D.C. The following day, he reported for duty, sutures in his scalp and all.

CHAPTER 34

"**L**ook, Chief, we have the murder of a gangland chieftain. He died with a bullet in his brain. It turns out he was the leader of the Caballeros, which has over five thousand members in it. If we don't find his killer soon, the Caballeros are going to go on a rampage against two of the rival gangs in the area. We'll have blood running down the gutters in East L.A."

"What's the problem here, Captain, don't you have enough men in your gangs division? What, do you need something more? Where do you stand in your investigation?"

"Yeah, we're overwhelmed, all right. Yes, I could use more men, more state of the art communications equipment, and I have only one SWAT team for all of East L.A. It's going to blow, Chief, and we better be ready. The mayor will come down on you, and you will come down on me. Feces flows downhill, and I don't like that. What I need the most, though, is information. What I need is some indicator of why he was killed. I need a motive; I need a reason. My people on the street say they have no idea why this hit was made. Rival gangs deny all knowledge of it. My sources are usually very good, so I think there is more here than meets the eye. If we don't crack this case soon, we could have twenty thousand Mexicans from half a dozen gangs battling twenty thousand blacks battling ten thousand Vietnamese and Koreans. At least, if it is narcotics related, which it most likely is. For the last two years, there has been a truce that has held. Everybody has been satisfied with their territory. Now, it looks like somebody is suffering growing pains. Our colleagues from the other municipalities tell me they haven't heard anything at all regarding a turf war. That's unusual. We usually get signals a couple of weeks in advance of anything happening. I want your permission to talk with the FBI to see if they can shed any light on this thing."

"All right, Captain, be my guest. You can talk to anyone in downtown L.A. or anywhere else you want. You can go to the Mayor of L.A. if you like. Just get this thing moving. You're right, feces flows downhill, and it might bury you."

Captain Frank Jacobi walked out of his boss's office straight to his unmarked sedan and made for the federal building in downtown L.A.

"Can I offer you a cup of coffee, Captain?" asked Wrangell's secretary. "No thanks, Ma'am, I'm fine." After a thirty minute wait, Captain Jacobi was escorted into the office of SSA Ed Wrangell.

"What can I do for you, Captain?" asked Wrangell, knowing full well why Jacobi was there.

"I need information on the Miguel Monzani murder. I am getting absolutely nothing off the street. If I don't come up with something soon, I am afraid that East L.A. will explode into gang warfare. I've brought our file on Monzani for your information, just in case we have something you don't. I would appreciate reciprocity."

Wrangell picked up his phone and asked his secretary to come in. "Copy the contents of this file and return it to the good Captain, please, Marilyn." She took the file and left, returning five minutes later with the original, which she handed to the Captain.

"Frankly, Captain, we don't have a lot on him. You probably have a lot more than we do. Our interest stems merely from the fact that he was a waiter who had frequent contact with an individual who is the object of a national security case. Your records might be of considerable value to us. I will go through your file and dovetail it with ours. If I find anything I can divulge that will be of interest to you, I will gladly share it. At the moment, that's the best I can offer you."

"Tell me, SSA Wrangell, do you FBI guys ever have a case that isn't national security associated? Do you ever share anything with us poor locals? After all, your resources are far greater than ours."

Wrangell smiled, "I can assure you, Captain, we want this Monzani case broken wide open as much as you do. I will do everything in my power to assist your investigation as long as it does not jeopardize ours. That's the best I can do."

"Well, thanks for the time. Here's my card if you ever find anything you can share." He handed Wrangell his business card and let himself out. Wrangell opened the file and began to read. He was surprised at the amount of information the East L.A. police had accumulated on Monzani. He had numerous arrests but no convictions. His gang was believed to exceed five thousand members. He had established a well-defined territory for drug distribution, believed to have several methamphetamine laboratories in operation, ran two chop shops and a stolen car ring, and kept street crime at modest levels in his district. His territory encompassed about four square miles of East L.A. The report stated that Monzani thought it was bad for business to have heists relieving his clientele of their money. He had several mistresses at various times and owned the restaurant where he worked as manager. Several lieutenants had been identified and had dossiers of their own. One of them was named Gomez, who disappeared from sight months ago. It struck him that many of the trucks and vans used by Gonzalez had been purchased by his gang members, the Caballeros.

The meeting was called by Monzani's lieutenants. It was a strategy meeting to consider a successor to Gomez and what actions to take regarding Monzani's murder. Signs of encroachment by rival gangs into the Caballeros' territory were beginning to appear. Gomez's presence was something of a surprise, but no one objected. Gomez leaned his chair against the wall along the side while the lieutenants expressed various opinions as to who had killed Monzani and why. After all had spoken, Gomez rose and quietly said, "You're all wrong. He was killed by a Chinaman. I don't know all of the connections of the Chinaman, but it was this Chinaman who set up Jesus Gonzalez in Mexico, had him raiding into the States, and supplied him with guns and supplies. When the Army knocked over Gonzalez's camp in Mexico, they caught Gonzalez. Gonzalez spilled his guts to the feds. The feds were closing in on the Chinaman. Miguel was a go-between for the Chinaman and Gonzalez. All those vehicles the gang bought went to Gonzalez. The Chinaman wanted to close the loop by eliminating Miguel. I don't know why the Chinaman wanted to cause all this trouble. Maybe the Chinaman had ideas about what was going on overseas. Maybe he worked for a foreign government; it seems so. I think Miguel said something wrong to the Chinaman. Maybe he threatened to expose him. I think that is why he died."

"And who is this Chinaman of whom you speak? Where do we find him to ask him?"

"I don't know. I saw him several times in Gonzalez's camp. That's why Miguel sent me there, to figure out what was going on. This Chinaman that killed the Russian in the whorehouse was one of the Chinaman's people. I recognized his picture. He was always with the Chinaman. The Chinaman left another babysitter with Gonzalez in Mexico. I don't know what happened to him. I came back just before the Army raided the camp. I saw the raid coming and told Miguel so. Miguel obviously did not tell the Chinaman, or if he did, the Chinaman did not tell Gonzalez, or Gonzalez chose to ignore it. I don't know which. We should find this Chinaman and ask him, as you suggest." With that, Gomez sat down.

"There was a Japanese who came into the restaurant and talked with Miguel and ate in the back room. I think his name was Ito, though. We followed him to the COSCO shipping company offices one day. We can point him out to you any day you wish to go, Gomez. If he is the Chinaman of whom you speak, we can ask him."

"Then, I will go with you early tomorrow. I will meet with you here at five o'clock in the morning and observe where he works. I don't want to be late and miss him. You will meet me here, and we will go?"

"Yes, I, Bernardo, will meet you here and we will go with binoculars tomorrow. In the meantime, we should all consider who we should elect to replace Miguel."

As they sat sipping coffee in an old Dodge pickup the next morning, Bernardo said, "There is his car" as it pulled into the reserved parking space. Gomez picked up the binoculars and watched Chan as he entered his office.

"It's him. He is the one who came to the camp in Mexico and supplied all the guns. He is no peon. He is someone who is important."

"We know where he lives. Now he has no bodyguards. They used to pick him up and bring him to work and then home again. We will have a talk with him, perhaps tonight before he can hire reinforcements."

The locksmith who unlocked the door of Chan's apartment early the next morning was indeed a registered locksmith. He did not drive his company truck with the signs painted all over it, but a fellow gang member took him to Chan's apartment building and gave him the number of the apartment. It only took him a few moments to unlock Chan's door, and then he left. Ten minutes later, Bernardo entered first, followed every five minutes by another until there were six armed gang members in Chan's apartment. They searched every aspect of it. They found nothing incriminating, so they waited for Chan's return. A gang member reported to Bernardo by cell phone when Chan left work. Another reported when Chan parked his car in the apartment building's lot.

Chan walked into the trap in complete surprise. He was intravenously injected with a dose of heroin so that he could be easily controlled. A minute later, he vomited on the floor. Two of the gang members left to drive their van to the rear door of the apartment. Chan was more or less carried by two gang members to the waiting van. Chan was driven to a secure house in East L.A. where he was handcuffed, gagged, and left on the floor in a closet for eight hours.

After the heroin wore off, the questioning began. At first, Chan declared he was only a shipping clerk. After the second heated needle was shoved under a fingernail, he began to talk. When he balked, a toenail was ripped off. His bowels autonomically released the contents from the pain. Chan talked some more. A tape recording was made of the session. Chan admitted that he supplied the arms to Gonzalez as a conspiracy to incite civil unrest in the southwest. He personally hoped to profit by the sale of many weapons and security services to the Anglo community of the southwest. Bernardo didn't buy it. They pulled a molar tooth with a pair of pliers. Chan talked some more. It wasn't enough. He denied any knowledge of the death of Miguel Monzani. Bernardo took one of Chan's testicles in the jaws of a pair of slip-joint pliers. Chan screamed as Bernardo slowly squeezed. Chan began dry heaving. He said he didn't know who killed Miguel, but that someone in his organization, COSCO, did out of fear that Monzani would talk. Further pressure on the pliers induced Chan to admit that he was a Chinese government agent. The involvement with Gonzalez and the raids were to tie down forces of the American Army along the Mexican border while North Korea invaded the south.

After a brief consultation, Bernardo and his men decided that the best course of action was to give Chan and the tape of his confession to the FBI. They bound and gagged him, wiped their prints off everything, placed the tape in a plastic bag, and took Chan to a deserted house in the barrio where they abandoned him. From a phone booth, Bernardo wiped his prints off a quarter and dropped it into the phone and dialed the FBI number. He played a tape recording for the FBI operator. "Turn on your tape recorders. I will only say this once." After a minute's pause, Bernardo played the tape that he earlier recorded through a voice scrambler. "At 3342 Margarita Avenue in East L.A., you will find a Chinese spy and a tape recorded confession by him describing his and the Chinese government's involvement in the raids from Mexico. I suggest you quickly find him before he dies." He turned off the recorder and hung up the phone after wiping it clean with an oiled cloth.

CHAPTER 35

The FBI requested the RCMP to investigate any travels Robert Wha Lee, aka Robert Zin Wang, had made in Canada in the last five years. A computer search revealed that one Robert Zin Wang had flown from Toronto to Japan fifteen months earlier. From there, he was traced to Taipei by taking a flight on Japan Airlines. The dates corresponded with a fishing vacation Robert Wha Lee had taken. He had not reported this trip overseas. Indeed, during that vacation, he reported that he was fishing in an isolated location in New Brunswick for Atlantic salmon and that he was not even taking his cell phone. American agents in Taipei were informed to check for any records, hotel, travel excursions, flights, or anything else they could find for Robert Zin Wang. Enlisting the cooperation of the Taiwanese authorities, they meticulously checked the computerized hotel records for the dates involved. It was discovered that he checked into the Taipei Hilton for a period of three days before returning to Japan on a JAL flight. Any other movements or activities on Taiwan were unknown. When the FBI received this information, a special detail was formed to monitor every movement of Robert Wha Lee.

During this excursion to Taipei, Robert Wha Lee had actually stayed in his hotel room the entire time. During that three-day period, Robert Wha Lee extensively briefed his superiors on the presidential candidate he had been guarding for the previous six months, the now President Jason Thornton. His superiors wanted critical insight into how Jason Thornton thought and acted and likely to react. They wanted into Jason Thornton's mind. Lee's assessment of Jason Thornton had been very accurate, to a point.

The political commissars of the People's Republic of China did not really expect Jason Thornton to win the election. They, therefore, considered it worth the risk to bring Robert Wha Lee to Taiwan for debriefing rather than debriefing him in the United States or Canada that might expose other agents. They underestimated the depth of the culture war waging in the United States, the war between the social welfare liberal left wing of the Democratic Party and the coalition forming between the Midwestern and western states. More and more blue collar Democrats were deserting the Democratic Party to the Libertarian or Republican parties. The Libertarian party almost cost Jason Thornton the election when it captured fifteen percent of the vote. It became a growing force, and the Republican Party realized it would have to woo or co-opt some of their issues.

Under pressure from the United States, Canada initiated an individual identification program for all people arriving or leaving on international flights. When the travelers stepped through the door framed metal detector, their digital photograph was automatically recorded. The door frame of the metal detector was numbered in meters on the left and feet on the right so that their height was measured in the photograph. Travelers then placed their right hand on a glass screen and looked into an apparatus similar to that used by ophthalmologists for eye examinations for three seconds. Their photograph, retinal scans and fingerprints were simultaneously and automatically digitally recorded and filed into a bank of IBM super computers funded by the United States from secret funds under the War on Terrorism program. Since it didn't cost the Canadian government any initial start-up costs, and the United States agreed to pay for the first three years of the program, Canada willingly went along with it. Each traveler's personal identification along with flights traveled were automatically recorded and filed along with personal data each time they traveled. Any discrepancies between previous name, address, photographs, fingerprints or retinal scans were immediately identified by the computers for investigation. Robert Wha Lee was among the very first to fly under the program. Since it caught him by surprise, Robert Wha Lee was forced to travel in Canada under the false identity of Robert Zin Wang on all future trips. The results of the program were astounding. In the first two years, more than three dozen significant discrepancies were found that identified foreign agents and would-be terrorists. Some of them were wanted in more than one country for terrorist activities. Most of them wound up in prison or extradited. A few foreigners against whom no charges could be filed were sent under guard to their native land under threat of prison should they return.

The President was informed of Robert Wha Lee's double identity. Lee was given two weeks convalescent leave after examination at Walter Reed Army Medical Center. The neurologist attending Robert Wha Lee expressed the opinion that Lee might have suffered a minor case of contrecoup. He informed the FBI agents that contrecoup is a bruising of the brain on the opposite side of the impact because the cerebral spinal fluid cannot rebound sufficiently fast enough to cushion the brain when it rebounds into the skull opposite the point of impact. Many individuals who have suffered serious head trauma have experienced slow mental deterioration, often to the point of idiocy or death. Thornton made the decision to have him assigned to other duties under the excuse that his injuries might have subtle but serious latent effects.

Fred Gateway, the Secretary of the Treasury and Ed McCluskey put their heads together. All were aware of a very good counterfeiting ring operating out of Taiwan. Their reproduction of U.S. Federal Reserve Notes in denominations of twenty and fifty dollar bills, including the bar chip, was extremely good. It was decided that if Lee were to be re-assigned to counterfeiting, it would only be a question of time until his Chinese superiors perceived this as an opportunity; certainly not as great as being the President's personal bodyguard, but an opportunity nevertheless. In this position, the Treasury Department could use him without his knowledge as a double agent. They could feed him partially factual information which he, in turn, would provide to his Chinese handler. It might be an opportunity to close down the counterfeit ring that was dumping several hundred million counterfeit U.S. dollars into the world markets each year. Lee's Treasury Department superiors assigned him to the counterfeiting division, explaining to him that they couldn't take a chance on a presidential bodyguard having a blackout at a crucial time. Lee accepted the assignment with resignation.

Lee began to take walks around the neighborhood, jogging around the local high school track when it wasn't in use, and moderate exercise on his home gym. While jogging one day, he made a phone call from a public phone booth one week after being re-assigned. The phone call was videotaped by an FBI agent sitting in a car two hundred yards away. Robert Wha Lee's body blocked the numbers punched into the phone. The video tape was examined, the time the call was made, the number and location of the phone all revealed sufficient evidence as to who was called. Checking with the telephone company revealed the call went to a Chinese restaurant that functioned as an establishment frequented by Chinese Embassy personnel.

Four FBI agents who were unknown to Lee were flown in from a Midwestern city and assigned to his case. They began to individually frequent the restaurant under various guises. One late afternoon, Lee was observed to abandon a newspaper on a park bench during a walk. A few minutes later, an elderly Chinese lady sat on the same bench, picked up the newspaper and began to read. After a few minutes, she folded the newspaper under her arm and left. She was photographed from four hundred yards away. She was identified as a matron associated with the Chinese restaurant that evening. Searching through their garbage cans late that night did not reveal the newspaper. A court order was granted, and the phone lines to the restaurant were tapped. A nearby apartment was rented by a black American couple, who just happened to be FBI agents. He posed as a stevedore and she as a sales clerk in a department store. They began to frequent the restaurant for evening meals once or twice a week. The owners of the restaurant were placed under twenty-four hour surveillance.

General Lui, Lien-chang was concerned, but not overly so, regarding the losses he had sustained. According to his staff's best estimates, they amounted to between 60 and 65% of his troops. He anticipated the Vietnamese would offer the stiffest resistance, and he was right. It was stiffer than he expected. Still, his armies had done as anticipated. The Malayan peninsula was essentially depopulated. Near as his staff could calculate, there were less than 10% of the people left in Vietnam, Cambodia, Laos and Thailand who lived there eighteen months ago. There were still small bands of survivors hiding out in caves, in the hills, in the jungles, but over time, these small groups would be eliminated. Most of these bands were in the hill country, where their survival without the support of the general population would be most difficult. He would assign the remnants of his armies to protect the incoming settlers. General Chang was pleased with his progress, and General Lui was always satisfied when he pleased his superiors. He decided that this was the time to request the settlers during his weekly radio report to General Chang.

The People's Republic of China was offering massive incentives to entire villages in the southern and southwestern provinces willing to move into the Malayan peninsula. They were promised modern farm machinery, new homes, wells dug to provide potable water, sewage systems with small but modern treatment plants, livestock, schools and medical clinics. They would be moved into the rich lowlands of Southeast Asia, where they could produce two, or perhaps even three, major rice crops a year. Villages of the higher elevations would be provided with what the Chinese government hoped would be the next generation of genetically engineered wheat as well as proven strains of rice and maize where feasible. Food security was paramount to the People's Republic of China. Since the 1990s, the Chinese agronomists had been experimenting with genetically engineered plants under uncontrolled conditions. The heads of the cereal grains had dramatically improved, but the stems were another matter. The heads were too heavy to be supported by the stems, and so with most of the newer strains of rice and wheat, the stalks gave way and bent over to the point that harvesting without damage was a serious problem.

Hundreds of small villages, living on the fringe of the twentieth century, gladly accepted the offer. Their land plots were small; in drought years they could only feed themselves. Their young people were being siphoned off into the cities of the eastern seaboard by the promise of modernity with the illusion of finding a better life than was offered by their parents.

Construction crews were detailed to construct new villages during the dry season. Military civil engineers were put in charge of districts. Land was surveyed. Tentative districts had been drawn on maps two years earlier. Civilian civil engineers were assigned one village at a time so that they would concentrate all of their efforts and energies on that single village. Their skills and progress in construction were graded according to design and quality. The civil engineers had overall responsibility, and the foremen of the crews of the carpenters, masons, electricians and plumbers were responsible to the engineer. An agronomist was assigned either to each village or district, according to the perceived necessity, productivity, terrain and experience of the agronomist. The terrain, climate, soil, potential agricultural productivity, and human necessities were thus all included and designed at the local level. Centralized planning with decentralized execution was the strategy. The typical village design was for fifty to one hundred families per village. Irrigation ditches and pumps were constructed. Concrete block homes with running water, indoor plumbing and electricity were raised with surprising rapidity. Each home consisted of a kitchen, a modest living room, bathroom, and two bedrooms. Each house was provided with a television, a radio, a computer, a fuel oil stove and a telephone. For many of the poorer villages, it would be a step up into paradise.

General Lui made the call. It went out on the microwave length, as on a cell phone. The Big Ear satellite had monitored all the weekly reports from the army fronts. The Chinese knew it but didn't care. What would the United States or Europe do about it anyway? If it was seriously detrimental information, it would be sent encrypted or by air courier. The Little Eye satellite recorded how the Chinese follow-on battalions quickly bulldozed graves about three feet deep for massive burial for the entire population of villages. Surgeon General Carolyn Weber expressed the possibility that the shallow graves would ultimately allow faster decomposition of the bodies resulting in more fertile soil, and allow the bones to be more easily recovered when they could be ground for fertilizer. Individuals murdered singly or in twos or threes were generally not buried but left for scavengers or to rot where they fell. Southeast Asia and the Indian subcontinent had several species of jackals, foxes, wolves, leopards, and vultures. She likened it to the slaughter of the bison on the American prairies.

"Yes, General Chang, we are ready for the engineers and their construction crews. We are doing most satisfactorily. I hope they can get started and completed before the monsoons come, which would make such efforts doubly hard and less than perfect. It would also allow the settlers to move in and immediately start their rice sets. The few remaining natives should prove no real difficulty, a minor nuisance at best. My staff is already designing defensive forces from my units to be detailed to each of the villages. It would most certainly help when the engineers and their staffs arrive so we can further fine tune these defensive units according the size of the village and the anticipated threat, if any. I am concerned about them getting started before the so-called 'dust rain' begins in the northern half of our new province of Vietnam. This persistent drizzle will begin two months from now, in February. The southern half of Vietnam is just starting its drier period which will last from this month of December into April. Perhaps it would be better to concentrate on the southern portion as a result of the climate. The engineers would have more time to complete their projects. The downside is the land line of communication that might be occasionally temporarily interrupted. As we earlier discussed, if things are brought by the sea, then they are much less likely to be interrupted by the few remnants of the Vietnamese Army who will probably attempt to wage guerilla war. It would certainly be cheaper to ship building materials and people into the southern ports as you suggested, General Chang."

General Chang disregarded the last bit of obsequiousness. "My congratulations, General Lui. You have made remarkable progress, and the Central Committee is as pleased as I am. I will inform the appropriate bureaus of your readiness. I anticipate that the construction crews have been alerted and should begin arriving in ten days to two weeks. We will ship the settlers to their assigned villages as soon as they are completed. The arriving engineers have been instructed to coordinate with your local troop commanders on the defensive aspects of each village and district. They will ensure there are adequate barracks and defensive positions incorporated into each village. Your troops will form the backbone of the future militia of each village. Are there any other things you wish to report?"

"No, General Chang, I am quite pleased overall. I thank you and look forward to the arrival of the engineers and their teams."

"Very well then, General. Continue as planned. Out here."

After they concluded the telephone conversation, General Lui sat at his desk and composed a message for encryption. "I have completed the necessary assignments of my troops who will form the Home Guard of the new areas for settlement.

"I have ordered a coalescing of the survivors of all units that are not necessary for devil defense duties, so that our battalions which depart for Africa will be at full strength. Each division is responsible to ensure that each of its surviving battalions will be at full strength, even though there will not be enough battalions to constitute a full division. Many battalion designations will, therefore, cease to exist, but that is what we expected. I have reduced or promoted officers as required to maintain appropriate lines of authority. After this is completed, I will initiate condensing of the undermanned regiments and, ultimately, divisions, so that the surviving divisions will be fully manned. This will maintain a nominal military structure. I will have these reconstituted battalions reporting to ports of debarkation in less than three weeks. Per our plan, they will leave as soon as our new ocean-going fleet of transports arrives at the designated harbors. My troops will be waiting there for re-supply and transportation. Many of my units are on reduced rations, so it is imperative that sufficient foodstuffs be included for immediate consumption. This is particularly important for those units now destined to function as Home Guard units. Those newly constituted for transport to Africa are also in need. They should be logistically supported for the inland march to the maximum extent possible. Sufficient truck transportation remains a major impediment, as there were insufficient trucks of suitable size obtained on the peninsula. Lui."

General Tsai's weekly report was not so favorable. His attack was launched several weeks later over radioactive terrain, against far larger and more formidable foes: the armies and peoples of the Indian subcontinent, India, Pakistan and Afghanistan. His southern armies assigned to clear the Indian Peninsula had been advancing very slowly, destroying as many people as they could. Corpses were everywhere. His disposal battalions could not keep up with providing mass burials in the areas of greater population density. Nuclear fires and the initial radiation sickness had killed tens of millions. Millions more succumbed over the ensuing months to prolonged radiation sickness that resulted from lower dosage, heat, dust, dehydration and exhaustion, and secondary infections while they fled southward in front of his armies. The southwest monsoon rains, blowing from June to September, had helped clear the air, but dust raised simply by marching and moving vehicles of all types resulted in its being inhaled, coughed up by the mucociliary apparatus of the respiratory tree and swallowed, only to exert its effect on the gastrointestinal tract. Many of his troops were suffering severe diarrhea from which they could not recover. His staff could not keep up with the specific number of casualties his armies were experiencing, so they merely provided best guesses as estimates reported by battalion commanders and assembled by the division level staffs.

His armies initially made rapid advancement along the southern boundary of the Himalayas. Two army groups, one leading westward, the other following, stretched one thousand miles from west to east. These two army groups simultaneously pivoted ninety degrees in a massive left flank movement to turn south when the advance elements of the westernmost reached the Great Indian Desert. The easternmost army corps of three divisions, he initially detailed to clear the nation of Bangladesh. Resistance was negligible. Civilian populations were not armed and so could offer little or no resistance. The Jain philosophy, especially in Gujarat, that all life is inviolate worked against the Indian civilians defending themselves as well. The swamps, marshes and rivers and tropical climate proved to be a far more formidable foe than the people. His troops were increasingly afflicted with malaria. Reports of cholera were becoming more and more common at the battalion level. Advancement was fairly rapid, up to five kilometers a day across the Indo-Gangetic Plain of the north. The two army groups were slowed, however, to progressing two to three kilometers per day through Madhya Pradesh. Now, the northeast monsoon from December through February was becoming a factor. The progress of his armies wasn't fast enough to suit General Tsai, but the Vindhya and Satpura ranges of low mountains could not be denied. The result was those armies on the flanks were proceeding faster in the lowlands so that his armies were in a great horseshoe formation. In effect, it was something akin to an unplanned trap for the indigenous population, as the people inside the horseshoe encountered the flanking units as they fled east and west. The larger towns and cities were more or less bypassed, leaving the inhabitants to starve and die of secondary effects of the nuclear exchange. General Tsai wanted to be at the southern tip of the peninsula by early March at the latest. He realized that early May was more likely. That was in the middle of the hot season, when the remnants of his army would board the ocean going catamarans. Strange in the eyes of many, General Tsai gave the order that no wildlife of any sort was to be killed, save for poisonous snakes, the kraits, cobras and vipers.

General Tsai was pleased with the compression of his forces accorded by the geographical narrowing of the Indian peninsula as they marched southward. It allowed the same concentration of his troops to accommodate some of the losses in personnel he was experiencing. His own deceased troops were placed in the mass graves along with their victims.

General Shen, De-ming was now at the western edge of Lake Balqash (Baikal) in eastern Kazakhstan. He had detached one army group to turn southward through Kyrgyzstan, Tajikistan, and into Afghanistan. He did not expect many of this army group to survive the combination of AIDs, the harsh winter, lack of adequate caloric intake, and harassment by the Pakhtun tribes. He hoped that there would be sufficient remnants of it left that he could invade Afghanistan from the west, thereby forcing a two front war for the Pakhtuns. Even though Afghanistan was assigned to Army Front II, he wanted to make contact with General Tsai's army group somewhere along the Afghanistan-Pakistan border if possible. He directed another army group to guard the flank, using an axis of approach through Uzbekistan and into Turkmenistan. This group was to halt operations one hundred and fifty kilometers from the Iranian border. This would tie down the armed forces of these Central Asian Republics and deny them the first army group's right, or western, flank. His third army group, he directed to continue the attack almost due westward, with their final objective as the northern end and eastern shore of the Caspian Sea. This group was not to proceed farther westward than Balyqshi and Atyrau, cities on the northern shore. General Chang and his staff felt that Russia and Iran should not be threatened with these boundaries. *Time will tell,* thought Tsai.

General Shen's subordinate generals were reporting increased resistance, particularly coming from the civilian population of Kazakhstan and Kyrgyzstan. The high desert of Kazakhstan was particularly suited for armored warfare. The Russians maintained a military college at Frunze, now named Bishkek, just inside the Kyrgyzstan border and on the southern edge of the desert when Kyrgyzstan was an autonomous Soviet Republic. It seemed that every male Kazakhstani and Kyrgyzstani had a semi-automatic rifle, usually an AK-47, and a considerable supply of ammunition. The rifle cartridges bore Russian head stamps, but the rifles seemed to come from several sources; among them Bulgaria, Rumania, Hungary, the Czech Republic, and Slovakia. A small number of M-16 type rifles, apparently of American manufacture, were also found on the bodies of resisting citizens.

Small bands of citizens, apparently uncoordinated, were attacking their flanks in areas of more rugged terrain, while regular army units were attacking the advance Chinese elements with artillery, armor and aircraft whenever they could isolate a unit up to a division in size. Kazakhstan army units would launch a frontal attack to slow the opposing unit, then strike at the flanks and then withdraw as quickly as they could. When the Chinese units advanced, the Kazakhstani squadrons on their flanks would renew their attacks with a vengeance. It was an effective tactic, slowing the Chinese, but nevertheless, grinding down the Kazakhstanis by overwhelming mass. The small bands of untrained citizens were usually annihilated when they did not practice good cover and concealment and strong discipline. If these bands survived a mistake, they did not make it a second time. They were becoming hardened guerillas that expected no mercy and granted none, in the most hideous ways on the few prisoners they captured.

Uzbek and Kazakh units began to attack from west to east, striking at the Chinese right flank and rear of the Chinese who turned eastward and were now attacking all along the western borders of Kyrgyzstan and Uzbekistan. The mouth of every valley into Kyrgyzstan and Uzbekistan was an avenue for attack for the Chinese. One night, several flights of Kazakh aircraft flew over, but apparently dropped their bombs only on the lead

2023: WORLD WAR III

elements. Other aircraft flew at an altitude of only a few hundred feet over entrained units, but did not release any ordnance, at least any that did not explode. Anti-aircraft missiles took their toll on the old Migs of the Uzbek and Kazakh air forces as they passed overhead. Those that flew over the entrained units were equipped with spray tanks. A persistent nerve agent, a close relative of the American nerve gas VX, settled on Chinese troops and equipment. Not equipped for gas warfare, nor provided pyridostigmine pre-treatment or atropine sulfate for immediate post exposure treatment, exposed Chinese troops died by the thousands within minutes. An entire division force equivalent succumbed within ten minutes.

General Shen, De-ming decided to respond in kind. He ordered a persistent nerve agent, a chemical variant of the American agent VX, identical to the one used against his troops, sprayed over the central part of the Kazakh capital of Almaty, a city of 1.5 million people. *It is just as well,* he thought. *It is a faster death than starvation. Since this nerve agent will remain effective for at least a week, it will cause panic among the survivors and force them out of the city and into the desert where we can more easily kill them with less loss of our own troops. Urban warfare is the most costly form of warfare, especially for the attacker. There will also be more room for mass burial for larger groups of them. The only down side is clearing the bodies from the city when we occupy it. We'll have to build a rendering plant to handle the dead. It will result in a great deal of fertilizer.* He gave the order, but it required several hundred tons of nerve agent disbursed from cargo planes equipped with oversized agricultural spray type equipment. Several soldiers assigned to the handling the fifty-five gallon drums of nerve agent died as a result of careless handling and pin holes in their protective suits.

General Shen was determined to have his troops on the Arabian Sea coast by early spring, at least what was left of them.

———————◦•◆•◦———————

Special Agent James Carter and Dr. Diane Foster were walking home after their fourth date. They went to dinner on the first two, then to an early dinner followed by a movie on the third date. The team had now added half a dozen new members to provide the additional security for Dr.

Foster. This time, they had a late dinner and went to a late movie. It was after 24:00 hours on Saturday night, and they were both tired but in good spirits. They were walking arm in arm. The night was cool, but a cold wind was blowing from the northeast. They held hands for a few minutes, then he sighed, smiled, squeezed her hands, and simply said, "Good night." He turned and walked away from the door of her apartment. He went home to his own apartment, somewhat morose. This was turning into something more serious than he had anticipated, and he wasn't quite sure how he should handle it. Equally as bad, he was uncertain how Diane Foster felt about him, or how far she would let her feelings develop. She was in her early thirties and had not had an affair for some years. Apparently, she had been romantically burned some years earlier. He sensed some caution in her. Carter knew the smart thing to do would be to talk to the Supervisory Special Agent, but that might result in his being removed from the duty. The consequence was that he might not see her as often, or if re-assigned to some demanding task force, perhaps not at all. He realized that privacy was out of the question for the time being. He decided he better let his superior know that he was developing something of an emotional attachment to Dr. Foster. After all, he was thirty-four years old. He was beginning to wonder what it would be like to have a family life.

Foster had returned to her work and buried herself in it. Many of her co-workers had noticed a subtle change in her, a cold attitude towards them that was not there before her shuttle mission. Carter had taken to calling her Di, and she called him James. They were becoming enamored with each other. At first, they had merely talked, almost on a daily basis. One day in the following week, she returned to her apartment to find that he had cooked dinner for the two of them. "Surprise, surprise," he said as she opened the kitchen door in a very cautious manner. She knew she was under surveillance, but that didn't lessen her apprehension when she discovered someone beating about in her kitchen. He was a pretty good cook and demonstrated it with an excellent Chinese dinner.

The following day, he dropped by after she arrived home. "I believe you like classical music. What do you say we take in the symphony this Saturday? I have two tickets to quite good seats."

She smiled, and said, "I'd like that."

He smiled back and said, "It's a date. I'll see you sometime later in the week. For right now, count on me picking you up around eighteen hundred. We'll have an early supper before the concert."

James Carter discussed his growing emotional attachment with his supervisor. The first question Supervisory Special Agent Congdon asked, "How is this threatening your guarding of Dr. Foster? Do you not detail your men to follow you on your dates at a distance that is both discreet but sufficient to offer one hundred percent protection?"

"I have never, and never will, jeopardize a witness regardless of the circumstances."

"Well, James, I suspect then that you better continue in your duties. Right now, it is an open-ended assignment, and you were instructed to court her. We don't know how long it will be necessary to maintain security for Dr. Foster, but make it unrequited love until the detail is over. Then you can have all the intimacy you two might desire, and it won't interfere with your duties. Just don't let me see or hear of any lapses in judgment. Now get out of here, Romeo."

Nine ocean freighters left the harbor of Darien, now called Dalian by the Chinese. They sailed through the Yellow Sea, the East China Sea, and the South China Sea and into Haiphong harbor. There, three of them offloaded people and construction supplies, such as cement, wire, reinforcing steel bar, lumber, concrete block and construction equipment such as bulldozers, road graders, ditching machines, pumps, backhoes, and trucks. General Lui's inventory of construction materials and equipment in-country revealed a dismal shortage of everything. The second group of three unloaded food, ammunition and fuel for the Chinese occupiers of what was Vietnam. The people were engineers and construction workers. One of the last three took on roughly eight hundred of General Liu's troops. The other two were filled with fresh troops from China. The three which unloaded cargo began retracing their route. Satellites monitored every mile as the three troopships steamed in a line. They sailed through the Straits of Malacca under the increasingly intense concerns of the rest of the world. As they emerged from the Straits of Malacca and entered the Indian Ocean, two U.S. Los Angeles class submarines, the USS Buffalo and the USS Louisville, were waiting and began to follow them at a distance of twenty miles.

Suspected but undetected by the two U.S. submarines and the rest of the world, a picket line of air independent propulsion system Chinese submarines were submerged into the depths in the Indian Ocean the previous week to guard their developing sea lines of communication.

Jason Thornton called his National Security Council together. "Opinions, people, as to their destination. I recognize that they could be heading for any port on the Indian peninsula or Karachi, Pakistan, or the Gulf of Kutch, or any other place in a gigantic pincer movement. The questions are just where are they headed, and why? These few ships don't even hold a division-sized force, so is this just a local maneuver or a harbinger of greater things to come?

"Admiral Stark, given the size of these ships, their capacities, the fact that they are each carrying from 500 to 1500 people, how far can they go before requiring re-supply and refueling?"

"Mr. President, they are of sufficient size and capability to land those forces anywhere on the Arabian Sea littoral if they make straight for their objective. They are moving at about twelve to fifteen knots, which is not all that fast. These ships are those which were confiscated during the fighting in Southeast Asia. I might add that, as of this morning, we have observed the departure of another small convoy of twelve Chinese merchant ships from Darien. We are not aware of their cargos. It would appear that this is a harbinger of things to come. A curious thing about this is that there are no accompanying warships to protect the convoy of which we are aware."

"General Leonard, as the ultimate amphibious warrior here, what's your opinion?"

"With a force that small, it is obvious that unless they rendezvous with a much larger force somewhere, they must anticipate unopposed landings. They can't steam around with 800 men, more or less, aboard ships forever. There are no other fleets in the area of which I am aware. They will have to make landfall, their objective, before too long, as Admiral Stark indicates, or be re-supplied at sea. That seems to be unlikely, as it would be a waste of time, energy and loss of surprise. There are still some ships of the Indian Navy in the Indian Ocean that, if they are aware of them, will undoubtedly attack them."

"That's an idea, General. Suppose we contact those Indian ships and inform them of the direction, speed, and possible destinations of this three-ship convoy and let the Indian Navy have at them. We should also inform the Iranians that the Chinese have begun moving troops by sea in their general direction. Maybe the Iranian gunboats and mines can become a modest factor. What do you think, Admiral Stark?"

"I think it would be a good idea to inform both the Indian Navy, or what's left of it, and the Iranians as well. If their objective is the Middle East, the sooner those characters in that region are aware of it, the better."

"Ed, what do you think?"

"Mr. President, I think we are witnessing the opening of another chapter in the saga of Chinese conquest. Now, just where that conquest is headed, I don't know. My best guess is still the Persian Gulf. They could put those troops ashore on the southwest coast of Pakistan without taking any fire or having to make an amphibious assault and march overland into Iran. I'll have our people check on possible routes of advance from southern Pakistan into Iran. Obviously, they are simply troop carriers and appear to require piers and a harbor since they are without amphibious assault vehicles."

"Jim, see to it that the word is passed to the Iranians and any Indian Naval vessels you can contact. Marge, what's your two cents?"

"I don't think they are stupid enough to invade the Middle East with just three ships. Now, maybe if they build a force, or develop a base nearby from which to launch an attack, that is something else. Spring (2023) is already here, Mr. President. The cherry trees are blossoming along the Mall, and the heat in that region builds very quickly. So, they will have to do something quickly, or the hot season will be upon them."

"Ralph, what do you say?"

"I say I don't like it, Mr. President. If we had some idea of the cargoes these ships are carrying, it might be an indicator. We know these troops that they picked up in Haiphong Harbor are exhausted. They are the remnants of forces that fought their way down the Malayan Peninsula.

This shipboard excursion will give them some rest and the opportunity to establish a logistical trail. They might be the advance guard to establish a base somewhere along the shore of the Arabian Sea, as Secretary Talbott suggests, or they might be decoys of some nature, although I am not sure over what. They might be floating them out there to see who will attack them and how. I have never trusted the Chinese to keep their word on anything. Their guarantee not to invade the Middle East is worthless so far as I am concerned. I think they intend to establish hegemony not only over East Asia, but the Middle East as well. If they control the classical land bridge that locks three continents together, with all its mineral wealth, they rule the world."

"Admiral Stark, how much time do we have before those ships commit to a course that reveals their objective?"

"We have about five days, Mr. President, before they will leave the Indian Ocean and enter the Arabian Sea, where we will have to either commit or passively accept their presence or wait until they are in littoral waters to make our move. I strongly recommend that we not wait until they are in littoral waters. That plays to our disadvantage."

"Alright, let's keep everybody here informed as to last minute developments around the clock. We will meet again on Wednesday, 07:30, for breakfast and briefing. Marge, brief Ms. Stearns on the situation and bring her next time."

The Chinese submarines strung out in a line across the Indian Ocean held their positions and did not reveal their presence as the USS Buffalo and Louisville cruised by at fifteen knots underwater, trailing the Chinese merchant ships. Their electronic officers and technicians recorded every noise each American submarine made. Even flushing the head resulted in digital analysis of the sound. They were under orders not to fire upon the Americans unless the Americans fired at any Chinese vessel, so they waited and listened.

CHAPTER 36

07:00 Wednesday, 14 April 2023

The staff came filing in, somewhat subdued, but everybody had now acquired the habit of a good breakfast at each of these meetings. Jason Thornton rather enjoyed the breakfast part of the meetings and hoped everyone else did as well. He did believe that they functioned better and thought better with an adequate level of blood glucose. They helped themselves to everything on the buffet table. The stewards had learned by now which beverage each of them preferred, coffee, tea, milk, orange juice, apple juice, grapefruit sections, or fresh fruit and yogurt. After fifteen minutes of eating, the President started the meeting.

"OK, Jim, what do we have for overnight developments?"

"Well, Mr. President, for starters, a convoy of twelve of those ocean-going catamarans they have been building left the East China Sea, accompanied by four of their new destroyers. From our satellite photos, their cargoes appeared mixed. It is believed that they were loading fifty kilo bags of food grains, such as rice and wheat, other food stuffs, crates of ammunition, vehicles, medical supplies, and fifty-five gallon drums of fuel. It appears a modest amount of each type of cargo was loaded on each ship. They have been moving at about twenty-five knots, as a convoy."

"What do you make of that, General Craig?"

"It suggests that each ship has a basic load for a specific function. That specific function appears to be re-supply and re-equip a light infantry battalion. The cargo suggests that each ship will take on more Chinese soldiers at Haiphong, Da Nang, or wherever. If so, that means that they are planning another military push somewhere."

"Admiral Stark?"

"At that speed, they could overtake the earlier convoy, or be just a day or two behind it, weather permitting smooth sailing. If they pick up more of their forces from Malaya, it looks like it might be a by-the-numbers drop off of the troops for an unopposed landing force. If they put a battalion on each ship, they have better than a division-sized force."

"General Anderson?" Thornton asked between mouthfuls of biscuit and sausage gravy.

"The lack of heavy weapons, tanks, armored personnel carriers, artillery, helicopters, and so on, strongly suggests that it is strictly a light infantry affair that will be without any support other than organic crew served weapons, such as mortars and machine guns. That means they aren't going up against anybody with any kind of modern weaponry. Given their tactics of slaughtering all the indigenous people, now known throughout the world, they really aren't expecting much resistance. That means somebody other than the Iranians or Iraqis or the Gulf States. The Middle Eastern states all have at least some modern aircraft that would blow them out of the water and heavy forces sufficient to repel an invasion force. So, where are they headed? My best guess, based on the information at hand, is the Pakistani coast, the western coast of India, or as an outside chance, Africa."

"What does Central Intelligence make of their radio traffic, Ed?"

"We aren't really getting any clues from that, Mr. President. They are practicing pretty good radio discipline in that regard. It seems that the Army Front Commander for the Malayan Peninsula, General Lui, is remaining there. He has established his headquarters in what was the Vietnamese Capitol of Hanoi. It seems that he is passing his troops off to a different commander, one General Fong, Cu-chen. There has been some chatter between their Chief of Staff Chang and General Fong. We don't know a lot about Fong. He was educated mostly in China, visited

France, England, and Germany. He's more of a technocrat, less of a liberal arts type. He studied mining, engineering, geology, earth sciences type of curriculum. He visited mines in Germany and England while he toured there. General Fong has been quiet since Monday; he hasn't sent any messages since then, at least not any that we have intercepted. He might be aboard one of those ships.

"Several clues here, Mr. President, if we think about them. Why would General Lui surrender elements of his Army? They do not need such a large number of troops for the occupation force. There is very little resistance, if any, left on the peninsula. Those that are shipping out are in need of rest and recuperation and re-supply. So why aren't they headed home instead of west? Next, the commander that General Lui is passing his troops off to is a mining engineer type. Is there some significance there, or is he just an engineer cum soldier? It seems that the people who disembarked on the first three ships are actually a bunch of grave diggers. They have started digging massive graves and collecting the dead to fill them. Then why all the construction materials? That suggests they are going to do some building as well. What, where, and why?"

"Has there been any change in the course they are steaming?"

"No, Mr. President, they are headed due west. Haven't changed a degree since they came out of the Straits and struck the equator. If they maintain that course, they will run into Africa."

"Let's do some critical thinking here, people. First, what is in Africa that would entice the Chinese? Second, where would they land, with how many troops? Third, who would resist them? Fourth, what would be the long-term consequences, especially for the United States and western Europe?"

No one spoke. Then Ms. Stearns calmly said, "Everything the Chinese want and need is in Africa south of the equator. Southern Africa is one of the world's last treasure houses of minerals. It is rich in tungsten, uranium, vanadium, platinum, nickel, gold, diamonds, cobalt, chromium, and a few other lesser known and underappreciated minerals. Additionally, if they go far enough west, they can tap into Angolan oil, a variety of timber, some fantastic grazing land. If they go far enough south, a mild climate and an agriculturally rich region. If they go all the way south to the Cape of Good Hope, they control another choke point. The Chinese have had more than a hundred thousand entrepreneurs, agents really, in a dozen African countries for over a dozen years. They know where everything they want is, how much is known in quantity, and what it takes to get it. There is no military opposition to speak of, they have bought off whole tribes with food and goods, supported both sides with small arms but no heavy weapons in civil strife and tribal wars, bribed officials, and came in through the back door all over the southern half of the continent. It makes very good sense to consider Africa as their objective."

"Ms. Stearns, I knew there was a reason I had you here today. Let's get a team effort here. I want a meeting this afternoon, at 16:00, all the people in this room to be briefed by your people Ed, and yours, Marge, and yours, Jim, to put together an overall picture on southern Africa. The thrust is what is in it for the Chinese, how easily can they militarily acquire it, and the long-term consequences of their seizing it. Let's take a fifteen minute break so you can make your phone calls to your appropriate personnel."

After twenty-five minutes, everyone had returned to their seats. "Alright, somebody fill me in on a few other details. Where do we stand on the possibility of invading the Canal Zone? Jim, how ready are your people?"

The flag officers all smiled at each other. Jointness among the services was at its best. Jim Neville looked at his people and smiled at the President. "We're ready, Mr. President. You just say the word. No one knows, or at least no one has been told, what the target is, although some might have guessed, particularly the SEAL teams involved, but everybody is keyed and chomping at the bit."

"Depending on the Chinese, I might say the word at any time, Mr. Secretary. If the Chinese steam a straight course into Africa, I'm much less likely to say the word. Marge, have you prepared statements and whatever you need to do on the diplomatic front when we, or if we, go into the Canal Zone?"

"I'm ready, Mr. President. About half a dozen of my people know the target and are people I trust. They have been ready for a month. I'm sure the useless UN will howl, especially the Panamanians who have become millionaires selling their country, and ours, to the Chinese. On that note, who cares? The fraudulence of the UN has tremendously disappointed our own left wing idealists so much that they don't say so much these days."

"Fred, what's the update on Robert Wha Lee? I can't believe my own bodyguard was a spy for the Chinese."

"We have him under intense surveillance, Mr. President. We are waiting for him to make a mistake so we can have hard evidence at his trial. We don't think he has spotted us, but he is very well trained, and that is always a possibility. We just hope he doesn't slip away on us. That leads me to the question of whether or not you want an open, public trial or a secret trial. We can do it either way, but we will have to work with the Justice Department very closely on it. If it is an open trial, there will be, obviously, a lot of bad publicity for your administration. On the other hand, there are no appeals on a secret trial, records are sealed for fifty years, and the penalty is usually death or life in solitary confinement. We anticipate he fed the Chinese everything that transpired in your office, everything you said, did, thought you did, ever since you became a Presidential candidate. Thank God the Canadians went along with our little investment in security.

"On that note, the Supreme Court should rule on the legality of installing the same system in all of our airports and overseas terminals in the next month or so. The ACLU has put together quite a team of legal eagles with some convoluted thinking in presenting their argument. The liberals appointed to the Supreme Court by your predecessor tilted the Court towards their perspective, so that does not bode well for its favorable ruling."

"I'm curious, Fred. In that same vein, do you have any idea how the Second Amendment case will turn out? Do you really think that the Supreme Court will rule that individual citizens in good standing do not have the right to own firearms? Will it become a privilege instead of a right in the eyes of the Court? If so, that might spark a civil war right here in River City."

"Mr. President, I can't say. One thing is for sure, with the news every night showing how the Chinese slaughtered millions of people who couldn't defend themselves, that just might hammer some common sense into the Court, but no guarantees. Some of them think the United States will never change, or that we couldn't be invaded because we have an ocean on each side of us. They refuse to recognize the invasion from the south, from Mexico especially, but tens of thousands from Central and South America as well, both legal and extra legal immigrants. It is a mess. Some of the eastern states have begun to falsify their criminal data the way the Brits have been doing for years, ever since they outlawed personal ownership of firearms of all types. They count ten burglaries on one block as one burglary. Ever since the raids from Mexico, everybody in the southwest is openly armed. I wouldn't want to be any law officer or officer of the court that ordered those people to surrender their arms. That law would be unenforceable. That might even lead to some states attempting to secede. Wyoming's Attorney General tells me that is being openly discussed in coffee shops across the state. Ditto for Montana and Idaho and both Dakotas."

"All right, then; Marge, tell our African embassies personnel to be ready to depart at a moment's notice. If the Chinese ships pass the 60th Meridian, they are going for Africa. We want our people out of there. Make sure there are no leaks to the press for the moment. General Shelton, plan for a military airlift for all our folks in Africa. On second thought, let's evacuate all non-essential personnel now. Give the order, Marge."

———————————

"The locals can get there a lot faster than we can. Call them. Have them get there as soon as possible, but not take any action other than guard whoever happens to be there. Have them dispatch an ambulance at the same time, just in case the guy is bleeding out or something. I'm on my way now." Ed Wrangell hung up the phone. The operator had immediately relayed the tape recording to him. He grabbed his sport coat and headed for the garage. He turned on his lights and siren in his sedan and headed for Margarita Street in East L.A.

The ambulance crew was loading Chan into the ambulance when he arrived.

"How is he?" he asked of the EMT crew chief. "Oh, he'll live all right, but they were pretty rough on him. He's dehydrated as hell, and in a lot of pain, but he will recover. He's got to be hurting real bad. We're taking him to L.A. General unless you specify otherwise. They're real good with these cases."

"L.A. General is fine." He turned to the uniformed sergeant standing adjacent to him. "Sergeant, the FBI has a very keen interest in this. Can you have a couple of your folks escort him there and keep him under wraps until we get squared away?"

The Sergeant, a twenty year street veteran, grinned, "Sure. We'll babysit him for you until you feds get there. If you like, I'll hold his hand all the way."

"That won't be necessary, Sergeant, but thanks." Wrangell put in a call to have an FBI photographer and fingerprinting authority meet the ambulance at the hospital. Upon Chan's arrival, the Emergency Department started an I.V. line, and after initial examination, the physician ordered a dose of intravenous Demerol for pain. They cleaned his face and propped him up so the FBI photographer and fingerprint expert could do their jobs. Wrangell then dug the business card of Jacobi out of his wallet, called him, and told him what transpired. He suggested Jacobi meet him in his office. Jacobi agreed to meet with pictures of Miguel Monzani and several of his lieutenants from their files. In Wrangell's office, they exchanged photographs. Wrangell called the photographic section to have them duplicate the photos provided by Jacobi and provided Jacobi with photos of Chan and Gonzalez.

Chan was identified from the photos by Gonzalez and several of the prisoners being held by the FBI in a special containment facility in the basement of what was supposed to be a warehouse. None of them recognized the photographs of Miguel Monzani or his lieutenants. Ed Wrangell called Fred Gateway to let him know they had a Chinese agent who was involved in the cross border raids.

That evening, Bernardo was elected by the Caballeros as the new leader. Gomez was appointed a lieutenant. The following day, Bernardo notified the gang leaders of the adjacent territories that he had been elected and would like to meet with them. At that meeting, Bernardo made it quite clear that the only thing that changed was the individual occupying the leadership position. Encroachment upon their territory, operations, or other endeavors would result in violent reprisals. Peace had existed for several years to everyone's satisfaction, and that should continue. The Council agreed.

Bernardo then called the local office of the Congressman for his district and requested an appointment when the Congressman was next in town. The nature of the meeting was to be discussion of support for the Congressman and La Reconquesta. When politicians and gangs unite, the gang becomes a private armed force for the politician, who in turn offers them political legitimacy. The gang metamorphoses into a quasi-political organization that begins to offer social services at the grass roots level. They constitute an ominous development for legitimate governments when they grow large and powerful.

Robert Wha Lee's mail included a flyer for 'luncheon specials' from a Chinese restaurant. Lee carefully trimmed the coupon for one out and wrote 'make it quick' on it. The next day, he visited the restaurant for a late supper, and gave the coupon to the waiter, instructing him to be sure that Mao took care of him.

When his meal was served, a note was written in Mandarin on the paper liner of his tray. Lee pretended to casually read it as he ate. It was a simple set of instructions that he should call the restaurant pretending not to understand or be inebriated and to order an "Antonio's Special Pizza" only in times of emergency. He would be met one hour later at the park bench in his neighborhood park. Lee finished his meal and left a generous tip. As soon as he stepped away from the table, his tray was whisked back to the kitchen. The note was fed into the stove.

Thirteen U.S. Treasury agents, one of which was Robert Wha Lee, and two FBI agents were hurriedly summoned to an emergency meeting. The two FBI agents were fully informed of the situation, but the Treasury agents were not. Nat Nash, head of Treasury's Counterfeiting Division, began the briefing.

"We just received word that a shipment of counterfeit U.S. Federal Reserve Notes in twenty- and fifty-dollar denominations entered the port of Baltimore yesterday. As we speak, it is going through customs for shipment to here in Washington, D.C. for distribution. We have an agent following the shipping container which is allegedly full of electrical supplies from Taiwan. We will intercept the shipment at the electrical supply distribution company receiving the container. It is due here late tomorrow afternoon. We have about twenty-four hours. Lights down please, camera." Nash pointed to the building projected on the screen as he assigned agents to cover the various entrances, where and how roads would be blocked, two ambulances that would be in the immediate vicinity for any casualties, and explained that it would be videotaped from an adjacent building which offered an excellent view of most of the operation. One Treasury Agent would be disguised as a taxi driver, another as a skid row bum. A van parked a block away would house a sound and film unit as well as three agents. At the appropriate moment, a helicopter from the FBI would be called on for possible support. A sniper was going to occupy the passenger's seat. Nash introduced the two FBI agents, elaborating that an FBI Hostage Rescue Team would be standing by as backup should any innocent individuals be seized as hostages.

"Since a foreign government is likely involved, the presence of the FBI is indicated. Our fellow officers of the Bureau think the FBI Hostage Rescue Team might be necessary, and I agree that it is better to have them and hopefully not need them. This way, the operation is kept entirely in federal hands. The local law enforcement agencies will be informed of the operation only at the last minute, when the shipping container arrives at the warehouse. We will meet here at 10:00 hours to draw equipment and review plans and make any necessary changes. We will have flash and bang grenades and smoke grenades and masks for those of us in uniform. I don't anticipate their use, but if necessary, we will deploy them. For those of you who will be very close to the building when it goes down, dress in the appropriate disguises according to your assignment. Everyone will be wearing communications equipment and a body vest regardless of assignment. The rest of us will be in highly visible lettered jackets. I know the vests and jackets are hot, but better to be sweaty than full of lead. Besides, no one will be close enough to see the earphones and mics until it is too late. Since I planned this, I'll personally lead it. Don Livingstone will be Number 2 if I should catch a round early on. Don, you will lead the front door team while I take down the loading dock at the receiving area. It's not all that big a building, with about twenty people usually inside. It shouldn't be anything big at all. We want to question all suspects, so watch the firepower. Don't hose down the place unless you have to. Many of the people inside are just ordinary employees, at least we think so. If there are no questions, let's call it a day."

———————•=●◆=•———————

In the park adjacent to his home, all but three of the park benches were being painted. Signs of fresh paint, do not use, were place on all four sides of each bench. Of the three not painted, a small microphone was taped to the underside of each. Each microphone had a different frequency and was voice activated.

That night, from a pay phone, Lee dialed the Chinese restaurant, and with a stutter, demanded Antonio's Special Pizza. "I need that pizza now, not tomorrow night, I want my pizza," he decried. "I'll come now to collect it." With that, he hung up and walked to the park with a newspaper under his arm. He sat on the appropriate bench and began to read. One block away, he was filmed by the FBI. The phone was tapped, and his pizza order and the number he dialed were recorded. One hour later, an elderly Chinese lady sat down on the bench next to him. Holding the newspaper over his face, he said, "There is to be a raid on the electrical supply house receiving the money tomorrow."

"We know nothing of that. What are you talking about?"

"A team was assembled today to raid the electrical supply company tomorrow afternoon when a shipment of ten million counterfeit dollars arrives."

"We know nothing of that. We are not involved in any counterfeiting operations. Our targets are political. I will, however, inform my superiors. They will know of such an arrangement and take the necessary precautions." With that, the old lady left. The entire conversation was recorded. She proceeded to a phone booth from which she called a minor clerk in the Chinese embassy. She invited her friend to meet her for drinks in an hour at a small bar in Silver Springs, Maryland at 21:00 hours. When she left, the FBI collected the coins from the phone and lifted fingerprints from all of them. A dozen FBI technicians proceeded to the bar over the next three hours and planted microphones in various locations around the bar, in places they thought the two women would talk, such as in the booths. Between 20:00 and 21:00 hours, half a dozen agents of both sexes and several ethnic nationalities drifted into the bar.

Over Rob Roy drinks, the elderly lady informed the younger woman of her conversation with Robert Wha Lee earlier that day.

"There is no such shipment arriving tomorrow. We have no such warehouse or contacts at any such business. We do not receive any shipments of anything at that place. There is something seriously wrong here. It smells of a trap to me. I suggest you immediately get ahold of your contact and let him know that he might be in serious trouble. As soon as you finish your drink, leave. I will leave a little later." One of the FBI agents was photographing the two women as they spoke with a tiny camera hidden in his attaché case.

Realizing that his apartment phone was probably tapped, the elderly lady ruled out a discussion of a possible trap over the phone lines. The only other way she could provide a timely warning was to stop by his apartment. That, too, she decided would be very risky, as it was undoubtedly under surveillance. Finally, she decided that the best way would be a simple phone call with the message, "Go see your Uncle Mao." He should be smart enough to figure out that she meant immediately proceed to the Chinese embassy because you are in immediate danger. She stopped at another bar and made the phone call. Lee was home reading when the call came in. As soon as he said "Hello," she said "Go see your Uncle Mao" twice, then hung up. Lee thought about it for a few minutes, then decided he should go for a walk. Perhaps he would be contacted as he walked.

As he walked, it dawned upon him that he should proceed to the Chinese embassy. He returned to his apartment and did a cursory search. He found a microphone behind a picture in the living room. He grabbed his coat and headed for his car in the parking lot. The FBI agent parked half a block away observed his movement, and radioed it to the command post. He followed Lee at a safe distance. Lee continually checked his mirror to see if he was being followed. The agent turned off after a mile, depending upon the transmitter in Lee's car to keep him informed. Lee's mind eased for a few minutes as he headed for the Chinese embassy.

Then he considered that his car probably had a transmitter in it as well. The Officer-in-Charge at the command post following his route on the computer screen determined Lee was headed for the Chinese Embassy. The OIC scrambled two cars with agents, radioing to them their instructions to intercept Lee immediately in front of the entrance to the Embassy so that Lee would not be able to find asylum.

Lee checked his rearview mirror and recognized the car that followed him from the apartment building was again behind him. He drove right up to the entrance of the Embassy and started out, but two men dashed from two different cars towards him. Lee delivered a roundhouse kick to the head of one that immediately rendered the agent unconscious. The second blocked a wheel kick as two more agents entered the fight. Lee connected with a high punch that shattered the second agent's jaw in three places. He went down. The third agent managed to deliver a solid body blow to Lee's lowest rib that broke it. It caused Lee a moment's hesitation from the pain. Lee delivered a low kick to the agent's patella, dislocating it. He went down. *One left to go,* thought Wha. At that instant, a 180-grain bullet from the third agent's Beretta in the .40 Smith & Wesson cartridge shattered Lee's left femur. He collapsed to the pavement as the proximal end of the distal portion of the bone ripped through the muscle of his leg. He started to pull his own sidearm, but the agent who shot him placed his Beretta against Lee's head and said, "If you pull it, you die." Lee lay still as the agent removed Lee's gun from the shoulder holster. The fourth agent rolled Lee onto his back and handcuffed him. The agent with the gun in hand handed his set of handcuffs to the standing agent and said, "You better cuff his ankles to keep him from crawling inside while you call for a couple of ambulances. This guy was really good. Jim is out, Dave is out, and I am in agony and can't stand." The fourth agent did just that, then called the command center with a request for two ambulances.

"Robert Wha Lee is in custody."

The OIC at the Command Center immediately put in a call to Fred Gateway and informed him of what transpired.

CHAPTER 37

"Very good news, Mr. President; the boys at DARPA, the Defense Advanced Research Projects Agency, just informed me that, in conjunction with the Japanese, we have built two new, identical satellites and have tested them. They named them SUBDUED I and II. It stands for Submarine Detection, Underwater Electromagnetic Distortion. It is based on changes in the magnetic field a submarine creates when it is underwater. The salt water environment interacts with the steel or titanium outer hull, even if it is an anechoic design. The distortion is greatest when the sub is moving, but they can still detect it even when it is lying still. There's enough distortion created by the chemical reaction between the salt water and the hull that it can be picked up from 125 miles up in space. We are planning to launch them, one here and one from Japan, next week. The Nipponese will use a rocket, while we will place ours in orbit from a shuttle mission. They will have two slightly different orbits, but they will both cover the southern Pacific, Indian Oceans and Arabian Sea.

"The two satellites will talk with one another, so to speak. This will allow an even greater detection and reporting capability. It is having two points of reference on the target. We have arranged a code from the two satellites that both we and the Japanese will monitor. Larry Corning and Diane Foster are the primary movers on this one. I must say, they are quite sharp people. By the way, a serious romance has budded between Dr. Foster and Fred Gateway's head FBI agent on her protection team."

What the DCI didn't tell the President was that a phony code was also shared with each of the suspect members in the laboratory. A slightly different part of the code was modified in each case, so that each suspect was provided with a copy of the code containing a unique identifier. Only Dr. Fisher knew the real, complete code. With nanotechnology, the satellites would identify whichever incorrect code was beamed to them, and report it to DARPA. Not even the Japanese were aware of this imaginative trap.

"That's very good news, Jim. I presume this technology and these satellites are aimed at detecting those air independent propulsion submarines we have all been so concerned about. Who else knows about this?"

"We're keeping it limited on a need-to-know basis, Mr. President. There aren't more than a dozen people in each country, outside the members at this table, and perhaps a similar table in Japan, who know about this capability. Other parts of the satellite were built independently; they are modular satellites and have to be completely assembled in order to function. These new detectors can be built in a matter of a couple of weeks. It is quite amazing. The circuits are actually built by bacteria in a complex web of connections. The satellites will be solar powered, but you can run them on a couple of D sized flashlight batteries as backup. We'll keep you posted as launch preparations proceed, Mr. President, but right now we're scheduling them for s shuttle and rocket launch one week from today.

"Other interesting news, Mr. President, is that the Chinese are sending one to three ships out of their harbors every twenty-four hours now. They are all steaming on the same course, or so it appears. They are headed for Malayan ports where they deliver a load of supplies, then pick up a battalion of Chinese troops. The first ships have made landfall on the East African coast, Mombassa, Kenya, to be specific. The troops are securing the ports right now. There is no opposition at all. Ed has more on this."

Everybody looked at Ed McCluskey, DCI. He nodded a thank you to Jim Neville and picked up the thread of conversation. "The first two shiploads of troops took over warehouses and acted as stevedores, unloading supplies in Mombassa after they established strong defensive perimeters around them. It looks like it will be an extended operation. Initially, there was some minor combat, skirmishes really, as some of the natives attempted to pilfer the supplies. They were shot for their attempts. Trucks are part of the offloaded supplies. The troops on the next convoy of ships loaded the supplies in trucks and started for the interior. It seems there are slight deviations in the courses of the following convoys, going north and south, to Mogadishu in Somalia in the north, Tanga and Dar es Salaam in Tanzania in the south. So, they are establishing four beach heads, roughly eight hundred miles apart by seacoast roads. It suggests that they plan to deliver roughly a battalion of infantry and logistical support every day to each of these three ports. They have a string of over thirty merchant ships now en route to Africa. Those catamarans are obviously built as ocean going fast freighters to deliver men and supplies for another invasion, this time, of Africa. Not a single ship has veered more than five degrees north of the equator, which supports that Mogadishu is their northern target port.

"This strongly suggests that they will drive westward from these three ports, probably with the Congo as their objective. Whether their final objective will be the Congo or the Atlantic coast, we don't know at this point. Given their previous behavior, it wouldn't surprise me if they drove completely across Africa, cutting off the entire southern portion of the continent.

"Another interesting development is that the Chinese are moving their regular armed forces off the coast, away from the Strait of Taiwan. We picked up on their movement twenty-four hours ago. They are headed west, but where they will stop, we don't know. A couple of analysts suggested that they might take over the drive in the Central Asian Republics. It's been eight months since the Chinese started moving, almost seven in the CARs. They have suffered tremendous losses but don't seem concerned about the loss of so much manpower, several tens of millions of people. They are closing down on the tip of the Indian peninsula. We have no idea how many people they slaughtered there, or how many troops they still have. Certainly, radiation sickness, diseases, and combat casualties should have depleted their ranks to skeleton proportions."

"Thoughts, ideas, people? What are they going to do with those troops they are moving away from the coast?"

Ms. Stearns thought for a moment, then looked around. Somewhat reluctantly, she said, "If they loaded those troops on ships from their eastern seaboard, it would be very easy for us to interpret them as an invasion fleet for Taiwan. If they shipped them elsewhere for boarding of ships, it would not raise anxiety here or in Taiwan. In fact, it should probably generate a feeling of relief. That means, it is either a massive diversion maneuver, or they are headed for conquered lands. They could replace the losses in India, the Malayan peninsula, or reinforce or relieve the forces fighting in the CARs. I don't know how much progress they have made in the Central Asian Republics, but I suspect they have had their hands full with winter weather and guerilla warfare. India is almost conquered, so my guess would be garrison duty in India and Pakistan, or a spring offensive in the Asian Republics."

"Why not fresh troops for the invasion of Africa, Ms. Stearns?" asked Ed McCluskey.

"That is quite possible, sir. Given the fact that they are taking battle hardened reserve troops that fought down the Malayan peninsula and using them for Africa suggests that they will do the same for troops that fought down the Indian peninsula. Fresh regular troops will be better used in garrison. They don't seem to mind losing the reserves. From what I have been told, the reserves are only trained in small unit infantry tactics with no heavy weapons training or capability whereas the regulars are. They shouldn't need troops trained in the use of heavy weapons to defeat the rabble of Africa. The Africans are three quarters starved to death, armed only with small arms, and absolutely riddled with AIDS. There are no trained armies there, only regional warlords ruling over essentially local tribal gangs of teenaged men and women. The Chinese have been supplying them with food and small arms for years to use against one another. They have killed each other off for the benefit of the Chinese. I'll bet that the Chinese shut down the supply line several months ago. That would further weaken resistance. They wouldn't waste well trained troops going into battle against such an enemy in such an environment as starving, AIDS and tropical disease ridden central and southern Africa. At least, it doesn't make sense to me to do so."

"We received communications from one of our people in Mombassa last night. He commented on how poorly nourished many of the Chinese soldiers looked. He said they looked like they suffered AIDS themselves."

"My God," said Roberta Stearns. "What if all of these Chinese reservists have AIDS? They are accomplishing massive world conquest, on two continents anyway, while they rid their nation of all their AIDS infected people, thus reducing the spread of the disease or perhaps even eliminating it, in their society. They are reducing their own population pressure, acquiring new lands for food production, destroying sources of economic competition from India and South Korea and competition for food from India and Pakistan, and acquiring new sources of raw materials, all at the same time. Do we have any data on how serious the AIDS problem is in China?"

"Yeah, as I recall, that's what Dr. Allison said a couple of months ago."

Jason Thornton pushed the intercom button on his desk. "Peggy, call Dr. Allison and tell him to have his people put together a couple of pages of facts on the AIDS situation in the People's Republic of China. We want to know how severe it is. I want it here by 15:00 today."

"Now, there is nobody to stop them when they control the wealth of southern Africa, Caspian Sea Basin oil, the minerals and oil of Southeast Asia, and they are in a springboard position to seize the Middle East with its oil reserves from two directions at any time they choose. They hold us in abeyance in the meantime, from the Panama Canal which they control. Magnificent! What a game plan," said General Anderson.

"Not only that, but Taiwan would now willingly join China out of intimidation. China would still have the world's four greatest markets for their goods and services; the United States, Western Europe, South America, and their own internal market. It will be a unipolar power world, and it won't be us," added Margaret Talbott.

"Marge, inform every African ambassador that we believe the Chinese intend to conquer every African nation south of the Sahara. Also inform every European nation and Russia. The world is going to be bipolar or tripolar. We are one pole, I hope Russia joins with Western Europe as the second pole, and China is the third. Ask them to consider what possible outcomes are the results of such a conquest, and what actions, individually and collectively, they are willing to do about it. Don't bother with the United Nations.

"Ladies and Gentlemen, they aren't going to hold us in abeyance for long. As of this moment, we are going to take back the Canal Zone. Put your heads together. I am going to stay out of it. The management of our seizure of the Canal Zone is up to you people at this table. Go when you are ready. Jim, as SECDEF, and you, General Anderson, as Chairman of the Joint Chiefs, have responsibility and total control. Go get the bastards."

"We will begin by pulling back our naval forces from the Indian Ocean and the Strait of Taiwan and the China Seas. That should put the Chinese at some degree of relief. We'll let them think we are withdrawing our forces for refitting, rest and recreation back to the west coast. We can take the Canal Zone within seventy-two hours after the operation begins." Jim Neville smiled as he spoke. Being a Ph.D. research physicist has its moments, but there is always the glimmer of playing the commanding Admiral in a major engagement in every naval officer.

Jason Thornton and United States Attorney General Hugh Collier struck a deal with the governors and Attorneys General of the southwestern states. They could have first trial rights on the suspects. "Why not," said Thornton, "let the states, in order of the raids conducted, try him first. Then, if all else fails, we will try him in federal court for whatever we can hang on him, from illegal entry into the United States, to gun running, to murder of federal officers." Hugh Collier ordered the FBI to assist the states in gathering and presenting evidence. He assigned a team of federal attorneys to assist in the prosecution with the strict admonition that the local prosecutors were in the lead. Photographs were taken of each of the prisoners and provided to witnesses. Dozens of witnesses and victims came forward with specific, individual identifications of the perpetrators. Cartridge cases collected from the raids were matched with individual AK-47s by the FBI ballistics laboratory. Fingerprints were taken, as were blood and DNA samples. DNA samples taken from semen collected from rape victims in Ruidoso alone matched more than two dozen of the raiders.

Jesus Gonzalez, whose real name was Jose Aguinaldo, went on public trial in Ruidoso, Texas. Reporters from around the world flooded into the little Texas town. Media networks broadcast the initial hearings live around the world. The Mexican government lodged protest after protest, but many Texas citizens, out of reach and earshot of the television cameras and microphones, whispered not-so-veiled threats into the ears of Latino journalists. Some were as simple as, "Get out of town or we will kill you." Others were only slightly more subtle. "Get on the right side of this or you will be put in a hole." Mexican journalists were specifically identified in most cases, but some threats were indiscriminately directed to all Latino journalists. Colombia, Venezuela, Ecuador, Argentina, Brazil, all had teams of reporters as did the Europeans. Everywhere, it seemed Anglo citizens of Texas openly carrying arms were televised.

The Latino journalists tried to hammer the point that with the withdrawal of the U.S. Army along the border, a wave of shooting of poor illegal immigrants trying to cross the border reached epidemic proportions. A wave of tens of thousands of immigrants waiting to cross had built up while the border was being patrolled. Camps holding hundreds of aliens formed in the desert along every possible water course and on every Mexican ranch that had a bank on the Rio Grande. When the Army withdrew, they advanced en masse for the next two weeks. Then, as word spread of mass shootings of illegal immigrants spread throughout Mexico and Central America, the number of those attempting to cross dropped off dramatically. County militias had been quietly organized by citizens all along the border but particularly in Texas. They consisted only of residents well known to each other. Local sheriffs' departments and small town police departments totally ignored them and officially denied their existence. In fact, many of the county deputies and city police officers of the small towns were among the militiamen. Hundreds of bodies were found from Brownsville to Tijuana.

Some Mexican journalist estimated on live television that perhaps only ten percent of the bodies were found. When queried as to how he arrived at that figure by a Fox Television News Team, he evaded the question. Women as well as men were found shot to death. It seemed that many Latino American citizens were also included in the carnage. It left the impression that sometimes revenge was indiscriminate. One Texan was asked why he carried both a rifle and a pistol. He retorted in a live television interview, "The range is long out here, four, five hundred yards sometimes, on a running target. That's why the rifle. I don't leave it in the truck for some wetback to steal. Wetbacks aren't welcome on my ranch. I sent all my Mexican vaqueros packing. A couple of them vowed revenge. Who are they to tell me I can't fire 'em? The handgun is for close-in work, in town, around the ranch buildings and in the truck where you can't handle a rifle as easily." Another armed Texan interviewed by a Mexican news team bluntly stated, "If I was you, I would stay real close to town here, except when you're packing back to wherever you came from." Another armed citizen smiled into the TV camera and said, "We have a rabies epidemic around here." Somebody in the local cafe where Latino reporters ate many of their meals said in a loud voice to no one in particular, "Around here, its shoot, shovel, and shut up!"

The Texas State Police provided a bodyguard of a dozen officers wearing bullet proof vests to surround Jesus Gonzalez. They huddled around him to prevent any sniper from having a clear shot that would blow his head off. They transported him in an armored car to and from the jail to the court house.

Jesus Gonzalez realized that he was going to be found guilty and that his only hope of living was that the Mexican government could persuade the Americans to turn him over to Mexico for lifetime incarceration. He realized he would be found guilty as charged, no matter what. The sentence was the only thing in doubt. He knew he could bribe his way out of a Mexican penal institution after several years. He wasn't naive enough to believe that Mr. Ito or his organization, unaware of Chan's death, would ever come to his defense, either in the U.S. or in Mexico. He had no doubts they would much rather have him dead. He decided that the only chance he had for leniency was to tell everything he knew. And talk he did. From the witness stand, he revealed the large cash deposits he received from Mr. Ito, all of the guns and the direction provided by the enigmatic Mr. Ito. He attempted to portray himself as a fool, a tool of some sinister organization whose representative was the evil Mr. Ito. He knew nothing personally of Mr. Ito. In Gonzalez's office however, the FBI found a file with pictures of Mr. Ito, his bodyguards and their vehicle. Blowing up the photograph revealed the license plate number of the sedan. The FBI immediately recognized Mr. Ito as Mr. Chan.

The FBI conducted a raid on the COSCO Shipping Company and seized all their records for the timeframes revealed by Gonzalez that they received the weapons. They found nothing of value. There were no records of any of the shipment of arms, ammunition or anything other than tractors and farm implements to Mexican implement dealers. According to COSCO, Mr. Ito never existed. No one in the COSCO offices recognized the photographs of Mr. Ito. Hugh Collier ordered a massive, close surveillance on COSCO shipping company executives.

The majority of the raiders were held in the temporary holding facility in the desert just north of El Paso, on a far desert corner of the Fort Bliss reservation. It didn't take long for the observant citizen to figure out where they were. The major question was to try them as individuals or collectively, and what punishment to mete out. It would presume that they were all equally guilty to try them en masse at a single trial. More than two dozen well known trial lawyers volunteered to defend them pro bono. It was more like a gathering of vultures for publicity. Hugh Collier anticipated a media circus would develop that would be overwhelming, out of control and make a mockery of the judicial system, as well as costing tens of millions of dollars. Jason Thornton made the decision to try them en masse at a secret trial.

Hugh Collier selected three volunteer attorneys to lead the defense team. He informed them that once they accepted the positions and formed a defense team, there was no turning back. There was no way they would enhance their legal reputations or make any money on this trial whatsoever. They had to accept the agreement up front without knowing the details or back out now. All of them objected. Collier then informed them that they would not be allowed to represent the raiders. Two acquiesced. Collier had the two sign the appropriate secrecy documents. He impressed upon them that the trial records would be sealed for fifty years. If any of them revealed anything about the trial, wrote any books, talked to their wives or girlfriends, or broke the secrecy agreement they just signed in any way, they would spend the rest of their life in prison, their possessions would be confiscated, legally or otherwise for tax evasion, and if necessary, bad things could happen to family members. *It's not the way I like to conduct business,* thought Collier. *I have just negated all that the law is supposed to stand for. On the other hand, I have a higher duty to protect the country and its citizens. This is the real world.*

Each of the raiders was undergoing a thorough interrogation. All of them denied ever having raped anyone or shot anyone. Those who were confronted with their fingerprints on cartridge cases claimed they were just shooting in the air to scare people. Those whose DNA samples matched those taken from rape victims claimed the tests were false and they were being framed. When confronted with testimony by the victims who picked out their pictures, they denied everything. Some were identified by their tattoos. Almost all claimed that they thought they were joining a guerilla army to resist the Mexican government, but once in, they went along with the raids out of fear for their lives.

"If they are found guilty, which they undoubtedly are, then how do you punish them? Do we incarcerate all one hundred and fifty of them at $50,000 a year expense for each of them? That's $7,500,000 a year burden on the taxpayers. If we execute them, it will be the largest mass execution in American history and most certainly will raise the cry against American barbarism. Sure as hell don't hear anything like that about the Chinese slaughtering millions, though. Perhaps we can execute those who are positively identified as rapists and or killers, and turn the rest over to Mexico and let them be their problem. They and the Mexican government will have to understand we will kill them on sight if they ever enter the United States again. Of those we execute, do we do it by firing squad or by hanging? The easiest way is to line them up and machine gun them into a mass grave. That would be a bloody business. If we hang them one at a time, that might be more dramatic, but time consuming. A firing squad is an option, if we can find the men who will man it. Lethal injection one at a time might be the way to go. It would deny any claims of barbarity. I suppose the question is how many will there be who receive the death sentence. I'll have to see what the President wants to do."

"No question about it, Hugh. We will invoke the death penalty. So far as I am concerned, those who raped and those who killed will get it. If Texas law doesn't string up the rapists, find a way to do it. Consider rape the same as murder. I have no problems with firing squad, hanging, or lethal injection. Lethal injection seems to be a slightly drawn out affair, firing squads would be a bit messy, and perhaps hanging them one at a time in front of all the others would be the best way to go. One gallows and hang them two or three at a time would be less bloody and faster than hanging them individually. We wouldn't have to be concerned about any firing squad members suffering psychological problems that way. Any idea how many will receive the death penalty, and what does the State of Texas say about it?"

"Well, Mr. President, I should think it will run about fifty of the one hundred fifty that we can definitely prove rape and murder. We can have the Army set up a temporary morgue and embalm the bodies and put them in wooden coffins and ship them back to relatives in Mexico, at least those that claim relatives. Many of them will likely deny any family whatsoever because of the shame of their crimes. We will probably wind up burying them here in the U.S. Alternatively, we can donate their bodies to medical science. Medical schools throughout the country could certainly use them in their anatomy classes. The Texas Attorney General wants their blood. He doesn't care how it is done. He will go along with any suggestions we are to make. By the way, he sends his thanks to you for all the federal involvement and letting his folks be the leaders in the investigation and trial. He very much appreciates the efforts of the FBI, BATFE, and INS Border Patrol participation."

"Does the Mexican government know how many we actually have and who they are, Hugh?"

"I don't think so, Mr. President."

"Good, then that is what we will do. The bodies will be donated to medical schools as John Does. Give the affected states first claims on the bodies. They might serve some useful function here in the good ol' USA after all. Make it mass hanging so as not to distort any anatomical features except their necks. Get on with it."

The Texas Attorney General ordered a gallows holding five prisoners at one time to be built in the desert adjacent to the holding compound, just meters away from the boundary of the Fort Bliss Reservation. He wanted the prisoners to see it, to think about it, and realize they were going to die on it. An agreement was struck between the Army, the State of Texas and the Bureau of Prisons. The Bureau of Prisons and the State of Texas would build a permanent facility in the desert to hold up to two hundred inmates for future contingencies. The Army would use its funds to maintain it once it was built and use it as an overflow facility for military installations in the southwest. It could be considered as an adjunct facility to that in Guantanamo Bay, Cuba.

"Admiral Stark, order our naval forces to withdraw to their home port of San Diego or wherever on the west coast. Send it in the clear so there is no confusion for the Chinese. When the carriers get within range of a UC-21M Greyhound, put sealed orders on them informing them of the battle plan and their part in Operation Recovery. They will provide backup for the Marine Expeditionary Forces. Give the order to sink any Chinese submarines in the area. The new satellites will provide their precise location. I don't want to have a single American ship torpedoed. If we have to strike the first blow at sea, so be it. We're going to take back the Canal Zone. They can then pass the word to the other ships in their groups. We don't want to tip our hand too soon to the Chinese, just in case they have cracked into our so-called secure internet transmissions. A quick review of our plans is in order for me. Run through it real quickly for me, General Craig."

"Mr. Secretary, General Anderson has assumed overall command for this operation. We have made some changes since our initial plan; fine-tuned it, so to speak. General Shelton's Air Force folks will be monitoring the radio traffic very closely from AWACS from the minute the carrier battle groups turn south, vectoring away from San Diego. General Leonard will attach two EA-6B Prowlers to General Shelton's AWACS, one to each AWACS. The second there appears any indication that the Chinese are figuring out what we are up to, they will attempt to contact the mainland. The AWACS can directly communicate with the Prowlers and jam their broadcasts. General Anderson, your Rangers are ready?"

"Yes, sir, General Craig, they were born ready. They are itching to go. Many of them have figured it out and are having a hard time sitting still. I have never seen so many men sharpening their fighting knives at one time."

General Craig continued, "Coordination and surprises will be the keys. It has to run like clockwork. We will set our timetables to the arrival of the forces from the Far East. We are going to seize everything at once, both ends and everything in the middle.

"The suspect warehouses in Balboa and Cristobal are the critical targets. That's where the missiles will be located. We have to take them before the Chinese can launch. We will assume they can launch within fifteen minutes of receiving a launch order. Two Brigades of the 82nd Airborne Division will make a night drop into the Pacific terminal of Balboa and seize the warehouses there. The adjacent old Rodman Naval Base on the Pacific side will be the objective of the 23rd Marine Expeditionary Unit in an amphibious assault. They will provide reinforcements and take out any resistance from the Panamanian Defense Force and Chinese units in the town of Balboa.

"On the Atlantic side, the 26th MEU will assault Cristobal in support of a third Brigade of the 82nd Airborne Division. We are using paratroopers to maximize the element of surprise. It will be a low-level flight group, five hundred feet off the deck, all the way from Fort Bragg in C-130s for these two airborne assaults. The 101st Airborne Division will be delivered to Howard Air Force Base on the Pacific side by massive airlift of Air Force C17s. I have ordered the 101st off border duty and ordered the reserves in place to hold down the fort in the desert. The 101st is martialing at Fort Bliss in El Paso as we speak. Things have really quieted down along the border, and I see no reason to maintain an active line division there.

"The 101st Airborne will assault and hold the air field. Our major concern is that it is going to require every Air Force Transport aircraft in the inventory. We are not aware of any enemy fighter or interceptor aircraft in the Canal Zone, but that doesn't mean there couldn't be any. Navy F-18F Hornets from the USS John C. Stennis will provide fighter coverage. One Marine airborne battalion will assault Ancon Hill where the old Quarry Heights Headquarters for SOUTHCOM used to be, while a second assaults the old Albrook Air Force Station. Galeta Island will be guarded by a battalion of Marines in a classic amphibious operation. Fort Sherman on the Atlantic side will be taken by Marines in a vertical assault from the USS Iwo Jima Assault Ship. The 101ˢᵗ Airborne will establish a holding facility for any Chinese and others that are taken prisoner at Howard Air Force Base. Army Rangers aboard ships will disembark at critical points along the entire length of the Canal. Navy SEALs will check all of the locks and dams. That's it in a nutshell, Mr. Secretary."

"Thank you, General. We received a report last night that the Chinese have DF-21A missiles in the warehouses at both ports. As we all know, these are cold launch missiles whose engines ignite in flight and can be launched very quickly. They can carry a 200-kiloton nuclear warhead for 1500 miles. They can reach any city in the United States. They are only thirty feet long and easily fit inside a standard ocean-going shipping container."

"We will have helicopter gunships in support of the assault units, Mr. Secretary. If any missile comes rolling out of a warehouse, those ships can fill it with enough holes that they will never initiate launch."

CHAPTER 38

The Chinese ambassador's phone rang at 02:00 hours. It was Marge Talbott. She politely requested the presence of his Excellency Kuan Sheng to meet with the President and herself in precisely one hour at the White House. Groggy from sleep and a bit too much alcohol from the cocktail party earlier in the evening, he grumbled as he quickly showered and dressed. His sedan was waiting for him as he emerged from the Chinese Embassy. At 02:55, the sedan pulled up to the White House.

Johnny Whittaker escorted the Ambassador into the Oval Office where Marge Talbott, Jim Neville, Ralph Gardner and the President were drinking coffee and animatedly chatting. They all stood when Kuan Shang entered the room. Kuan Shang politely bowed to the President first and the others in turn without speaking.

Jason Thornton waved Kuan Shang into a chair with his hand and said, "I'm sorry to awaken you at this hour, Mr. Ambassador. I have some critical information for you that you will wish to communicate to your government as soon as possible, I am sure."

Now fully awake, Kuan Sheng leaned forward in his chair, a furrow appeared in his brow, and he grasped both arms of his chair.

"As of this moment, Mr. Ambassador, we are launching an attack upon the Republic of Panama. Our objectives are the warehouses that house your missiles. We are aware of your submarines in the area. We have pinpointed them precisely, and I have given the order that if they open the outer doors of their torpedo tubes, they are to be immediately sunk. There is no recourse. Additionally, I have ordered all of our ICBMs to target each Chinese city on the coast as well as Peking, Darien, and a number of others. If you launch a single missile in our direction, attack a single American ship, you will launch a new phase of World War III. In effect, with our MIRVs, the design which you stole back in the 1990s, with six warheads per missile, we will obliterate your hopes of world domination and a modern China. You are probably not aware that instead of the original twenty-five kiloton weapons in each independent re-entry vehicle, due to miniaturization, we have upgraded them to one hundred-kiloton warheads. We do have a few with warheads in the megaton range for your larger cities.

"Look at me, Mr. Ambassador! I am not bluffing. I will order the destruction of your nation in the blink of an eye if China so much as twitches. Here is the position of all of your nuclear submarines capable of launching any kind of missile against United States territory as of one hour ago. You can confirm their positions when you communicate to your Government." He handed Kuan Sheng a piece of paper with the names and locations of forty submarines listed.

Kuan Sheng took the paper very carefully and read down the list. He realized that he did not know the accuracy, but he recognized the names of many of the submarines. He looked up at Jason Thornton, then looked at the others in the room, but said nothing. They were as inscrutable as he was. Inwardly, he was absolutely seething. If the United States seized the missiles in Panama, it would reveal not only the state of their nuclear defenses and rocketry, but the massive biological weapons program.

"In addition, Mr. Ambassador, if there is a single outbreak of some exotic disease in the United States, be it against humans, our crops or domestic animals, we will retaliate. You are not the only one who knows how to genetically engineer viruses and bacteria. While President Richard Nixon ordered the destruction of our entire biological and chemical stocks in 1969, I have directed the appropriate institutions to initiate research into possible biological weapons once again. Offensive weapons, Mr. Ambassador, to retaliate against any nation that uses biological weapons against us. We both know that these pose a far greater threat in the long run than nuclear weapons. We will ensure that our own population, every man, woman, and child, is vaccinated against any biological weapons that we select for deployment. I will candidly admit that right now we have no such capability, so our response for the immediate future will be nuclear. I would prefer to avoid any environmental destruction such as we have recently witnessed on the Asian continent. I don't know how accurate a nuclear winter scenario is, but it is something I would prefer not to risk. Therefore, I will proceed with such research on biological weapons and their defense as I deem necessary to protect our country through a balance of, shall I say, biological power?"

"As regards to your invasion of the Central Asian Republics, Southeast Asia, and of Africa, I can only say this. It is too late to stop you in Southeast Asia and the Indian subcontinent. You already own them. The west was not at all prepared for such an explosion of your conquests. I have communicated with the nations of Western Europe. That includes Russia. We agree that it is necessary for you to withdraw from Africa. It presents you with too much of an advantage to launch an attack on the Persian Gulf and the Middle East. Therefore, you must withdraw your forces from Africa. Your daily convoys of troops and supplies must cease within twenty-four hours. If they do not, we will engage you in submarine and other forms of naval warfare. We will first sink all your submarines that you have on picket duty in the Indian Ocean and Arabian Sea. Then we will assault your convoys from the air, land and sea. Should you attempt retaliation against any nation participating in this coalition, of the naval and air forces conducting such interdiction, we will be forced to conclude that you desire to expand World War III into nuclear war. Therefore, I strongly urge your government to withdraw all your naval and land forces now on or in the Arabian Sea and Indian Ocean.

"The government of Iran has suddenly seen the light. They are now actively seeking coalition partners with Europe and the United States. We are no longer the Great Satan. They now regard China as a re-incarnation of the feared Mongol Hordes of the twelfth and thirteenth centuries. You have turned Islam, or what's left of it, against you. Even the hordes of your Asian brethren in Indonesia and the Republic of the Philippines now regard you as a far greater threat to Islam than western democracy and their materialistic decadence.

"Russia is now seen as the front line of battle. What is left of Kazakhstan, Uzbekistan and Turkmenistan are scrambling to rebuild their ties with Russia and inviting western powers to build bases to ensure that there is no further encroachment on their territories. Indeed, they are asking the European Union, NATO and the United States to go to war with you on their lands. We will not engage you in a conventional war upon the Asian continent at this time. Rather, weapons of mass destruction are our only option. I cannot guarantee what the future holds; that depends a great deal upon you. You have eliminated hundreds of millions of the peoples of the Asian subcontinent, destroyed cultures foreign to your own, launched the destruction of nuclear wars, and earned the enmity of the world. As far as your being the manufacturing center of the world, that cannot be denied. If the rest of the world imposes tremendous tariffs on your goods and re-institutes manufacturing in their own countries, your economy could collapse in a relatively short time.

"Within twenty-four hours, the rest of the world will know of our invasion of Panama and what we have seized in your warehouses of the Hutchison-Whampoa and COSCO shipping companies. We will make the results public. We are taking journalists embedded in our forces into those warehouses for independent confirmation. The nations of Western Europe are having similar conversations with their ambassadors from China as I am having with you. The only difference is that they are not knowledgeable of our invasion of Panama at the moment. They will know it as soon as we are finished here.

"Your government has some hard choices to make, Mr. Ambassador, and precious little time in which to make them. If you do not withdraw as I have outlined, the United States Navy will initiate maritime war. All warships have already received their instructions to proceed into combat unless otherwise countermanded. That includes nuclear launch from our Ohio and Trident nuclear submarines. That is just in case you decide to try and take out the U.S. leadership, meaning myself and the rest of Washington, D.C. I pray that your government makes the right choices.

Secretary Albright has a detailed list for you to ensure that you don't overlook anything in your communications."

Marge Albright handed the Ambassador a single sheet of double spaced typed paper.

"Do you have any questions, Mr. Ambassador?"

"No, Mr. President. I will immediately contact my government and inform them of what you have said."

"My aide, Johnny Whittaker, will provide a tape recording of this conversation for you on your way out. In that case, Mr. Ambassador, I must apologize once again for disturbing your sleep. I hope that we can all sleep well, tonight and in the future. Good night, sir."

Johnny Whittaker escorted the Ambassador into the foyer where he was handed the tape. Then he escorted the Ambassador back to his sedan. Whittaker noticed that Kuan Sheng was slightly trembling. He had never seen the man with a visible expression of being upset before.

"Marge, send our prepared communiqué to all our friends and acquaintances in Japan, the Middle East and Europe, as we planned. We'll see what they have to say. I expect we will hear from most of them by 09:00 this morning. I am going to get some sleep. I suggest you all do as well. We'll have a breakfast meeting at 09:00 to see what the responses are. Good night to all."

Jason Thornton rose from his desk and went to bed, feeling better than he had since he won the election.

"American warships are immune from being searched and tolls paid. If that Panamanian pilot and his Chinese sidekick give you any crap, Captain, tell them to send the bill to the Department of the Navy, Washington, D.C. If they don't buy that, you tell them they are going through the locks if you have to seize them and operate them yourself. You have the Marines aboard, and that's no bull." The US Navy transport ship carried a battalion of Rangers and ten SEAL Teams. They were allegedly en route to California to participate in amphibious war games. Each SEAL Team was assigned one set of the locks on Gatun Lake. Their mission was to check for underwater explosives on the gates and chains and then guard the locks at the hinges. Bravo Company, 1st Ranger Battalion would provide security for the remainder of the facilities: the electric locomotives, the tracks, the controls and the approaches to the locks. They would quietly slip over the side at 01:00 and carry out their missions.

The year of 1970 saw the highest number of transits through the Panama Canal. That year, 15,523 vessels passed through the Canal. Now, because of larger ships, the total was less than 10,000 vessels per year. Still, it is the second most critical waterway in the world. The Suez Canal ranks first, and the Malacca Straits ranks a close third. It saves the United States Navy, and all ocean going trade between the east and west coasts, and the Pacific Rim to the east coast of North America, over eight thousand extra sea miles when going around the Straits of Tierra del Fuego, often in very stormy seas.

Captain Sabata woke his company at midnight, 00:00 hours. He saw that they had a hearty meal in the mess, then final gear check, faces and hands blackened, rifles loaded and locked on deck. Quickly and quietly, they inflated the Zodiac rubber rafts with CO_2 cartridges. The onboard Marine complement secured the Panamanian pilot and his Chinese colleague on the bridge. When they objected to the activity on deck and threatened to radio the shore installations, the Marine Sergeant in charge of the detail slapped the Chinese pilot alongside the head with his Beretta. It sent him to the floor holding his head; while it didn't render him unconscious, it did get his attention. He made no further objections. Alpha Company, First Ranger Battalion and three SEAL Teams slipped out of the loading well of the assault ship in their boats and made for their assigned sides of the locks. The SEALs slid into the water with their SCUBA gear on to explore the locks beneath the surface, leaving the two Rangers in each of their Zodiac boats to paddle them to shore and secure them. In thirty minutes, the Rangers had surrounded the locks and secured a four-hundred-yard perimeter on both sides. They encountered absolutely no opposition. There weren't even any guards on duty. Captain Sabata radioed the 'all secure' code to the battalion commander.

When the warship entered the lake channel through the cut at the continental divide, eight miles downstream where the Pedro Miguel locks that lower ships thirty-one feet to Lake Miraflores were located, SEAL Teams Eight, Nine and Ten repeated the scenario in the company of Bravo Company, First Ranger Battalion. They slipped over the side with their Zodiacs equipped with outboard motors, and while the SEALS explored the gates, the Rangers seized the controls without firing a shot.

SEAL Teams Two, Three, and Five had the same mission at the Milafores Locks on the western side of the continental divide.

At 02:00, the C-130s began to drop the 82nd Airborne on their objectives. At 02:30, the first C-17A landed on Howard Air Force Base. There was minimal opposition. The few Panamanian Defense Force Guards present decided that deserting their posts was the better part of valor. Landings continued for the next ninety minutes. As soon as the troopers evacuated the aircraft, it lined up for takeoff. Landings and takeoffs were three minutes apart. Some pileup of aircraft occurred, with those waiting to land circling at three thousand feet while those taking off exited the area at one thousand feet. The tremendous noise of the aircraft woke almost the entire population surrounding the Canal Zone.

A platoon of Chinese soldiers guarded each large warehouse. Chinese guards at the warehouses resisted but were quickly overwhelmed. There were no survivors among them. Using black parachutes, elements of the 82nd were on their objectives before the Chinese guards had any significant reaction time. The 82nd Airborne soldiers were equipped with night vision goggles and sights on their rifles. It wasn't much of a firefight. There were two battalions of Chinese at both Balboa and Cristobal, but the warehouses were in American hands before their full weight could be brought to bear. As soon as a Chinese company formed to counterattack, it came under fire from an AH-64 Apache helicopter equipped for night attack. When troops began to pour out of the Chinese barracks, the Warrant Officers flying the Apaches decided to spray them with machine gun fire. One intrepid Chinese soldier fired a shoulder fired rocket, a Chinese copy of the Stinger missile, at an Apache, and scored a hit. The Apache exploded in a massive ball of light. The other Apaches in the section then laid down a field of fire that covered a football-field-sized area. When they withdrew, a Joint Strike Fighter put improved conventional munitions bombs on the area of their barracks to ensure there would be no further resistance.

Companies of the 101st Airborne quickly moved to cordon off the entire area of the Balboa docks and warehouses while the 82nd secured the warehouses themselves. A perimeter was established that provided overlapping fires from mortars and machine guns should any Chinese or Panamanian Self Defense Forces be foolish enough to counter attack.

The USS Bataan of the 26th Marine Expeditionary Unit launched amphibious Assault Vehicles loaded with Marines for an over the beach assault on Cristobal. From her decks, OV-22 Ospreys loaded with two squads each of Marines took off for vertical envelopment. The 23rd Marine Expeditionary Unit made a similar assault on Balboa to act as reinforcements from the sea. The massive assault from the air and the sea ensured that no significant resistance was offered.

By dawn, all objectives were secure. The remaining Chinese who were alive were held under close guard until trucks could be unloaded and they could be transported to Howard Air Force Base, where the Engineering Battalion had constructed a hasty prison camp. One C-17A had a cargo of eight foot fence sections that quickly bolted together, along with dozens of rolls of razor wire that was quickly strung along the top and on the outside bottom of the fence.

At 08:00, upon receiving the all-clear signal, Army rocket experts from Redstone Arsenal, Alabama aboard the USS Iwo Jima were in the Balboa warehouses to inspect the intermediate range DF-21A rockets while physicists from DARPA were examining the warheads. Some warheads contained multiple re-entry vehicles with nuclear devices. It appeared that several rockets carried two MIRVs with nuclear bombs in the two-hundred-kiloton range, while others carried four smaller bombs that the experts believed were in the twenty-five to fifty-kiloton range. These were carefully disarmed and flown in Blackhawk helicopters to waiting C-130 aircraft at Howard Air Force Base, where they were flown back to the United States. Their guidance systems were also removed and placed in shielded containers so that their guidance could not be scrambled. Later analysis would reveal their flight paths and their targets.

The rockets at Cristobal, however, were different. They really weren't rockets, but cruise missiles launched by a rocket booster. They contained a different kind of warhead. These were found to carry multiple re-entry canisters of an unknown substance. Samples of these were removed by trained NBC (Nuclear, Biological and Chemical) specialists wearing containerized suits. These canisters were placed in biochemical hazard bags, then in padded containers, then in rigid aluminum lock boxes and transported by helicopter to a waiting C-130H Hercules at Howard Air Force Base. From there, they were flown to Dover Air Force Base and transported in military convoy to the U.S. Army Medical Institute of Infectious Diseases at Fort Detrick, MD for examination. Round the clock research revealed seven days later that they contained a genetically engineered strain of influenza A virus of very high morbidity.

The rockets themselves, with their guidance systems and warheads removed, were taken to the docks for loading aboard a US Navy fast sea transport vessel.

General Anderson personally called upon the President of Panama at his residence at 08:00 that morning. His helicopter, covered by two Apache gunships, landed in the front yard of the Presidential Palace. General Anderson politely informed the President that the United States had assumed control of the Panama Canal, effective immediately. Any attempts to re-take the Canal by anyone would be met with the greatest of violence. Protestations by the President resulted in a smirking General Anderson remarking, "If you bastards hadn't sold your country and offices out to the Chinese, if you had lived by the Treaty, if you had maintained the Canal in a satisfactory manner, none of this would have happened. We built it, we paid for it, and we are going to keep it this time. If you don't like it, we'll re-attach the eastern half of Panama to Colombia where you really belong, and give the western half to Costa Rica or maybe keep it for ourselves. We really do need new bombing ranges and jungle warfare training grounds." With that, he turned abruptly on his heel and departed.

———————— •◦•◦• ————————

The satellite SUBDUED I received a coded radio message. It was relayed by the satellite to a DARPA laboratory in the western American desert. The DARPA engineer made a copy of the recorded signal and placed the tape in a supercomputer. He picked up the phone and reported the receipt of the signal to his superiors in the Pentagon. Twenty minutes later, the computer identified the specific code, the location and time from which it was sent. The technician then sent a secure fax with that information to the Pentagon and to DARPA Headquarters.

Diane Foster was asleep on the arm of James Carter in his modest suburban home when the call came through. He had specifically insisted that his home not be wired with hidden cameras or microphones. His superiors gave their word that they would not, but bugged the entire house except for the bedroom. Fred Gateway figured he was entitled to at least that much privacy. Dr. Foster was to report to her laboratory immediately. She and Special Agent Carter hurriedly dressed, giggled, and decided that they were hungry. Ignoring the agents assigned to guard them as they left the house, Carter drove them to an Arby's that was open all night. At the drive-up window, they each ordered a breakfast sandwich with hash browns and an extra sized coffee. Then they proceeded to her office.

The laboratory director, Larry Corning, and Fred Gateway were already there. They entered with their breakfasts in sacks and began eating after the customary greetings. Larry Corning began to brief everyone.

"Each individual received a copy of the code for the SUBDUED I satellite. Only, each team member received a different copy of the code. There was just enough of the real code present in each one for the satellite to receive it and re-transmit it, to us. Only Diane and I had the complete and unaltered codes. Each member's code contained a unique section that would identify it. The decoded signal revealed which code had been supplied to whom and therefore who had supplied it to a foreign source, or attempted to send it themselves. In this case, the signal was generated from China. It came from the Chinese research laboratories at Tien Shan. In other words, the Chinese government sent the signal. This particular signal had been sourced to Choi, We Hin, in our laboratory. Of that there is no question. How he supplied the code to the Chinese is out of my realm. I can only state unequivocally that he, and he alone, had that particular code. There can be no mistake, as each code contains almost two and a half million lines. There would be no way to search through them and identify which are valid and which are not, nor any way to compare them with anyone else's code. I am certain, therefore, that Dr. Choi supplied his copy of the code to the Chinese and is, therefore, a traitor in our midst.

"I might add that, based upon the reports from our anti-submarine forces that have come in over the last forty-eight hours, SUBDUED I and II are an enormous success. They pinpointed the Chinese submarines on the nose. They were simply too big to miss."

Fred Gateway rose from his chair and picked up the phone. He called Hugh Collier. "Sorry to arouse you, Hugh, but we have conclusive evidence of our spy. I want a warrant for a wiretap and complete surveillance and all the other paperwork for a complete activities trace and investigation, for one Choi, We Hin; C H O I is how he spells it. I'll have one of our people deliver the details to your office promptly at 08:00 tomorrow. In the meantime, if you don't object, I will order complete surveillance for him as of right now."

"No, Fred, I don't object. Go for it. We won't let him slip through the net because of three or four hours delay in paperwork. Congratulations on the make."

Fred Gateway smiled. "Hell, Hugh, I didn't do it. A couple of computer sharpies in DARPA did. See you sometime tomorrow." He hung up the phone. "I'm sorry to rouse everyone, but we don't want to waste any time, do we? We don't want this fish to slip out of the net. We'll see what other fish he leads us to. Agent Carter, I think you have earned a two week vacation. We'll see if we can find you some temporary duty in Bermuda or something. If I might speak for DARPA, Dr. Foster deserves a simultaneous two weeks as well."

An Aegis destroyer, cruiser, or DDX destroyer or frigate parked directly over each missile carrying submarine located off the west coast of the United States and in the Indian Ocean and Arabian Sea. Sonar operators aboard the Chinese submarines listened with increasing anxiety as the warships approached, slowed and then came to a halt immediately over them. They heard sonar buoys dropped in the water. Then, they were pinged. A recorded message was sent to each submarine. "Immediately surface and contact your government for further instructions. Failure to comply will result in initiation of hostile activities. Opening your outer torpedo tube doors or missile hatches or any indication of preparation to fire any weapon will result in your being immediately attacked with guided torpedoes. Rise or be destroyed."

The submarines slowly surfaced with their bows pointed towards the American warships. U.S. Navy Sikorsky SH-60B Seahawk helicopters hovered over them, with anti-submarine torpedoes suspended beneath them very visible. Within the hour, all submarines set a course for China. The catamaran convoys reversed their courses. Those which had picked up troops in Southeast Asia returned them to their embarkation points.

All of Pakistan except a one hundred fifty kilometer strip along the Iranian border was occupied by Chinese. The eastern half of Afghanistan was occupied in a northeast-southwestern orientation. Kyrgyzstan, Tajikistan were wholly occupied but not conquered. Chinese forces in Kazakhstan withdrew to the eastern shore of Lake Baikal. Chinese troops in Uzbekistan and Turkmenistan withdrew towards Lake Baikal. Russian forces moved south into Kazakhstan to the northern and western shores of Lake Baikal. Intelligence reports filtering out of the occupied areas indicated that the Chinese troops were in very poor physical condition, short of food, medical supplies, and fuel and with very low morale. Surveillance flights every six hours, day and night, monitored the Chinese withdrawal. In most cases, the retreating Chinese were severely harassed by guerilla forces along their flanks and rear without respite. No prisoners were taken, and those that were captured alive lived, albeit shortly, to regret it. Russian troops were invited into the former member republics of the Union of Socialist Soviet Republics of Georgia and Azerbaijan. Spetsnaz troops guarded the Caspian oil fields. The Iranian government was extremely quiet, with all its armed forces deployed to their western border.

Everyone was present at the breakfast meeting. During the Presidential Daily Briefing, Ralph Gardner recounted the success of the Panama Canal invasion with glee. He couldn't restrain himself. Reports were still coming in regarding the number of prisoners taken, the number of wounded, both Chinese and American. All in all, casualties were considered remarkably light on both sides.

"Marge, tell the Chinese ambassador that they can send one of their new ocean-going catamarans to the Panama Canal Zone to pick up their people, to include those who are not seriously wounded. Tell him we are providing the best of medical care to those who are seriously wounded, and they can follow at a later date. The deceased will be prepared for shipment home as well. All should be ready by the time of arrival of one of those fast ships. It will give us a chance to look at one of them up close should they send one instead of some old tub." Marge Talbott nodded in agreement.

"Then call our Ambassador to Panama and give him my personal apology for not bringing him into the loop. Tell him it was my decision out of concerns that the word of our invasion might leak out one way or another. Let me know how diplomatic he is about accepting my apology." Marge Talbott just smiled. She didn't care much for the Ambassador to Panama anyway. She regarded him as a rather wishy-washy excuse for a man, let alone a diplomat.

When Gardner finished, Fred Gateway motioned that he had something to say. "We lucked out yesterday on another front, Mr. President. DARPA didn't get the decoding finished until the middle of last night, but they called us as soon as they did. We found our spy in DARPA. Ed and I got with the DARPA folks last night and had a chat. The signal was sent to China, which then attempted to influence our satellites. The code revealed it was one Dr. Choi, We Hin. We need to get with Hugh Collier today to see what we can do about prosecution. There is absolutely no doubt Dr. Choi is the man that provided the codes that screwed up our satellites many months ago. We don't know how he got those codes to the Chinese, but he did. I have ordered complete surveillance of him as of last night. The paperwork regarding the wiretaps and his rights is on its way to Hugh's desk as we speak. The question now is one of prosecution. Those people over at DARPA deserve a big pat on the back, Mr. President."

The President picked up his phone. "Peggy, get Hugh Collier over here, along with Fred Gateway and Ed McCluskey, Jim and Ralph here, for a meeting. Give it thirty minutes." He hung up the phone without waiting for an answer. Peggy began to put through a conference call with their secretaries to set it up. It was routine for her. Itineraries were changed on a daily basis for all concerned.

"Any indication that the Chinese ships have reversed course, or have any more left their ports? What do we have on their movements, Ed?"

"As of thirty minutes ago, Mr. President, there hasn't been any change in their activity. I imagine the Supreme Council is still debating the issue. Until they do make a decision, I expect they will continue with their game plan. Four more ships left their ports within the last twelve hours to form a convoy in the South China Sea. I have left word for our monitors to call me as soon as they have any indication of reversing course or halting their advances on land. I'll be surprised if they completely abandon their plans for an overland march for the Persian Gulf oil, especially since they didn't even get the Caspian Basin. They are getting pretty close to the line Russia has drawn. If our satellites pick up any more nuclear blasts, we are all going to be hurting. There's a lot of desert there that will be easily sucked up into the atmosphere, adding to more global radioactive dust."

"Is there any other way to stop them?"

"Short of use of biological weapons, no, Mr. President. Nobody has the mass of men, weapons and materiel to meet them head on. Chemical agents are really tactical in nature, not strategic. It would take thousands of tons of chemical weapons to cover so wide an area. There are some biologicals out there that would do a very good job of it, that are not transmissible person to person but are still highly infectious, such as certain strains of tularemia. You would have to dust tens of thousands of square miles with that agent in order to bring all of their fronts to a halt. Nobody wants to contaminate their own environment for God knows how long. Tularemia is known to infect over one hundred and thirty species of animals, including most livestock species. If a transmissible agent is used, it will probably spread around the world to really put mankind in a hurt." The President reflected again on his conversation with the physician from the Medical Intelligence Unit, Colonel Burgess.

Peggy called on the President's phone. "Mr. President, the only time today they are all free is on their lunch hour, 12:30 to 14:00. Shall I confirm that?"

"Yes, Peggy, do that. We'll have a working lunch here. 12:30 to 13:30 then. Have their secretaries write it in. Then call the kitchen and tell them we are having guests for lunch today. Make it a choice of two entrees. I really don't care what's on the menu. Everybody can eat whichever or claim they are on a diet."

"Jim, do we have any idea of the size and quality of the Russian tactical nuclear arsenal? Have they really been truthful with us? If push comes to shove, do they have enough that will go bang when they push the button to bring the Chinese to a halt? Do we need to loan them any if it goes that far? What will China's reaction be to nuclear weapons on their field armies? Will Russia also attack Chinese soil, especially the coastal cities? I have been trying to weasel that out of Vassily without success. As soon as it is 18:00 Moscow time, I will give him a call today. The Russians are going to have to make a hard decision. I wouldn't count on the Europeans and their European Union for anything but tears and gnashing of teeth. They haven't done anything to prepare since the Chinese first started moving. Maybe if the Chinese knock on the door the way the Mongols did when they laid siege to Vienna in the fifteenth century, they will remove their heads from their rectums."

Everyone was rather stunned by the President's phraseology. He certainly did not usually speak in such a vulgar manner. "All right then, if there is nothing else of catastrophic news, those of you involved with our traitor, be back here at 12:30 with appetites and ideas."

In spite of the President's comments on lunch, the kitchen served up a variety of cold cuts for sandwiches, with a half dozen spreads. Roast beef, ham, chicken breasts, turkey slices, salami, pastrami, five different kinds of cheeses, tossed salad with four choices of dressings, soda, milk, juice, water, coffee, tea, and wine, with white, rye, wheat, pumpernickel breads, completed the menu. *Not bad,* thought Jason Thornton. *My authority around here is eroding fast, but not bad.*

"OK, Hugh, what do we have for this DARPA traitor?"

"Mr. President, I believe we should build a stronger case than we have right now for several reasons. First, we cannot prove he passed his code to China. We don't know how he did it. That is something we must be able to prove. Even though two and a half million lines of code were fed in the satellites, and his code came up, that doesn't prove he gave it to the Chinese. Second, the defense will claim that it is impossible to get a fair trial anywhere in the country because of Chinese aggression all over Asia, and he is a Chinese American. I have absolutely no doubt that he is guilty; we just can't prove it beyond a satisfactory doubt at this time. The only other alternatives are to either go public and fire him, in which case, he will probably sue for re-instatement, or to eliminate him, and I mean remove him from planet earth in the latter case. In the meantime, we can keep him under intense surveillance and see if he will tip his hand. I suggest we do nothing to indicate to him that he is a suspect. Perhaps DARPA can assign him to some other project or area that is not so sensitive but would not suggest that he is under suspicion."

"What do you say, Jim?"

Jim Neville looked at his boss and simply said, "Kill him. Make it look like a hit and run. I'll tell you why. We are on the verge of constructing a common software architecture for network centric military operations to share with our so-called military allies. We will have it this year. If he passes it to the Chinese or implants a sleeper virus in it, to be activated on command within our computer systems, especially our logistical systems, we've had it. Our acquisition systems aren't fast enough to keep up with commercial development of computers and communications systems. By the time our acquisitions process procures our C4I systems, computers, and communications, and control, command and intelligence systems for us, they are already several years out of date. Therefore, we are building on commercial, off the shelf technology. Most of our computer software has been manufactured in Asia, especially China, for many years. Thank God he hasn't already done this, or perhaps he has, and the Chinese haven't activated it. They might be waiting for the next round. Imagine what happens if all of our transportation, communications, electrical power grid, nuclear power plants, water and sewage treatment plants were hit with a virus or viruses that destroyed the controls or shut them down for days to weeks. You want to see urban riots? Just see what happens when our cities can't get food and water on a daily basis."

"Ed, what does the Central Intelligence Agency have to say?"

"I agree with Jim. The man put the security of three hundred million Americans in jeopardy, and we are worried about violating his rights. What would have happened if China had those submarines launch ballistic missiles at us right off the bat to make sure we didn't go to Korea's aid, or Southeast Asia's or to the Caspian Sea basin nations? They still could, if we go to their aid or assist Russia. We could have been hurt, real bad.

"What if, thanks to Choi, We Hin, China establishes a number of small, but highly complex computer bases in various places around the world and the US to conduct cyber warfare against us? Targets could include traffic management systems, air, rail, naval, banking, merchant marine, telecommunications radio attacks on satellites, computer and telephone systems. He can hurt us bad, where he now is."

"Marge, I asked you to sit in on this because you are the most liberal individual in our inner circle here, what do you say?"

"Mr. President, I cannot condone the assassination based on what you have told me. The chances of his being guilty are obvious, but there is just that one chance in a million somebody else copied his code, or used it somehow without his knowledge. Until there is definitive proof that he is the individual who gave it to the Chinese, I say, wait. Wait until he betrays himself, which he will do, sooner or later."

"Fred, what say you?"

"I see both sides, Mr. President. As a former practicing attorney, I would say we wouldn't win in court. On the other hand, the man is an absolute threat to the security of our country. No telling what other projects DARPA is working on that this guy has handed to the Chinese. He could be costing us billions of dollars, decades of time, and ultimately, thousands or tens of thousands or even millions of American lives. What has he cost us? What is his life worth, what is his work in DARPA worth, and how can we trap him if he is their spy? Those are questions I would like answers to before I vote one way or the other."

Jason Thornton said nothing. He ate his lunch as everybody else made small talk, mostly about the success of the invasion of the Canal

Zone. Details were still coming in, and most were slightly excited. Finally, Jason Thornton spoke. "I'm going to have to think on this one for a while. I thank everyone for coming. If anyone has any more information or developments on Dr. Choi's case, let me know immediately. It might influence my decision. Everybody is free to go after they finish their chow on the White House budget." The secretaries and staffers drifted out as they finished their meals.

At 16:00, Ed McCluskey, Jim Neville and Ralph Gardner came walking in, practically arm in arm, and all smiles. Almost in unison, they said, "Mr. President," then Jim Neville said, "OK, Ed, give it to him straight."

"Mr. President, the Chinese convoys are turning around. Their ground forces have halted. We have intercepted communications that they are ordered to remain in place indefinitely. The Russians informed them at 12:00 hours Eastern Standard Time they would launch nuclear war against every major Chinese city with a population of over one million if the Chinese continued their attack past 18:00 hours Eastern Standard Time. That's over two hundred cities, Mr. President. They have the rockets and nuclear warheads to do it, and the Chinese knew they would do it. It's over, Mr. President, at least for the time being."

CHAPTER 39

"The question now, Mr. President, is what to do about Panama."

"What do you suggest we do, Marge?"

"Well, there are several options. This nation building concept has never worked very well for us; therefore I would not suggest we occupy the entire country and try to bring them up to snuff as a democracy. The concept of graft is simply too much for them. They have the concept so common in second tier nations that bureaucrats should get rich at the expense of the people by selling their offices that we'll never overcome it. Therefore, unless we want to absolutely heavy hand that little nation, we don't want boots on the ground down there. Let's get out of there and leave it to the Panamanians."

"Secretary of Defense Neville, what say you?"

"Mr. President, we have already seen the threat that can be posed from the Panama Canal Zone. I agree with Secretary Talbott that we don't want to occupy the country, but the Canal is still vital to our wellbeing. Therefore, we should occupy the Canal Zone as we used to do. I admit this will cause problems, but if we share the wealth of the Canal, I don't think the resistance will be anything that we can't overcome."

"Ed, your turn."

"Mr. President, I tend to agree with Secretary Neville, but I admit that we will have problems if we try and control the Canal ourselves. Rather, I think we should control the bureaucrats who control the Canal.

Admittedly, the Canal Zone, while still functional, has fallen into a serious state of disrepair, and it needs tens of millions of dollars to upgrade and repair it. I don't see any reason we can't do that. We should make it absolutely clear, though, to the Panamanian Government that we will hold them responsible for its maintenance and security. If we don't actually control it, we should make them understand that their very lives depend on it. I am not above, shall I say, dirty business, in making sure the bureaucrats don't sell their offices and the Canal Zone again. I am suggesting that we make perfectly clear to them that we will go to any lengths to make sure they fulfill their functions without any foreign interference except ours. Their health and wellbeing depend on it. Essentially, what I am saying is that we should control it from behind the scenes."

"And if these Panamanians resort to their old tricks, are you suggesting we assassinate them, Ed?"

"Mr. President, that is exactly what I am suggesting. There are all kinds of accidents that can happen to people in a tropical environment. Then, too, our behind the scenes presence would help reduce the flow of cocaine, other illicit substances, and arms into the United States. It is a natural choke point."

"General Craig, what is your opinion?"

"I can see both edges of the sword, Mr. President. There is a lot of fact in what has been said by everyone so far. My concern with Secretary McCluskey's suggestion is that ultimately it will come to light that we are engaging in assassinations, dirty tricks, and so on that will make political hay for political opponents of your administration and the congress will threaten funding reductions, outright attempts to prevent it through legislation, and so on with the hypocrisy of the Almighty. On the other hand, the Panamanians cannot be trusted to behave on their own. It is a lesser of two evils. I would prefer that we write a strong treaty with Panama and remain in control of the Canal Zone ourselves. It is the only way we will be able to maintain it and prevent a recurrence of the scenario we just experienced. If we share the wealth, then perhaps we can keep the local resistance to a tolerable level. Of course, that means we will have our noses in Panama's books, to make sure the people get the benefits of the Canal Zone and not enrich the bank accounts of the politicians and bureaucrats.

It might be necessary to do a little of the DCI's suggested arm twisting, so to speak, but hopefully it could be kept to a minimum. In effect, we would have to re-create the Panama Canal Zone Company backed by armed force and political intrigue as necessary."

"Would this Panama Canal Zone Company be a U.S. Government enterprise or a private one, General?"

"There's no reason it couldn't be a public company, Mr. President. The Canal Zone Company can sell stock on the New York Stock Exchange to make it open to international business as long as the controlling interest remains in American hands. Panamanians themselves could own stock, giving them a voice in its operations, as long as it is not too strong a voice. Of course, we would have to present a legitimate appearance on such an action by sitting down with representatives of the Panamanian Government and making them agree to the formation of such a company. That way, Panamanians could share in the profits. Everything could be published in the public domain, in the Panamanian papers, as a quarterly report on the status and operation of the Canal, and give them a sense of pride of ownership. They could see where the money goes: into roads, hospitals, water and sewage works and other public infrastructure."

"Are there any other opinions on this subject? If not, I'll ponder it, and we will rehash it later. If anyone wants to write a position paper on it for the record, please do so.

"The next item I want to discuss is the military budget. It is going to have to be expanded considerably if we wish to remain a power in the Pacific and Indian Ocean littorals. We are going to have to greatly increase funding for the Navy. Admiral Stark, please prepare a budget request for Secretary Neville to reflect what it will take to contain the Chinese from expanding and dominating the Indian and Pacific Oceans and the Arabian Sea. We can't let them control those vital waterways. Don't be modest about it. The public will support it, I think, when all the facts are out. We will make the facts public over the next few weeks and months as to how severe the threat really was. We'll build public opinion for a dominating Navy to ensure we are not threatened like this again. We will also try a little arm twisting on our so-called friends and allies of the European Union to do their share. Perhaps if we agree to handle the maritime threat, they will agree to handle the land massed threat. They can put boots on the ground in Central Asia and the Middle East and take the heat from the idiots whose soil they are on. After all, those massed Chinese armies directly threaten them, not us.

"In the meantime, I want everyone to start thinking about a 'Build it in America and Buy American' campaign to restore our manufacturing and services economies.

"Let's go to work, folks."

EPILOGUE

General Craig decided that he had had enough. He could retire at the rank of full general. He willingly stepped down and supported General Anderson as his replacement for the highest military position in the Pentagon: Chairman of the Joint Chiefs of Staff.

Legislation was passed for the inclusion of the Chiefs of Staff of the military services to be an integral part of the National Security Council. The legislation to change the Constitution requiring the President to have active military service did not. Senator Kennely decided to hold Senate hearings to determine the responsibility for the poor condition of the United States military forces. He publicly railed that he wanted to know why the current administration did not see the developing problem of Chinese aggression and plan accordingly.

The European Union requested that NATO be dissolved. The European Union would assume full responsibility for the defense of Europe to include Russia, the Balkans, the Caucasus and Turkey without involvement of the United States. Those European forces previously assigned to NATO were requested to be assigned to the EU by the EU High Commission. Any ethnic rivalries on the continent of Europe were to be decided by the vote of the High Commission. Regions were allowed to become nations if the separatist move was strong enough. No use of force would be allowed to either retain a breakaway region or to establish independence. If negotiations between the antagonists could not be reached by those involved, then the European Union retained the right to impose a settlement. No citizen of the antagonists could participate as a member of the High Commission if their native land was involved. Only the High Commission could employ force if necessary. Balkanization continued as political entities as small as provinces declared their independence.

Governance of such a political mosaic was predicted to be such a quagmire that many wondered if Europe shouldn't return to something like the Treaty of Westphalia in 1648 that declared nationhood in Europe.

The Islamic nations of the Middle East requested that the United States and the European Union provide naval and air forces for their protection. Basing rights to be granted under whatever conditions the providing contingents desired. Turkey reached an uneasy truce with its own Kurdish population and that of northern Iraq. Ultimately, the independent nation of Kurdistan became reality. Turkey grimaced as the Kurds seceded with the southeastern quarter of Turkey as an independent Kurdistan to join with those of northern Iraq.

France established bases in the center and southern portions of Iraq. Iran remained sufficiently truculent to remain outside any public form of coalition. In secret treaty, however, they agreed that the United States would come to their aid with conventional forces should China's westward expansion continue. The use of nuclear and chemical weapons is still being debated. The Trucial States and Saudi Arabia agreed to open their societies in conjunction with naval and air bases on their soil. The Royal Saudi family agreed in principle, and grudgingly committed to a formal plan for a greater role of women, and ultimately, a secular rather than a clerical government. Certain hard line Islamic clerics who protested disappeared from the scene in Iraq and Saudi Arabia.

The Chinese invasion of Africa was relatively limited. China did not even attempt to evacuate their forces from the continent. Those Chinese abandoned there ultimately succumbed to guerilla warfare, AIDS, starvation and a plethora of diseases. Africa continued to smolder and burn as petty tyrants fought for control of its wealth. They usually followed tribal and ethnic lines. Mineral extraction companies from Europe, China, Japan, Australia and the United States continued to do economic battle with each other for the mineral wealth of southern Africa. Companies such as Executive Outcomes continued to do a thriving business, approaching de facto governments in some cases.

The end result was a quadri-polar world of the United States, the European Union, Japan and China. No one knows how many died; estimates from various sources widely varied. That two billion people died was the minimum in all estimates. Several considered the total to be as high as three billion, perhaps one third or more of the human population. The long-term harm to the environment by limited nuclear war remains to be seen. Radioactivity in the estuarine environments, the nursery beds of most of the world's sea foods, is a major concern.

Choi, We Hin is still employed as a mathematician and computer scientist at DARPA. He suspects that he is under surveillance, and so continues his work without any hint of betrayal to his adopted country.

Major Bradley finally made it to Seoul. Ultimately, he was evacuated along with several other Americans who survived the second Korean War. He suffered mild to moderate radiation poisoning, receiving less fallout because his activities were in the mountainous eastern portion of Korea. He was decorated by both the Korean and American governments for his actions in Korea. The American government awarded him the Distinguished Service Cross, the Purple Heart, and promotion one grade.

Colonel Matthews was finally evacuated from Pusan. He suffered moderate radiation poisoning which resulted in his early retirement. He was awarded the Purple Heart and the Legion of Merit.

President Jason Thorton continued to lead the United States of America with the resolute certainty there would be no more WWIII in 2023.

China watches..............and waits.

Lightning Source UK Ltd.
Milton Keynes UK
UKHW012011301222
414659UK00019B/337/J